We all lived happily ever after
This story has many endings but we like this one the best

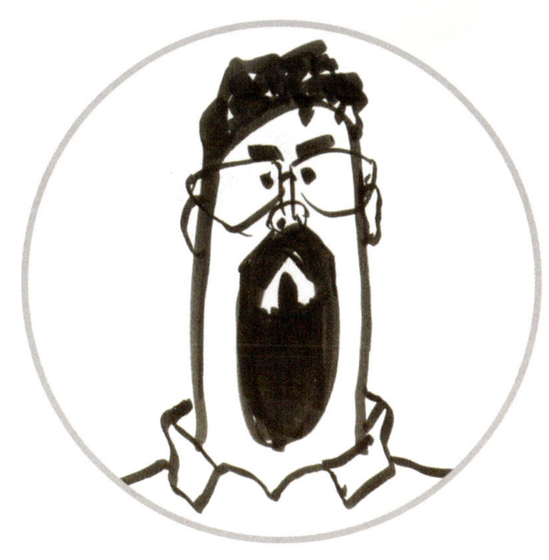

Two Guys Named Joe

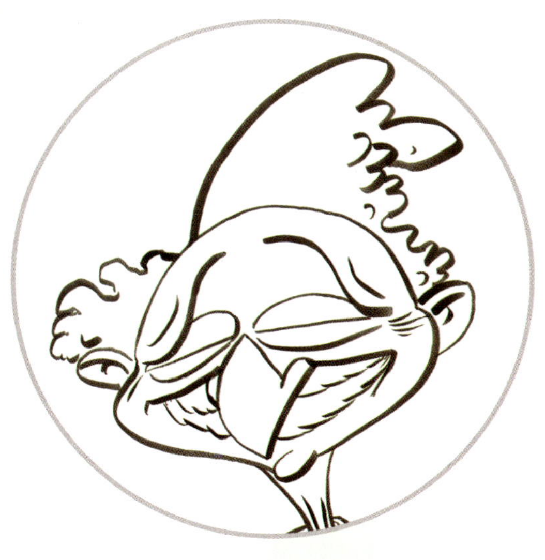

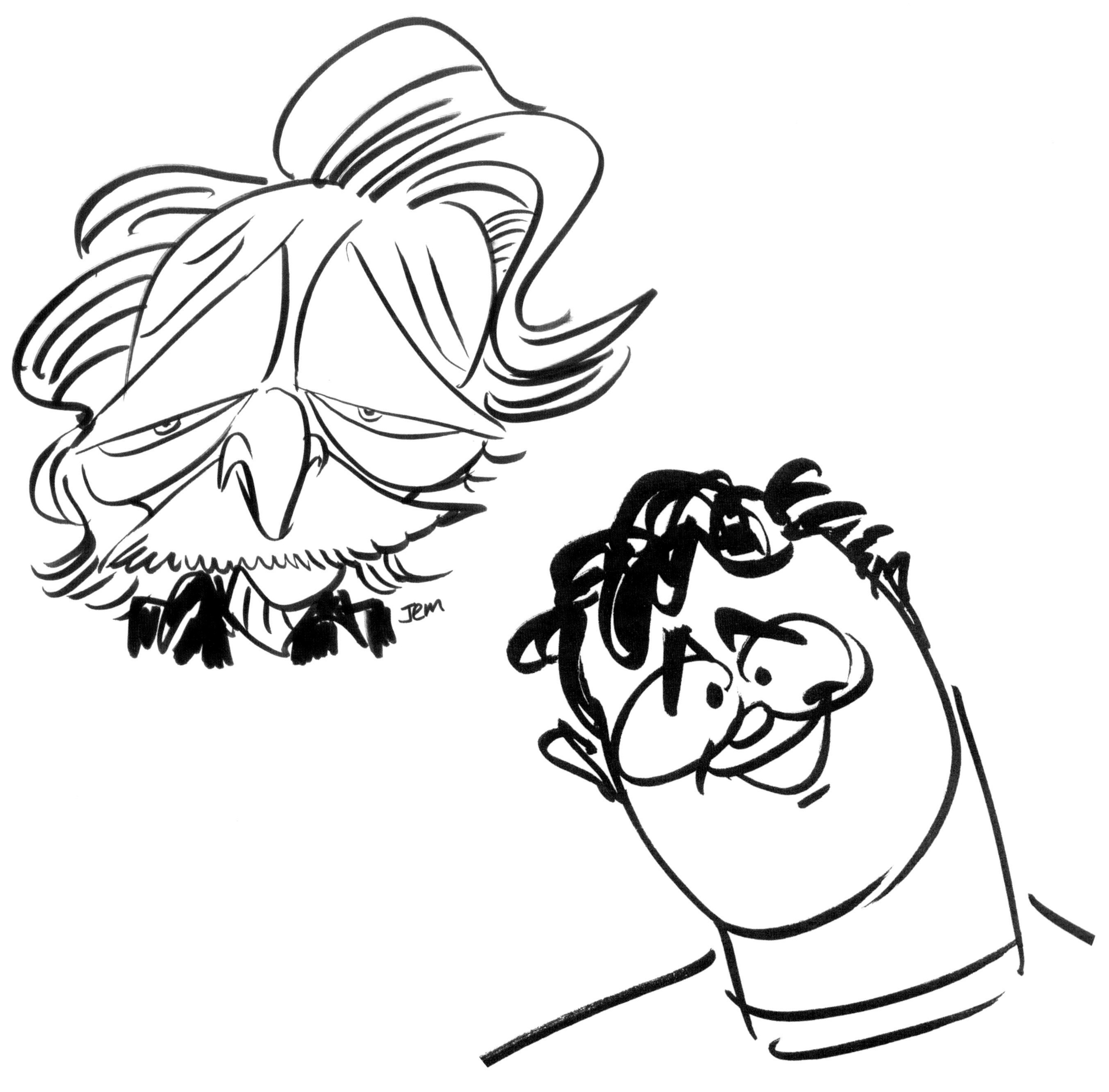
JEM

Two Guys Named Joe

MASTER ANIMATION STORYTELLERS **JOE GRANT** AND **JOE RANFT**

by John Canemaker

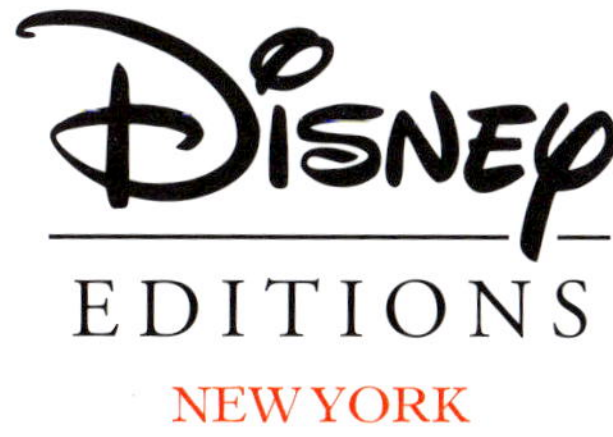

OTHER BOOKS BY JOHN CANEMAKER:

The Animated Raggedy Ann & Andy (1977)
Winsor McCay: His Life and Art (1987; revised 2005)
Felix: The Twisted Tale of the World's Most Famous Cat (1991)
Vladimir Tytla: Master Animator. Katonah Museum of Art catalogue (1994)
Tex Avery: The MGM Years (1997)
Before the Animation Begins: The Art and Lives of Disney Inspirational Sketch Artists (1997)
Paper Dreams: The Art and Artists of Disney Storyboards (1999)
Walt Disney's Nine Old Men and the Art of Animation (2001)
The Art and Flair of Mary Blair (2003)
By John Canemaker and Robert E. Abrams: *Treasures of Disney Animation Art* (1982)
By John Canemaker and Joseph Kennedy: *Lucy Goes to the Country* (1998)

For information please address Disney Editions, 114 Fifth Avenue, New York, New York 10011-5690.
Editiorial Director: Wendy Lefkon
Assistant Editor: Jessica Ward
Library of Congress Cataloging-in-Publication Data on file

Reinforced binding
ISBN 978-1-4231-1067-5
First Edition
10 9 8 7 6 5 4 3 2 1
F850-6835-5-10121
Printed in Singapore

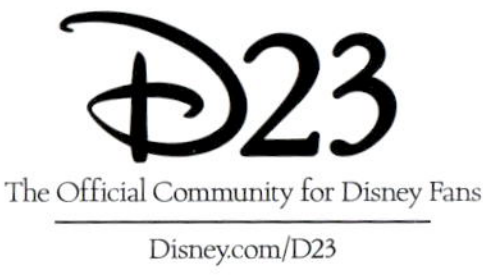

Caricatures on first page by Brad Bird (LEFT) *and John Musker* (RIGHT). *Title page art is by Musker.* OPPOSITE: *Drawing by Joe Grant.*

PHOTOS AND ILLUSTRATION CREDITS

Courtesy of John Canemaker, pp. 45, 110, 126 (left), 148, 170 (middle), 179 (middle), 180 (bot.), 208; courtesy of Brad Bird, p. 1 (left); courtesy of Mike Gabriel, pp. 5, 40 (bot.), 144, (bot.), 182, 186 (left), 187; courtesy of Howard E. Green, p. 8; courtesy of Carol Grant Grubb, pp. 106 (top), 112 (right), 166, 178, 179 (top, bot.); courtesy of Al Holter, pp. 24, 29, 31; courtesy of Joseph Kennedy, pp. 102 (top left), 106 (bot.), 108, 109, 114 (top), 117, 118, 119, 120, 121, 122 (bot.); courtesy of Leonard Maltin, pp. 122 (top), 123; courtesy of John Musker, pp. 1 (right), 2, 16, 19 (top), 33, 34, 35, 36, 37, 39, 41, 44 (bot.), 52 (bot.), 77, 97, 101; courtesy of Pixar Archives, pp. 7, 10, 11, 12, 13, 17, 18, 20, 21, 42, 43, 44 (top, © 2010 BLT Venture), 54, 58 (top), 60, 61, 62, 63, 64, 65, 66, 67, 68, 69, 70, 71, 72 (left), 72, 73, 78, 79, 80, 81, 84, 85, 86, 87, 88, 89, 90, 91, 92, 93, 95, 96, 97; courtesy of Su Ranft, pp. 15, 28, 40 (top), 45 (circle), 55, 56 (top), 57 (circle), 58, 59, 75 (top), 83; courtesy of Ranft Family, pp. 19 (bot.), 22, 23; courtesy of Tom Schumacher, 181, 184 (bot.), 187, 189. 191 (top), 207; courtesy of Charles Solomon/Scott Johnston, p. 177 (bot.); courtesy of Adrienne Tytla, p.128; courtesy of Walt Disney Animation Research Library, pp. 6, 27, 53, 56 (bot.), 57 (top), 74, 75, 76, 103, 104, 105, 111 (top), 126 (bot.), 127, 131, 132, 134, 135, 136, 137, 138, 139, 140 (top), 141, 145 (top left and bot.), 146, 149, 150, 151, 153, 154, 159, 160, 161, 167, 168, 171, 175, 183 (top), 184, 185 (left), 190, 191 (bot. left), 193, 194, 195; courtesy of Walt Disney Photo Library, pp. 14, 26, 41 (bot.), 51, 52 (top), 98, 99, 100, 102 (top right and bot.), 114 (bot.), 124, 125, 129, 130, 133 (bot), 140, 142, 143, 144 (top and middle), 145 (top right), 152, 155, 156, 157, 158, 162, 169, 170 (top and bot.), 172, 173, 174, 176, 177 (top), 180 (top), 183 (bot.), 185 (right), 186 (bot. right), 191 (right).

For Howard E. Green,

Patron Saint of Animation Historians

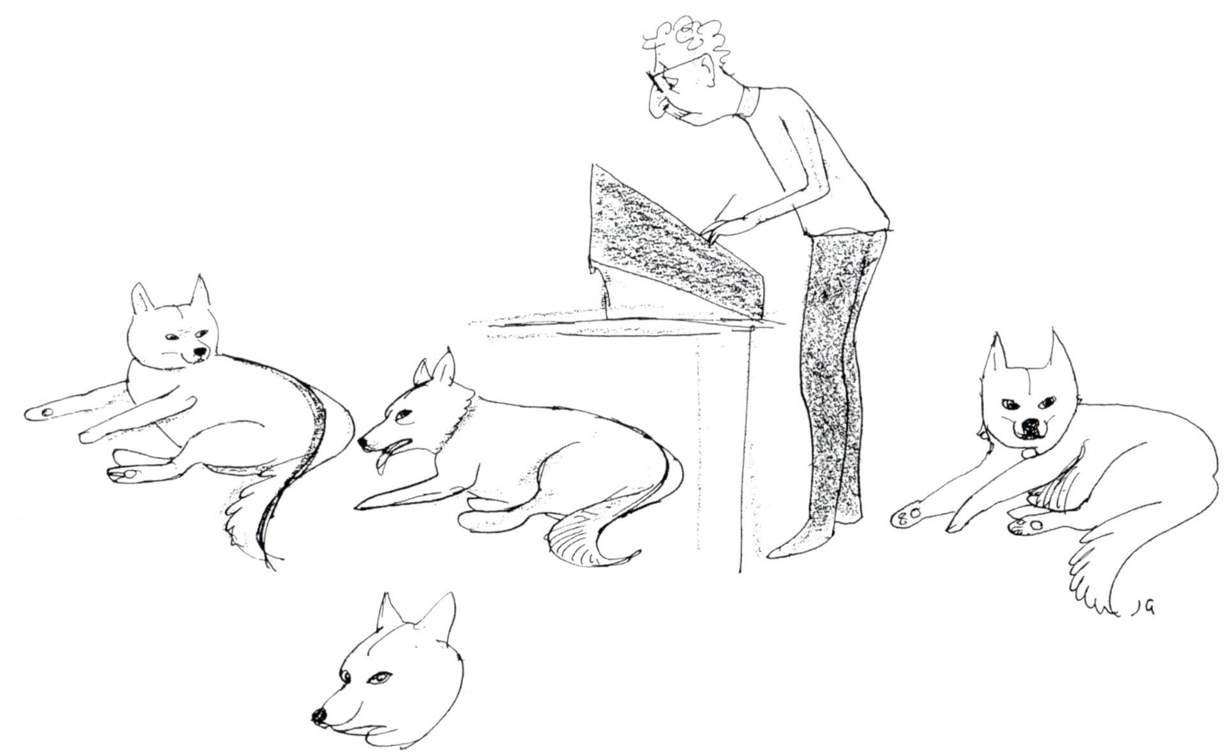

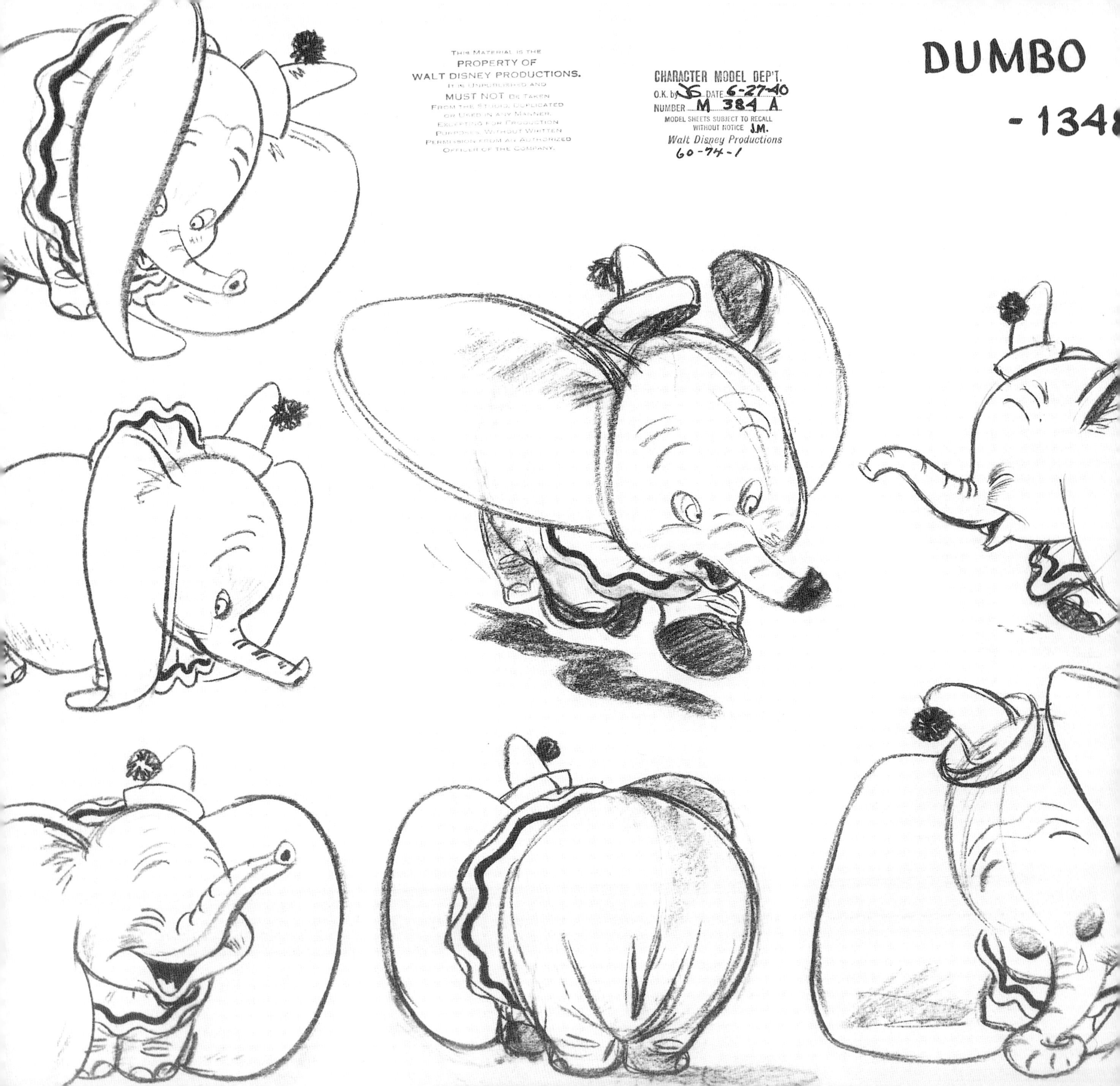
THIS MATERIAL IS THE
PROPERTY OF
WALT DISNEY PRODUCTIONS.
IT IS UNPUBLISHED AND
MUST NOT BE TAKEN
FROM THE STUDIO, DUPLICATED
OR USED IN ANY MANNER,
EXCEPTING FOR PRODUCTION
PURPOSES, WITHOUT WRITTEN
PERMISSION FROM AN AUTHORIZED
OFFICER OF THE COMPANY.
CHARACTER MODEL DEP'T.
O.K. by JG DATE 6-27-40
NUMBER M 384 A
MODEL SHEETS SUBJECT TO RECALL
WITHOUT NOTICE J.M.
Walt Disney Productions
60-74-1
DUMBO
-134

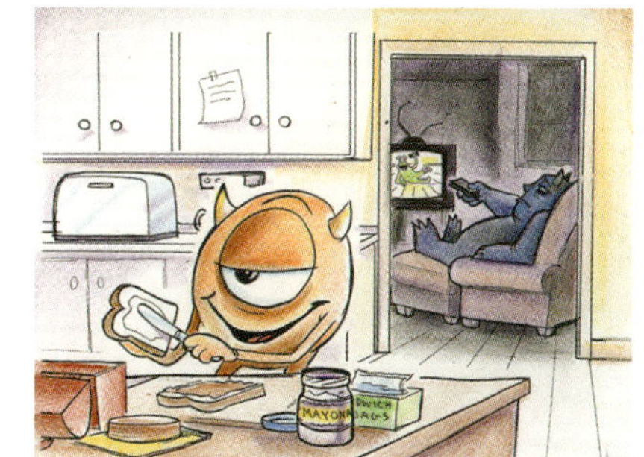

INTRODUCTION

One Joe was in his ninety-seventh year when he died in 2005; the other Joe died the same year at age forty-five. Both left us before their time.

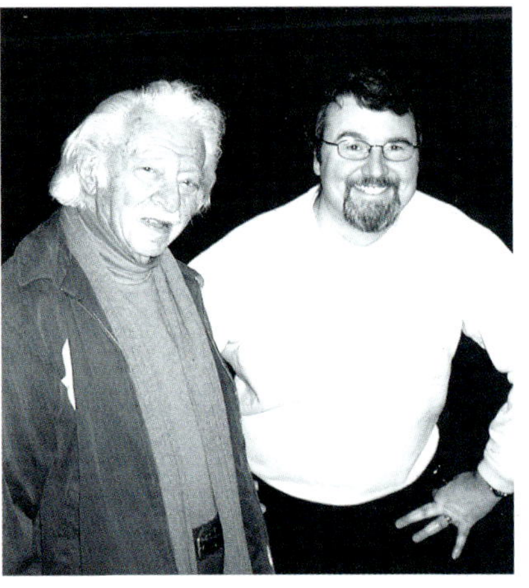

Joe Grant (LEFT) *and Joe Ranft. Photo by Howard E. Green.*

This book explores the interplay between personal creativity and the craft of animation storytelling, as seen through the lives and art of two of its greatest practitioners: Joe Grant and Joe Ranft.

Inventive and imaginative, with keen insight into characters, they inspired colleagues and entertained audiences around the world. Although their combined careers span the Golden Age of traditional animation beginning in the 1930s at The Walt Disney Company and continuing into the present digital age at Pixar Animation Studios, their extraordinary contributions remain largely unknown to the public.

Walt Disney believed the Story Department was "the heart" of his organization, and Pixar echoes the sentiment that "story is king." Unlike live-action movies, the "stars" of animated features do not appear directly on-screen, and, for the public, the process by which stories and characters are created for animated films remains mysterious. While many people know that animators breathe life and motion into cartoon characters, few understand the equally important role that story artists play—creating characters' personalities, relationships, appearances, and emotions, and a film's entire narrative thrust.

Animation stories may begin with a script or story outline. Long before any animation is done, visual development artists begin a pictorial exploration of design, emotion, mood, dramatic story moments, character relationships and conflicts, settings, color, and costumes. Their conceptual drawings, also called "idea" drawings, serve to inspire the entire crew of a production, including the storyboard artists, specialists who visualize a film's narrative—emotionally, cinematographically, structurally—and its overall direction through sequential drawings that resemble the panels of a comic strip.

Although Joe Grant and Joe Ranft could function well as either visual development or storyboard artists, each had his specialty. Grant excelled as a brilliant, freewheeling idea man, adventurously exploring concepts and characters in sketches that others brought into a cohesive story line. Ranft was capable of improvisation and creative invention, but his forte was masterfully storyboarding emotions and action into compelling narratives.

Of all the conceptual artists and storyboarders through the years at Disney and Pixar, why focus on these two?

Grant and Ranft were unique influences on storytelling at two major studios during important periods in the history of animation. Joe Grant, in fact, straddled two eras. A gifted newspaper caricaturist, he contributed ideas for Mickey Mouse and Silly Symphony shorts and classic masterworks such as *Snow White and the Seven Dwarfs*, *Pinocchio*, *Fantasia*, and *Dumbo*. As Walt Disney's confidant, Grant played a leading role in defining Disney's pioneering animation legacy. After a forty-year hiatus, he returned to the studio in his eighty-first year, his creative spirit and abilities undiminished, and made significant contributions to *Beauty and the Beast*, *Aladdin*, *Mulan*, and *The Lion King*, among others.

Joe Ranft built on the traditions of the past forged by Grant and others to become the top animation storyboard artist of his generation for *Tim Burton's The Nightmare Before Christmas*, *The Brave Little Toaster*, *Who Framed Roger Rabbit*, *James and the Giant Peach*, *The Little Mermaid*, and *Beauty and the Beast*, among other films. As one of Pixar's creative founders and a close friend to John Lasseter, Ranft had a major influence on the studio's signature originality, warmth, and irreverent humor, through his contributions to *Toy Story* (1 and 2), *A Bug's Life*, *Monsters, Inc., and Cars*, to name a few.

While the two Joes never worked directly with each other, their participation in projects at Disney and Pixar sometimes overlapped. They shared a deep love of animation and its limitless possibilities and became mentors to numerous story artists.

Grant and Ranft inspired others by working through difficult personal and professional obstacles in order to express their creativity. "Neither one was satisfied with their God-given talents," observes director Pete Docter. "They took what they had and they saw what they wanted to be and they worked. Both of those guys showed that through persistent hard work, you could become whatever you needed or wanted to be."

I believe future cinema scholars and fans of animation will want to know how masterworks like *Snow White* and *Toy Story* were made and who in the trenches contributed to them, much as we wish we knew more about the actual builders of the pyramids or Chartres, or individual artists within fifteenth-century Renaissance workshops.

To that end, here is the story of two special twentieth- and twenty-first-century storytellers in a still-young art form—two guys named Joe.

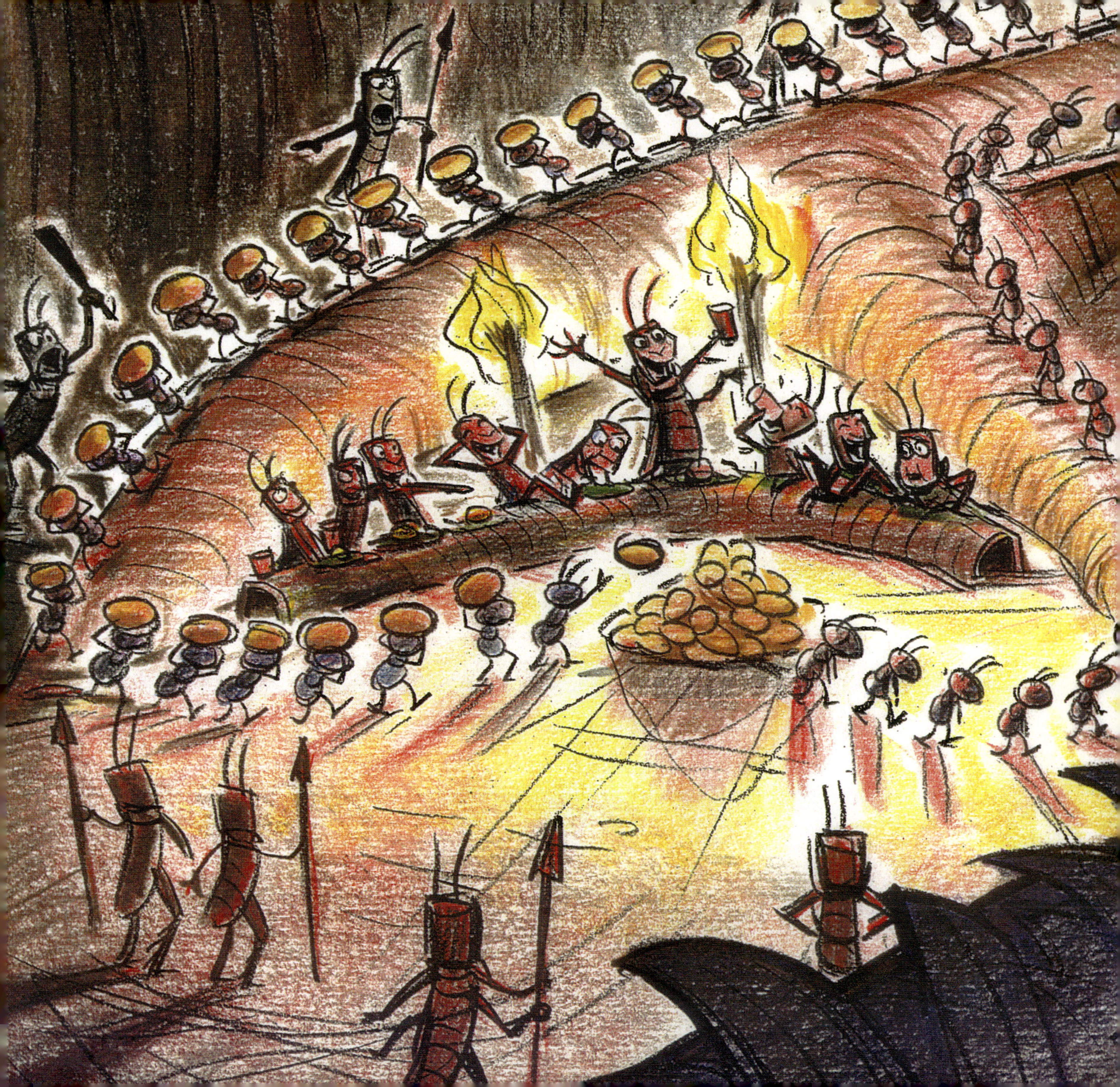

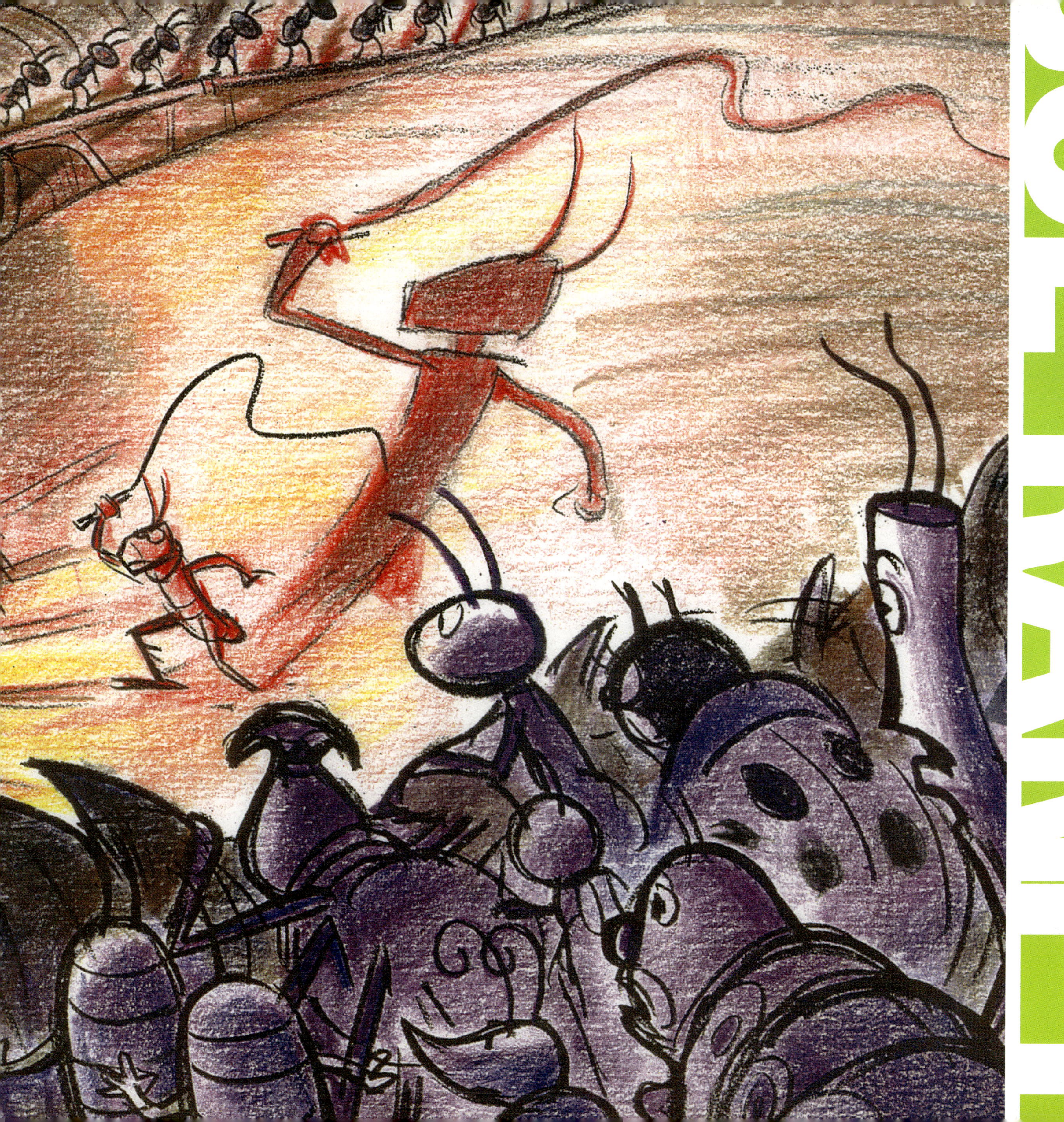

JOE RANFT

Joe! Put in the Teeth!

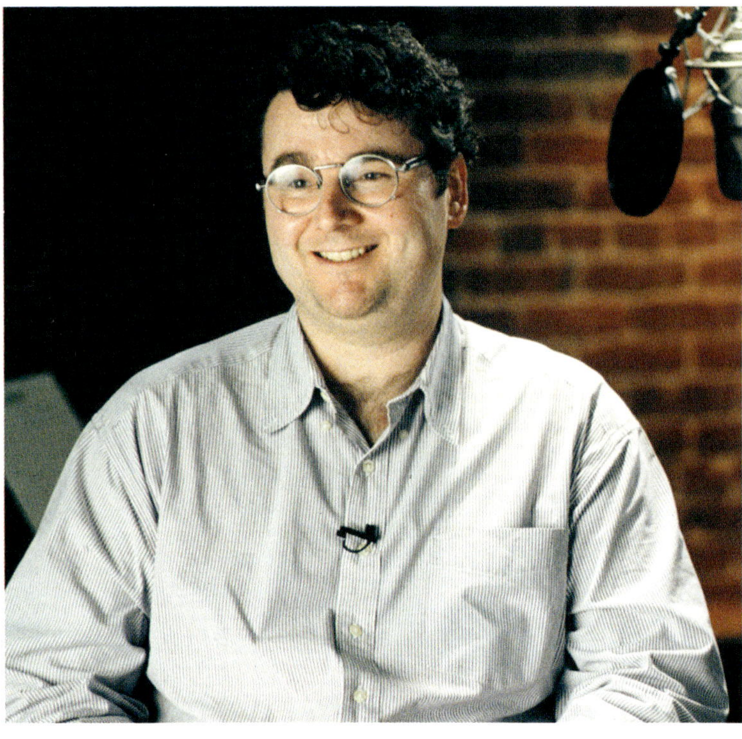

ABOVE: *Joe Ranft during A Bug's Life recording session, c. 1997.* OPPOSITE: *Ranft's storyboard of the Pixar storyboarding process.*

In late 1997, John Lasseter and Joe Ranft, top creative talents at Pixar Animation Studios and longtime friends, flew to Los Angeles to supervise final recording sessions for *A Bug's Life*, the follow-up film to *Toy Story*.

Toy Story, the first animated feature created entirely using computer-generated imagery (CGI), made movie history in 1995. Utilizing innovative technology, Pixar artists told a funny, endearing, and original tale about friendship among memorable personalities who happen to be toys.

The movie's spectacular box office success put Pixar on the map and caused a seismic shift in how animated movies are made. Pixels soon replaced pencils and paper in studios around the world.

Today it seems odd that *Toy Story*'s triumph surprised its distributor, The Walt Disney Company. But initially there were script problems and Disney considered the story "a weird idea."[1] That is, the narrative was original, not a famous fairy tale, and involved unproven technology in a studio across the San Francisco Bay, far from Disney's Burbank, California, base. Also, none of the filmmakers (except Joe Ranft) had ever supervised an animated feature from start to finish.

"They weren't expecting [*Toy Story*] to do anything," recalls Pete Docter, one of the principal creators along with Lasseter, Ranft, and Andrew Stanton. "Consumer Products said we don't see any potential in the marketing of this film!"

The filmmakers were also myopic. "The summer before *Toy Story* came out, we suddenly realized it was going to work," says Stanton, codirector with Lasseter. "Oh my gosh! We may get to make another movie!"[2]

The young studio tumbled into what Steve Jobs, Pixar cofounder, called "the whole sophomore-effort thing."[3] "It was a classic case of having a successful film and doing a big epic film as a follow-up," explains Lee Unkrich, editor and a major creative contributor.[4]

A Bug's Life, a Ranft and Stanton idea, called for a large cast of insects (mostly ants and grasshoppers) and myriad special effects. The "scope and scale was a much bigger bite than we could chew," Stanton says. The production soon became "a big harrowing journey," Unkrich concurs.

"Are we going to be a one-shot wonder?" producer Darla Anderson wondered. "We worked really hard. We were terrified. And the whole *Antz* thing didn't help."

The "*Antz* thing" was another CGI feature in production also starring a cast of insects. Former Disney executive Jeffrey Katzenberg produced it.

In 1984, Michael Eisner, Disney's new CEO, invited Katzenberg to head the motion picture division. Under Katzenberg's supervision, Disney animation revitalized, enjoying box office hits such as *The Little Mermaid*, *Beauty and the Beast*, *Aladdin*, and *The Lion King*; and he brokered the deal between Disney and Pixar for *Toy Story*'s production and distribution.

STORYBOARDING THE PROCESS!

(in rough storyboards)

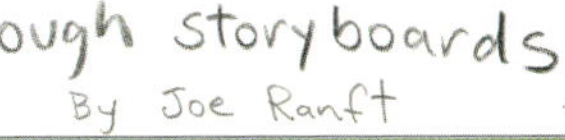

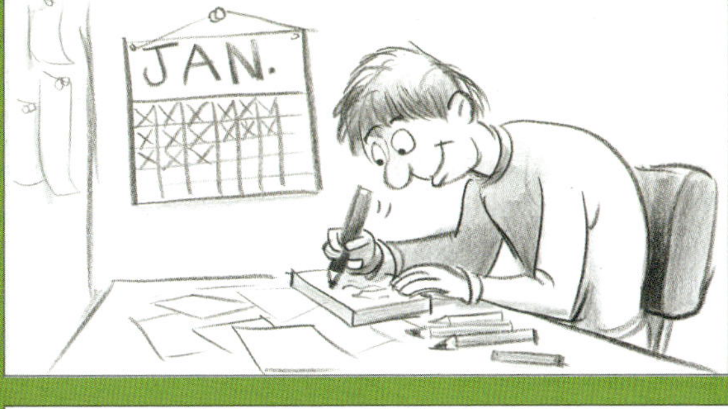

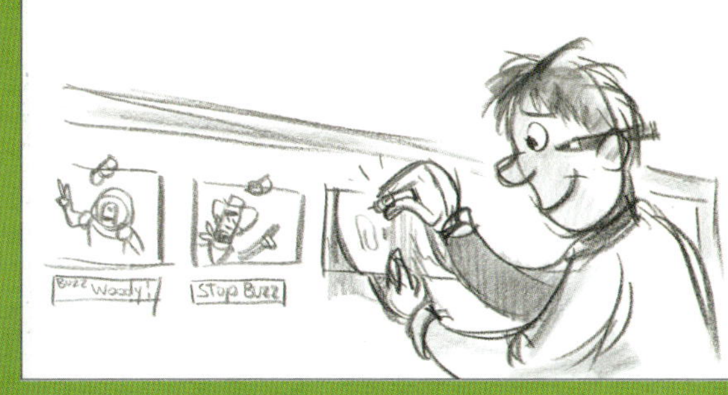

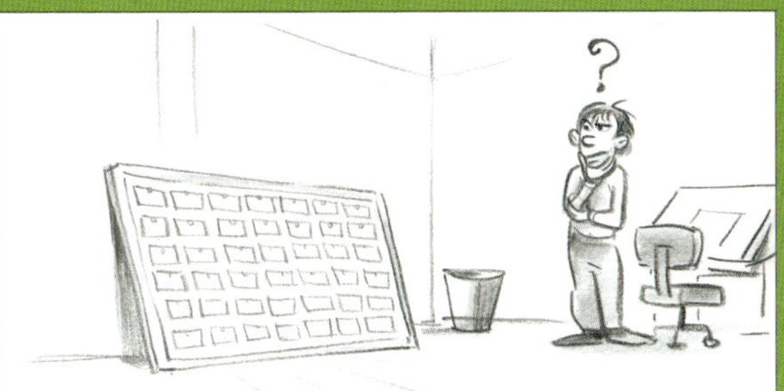

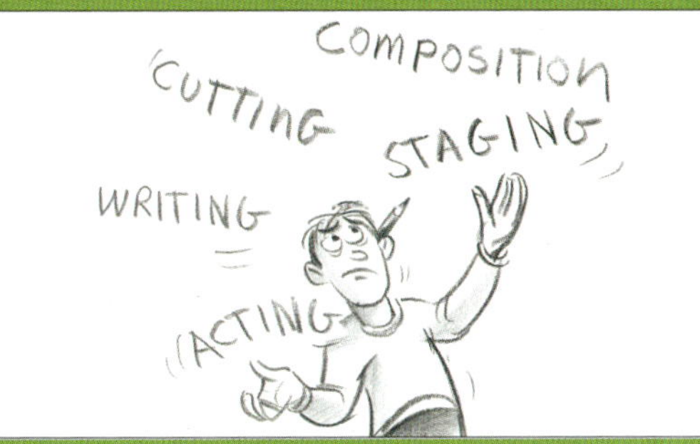

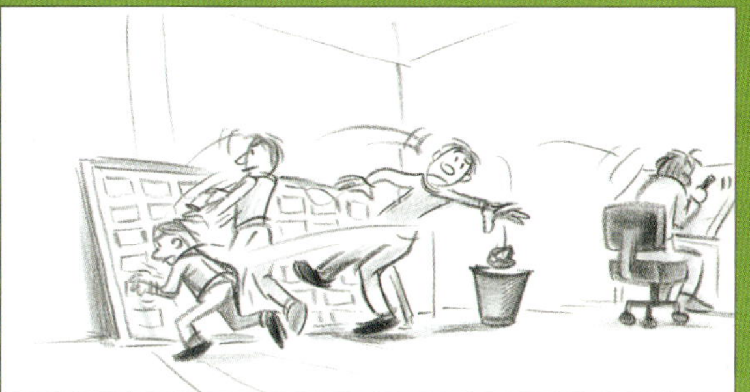

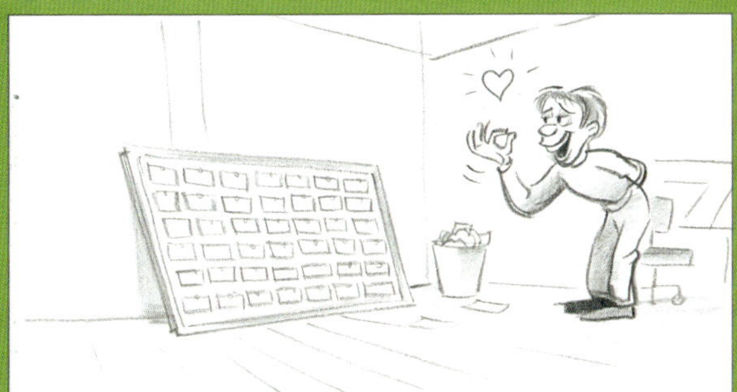

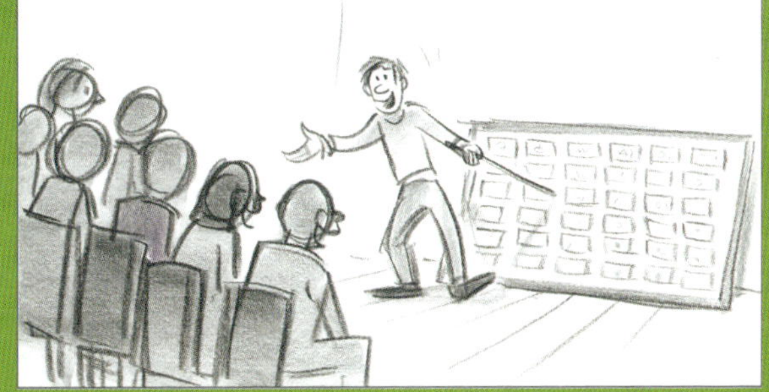

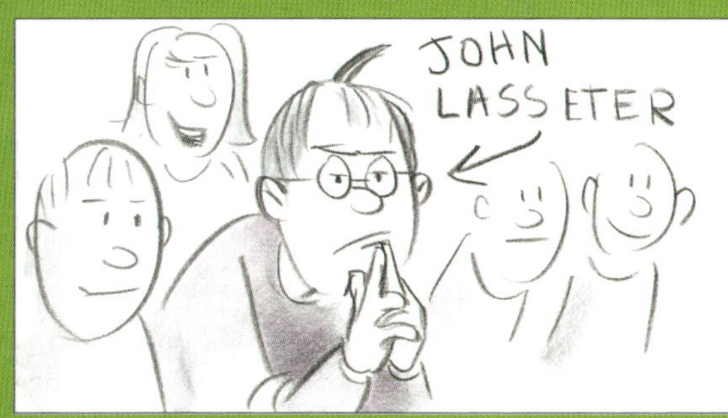

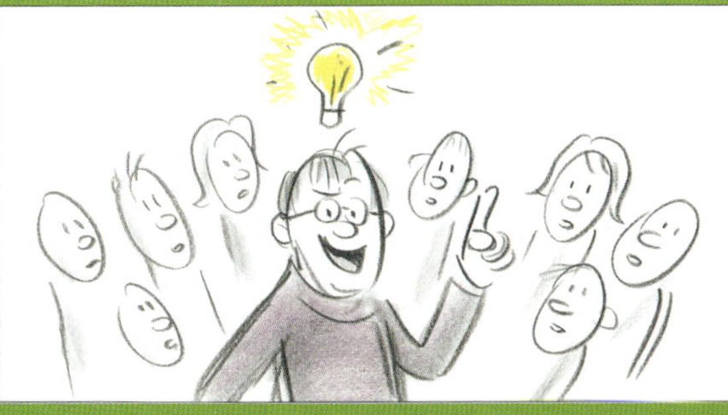

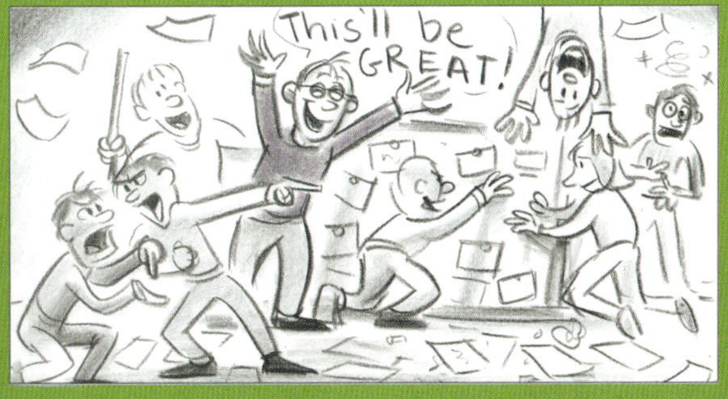

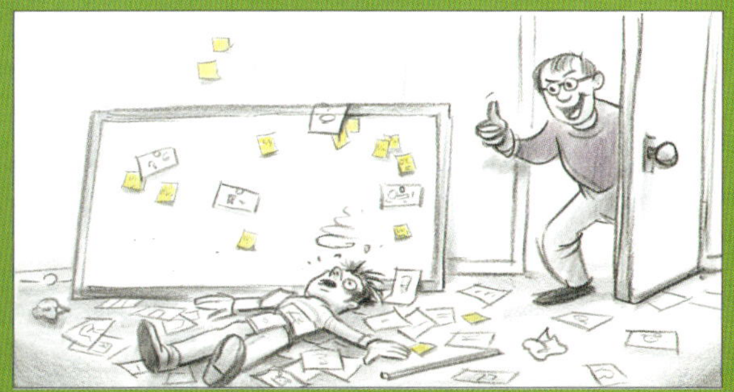

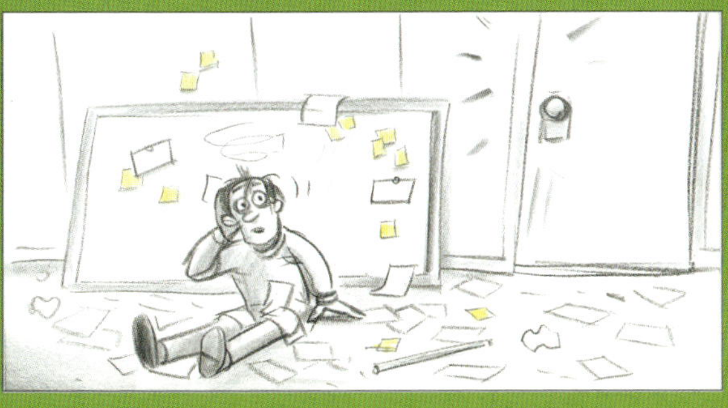

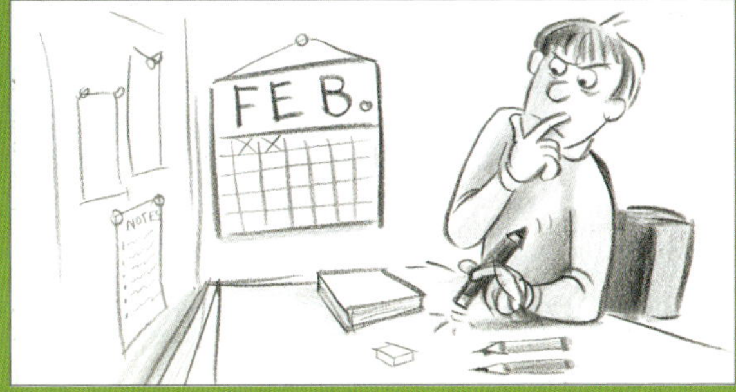

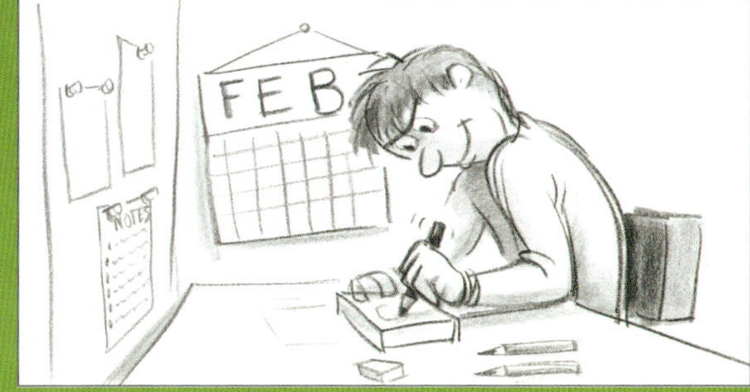

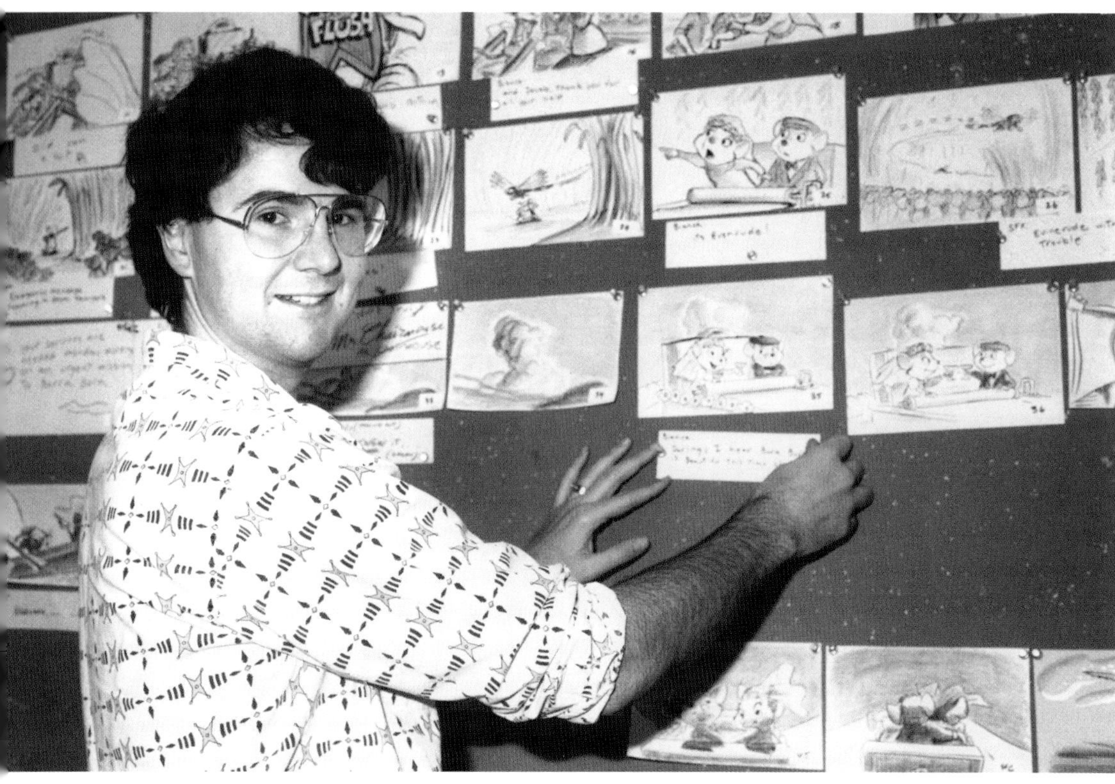

Joe Ranft as story supervisor for The Rescuers Down Under *(1990).*

After an acrimonious falling-out with Eisner (which eventually led to an expensive lawsuit settled in Katzenberg's favor), Katzenberg left Disney in 1994 to cofound DreamWorks SKG, a new studio with an animation division.

How and why two rival studios happened to be producing CGI features, with ants, that would both premiere in the fall of 1998 remains a matter of smoldering anger among Pixarians. On top of besting themselves, Pixar was now racing against the clock because they inadvertently became enmeshed in the Eisner/Katzenberg rivalry.[5]

"We only had two and a half years to make the movie," Anderson remembers. "We felt the weight of the world on our shoulders." The biggest problem was "we never knew what the movie was about," Unkrich says.

Onto the hefty shoulders of story supervisor Joe Ranft fell the daunting task of visualizing the narrative. *A Bug's Life* proved to be a most difficult film to work on, full of long hours with a story crew twice the size of *Toy Story*'s, but mostly inexperienced.

"Story at Pixar is not easy," according to Jerome Ranft, Joe's youngest brother, a gifted character sculptor. "It's brutal, a meat grinder."[6] Pixar story heads and their crews draw, redraw, and pitch new ideas every day. They listen to criticism and suggestions from the films' directors, plus a roving group of directors and producers nicknamed "The Brain Trust." Then they start all over again.

At one point, *A Bug's Life* had five different endings. Eventually, nearly forty thousand story sketches were drawn during production.

Ranft, however, was unflappably optimistic. Stanton recalls, "He had a way of making you feel like anything was possible, and any problem could be overcome. He brought out the best in you."

Throughout his career, Ranft repeated three mantras to himself, his crews, and his colleagues to encourage them: "Storyboarding is story reboarding." "The journey is the reward." And, most important, "Trust the process."

The latter means, "If it's a good idea, it will make its way back," explains Stanton. "Don't be afraid to throw it out. Everything has its moment in time. [Joe] persevered with inhuman patience."

"As story supervisor I work with the whole team," Ranft said in 1998. "To make sure that what [the story crew is] working on gets on the green, to use a golf analogy. To get [storyboards] in shape enough to get it in front of the directors."[7]

Eventually, all problems were solved and *A Bug's Life*'s became one of Pixar's most delightful offerings. *The New York Times* review said, "*A Bug's Life* makes jaunty, imaginative use of both extraordinary technology and bold storytelling possibilities within the insect world."[8]

When Ranft and Lasseter flew into Los Angeles to record the final voice tracks, however, a year's worth of animation and technical problem-solving lay ahead. Storyboards had finally been approved and, to mark the occasion, Ranft fulfilled a promise to the exhausted, loyal crew he'd led for nearly two years: he shaved his head.

Ranft crammed his bulky, six-foot five-inch frame and baldpate into what Lasseter called a "cheeseball" rental car and they drove down Sunset Boulevard. Both were tired and worried about the film as they turned into valet parking at the Mondrian Hotel.

Disney booked them into hotelier Ian Schrager's new $32 million "surreal stage set" (diaphanous curtains, glass walls) with a staff of high-energy, Armani-clad, model-perfect young men and women.[9] As their small car sidled up to the hotel's gleaming Mercedeses and Ferraris, the mood of the two men blackened.

Suddenly, inspiration struck Lasseter.

"Joe, Joe, Joe, Joe! Put in the teeth! Put in the teeth!"[10]

The teeth were a set of distorted false incisors ("Billy Bob teeth") Lasseter bought for Ranft. His pal Joe could always make Lasseter laugh with his zany, satirical, often black humor and spot-on impressions of colleagues and imagined characters.

"During times of pressure when I needed a laugh," Lasseter says, "I'd say, 'Joe, do the little English boy!' And he'd immediately become the character. It's no longer Joe Ranft! It's this little proper English boy talking about having peas and carrots for lunch. And you're rolling on the floor." Sometimes Ranft imitated a film executive with hooded eyes by taping his eyelids to his cheekbones and talking out of both sides of his mouth.

No character made Lasseter laugh harder than the dim-witted hillbilly who came out whenever "the teeth" went in.

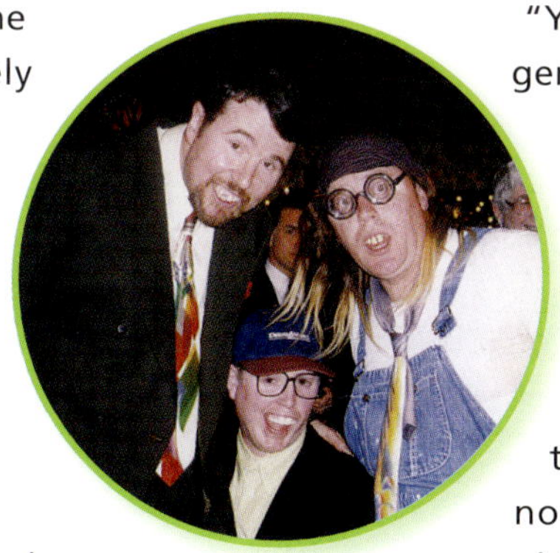

Joe Ranft (LEFT) *and friends wearing "Billy Bob teeth."*

An unctuous valet approached. Ranft inserted the dilapidated dentures and rolled a window down.

"Welcome to the Mond . . ." was as far as the valet got before being confronted by a large, bald redneck at the wheel, grinnin' wide with amazingly bad teeth and talkin' loud!

"Is this *hee-ah the Mun-dar-eee-aaann Hoe*-tel?"

The valet attempted to keep Ranft in the car. "I'm sorry, sir. Do you have a reservation?"

Lasseter suppressed his laughter, wondering "How's Joe going to get out of this?"

Ranft opened the door, his huge frame towering over the valet. "Yeah. Muh name's *Eisner.* Chucky Eisner! My uncle Michael's gonna let me make a moooovie!"

"Chucky" flashed a sweet, gaggle-toothed smile at the horrified and confused valet. Lasseter lost it.

Ranft was not finished. Ignoring icy glances from tailored women and men, Chucky marched into the grand hotel's lobby, marveling loudly:

"Gaw-damn! The Mun-daaar-eeean Hoe-tel!"

"He went all the way up and he checked in," says Lasseter, who followed laughing spasmodically. Chucky pointed out his "lucky tooth," a moldy molar stuck way up in his gums, to the concierge.

"Ya wanna rub it?" Chucky generously offered.

"That's what I love about Joe," Lasseter said, still talking in the present tense in his eulogy at Ranft's memorial service on August 21, 2005. "He would take something to the end. I made him promise to take those teeth everywhere. 'Cause no matter how awful a situation would be, you knew you had a secret weapon. Everything was going to be okay as long as Chucky Eisner came to visit you."

CHAPTER TWO

The Best Storyboard Guy in the Business

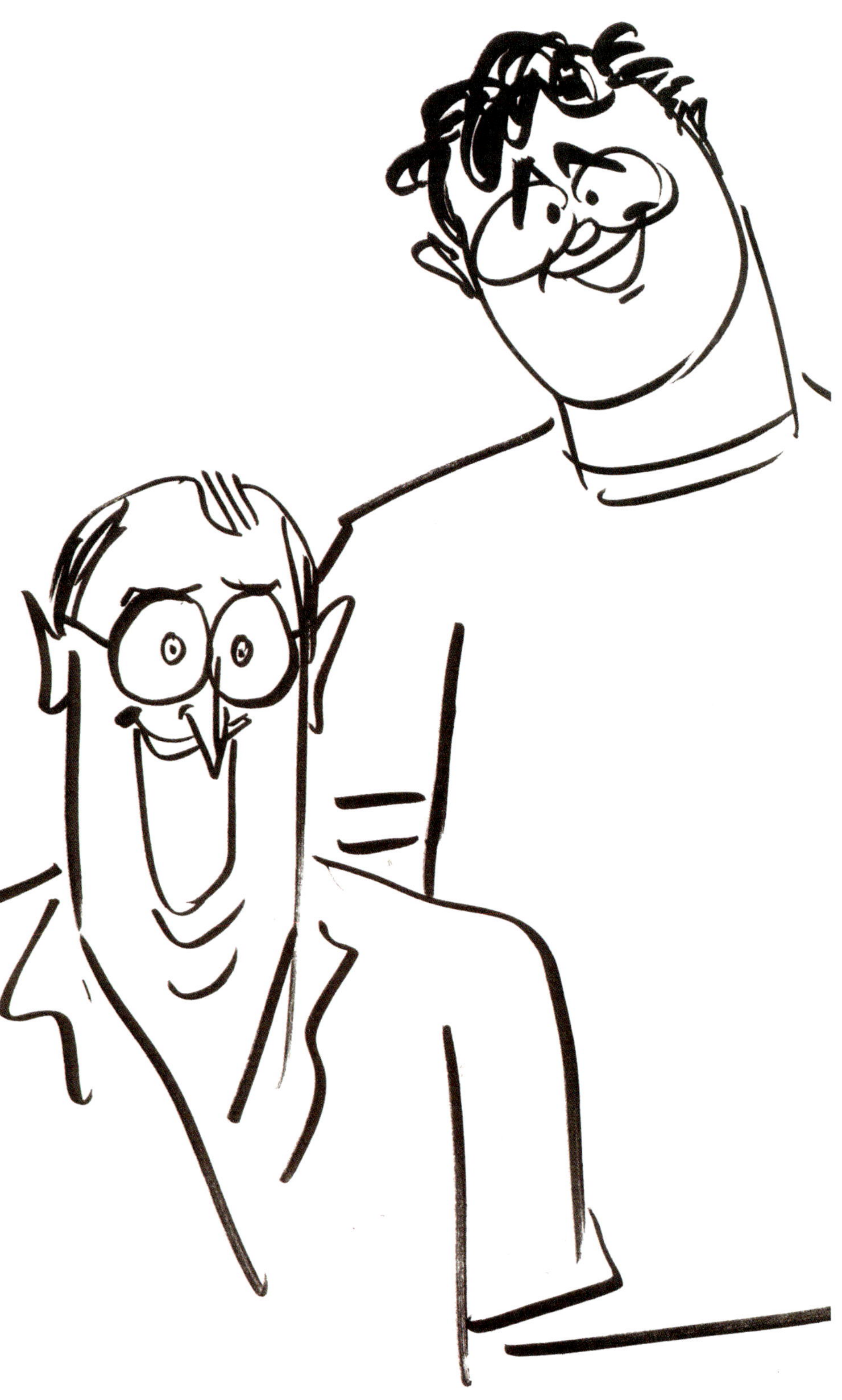

For nearly thirty years, Joe Ranft made funny, heart-tugging, irreverent contributions to storyboards, scripts, and sound tracks for animated films. He was his generation's go-to guy for narrative problem-solving, imaginative gags, and personality touches—from student films at CalArts (California Institute of the Arts) to *Cars*, the Pixar feature he cowrote and codirected with John Lasseter, released in 2006 the year after Ranft's death.

His peers consider him "the best storyboard guy in the business," according to Pete Docter. Lasseter praised him as "funny, poignant, original, [with] an infallible sense for how to structure a story."[1]

Ranft was intimately involved in some of the most significant animated films of his time. He was a major contributor to story and animation for *The Brave Little Toaster*, a breakthrough 1987 cartoon feature launched by a group who became acclaimed filmmakers. He was an important part of the Disney animation renaissance in the late 1980s to mid-1990s, contributing to *Who Framed Roger Rabbit*, *The Little Mermaid*, *Beauty and the Beast*, and *The Lion King*, among others.

He supervised the story for the 1990 Disney feature *The Rescuers Down Under*, as well as *Tim Burton's The Nightmare Before Christmas* in 1993 and the 1996 adaptation of Roald Dahl's *James and the Giant Peach*, two stop-motion features directed by Henry Selick.

Ranft cofounded the creative legacy of Pixar Animation Studios and its signature narrative style: sincere, inventive, original stories with appealing characters, and a sunny irreverent humor. "Joe helped to make Pixar what it is today," Lasseter confirms, "and he helped us elevate the craft of storytelling."[2] "Joe was really a major part of Pixar's soul," Docter says.

Many think he was the company's very heart.

"Joe had the heart," concurs Ed Catmull, Pixar

cofounder and president of Pixar Animation and Walt Disney Animation. "An extraordinary storyteller in getting the points across. Knew exactly what he wanted and needed."[3]

Throughout his career, Ranft came to the aid of filmmakers in need of a storyboard, a few good gags, a voice-over, or just a fresh eye and advice. Because of his generosity, his name appears in the credits for many films. "Andrew Stanton and I would tease him," Darla Anderson laughs. "'You're *not* that helpful,' we'd say. 'You're just a credit whore!'"

What elements made Joe Ranft the best story man of his generation?

Important was his natural acting ability and unfettered sense of humor, and skill for improvisation. Early on, Ranft enrolled in improv classes to help him develop empathy for personalities and situations.[4]

His pitches—talking through a storyboard using a pointer—held an entertainer's energy and timing. His test recordings often became part of the final sound track. Ranft was the voice of Heimlich, the ravenous Teutonic caterpillar in *A Bug's Life*; Lenny the Binoculars in *Toy Story*; Wheezy, the asthmatic squeeze-toy penguin in *Toy Story 2*; and Jacques the fastidious shrimp in *Finding Nemo*, among others.

His open-mindedness made him an invaluable team player and creative leader. He believed story artists must "develop flexibility, speed, teamwork, the ability to take direction, and work under pressure," and deal with constant "Changes! Changes! Changes!"[5]

Ranft strove to make "a drawing that lands you directly in an emotion."[6]

His draftsmanship was "a little lumpy and not as polished as others," Docter observes, but "when you look at his drawings with more wisdom, they all 'read' incredibly well, including what's going through the character's head."

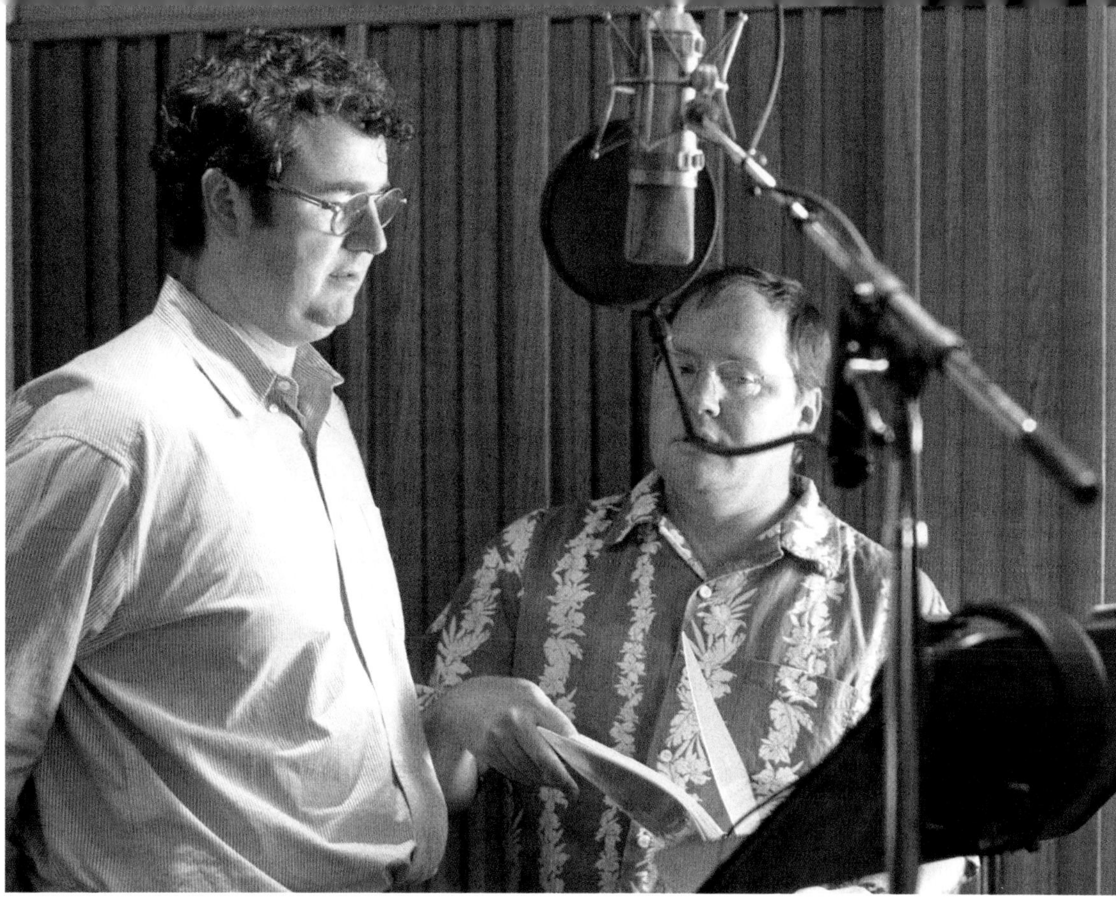

OPPOSITE PAGE: *John Musker's caricatures of John Lasseter and Joe Ranft.* ABOVE: *Lasseter and Ranft during a recording session.*

Brad Bird, director of *Ratatouille* and *The Incredibles*, says, "He could quickly conjure up a feeling and an attitude."[7]

Ranft was driven to perfect his art—and himself. "I don't think it came easy for him," Docter notes. "He really worked at it, pushed himself to make those drawings get his ideas across." Ranft studied sketches of great story men such as Bill Peet, Vance Gerry, and Joe Grant for inspiration. John Musker, cowriter/codirector of *The Little Mermaid*, sees similarities between the two Joes (Grant and Ranft) in their "thinking visually, thinking in terms of entertainment, letting the story grow out of character, not imposing but keeping it light." Both men sought whimsy in stories.[8]

Ranft drew every day: people at work, in his neighborhood, his family, his travels, and his surreal, dark dreams. He drew in scores of sketchbooks to improve his draftsmanship and observational skills, to refresh his imagination, and to discover more about Joe Ranft. He felt he was a work-in-progress.[9]

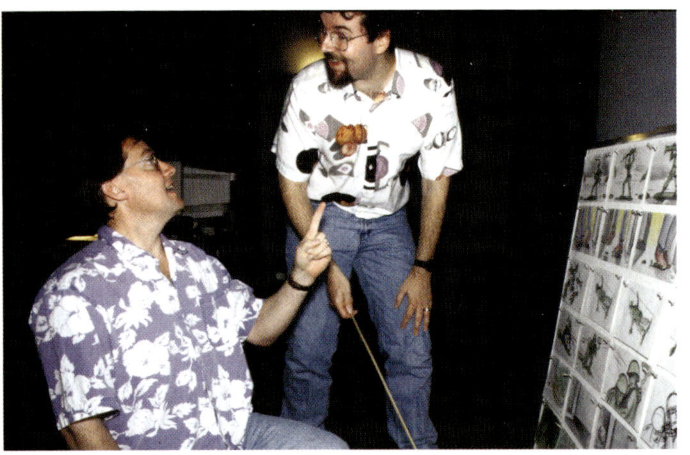

"I've never seen anyone try to improve himself as much as Joe," Henry Selick says.[10] Because he rarely discussed it, few knew Ranft "had a few dragons to slay leftover from his younger life," Su Ranft, Joe's wife, says. They stemmed from a difficult childhood as an overweight, prematurely tall, hyperactive, angry, often violent kid who felt freakish and out of place.

Animation anchored him. He channeled and controlled his feelings through macabre and outrageously funny imagery he drew professionally and in personal sketchbooks.

He also vowed never to get that violent or angry again. Ranft literally "changed directions," Andrew Stanton says. "There's a real before and after stage to Joe's life."

"He didn't get nice till later in life," says Jerome Ranft, his youngest brother, whom Joe "tormented" when they were kids. "Everyone thought he was such a saint—and he *did* become a really fantastic man—but early on he was tough." The laudatory tributes after Joe died were "half the picture," Jerome believes. "Because he still had that dark side he didn't share with everybody."

Bird recalls Ranft as a "relentlessly positive presence. It wasn't a Pollyannaish positive because he could be as dark and dirty with his jokes as you wanted to go—and he would go there if he sensed that you were ready for it. But his soul was positive and upbeat, and he could lift any room he entered."

He was "the kindest man I've ever known," Stanton says.

When Ranft decided to change his life, he joined "human potential" groups and focused on small personal gestures: conscious sensitivity toward others' feelings and striving for a positive approach to problem-solving at home and work. Eventually, Ranft moved on to bigger actions, donating considerable time, energy, and money to "cultural healing" organizations aiding and comforting society's less fortunate.

His tragic death deeply touched people from all walks of life. It wasn't just the loss of a great talent in his prime. To those who knew the man, worked with him, played and laughed with him, he had an easy warmth, a joy, and a magic based on his secret quest to help others.

"I would not be who I am, what I am, if it were not for Joe," Brenda Chapman, Pixar story artist and director, attests. "And I know there are an amazing amount of people out there who would say the same."[11] Bob Peterson, another Pixar story artist/director, considers Ranft "a huge mentoring influence" with "something special. He was like an angel" who "balanced [Pixar] and brought joy every day."[12]

"He really worked at who he was and doing what he wanted to do," Anderson observes. "People say nobody can do it like Joe did it. Well, he would disagree with that. He would say, look what I did with my life. You should try to do the same.

"In that regard he should be an inspiration to all of us."

LEFT AND BELOW: *John Lasseter and Joe Ranft discuss* TOY STORY *storyboards.* OPPOSITE PAGE, TOP: *John Musker drawings of Ranft versus nuns.* INSET: *Ranft in grade school, c. 1967.*

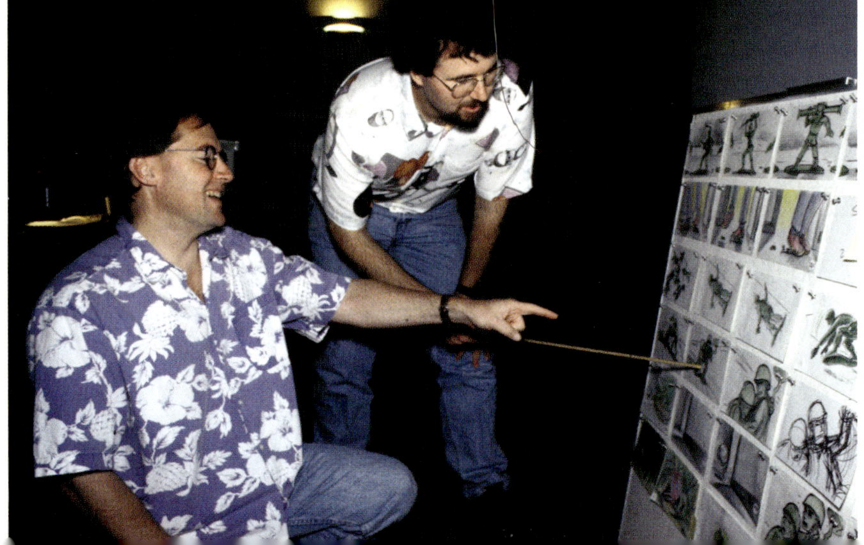

CHAPTER THREE

Spitting at Nuns

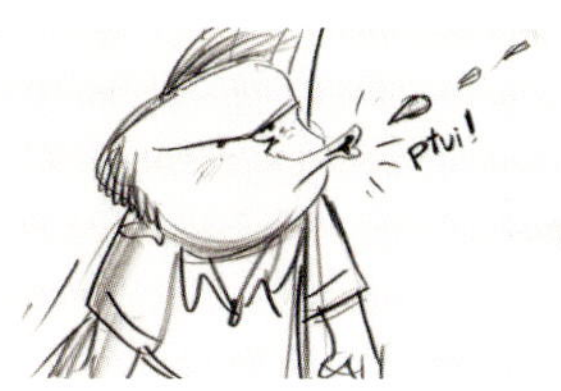

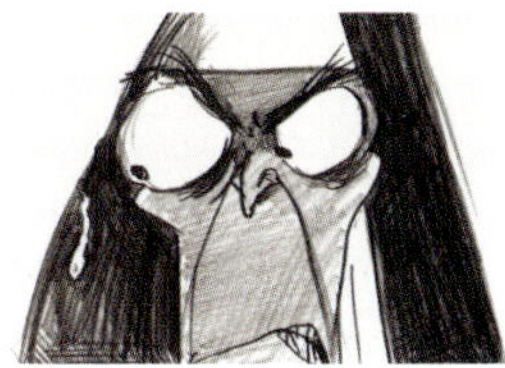

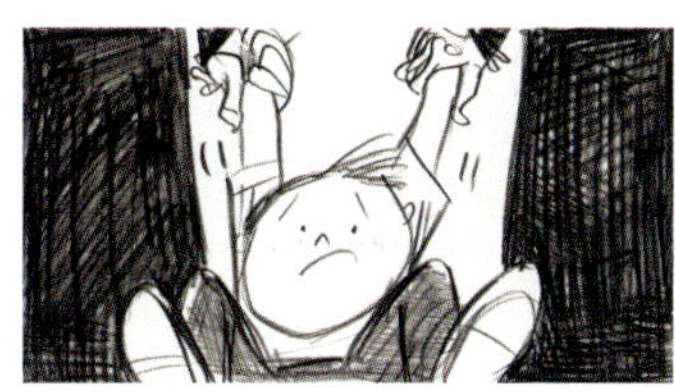

Joseph Henry Ranft was born on March 13, 1960, in Pasadena, California, and raised nearby in the middle-class suburb of Whittier, which coincidently was also the birthplace of John Lasseter.

Lasseter and Ranft did not know each other growing up—they met in 1978 at CalArts when Lasseter was a senior and Ranft a freshman. But "that little connection," Lasseter says, "made the bond for us."[1]

During the Revolutionary War, a Ranft from the German province of Hesse fought in America for the British as a mercenary. "The Hessians all stayed after the war saying, 'This is a pretty good deal,'" Ranft once cracked.[2]

James Joseph Ranft, Joe's father, born in 1924, was a mechanical engineer/designer of boiler feed pumps for Pacific Pump. Joe's "one-hundred-percent Irish" mother, Ruth Jordan, born in 1929, was a U.S. Army nurse for seven years. She served in Austria and Italy, attaining the rank of captain before leaving the service to marry on June 20, 1959.

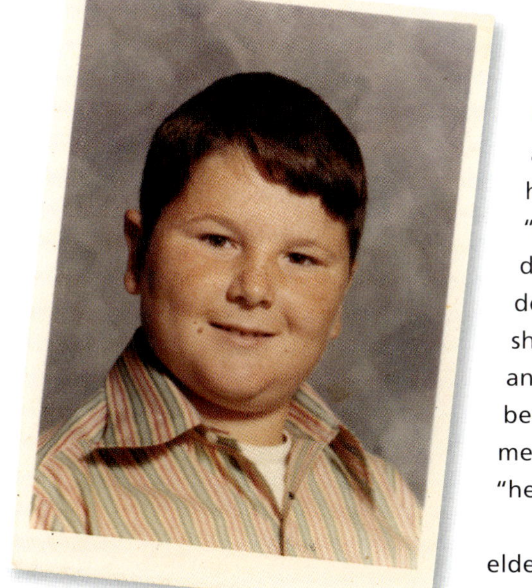

It was a big decision. Ruth enjoyed her independent life traveling and caring for soldiers and had only thirteen years before retirement. But Ruth was pushing thirty and in those days "if you weren't married by the twenty-eighth [birthday], you were an old maid," she recalls.

"I always say I got married and sentenced to forty years of hard labor!" she laughs, and her joke holds a kernel of truth: within eight years, Ruth gave birth to four children: Joseph, James, Ruth Ann, and Jerome.[3]

Joe was a "honeymoon" baby. Ruth looked forward to cuddling him, but Joe didn't like to be held. Inconsolable, he cried constantly.[4] He was also big—twenty-nine pounds at nine months—and hyperactive.

While Ruth was pregnant with Joe, her father *and* father-in-law died, so "she was under a great deal of stress," Su Ranft, Joe's wife, says. "She went from being this totally independent woman to being a wife, pregnant, her mother-in-law moves in, and there's this screaming baby."

Joe developed rapidly, but was uncoordinated because he was so big for his age.[5] "He wore size two toddler at nine months," Ruth says, and was late getting his teeth. "So here was this huge kid with one tooth in his mouth."

On Joe's first birthday, Ruth gave birth to his brother James, another large handful. At ages three and two, both were in harnesses and on leashes.[6] "Rambunctious" and "a dynamo" is Ruth's loving description of Joe, although she had some insight into his antics because she too had been a high-strung kid. "Let me put it this way," she says, "he was a challenge."

Neighbors thought her eldest son was a crazy boy and a hard-to-handle devil.[7] "Mischievous" is how John Tschudin, Joe's six-years-older neighbor, remembers him. He was in constant trouble because he teased his family relentlessly and at school "drove the nuns absolutely crazy!"[8]

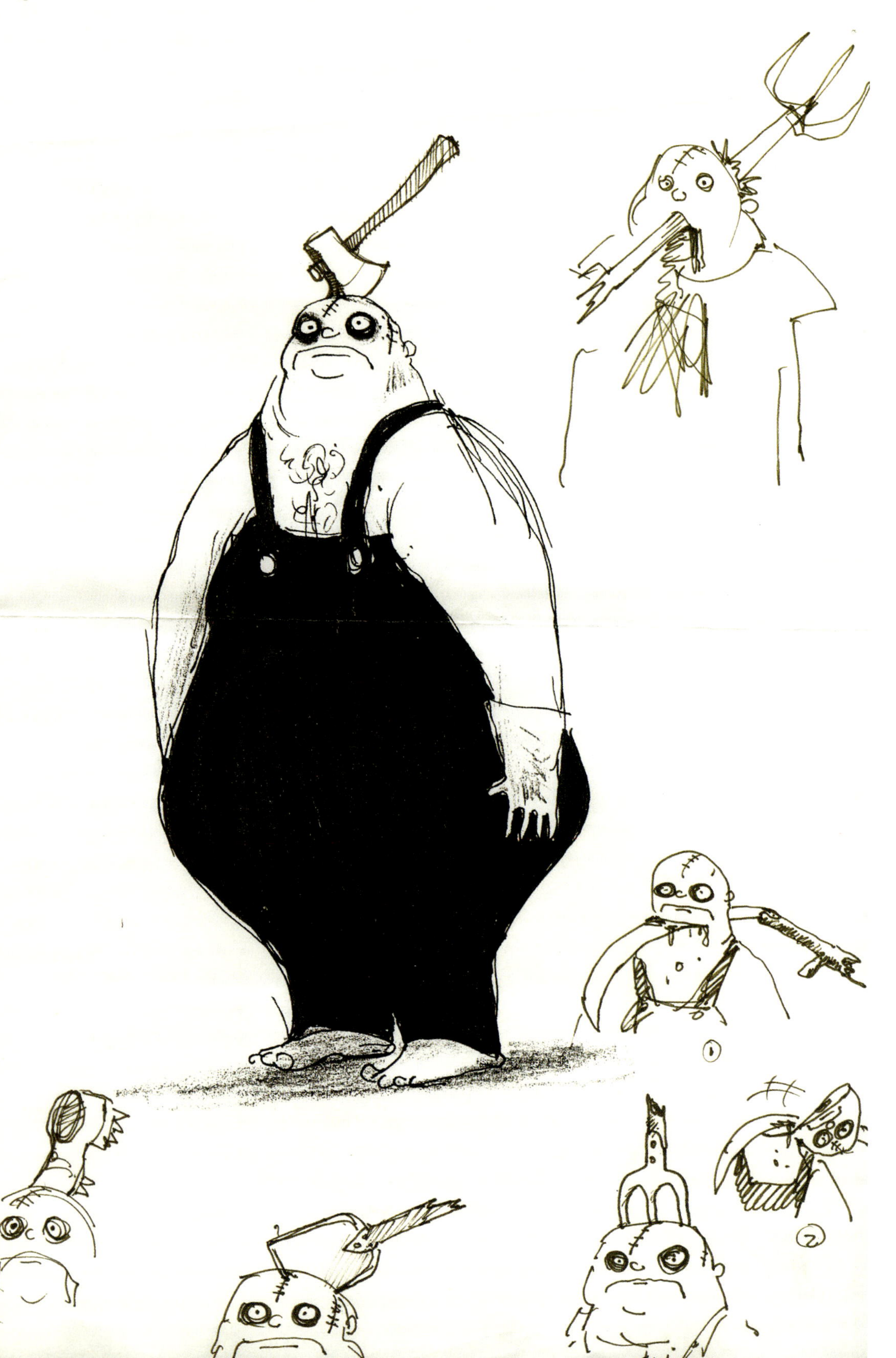

LEFT: *The dark side of Joe Ranft's imagination.*

In fact, Joe was expelled from parochial school in the second grade. Ruth and James, devout Catholics, wanted their children to have a solid religious education. Joe's uncontrollable energy, however, overwhelmed the good sisters. The big kid talked back in class with wisecracks. When a large Irish nun caught him sliding on a banana peel, she said his mother should give him a spanking. "Oh, she gave me one before I left," he shot back.[9]

When a teacher put Joe outside the door to literally remove the disruption in her classroom, the chubby disruption walked away. Frantic nuns phoned his mother, who combed Whittier looking for her missing seven-year-old. Meantime, Joe boldly walked the mile from school to home.

"He was so proud," Ruth warmly recalls. "He broke into his bedroom, and when I drove up he wanted a gold medal for having changed his clothes. You train your children to change their clothes when they come in from school. And he was very happy."

The incident that finally pushed the sisters beyond their not-so-infinite patience is unknown. It might have been throwing a cat onto the school's roof. Or his nasty practice of spitting at the nuns. In any event, six weeks before the term was over, he was in public school. After the first day, Ruth anxiously asked, "Joseph, did you like school?"

"Oh, Mom," he answered, "that Salisbury steak was out of this world!"

Ruth laughs because "at parochial school they had to carry their lunch. At public school they could buy their lunch. So he didn't mind the school."

Neither did his three siblings. Thanks to Joe, none had to attend Catholic school. "If you don't take him, you don't get any of them!" declared Ruth Ranft.

Today, Joe's behavioral problems and short attention span would be diagnosed as ADD (attention deficit disorder) and perhaps treated with

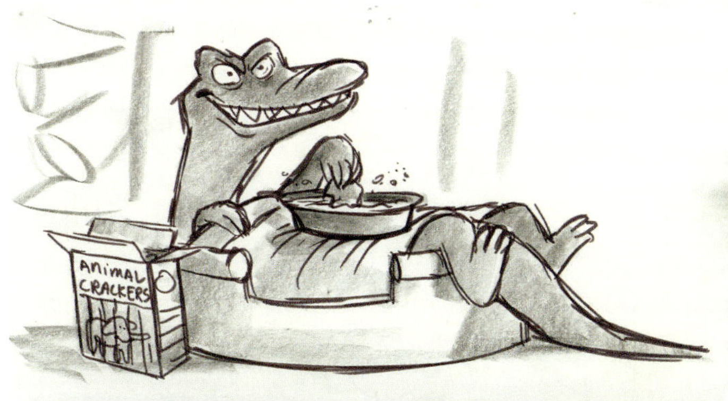

Ritalin. Studies suggest that ADD children "suffer primarily from a delay in brain development, not from a deficit or flaw," and kindergartners identified "as troubled do as well academically as their peers in elementary school."[10]

"They didn't have that diagnosis in those days," Ruth says. A conservative pediatrician prescribed twenty-five milligrams of Atarax, an antihistamine, to relieve Joe's tension and anxiety. He took the mild medication for four years. As his body weight grew to "man size," the dosage remained ineffectively low. "That doctor was just giving him the medication to shut me up," Ruth figures.

Physical ailments fueled Joe's angry hyperactivity. He had visual problems and couldn't write in first or second grade. "He was very frustrated 'cause he was very bright," Ruth says. "Therefore, he thought his job was to entertain the class." His parents gave him vision-therapy sessions.

Rapidly becoming taller and heavier, Joe developed a condition in which bones grow faster than the blood's circulation. Overusing the knee causes damage, so he couldn't run or ride a bike. His mom bought him wood-carving sets and magic kits containing playing cards and coin tricks, "things to do to keep him off his legs."

A strong, can-do woman whom the neighborhood kids affectionately called "Sarge" (after her Army experience), Ruth doted on all her children; but she was fiercely protective of her firstborn. Fearful that his peers would call him "Dumbo" because Joe's ears stuck straight out "like elephant ears," she had them surgically pinned back when he was four. But the kids made fun of him anyway.

"He was larger than everybody but wasn't athletic," John Tschudin recalls. Magic was his thing and he constantly practiced coin and card tricks. "Bullies picked on him 'cause he was geeky, a big gentle giant," says Tschudin, who "ran the block" and protected Joe. When a bully held him on the ground giving him "noogies," Tschudin hopped off his bike, put the bully in a headlock, and made him eat grass as "punishment for pickin' on Joe."

Joe, in turn, tormented his younger sister, Ruth Ann, and brother Jerome, the youngest of the Ranft kids. "He was an excellent tormentor," Ruth Ann says. "No meanness. Just a sick sense of humor."

Sometimes he and James teamed up against their younger siblings. When Tschudin babysat the Ranfts, little Ruth Ann "headed for the hills" because the babysitter allowed the boys to wrestle in the living room. "You wouldn't believe the demolition and calamity from these three huge man-kids. Wrecking furniture, pummeling, and throwing each other down. I used to sit there laughing!"

Joe's solo turns at terror were "more mental" than physical. Ever the performer, he staged "séances" for Jerome and Ruth Ann in a darkened hallway. Seated at a table, he did magic tricks for the captive audience of two, who were duly shocked when an illuminated skull (from Disneyland's Jungle Cruise attraction) appeared from thin air.

Sometimes, ketchup dribbling from his mouth, Joe rolled on the living room rug pretending to have convulsions. And Jerome would cry. Often while he was babysitting Ruth and Jerome, Joe let his large frame fall to the floor, remaining still so long "we actually got nervous," Jerome recalls. Suddenly, Joe flipped his eyelids inside out and became a zombie. "Scared the crap out of us!"

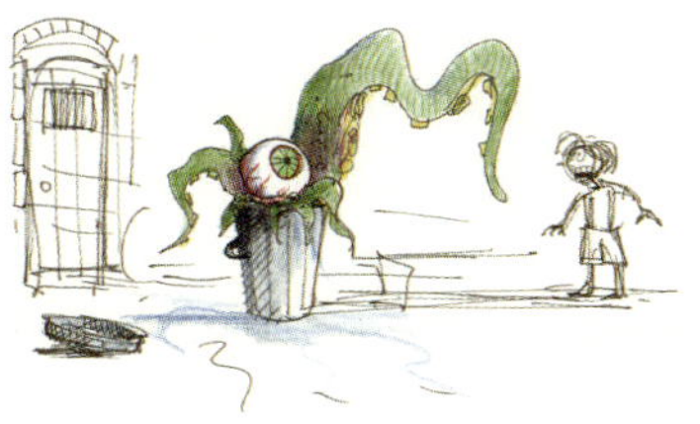

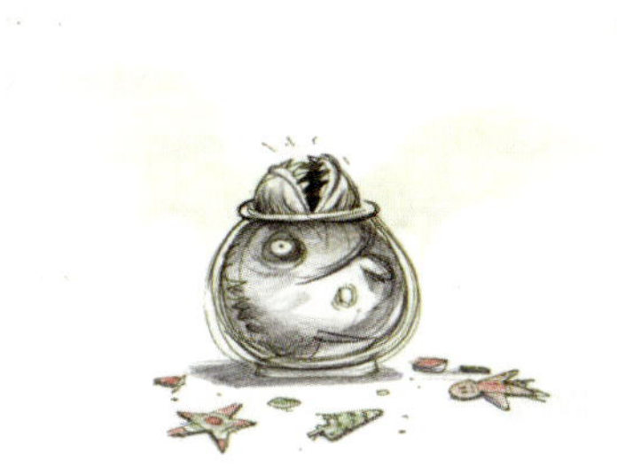

ABOVE: *More of Joe Ranft's free-range nightmares.*

What would become of Mrs. Ranft's overweight, overgrown, hyperactive, troublesome boy who seemed interested only in magic tricks and sick pranks?

There were some hopeful glimmerings. For example, Mrs. Brownfield, a fourth-grade teacher, actually *liked* Joe. "Your son is going to do you proud one day," she told Ruth. Her prediction was based on the fact that, in all of her years of teaching, Joe was the only student who read books she recommended and asked questions about them in class.

In seventh grade he won a prize in a classroom speech contest for "Humorous Interpretation," reciting an original story from the viewpoint of "the Persecuted Pencil."

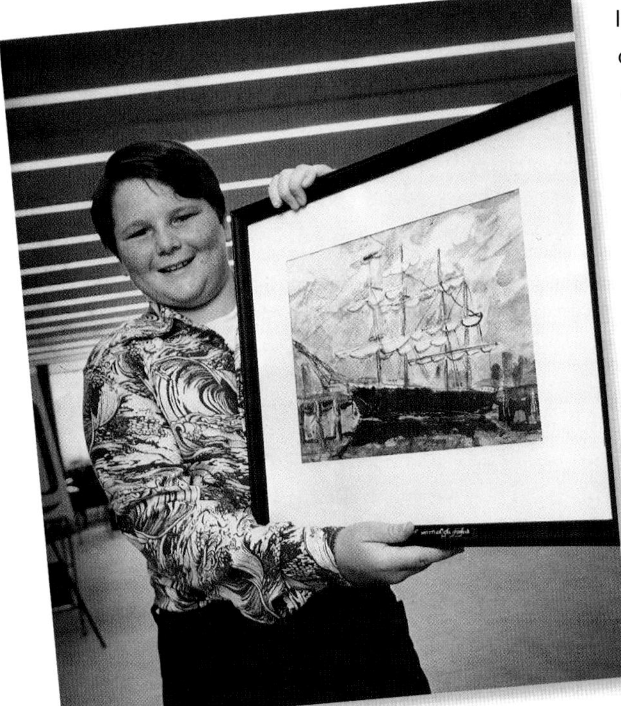

A thirteen-year-old Joe Ranft displays his prize-winning painting.

> I was . . . owned by this girl named Gertrude who passed notes to another girl in class. I didn't have much patience with her and commented on the situation. The drama was that the teacher was going to discover them. I laughed when she got caught. The big punch line was "It's detention time for Gertrude!" All the kids laughed and she got so upset, she breaks me. The spunky pencil got the last line: "Just call me Shorty!"

Ranft's talent for drawing blossomed despite banishment from school art classes because, as Ruth puts it, "he was so naughty." One day he brought home a realistically drawn and shaded banana.

Surprised and delighted, his parents bought expensive art materials *and* magician's paraphernalia. "You could tell he had talent," his proud mother says. "We encouraged him in any way."

It was a wise investment. In 1973, thirteen-year-old Joe's oil painting of a sailing ship was selected in a national competition among sixth graders for an Equitable Life Society calendar. A news photo shows the smiling rotund artist wearing a psychedelic shirt, pointing to his painting, as three teachers (or contest judges) grin at his gesture. The picture predicts the future: Joe Ranft amusing an audience with a storyboard pitch.

"I wasn't doing so good in school," he said years later. But after winning the calendar contest, he "decided to become an artist."

At Monte Vista High School in Whittier, he enjoyed drawing, appearing in school plays (small parts in *My Fair Lady*), acting classes, and "goofing around and doing voices." He and a partner performed magic shows at grade schools and Joe became a junior member of the Hollywood Magic Castle, a private clubhouse "devoted to the advancement of the ancient art of magic." Ranft's graceful hand movements held the pantomimic expressiveness of Marcel Marceau or Fayard Nicholas.

His skewed sense of humor was reinforced by devoted listening to recordings of The Firesign Theatre satire troupe and by watching *Monty Python*. He became a self-described "movie nut," obsessed with horror films featuring Dracula, the Wolfman, and Frankenstein. At age fifteen, Joe found his taste in cinema expanding when he and a friend discovered an art-film house "run by a motorcycle guy" that showed triple features. One summer he "clicked into" three films starring Malcolm McDowell, all of them about rebellious youth, counterculture violence, and surreal black humor: Stanley Kubrick's *A Clockwork Orange* (1971) and Lindsay Anderson's *If* (1968) and *O Lucky Man!* (1973).

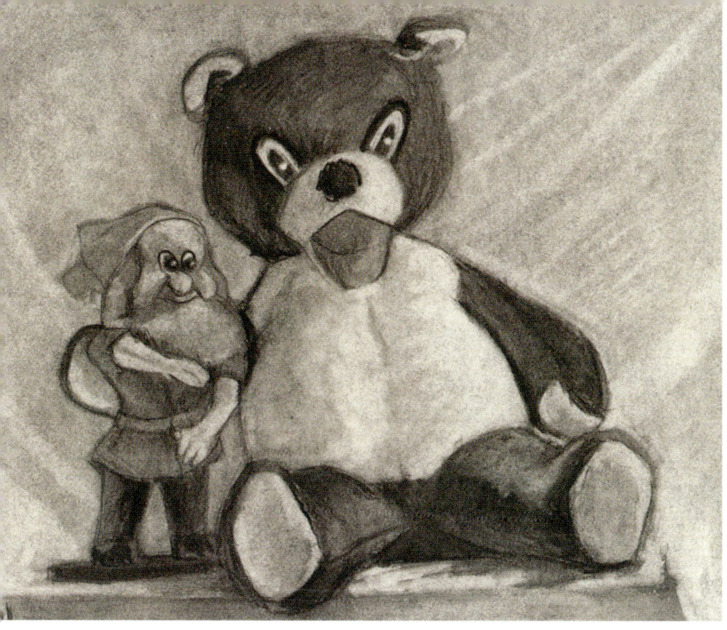

"I was just soaking it in," he said. "I didn't analyze it too much. Just looked at all these ideas expressed in these weird ways." He also watched "tons" of animated cartoons.

In 1977, a short-lived PBS series hosted by Jean Marsh called *The International Festival of Animation* fascinated him. The shorts were in various styles and techniques by independent animation filmmakers, and Ranft loved the personal quality in the artwork of National Film Board of Canada films. In Caroline Leaf's *The Street*, for example, sequential images were painted on glass and photographed frame by frame; so the hand of the artist was apparent throughout, and the process of animation itself was revealed.

"I could see someone did that," Ranft remembered. "You could see the drawing in it. I said, 'Wow! I'd like to do this. Make my own animated films.'"

He had no idea how to learn animation. He agreed with his parents: "I have to make money from this art pursuit thing." His mother encouraged him to become a commercial artist and paid for Saturday art classes for teens at Pasadena's Art Center College of Design. Charcoal still lifes of flowers and statues soon filled the Ranft home.

He never took life or figure-drawing classes, which would have strengthened his basic draftsmanship skills. As a result, Ranft "struggled to draw my whole life. I had more ideas than the ability to draw them."[11]

His Art Center teachers advised him to attend state college to get "some craft of drawing" under his belt before applying to their intensive college program. Then one night, while watching TV's *The Midnight Special* (hosted by Wolfman Jack), he saw an animated short made by a student (Mark Kirkland) at the California Institute of the Arts.[12]

So there was a *school* where you could learn how to do animation. Excited, he sent for the CalArts brochure, which offered programs in both experimental and character animation. He applied to the latter because "I just knew. Oh, there's these expressive drawings of characters and they're thinking, and I said, 'Oh, I want to do that!'"

Ranft connected his love of magic with animation. "I liked the whole thing of evoking a response from audiences through magic, the whole thing of illusion. Animation's kind of the ultimate illusion, of life, of a character that doesn't really exist."[13]

As summer ended, he quit his part-time job as a soda jerk at Farrell's Ice Cream Parlour with a spectacular sick joke. On his final night, while he was cleaning the soda fountain and counter, twenty people walked in demanding sundaes. Ranft obliged: he filled his mouth with strawberry syrup, walnut toppings, and whipped cream, then spat it out onto himself and, for a finale, faked a huge seizure on the floor. People fled. The manager warned: "That Ranft better not ask for a reference!"

In the fall of 1978, "that Ranft" arrived at CalArts in Valencia, California.

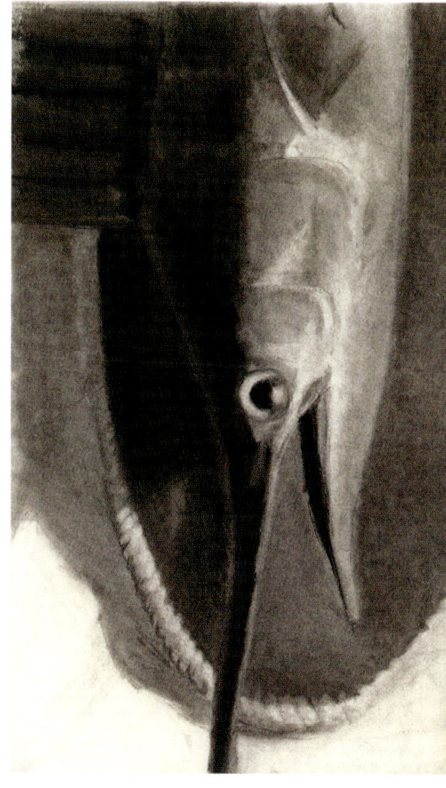

THIS PAGE: *Charcoal still life drawings by a teenage Joe Ranft.*

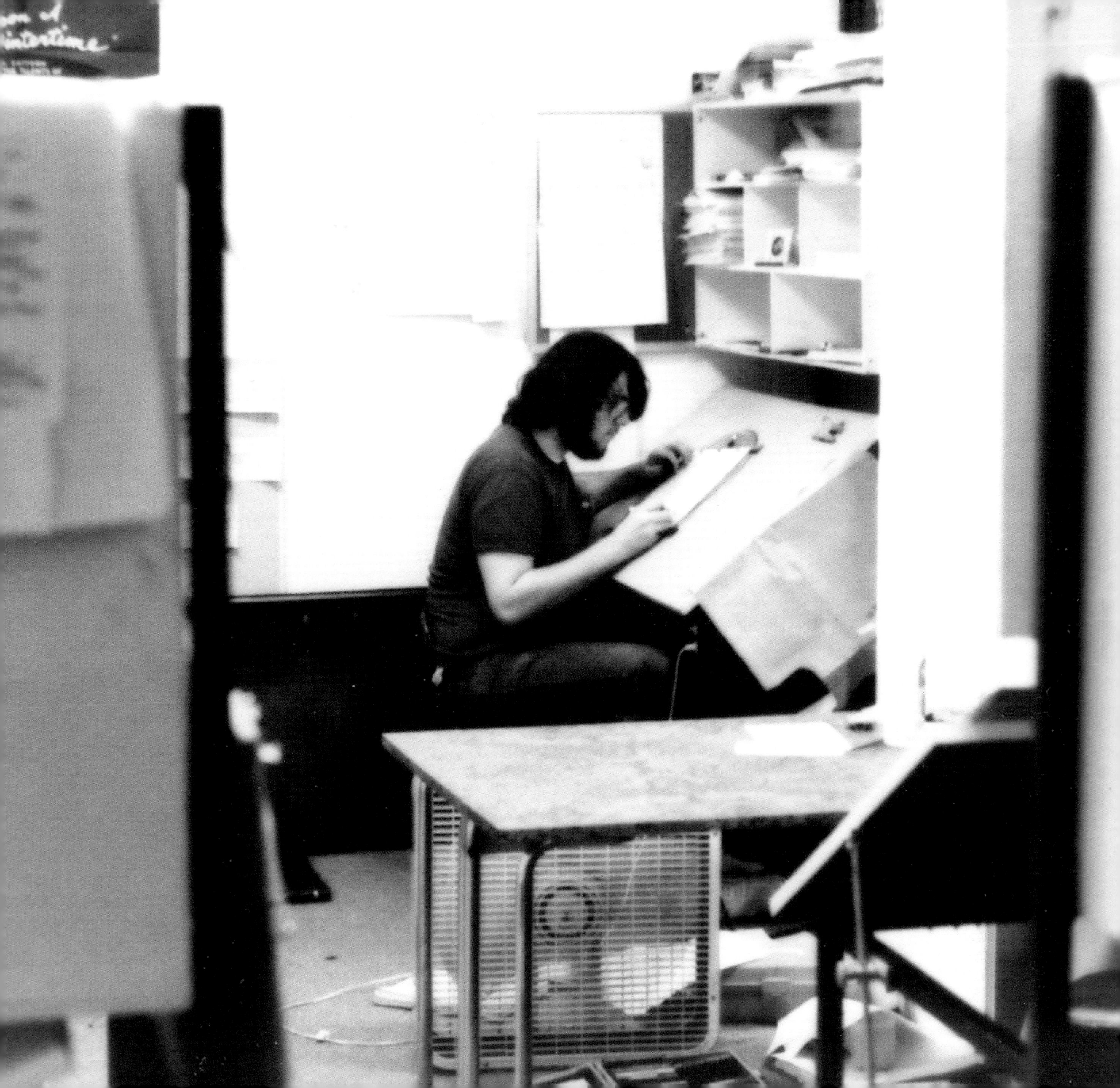

Walt Disney (1901–1966) was the catalyst and financial backer of CalArts, an arts education experiment that merged the Los Angeles Conservatory of Music and the Chouinard Art Institute. Disney's interest in arts-education began in the 1930s when his animators studied at Chouinard. Later, Chouinard faculty members taught classes on the Disney lot in a unique "school" where old and new films were analyzed, lecturers discussed color theory and animal and human anatomy, and field trips were organized to attend dance, music, and theatrical performances.

Intermingling graphics, painting, dance, music, film, and sound fed Disney's dream of merging the creative arts into a Hollywood manifestation of Wagner's theory of *Gesamtkunstwerk* ("total artwork").[1] Ultimately, this led to *Fantasia*, the 1940 animated concert feature combining classical music, choreography, color, and art with innovative technology such as stereophonic sound.

Disney's wish to blend the creative arts in a learning environment found ultimate expression at CalArts. "I like the workshop idea, with students being able to drop in and learn all kinds of arts," he said in 1964. "You know, a kid might start out in art and end up as a talented musician. A school should offer a kind of cross-pollenization that would develop the best in its students. . . . Students will be able to take anything—art, drama, music, dance, writing. . . . We don't want dilettantes at CalArts. We want people with talent. That will be the one factor in getting into CalArts: talent."[2]

In 1970, CalArts founded an experimental animation department, which Jules Engel headed for thirty-three years until his death in 2003 at age ninety-four.[3] An abstract painter and filmmaker who worked on *Fantasia*, *Bambi*, and the innovative United Productions of America (UPA) shorts (featuring Gerald McBoing Boing and Mr. Magoo), Engel was an inspiring teacher. He nurtured several generations of film artists interested in personal expression in animation, and his program earned an international reputation as an incubator of avant-garde filmmakers.

The Disney studio, however, was unhappy because CalArts was not graduating talents specifically trained in the "art of acting animation." And the studio had a dire need for young blood. It struggled to complete *The Aristocats*, released in 1970, the first cartoon feature completed without the guidance and input of Walt, who died several years earlier. If it failed, the animation division would close. Though a minor effort, the film became a box office hit, which convinced Disney management that a continuing audience—and revenue stream—for Disney cartoon features existed.

If the spirit was willing on the part of executives, the flesh of the aging Disney animation staff was weak. Creatively exhausted veteran animators, story artists, designers, and craftspeople were retiring or dying at an alarming rate. Second-tier talents moved into power positions; like the execs, they were unwilling or unable to make innovatively creative decisions. They remained stuck in the tried-and-true.

The studio decided CalArts needed a "feeder" school like Chouinard in the 1930s, one that could train gifted young talent in traditional character-based animation techniques for features and television shows aimed at a general public. In 1974, Character Animation was added to the CalArts curriculum. The new department, separate from Engel's, was headed by Jack Hannah, a Disney veteran of nearly thirty years' experience as the writer of twenty-one Disney shorts and director of ninety-four more, most starring Donald Duck, Chip 'n' Dale, and Humphrey the Bear.

LEFT: *Joe Ranft pulls an all-nighter animating at CalArts in January 1980. Photo by classmate Al Holter.*

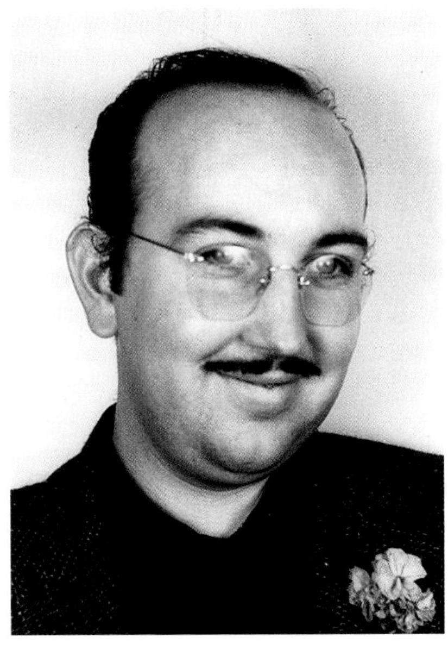

Story man/director T. Hee in the early 1940s.

Augmenting the faculty were other gifted former Disney artists. Bob McCrea and Hal Ambro taught animation; Elmer Plummer taught figure drawing; A. Kendall O'Connor taught layout; the onomatopoetically named T. (Thornton) Hee taught caricature and storyboarding. Bill Moore, a legendary Chouinard teacher (from 1936 to 1970) of color and design, was the only non-Disney staffer.

"The curriculum was tough and the teachers acted more like directors," says animator Nancy Beiman (*Hercules*, *Treasure Planet*), a student in the first class (1975 to 1979), which included John Lasseter, Brad Bird, Jerry Rees, Darrell Van Citters, and John Musker.

"They weren't there to make you feel good; they were there to help you work. When Elmer Plummer told me that I wasn't drawing as well as the boys, I was mad—but not at him—and decided I was going to make sure that I caught up. I worked two hours a day on my sketchbook and did a minimum of ten pages each day, and I did improve. Mr. Moore's design class was a particular torture since none of us had any training at all," recalls Beiman. She continues, "Moore was brutal in his critiques, which sometimes led to a student (this one) having to leave the room suddenly. Once again, I was mad . . . but not at him. (Well, sometimes at him.) I worked until I understood the basic principles of design that he was describing. It was ultimately the most important class of them all; if you don't know good design, you can't do a good pose or background. It's the core of everything else. Ken O'Connor and T. Hee were not as aggressive in their critiques but could be just as determined. All of them loved this art form and did not want to see it die with them."[4]

Animation luminaries frequently dropped by to lecture, including Disney animators Frank Thomas, Ollie Johnston, Ward Kimball, and Milt Kahl; and, from Warner Bros., director Chuck Jones, story man Mike Maltese, and designer/layout artist Maurice Noble.

When Ranft entered CalArts in 1978, Tim Burton and John Lasseter were seniors. Among his twenty freshmen colleagues were Brian McEntee (future art director of *Beauty and the Beast*), Rick Heinrichs (future production designer of *Pirates of the Caribbean* and several Tim Burton films), Mark Henn (future supervising animator on *Lilo & Stitch*, *Mulan*, *The Lion King*), Mark Dindel (future director of *Cats Don't Dance*, *The Emperor's New Groove*), and Tony Anselmo (future animator on *The Little Mermaid* and *Tarzan*, among other films, and, since 1987, the voice of Donald Duck).

Ranft absorbed the CalArts experience enthusiastically and was well-liked by classmates and teachers. Even the prickly Moore praised Ranft for his quick grasp of design principles.

One day O'Connor brought in Bill Peet's exemplary story sketches for *Song of the South*. Peet being arguably Disney's greatest story artist, his expressive drawings in pastel had an electric effect on Ranft. "They just knocked me over! I knew that's what I wanted to try to accomplish, wanted to learn how to do that," he said. "They were so alive. They were still drawings screaming to be animated. They're lean and the stories really move."

Inspired, Ranft shifted focus from animator to story man. In his own boards he sought to "work out something that would be good to animate. An animator's gonna say, 'Give me that scene!'"

"From the outset," Anselmo recalls, "Joe was a natural with story."[5] When Anselmo was stuck for an ending to his thesis film about a baby hyena who couldn't laugh, he took the storyboard to Hannah for advice. The gruff, kindly former boxer looked it over and paused for a long time.

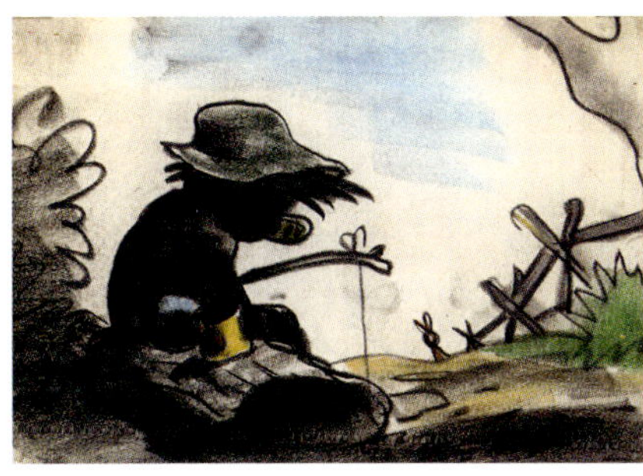
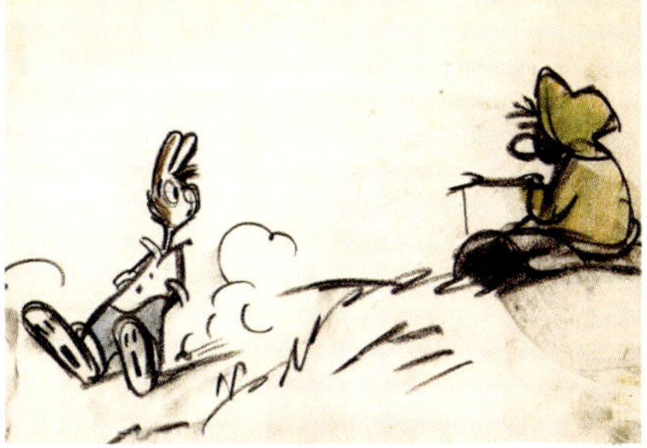
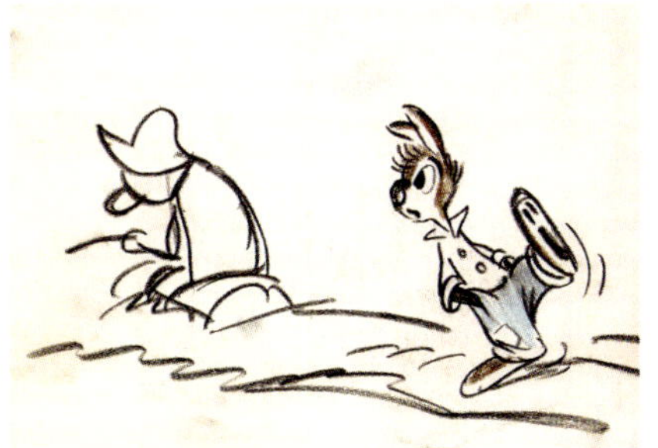
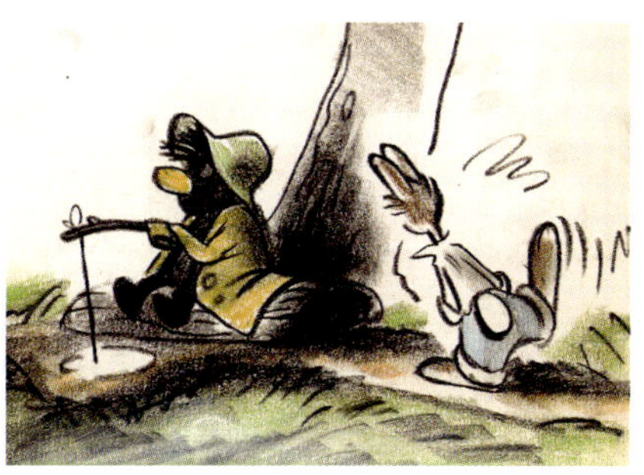

THIS PAGE: *Bill Peet's legendary storyboards for* SONG OF THE SOUTH *(1946).*

"Say, at the end," he finally suggested, "why don'cha have a little inchworm inch his way into the shot, tip his little top hat, and then iris out?"

Forcing a smile at the non sequitur, Anselmo thought, "That's it? An inchworm? I've just gotten myself into a corner 'cause if I don't use Jack's ending he'll be offended."

He ran for help to Ranft, who, upon hearing Hannah's suggestion, "laughed out loud hard for about ten minutes." Then he snatched some paper and in seconds sketched out six panels for a perfect ending: a stork doctor, after all medical attempts fail, puts on a clown suit and performs old vaudeville gags, which induces a laughing jag in the baby hyena. Iris out.

"Redraw it in your hand," Ranft instructed Anselmo. "And tell Jack you wanted to run this new idea by him."

Hannah looked over both versions and smiled broadly. "Gee, that new idea is a keen ending. Much better than mine. Use that new one!"

"Joe had saved my film anonymously," says Anselmo. "Without offending Jack."

On free evenings, Ranft and his colleagues went to see cult movies. "Joe exposed me to a whole new genre in motion-picture history," Anselmo says, "such as *Harold and Maude* (1971) and *Pink Flamingos* (1972)."

Sometimes Ranft sat in on Engel's lectures. "He'd show experimental films made with pinscreens," Ranft recalled, referring to an obscure technique using hundreds of tiny pins pushed frame by frame through a screen to create textured imagery. "Jules knew we were from Character Animation, and he'd throw glances at us and say, 'Of course, this isn't Donald Duck!'"[6]

Ranft hung with the experimental film kids, feeling akin to their thinking outside of cartoon formulas. When Ranft pitched the plot of his second-year film, he (like Anselmo) got stuck in Hannah's thick sensibilities.

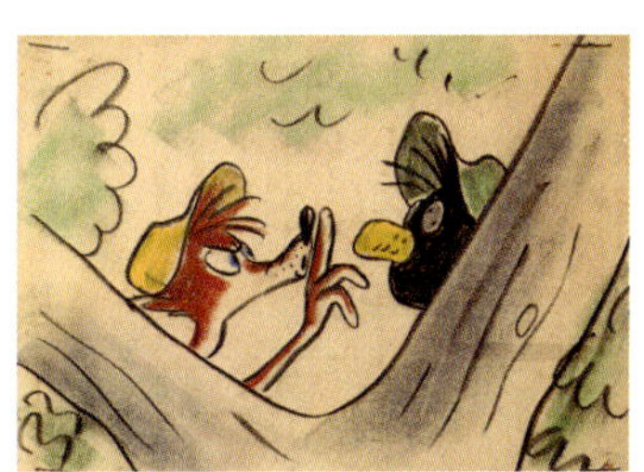
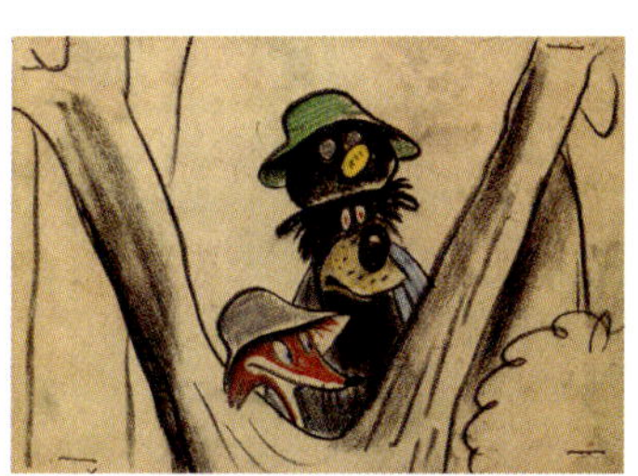
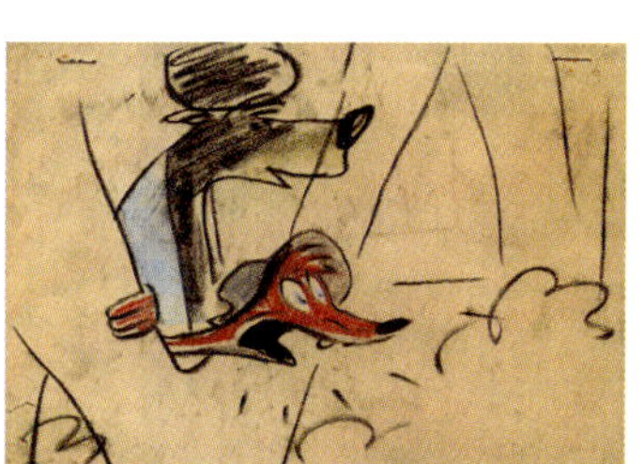
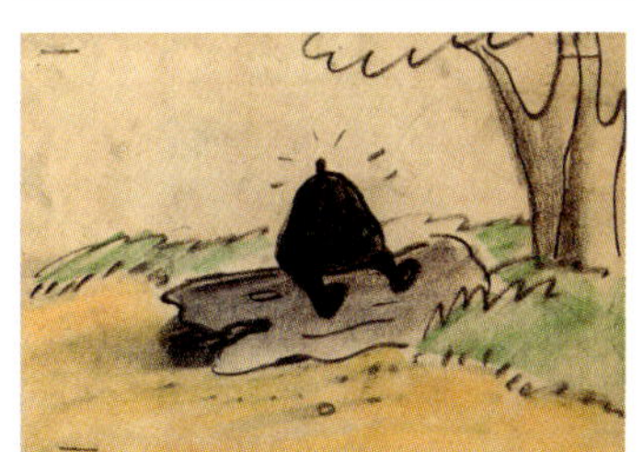
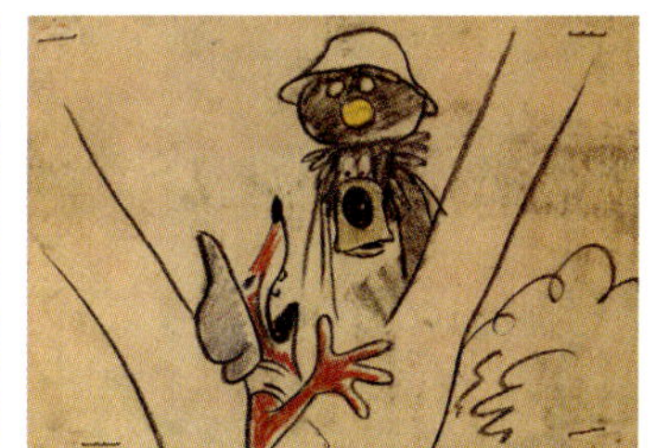
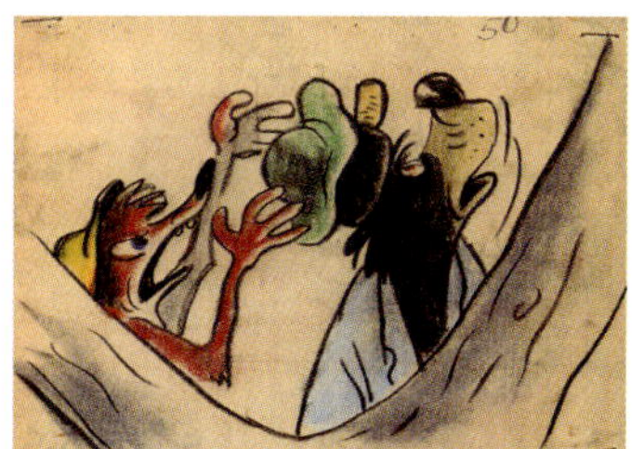
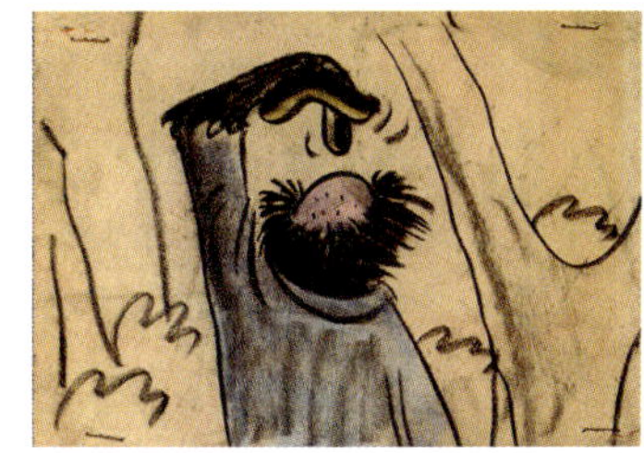

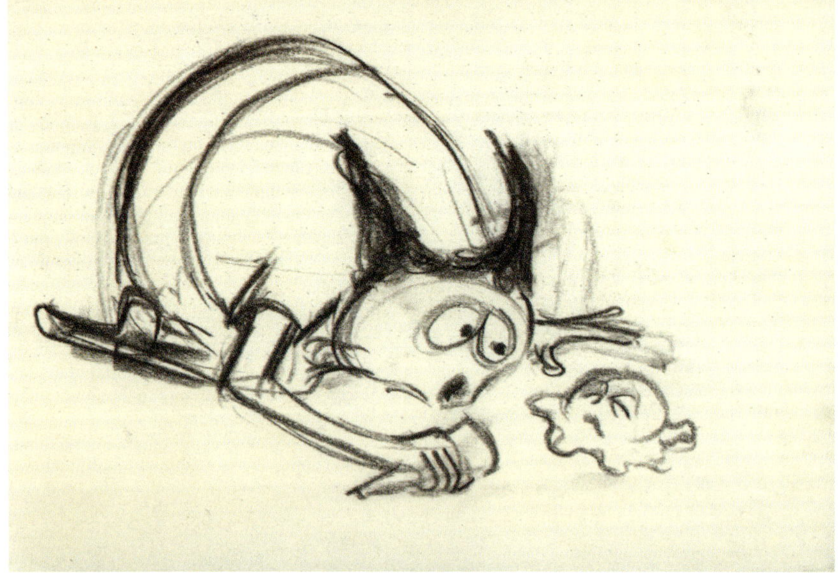

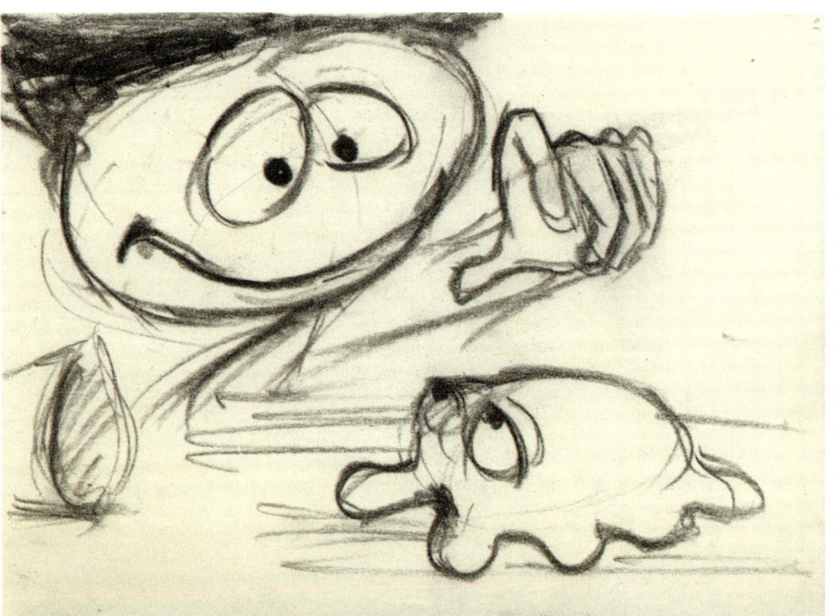

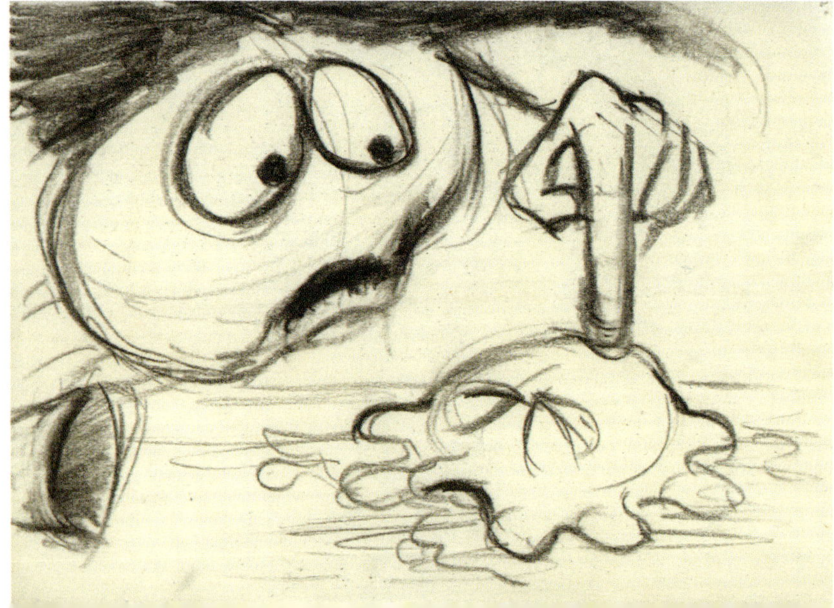

Good Humor, Ranft tried explaining, is about an anthropomorphic ice cream cone and a "crazy manic kidlike character that was like a monster." The kid licks the ice cream, which comes alive and begs not to be eaten. The monstrous kid persists and the bloblike ice cream faints and falls to the ground. The ending is a race to the refrigerator.

Ranft transferred aspects of himself into the story—his obsession with junk food, love of monster movies, and ability to make common objects human and empathetic.

Hannah looked at the storyboard. "Now what is this thing? Is he an alien?"

"He's sort of like a hungry side of a kid," Ranft replied.

It was all too oblique for Hannah.

"He's got some weird thing . . ." he said, turning the chubby student over to T. Hee.

Hee was the perfect choice to encourage young Ranft. A true out-of-the-box thinker, Hee encouraged students to let their minds "go to a place creatively we otherwise might censor," Anselmo recalls. Hee advised students to take different routes to school each day in order to be open to new experiences and not get in a rut. His philosophy profoundly affected Ranft, who developed "a unique perspective of his own," John Musker says. "Not beholden to some formula regarding character or story or entertainment."[7]

At the age of sixty-eight, Hee's animation experience was eclectic. Starting as a stylish caricaturist for Warner's 1936 short *The Coo Coo Nut Grove* and Disney's 1937 Silly Symphony *Mother Goose Goes Hollywood*, Hee became a sequence codirector on *Pinocchio* and *Fantasia*; a Bob Hope comedy writer at Paramount; writer and designer at UPA; and co-creator of *Noah's Ark* (1959), Disney's first stop-motion film, with characters and scenery made of pipe cleaners, clothespins, corks, and other household items.

OPPOSITE: *Joe Ranft's storyboard drawings for his CalArts student film* GOOD HUMOR *(1980).* RIGHT: *Ranft with mentor T. Hee at CalArts' Producers Show, May 1980. Photo by Al Holter.*

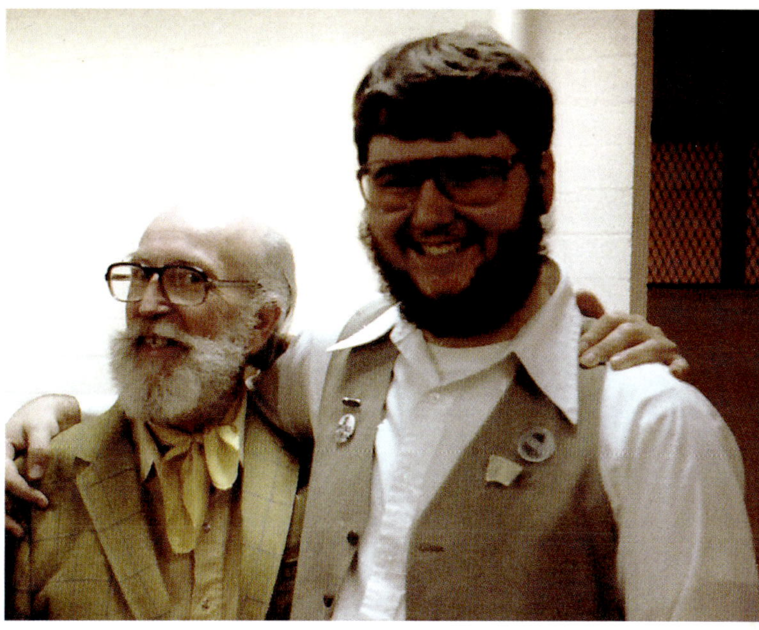

"Oh, you could have a lot of fun with this character," Hee said of Ranft's *Good Humor* storyboard. Ranft remembered that "T. did nothing but encourage me. He said, 'You've got something here that's unique. And you know what you think is funny, and you should do it!'"

In Hee's classroom, Ranft was encouraged to express verbal humor as well. Once Hee recited a poem from the 1941 Disney version of *The Reluctant Dragon*:

Sweet little Upside-Down Cake
Cares and woes, you gottem.
Poor little Upside-Down Cake.
Your top is on your bottom.

Then he prompted Ranft to make up a poem off the top of his head, resulting in:

Head is on your shoulders.
Head as big as boulders.
Head is hard to dent.
Head is like cement.

Encouraged by the laughter of his mentor and classmates, Ranft uninhibitedly improvised a dark, free-form verse in a weird accent about bloated dead bodies releasing gasses in the streets of Pakistan.[8] Again the class laughed, as much at the gross imagery as Ranft's over-the-top delivery.

Ranft spent considerable time with Hee and his wife at their Lancaster, California, ranch. "I was a fat kid and T. looked at me and said, 'I used to be real heavy like you. You know, you shouldn't eat so much.'"

In 1937 when Hee arrived at Disney, he weighed 260 pounds. Over the years he slimmed down to a skinny beanpole through a diet of low-fat vegetarian foods and yoga. "He got into health food and encouraged me in that direction, which was good," Ranft said. "T. was more than a teacher with me."

Ranft dove into *Good Humor*, asking Anselmo to provide the melting ice cream's voice. In turn, Ranft voiced Anselmo's hyena. "Decades later," Anselmo says, "Joe and I performed voices again at a recording session for a new parade at Disneyland—Joe as Heimlich the caterpillar and I as Donald Duck. That was the last time I ever saw Joe."

At the annual screening of student films for talent-scouting Disney studio bigwigs, *Good Humor* attracted attention. Ranft was asked to join the Disney studio after only two years at CalArts.

"Mom was quite upset about it," brother Jerome recalls. "She wanted him to get a degree." But Joe argued, "Look, Disney wants me and that's better than any degree is. Working in a studio."

"CalArts gave him direction," Jerome says. "He was following his passion, made a bunch of friends who loved the same thing he did, and he found story. It was an outlet, a way to explore the world, a filter to see the world through."

Ranft rented an apartment with other youngsters on South Brighton Street in Burbank, within walking distance of Disney. On July 2, 1980, he strolled through the studio's West Alameda Avenue gate to begin his professional life.

Joe Ranft and the other CalArts recruits were eager to get to work, but first came two months of training and testing. Disney needed to assess where to place the new talent within the studio system.

Their tutor was seventy-five-year-old Eric Larson, who began at the studio in 1933 and became one of Walt's legendary master animators known as The Nine Old Men. "Eric had a real calm manner," Ranft recalled of the gentle man who animated Figaro the kitten in *Pinocchio*, the old owl in *Bambi*, and Peg the canine chanteuse in *Lady and the Tramp*, among others.[1]

"Remember," Larson would say, easing his bulk behind a drawing table and placing a clean sheet of paper over a student's drawing, "the audience only gets one shot to see this. So you've got to be super clear." He then carefully drew diagrammatic improvements in staging or strengthening a character's pose.

With its manicured lawns and shady trees dotted among low-rise pastel buildings designed by Kem Weber in 1939, the Disney lot resembled a relaxed college campus. In 1980, however, the film studio seemed frozen in time, and a good deal of discontent bubbled beneath its sleepy surface.

The movie division was neglected for years by management, which poured money, time, and energy into the theme parks Disneyland, Walt Disney World, and the then-upcoming Epcot. When it came to making films, Disney executives demonstrated complacency and reluctance about trying anything new or dynamic. The question "What would Walt have done?" preceded and stultified creative discussions.

In the 1970s and early '80s, the "studio was still stuck in a time warp, technically and creatively," says animator/director Bill Kroyer. "If you asked them why they were not innovating, they'd say, 'Because we do what we do best,' which meant they just didn't dare touch the formula that Walt had left behind."[2]

Boring formulaic live-action comedies and animated features dull in concept and storytelling were the studio's fare, such as *The Aristocats*, *Robin Hood*, *Pete's Dragon*, *Herbie Goes To Monte Carlo*, and *The Cat from Outer Space*. Other studios made innovative fantasy films that Disney should have made, the most glaring example being George Lucas's *Star Wars* in 1977.

"It seemed like a company stuck in puberty," Tim Burton says. "They realized they needed to come into the twenty-first century but they didn't quite know how to do that. The movies that they made then were awkward. My impression was of a company being run by people who were the third or fourth on the tier—when the talented people left, retired, or died, they were left in charge."[3]

By the end of the 1970s, film represented a meager twenty percent of the total revenues of Walt Disney Productions, half of which came from reissuing the animated classics periodically, *Cinderella*, *Pinocchio*, and others.[4]

Despite weak, bland narratives, the animated features of the period (*The Aristocats*, *Robin Hood*, and *The Rescuers*) performed well at the box office. They contain excellent character animation, principally by the surviving Nine Old Men (including Frank Thomas, Ollie Johnston, Milt Kahl, and Wolfgang Reitherman), all of whom had reached retirement age. The main reason for their popularity was that there was little competition. Disney's brand name attracted moviegoers who had few options for animated family fare.

In the early 1970s, the studio belatedly started nurturing this vital revenue source by replenishing the pool of older animators, designers, directors, and storytellers with young talent. At first, Larson scouted colleges and art schools around the country. Then CalArts' Character Animation program became

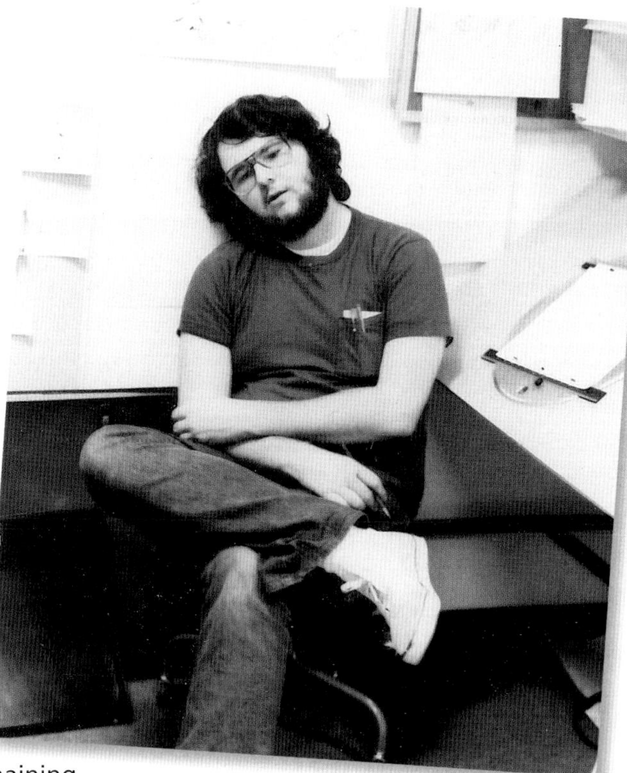

Joe Ranft in 1980. Photo by Al Holter.

a steady source of personnel. Between 1970 and 1977, twenty-five new artists were hired and the first real collaboration between studio old-timers and new recruits occurred on *The Rescuers*.

The studio's Animation Department soon became split three ways: there were "Walt's Boys"—the remaining Nine Old Men plus a second tier of veteran animators, story men, and directors who had also worked with Walt and were finally getting their shot at creative power; there were the energetic, ambitious, outspoken trainees from CalArts; and, finally, there were "Bluth's Boys": older, former trainees recently advanced to positions as animators and assistant animators.[5]

Don Bluth, a gifted animator who was forty in 1978, had emerged as the latter group's leader; his directing potential was encouraged by management, including Ron Miller, president and chief operating officer of Walt Disney Productions, and Ed Hansen, animation production manager.

"I think Ron Miller felt that Bluth was going to be the Second Coming of Walt and really take over the whole thing," Burny Mattinson, veteran story artist, commented.[6] Bluth, animating on the feature-in-progress *The Fox and the Hound*, was given directorial duties for the animated portions of *Pete's Dragon*, a live-action musical, and *The Small One*, a short. He was being groomed for an important position on a planned feature based on Lloyd Alexander's *The Black Cauldron*, which it was hoped would reach teenage fans of fantasy novels and give studio newcomers their own *Snow White*.

Bluth and his followers were unhappy with the cost-cutting of recent features. They sent pointed memos to Miller and Hansen saying in essence "we can do better movies." By that they meant a return to the lavish, expensive production values and special effects of the *Pinocchio* era.

"He thought [the current film quality] wasn't 'Disney' enough," commented designer/animator Dan Haskett, then a trainee. "From my viewpoint, he wanted to bring back the 1930s in a big way." That meant a continuing emphasis on animation and effects, rather than storytelling or exploring properties other than traditional fairy tales.

When Bluth replaced the beloved Larson as *The Small One*'s director, the CalArts contingent suspected a "palace coup" and openly questioned Bluth's authority and creative decisions. Bluth called the large bull pen housing CalArts trainees a "rat's nest" of innuendo and rumor. The "rats" accepted the designation "as a badge of honor," says John Musker, who was one of them along with Haskett, Jerry Rees, Henry Selick, and Brad Bird.

"[The rats] said there was too much emphasis on motion rather than acting" in the animation, recalls Darrell Van Citters. They protested the lazy habit of "pirating old scenes from past Disney movies, instead of thinking about animating a new one from scratch."

Bluth's condescension toward the CalArts kids and their opinions didn't help matters. "He said, 'These guys have got to learn. There's always been a system of kings and serfs at this studio. They have no right to complain,'" Musker recalls.

The most outspoken "rat" was Brad Bird, future director of *Ratatouille*. "It felt sometimes like we were all retarded," he said recently, "and that somehow animation had lost the ability to judge what good color was, what good acting was, and why we don't feel anything at any moment in these films."[7]

In 1979, the year before Ranft arrived, the situation exploded. In September, Bluth abruptly quit Disney to form his own studio, taking eleven animators with him. The departure shocked management, and *The Fox and the Hound* was delayed for months.[8] "Don had a cult of personality" around him," Van Citters says. "There was big discontent. [When he left] management said, 'Oh no! We've lost what we thought was our future.' Our viewpoint was, 'good riddance to bad rubbish.' None of us took it that seriously. It was our chance to step up to the plate."[9]

Ranft expected to work his way up through the animation hierarchy and, after years of toil, gain entry into the Story Department, his ultimate goal. However, by late 1980, based on his CalArts short and studio tests, he was assigned to develop gags for Epcot television specials.

"They basically put me in a room and said, 'Make it funny!'" he remembered. "I didn't have anyone training me."

Walt Disney dreamed up Epcot (Experimental Prototype Community of Tomorrow) as a planned and *totally controlled* utopian city under a glass dome. After he died, his impractical urban planning scheme was radically altered. When Epcot opened sixteen years later in fall 1982, it had turned into the second theme park built at the Walt Disney World Resort in Orlando, Florida, and was dedicated to "world culture and technological innovation," not social experimentation.

Four one-hour TV specials were planned to promote the opening of Epcot, much as Walt used television in 1955 to prime America for Disneyland. Van Citters and Michael Giaimo, two CalArts alums who joined Disney in 1978, worked with Ranft on humorous animation segments within the live-action series.

Van Citters remembers Ranft as "a big giant kid" with an "extraordinary positive outlook about everything and a great sense of humor." Giaimo found him full of energy with a subversive and dark sense of humor "more layered and complex than zany."

Ranft's irreverent humor gave him a reputation with Disney production executives, including Ron Miller, president and COO. A former tight end for the Los Angeles Rams and Walt Disney's son-in-law, Miller was known for not showing emotion during story pitch sessions.

At the Epcot meeting, Ranft cheerfully pitched storyboards on the effects of climate change and the "greenhouse effect." His visualization of a new ice age—the Statue of Liberty sticking out of a glacier with a tiny Eskimo gaily dancing and singing next to it—caused Miller to "fall on the floor laughing," Ranft recalled.

Van Citters, the film's director, confirmed Ranft's soon-to-be-legendary gift for provoking laughter. "He could put unusual things together. I never laughed harder than when Joe presented a gag. One of his crisp little things."

Suddenly, Hansen and other smiling executives told Ranft, "You're in story forever!" Overnight, Ranft said he "became the 'Oh, he's a funny guy!' A gag person."

"Joe was a wild boy," recalls Henry Selick, who later worked with Ranft on *The Nightmare Before Christmas.* "He was huge and red-faced and full of laughing gas and jumping beans." Selick remembers attending punk rock concerts with Ranft, who slam-danced with such abandon in the mosh pit that he spent half the time politely helping kids back to their feet after he'd knocked them to the floor.[10]

The Epcot specials were shelved, but a ten-minute satiric short, *Fun With Mr. Future*, was cobbled together from the animated bits. The filmmakers (Van Citters, Ranft, Giaimo, and Ed Gombert) connected the animation with a talking demo head of "Mr. Lincoln" from a Disneyland exhibit (a cranium of exposed wires and lights wearing a polka-dot bow tie). Released in October 1982, it played with *Diva* (1981) at L.A.'s Cinerama Dome to qualify for an Academy Award. Not nominated, it disappeared into the Disney vaults.

However, the film's irreverent raw creativity is fondly remembered by many, including Bird. "It was this tiny pocket of goodness in a very dark time. It was coming out of a really horrible atmosphere at Disney. Like an air bubble in an undersea wreck."

Fun With Mr. Future was produced because of the intercession of Tom Wilhite, who would play a pivotal role in the careers of several new talents, including Ranft. Wilhite was the studio's twenty-seven-year-old publicity director whom Miller promoted to vice president of creative development for movies and television.[11] Miller hoped the energetic, well-organized young man from Iowa would revitalize the studio's live-action family entertainment.

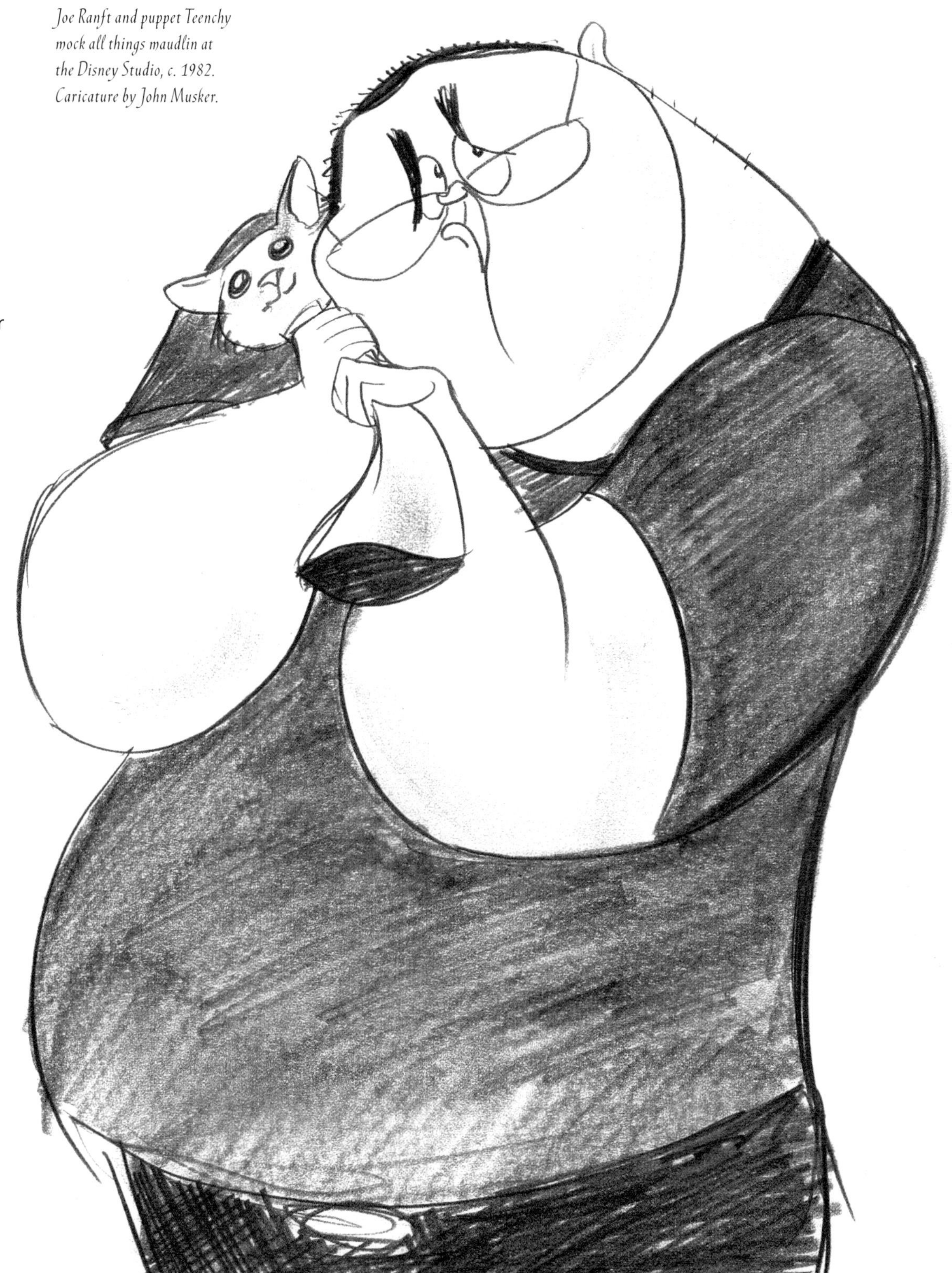

Joe Ranft and puppet Teenchy mock all things maudlin at the Disney Studio, c. 1982. Caricature by John Musker.

Wilhite realized "family entertainment" needed redefinition to include young and older adults as well as children. His most ambitious project was *Tron*, a $21 million science fiction adventure with computer-generated animation about a software programmer trapped in his own video game.[12] Released in 1982, the film boasted minimal but elegant computer graphics that were a dazzling breakthrough in the evolution of CGI in features.

Wilhite's duties did not include the Animation Department, but he became friends with several of the young animators "because I was essentially their age and someone they could talk to." All shared an interest in expanding Disney animation's creative horizons rather than sticking with the status quo.[13] Wilhite became interested in their ideas and often found money for their projects, which led to an escalating conflict with the animation division's manager.

BELOW: *Joe Ranft's 1983 over-the-top* BASIL OF BAKER STREET *story sketches included a* CITIZEN KANE *parody.* OPPOSITE: *Dr. Dawson as a nun and Holmes as a violent manic-depressive.*

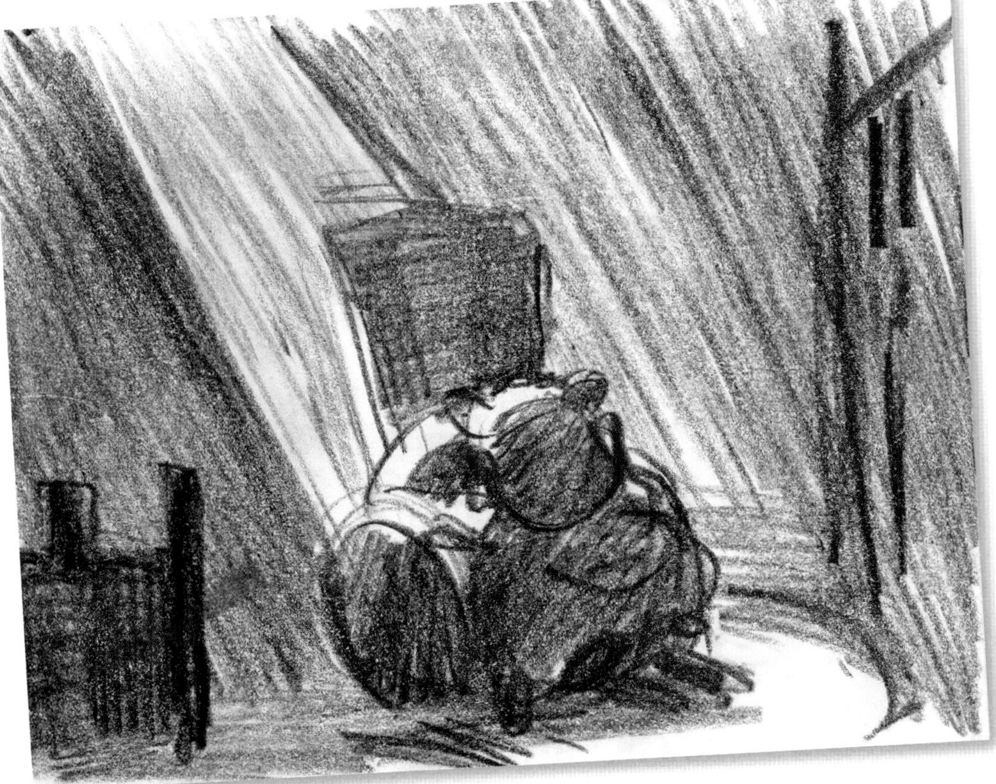

Tim Burton's short *Vincent*, for example, "was something that we just found a charge number for in the live-action department, called it a stop-motion experiment, and that's how we made it," Wilhite says. "When the Animation Department found out, they went crazy!"

Burton compared his time at Disney to "Chinese water torture." He was an assistant animator on *The Fox and the Hound*. "Imagine drawing a cute fox with Sandy Duncan's voice for three years," he groans. Then his "weird" personal drawings of monsters got him assigned as a conceptual artist on *The Black Cauldron*, but "they didn't use one single concept of mine."[14]

Meanwhile, Ranft was experiencing a comparable round-peg-in-a-square-hole feeling. "Basically the first five years I worked at Disney, nothing I worked on got made."[15] He commiserated with Burton and identified with his strange drawings, dark in tone like his own. A circa-1983 snapshot shows pumpkin-faced Ranft grinning manically next to thin, short-haired, sleepy-eyed Burton with (allegedly) fake blood dribbling from his mouth and spattering on his white shirt. It is easy to see these two simpatico imps collaborating on future ghoulish projects like *The Nightmare Before Christmas* and *Corpse Bride*.[16] "I like Tim's world," Ranft said. According to Giaimo, Ranft "idolized" Burton.[17]

After the Epcot series imploded, John Musker recruited Ranft to draw storyboards for *Basil of Baker Street*. Based on a five-book series by Eve Titus about a Sherlock Holmes–type mouse, the film eventually reached the screen in 1986 as *The Great Mouse Detective*.

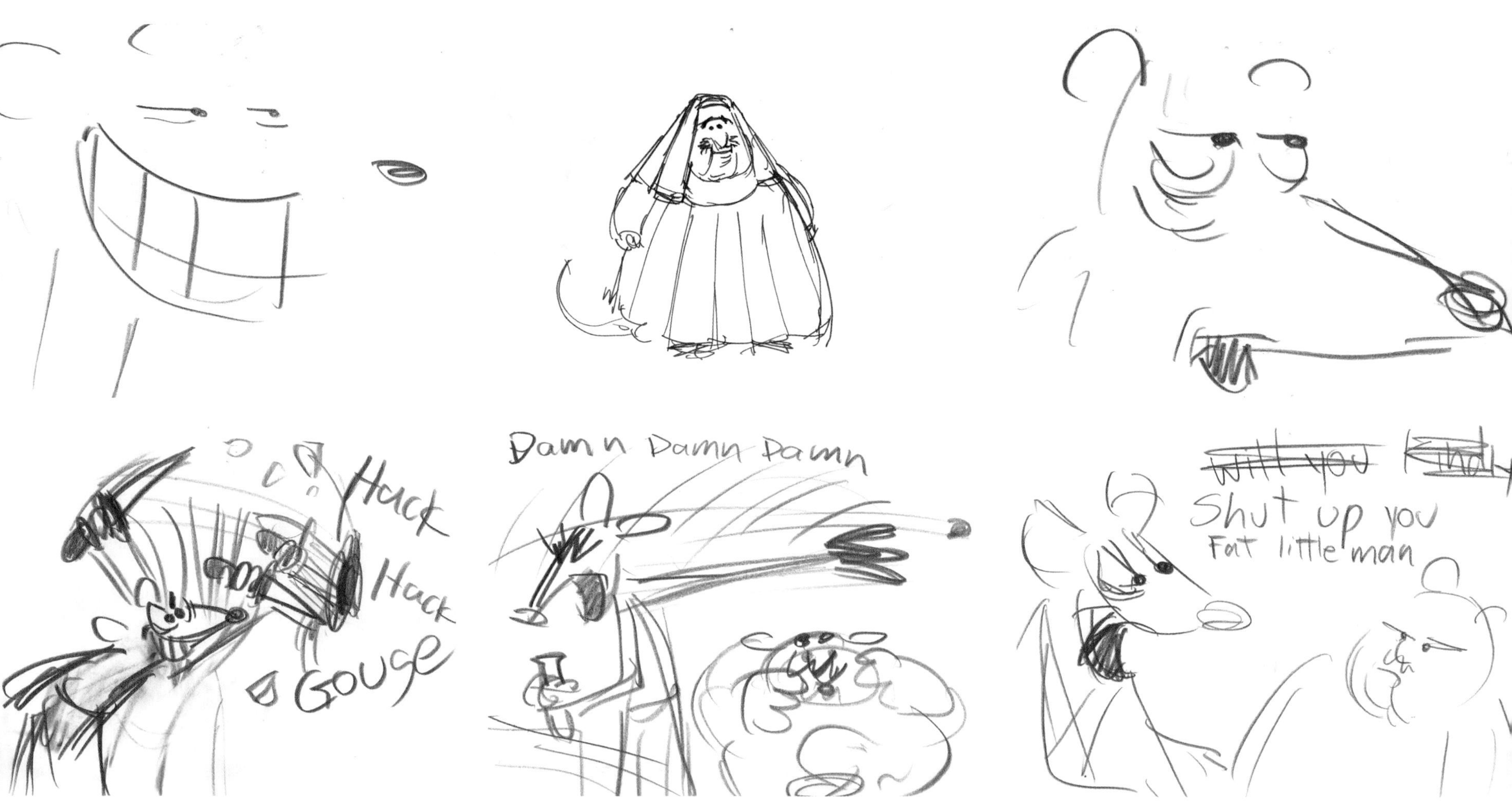

This was Ranft's first opportunity to fashion a feature film narrative. "They told John, 'You can do anything you want,'" Ranft said.

"Big highs and lows appealed to Joe," says Musker, one of the film's four directors. "The caricature aspect. He brought this great sense of humor and entertainment." In Ranft's version, the wiry Basil was manic and excitable, contrasted with heavyset Dr. Dawson (representing Dr. Watson), whose courtly manner and twinkle in his eye was modeled on Eric Larson.

Ranft concocted a *Citizen Kane* opening with old Dawson living in a hospital ward for shell-shocked veterans of the Victorian-era Afghan war. In a shaft of light, he sits in a wheelchair relating how he first met the famous Basil of Baker Street. Suddenly, a disturbance in the ward sets the veterans ricocheting off the walls, while an orderly (based on Ken O'Connor, a deadpan Australian with a dry wit) barely moves amidst the chaos. "That was Joe's sensibility, playing off people we knew. And this craziness against deadpan static. I wouldn't have thought of it," Musker

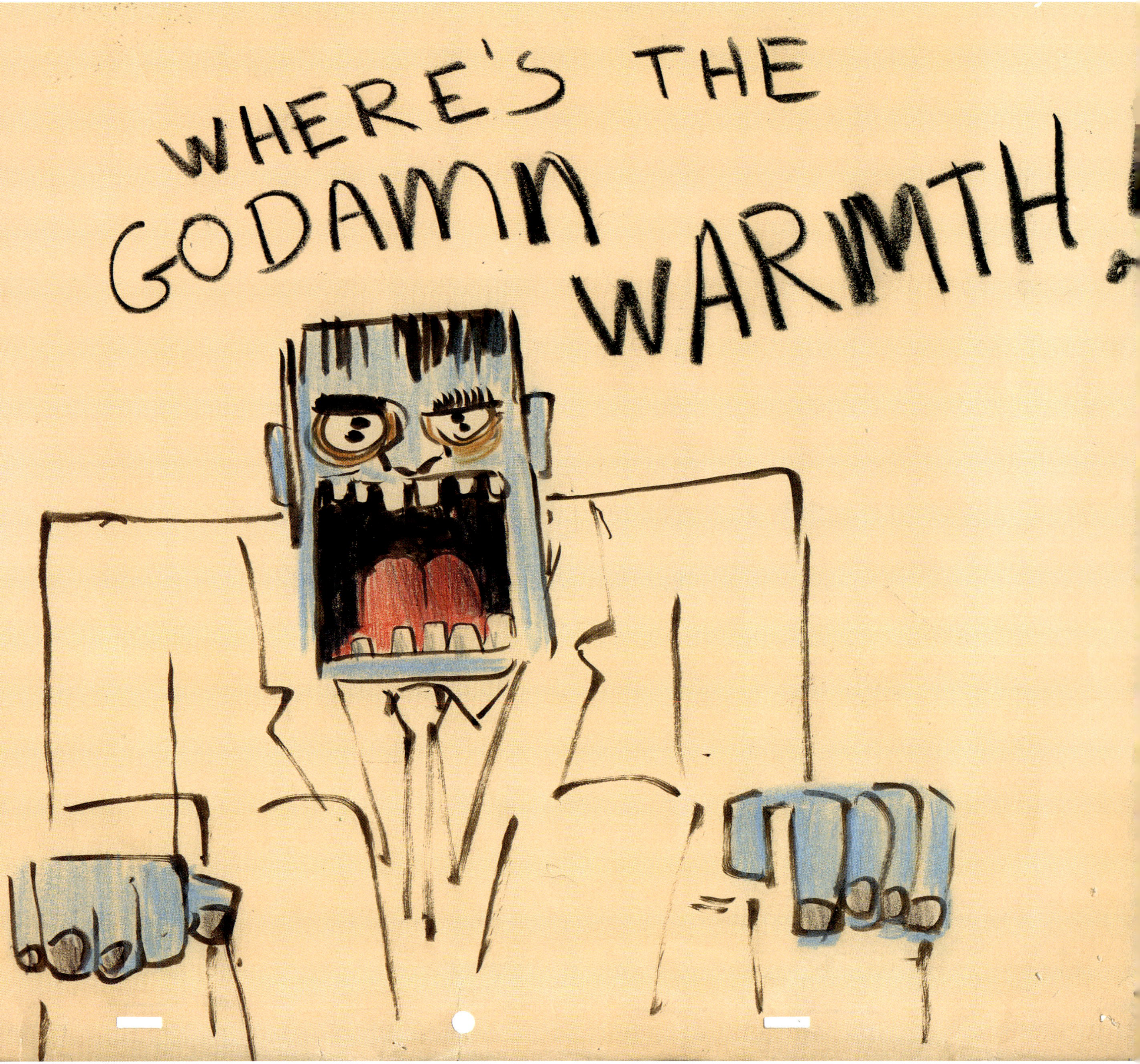

WHERE'S THE GODAMN WARMTH!

says. "We were listening to the Goon Shows and watching *Monty Python*," Ranft said of his influences. "The first pass was really wacky."

After six months of work, Ranft and Musker pitched the boards to Ron Miller. This time he didn't laugh. Instead he asked angrily, "Where's the warmth?"

Ranft was replaced. "Get Joe off of that!" Ranft laughed years later. "When the story's working, have him come back and do gags."

Ranft expressed his disappointment by drawing Miller as a blue-faced, huge-shouldered Frankenstein yelling, "Where's the godamn [sic] warmth!" Fearlessly, Ranft displayed the sketch in a studio caricature show. When Miller saw it, he filled the halls of the animation building with booming laughter, then walked away smiling and muttering, "That big crazy kid!"[18] Musker kept the sketch over his desk for twenty-five years.

Ranft continued bouncing from project to project. He worked briefly on story for *Oliver & Company* (released in 1988, it became the first feature of the Eisner/Katzenberg era) and earned a screen credit. Hungry to develop his storyboarding skills further, he received excellent lessons from story artist Pete Young. "Pete had a way of roughing a board with super-simple stick figures of what you're trying to tell," Ranft said. "Just get the whole thing up and then just go into it and clean it up. A quick way to work."

He also learned from Young not to introduce a new story element if the director wasn't ready for it. "Good ideas presented at the wrong time stood a chance of being rejected," explains animator Floyd Norman. "At Disney, the politics of story can be as important as creative skills."[19]

Ranft and Van Citters began developing storyboards based on galleys for a soon-to-be-published novel titled *Who Censored Roger Rabbit?* No director was assigned, so the project was delayed. "I was spinning my wheels," Ranft said.[20]

Tim Burton's film *Vincent* jump-started his directing career, but Ranft had no personal project to pitch. He was becoming lost within the slow confines of a convoluted and frustrating system.

With no immediate projects for his talents and not knowing what to do with him, the studio consigned Ranft to busy work as a special effects "inbetweener." He made incremental sequential drawings *between* animators' main poses on *Mickey's Christmas Carol* (a 1983 "featurette"), and he was miserable.

"The worst part," he cried, "was inbetweening Marley's ghost's chains. Someone had keyed every twelve frames of chain, and I had to make every link not jitter. I wasn't that fast or that good."

After six months, he was switched from "tweening" rigid steel chains to smoke and steam effects. Like the amorphous shapes on his drawing board, he felt he was drifting.

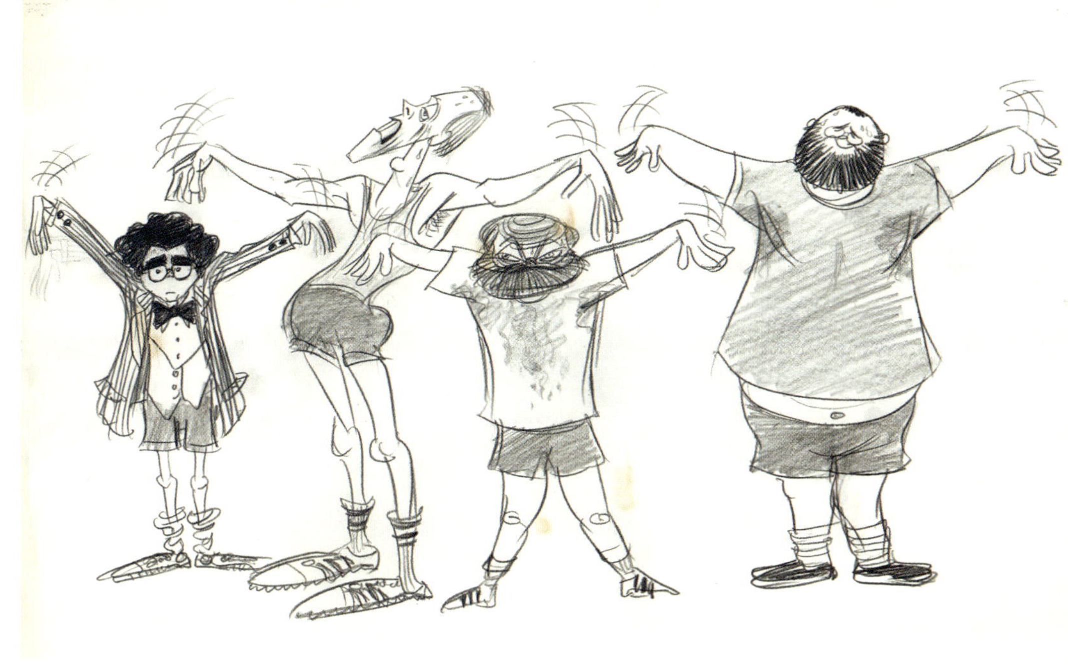

OPPOSITE: *Joe Ranft's caricature of Disney Studio president Ron Miller reacting to Ranft's* BASIL OF BAKER STREET *storyboard.* ABOVE: *an aerobics class with* BASIL OF BAKER STREET *crew members* (LEFT TO RIGHT) *Chuck Richardson, Steve Hulett, Ron Clements, and Ranft. Caricature by John Musker.*

"Learning the politics of working on a film or being part of a big studio system, Joe started taking life more seriously after three or four years in the business," brother Jerome observes. "And having some illusions shattered about working at a film company."

Despite Ranft's feeling frustrated, his irrepressible creativity found extracurricular outlets along with other Disney malcontents. There was *Luau*, an elaborate 1982 Super-8 home movie produced, written, and directed by Jerry Rees and Tim Burton that parodied the inane beach-party movies of the period. Various young artists participated as actors and technicians, including Mike Gabriel, John Musker, and Randy Cartwright. Ranft played I.Q., the surfers' thick-witted mascot. Burton acted The Supreme Being, a space alien dissatisfied with being a floating head. After separating I.Q. from his body, The Supreme became a new character named Mortie.

Then there were "the Eddie Shows."

Ranft with other dissatisfied colleagues of like mind and humor poured considerable energy, effort, and imagination into what were essentially giant puppet shows performed for their own amusement.[1]

In 1981, full-size photo blowups of Eddie Fisher, Doris Day, Marlon Brando, and Zsa Zsa Gabor, discarded from the film *Beatlemania*, somehow found their way into the G-wing of the Animation Building to become office décor for Giaimo and Ranft. Soon Eddie, Doris, Marlon, and Zsa Zsa, outfitted with hinged mouths, appeared in office windows waving and talking to employees heading home through the nearby gate.

Before long, the Eddie Shows became extravagant with props and costumes and kitsch musical sound tracks for lip-synching (or rather hinged-jawing). As the zany shows grew, so did their reputation. Expectant crowds gathered whenever the well-rehearsed performances occurred, encouraging the puppeteers to further heights. "Mike and Joe were a deadly combination," says Van Citters. "They just got crazy!"

The Eddie Shows' campy apotheosis was a Christmas spectacular, which became studio legend. "I swear there was more creativity in that thing," Musker says, "than in our films of the time." The ten-minute paean to Christmas kitsch starred the usual cast decked out in Santa hats and coats. Lip-synching to "Ring Those Christmas Bells," the puppeteers' cut-out bells became absurdly larger with each chorus, as the old ones were casually tossed away. Suzy Snowflake (Miss Day) "dressed in her snow white gown" cheerfully warbled while passionately caressing cardboard Eddie.

The show's highlight—Santa Claus's appearance on the Animation Building's roof—was Ranft, of course, in a red suit and hat and flowing white beard, vigorously gesticulating to lip-synched dialogue. Two stylized reindeer cutouts danced at Santa's side as he encouraged the audience below to "laugh and be happy! Ho-ho-ho!"

Then, in a magician's quick switch, Ranft cut through the forced jollity and sentiment. Disappearing beneath the parapet, he hurled a dummy of Santa over the building. The audience gasped as jolly Saint Nick sailed through the air (sans reindeer) and hit the ground—thud! Two "medics" carried Santa away on a stretcher as sirens wailed and the crowd laughed nervously.

The mood shifted as "Marlon," costumed as a demented elf, crooned "I Want a Hippopotamus for Christmas" atop said smiling amphibious mammal. This distraction allowed "Santa" Ranft to don bandages and open the frost-decorated window to assure the crowd not to worry. He was ho-ho-ho-okay!

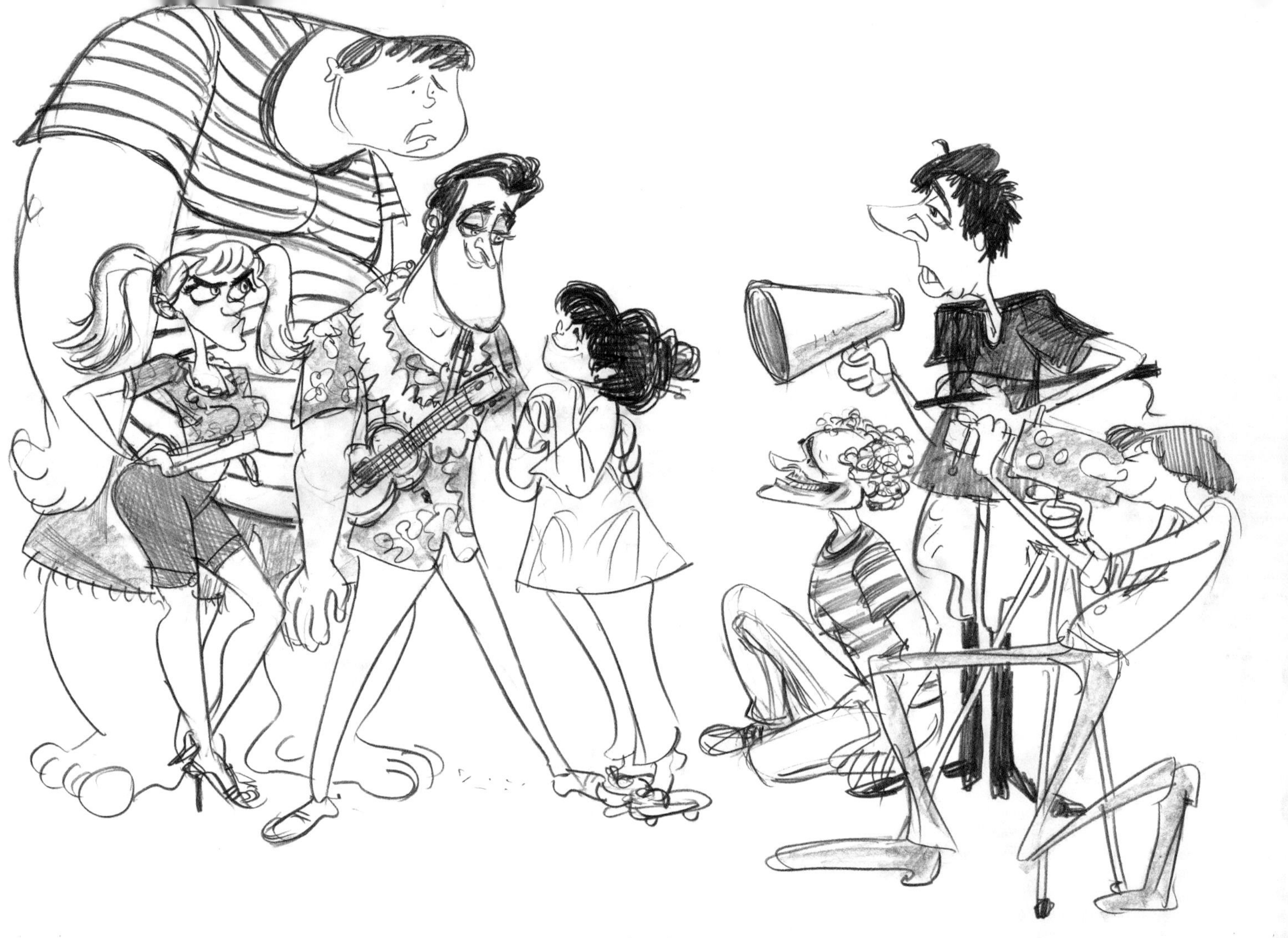

Cast and crew of Super 8 featurette Luau *(1982); (*LEFT TO RIGHT*) Joe Ranft (as gentle giant I.Q.), Sue Frankenberger (as diva star), Mike Gabriel (as Elvis-like hero), Terrey Hamada (as potential girlfriend), writers/directors Jerry Rees and Tim Burton, and cameraman Randy Cartwright. Caricature by John Musker.*

"We had a lot of time on our hands," Van Citters says, laughing at the memory.

By late summer 1982, the animation industry had time on its hands. Screen Cartoonists Guild Local 852 called a strike to protest "runaway productions": studios sending work overseas (primarily Asia) to defray costs.[2] Although targeting television producers, the union asked the entire industry to share the pain. "They said, 'You're gonna get fired if you don't go on strike,'" Ranft remembered. "I didn't understand it at all." The strike, which proved futile, lasted ten weeks.

During his layoff, Ranft channeled his anger and boredom by writing and illustrating a nightmarish series of Grand Guignol stories featuring a child with a large cankerous hole in his head. In the *Billy* stories, nothing is sacred—not childhood, small fuzzy animals, parents, or any authority figures. The fearsome tales of a put-upon innocent's gruesome revenge pushed Ranft's unbridled imagination to extreme lengths.

The crude faux-naïf drawings—thick black lines on white paper accented by rust-colored blood—display mutilation, decapitation, blood, gore, and altered forms. In one episode, Billy's avenging eye becomes a lethal piercing sword seeking payback for numerous slights.

In another, Billy adopts and nurtures a pet duck in his bedroom. Suddenly the duck starts talking and then possessing him Svengali-like, ordering him about. "One day Billy snapped!" reads the text of a drawing of Billy's eyes narrowing to pinpoints. He grabs a gun, and the rest is pure mayhem for both duck and reader.

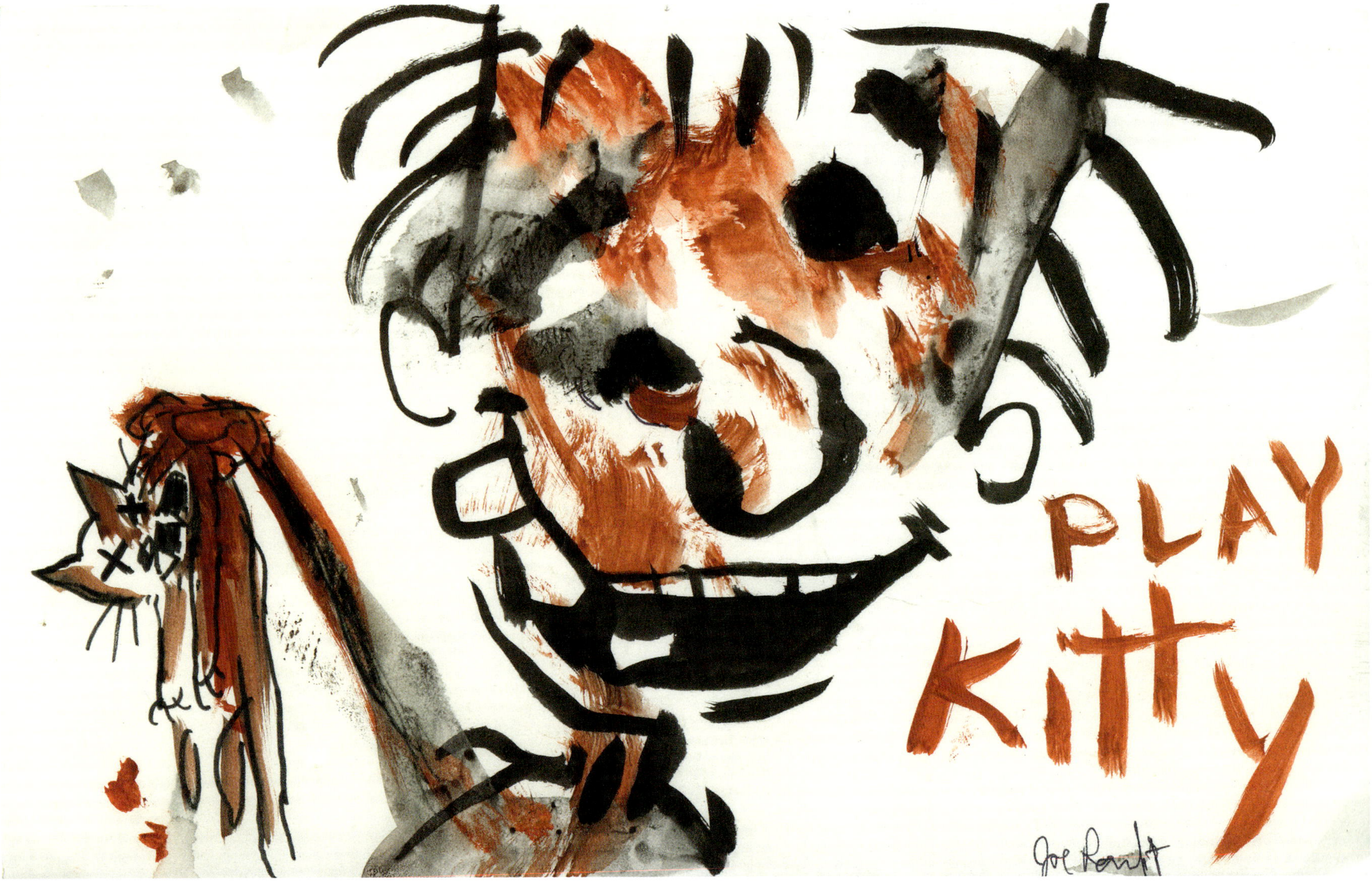

In yet another, Billy's mother's head is attached to the family dog, foreshadowing Sid the malevolent child in *Toy Story*, who cuts up toys to "artistically" reconstruct them. Ranft didn't show *Billy* to just anyone.

He selectively chose readers he thought were receptive to his outrageous humor. The nihilistic *Billy* stories fascinate because, within the frustration and rage, Ranft posited sensitive details and childhood memories readers could relate to. When Billy's mother sends him to the barber, she instructs him to "ask for a regular boy's haircut," a resonant line for many men. Ranft evocatively describes how Billy could "feel the breezes through his new haircut." Of course the haircut reveals the hole in Billy's head, leading to inevitable chaos. *Billy* shows Ranft's Jekyll/Hyde ability to charm/repulse simultaneously.

"I shared that dark side with him, that was something I always liked," says Lee Unkrich, whose Pixar office of stuffed animals rivals a taxidermist's shop. "He could do the heartfelt stuff and do it well. But left to his own devices, I think Joe had a lot

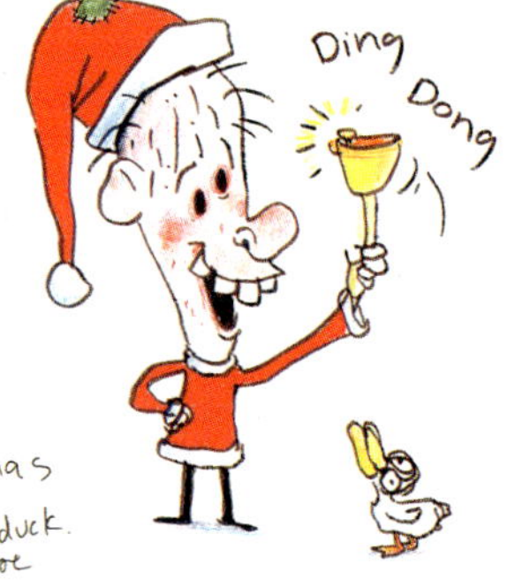

of demons. And that got worked out through some of this dark humor. His private work, the comic books, storybooks, the Billy character, that's pretty twisted stuff. That comes from somewhere. He was always talking about dreams and dream analysis. He read Jung."[3]

"I think the *Billy* stories were a release for him," Giaimo says. "He was frustrated. At the studio, we were working on inane featurette ideas for Mickey, Donald, and Goofy. For that certain faction of us who were less mainstream, those projects were difficult to wrap our heads around. We wondered, 'When are we going to grow up creatively?'"

Ranft's optimistic side shone through during this period. As he began investigating how to improve professionally, he attended classes in improvisation at The Groundlings, a Hollywood performance troupe, whose alumni included future *Saturday Night Live* regulars Phil Hartman, Jon Lovitz, Julia Sweeney, and Paul (Pee-Wee Herman) Reubens.

"We do not teach acting. We teach improvisation," states the group's mission statement, through "classes that are uninhibited and encourage self-growth."[4]

> "I first enrolled in The Groundlings improv classes because I thought it would be fun, and perhaps help my storyboard pitches. What I got out of them was much more," Ranft wrote in 1995.
>
> The classes were taught by working improv actors. These teachers had a direct connection to a live audience on a weekly basis. I found that this audience-informed teaching was invaluable. Their stories about what worked or didn't work in front of a live audience taught me a lot. One exercise—the "Yes And" game—was worth the price of the class alone. I learned that the same thing that kills an improvisation on stage (denial) also impedes any form of creative brainstorming.
>
> . . . Rather than judging or waiting for a seemingly better idea to come along, I was taught to commit in that moment and see how far a suggestion would go. . . .
>
> Other valuable lessons from the classes were:
>
> - Trust
> - Teamwork
> - Risk Taking
> - Concentration
> - Pantomime/Space Work
> - Character Work
> - Scene/Sketch Writing
>
> The key aspect of the class is that it's experimental, you learn by doing. I highly recommend this type of improv training to anyone interested in animation story.[5]

Observing Ranft in a Groundlings class, Giaimo was "amazed how this guy was open and free, free with his body, his sense of humor, and where he could apply all this timing and everything he knew in our business on stage."

At Disney, he soon put his new improv skills to good use. Shortly before the strike, John Lasseter read a novella about household appliances by science fiction writer Thomas M. Disch. He asked Ranft to help him develop the project.

"I looked at the title *The Brave Little Toaster*," recalled Ranft, "and thought, 'Awwww!' But then I read the story and it was really fun! This could be great!"

The film would prove important for Ranft because it cemented his relationship with Lasseter, who never forgot "the unbelievable talent I saw in this guy." Ranft was forever grateful to Lasseter for rescuing him from his Disney doldrums by jump-starting his career as a story man.

"John Lasseter said 'Read this.' He saved me."

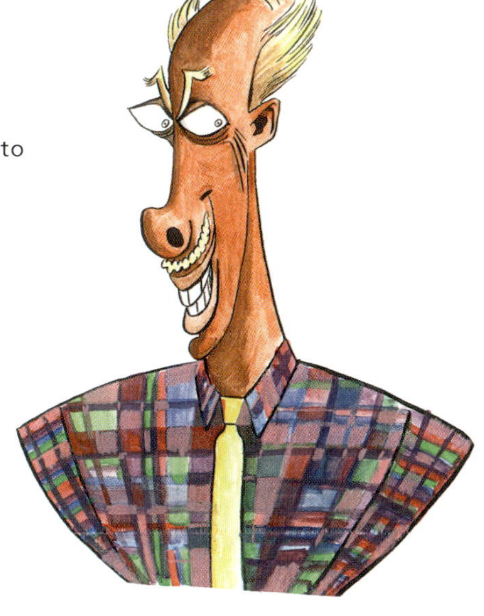

OPPOSITE: *Joe Ranft's comic book child from hell, Billy.* ABOVE: *designer/story artist Michael Giaimo, caricature by John Musker.* BELOW: *John Lasseter, c. 1983.*

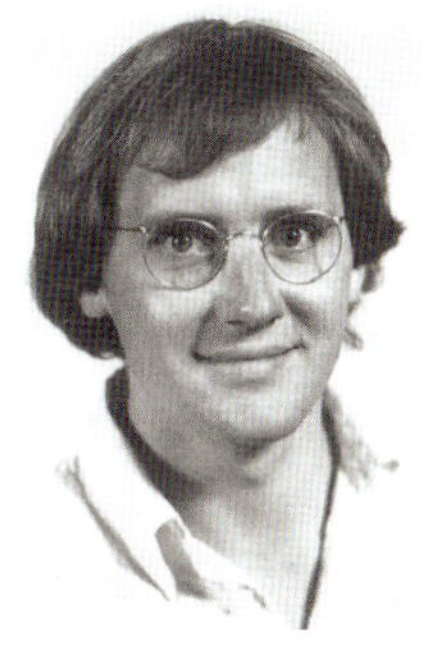

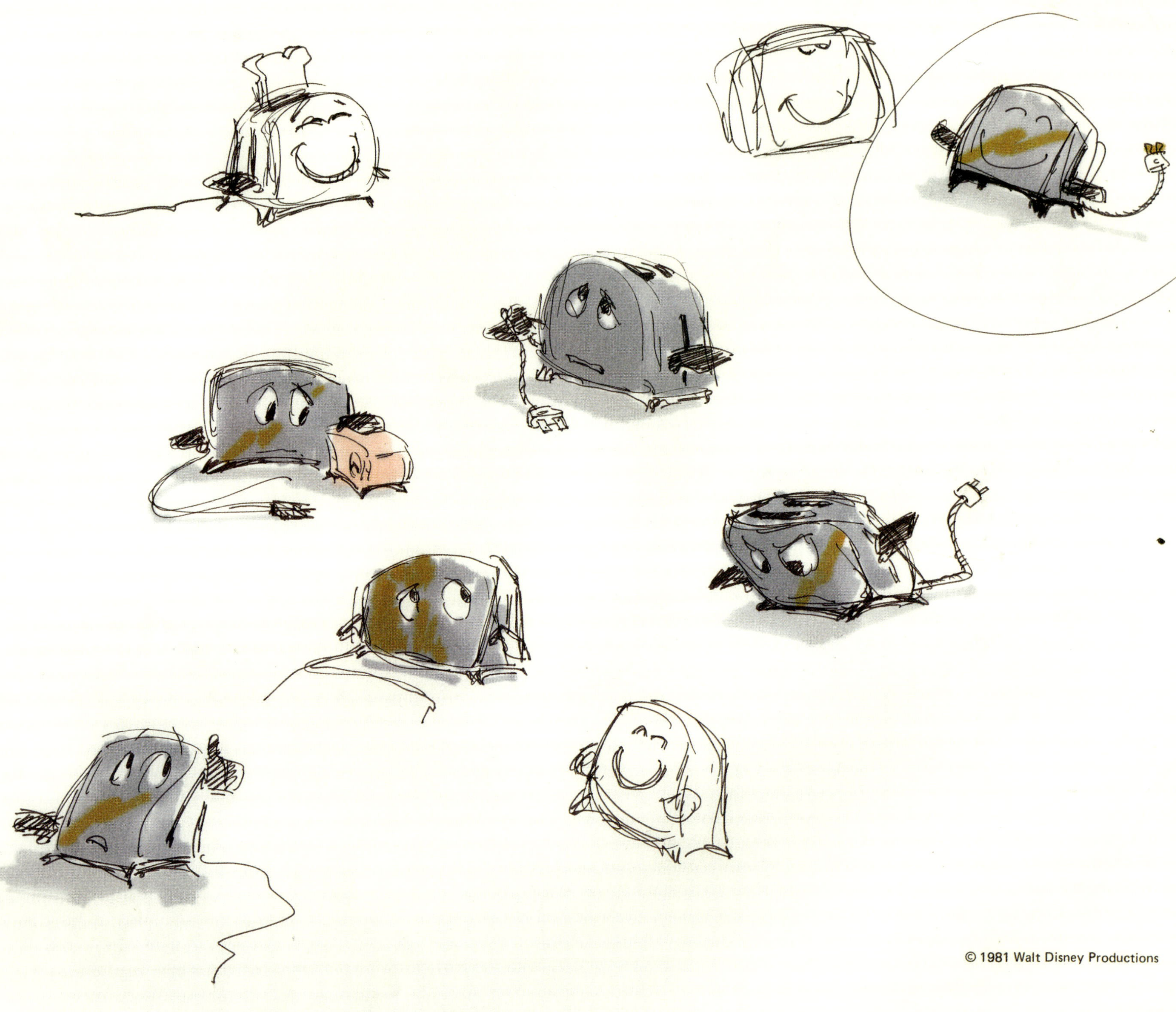

CHAPTER SEVEN

Love and a Toaster

"John [Lasseter] was always what I'd call a floater," Tom Wilhite recalls. "He would move around the Disney Studio, always seemed to know what was going on. He introduced me to Tim [Burton] and Joe [Ranft] as well."[1]

Although Wilhite was in charge of live-action production on films such as *Splash*, *Tex*, and *Tron*, Lasseter recalls Tom as "the one executive who seemed to look at us young [animation] whippersnappers that were stirring the pot at Disney in those days and gave us opportunities."[2]

Lasseter had knocked around Disney on various uninspiring assignments—*The Fox and the Hound*, *Mickey's Christmas Carol*, and two abandoned projects: a *Fantasia*-like film called *Musicana* and *The Emperor's Nightingale* starring Mickey Mouse. Like his peers, he was dissatisfied and eager to keep pushing Disney animation to another level.

Between assignments, "Disney paid us to stay there," Jerry Rees says. "Nobody was laid off." Drawing classes were available, but the young eager beavers' ideas were ignored and their talents wasted. "The powers-that-be went 'No! No making films together. Must stay separate and sit at your desk.' Jeez!" cried Rees, who "knocked on Tom Wilhite's door."[3]

Wilhite continually crossed the line between his duties in live-action and those within the jurisdiction of the Animation Department. "Whenever the animation management saw me coming, they got extremely defensive," says Wilhite, who funded Tim Burton's short *Vincent* and hired Rees and Bill Kroyer as *Tron* storyboard artists and "computer image choreographers."

Lasseter saw the nascent computer imagery his friends were cooking up for *Tron*. "It absolutely blew me away!" he says. "A little door in my mind opened up. I looked at it and said, 'This is it! This is the future!'"[4]

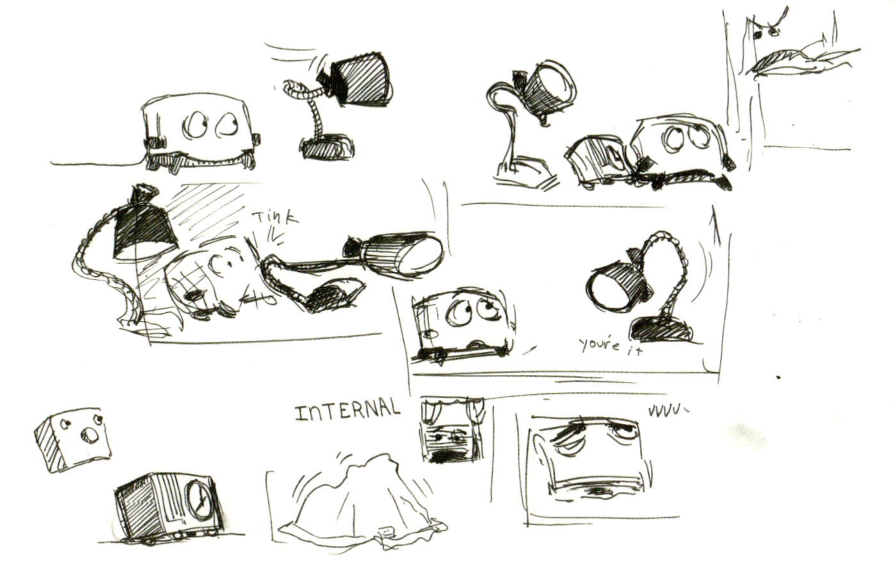

OPPOSITE AND THIS PAGE: *Joe Ranft's charming concept sketches of the star of* THE BRAVE LITTLE TOASTER *(1987).*

On fire about CGI's possibilities, Lasseter enlisted Wilhite's help in making a thirty-second test combining hand-drawn character animation with computer-generated backgrounds. For the test, Wilhite asked his friend Maurice Sendak for permission to use the character of the boy Max from Sendak's celebrated book *Where the Wild Things Are*.[5]

Lasseter directed the test. "It was exciting," he says of the result, "but at the time, Disney was only interested in computers if it could make what they were doing cheaper and faster. I said, 'Look at the advancement in the art form. Look at the beauty of it.' But they just weren't interested."[6]

Indefatigable, Lasseter next brought *The Brave Little Toaster* to a sympathetic Wilhite, who acquired rights to the novella for the studio. *Toaster*'s cast of discarded appliances (a toaster, lamp, radio, vacuum cleaner, and blanket in search of their owner) with individualistic personalities and an emotional story—about feeling unwanted and obsolete and needing to be useful and loved—were themes later echoed in *Toy Story*.

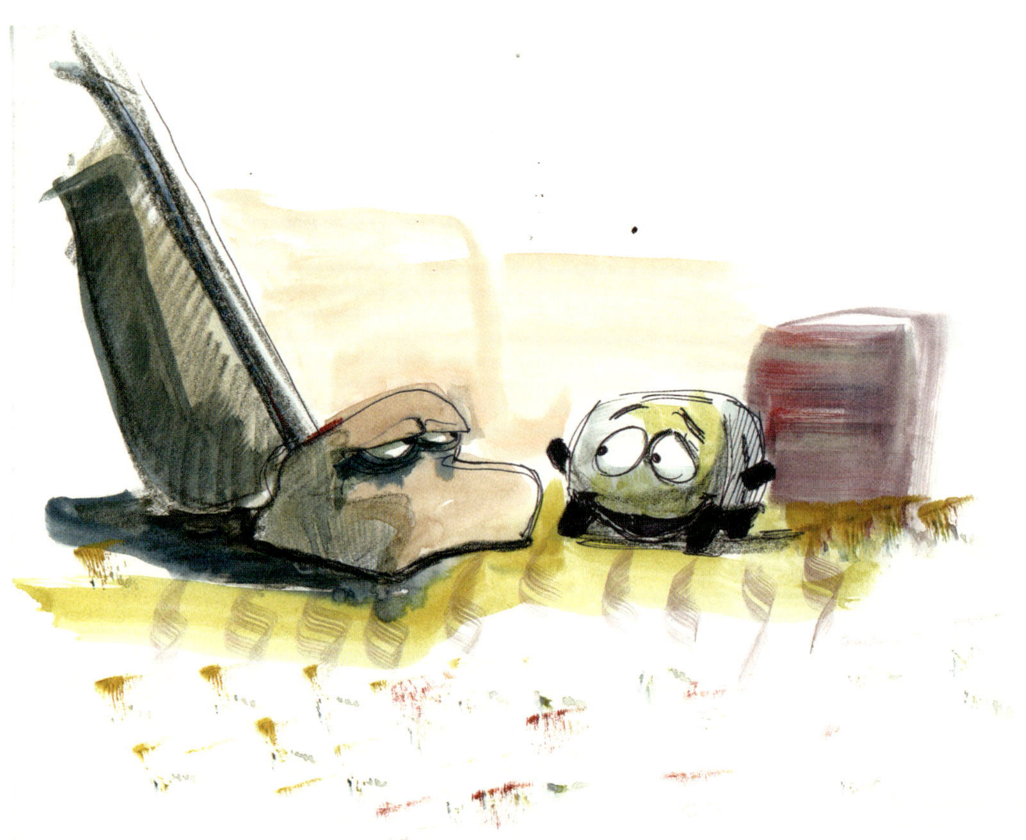

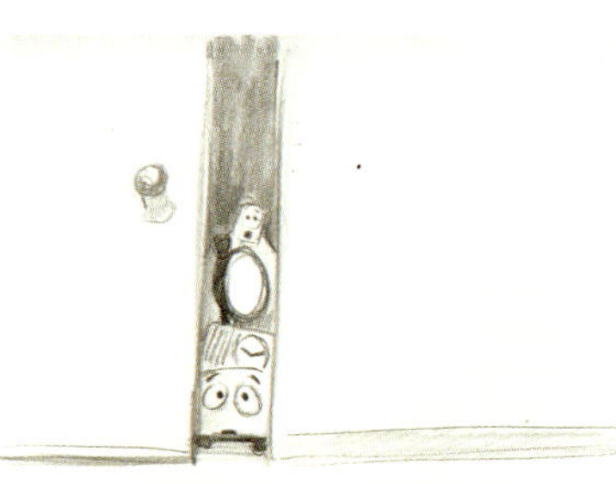

ABOVE: *Toaster and companions.* RIGHT: *Joe Ranft, John Lasseter, and Brian McEntee present their* TOASTER *storyboards to Disney execs, and are rejected. Caricatures by John Musker.*

"To me there's no object that can't become a personality," Lasseter once said.[7] "I've always loved animating inanimate objects, and this story had a lot of that."[8]

For *Toaster*, Lasseter's sunny optimism and empathy toward inanimate objects blended well with Ranft's similar qualities; plus, Ranft's dark, iconoclastic side provided a leavening balance to the narrative and its quirky personalities.

"Joe was fundamental to the story process," Wilhite says. "He was absolutely key to the success of that movie in terms of the emotion. And the gentle comedy and sweetness that came out of the characters came heavily from him."

"We always talked and dreamed of things we wanted to do that were bigger and better," Lasseter says. "So every time I had an opportunity, [Joe] was the first one on my list to join me."[9] "John and I had this sort of pact that when John directed his first feature, I was definitely going to work on it," Ranft said.

Lasseter, Ranft, and Brian McEntee spent nearly a year developing *Toaster* under Wilhite's supervision. When they finally pitched their concept sketches, storyboards, and budget to Ron Miller and Ed Hansen, all hell broke loose.

Wilhite and Hansen had a confrontation in front of Miller. "Because," Wilhite explains, "it was a picture *I* wanted to make. If it got made it would be a wedge in the Animation Department, a project developed outside their purview in a very different way, probably more efficiently, and it became something they couldn't tolerate. In Ron's defense, as a good CEO he had to support his division heads and animation wasn't my area. So I lost that one."

Lasseter lost his job. "Ten minutes after the studio head left the room," he says, "I get a call from the superior who didn't like me, and he said, 'Well, since it's not going to be made, your project with Disney is now complete. Your position is terminated, and your employment with Disney is now ended.'"[10]

Lasseter went north to the Bay Area to follow his dream. "But I never forgot Joe."

Meanwhile Ranft was assigned with Mike Giaimo to do preliminary story work on *Captain Eo*, a 3-D movie for the theme parks starring Michael Jackson, and storyboards for *Mickey Columbus*, yet another Mickey/Donald/Goofy vehicle. No matter how ridiculous the project, Ranft was able to be optimistic while simultaneously disliking it.[11]

Ranft's improv classes helped with story work, but The Groundlings instructors felt he was holding back with a lot more to give. Ranft agreed and sought a way to allow his full potential to be expressed both professionally and personally.

He also yearned to experience love and romance. The twenty-five-year-old rarely dated and never had a girlfriend.[12] "Like many of us in animation, Joe had a pretty severe case of arrested development in terms of dating, just being with women," observes Giaimo. "I know Joe's physical size often made him feel like an outsider. I think the whole thing that spun Joe was a deep desire for acceptance and to improve himself."[13]

Ranft, Giaimo, and friends often attended Largo, a music club on Fairfax Avenue in Hollywood, to see a cabaret singer named Weba Garretson. "Her performances have both the softness of Brazilian jazz and the sultry, sharp devastation of Bertold Brecht and Kurt Weill," a reviewer wrote.[14]

"Weba was not for the masses," Giaimo says. "You had to be creative to truly appreciate her oblique but entertaining, slyly humorous performances. She was rather exotic-looking, beautiful in a peculiar way."

Ranft was fascinated with her. He sent her a drawing capturing her eyes and essence. On it he wrote how much he loved . . . the show. "He wrote it in a childlike way," Giaimo recalls, "but it was hopefully an entrée to getting to know her."

Garretson responded with enthusiasm over the drawing, and Ranft was delighted but "disappointed," says Giaimo, that "he didn't know how to carry it further at that point."[15]

A friend suggested he join Lifespring, a New Age/human potential organization Ranft described as "a sister to [Werner Erhard's] est kinda stuff." Ranft signed up for one session, little knowing it would change his life.

In 1974 John Hanley, a former member of Mind Dynamics with Erhard, founded Lifespring. The seminar-based group focused on introspection and empowering people to take control over their lives. Exercises included sharing and confrontation, neuro-linguistic training (redefining words), behavioral modification, and team-building. Each intensive session attracted as many as 300 participants in the mid-1980s, mostly businessmen and women interested in improving their performance at work.[16]

The group was often labeled a cult, but many participants found the experience enriching and valuable, including Ranft.[17] However, some colleagues felt his rough, subversive edges were softened. "Joe was *the* guy at the studio who was a unique artist with an outrageous sense of expression," Giaimo says. "The Joe who introduced me to *Pink Flamingos* and Divine eating dog shit. Joe's true sensibility was not always populist, like Tim Burton's was. Joe was always our champion of all things subversive. To see him soften was slightly disappointing at that time."

Joe Ranft was evolving, changing his thinking and his physical self (he had slimmed down considerably). "That big crazy kid" was growing up emotionally and moving forward.

Whether or not his friends were ready for it, he would soon make even bigger changes in his life, including leaving Disney and getting married.

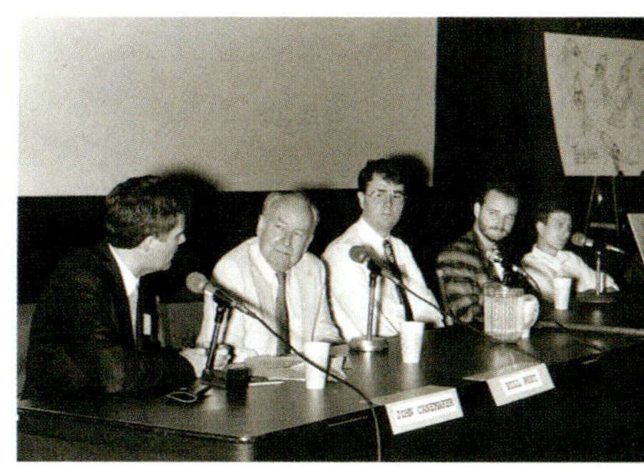

ABOVE: *June 11, 1988, AFI Conference on Storytelling in Animation, hosted by John Canemaker* (LEFT), *with panelists* (LEFT TO RIGHT) *Bill Peet, Joe Ranft, Jerry Rees, and Peter Schneider.* LEFT INSET: *Newlyweds Su and Joe Ranft, September 28, 1985.*

We Gotta Get Out of Here

"I wonder what would happen if I hadn't met you?" Joe Ranft once wrote to his wife during their twenty years of marriage. "I've done so many brave things since I met you. I wonder if you're my muse or if you just make me feel brave?"[1]

When Joe met Susan Elaine Barry (known as Su) at a 1985 Lifespring session, it was (as Henry Selick described it) "like two messy comets colliding in space to form a new planet!"[2]

Five years older than Joe and the survivor of a brief unhappy marriage, Su, a beautiful blonde with penetrating blue eyes, is a strong-willed, independent woman filled with good humor, warmth, and outspoken opinions. Honest and direct to the point of bluntness, she lets you know exactly what's on her mind and where you stand with her.

"Joe finally met his match when he met Su," Selick and their friends agree. "Su helped Joe focus his ADD energy and raw talent." They *were* perfectly matched in high energy, quest for spiritual meaning, and the sweet, bold way they approached life's challenges.

Su was born in San Francisco in 1955 and raised in Sacramento, the middle child of three daughters whose father was an energy-resource developer in Las Vegas. While attending the University of Las Vegas as an art major, she married against her parents' wishes. When the marriage failed within a year, she was disinherited and unable to return to school. Divorced, Su left Las Vegas ("a horrible place to live") for Los Angeles, where she worked two jobs as a waitress and developed many new friends. "I knew how to deal with people, make 'em laugh. When you're a waitress every table is an audience," she explains. During an L.A. housing boom, she trained as an escrow agent. Eventually, she became an executive administrator for a property entrepreneur in Redondo Beach.

"I was doing well, took care of myself, had my own apartment, didn't have any bills," she says. "Really very happy. But I wanted a kick in the ass. I knew this guy who was a complete jerk and he took this [Lifespring] class and came out of it completely different. I thought, well, if that could happen to a jerk, what would happen if somebody good and nice went in there?"

Su found the seminar "absolutely wonderful!" and stayed on to conduct advance-course interviews. One of her interviewees was Joe Ranft.

Both were immediately attracted to each other. "And I got his phone number," Su says. "But we weren't allowed to date as long as he was taking the classes. So we became pretty good friends. And then we fell in love. And then he decided to go to Taiwan!"

In March 1984, the Disney Studio was in a major upheaval. Notorious corporate raider Saul Steinberg "took a position in Disney," leading Wall Street to anticipate a takeover. The corporate fight led to the replacement of Ron Miller and others with Michael Eisner, Frank Wells, and "Team Disney," including Jeffrey Katzenberg, revitalizing the movie/television departments. A new chapter for Disney animation began.

"It was an interesting time to be there," Ranft noted of the takeover period. He could have waited it out but was tired of "sitting on my hands." He accepted an offer from Tom Wilhite, who left to set up Hyperion, his own production company.

Wilhite took the rights to *The Brave Little Toaster* with him and asked Ranft and Brian McEntee to make the film. "I had been integral in developing it and I just wanted to work on something that's getting made," Ranft said.

It took a year to finance the project. In pre-PowerPoint days, whenever Wilhite, Ranft, and McEntee pitched *Toaster*, eight large storyboards were loaded into a pickup truck and then unloaded in studio offices. Ranft did most of the pitching. "He was a great storyteller, performer, impressionist, really terrific at it," Wilhite recalls.[3]

Finally, a miniscule budget of $2.3 million was cobbled together, at a time when Disney's in-house budgets started at $18 million. Four companies contributed funding, including Disney, which acquired television rights.

Jerry Rees became the film's director, with Ranft and McEntee as his story team. "Joe had a wealth of different things he could do," Rees recalled. "He could perform a voice [shop-owner Elmo St. Peters], do character model idea sketches, and talk about raw-story structure. He'd roll up his sleeves and go with new ideas. He never got stuck in a rut."

The team dug for motivations within the characters. "We'd sit together and go, 'Well, the toaster is warm because toasters *are* warm,'" Rees says. "You'd feel comfortable with a toaster 'cause you can see yourself reflected back, so all the characters would feel a comfort just being around this character. [Joe] would completely accept that as real.

"And what I loved about Joe," Rees continues, "he'd never lapse into saying 'What would a kid like?' Or, 'What would market well?' It would come from his heart. If it touched him or made him smile, he would go with it!"

Wilhite credits Ranft with pioneering a pre-production technique often used today in animated features to improve the story: bringing in actors to riff on a film's script. He invited Groundlings (including Phil Hartman and Jon Lovitz) to view storyboards and "play" with the story and dialogue. "Much of that session," Wilhite says, "was incorporated by Joe and Jerry into the final recording script. This kind of comedic, emotional, and character spontaneity seems to infuse the later Pixar movies."[4]

Rebecca Rees—a directing animator along with her husband, Jerry, and Ranft—remembers Joe as "so different from anyone I had ever known." During pre-production, a crew member was teased because a nightmare about a black cat so upset him he could hardly work. Ranft became a gentle mediator. He drew a white kitty that, he said, would cancel out the black kitty. "And it worked!" says Rebecca. "The guy calmed down. Joe was always trying to solve problems in a good way and be helpful."

Finances necessitated that pre-production (storyboards, character models, and layouts) be done in L.A., while animation, backgrounds, cel ink and paint, and photography be produced in Taiwan, 140 miles off mainland China. As part of the deal, several Americans would spend six months supervising Taiwanese animators while serving as their mentors.[5]

Ranft was eager to go, though friends "thought he was crazy," Su recalls. She and Joe had been together for only six months, but they didn't want to go to Taiwan unmarried. So they "snuck off to Vegas to make it legal" on September 28, 1985. Joe knew his mother would be sorely disappointed if he married outside the Roman Catholic Church—and to a woman who was five years older, "kinda Episcopal," and a divorcée. "So we eloped," Su says.

Joe was estranged from organized religion, but promised his mother it didn't mean he abandoned spirituality or morality. He was "on his own spiritual quest," which over the years included Zen retreats and self-actualization workshops.[6]

In November, Hyperion hired Su to precede Joe and the others to Taipei to set up apartments with electricity, pots and pans, blankets, and so forth. She had everything ready for the American crew when they arrived just before Christmas.

But by then Su was "the invalid bride." A ruptured disk in her lower back put her in traction.

"Joe started working six, seven days a week in a foreign country, and I was basically incapacitated," she says.

Ruth Ranft to the rescue! She quickly got a visa, flew to Su's side, and became her private nurse. She cooked for her daughter-in-law, bathed her, and when emergency spinal surgery became necessary, Ruth grilled the doctor about his qualifications and slept in Su's hospital room to monitor her post-op treatment.[7] "Boy, she's a woman for an emergency," Su says. "She's a saint! She'll give you the shirt off her back. We got to eventually know each other very well."

"My children are my most precious assets," says Joe's mother.[8]

Su's predicament was in addition to Joe working long hours and trying to adjust to a strange new place. "It was exciting and fun when we got there, but that went away really quick," Jerry Rees recalls.

It was the rainy season, and mosquito bites took a toll. One closed one of Joe's eyes and another swelled his lip to baseball size. "We were working seven days a week, even through the Chinese New Year. Everybody got sick, food poisoning, flu. Joe, too," Rees recalls.

"*Blade Runner* exists," Rees says of Taipei, a large city with a dizzying mix of Chinese, Japanese, and Western influences. Industrial plants and heavy traffic have raised air pollution to dangerous levels. Face masks were recommended. In Snake Alley, the oldest district, cobra and mongoose fights are staged on the sidewalk, and whiskey containing snake and turtle blood is hawked as male enhancement medication. Rees saw open sewers gurgling in front of a new McDonald's, near a high-rise modern hotel sitting next to a tin shack where a large family lived and sold bootleg videos. Nearby, a 150-year-old temple offered a time trip to a distant, more peaceful world.

Ranft developed welts on his head from hitting it so often on low doorways. Eventually scar tissue developed, which he showed off as his "Taiwan knot." He and the crew compared working on *Toaster* to combat and his knot was "my Purple Heart."

One shining memory of "the battle days" on *Toaster* was working with the Taiwanese animators, "the nicest people you'd ever want to meet," Rees says. Ranft, who learned some Mandarin ("I was fascinated by the language's structure"), agreed. "The people were great."[9]

The feeling was mutual. "They were so willing to learn," says Rebecca Rees. "Everybody loved Joe. He was so big, too. They looked up to him like he was a god."[10]

"Joe was a giant to the little kids in Taiwan," Jerry Rees says. "A giggling group followed behind him. He got dismayed. 'They think I'm weird. I'm too different.' He thought they looked at him as a freak. I said, 'No, Joe. You're magical to them.'" In social settings Ranft often used magic (cards, coins, cigarettes) to "converse" without interpreters.

The production was a labor of love for both the Americans and the nearly 200 Taiwanese artists. "They put in as much work as we did," Rebecca says. "The reason we could get it done in the time and the money we had is because everybody believed in the movie. It was the very first time we were given absolute freedom to perform at our full potential."

"For a lot of animation stars of today who are now the backbone of the animation business," Wilhite says, "*The Brave Little Toaster* was the Roger Corman movie of their time," alluding to the low-budget producer whose films provided early showcases for directors such as James Cameron, Peter Bogdanovich, and Francis Ford Coppola, among others.[11]

Back in the States, an exhausted Joe Ranft said he "didn't want to touch a pencil" ever again. He and Su lived in a "little bitty" apartment in Glendale, drove used cars, and didn't have credit cards. "Joe was very good with money," Su says. They never had a honeymoon, so they took a road trip visiting relatives "all over the place" and went to Expo '86 in Vancouver.

A doctor said that if they planned to have children, Su would need a spinal fusion to prevent her back from collapsing. Which meant Ranft needed insurance; which meant he needed to get a union job. Fortuitously, producer Don Hahn offered Ranft a return to Disney for *Who Framed Roger Rabbit*.

"If you want to get ahead at Disney," Ranft advised his brother Jerome, "you've got to leave and come back. And then they think you know something they don't."[12]

Roger Rabbit was coproduced by Disney and Steven Spielberg's Amblin Entertainment. For four months at the end of 1986 in a trailer in Universal City, Ranft worked with animator/historian Mark Kausler alongside the film's art department, including live-action storyboard artists.

Ranft and Kausler supplied gags for the film's opening, a takeoff on Tex Avery cartoons. Richard Williams, the animation director, partially boarded the sequence before leaving to set up the production's animation studio in London. Ranft's fondest memory: "We were doing stuff that was character-oriented and kind of tame—oh, what's Roger thinking and feeling? [Robert] Zemeckis [the film's director] looked at it, laughed, but said, 'Now fuck the rabbit up! Keep him in the air. I want you to beat him up and . . .' It was like, *Yesssss!* And we just went crazy! Violence for its own sake."

Ranft noted the differences between storyboarding for live-action and animation. Live-action involves "solving logistical problems for the director," determining how many camera setups are needed and can be budgeted for. Animation storyboards in the Disney tradition reveal the characters, or, as [story man] Vance Gerry said, "We're looking for the gold," moments revealing character that can be best expressed in animation.[13]

In 1987, CalArts invited Ranft to teach storyboarding, which he did for three years. The seeds of his Pixar mentoring were sown there. A first syllabus, put together by a nervous Ranft, flew over the pupils' heads. Within two weeks he revamped it to provide "what they needed."

First, students stood and told a story, an icebreaker that helped Ranft ascertain their communication skills. Then, he "broke down the basics of screen direction for one assignment. Another class was about 'silhouette value' in a drawing—if you blacken in a figure, can you decipher the character's attitude? Another on logistics of filmmaking and acting. One class dealt with composition in staging a drawing to make its meaning clear—does it read? Can you tell what's going on here? Are we seeing in the drawing what you're saying? If not, how do you get the drawing to tell you that?"

Viewing Chaplin and Keaton films reinforced discussions of body language and physical expressions of emotion. Drawings by Daumier, Rembrandt, and Dore showed how tones and values focus and direct the eye. Artwork by Bill Peet, A. B. Frost, and Hokusai reveal how caricature makes drawings "seem to be alive." In each class Disney storyboards were compared with the final film.

Ranft formed specific "rules" for storyboarding, such as:

- Show rather than tell.
- Communicate one idea at a time.
- Stage it so the audience can see it clearly.
- Clarity in the shot's composition.
- Clarity in staging the acting or pantomime.
- The story drawing's job is to communicate: an idea, feeling/emotion, mood, an action.
- Imply animation in your drawings (through caricature, use of animation principles, i.e., stretch and squash, exaggeration, etc.)
- Imagine ourselves in our character's shoes/place.
- Leave an impression, an impact (visual and emotional) that affects the viewer.

He challenged students to show a character's state of mind using contradictions (a character covered in garbage who maintains an inner dignity).

Ranft shared screenwriting guru Robert McKee's prayer to the storyteller:

> Please, make it good.
> Let it give me an experience I've
> never had, insights into a fresh truth.
> Let me laugh at something I've never
> thought funny. Let me be moved by
> something that's never touched me before.
> Let me see the world in a new way. Amen.[14]

One of Ranft's students was a twenty-one-year-old Minnesotan, Pete Docter. "Joe would look at your work and figure out who you were underneath," Docter says. "He tried hard to be encouraging to everybody, whatever their level. He really went out of his way. As important as animation was, helping people was equally important."

Impressed by Docter's films, Ranft invited him to the Disney Studio, showed him professional storyboards, introduced him to Thai food and iced tea, and eventually recommended him to John Lasseter when he began expanding Pixar. "In part that's why I'm here [at Pixar]. Because of Joe. He was a real connector," says Docter.

One night Ranft happened to see storyboards by a student who was not a member of his class. "Hey! Those are pretty good. Did you ever think of going into story?" he asked Brenda Chapman, in a casual encounter that changed her focus from animator to story artist. She became one of the few women to reach the top ranks of story at Disney and (even rarer) became a feature animation director, first at DreamWorks and currently at Pixar.

"I would not be who I am, what I am, if it were not for Joe," Chapman says.[15] "Joe was so encouraging. I've never met anyone like him and his ability to criticize someone's work and yet make them feel like a million bucks."[16]

At Disney, Jeffrey Katzenberg led an animation team populated with CalArts alums, and the studio was suffused with new energy and creativity. Ranft's colleagues knew and valued his talent and invited his participation as a roving idea man. "At a certain point," he once explained, "they'd have a 'ten-gag' meeting. Okay, the story's working. We just need some gags, really funny things peppered throughout."

For *The Little Mermaid*, "Joe did great drawings of a sequence with Scuttle [a seagull] and [mermaid princess] Ariel," John Musker recalls. "Joe had a lot of charm in the way he drew Ariel, though it didn't look like her. The heart, warmth, the wide-eyed-ness of her. Wow! Her enthusiasm. Very Joe. Even the printing style [for storyboard captions] looked like an eight-year-old. Block printing style, naive."

On June 11, 1988, Ranft participated in "Storytelling in Animation" at the Second Annual Walter Lantz Conference on Animation at the American Film Institute in Los Angeles on a panel that included Jerry Rees, Peter Schneider (then vice president of Walt Disney Feature Animation), and master story artist Bill Peet, Ranft's longtime idol. Ranft found sustenance in Peet's opening statement: the first thing an animation storyteller must have is "a set of characters that can carry you through the story once they're established." Without them, Peet asserted, it's "like a train leaving the station without the passengers."[17]

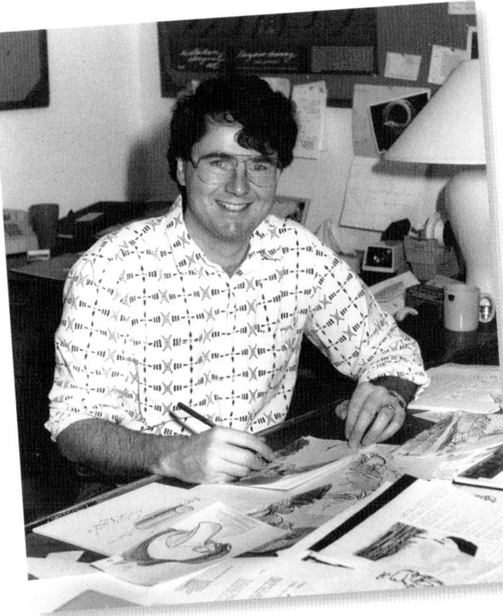

LEFT: *Joe Ranft, as a twenty-eight-year-old head of story for* THE RESCUERS DOWN UNDER.

Ranft politely spoke of the script as "a jumping-off point" and maintaining "fidelity to the original material in spirit" while "exploring the possibilities of entertainment," including going "to the edge." He preferred collaborating on stories in "one large room where everybody works together," he said, "kibitzing and commenting on each other's work," a technique he later encouraged at Pixar. "Notwithstanding Bill doing it all by himself," Ranft said, deferring to Peet, who wrote the script *and* drew the storyboards for *One Hundred and One Dalmatians* and *The Sword in the Stone*. Ranft, clearly in awe of the seventy-year-old legend, expressed how exposure to Peet's *Song of the South* story sketches at CalArts had greatly inspired him.

Back at the studio, Ranft was developing a short (*Aladdin Mickey and the Lamp*) when he was drafted as story supervisor for *The Rescuers Down Under*, Disney's first animated feature sequel, based on 1977's *The Rescuers*. "Joe was at the very center of *The Rescuers Down Under*," Thomas Schumacher says. Schumacher, who became the head of Disney Feature Animation and is currently president of Disney Theatrical Group, was, in 1988, the newly hired producer of *The Rescuers Down Under*. Ranft was chosen as the film's story head because Schumacher believed "he had the ability to change and transform through excellence of idea. Never through argument. Joe Ranft would never argue you into anything."[18]

On August 16, 1988, Joe and Su left for a brief summer vacation to Ireland and England with a little money they had saved. "My life is going really well right now," Ranft wrote to a friend.[19] "I've also been promoted to storyboard supervisor on *The Rescuers* sequel which takes place in Australia, so right after my Europe trip I'm going to Australia for twelve days (on the company)."

Schumacher recalls how in September he, Ranft, and the film's young directors (Mike Gabriel and Hendel Butoy) climbed Uluru/Ayers Rock in central Australia and visited desert Aboriginal centers, where they took turns around a campfire playing the digeradoo, and Ranft taught magic tricks to the children. "Joe could deal with anybody. Joe was naturally a teacher. I've never met a person who didn't love Joe."

The Australian research trip was the bright beginning for what became a hard two-year slog for Ranft. As story supervisor he continually bolstered the spirits of his crew, but rarely got to draw storyboards himself. And there were disagreements with studio management and marketing executives on creative matters.

"What was difficult," says Chapman, who was on Ranft's crew, "was a sense of wanting to be true to Australia. We wanted to use an Aboriginal little boy [for the lead] but were forced to go with a little white blond kid. It may as well have been Arizona by the time it was finished. That was frustrating to all the artists who started out with incredible development artwork and concepts."

Ranft stood up for things he believed in, "but kept a level head," Chapman says. "He created a great working atmosphere, even when we were frustrated with some of the creative decisions. We still had great times working together. Fun." In a variation on the

BELOW: *Joe Ranft's caricature of Jeffrey Katzenberg.* ABOVE RIGHT: *THE RESCUERS DOWN UNDER film frame.* OPPOSITE: *two Ranft story sketches from THE RESCUERS DOWN UNDER.*

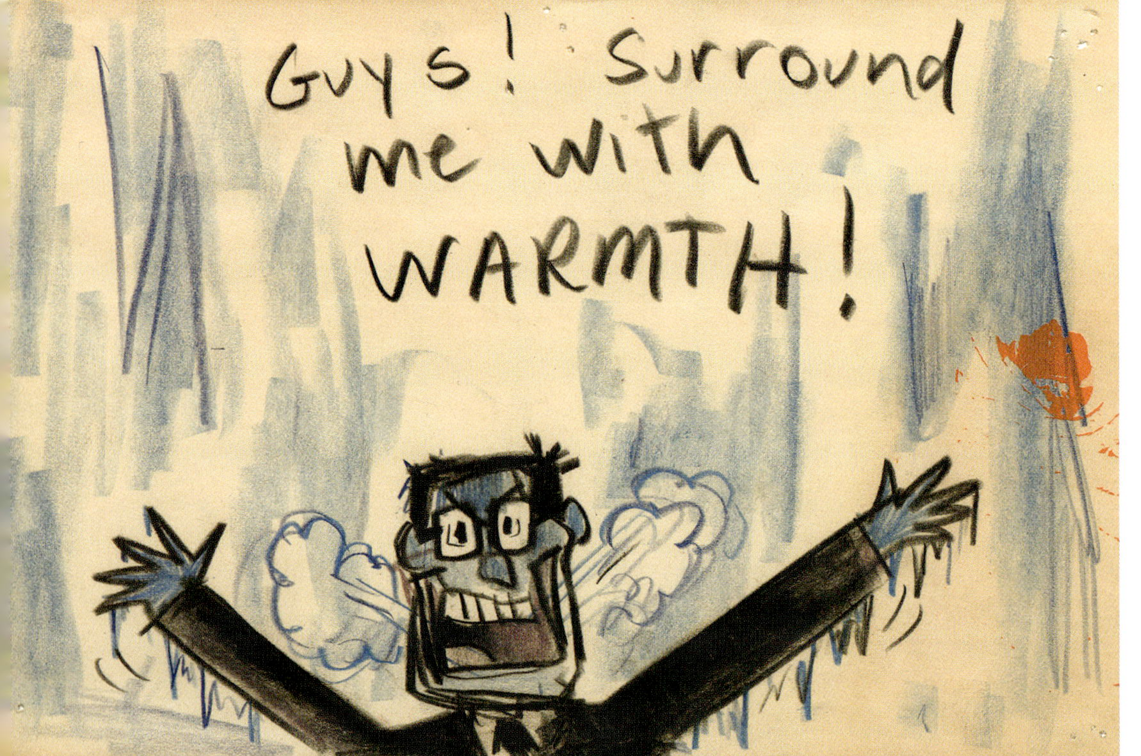

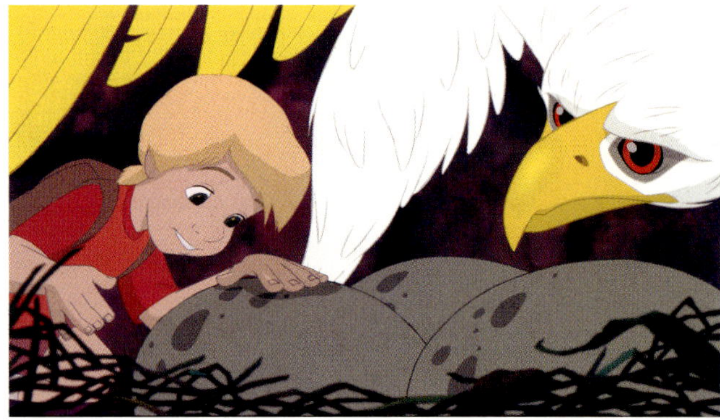

caricature he drew of Ron Miller, Ranft caricatured animation boss Jeffrey Katzenberg, blue with icicles hanging off his suit, rallying the Story Department with: "Guys! Surround me with warmth!"

Critiquing the story artists' work was part of Ranft's job. But first he'd always point out something he liked. "No matter how miniscule it might be. It really validated what you'd done," Chapman says. "Then he'd zero in on a problem area: 'But you might try something like this here.' He always had a positive spin even when he was telling you he didn't like something."

During the film's production, Ranft supported Su's return to college for a teaching certificate. "Then *I'll* be able to go back to work," she told him. By the time she graduated, however, "he smelled something bad at Disney," Su says.

The positive face he showed at work was at odds with how he really felt. He always felt remaking *The Rescuers* "was lame," Su says. "He was embarrassed about it. Joe could not tolerate formulas, lack of spontaneity, gearing it toward the money rather than the people."

Ranft said the story work on *The Rescuers Down Under*, released in November 1990, was "the weakest thing in it," and he blamed himself. "I was depressed about that," he said.[20] Su knew he wasn't happy. "So when I got out of college, I said thanks. What do *you* want?

"He says, 'We gotta get out of here. We gotta get out of Disney.'"

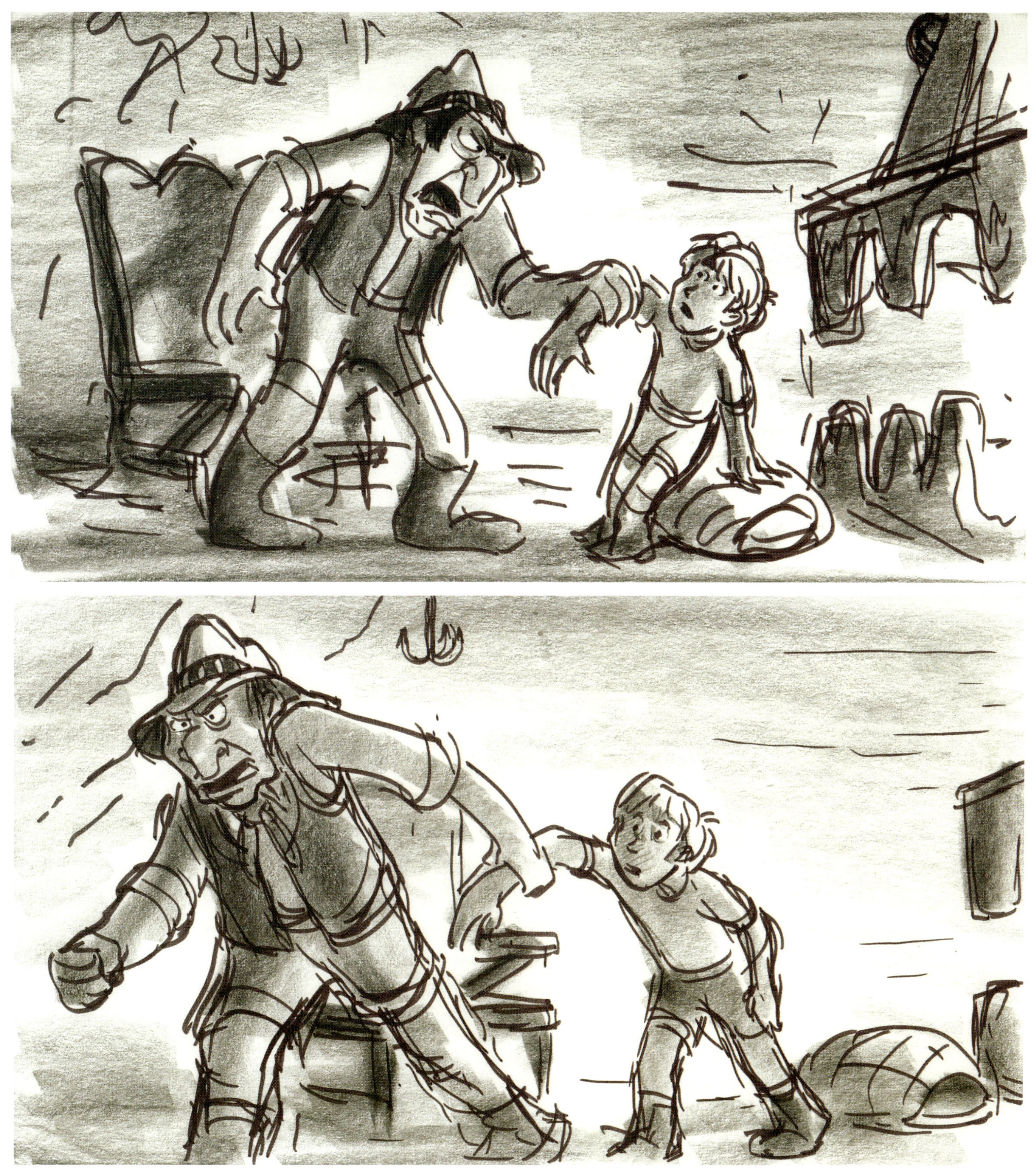

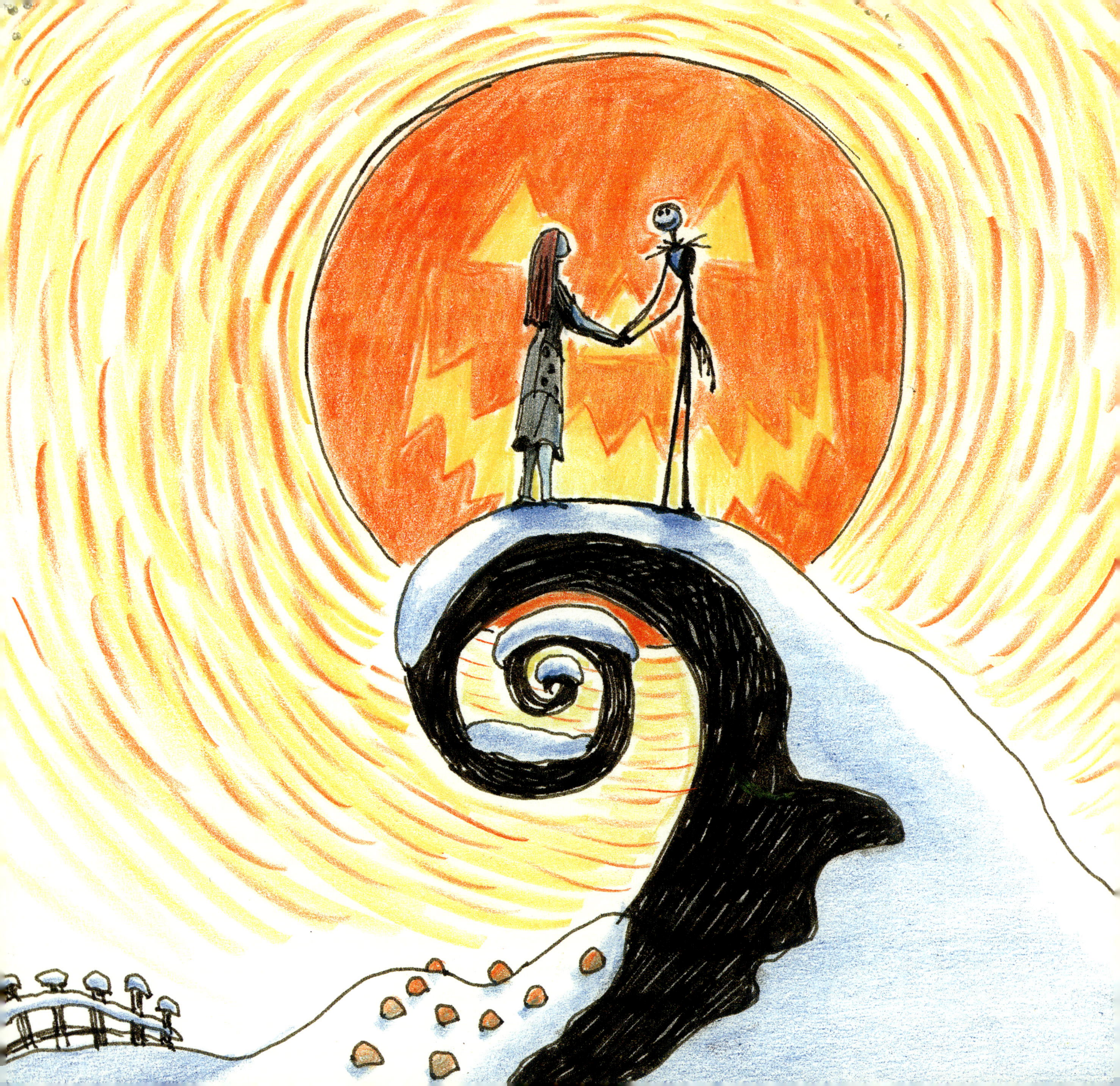

"Hello from Seattle," Joe Ranft wrote to a friend New Year's Day 1991 in his familiar childlike lowercase print style.

> Yes Seattle. In September my wife and I move[d] out of LA to the Great Green Northwest. So here we are now. The move thus far has proved to be very rewarding as well as challenging. We're attempting to live a more frugal life style and keep our lives simpler. We find ourselves experiencing some withdrawl [sic] symptoms as well as fear of the unknown.

Inspired by Bill Peet, he planned to switch from animation to children's books. "My goal is to get one published at least, so keep your fingers crossed for me."

Ranft explained candidly why he left Disney:

> I'm recovering from a period of creative burn out and on coming cynicalness [sic] brought on my last few years at Disney and becoming one of the "key players" as they like to say. The wounds are healing nicely. I love the people at Disney mostly fellow artists that I worked with there. I'm completely fed up with the "panic" management style and lack of originality in their choice of projects. Perhaps in the future I'll return for more abuse but I think if that happens I'll be playing the game in a different way. Anyway my challenge creatively right now is working on my own. Something you are very familiar with. I've always had the crutch of a lot of other creative people around to bounce ideas off of and run to whenever the inevitable blocks or depressions arrive. Ah but no more. I get to wade into those blocks hip deep, all by myself right now and it's not the easiest thing to do. I feel in my gut it's what I really need right now. . . .[1]

OPPOSITE: *Joe Ranft story sketch for* TIM BURTON'S THE NIGHTMARE BEFORE CHRISTMAS. RIGHT: *Ranft as Buttocks the Clown, "a Cirque du Soleil reject."*

During his first month in Seattle, he corresponded with several "fellow compatriates [sic]" on *The Rescuers Down Under*, including a January 25 letter to Tom Schumacher:

> I would just like to say thank you for all the gifts you brought to the crazy party called *The Rescuers Down Under*. . . . I feel that I learned a lot from being around you during the production and I just wanted to express my gratitude. You're a good guy Tom.

He attended a recycling/composting class, started a twenty-six-day intensive 7:00 A.M. yoga class, and found inspiration in *Iron John: A Book About Men* by poet Robert Bly. He looked forward to a retreat led by Bly and storyteller/mythologist Michael Meade. "That was what launched Joe into all this mentoring, the *Iron John* thing, a man taking responsibility for himself. It became a huge thing for him," Schumacher says.

Joe and Su moved what remained of their furniture into a rented room in a Seattle house owned by Ranft's cousin. Su found work at the local U-Haul, then as a waitress at "a swanky country club." Joe rested and worked on his kids' book. In January, he and Su participated in a fund-raising party to benefit the Seattle Hospice Co-op, in full clown drag as their scary clown personas Buttocks and his partner Bimbo.

Buttocks was "born" in 1988 when Su sewed a costume with yards of material and foam rubber to Joe's specifications ("Can you make a big butt that sticks far out in the back?"). Introduced as Cirque du

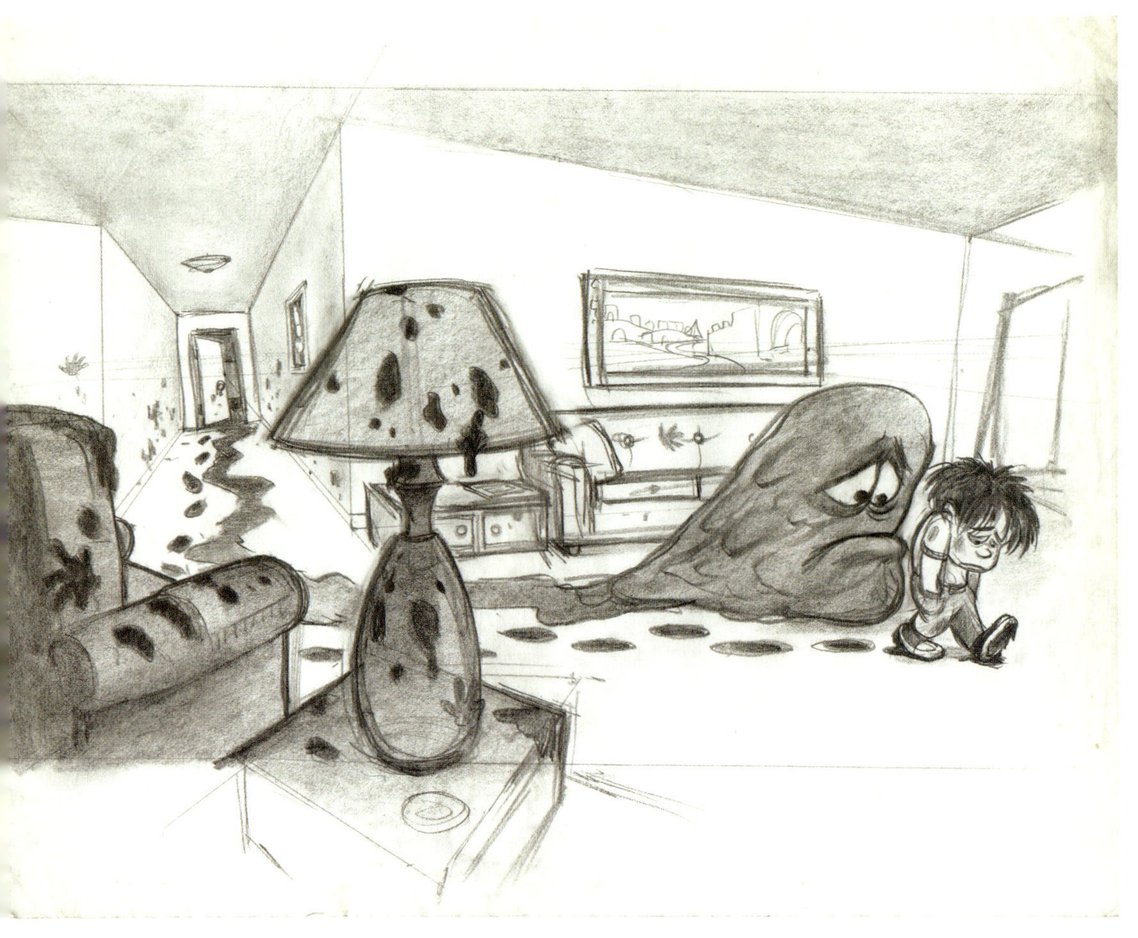

ABOVE: *Joe Ranft's illustration for* MUD, *a kids' book.* RIGHT: *Ranft's ideas for clock and candelabra rivalry in* BEAUTY AND THE BEAST.

Soleil rejects, Buttocks and Bimbo played L.A. charity gigs and marched in Pasadena's Doo Dah Parade, the staid Rose Bowl Parade's twisted sister; they then brought their zany act to Seattle (and later Pixar). "Let me tell you," Su says, "when [Joe] got the whole thing on and added the makeup, we are talking one helluva clown statement. Sometimes he would make little kids cry . . . overdosing on too much visual clowness."[2]

Every morning in Seattle, Joe walked around a lake communing with the animals as he went into town. During the next ten months, he read books, took drawing and yoga classes, met people, and made friends. He participated in "a Vision Quest thing" (fasting and living off the land); occasionally the Ranfts attended a spiritual retreat in Los Angeles, where invariably they asked themselves, "What are we doing?" in awful L.A.

In April, Ranft reported that while "things have been a little tough," the Seattle move has so far been "a fulfilling growth experience."[3] Su's unoccupied car was totaled by a drunk driver one night outside their house, and the couple was forced to share one car. "We're just a couple of fossil fuel addicts going through withdrawal," Ranft cheerfully wrote.

He completed two children's books—*Mud* (about personified muck and a kid) and *Baby Go Bowling*. He wrote a treatment for an animated feature. "I've been writting [sic] fast and just sort of puking out lots of ideas without regard for spelling, syntax punctuation etc. (Kind of like this letter)," he wrote with endearing self-awareness.

The recession of 1990–1991 hit hard. "Gee, savings going down a bit," Ranft noted. To help pay the rent, he accepted freelance jobs. He designed titles for the 1991 feature *Drop Dead Fred*, drew storyboards for the Saturday morning TV series *Back to the Future*, and designed titles for the TV series *Family Dog*, a 1993 spin-off based on a 1987 episode of *Amazing Stories* written and directed by Brad Bird.[4]

Ranft even worked for a week at Disney contributing gags to *Beauty and the Beast*. In the "Be Our Guest" musical number, he brought life to the antagonistic relationship between Cogsworth, a

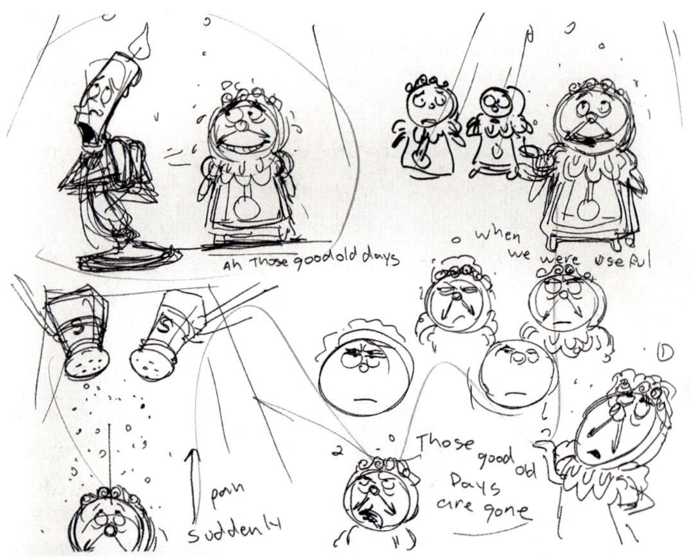

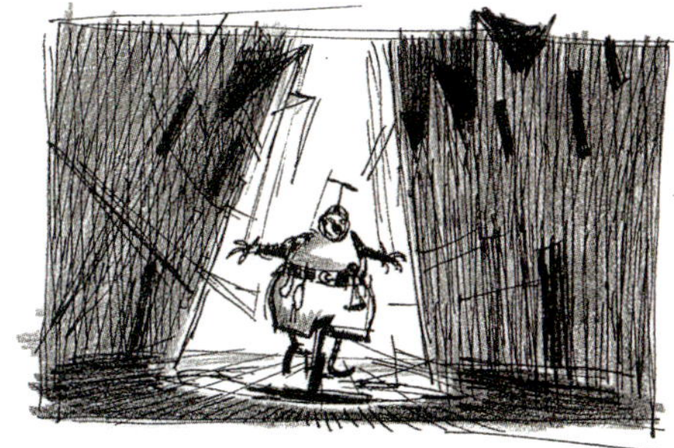
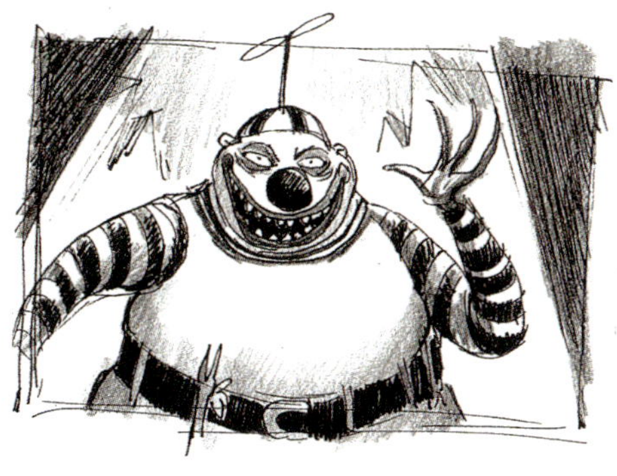
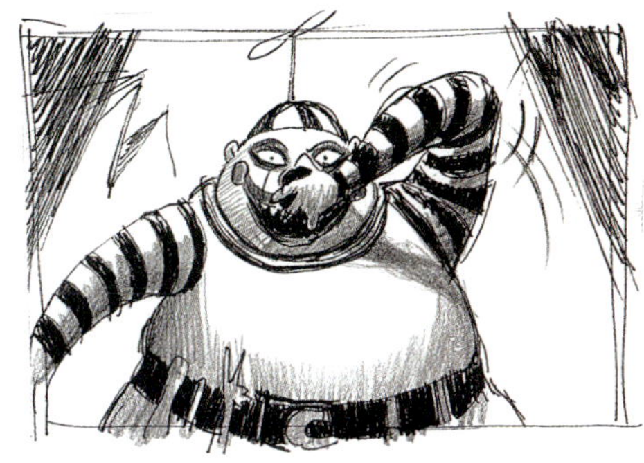
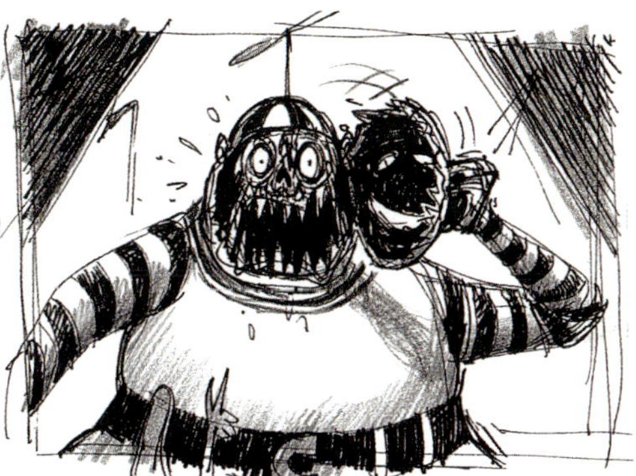

ABOVE: *A monstrous clown, and Joe Ranft* (LEFT INSET) *on the* NIGHTMARE *puppet set.*

stage-shy clock, and Lumiere, a hammy candelabra. Cogsworth ends up head-first in a bowl of Jell-O. "Pure Joe!" laughs story artist Brenda Chapman. Another charmingly inventive Ranft sight gag is the teacup child, Chip, showing off by blowing bubbles from the top of his head. "When you're burned out," Ranft said, "you don't have stuff to give. You go away, you replenish, and it's a joy!"[5]

Ranft stayed in touch with John Lasseter. In February he flew to Pixar, then located in Point Richmond, California, to discuss a TV special (*Tin Toy Christmas*), based on Lasseter's 1988 Academy Award–winning short *Tin Toy*. The special never happened, but ideas generated about a mechanical one-man band named Tinny—a toy discarded by a human baby for another plaything—eventually blossomed into *Toy Story*.

At a party in San Francisco, Ranft ran into Henry Selick. "Have you been contacted?" Selick asked regarding a puppet feature based on a Tim Burton story. *The Nightmare Before Christmas* would be designed by Burton, directed by Selick, distributed by Disney's Touchstone Pictures, and produced in the Bay Area by Skellington Productions. The company was named after "Jack Skellington," the film's skeleton "Pumpkin King" who, bored with Halloween, discovers the joys of Christmas.

Next day Ranft met with Burton, Selick, and visual consultant Rick Heinrichs and was offered the job of storyboard supervisor. "It looks like we may be moving to San Francisco this July," Ranft wrote in an April 4, 1991 letter. ". . . I'd move to the armpit of Aisa [sic] to work on it. San Francisco is not that bad," he joked.[6]

Nightmare was a perfect project for Ranft, not only because of the production's location. It reunited him with his idol Burton on an original story that allowed Ranft to display his full creative range—from cute and irreverent to monstrously ghoulish.

Stop-motion, animation's oldest technique, fascinated Ranft, who loved Rankin/Bass TV specials and shorts by Czech master Jiri Trnka. And, of course, Burton's *Vincent*. "There's nothing cooler than going to a stop-motion set," he said. Rows of black curtains surround miniature sets hovered over by animators listening to music on headphones, their faces studies of fierce concentration as their fingers manipulate puppet actors incrementally and photograph them frame by frame. "It's all lit and all there," Ranft marveled. "I love taking relatives, friends there. A window into another world."

Jerome Ranft, a *Nightmare* model maker, remembers the first time he watched his brother "do his thing"—storyboard the entire song "What's This?" "It was shocking how good he was! Wow! You know what you're doing!"

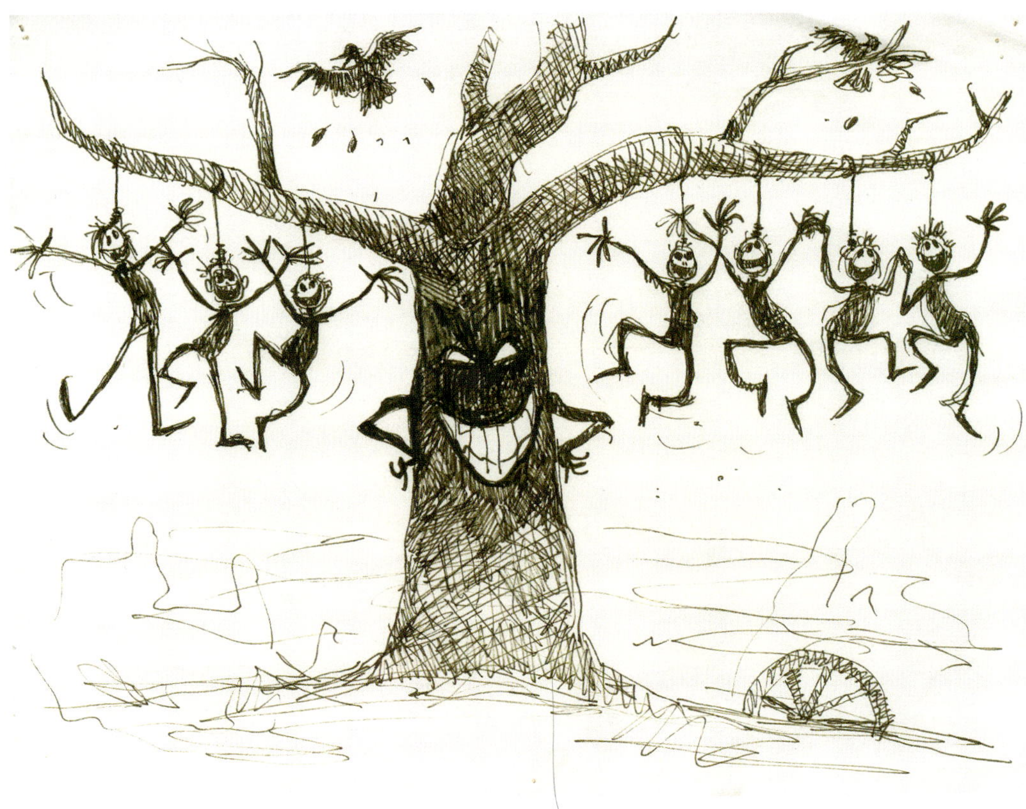

A card bearing a cartoon Santa Claus stork flying over Redwood City, California, with a bundle in his beak labeled "Ranft" announced their son's arrival on Christmas Eve 1991. Jordan James Ranft was named after Ruth's maiden name and Joe's father's first name.

The Ranft and Lasseter families lived around the corner from each other in Redwood City and shared many barbecues and birthday and anniversary celebrations. "We were so blessed," Lasseter says of their close friendship.[7]

Each day, Ranft took Caltrans public transportation to Seventh and Harrison streets in San Francisco to work at Skellington Productions, and Lasseter commuted by car to Pixar across the bay in

ABOVE: *A jolly hanging tree by Joe Ranft.*

On November 5, Ranft wrote:

Sue [sic] and I are relocated in the Bay Area. I'm busy at work on *The Nightmare Before Christmas*. And buisy [sic] is the word. But it's a lot of fun too. Sue and I are expecting a baby at the end of December. So as you see, we've got a lot of projects in development. After the story reel is complete on *Nightmare* I'm scheduled to go to work for Pixar on John Lassiters [sic] *Tiny Toy* feature.

Thanks so much for your words of encouragement. My sabbatacle [sic] in Seattle was so valuable to me in a lot of areas. Career wise I got back in touch with my old enthusiasm for animation like when I first went to CalArts. It was also very humbling working on my own. It made me realize how much I like being on a team. Though I think I'm a better team player after having spent ten months working on my own. More self discipline.

. . . We'll send you a birth announcement when the baby arrives. We don't know if it's a boy or girl yet. We could have found out but chose to keep it a surprise.

SeQ 802

3. new Dialog for santa grumbling more to himself or more interactive Dialog between Santa and LS + Barrell.

4. Grumbling becomes higher key ~~bef~~ when LS + Barrell approach Their tree house

5. perhaps we establish fog comming over hill as LS + Barrell enter Treehouse area.

SeQ 900 - Jacks send off

We need To re examine The Board.

1. mayor christens Jacks coffin Sleigh with a bottle handed to him by The corpse mom

2. Do ~~a~~ Long shot of halloween hill with fog creeping up

3. whole scene feels rushed and Dictated by mayors speech instead of storytelling.

Jack

snow first → Then Train
Holding snow cone
—Ice skaters

Jack

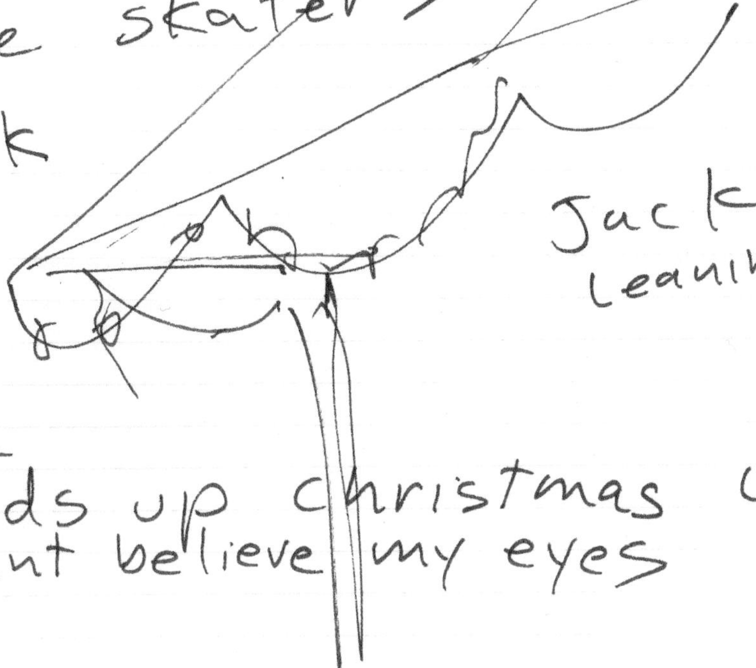

Jack
Leaning

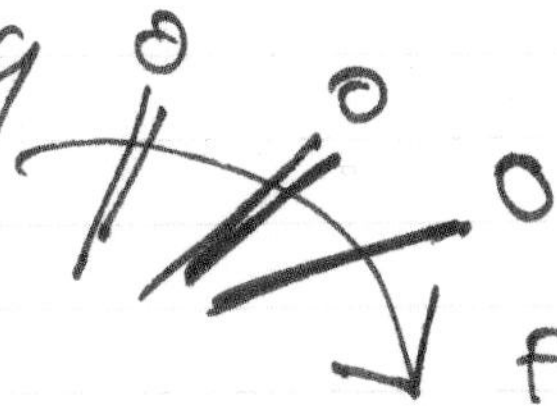

Falls

Jack
Holds up Christmas Lights
cant believe my eyes

Jack has Lights behind
him Then notices
snow.

Drag Jack Towards
cakes + pies

Jack more -3D

Jack
straight
profile

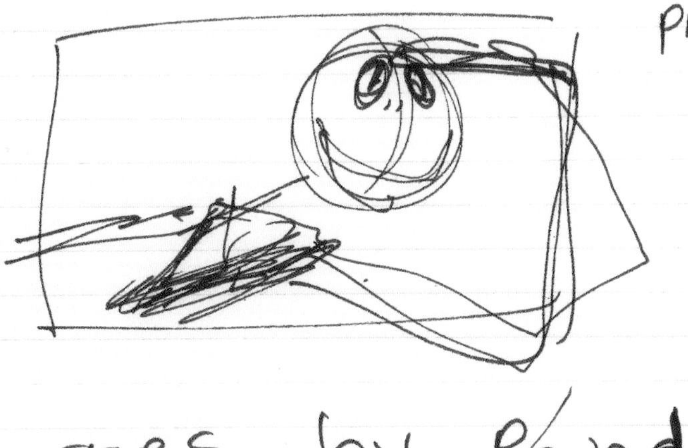

Jack goes by Reindeer

Seq 702 making Christmas cont.

③ Jack Says "Interesting" To
MR Hydes Russian Nesting
Vampire Doll.

④ cut out corpse kid w Truck
Jack Just points o.s. for
Uh huh?

⑤ characters Dancing on Table
Tops when ghosts enter at
end Restage final Tablea
before Reindeer Skelletons enter

Seq 800 Santa kidnapped
① Dialog for Santa
"Naughty nice naughty nice...
I wonder who that could be?
② Mrs clause Dialog? could you get That
Dear I'm Buisy
③ Santa smiles down at children LSB.

Seq 801 Jack Tries on santa suit

① Sally Distracted by new creation
pokes Jack with pin?

② Santa muttering Dialog Befor LS+B
open Bag.

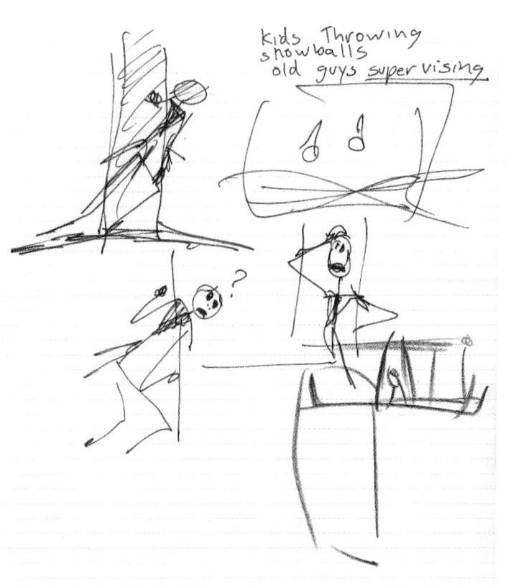

OPPOSITE AND THIS PAGE: *Joe Ranft's notes for NIGHTMARE ideas and story points.*

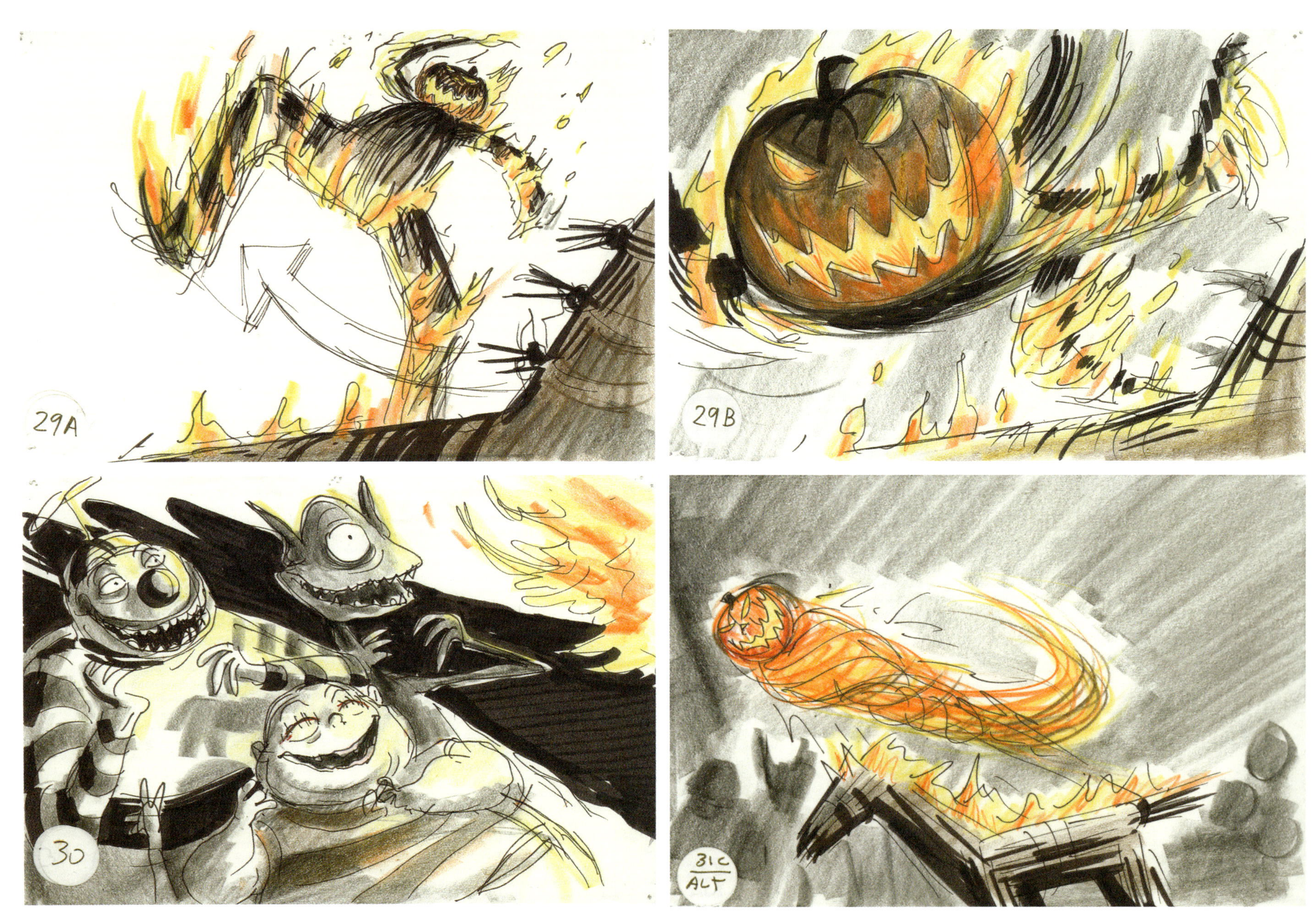

ABOVE: *Cinematic shot variations in Joe Ranft's boards for a* NIGHTMARE *musical number.*

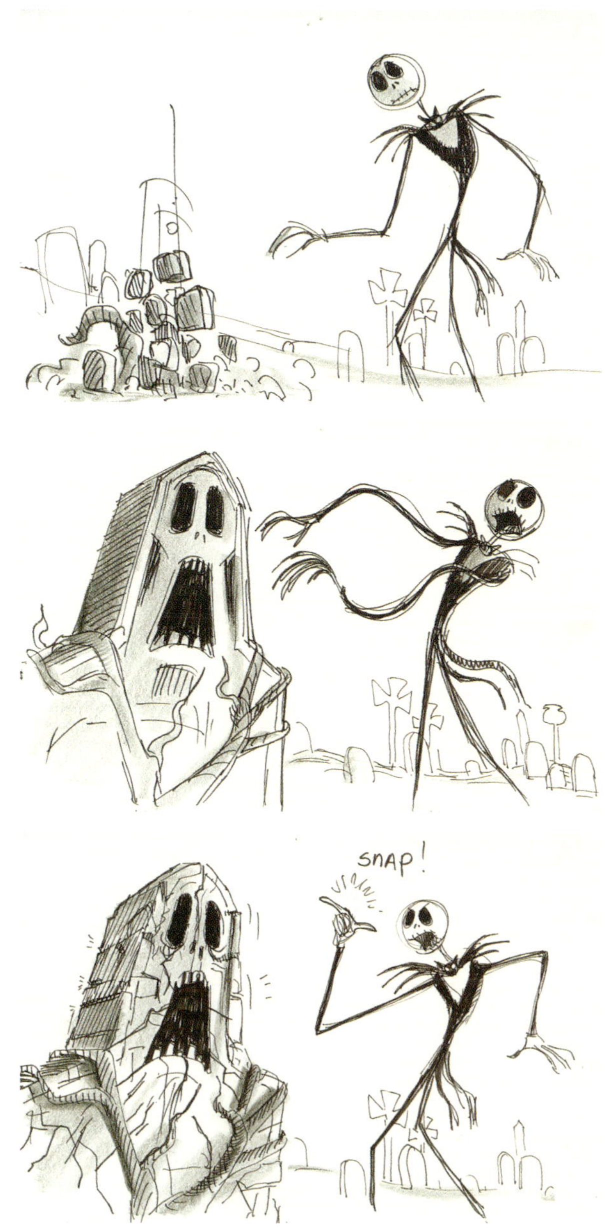

Point Richmond. For years, each time Lasseter completed another award-winning short or commercial, Disney attempted to woo him back. But he preferred Pixar and living in the Bay Area.

"Why can't I do a film for you up here?" Lasseter asked the company. "We have this brilliant technology, it's a great setup." Disney became more interested after Burton's *Nightmare* broke the precedent that all Disney films must be made in-house. "It was obvious that animation had become so profitable that Disney knew they couldn't turn out as much work as they could sell," Lasseter says. "They started looking for other producers that could do films within the Disney framework."[8]

Lasseter insisted that Pixar wanted to make a different kind of feature using only CGI, and an original story, not a familiar fairy tale. Characters wouldn't burst into song à la musical comedy formula; the score would be "cohesive" (sung by an off-screen voice commenting on the narrative). Further, there would be no villain, no comic sidekicks, and the leads could be funny as well as serious.

"They said great!" Lasseter recalls. In July 1991, Pixar signed a three-picture deal with Disney and began developing the story and design for the film that became *Toy Story*.

After *Nightmare*, Ranft planned to move across the bay to work full time at Pixar. Meantime, he helped Lasseter, Docter, and Andrew Stanton get going on *Toy Story* by coming in for a day or two and a phone call here and there as the story developed.

Su and Joe continued attending spiritual retreats, yoga empowerment return-to-the senses meditations, such as Inward Bound ("Those who don't go within, go without."), and other self-actualization/marriage retreats. They attended the nondenominational Church of Religious Science (also known as Science of Mind) to feed their spiritual sides. "It was really strong in our relationship," Su says.

"Joe had this idea that when we left L.A., if we really believed that we were following our hearts, that the universe would open doors that you don't see. There was no *Nightmare Before Christmas* or *Toy Story* when we left L.A. So it's a little weird. There was no way to make a living in Seattle, and we couldn't tolerate L.A. anymore. So the universe said, well, how about the Bay Area? I was born here and came back in time to have my son. Isn't that amazing?

"It's amazing!"

Sequential boards by Joe Ranft for NIGHTMARE.

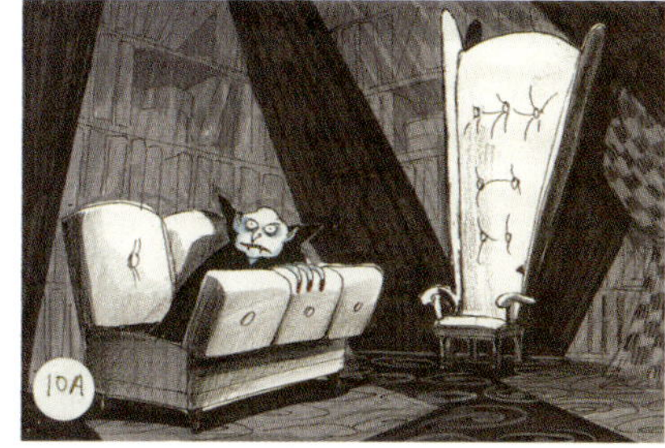

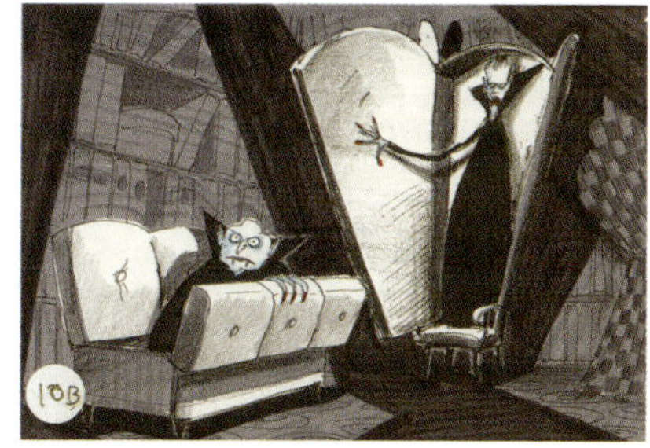

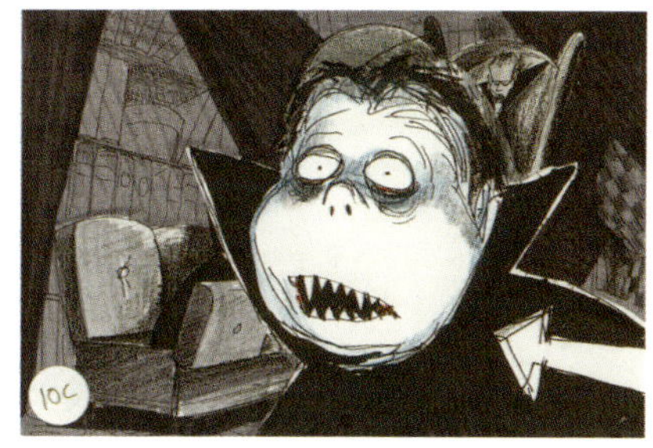

CHAPTER TEN

Toy Stories

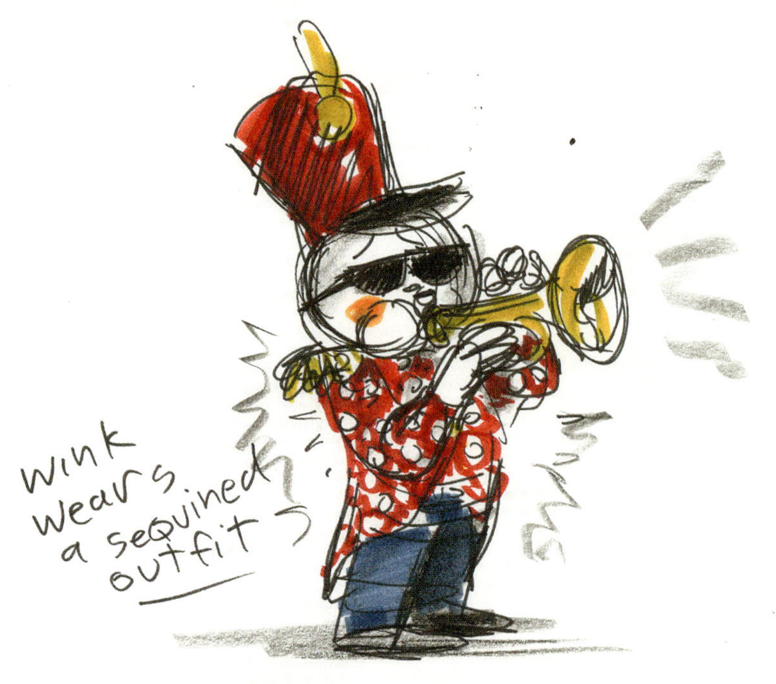

ABOVE: *Tinny, a toy one-man band.* RIGHT: *Animation legend Chuck Jones* (CENTER) *visits the Pixar "Brain Trust"* (LEFT TO RIGHT), *John Lasseter, Pete Docter, Andrew Stanton, and Joe Ranft.*

One of Su Ranft's favorite memories during the making of *Toy Story* is of her husband washing dishes in the kitchen of their two-bedroom rental in Point Richmond. Smiling contentedly, he glanced at his reflection in the window over the sink and quietly said, "I just *love* my fuckin' job!"

"It was the best time of our lives," Su says.

At the beginning of the 1990s, Pixar was a small company blazing new trails in animation. "There were only a hundred of us in the building," Darla Anderson says.[1]

The studio's original creative core—nicknamed the "Brain Trust"—included John Lasseter, Pete Docter, Andrew Stanton, and Joe Ranft. "We traveled everywhere together, had meetings, and we'd write together, a very collaborative group," Docter says. The four individualistic personalities meshed well, and Joe Ranft had a particular gift for moving ideas forward if things got bogged down.

The journey to success for *Toy Story*, however, was neither short nor painless. "Inevitably, these movies have to go through a death and a rebirth," Ranft later commented. "I don't know why, but I've never seen it where there's one pass and everybody says, gee, that was easy."[2] The film was green-lit in January 1993 and development began on the *Tin Toy* idea by Lasseter, Stanton, and Docter. Ranft contributed whenever he could get time away from Skellington. "John wanted to pull on Joe's story strength," especially his talent for brainstorming, Stanton says. And "Joe was always [Lasseter's] confidant." By fall, Ranft joined Pixar's Brain Trust full-time.

Becoming a "buddy picture" enhanced the initial idea—making toys come alive. Tinny, a one-man-band toy, is lost by his young owner at a rest stop during a family vacation. A junk man finds him and tosses him into the back of his truck, where he meets an old ventriloquist's dummy. The two stick together sharing adventures and end up in a preschool "toy heaven" where they'll never again be lost or outgrown.

When the story line evolved into a boy receiving a new toy for his birthday and bringing it into his toy-filled bedroom, critical character changes occurred. Tinny now seemed old-fashioned and was replaced

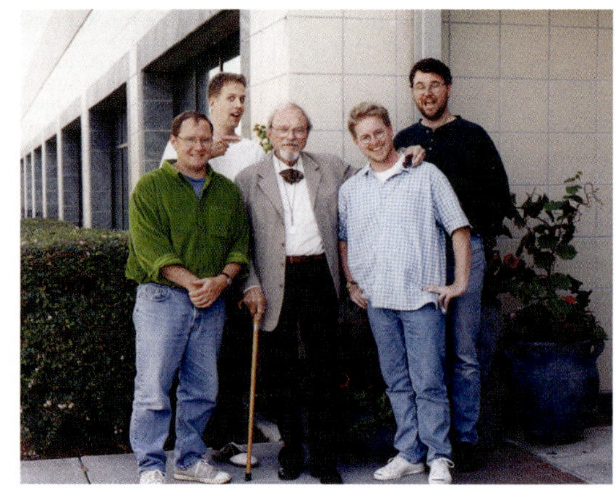

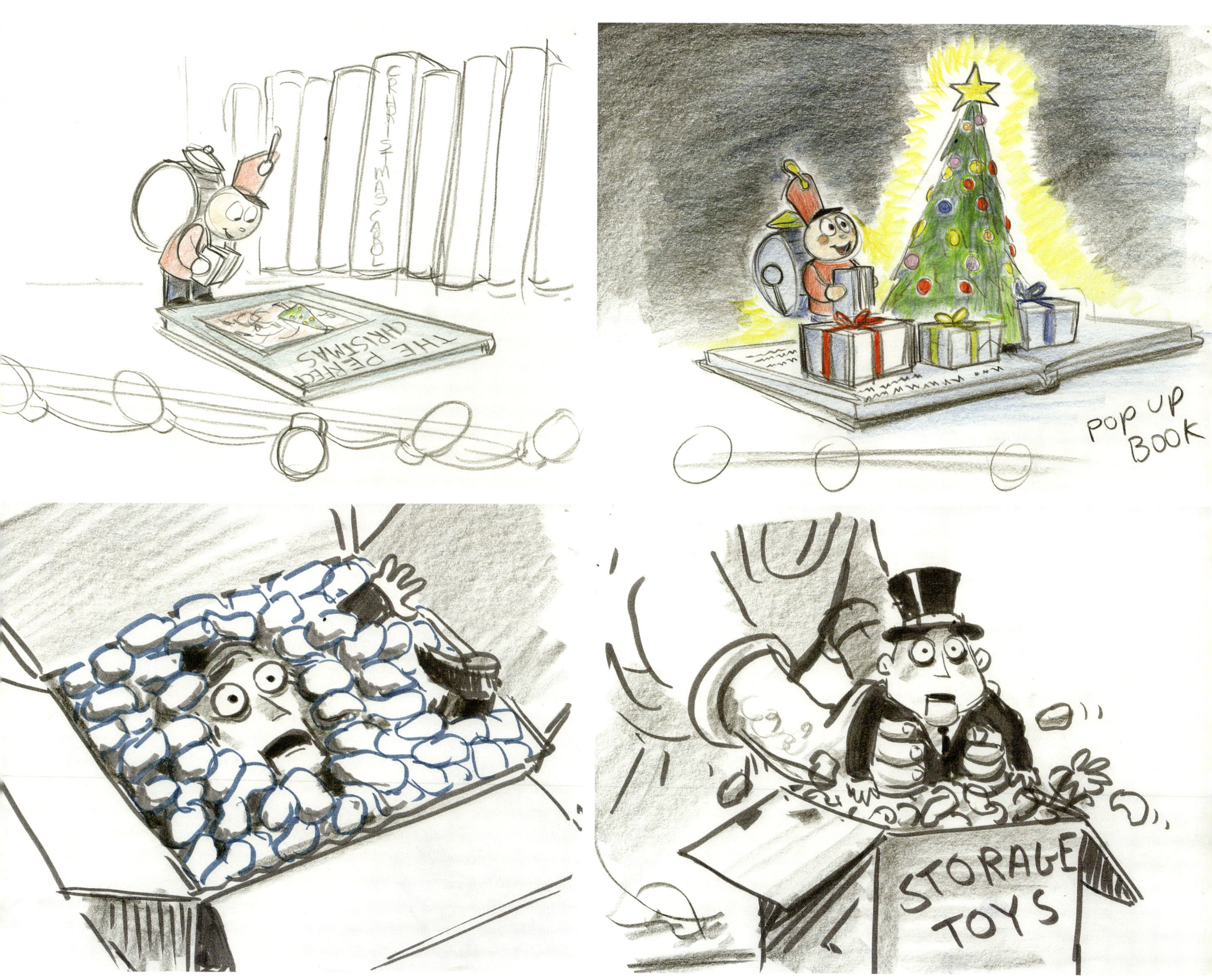

Joe Ranft story sketches for a Tin Toy *Christmas special c. 1993, which evolved into* Toy Story.

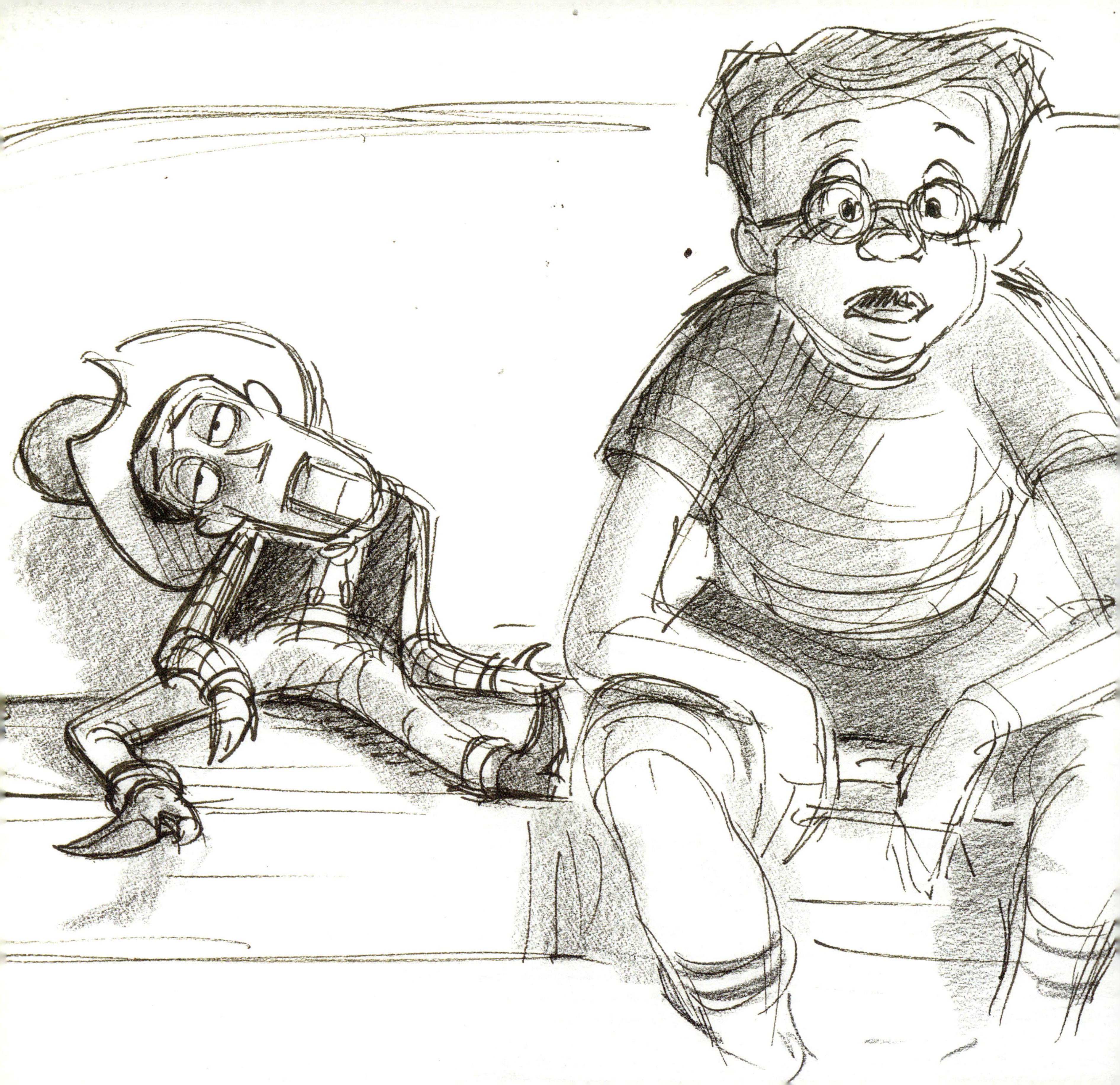

by a futuristic action figure ultimately named Buzz Lightyear, Space Ranger. The dummy concept morphed into a pull-string rag doll cowboy named Woody.

Buzz and Woody were contrasting yet complementary types, one symbolizing the frontier of space, the other an icon of the Western frontier; both perfect for a buddy film. The four Pixarians, believing this would be the only feature they would make, based it on their own sensibilities, humor, and memories of childhood. Determined not to conform to Disney's formula, they had a ball.

For research, a slew of Toys "R" Us™ playthings were bought for inspiration. All day and late into many nights, the four men shared loud arguments and laughter over story points around a single table, finishing each other's sentences while scribbling rows of storyboard drawings that barely contained the profusion of ideas spilling forth.

Lasseter and Docter identified with Andy, the sweet-natured kid who owned Buzz and Woody, while Stanton and Ranft saw their child selves in Sid, a "bad" kid who makes "mutant toys" and plays with fire. Ranft recalled that he and his brother Jim burned tiny plastic green army men with magnifying glasses "just to see how they melt." The Ranft boys also challenged a TV commercial proclaiming an elephant could sit on a Tonka truck with no resultant damage. Then seven-year-old Joe and six-year-old Jim pushed a cinder block out of a wall onto a toy Tonka, which destroyed it and the kids' belief in truthful advertising. "Aw, that's baloney!" they surmised.

Ranft masterfully storyboarded one of *Toy Story*'s most memorable sequences: a squad of tiny green plastic soldiers set up a reconnaissance to spy and report back to the toys when Andy opens his birthday presents. In Ranft's hands it became a brilliant, entertaining parody of Hollywood war-movie bravery, complete with selfless wounded soldiers and a gruff bighearted commander.

Staged with dramatic cinematic camera angles, the sequence sailed through the production with minimal changes, "a magical thing [that] happens with Joe Ranft in every one of our movies," Lasseter says.

"He would present this thing production-ready, it would be gold," says Stanton. "You wouldn't want to touch anything."

Pixar prepared a finished animation test of Woody and Buzz exchanging dialogue to placate worried Disney executives who feared audiences—used to hand-drawn animation—would not sit still for eighty-plus minutes of computer imagery. The suits were reassured when they saw Woody and Buzz interacting, perfectly modeled and lit "like you could reach up and touch those toys," Lasseter said. "All doubts went away."

Not completely. Doubts persisted about the narrative and the Pixarians were peppered with memos full of advice from Disney management, including Jeffrey Katzenberg. "This is too juvenile" and "make it more edgy" was the gist, with demands for more one-liners, put-downs, and zingers.

Pixar "jumped through hoops" to accommodate the suggestions, deferring to Disney's long experience. "They know what they're talking about," Lasseter said. "They've been so successful, we'll just learn from them as best we can."

On November 17, 1993, the Pixar gang of four flew to Burbank to screen the work-in-progress for Disney executives. It was a disaster. No one laughed, and the suits left the screening room in ominous silence.

Pixar's effort to accommodate Disney's desire for "edginess" stuffed the story with smart-ass gags and no narrative flow. "The characters were basically jerks to each other and completely unlikable," says

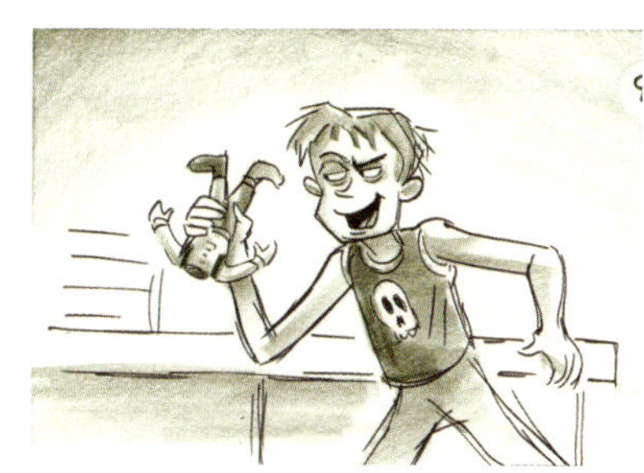

OPPOSITE: *An early version of Woody, the cowboy toy, and Andy.* ABOVE: *Sid, the sadistic bully. Drawings by Joe Ranft.*

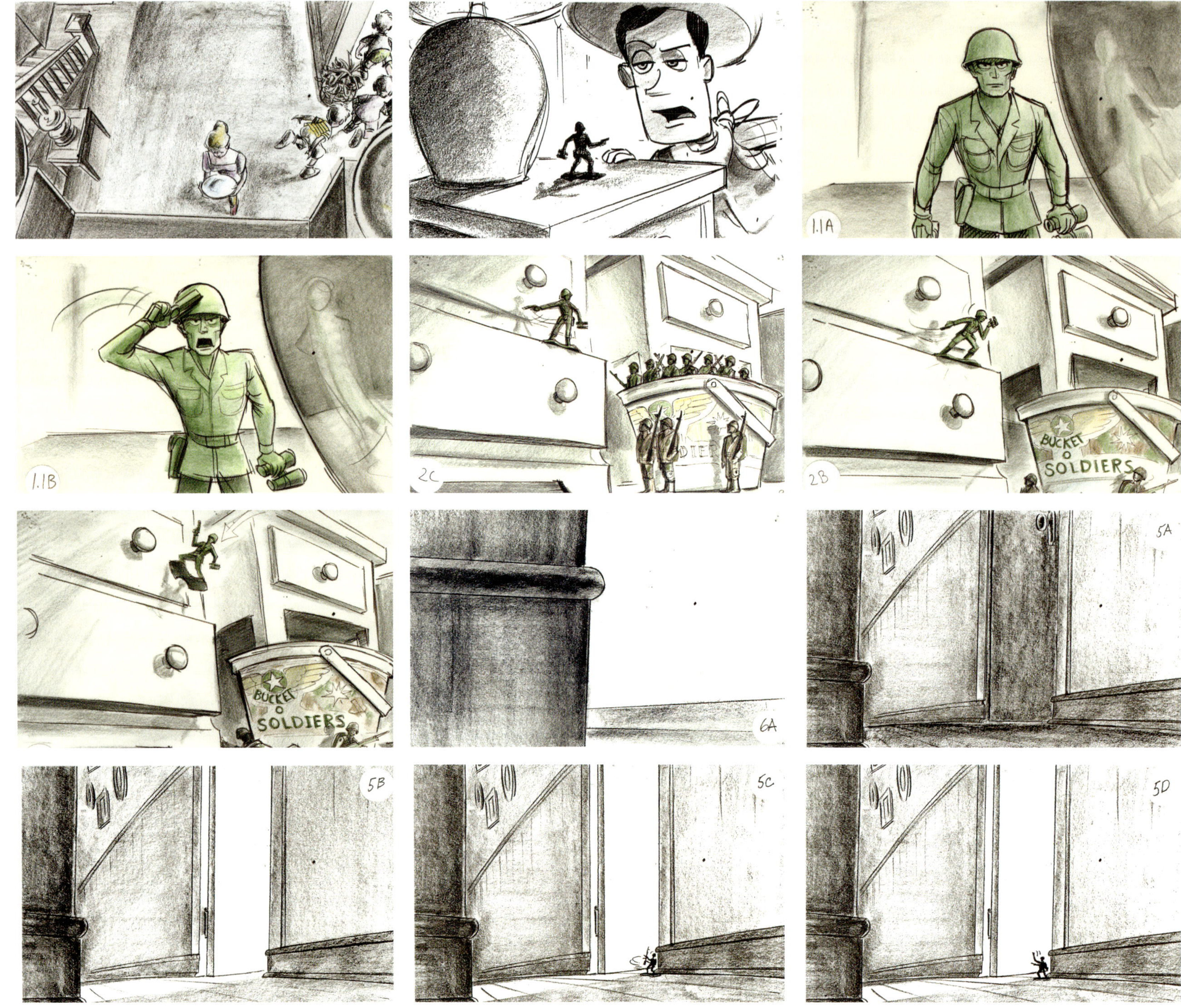
1.1A
1.1B
2C
BUCKET O SOLDIERS
2B
BUCKET O SOLDIERS
6A
5A
5B
5C
5D

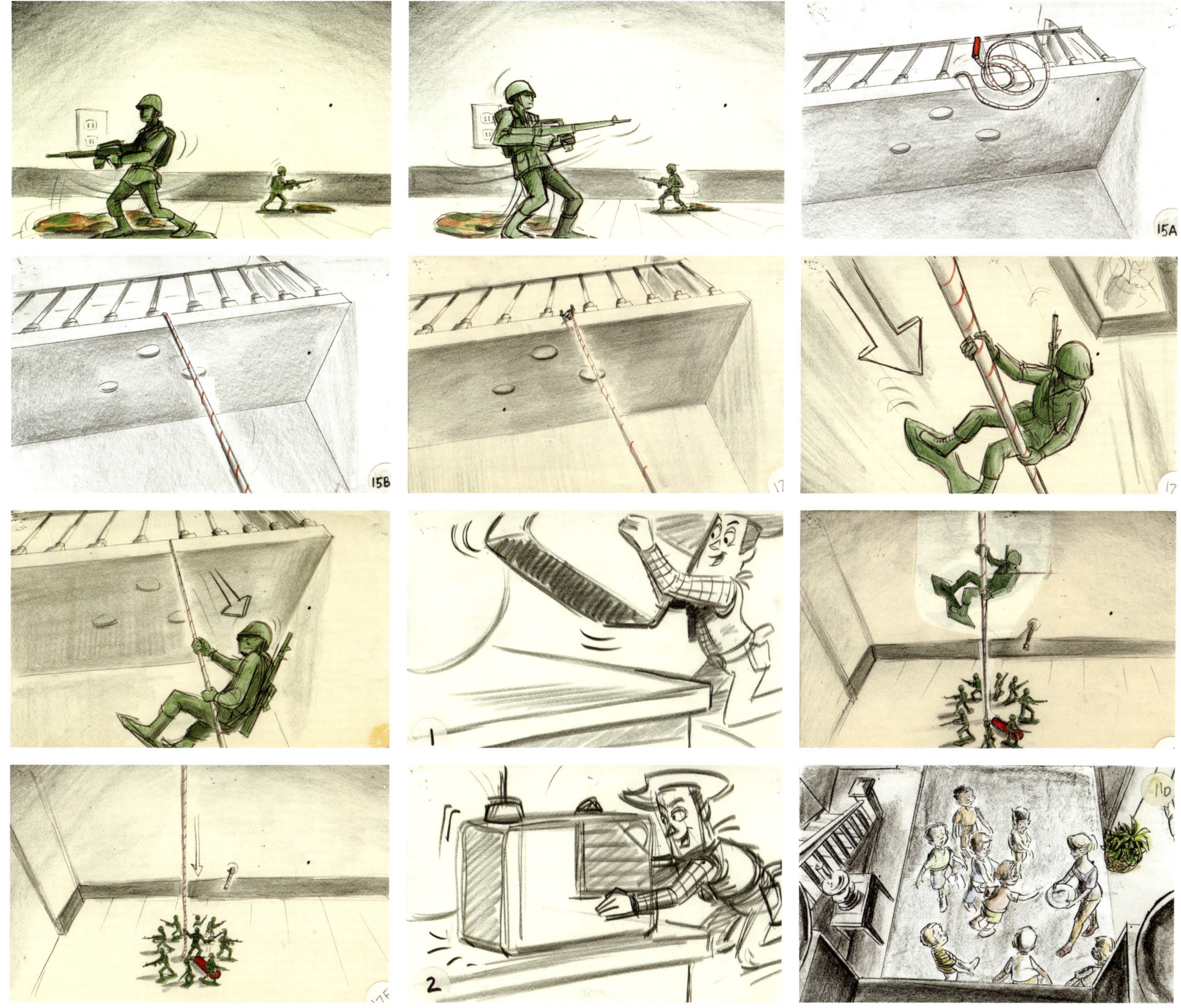

Joe Ranft

ARMY MEN

ON THE MOVE

BOARD 1

THIS PAGE AND FOLDOUTS: *Joe Ranft's classic* Toy Story *storyboard of the green army men "on the move."*

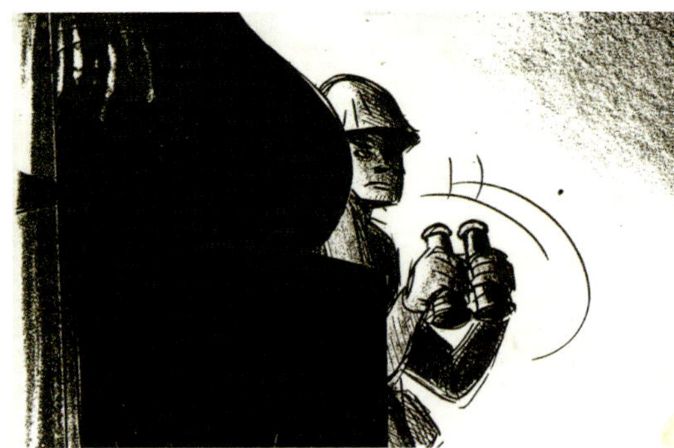

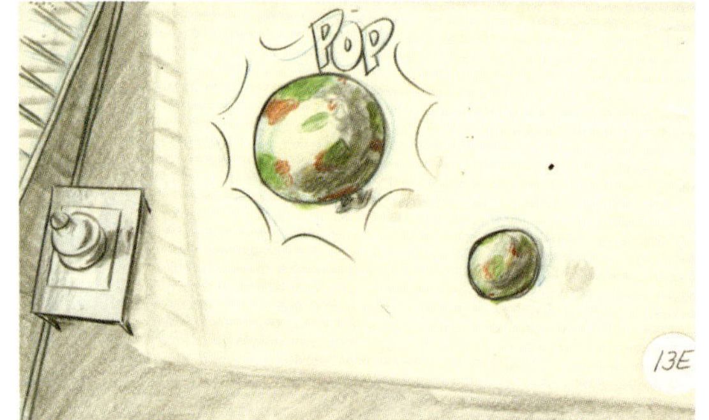

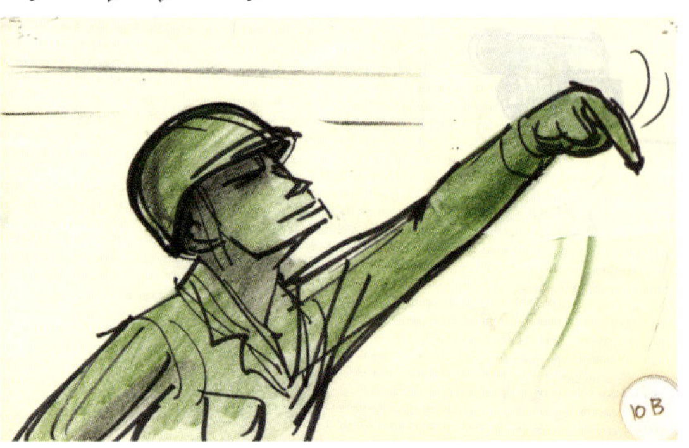

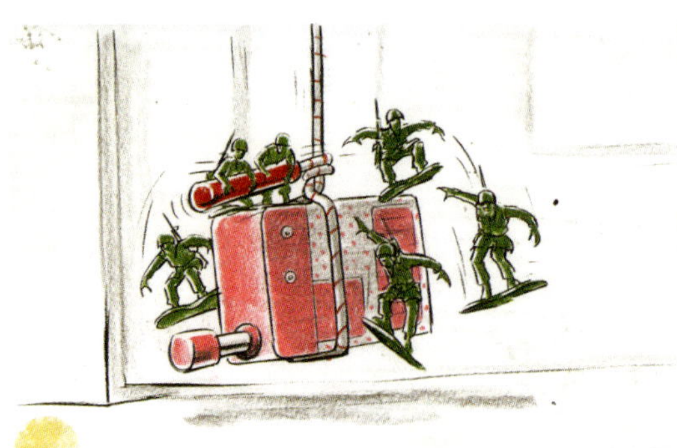

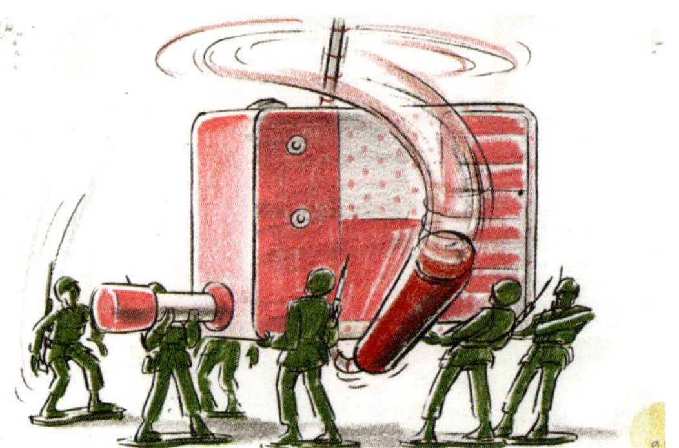

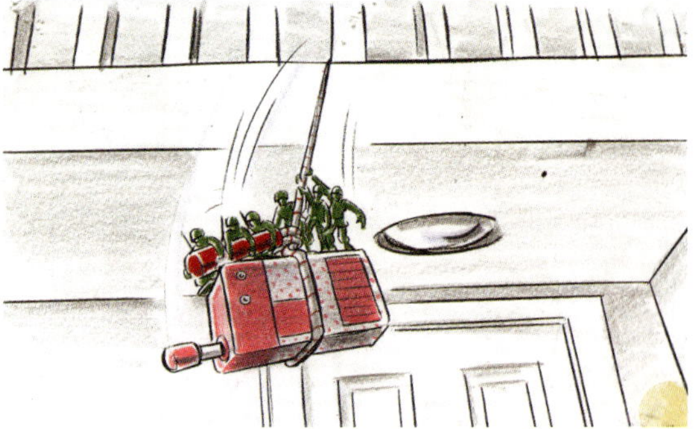

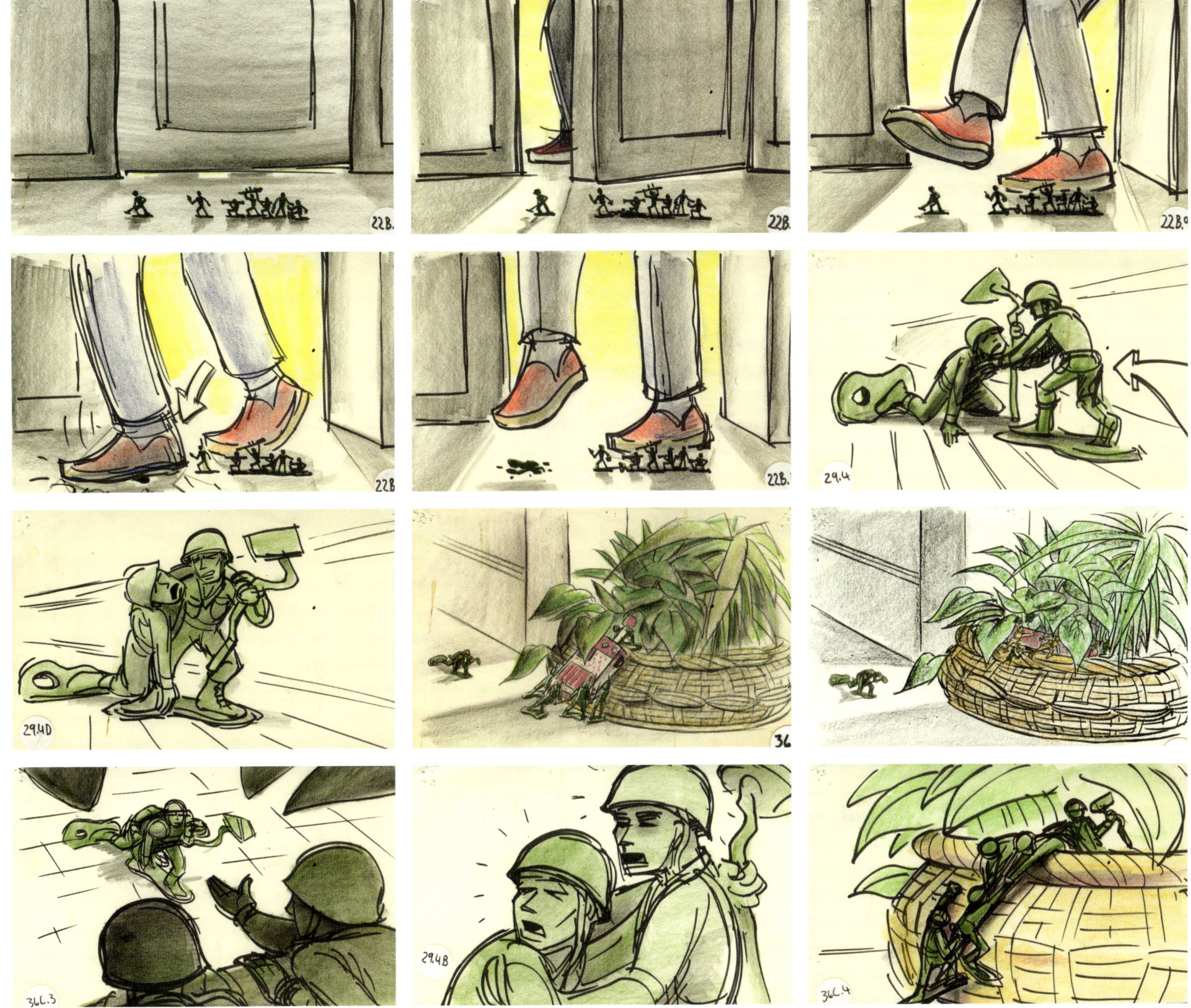

22B.
22B.
22B
29.4
29.4D
36
36C.3
29.4B
36C.4

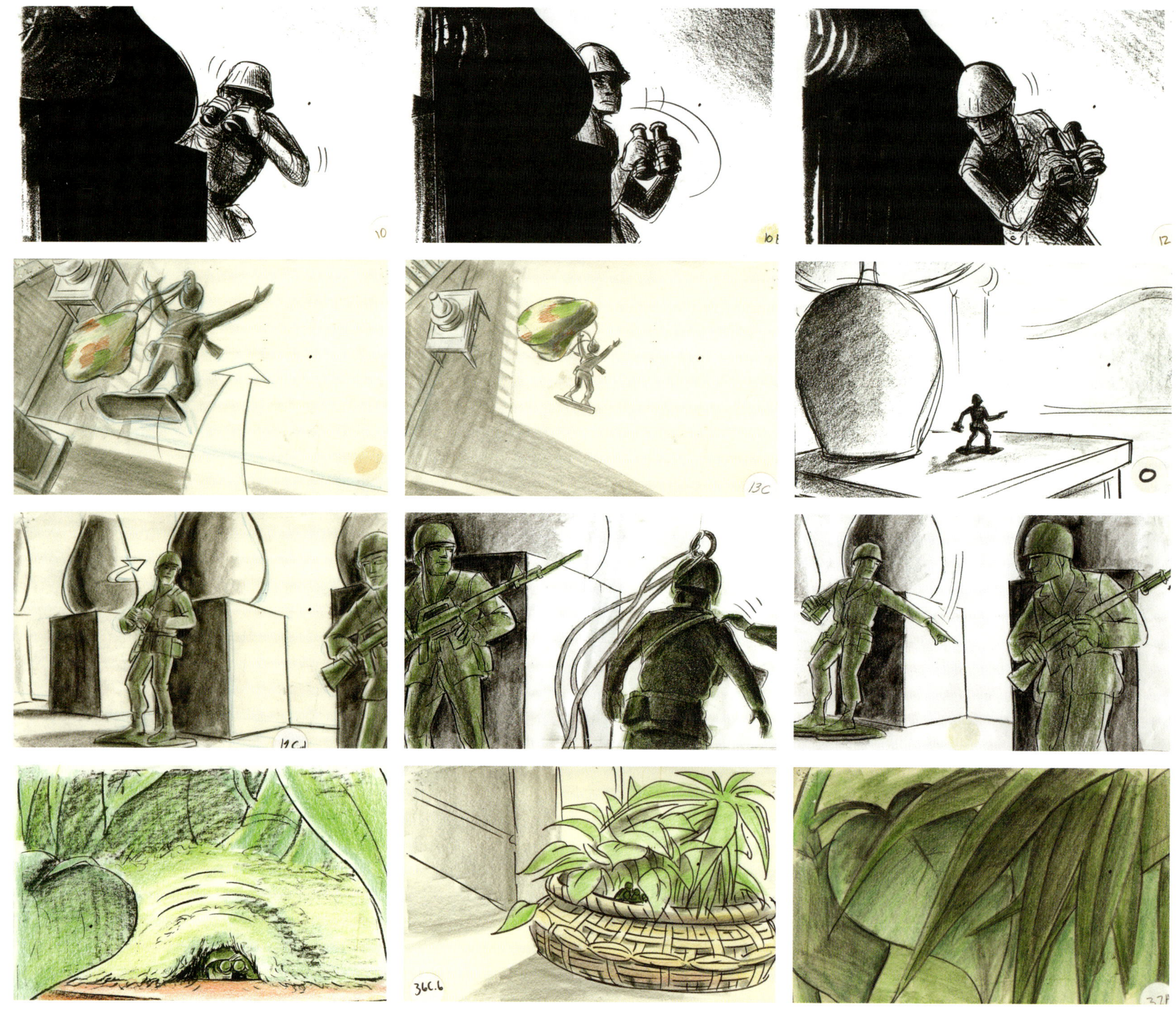

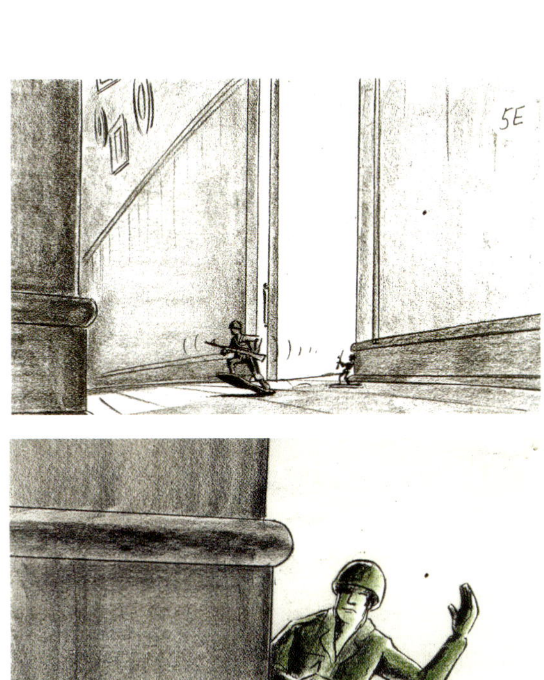
5E

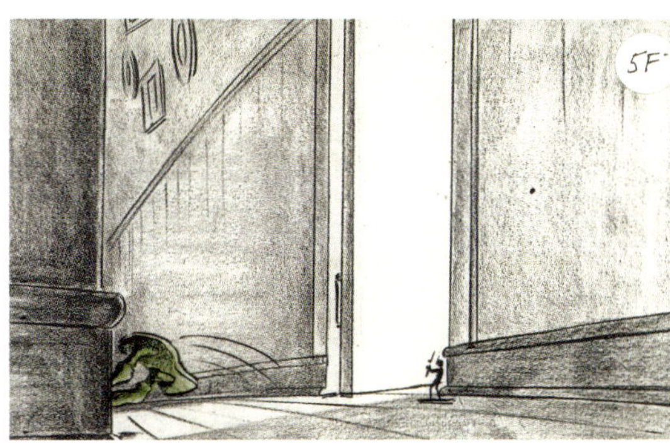
5F

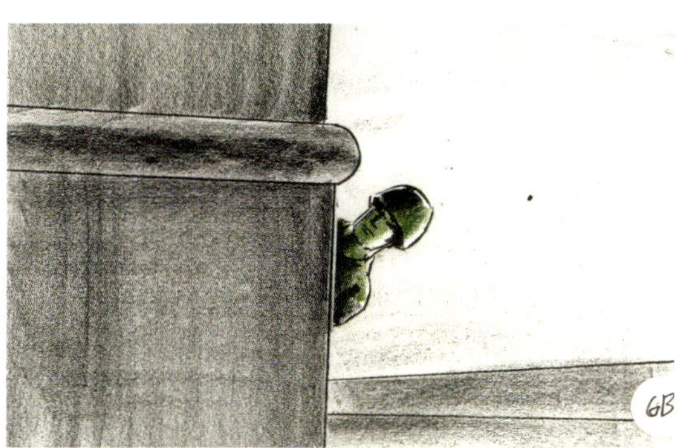
6B

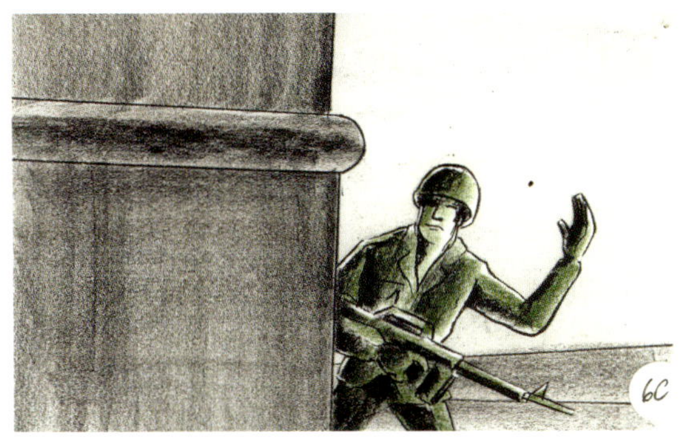
6C

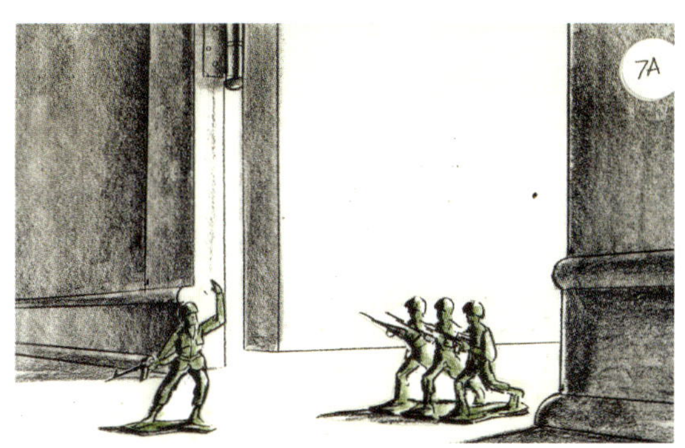
7A

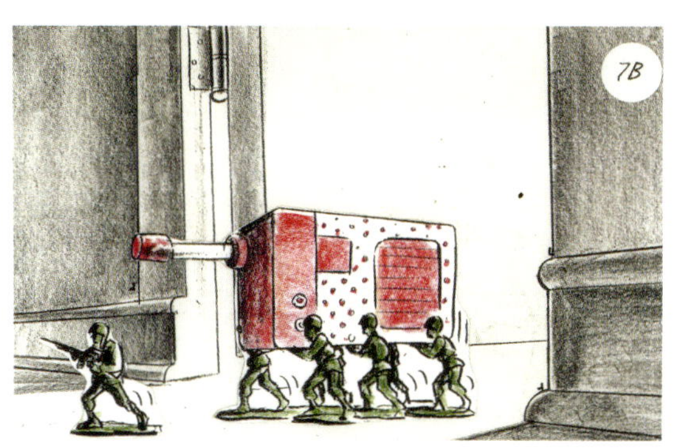
7B

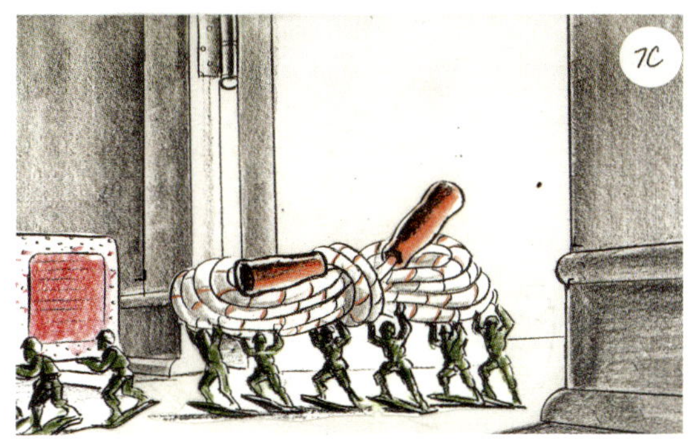
7C

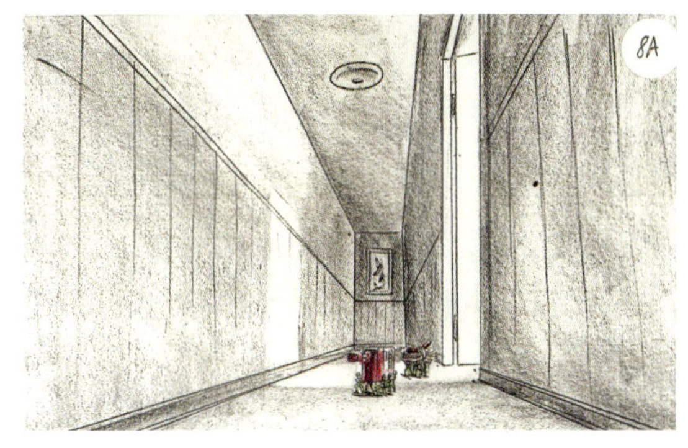
8A

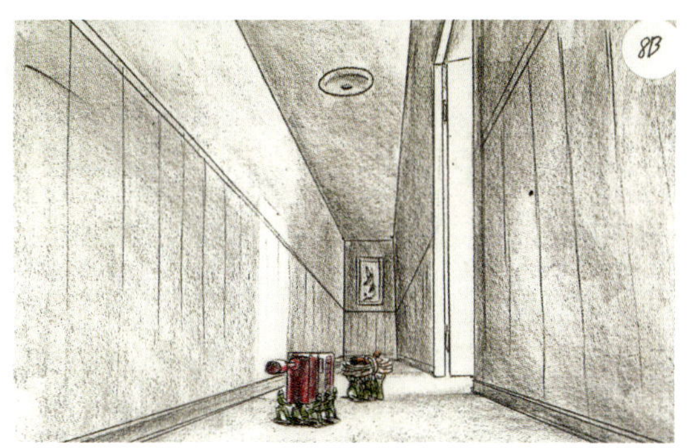
8B

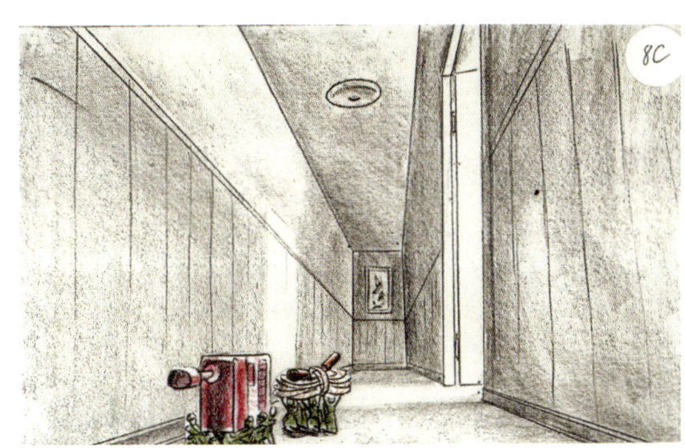
8C

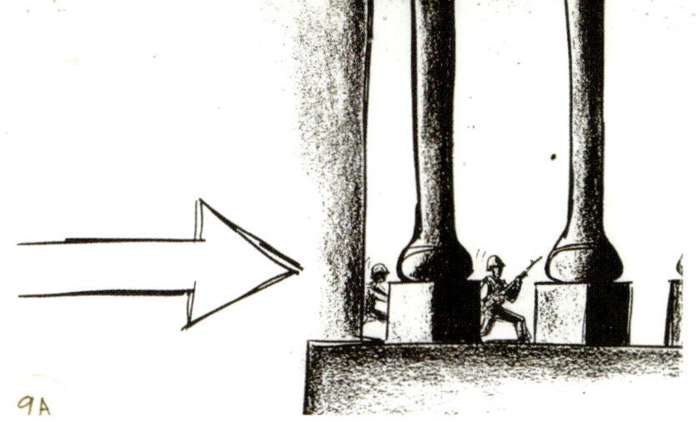
9A

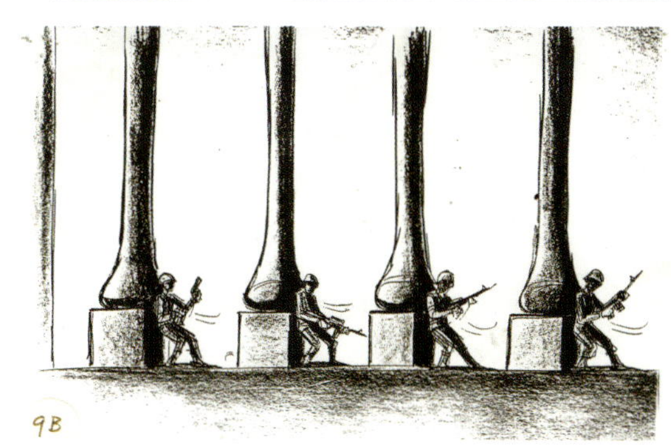
9B

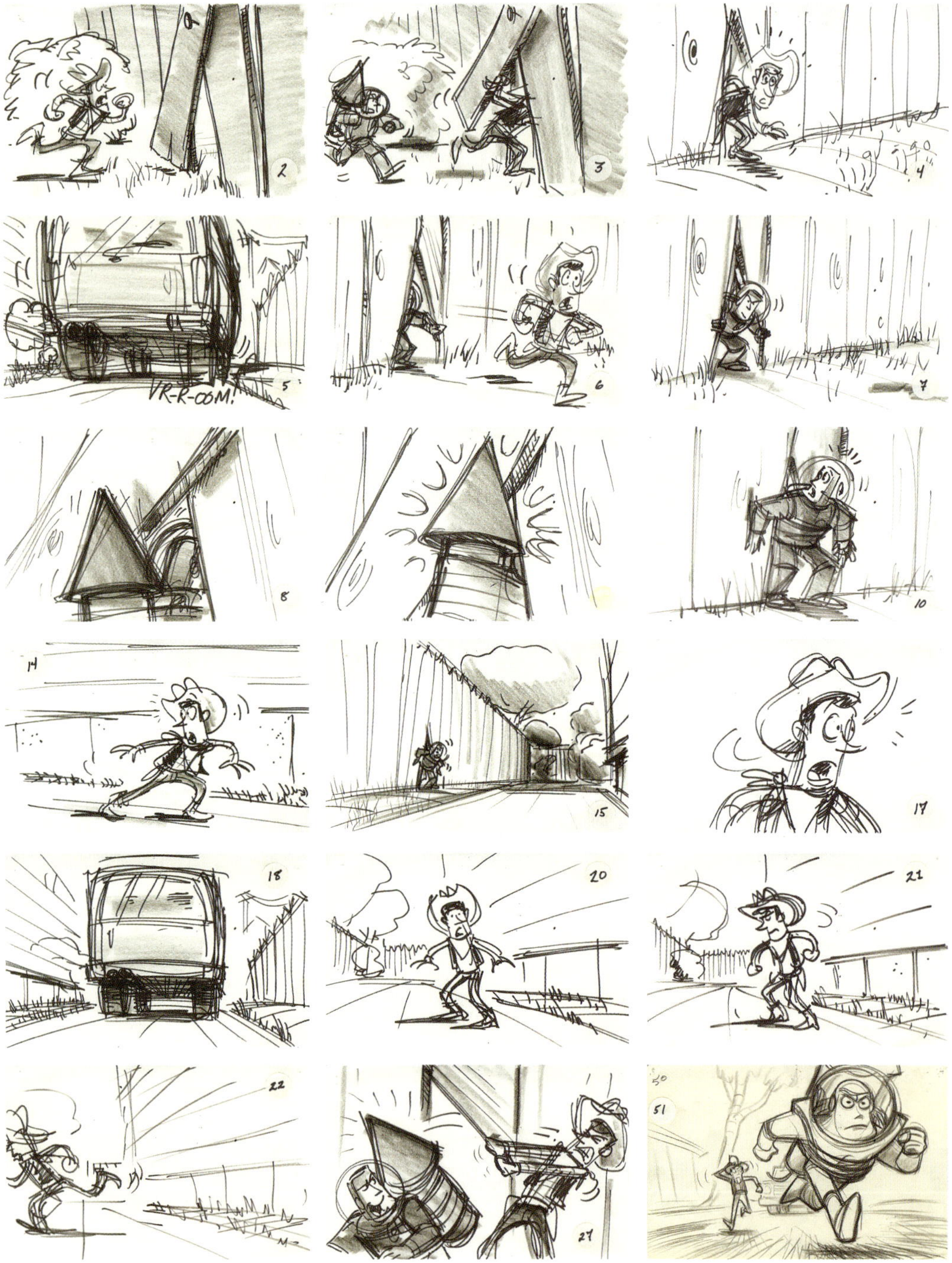

Docter. "I was so embarrassed for what was up on the screen," Lasseter admits.

The production shut down, and twelve newly trained animators were placed on hold. Since Pixar's story crew apparently couldn't cut it, Disney insisted the production move to Los Angeles so the studio could oversee things. "And give us more notes," Ranft lamented.

Lasseter, whose "heart was broken," begged for a two-week reprieve to turn things around. After obtaining Disney's skeptical permission, Lasseter, Ranft, Docter, and Stanton resolved to "make the movie we want to make!"

The story revision, Docter recalls, "was where Joe Ranft really sang. He was the only one of us who'd worked on a feature film all the way through. Joe would always say 'trust the process,' which means stick with it. He was amazing at this. Joe would leap one hundred percent with his heart and say, 'I believe in this! We're gonna go!' So he would commit everything to making it better. Joe was really brave in that."

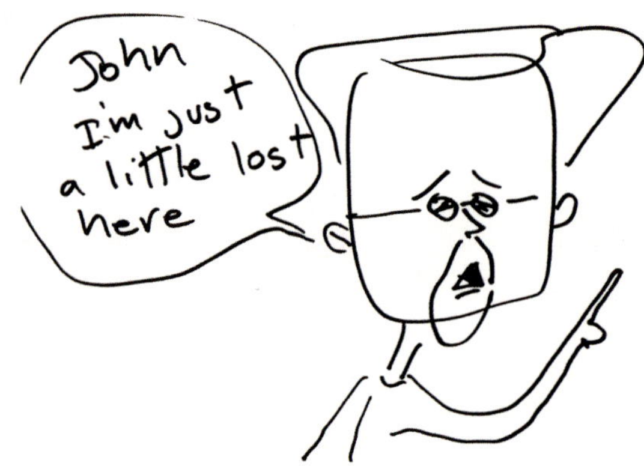

LEFT: *Joe Ranft story sketches for* TOY STORY *finale.*
ABOVE: *Ranft's caricature of Disney executive Tom Schumacher during a* TOY STORY *meeting.*

The process included writing, gathering more material, constant meetings, weeding out, refocusing, and . . . more meetings. "Two or five heads are better than one," Ranft believed. "If you can work together without killing each other, you can accomplish a lot."

"The great thing about Pixar," Ranft reiterated, "is that everybody is in on the story. Dozens of people here have read screenwriting books and gone to screenwriting conferences, and we collaborate in a form of oral storytelling, with people trying to top each other, acting out parts. I imagine it's what it must have been like in the Mack Sennett silent-clown days."[3]

Lee Unkrich was hired during *Toy Story*'s revamp. "Editors are huge contributors," Ranft commented in 1997. "You can turn something in and look at it on the reels. It's slow, it's boring. What's not working? Oh, that little part, one little thing and you build around that. . . . Once you start boarding stuff, especially the first time, you immediately start uncovering all the problems no one thought of . . . All kinds of unforeseen problems just emerge. *Boink! Boink!* They come jumping up like Jack-in-the-boxes when you first board a scene. . . . Storyboarding is just re-boarding."

Unkrich remembers "a rush of lots of ideas and excitement and hope that they could turn this around. Not everything I saw was working great. But I watched the earlier reels and they'd gotten over that hump. So my memories of those early days were being in an editing room with John, Joe, Andrew, and Pete, everybody excited. It wasn't gloomy. It was the excitement that they were onto something!"[4]

Two weeks later, Disney executives filed into a screening room expecting nothing. Instead, the new reels were received with amazement. "What did you guys take? Funny pills?" someone asked Lasseter.

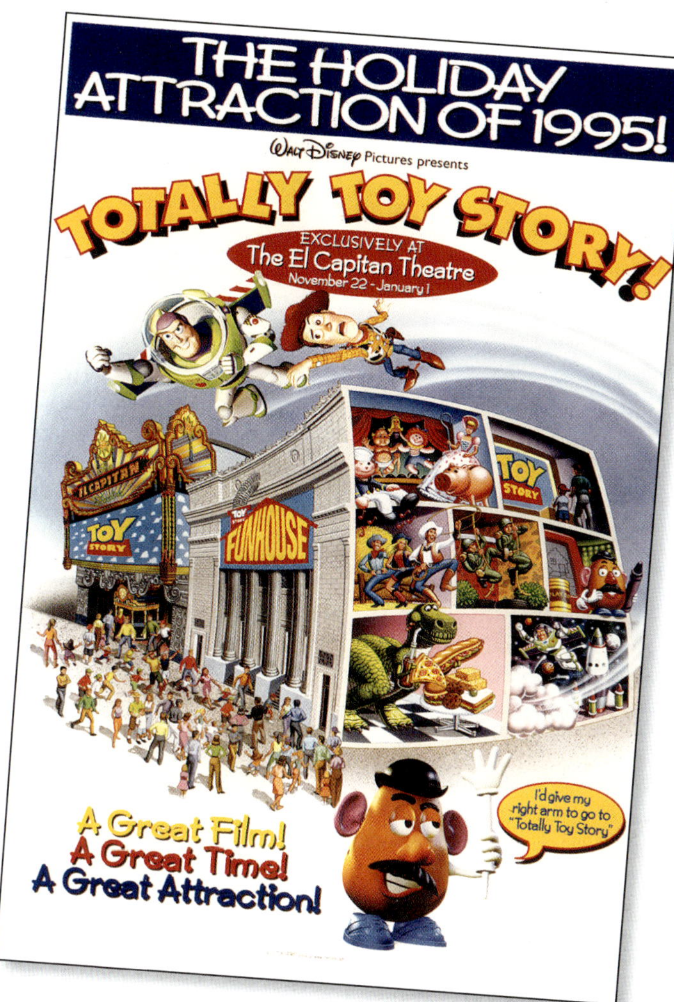

A 1995 TOY STORY poster.

Going forward, Pixar gladly accepted notes from Disney and welcomed participating in brainstorming sessions with their artists. "But," Ranft said, "we'd go away and really think about [the notes]. A lot of times we'd go, 'No. Here's the real problem!' And it was even deeper than the notes. 'And here's how we're going to fix it.'"

Regarding the creative process, Ranft once said, "It's a challenge. The final product is the goal you're searching for. [Your little sequence is] gonna get smashed, trashed. It's gonna come apart for the good of the final film . . . it's a paradox. You've got to put yourself into it, and then you've got to take yourself out of it. Be objective and not be hurt."

"Everything I learned about storyboarding a film and rewriting scripts," Stanton says, "was with Joe Ranft on *Toy Story*."

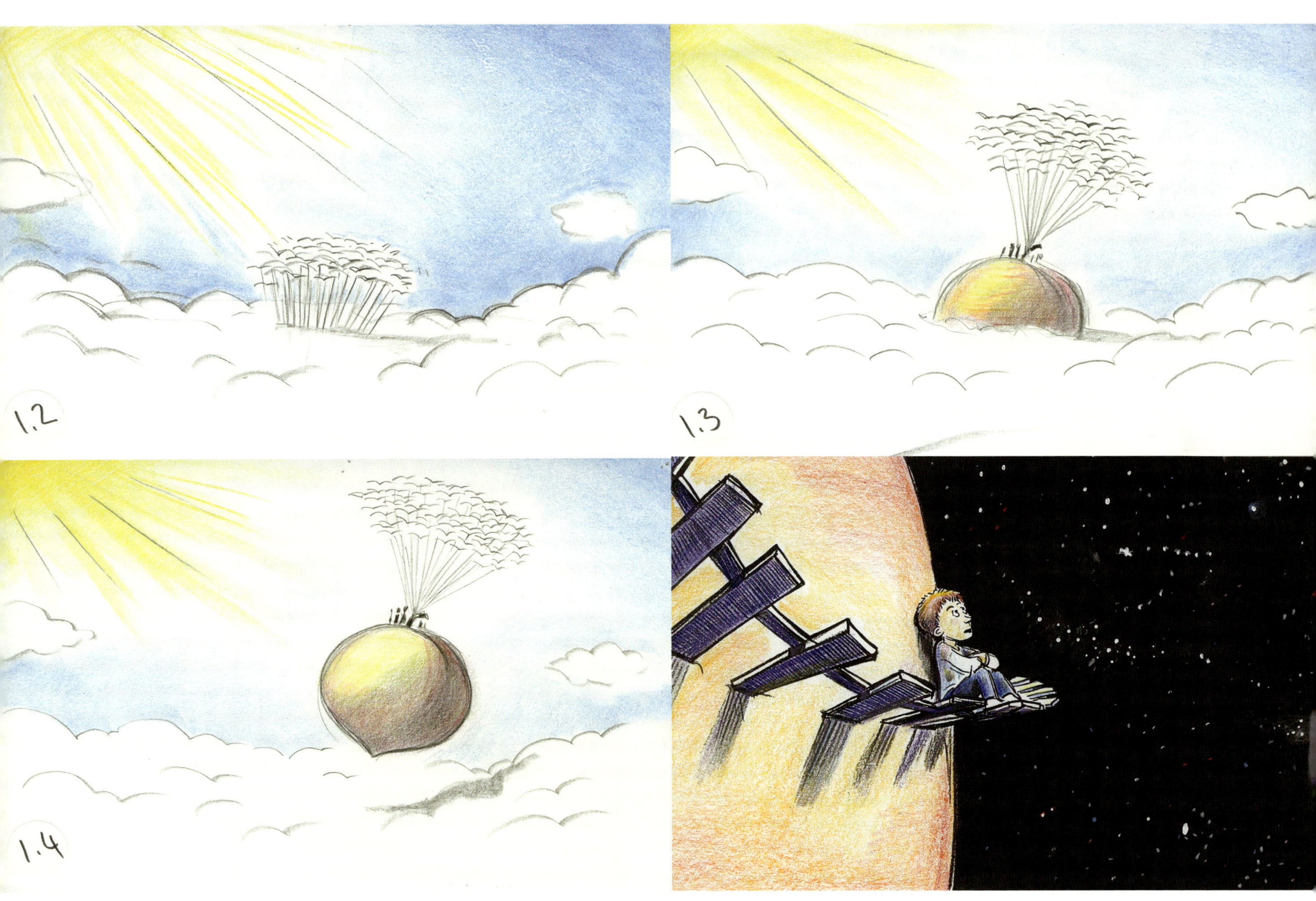

Joe Ranft story sketches for James and the Giant Peach.

Toy Story opened on November 22, 1995, to unanimous praise. *The Washington Post* found its "enormous humanity and heart" a "nice change of pace" from Disney fairy tales because it found "magic from this modern tale about ordinary 20th century kid Andy and his eager-to-please playthings."[1]

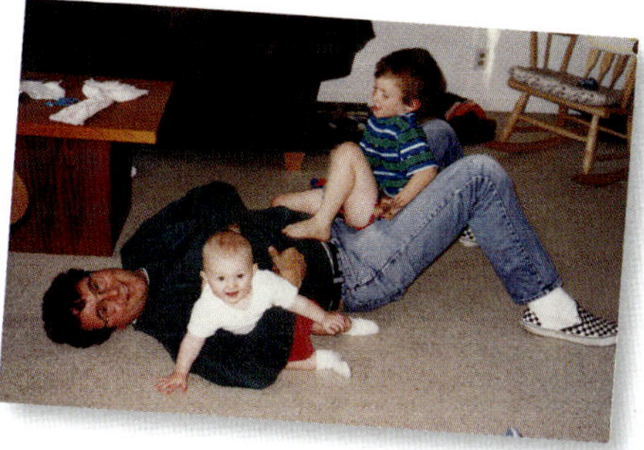

ABOVE: *Joe Ranft plays with his children, Jordy and Sophia.* RIGHT: *James and the Giant Peach's evil aunts, Spiker and Sponge. Sketch by Ranft.*

The *San Francisco Chronicle* called it "a gem of fast action, sophisticated wit, and inspired comedy" that "gets beyond cute and takes on wonderful shadings and moods." "Scriptwriters" Lasseter, Docter, Stanton, and Ranft were singled out for special mention.[2]

Toy Story made back its production costs after one week in theaters and eventually earned nearly $400 million worldwide, making it the highest-grossing film of 1995.[3] For the Ranft family, *Toy Story* was the second celebratory debut in a week. On November 13 they welcomed a daughter, Sophia Jo. "A very pretty baby indeed" read Joe's announcement, which noted the Ranfts' new house in Corte Madera, California, near Point Richmond.

Ranft was now reverse commuting across the bay, working on another Henry Selick–directed puppet film for Disney, *James and the Giant Peach*, which was adapted from Roald Dahl's 1961 book of the same name. His *Toy Story* duties ended months before, and for all anybody knew, Pixar might never make another feature film. With a second child on the way at the time and a mortgage, Ranft needed a job. A prior commitment to *James* filled the bill from spring 1994 through fall 1995.

"You start looking at his notes," Su says, "and it's about buying a house and saving up. He did that whole responsibility thing."

Ranft shared storyboard supervision duties on *James and the Giant Peach* with Kelly Asbury, who later directed *Shrek 2*. "Joe's creative hand touched every aspect on *Peach*," Asbury says. "As with every film he worked on, his impact was immeasurable. Joe possessed firm grasps on structure, character, emotion, and entertainment, and always kept the big picture in mind. He himself was a born entertainer—on and off the storyboard—and that talent prevailed in everything he did."[4]

The film was a rocky road. "We shut down [while] doing rewrites," Selick told *Entertainment Weekly*.[5] "We laid off people. But I've never heard of great movies coming from Party Atmosphere Productions."

There were battles with Disney over content. Selick refused to "manufacture a happy ending in which James's parents would come back to life," although Disney made him remove the evil aunts' "too frightening" glowing red eyes. Selick himself balked at the notion of a certain storyboard artist (guess who?) having "James scrub Aunt Sponge's back and clip Aunt Spiker's toenails."

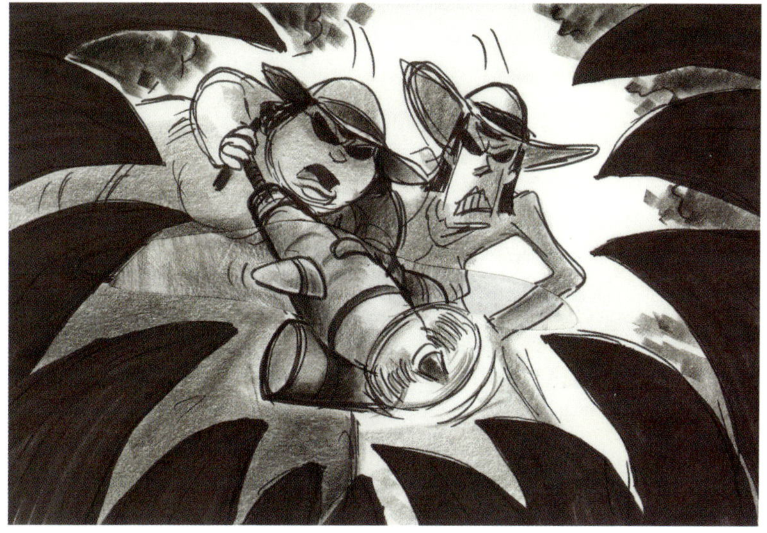

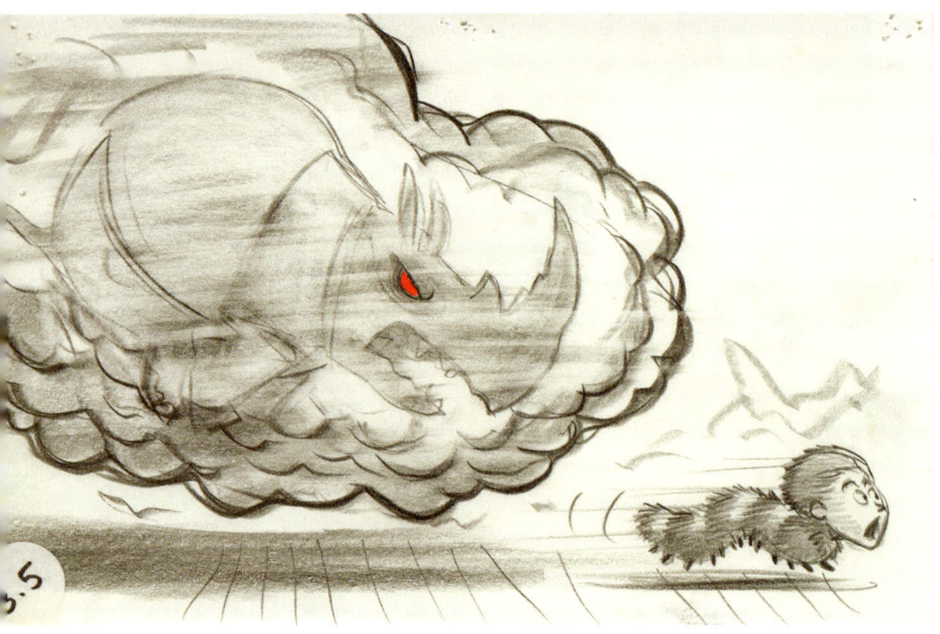

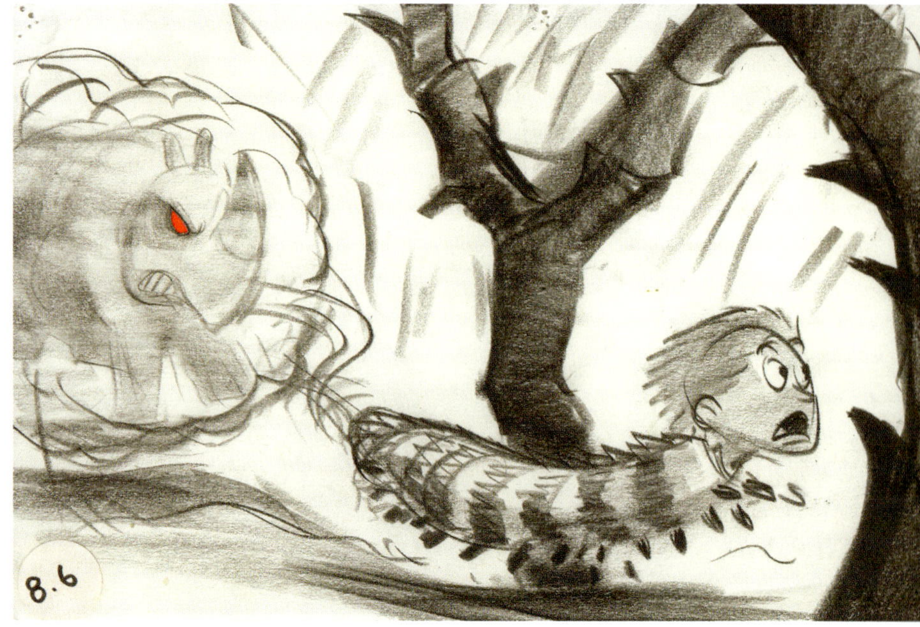

An altered James escapes a nightmarish rhino. Art by Joe Ranft.

"Too kinky," admitted Ranft.[6]

Still, the PG-rated film gave him many opportunities to indulge in scary imagery, including James (transformed into a bug) being chased by a rhino that killed his parents. He showcased his lyrical side, too, in lovely pictures of James precariously seated on the side of a huge peach gazing at stars.

Lane Smith, the film's conceptual designer, remembers Ranft as "the nicest guy I ever met in the business." He recalled an incident concerning a deranged street person who occasionally sneaked into Skellington Studios. One day he ran upstairs to the Story Department, screaming and threatening violence. Smith and others fled in fear for their lives, but "Joe sat there with the guy and talked him down and gave him money. Then security took him away. I thought," says Smith, "that's Joe in a nutshell: a great communicator and just a really sweet guy."[7]

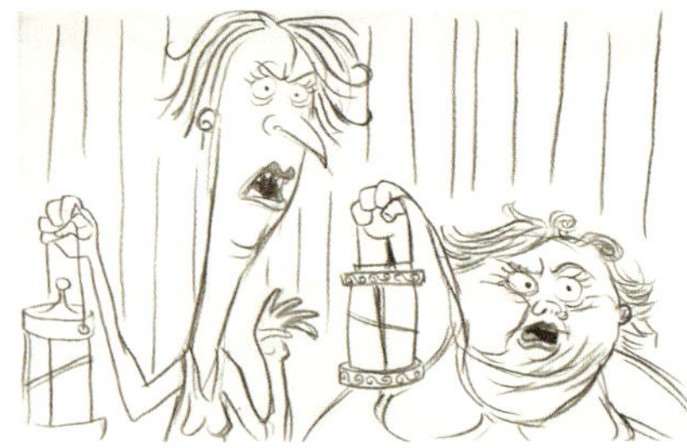

Toy Story's extraordinary financial and critical success surprised its creators. But a year before the film's premiere, they suddenly realized it was going to work as a film. It became likely Pixar would be offered a follow-up feature.

In the summer of 1994, the Brain Trust met at Hidden City Café, a Point Richmond sandwich eatery, to brainstorm future projects. It turned out to be a most fortunate lunch for Pixar and for audiences. Stanton talked about possibly doing a film in the ocean environment, which eventually led to *Finding Nemo*. Docter suggested something about dealing with childhood fears, which evolved into *Monsters, Inc*. Lasseter expressed his love of automobiles, which became *Cars*. And an idea about a Robinson Crusoe robot on an earth abandoned by humans reached theaters more than a decade later as *Wall-E*.

Ranft and Stanton's concept really had legs, lots of them: using a bunch of bugs as characters. "'Cause we were thinking about the strengths of the computer, which was limited at that time," Docter remembers. "Insects seemed like a natural with their hard exoskeletons and rotate joints, which computers do well." It was decided to move ahead with the insect film. Lasseter and Stanton would direct, Ranft would story supervise after his Skellington duties.

For nearly a year, *A Bug's Life* focused on a character lacking empathy. "After six or eight months of boarding and putting it up on reels, we realized there was just no gas in the story for this main character," Ranft said.[8] Having corrected the story's course, Ranft and crew still had to deal with a large cast, including a troupe of eccentric circus bugs, marauding grasshoppers, and an ant colony. "There were moments," Ranft said, "where they were all at the same level and all competing with each other story-wise. We had to find the hierarchy and find the right moments for each one of them. We explored stuff for each of the circus bugs where they'd each have their own moment and their own payoffs, separate from one another. It made for a long movie, and we had a lot more characters to make errors with."

The story crew worked through three plot revisions. "We've delivered more than 27,000 drawings to editorial [for the story reels]," Ranft said, and this did not include thousands of rejected sketches.[9]

Ranft was "the ultimate collaborator," according to Lee Unkrich, meaning he was the first to discard an unworkable idea for another approach. He was a role model for those who became fiercely attached to their ideas.

Ranft also needed to percolate ideas—give them their full due—before abandoning them. When others moved on from a blind alley idea, Ranft often steered them back for another look from a different angle. "He did this all the time," Unkrich says, "see something special. Same way he saw something special about people."

In picking story crews, Ranft had a "green thumb for finding raw talent," says Stanton. Sometimes he'd meet someone in another department and say, "That person should be in story." Sometimes he discovered talent in a job seeker's portfolio. Stanton, who admits to impatience when viewing portfolios, was "always amazed" that Ranft would "find that one page or one drawing and say, 'Look at this!' He really had an eye for people's potential."

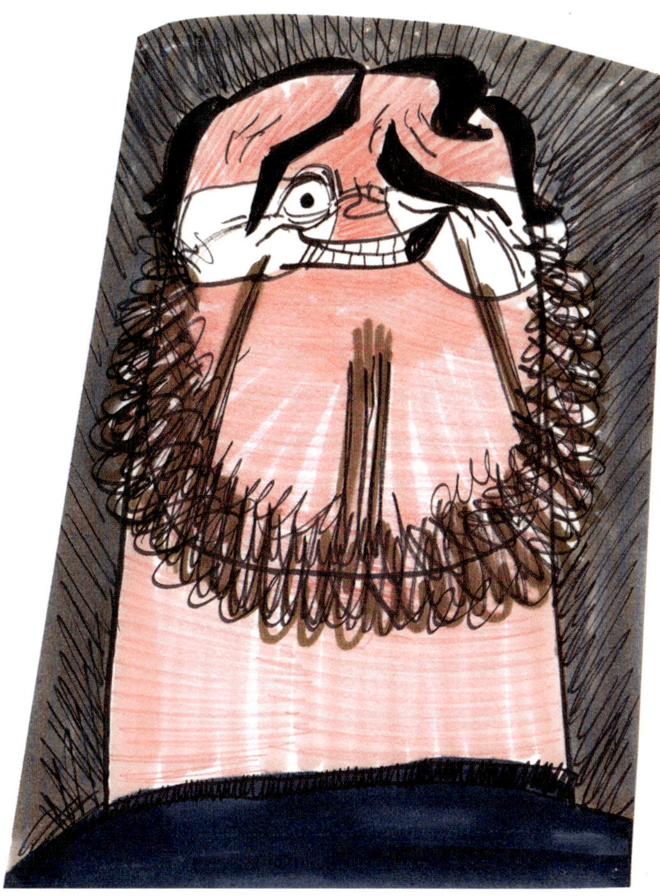

"Joe [Ranft] used his eyebrows asymmetrically when he smiled," says caricaturist John Musker, who used Ranft's expressive brows here for "more of a 'Joe' look."

The *Bug's* story crew was twice the size of *Toy Story*'s and mostly new to the story process. Bob Peterson was a former 3-D graphics software trainer and sports graphics animator before coming to Pixar in 1994. After starting on shorts, he did ninety layouts and animated seven shots of Sid in *Toy Story*. Ambitious, Peterson pitched ideas to Stanton, who brought him onto *A Bug's Life*'s story team. There, Ranft "took me under his wing" and became "a huge mentoring influence."[10]

When they met, Ranft asked Peterson to make a drawing just to define who he was. Peterson responded with a self-caricature in a Betty Grable World War II swimsuit pose with hairy legs, which made Ranft laugh. "I immediately hit it off with him," Peterson says.

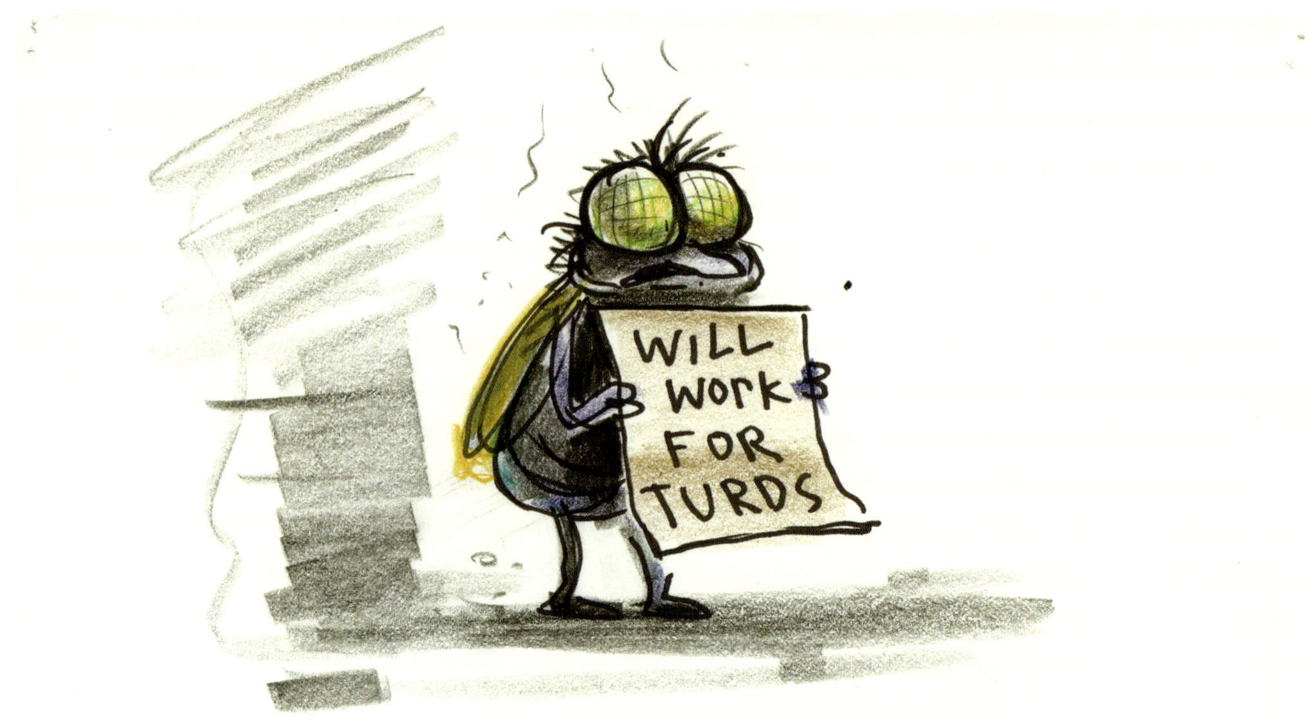

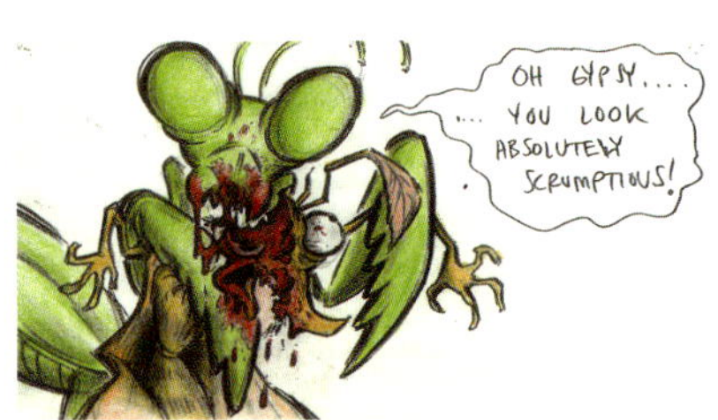

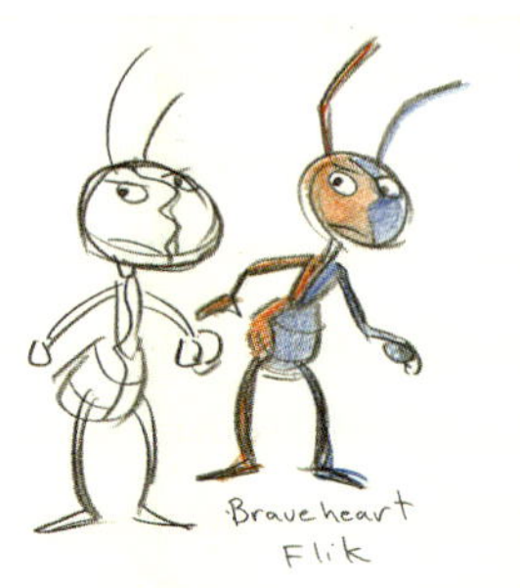

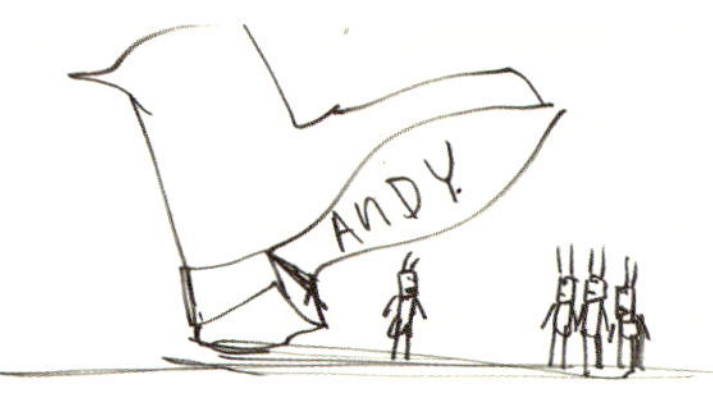

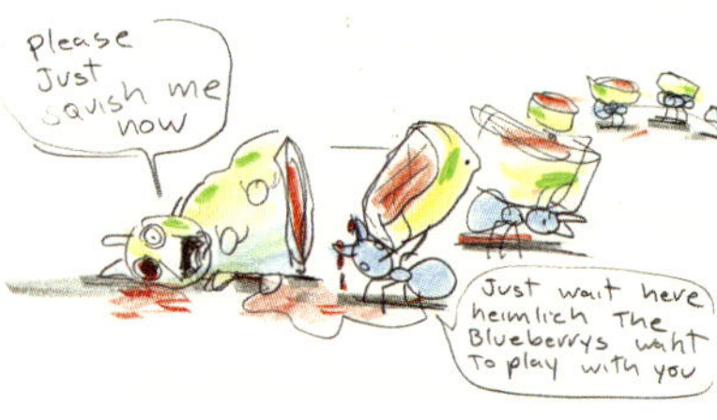

Joe Ranft's irreverent riffs on A Bug's Life characters.

Peterson's drawings look like warped *Far Side* cartoons, Stanton says. "Bob would be the first to say he couldn't draw worth beans." But Ranft thought he was the funniest guy in the room and "immediately recognized the value in those weird goofy-looking drawings." So did the animators, Stanton says, who all wanted to animate Peterson's storyboards "'cause they ooze character and potential."

Peterson, an admitted ham, was fearless pitching ideas but terrified to show John Lasseter his drawings. His sketches had several things happen simultaneously, no focus and unclear acting. "I needed Joe's help."

Ranft taught him that story art is different from the cartoon strips Peterson drew in college. "Focus the eye," Ranft explained. "You want one thing to happen at a time in your drawings."

Ranft brought his sunny personality to the production's grind. "We drew thousands of drawings and I wasn't used to that number," Peterson says. "And I got very tired. We pulled a lot of late nights. But it was a fun crew. Just sitting and brainstorming with Joe was a joy. He always welcomed ideas and being an improv man, it never hit a wall. Always, whatever was said seemed to drive the idea forward."

The story crew worked behind half-wall cubicles. "You could hear everybody," Peterson remembers. "We'd be drawing away and somebody would fire off something funny and people would build on it. And Joe was always over there making jokes, making us laugh."

In critiques, Ranft might diplomatically suggest, "Here's another way this will communicate better." Or, "The moment doesn't call for this." Or, Peterson recalls, "He'd say, 'Bob, you have this alternative idea. Pitch it or pin it up. We can do this which is in the script, or we can give the directors options.'"

Ranft often supplied "scratch" or temporary voice tracks for films in progress. He voiced bit parts going back to *The Brave Little Toaster.* As Igor in *The Nightmare Before Christmas*, he salivated and said, "Master, the plans" and was thrown a dog biscuit.[11]

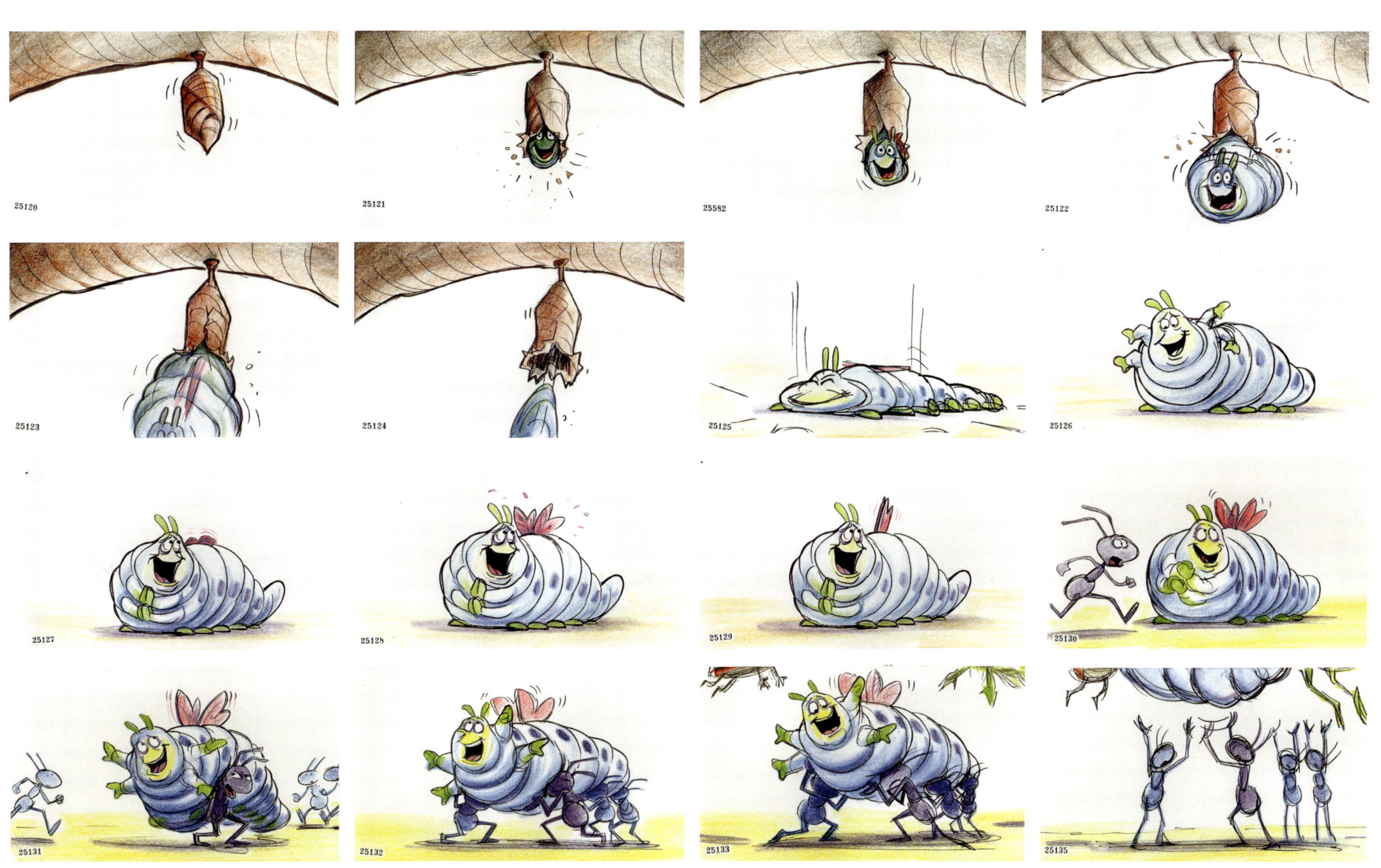

Ranft's storyboard for Heimlich the caterpillar's heavy transition into a butterfly.

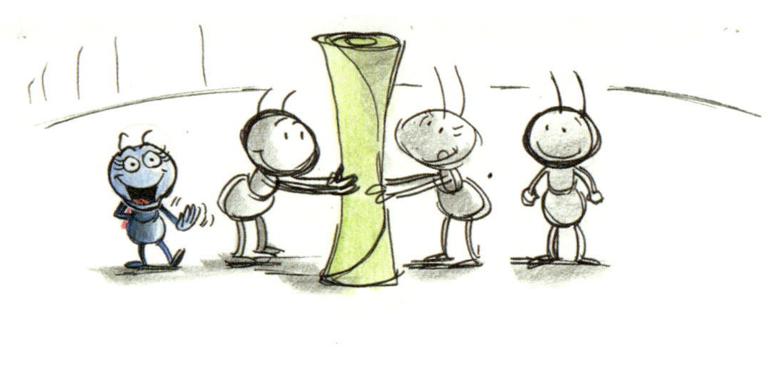
20997
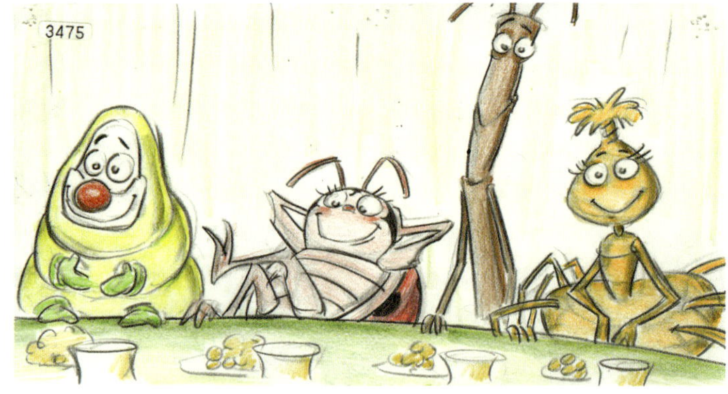
3475
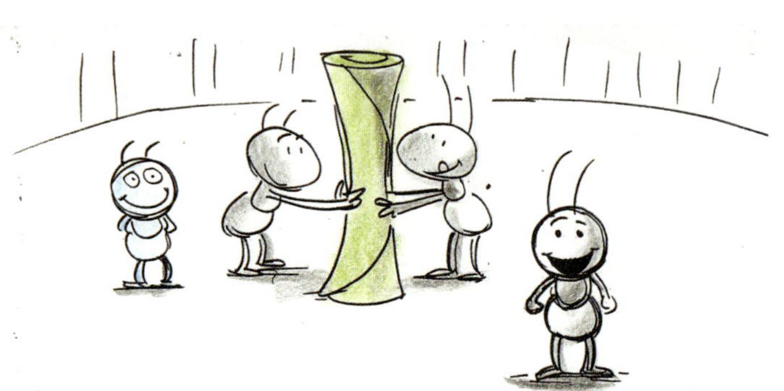
20999
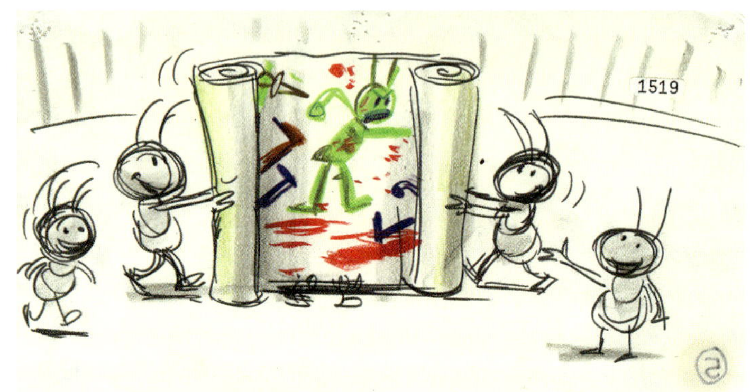
1519
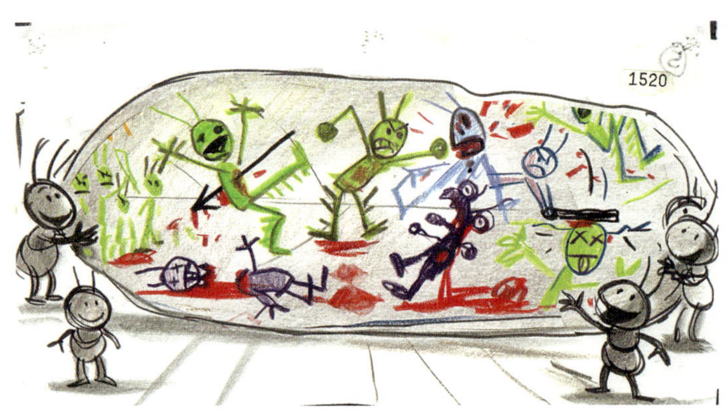
1520
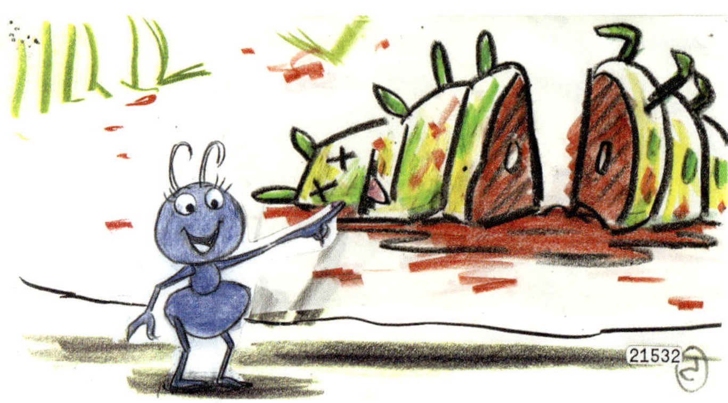
21532
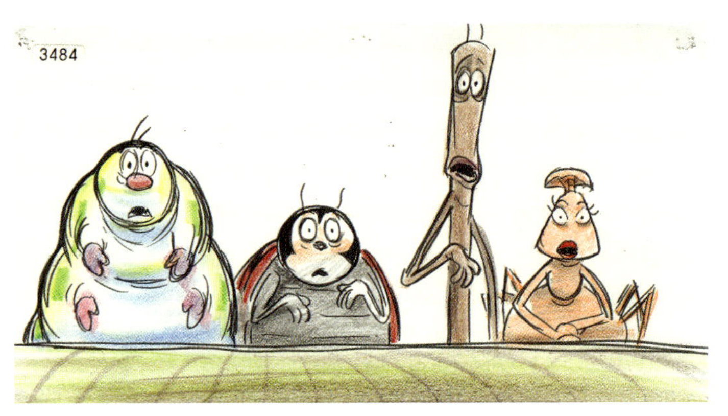
3484
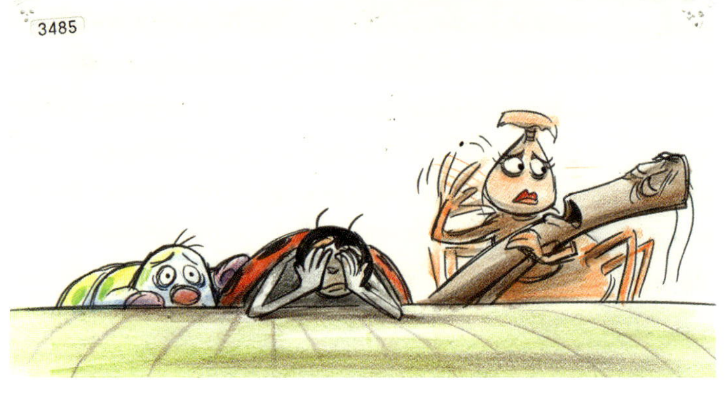
3485

OPPOSITE: *Gruesome innocence in a children's mural: story sketches of baby ants by Joe Ranft; reaction drawings of other bugs by Bud Luckey are also displayed.*

Ranft loved getting a call from editorial when a scene was turned in and he was needed "to come to the recording booth and do scratch. Ooh, I'm never going to finish [storyboarding] this scene. Okay, I'll come in fifteen minutes, whatever. I'd go through, read the scene, maybe get to be five different people in a half hour, and it was like a great mind sweep! Goofing around before a mike, doing improv takes, making impact sounds if they're getting hit. Getting to play as an actor, I would be totally refreshed by the time I went back to my boards."[12] Often his scratch voices ended up in the film. He had five lines as Lenny the Binoculars in *Toy Story*, but his first "star" part was Heimlich, *A Bug's Life*'s jolly, gluttonous Bavarian caterpillar who yearns to fly. A professional actor had been cast, but Nancy Lasseter (John's wife) "laughed really hard at my scratch over the other guy's stuff," said Ranft.

"When he did Heimlich he gave us all hope that we might be able to do the same thing," says Peterson, story supervisor on *Monsters, Inc.* and codirector of *Up*, who recorded the voices of Roz the office manager in *Monsters, Inc.* and Mr. Ray in *Finding Nemo*.

Peterson said he learned how to direct actors during voice-recording sessions from Ranft. "There's a real art to reading opposite the professional actor. Reading all the other characters, doing it *in* character, timing it correctly, but also leaving a little bit of space so he didn't step on, say, Tom Hanks's performance. He was a great partner on the other side."

As with *Toy Story*'s army men sequence, Ranft quietly picked a *Bug's Life* section and made it his own: it's when ant children unveil a mural depicting the circus bugs "helping us fight the grasshoppers away." The childish drawings depict a gruesome scene of gore and body parts. Poor Heimlich is cut in two like a side of beef. "It's perfect Joe!" Darla Anderson laughs when recalling the moment. "Totally sweet and endearing, but hilariously macabre at the same time. He was perfectly in touch with his shadow side."[13]

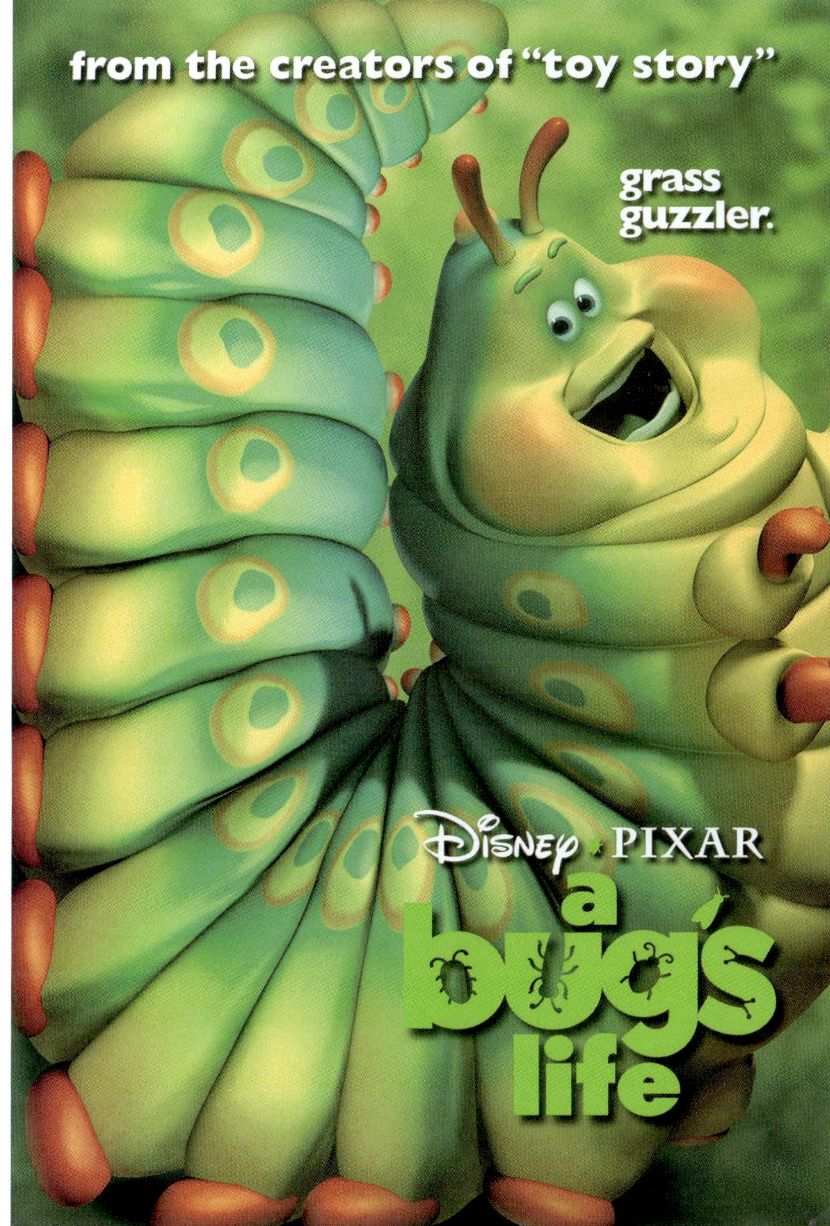

Heimlich (voiced by Joe Ranft) starred in his own poster.

Like all of Ranft's colleagues, Peterson deeply misses his welcoming presence. "This amazingly generous giant soul had something special," he says, tearing up during an interview. "He was like an angel. He took joy in things, and it rubbed off on all of us."

In the mid-1990s, animation feature production increased and competition among studios for key personnel set off an industrywide bidding war. Several studios wooed Ranft between *James and the Giant Peach* and *A Bug's Life*, including DreamWorks.

Always concerned about supporting his family, Ranft took meetings in L.A., and he and Su scouted houses in La Cañada, a Pasadena suburb. "That's how close he came to working on *Prince of Egypt*," DreamWorks's first animated feature, released in 1998, Su recalls.

Alarmed, Disney Feature Animation heads Tom Schumacher and Peter Schneider flew to San Francisco to lunch with Ranft. "They said 'You're a hands-off guy, we get that,'" recounts Su from what Joe told her later. "'You don't like to be pressured. We've offered you directing jobs [but] you're not interested. But we never thought you would go someplace else. What do you want?'"

"Um, I don't want to sign a seven-year contract," Ranft said.

"They said, 'Okay. Four.'"

"'I don't want to go back to L.A. I want to stay up here in the Bay Area. Whatever Pixar, Skellington does next.'"

"'Fine. No problem.'"

"'I really want to buy my wife a house.'" (At the time, Su was pregnant with their second child and they were living in a two-bedroom rental.)

"So," says Su, "they gave him a bonus of $300,000 like they do sports stars. They ponied up. They said, 'Anything else?' 'No, that's it.' So he went to work on *Bug's* and then *Toy Story 2* and then his contract ran out again, and he [finally] became a Pixar employee.

"So, this is the house that *Bug's Life* bought," Su says of their Corte Madera home.[1]

After the release of *A Bug's Life*, Ranft received two $50,000 bonus checks with a note from Schumacher saying, "You've done it again."[2] Eventually, Ranft participated in juicy Pixar stock options; with more bonuses, supplementary income from voice work, and an ever-rising salary. "Next thing we know," says Su, "he's a millionaire."

But the more material wealth Ranft acquired, the more uncomfortable he became with it. "It wasn't his nature to flaunt it or want people to be aware of it or think of him differently maybe because he has more money," Lee Unkrich says. "He was very humble. In his neighborhood, he didn't like being thought of as the guy from Pixar. Joe never wanted the spotlight."[3]

"The Academy Awards was the most surreal, fakest and disappointing event," he wrote in his diary after attending the 1996 ceremony when *Toy Story* was nominated. "Love is not necessarily found in success."[4]

"Joe had this Catholic-guilt thing," says his wife. "'How dare I enjoy my success when people are suffering?'" He joined a men's group that met every Monday night for nearly nine years. "Overtime? No matter. He was there. They did a lot of good works," Su says. It was also a place to talk where it wasn't business. One guy was a piano tuner, another an insurance salesman. Friends not involved with the industry. "It gave him peace."

He meditated in the morning for more than sixteen years. He did Hatha yoga because of a bum hip. He became interested in Celtic legends and Irish myths, Russian fairy tales. "But it's not about the movies," says Su. "It's about teaching and healing."

He became involved in community outreach programs with prisons and neighborhoods like Watts in L.A. and Hunters Point in San Francisco. "And that really appealed to Joe," says Su. At Ranft's suggestion, Steve Jobs donated computers to a Watts organization.

Eventually Ranft contributed considerable amounts of his money and time to Michael Meade's

Mosaic Multicultural Foundation and attended their annual retreats "for movers and shakers and connections to hook up with the community leaders in depressed areas," says Su.

"Giving back to humanity makes it sound really grandiose," his brother Jerome Ranft says. "He was super successful, and he was worried about that success and how to be a contributor to the bigger story of the world, of life."

After *A Bug's Life*, Ranft was tired. "By the time it was over," Jerome says, "his daughter was three and he had worked overtime every weekend for those three years. So, they'll take as much as you're willing to give, I guess."

"They kept offering him directing jobs," Su remembers. "He didn't have a desire to be a director because you have to give your life away. And I was already pissed about the overtime as bad as it was. 'Cause he was gone a lot. He had a very strong work ethic. He would never leave his crew alone and come home. I said, 'I'll make this very easy for you. Tell them that your wife said no!'"

Unkrich noticed the toll it took on Ranft. As a result, "he was never willing to put in those kind of hours working that way again." Ranft intended to fully participate in the production of Pixar films, but he would spread himself and his storytelling gifts in wider circles. "It meant he wasn't [story]boarding as much after that," Unkrich says. "After that movie it was the beginning of Joe rising into more of a mentoring role."

He took mentoring very seriously. In a December 18, 1995, memo to Disney executives, he presented ideas for the training of "the storyboarders of tomorrow." The document is a detailed, cogent blueprint of instruction based on Ranft's practical experience in the trenches.

In it, Ranft identifies five fundamental skills necessary for story work. "Drawing is the number one skill," he wrote, that "permeates all the skills that follow."

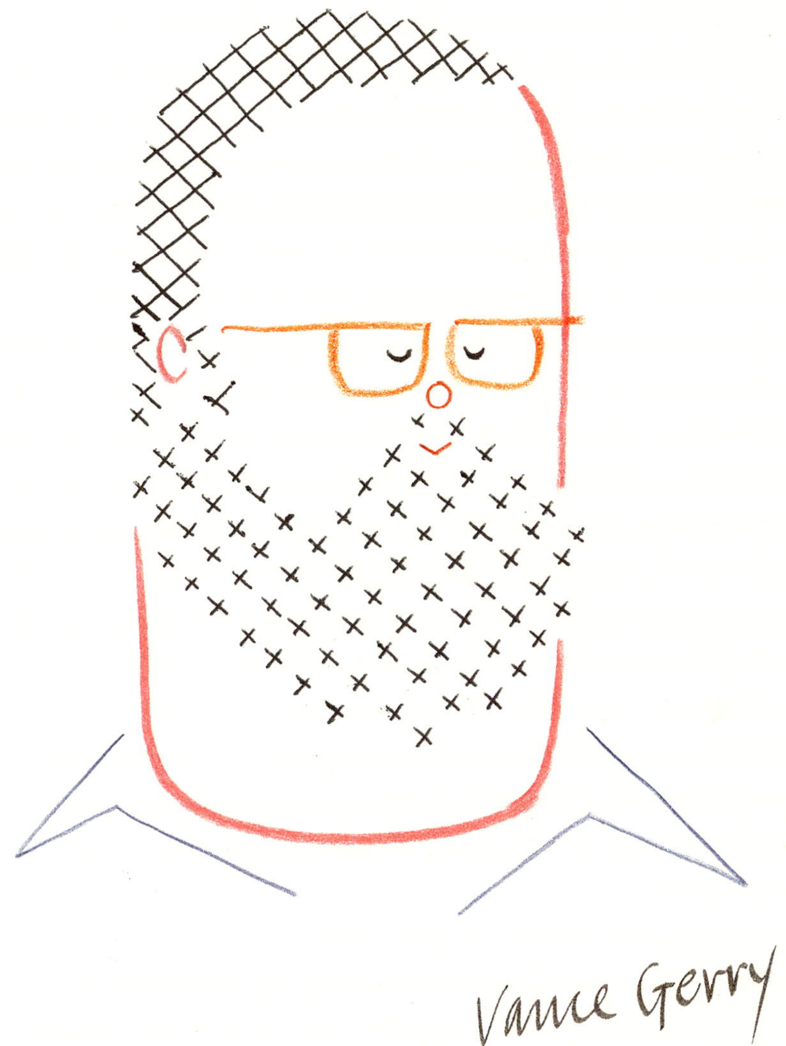

Story artist Vance Gerry's caricature of Joe Ranft, c. 1981.

Other skills include fundamentals of acting and improvisation training; a basic writing workshop (with Robert McKee's story-structure seminar "a must!"), and a class analyzing Shakespeare "could do nothing but help"; and fundamentals of composition and staging, with guest artists and discussions of the theories of Donald W. Graham, Disney Studio art teacher in the 1930s, based on his 1970 book *Composing Pictures*.

Ranft encouraged students to study classic films by freezing film frames on laser discs (the day's

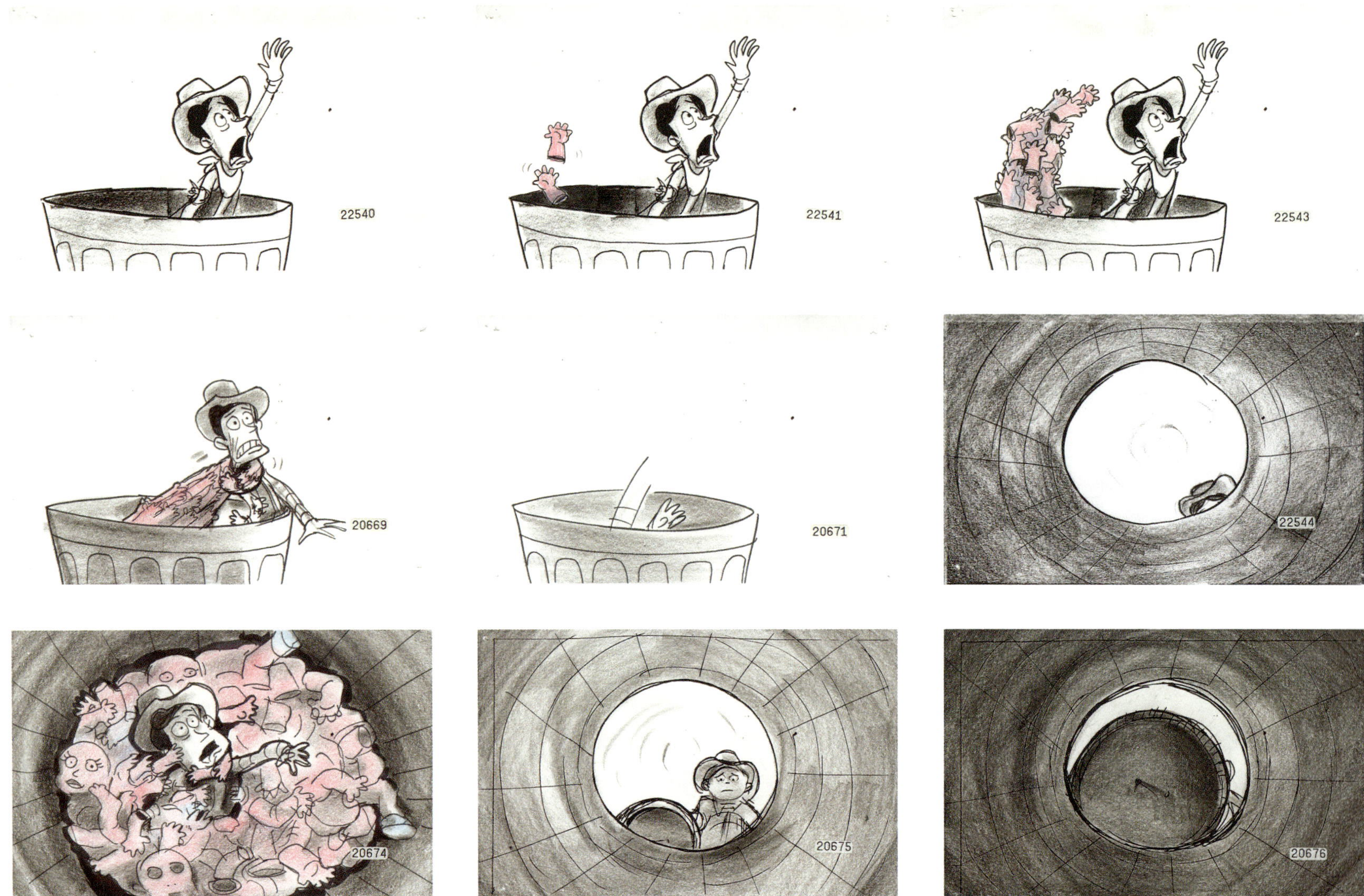

Joe Ranft's surreal sequence for Toy Story 2.

high-tech format) and drawing scene compositions from films by David Lean, John Ford, Akira Kurosawa, and Steven Spielberg, among others. He suggested bringing in "a good editor" to instruct in "storytelling through montage, match cutting, pacing, avoiding jump-cuts, what makes a good cut, eyelines, screen direction, etc."

He outlined a plan for an intense two-week Story Boot Camp for novice storyboarders to develop flexibility, speed, teamwork, and the ability to take direction under production pressure. "There would need to be a Story Drill Instructor to keep the pressure on, delegate assignments, and ask for CHANGES! CHANGES! CHANGES!"

Possible Boot Camp assignments might include, he noted:

> 1. Pitching three ideas for a Pluto 60th anniversary short tomorrow at 1700 hours.
>
> 2. Rough-board a scene from 2–3 pages of written script within a 24-hour period.
>
> 3. Make several sets of revisions to the same scene as per the Drill Instructor's instructions, have it in shape as

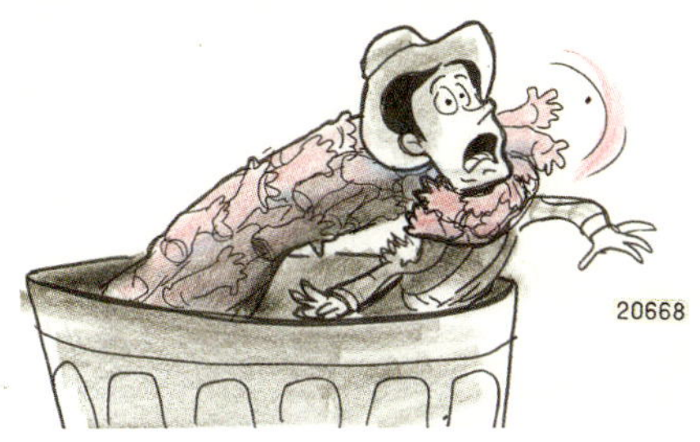

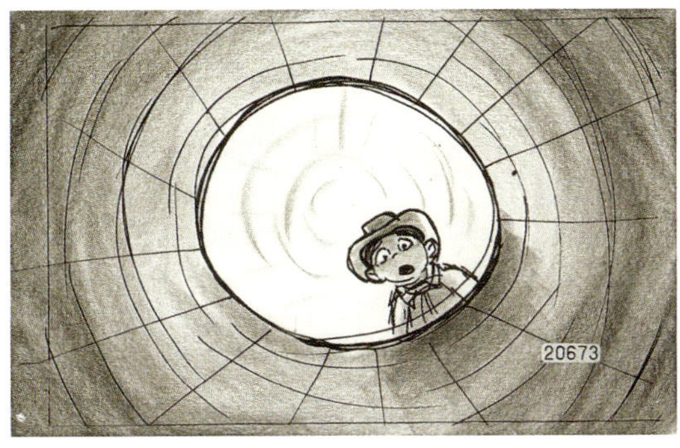

if it were going to be pitched to Michael Eisner by 7 A.M. Monday morning. (Use four pins and judicious use of color.)

4. Switch rough boarded sequences among trainees and have them clean up each other's work.

5. Team trainees in groups of two and three per assignment.

6. Trainees should have the experience of seeing their work cut into reels. Do their own scratch dialogue and hand their work off to an editor.

7. They should have to work over the weekend, pull at least one all-nighter and have pizza brought in.

Finally, Ranft's manifesto demands that the "motto of the boot camp should be CHANGES! CHANGES! CHANGES! CHANGES! Changes to improve gags, clarify characters, correct screen direction, improve staging, strengthen poses, and more clearly communicate the ideas."

By June of 1998, there was enormous demand for Joe Ranft's Story class. A memo noted that he taught two different classes. Story Development (also known as Joe's Story Class,"much celebrated in legend and song") was by invitation only with a maximum of fifteen students chosen by management. The full-time ten-week course ran like a story department with "real projects, real deadlines, real work" focusing on creating material that could go into production using existing Pixar characters, props, and sets. The intention was to create a new Pixar story team. Successful students "may be asked to change careers in the Studio" and work in story full-time.

For Story 101, a more modest and flexible second class, a maximum of thirty students met once a week for three hours to learn story-building and storyboarding techniques. The goal was to enrich their other work and "better prepare them for the next offering of Story Development." Particularly promising Story 101 students "may be added to the Story Development class during the first two weeks."[5]

"He was certainly an amazing mentor," Darla Anderson says. "Anybody who'd worked with Joe after he put his focus on them and helped them," she notes, "[well] now they're the most sought after people in the company."[6]

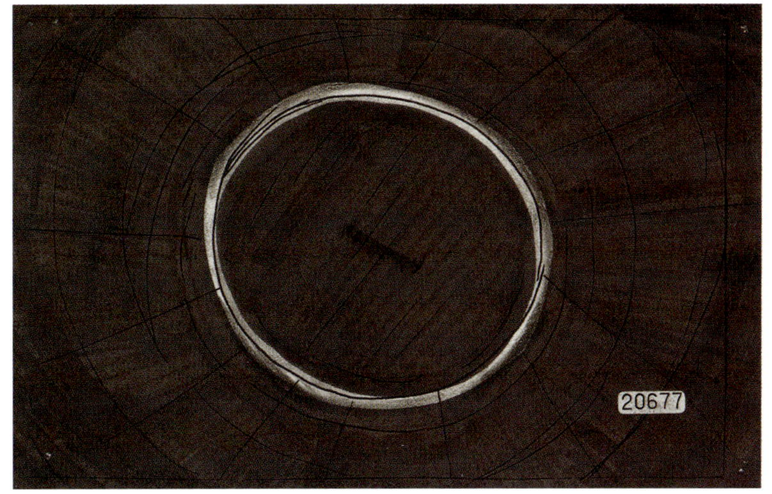

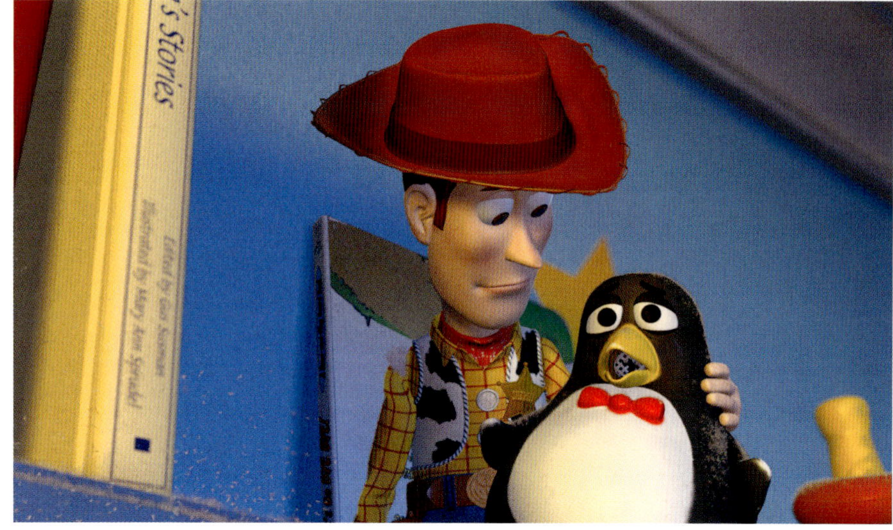

ABOVE: *Woody and Wheezy the Penguin.* OPPOSITE: *a Joe Ranft sketch for* MONSTERS, INC.

Formal teaching was one way Joe Ranft influenced future Pixar films. He was also a floating resource, a mobile vessel of knowledge and mirth always willing to contribute to others' films.

After *A Bug's Life* and a brief vacation, he joined a group effort to expand *Toy Story 2* from a direct-to-video sequel to a theatrical feature. Sequences concocted for the first *Toy Story* were overhauled, including an over-the-top Buzz Lightyear adventure in space. "We murdered that darling on the first one, but it came back in a different way in this film," Ranft said.[1]

Also resurrected: a creepy Ranft sequence about rejection when Woody dreams that his owner discarded him in a trash can. It was revived when Ranft's CalArts students viewed the original story reel and it got big laughs. "It made us realize," Ranft said, "that if people already know and love your characters, you can get away with things that are a little darker. In [*Toy Story 2*] it was cool to push toward surreal nightmare limits."[2]

Ranft's idea for Wheezy, an asthmatic penguin squeeze toy, existed even before the creation of Woody and Buzz; he also provided the bird's voice.

By this time the key Pixar creatives worked so well together, it "was like finishing each other's sentences."[3] "When that group was in a room together, it was phenomenal," Ed Catmull recalls. "It was a great privilege to be in the room. They were funny, focused, professional. They were filmmakers. Amazing to watch."[4]

"I call them the 'Beatles of Pixar,'" says Jorgen Klubien, Disney/Pixar story artist/animator and a friend of Ranft and Lasseter since CalArts. "It was a sometimes difficult group to feel part of because they were so much of a group."[5]

Pixar's success demanded more films, necessitating the foursome split up to work simultaneously on separate projects. *Monsters, Inc.* was the first Pixar feature not directed by Lasseter. "We assembled a whole other team to put it together," says Pete Docter, who codirected with Lee Unkrich and David Silverman. As the team expanded, "we were floating off by ourselves" in another building, Docter says. "We were really isolated. Joe was a tie-back to the mainland. He would come over once in a while to look at what we were doing."

In addition to throwing out ideas, Ranft volunteered his time as a *Monsters, Inc*. storyboard artist. ("I'd love to do that for you.") He worked on the opening scenes and one of the many versions of the surreal Himalayas sequence. He boarded emotional scenes of big blue monster Sully saying good night to little girl Boo. "There's a lot of his staging in there," Docter notes, "and certainly a lot of his emotion. He didn't have to do that. He was a big cheese, but he just had this sense these guys need my help. So he came in."

Finding Nemo was Andrew Stanton's first time making a movie without the direct day-to-day support of "the gang of John, Joe, and Pete." For him, Ranft turned into "a mentor-slash-personal

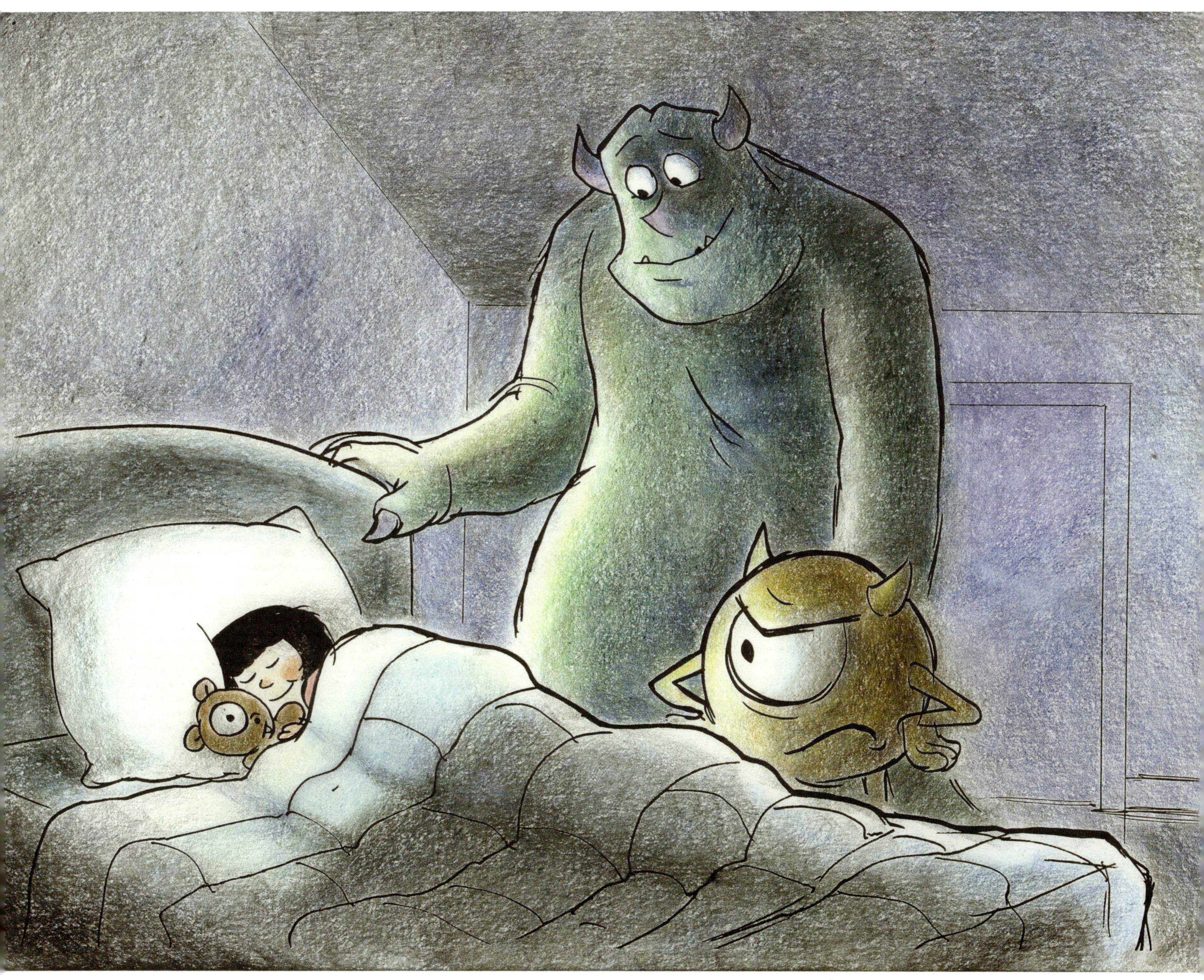

Joe Ranft

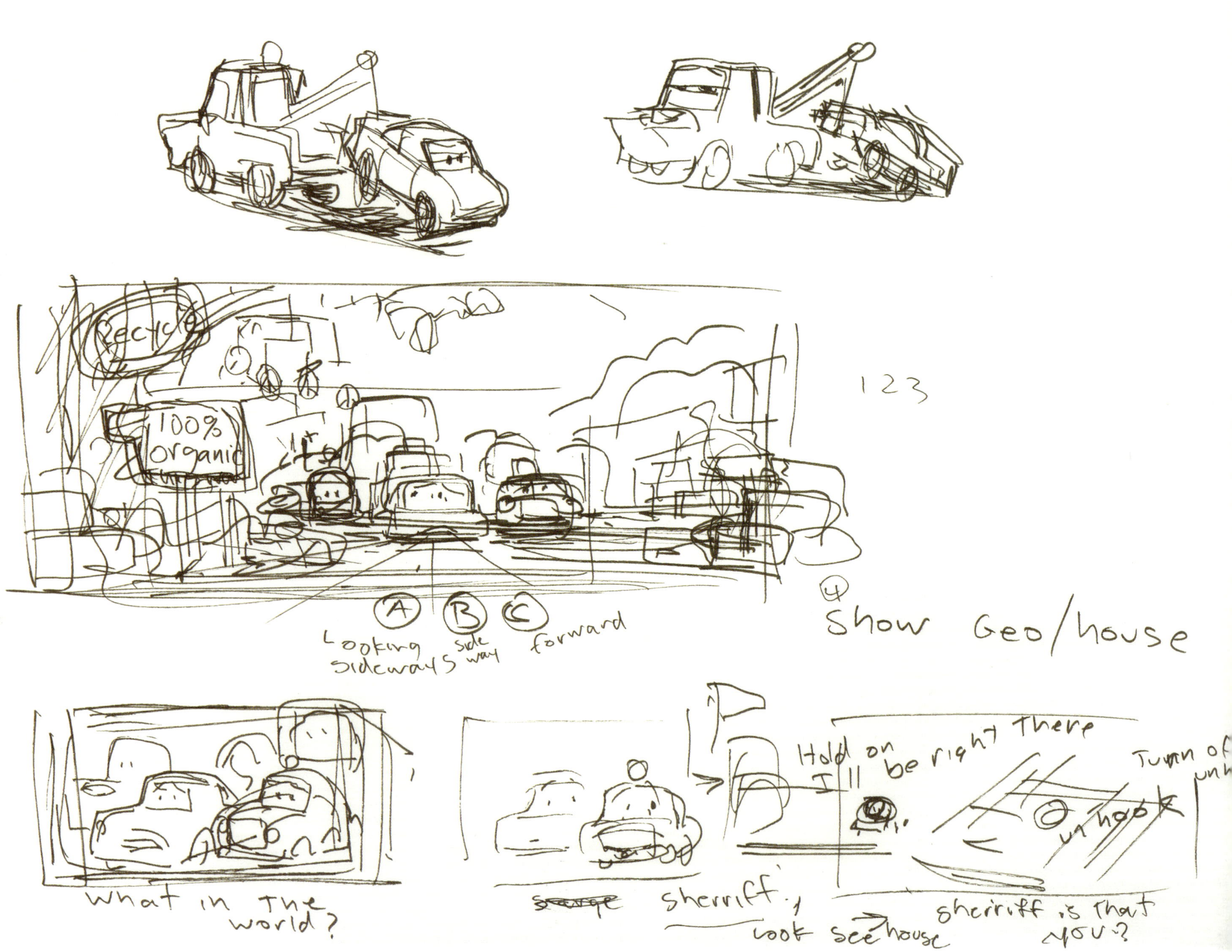
Recycle
100% organic
123
A
B
C
Looking sideways
side way
forward
4
Show Geo/house
Hold on
I'll be right there
What in the world?
sherriff.
look see house
sherriff is that you?

confidant. Your buddy-slash-therapist," Stanton says. "I'd say I was having this problem, what do you think of this? I'd always want his opinion."

Stanton saw Ranft as "almost a guidance counselor" who did "rounds," walking around the studio knocking on doors and asking how people were doing. "That made Joe very special, and I've never seen anybody do it before or since," Stanton says. "It wasn't his role, wasn't his job. Which made it all the more effective because you could tell that as a friend and artist, he just cared and wanted to know how you were. It was always such a breath of fresh air to get that knock on the door from Joe.

"In a very removed sense, he was incredibly beneficial for me on *Nemo*," Stanton notes. "Like your big brother, reminding you he was still there, you could rely on him if you had to." For *WALL-E*, released to great acclaim in summer 2008, Stanton received a set of notes from Ranft after the film's first rough cut in 2004, which he frequently referred to. "Joe was such a collaborator."

The original Brain Trust did converge at all works-in-progress screenings every twelve weeks or so. Darla Anderson remembers Brad Bird coming in with "amazing" work reels for *The Incredibles*, yet the Brain Trust still gave him "a million notes." It was considered "the biggest compliment you can get." It meant, Anderson says, "they care about you and the movie that much." Ranft "helped set a lot of the tone for this—that everybody sincerely wants that film to be better."

Bird is now part of the current Brain Trust, which includes John Lasseter, Andrew Stanton, Pete Docter, Lee Unkrich, Brenda Chapman, Bob Peterson, Gary Rydstrom, and Michael Arndt. Bird sought Ranft's input on *Ratatouille*. "The last time I ever saw Joe was as we were leaving the back of Pixar on the steps near the parking lot. We were talking about problems with the rat movie. He's the kind of guy who would set aside whatever he was doing to help."[6]

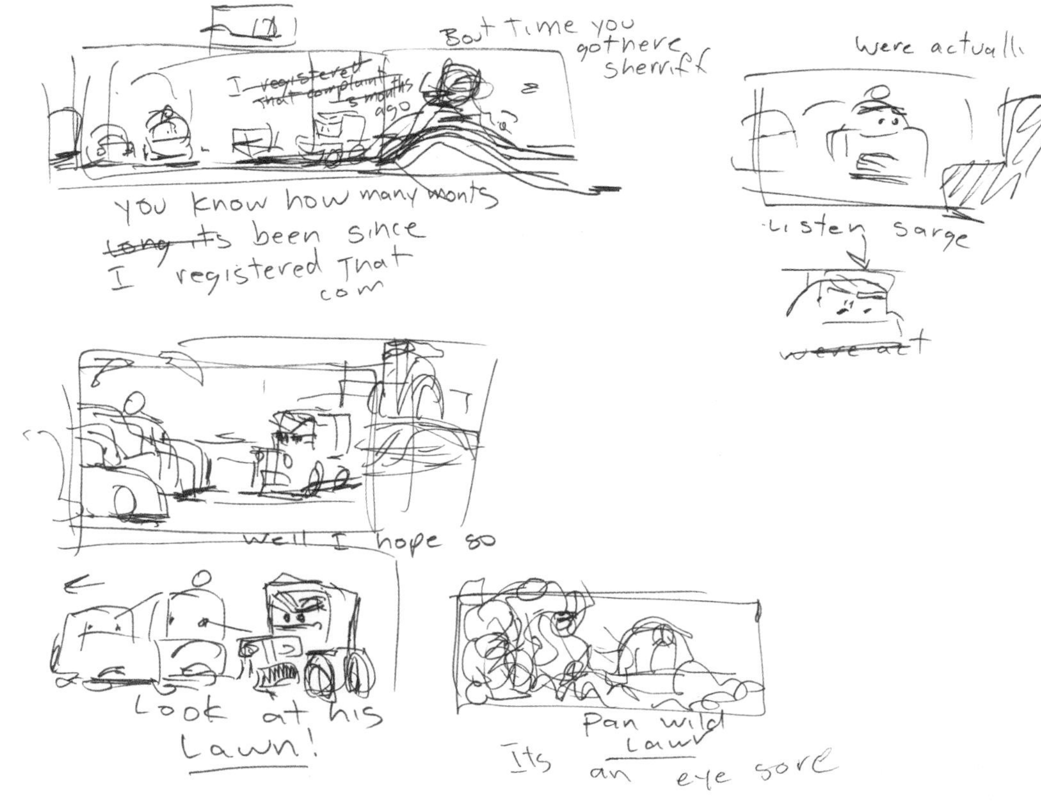

OPPOSITE AND ABOVE: *Joe Ranft's rough idea drawings for* CARS.

Ranft's greatest loyalty, however, was to Lasseter. He spent a goodly portion of the final five years of his life helping Lasseter realize his vision for *Cars*. "Joe is in every frame of that film," Lasseter acknowledges.

The film emerged from a 1997 treatment with text and a hundred drawings by Klubien. He pitched a story about an electric car ostracized in favor of a race car called Hotrod by a gas-guzzling small town (modeled on Point Richmond, which is surrounded by oil refineries) populated only by cars. The treatment coincided with Lasseter's interest in anthropomorphism and the subject matter; he loves antique cars,

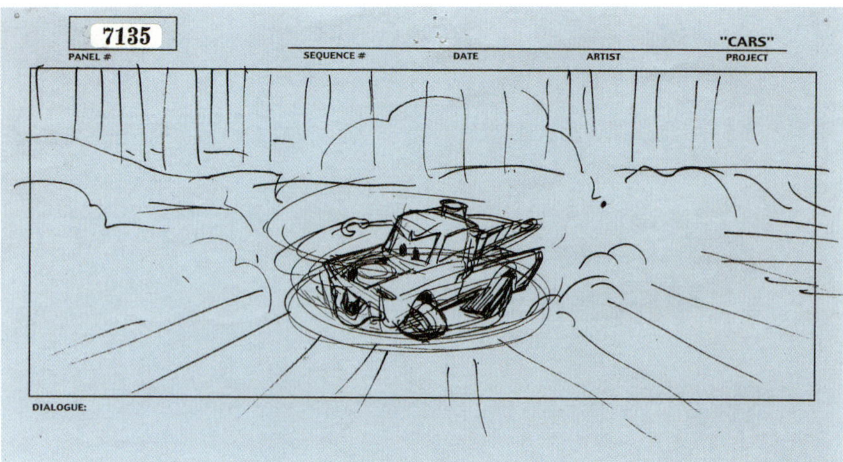

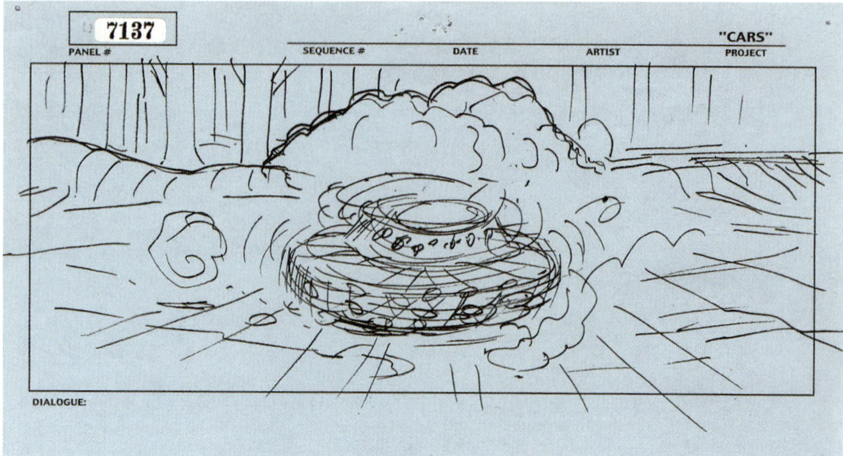

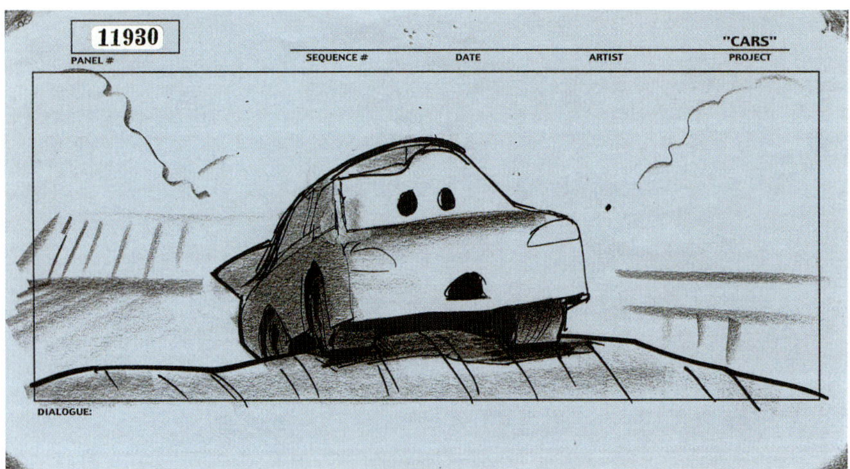

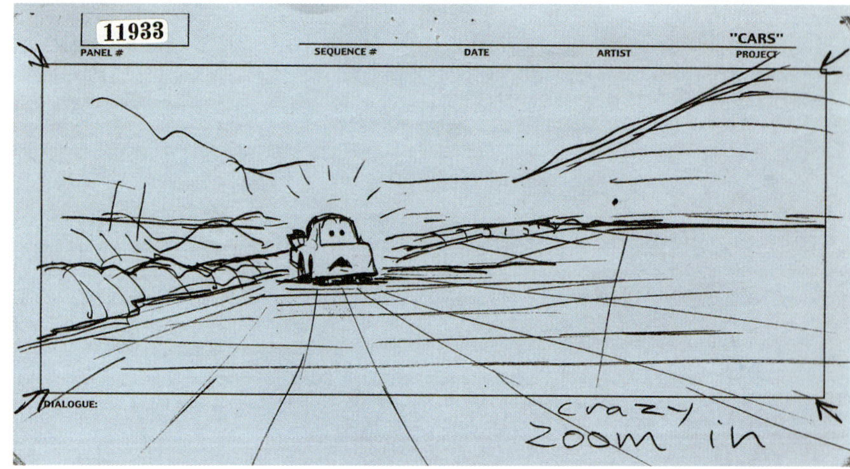

ABOVE AND OPPOSITE: *Two Joe Ranft sequential story sketches for* CARS.

and his father was a parts manager at a Chevrolet dealership.

He, Ranft, and Klubien wrote the first script, and the film was scheduled for release in 1999 after *A Bug's Life*. However, *Toy Story 2* was green-lighted in November 1997; story work took about nine months, and the film was released in November 1999.

Cars went into full development in fall 1998 with Lasseter as director and Ranft as story head and codirector. The film now starred a smart-aleck race car (Lightning McQueen) whose fast-lane life changes radically when he gets sidetracked in a slow, small town called Radiator Springs along Route 66.

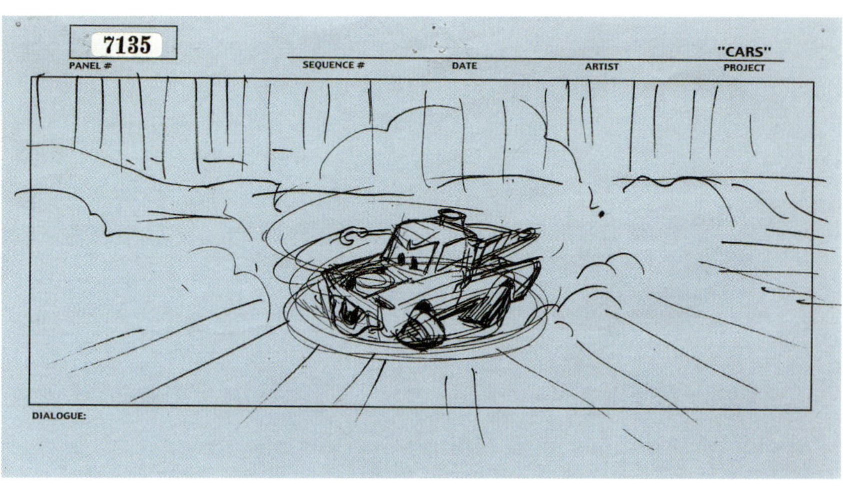

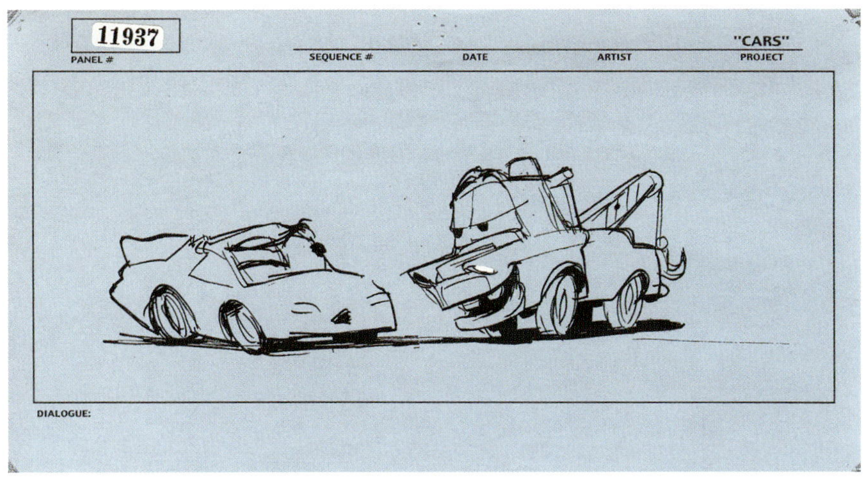

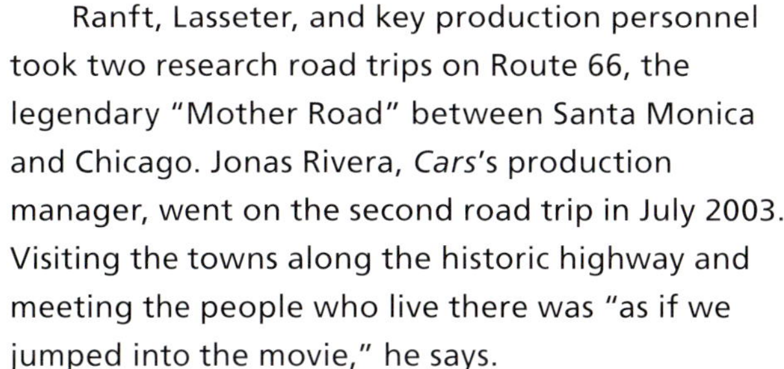

Ranft, Lasseter, and key production personnel took two research road trips on Route 66, the legendary "Mother Road" between Santa Monica and Chicago. Jonas Rivera, *Cars*'s production manager, went on the second road trip in July 2003. Visiting the towns along the historic highway and meeting the people who live there was "as if we jumped into the movie," he says.

"We saw so many characters and spent such good times on the road. All this camaraderie and friendship we established out there. Joe said if we

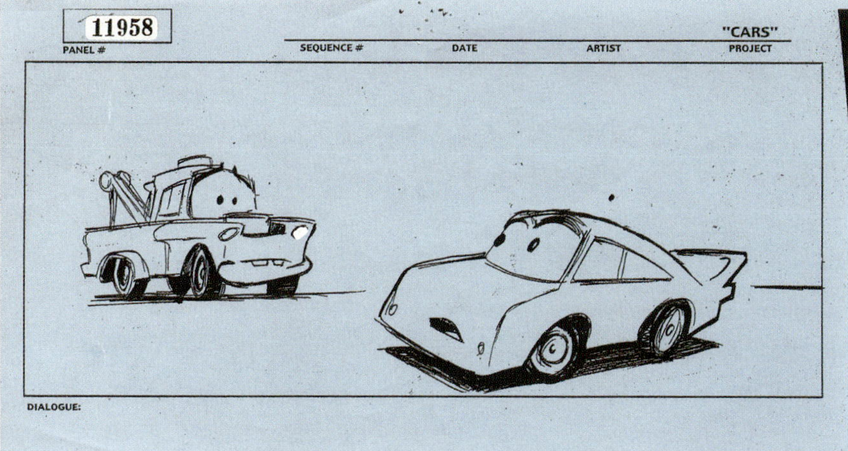

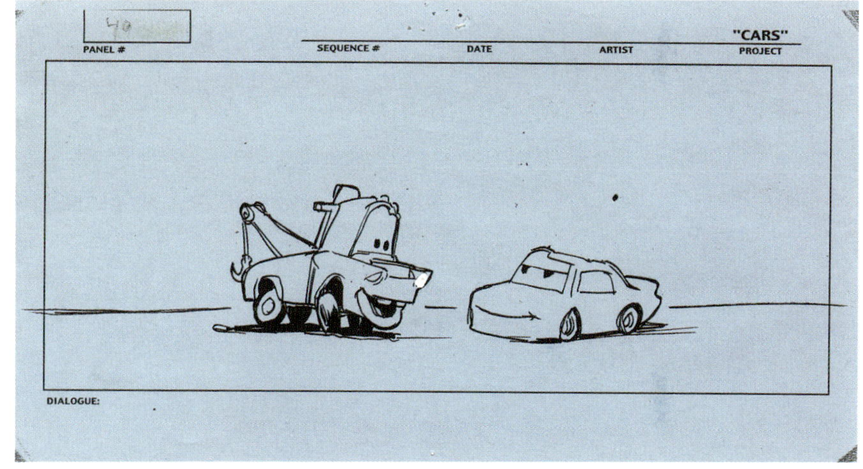

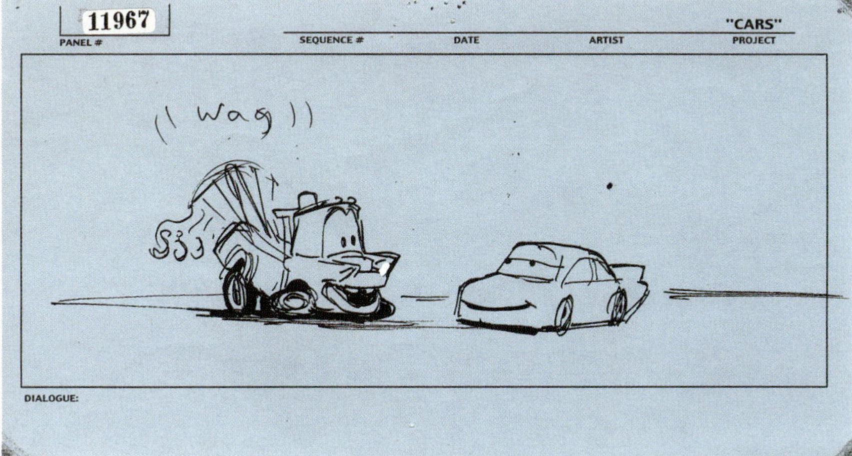

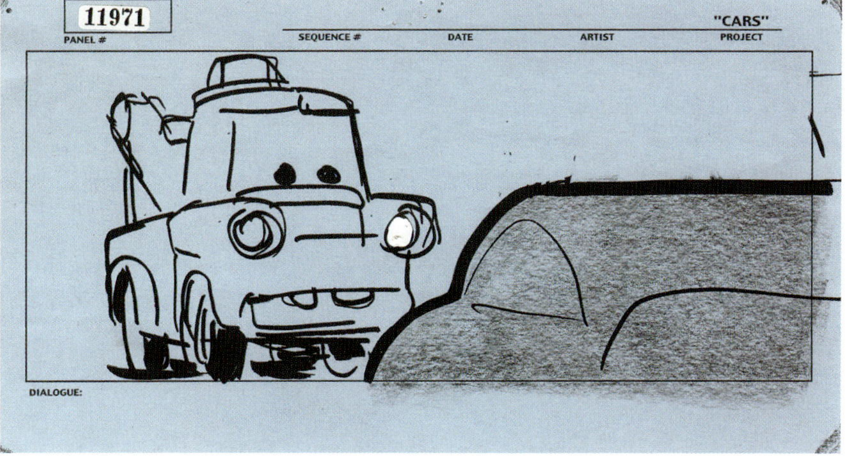

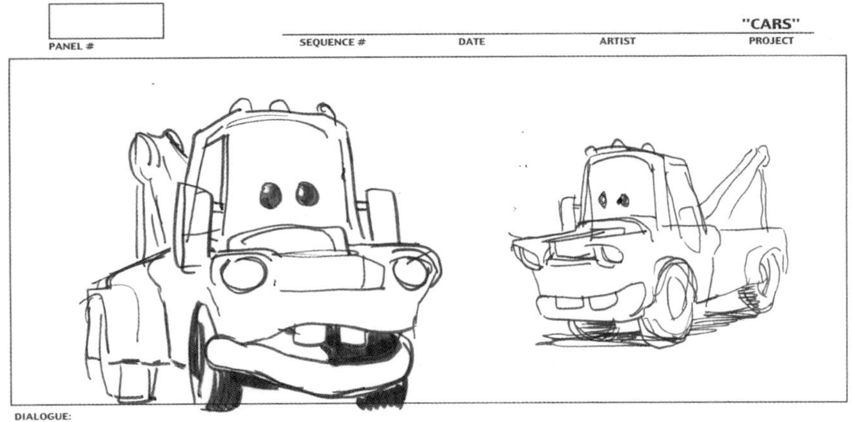

could get ten percent of what we're feeling into this movie, we're going to have a great movie. Because it was just so fun."[7]

It was a sad journey, too. Interstate highways constructed in the 1950s bypassed the towns and absorbed Route 66's traffic and commerce. "These towns are gone or hanging by a thread," Rivera says. "Only thing keeping it alive are these people. Really good and smart people, with a sense of family and pride about where they live and working hard to keep their towns. We tried to get that into the film."

Ranft befriended many Route 66 denizens. But there was one "good ol' boy" in the middle of Oklahoma who invited him to his home, took him fishing, fed him baloney sandwiches, and gave him ice water out of a jug. This fellow's claim to fame was his ability to turn his double-jointed leg backward 180 degrees. "I kick *muh* leg," he said, demonstrating proudly.

It was like a magic trick, and "Joe thought this was the greatest thing he'd ever seen," says Rivera. From this odd encounter, Ranft created what Lasseter calls "the single greatest" Pixar character: Mater, a rusty tow truck/good ol' boy with a deep-fried accent.

On the surface, Mater seems a stereotypical hillbilly, not far removed from toothsome Chucky Eisner. But "Joe was sensitive to not doing a parody," Rivera says. "He didn't want to make fun of the people he met. He wanted to celebrate them as individuals."

As the film unfolds we discover hidden facets in Mater, such as a sly humor born of quiet intelligence, sensitivity, and honest appraisal of people and their foibles; plus there's a joy of life exuberantly expressed by wildly driving backward through the town (adapted from the Oklahoma fellow's trick leg). There is Mater's endearing loyalty to friends and childlike willingness to find the good in people and seek their friendship openly. There is his warmth mixed with mischievousness and forthrightness.

Ranft put a lot of himself into the endearing Mater, which Lasseter appreciated: "I realize it's Joe. This is pure Joe." Mater's loyal friendship to McQueen, whom he considers his best friend and can make laugh and appreciate life, mirrors Ranft's longtime relationship with Lasseter.

The driving-backward sequence in *Cars* is another example of Ranft's ability to pick a key moment and storyboard it definitively. The sequence "made it all the way through without comments to the final movie," Lasseter notes.

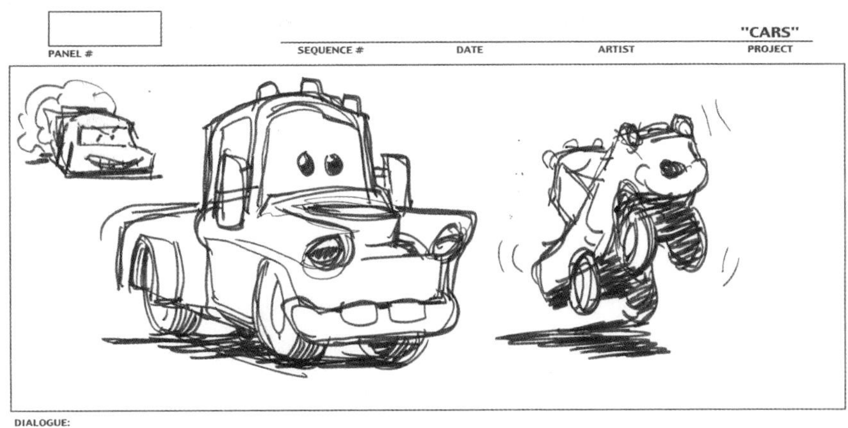

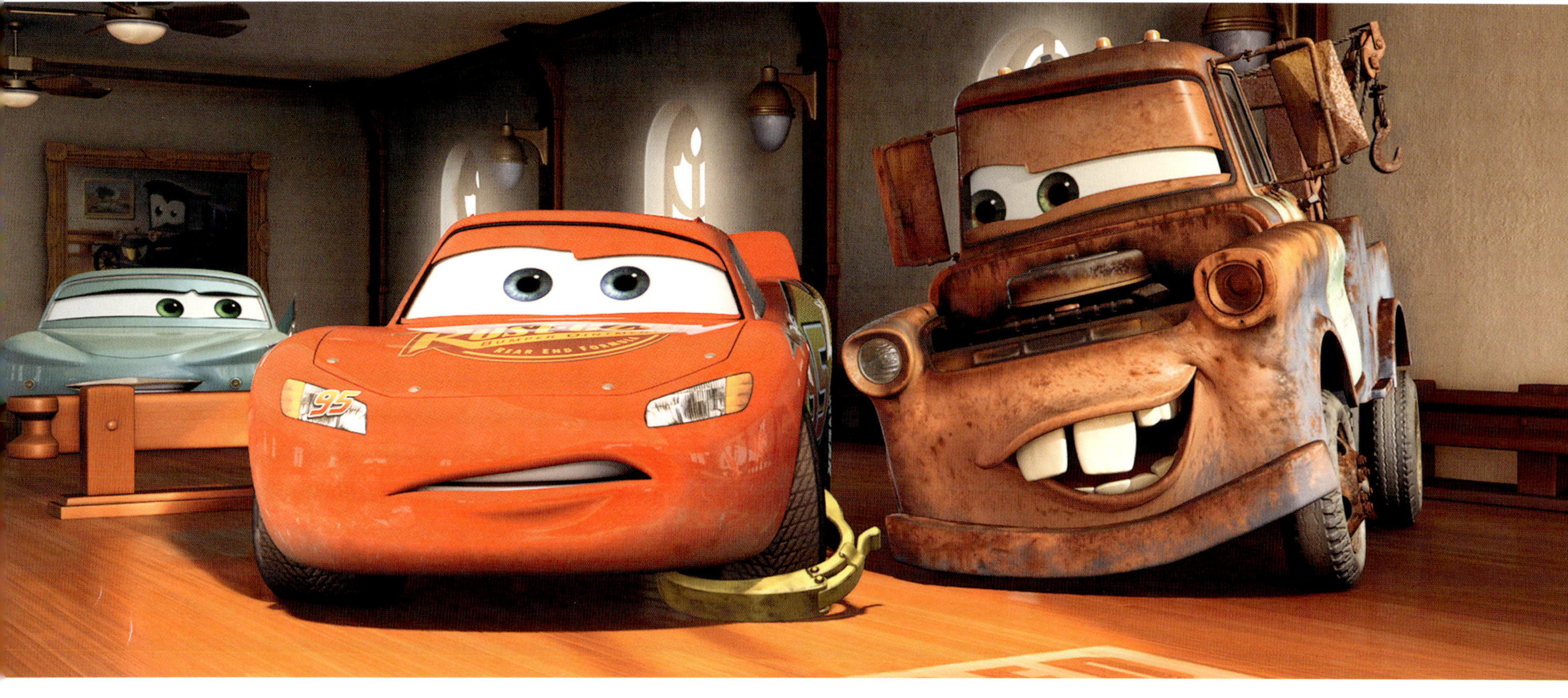

ABOVE AND OPPOSITE: *Mater, a good ol' truck and best buddy of race car Lightning McQueen.*

"*Cars* was really tough," Darla Anderson, the film's producer, says. Ranft was (again) guiding a crew of mostly neophyte story artists, and there were his increasingly heavy codirecting duties.

"John was running the studio *and* directing the film, so it was a difficult schedule," Anderson says. Lasseter was also deeply involved with the design and construction of a new Pixar studio complex on sixteen acres in nearby Emeryville, between Berkeley and Oakland, into which the company moved in 2000.

"Then in the middle of all that," Anderson continues, "behind closed doors the deal was going on." "The deal" was an attempt to renegotiate the Disney/Pixar contract, which continued for several years. Eventually (on January 24, 2006) The Walt Disney Company purchased Pixar for more than $7 billion, and Lasseter became creative overseer of both Disney and Pixar animated films.

"Poor John," Anderson says. "Talk about having your mind in one thousand different places in a tense situation. Just getting enough director time in a world where John is John. He's got a big, big life and a lot of responsibilities. Without question, genius director. So it's a question of focus and time."

Ranft "was the rock of *Cars*," Anderson says.

"You could see *Cars* wore Joe down," Docter observes. "That was a monumental project. Usually as head of story there's always a lot of weight on you. Now all these people were reporting to [Ranft as codirector] and him carrying the torch while John was away."

An animation director supervises all aspects of a film's production processes, including concepts, design, color, story, layout, timing, editing, animation, sound, and music. He or she guides the crew (especially animators' performances) using drawings and/or daily one-on-one critiques. The director is a cheerleader, a troubleshooter, and a film's ultimate decision-maker.

Ranft was again working long, late hours through weekends, which he had vowed he wouldn't do after *A Bug's Life*. "I think what happens with these movies," Anderson says, "when you're head of story, when you're the director or producer, there's different pressures. I feel like the movie is constantly playing in their heads. So, even when they're not working the long hours, their spouses complain they're not there. They're elsewhere. They're thinking of their movie, until the nut is cracked and they can put it to bed. Sometimes it's the hours. Sometimes it's just the presence of mind, body, and spirit. 'Cause they're just trying to figure it out. I know Joe struggled with that, like we all did."[8]

Late in the story process, Ranft brought Brenda Chapman onto the production. "'Cause he was feeling they needed some female perspective on their female characters. That's my lot in life," she jokes. "'Oh, we need a girl. Call Brenda.'"

Ranft called Chapman because of her accomplishments in developing standout sequences in *The Rescuers Down Under* and *Beauty and the Beast* and her story supervision of *The Lion King*. In 1994, she joined DreamWorks to become one of the few women ever to direct a feature film (she shared codirection of *Prince of Egypt*).

But Chapman left DreamWorks for the same reason she left Disney. "It was so over executive-managed, the whole story process, that the artists weren't being trusted anymore. So, I was depressed and pretty disillusioned about the industry in general."

Ranft convinced her to join Pixar in spring 2003, where, he said, "story is king." "It touched me," she says, "that he loved his craft and art so much and had found a place to nurture it. I think he knew I was pretty wounded from my experiences at the other studios, and he thought it was a good place to come and heal. He was very right."

Chapman worked nine months on *Cars*. Then she was asked to direct a feature based on her own idea (*The Bear and the Bow*) and for which Ranft would be executive producer.[9] "I'm very happy at Pixar and I owe that to Joe," she says. "He was always there in my darkest moments with either inspirational advice or a hug or the invitation to come work with him again."

On *Cars*, Chapman observed how Ranft was "pulled in many directions" and "carried a lot of the weight. John [Lasseter] trusted Joe implicitly, so a lot of the responsibility was on Joe's shoulders."[10]

"He was so exhausted," Su Ranft says. Despite his fatigue, at the beginning of 2005 he quietly flew to London with his brother Jerome to meet with Tim Burton on the set of *Corpse Bride*. "Joe wasn't supposed to do this, he was working for Pixar, but he couldn't help himself because it was his baby," Jerome explains. Ranft had pitched the idea for the puppet film to Burton a decade earlier. The two friends met and watched reels all day. "Joe gave notes. All good ideas," Jerome says.

Eventually, his *Cars* duties were completed, and "after twenty-five years in the animation business, he was ready to take a break," Su says. In the future he would "be the teacher, the mentor. That's what he wanted to be. And have more time for his humanitarian work."

He asked for and got twelve weeks off. He began making plans to publish his children's books and direct a short based on *Baby Go Bowling*. He got together with friends again, attended magic seminars, and worked out at the gym. He started taking anti-depressants. "It was like he woke up," Su says. "He didn't even know he was depressed. *Ex-haus-ted!*" The couple made plans to celebrate their twentieth wedding anniversary in September at the Miraval Life in Balance Resort in Tucson, Arizona.

In June, I received an e-mail from Joe:

> Hi John,
>
> Sue [sic], Sophia and I are going to be in your neck of the woods [New York City] June 30 through July 4th, for a fun-filled week of Broadway shows and culture. We're going to see *Beauty and the Beast*, *Wicked*, and *Spamalot!* We would love to see you if you're in town. I wanted to pick your brain about seeing fireworks on the 4th. We're staying in a hotel in Times Square. Story is winding down on *Cars* and life is good. I'll have several of my drawings from *Toy Story* exhibited in the upcoming MoMA show ["Pixar: 20 Years of Animation" December 14, 2005–February 6, 2006] which is pretty cool. Never thought I'd ever have any of my work in the Museum of Modern Art.
>
> I hope all is well with you.
>
> Best, Joe[11]

I'd last seen Joe the previous year for dinner when he, Lasseter, Anderson, and others came east for a *Cars* recording session with Paul Newman. Now, on a hot July Fourth, we met on the steps of the American Museum of Natural History. Su and Sophia were nursing summer colds at the hotel, so Joe went alone to view a special dinosaur exhibit. It was easy to spot him, tall as an apatosaurus, among the holiday crowd.

At lunch at a nearby Columbus Avenue restaurant, Joe was relaxed and happy and expressed how proud he was of *Cars*. I teased him saying I hoped there weren't too many fart jokes in the film. He gave a coy butter-wouldn't-melt-in-his-mouth smile and murmured, "Well, maybe a couple."

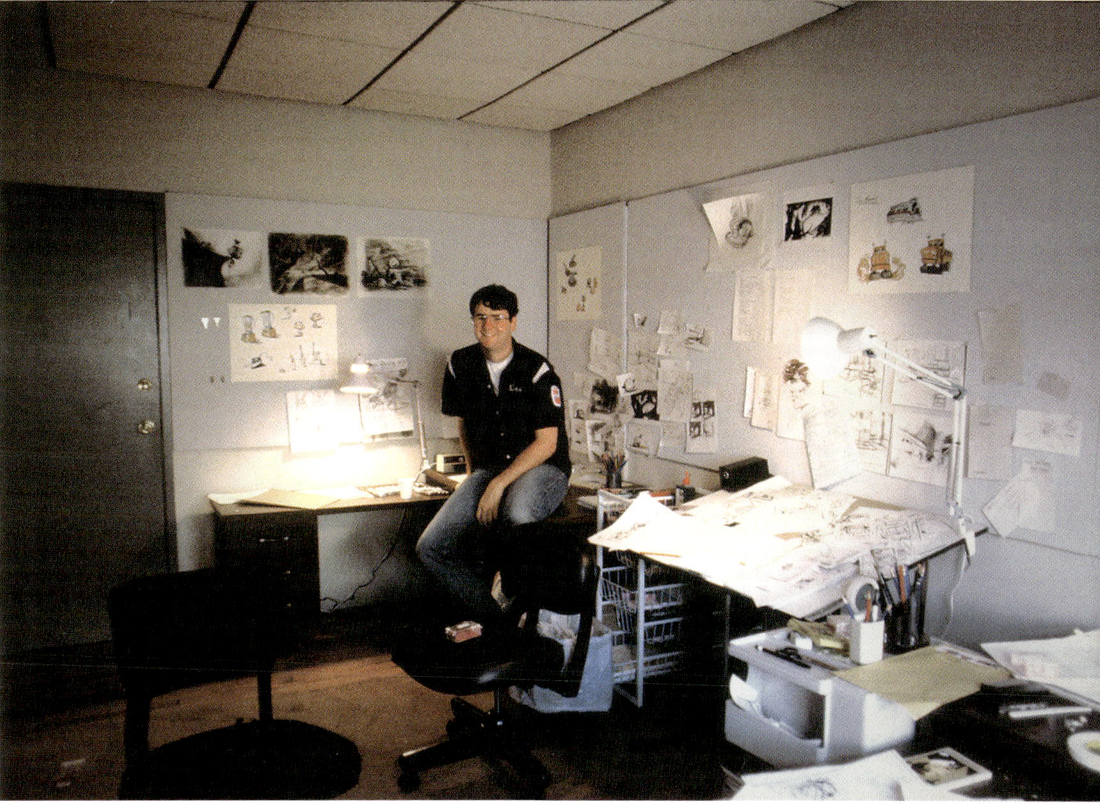

Joe Ranft takes a break in his Pixar office.

Afterward we spent about three hours at my apartment looking through old children's books and vintage animation art. Then off he went to meet his family and watch the fireworks over Manhattan.[12]

During that last visit to New York, the Ranfts lunched with Tom Schumacher. "It was so great to see them," Schumacher says. Before the meal was over, Ranft said, "We just wanted to make sure that you know how grateful we are."

"For what?" Schumacher asked.

"You were so generous with us. You helped us get our first house. I've never forgotten it."

"He went on and on and got very teary-eyed, as did Su, who is a tough bird, you know!" Schumacher says.[13]

On August 16, Joe Ranft drove his 2004 Honda Element to the Mosaic Foundation's annual spiritual

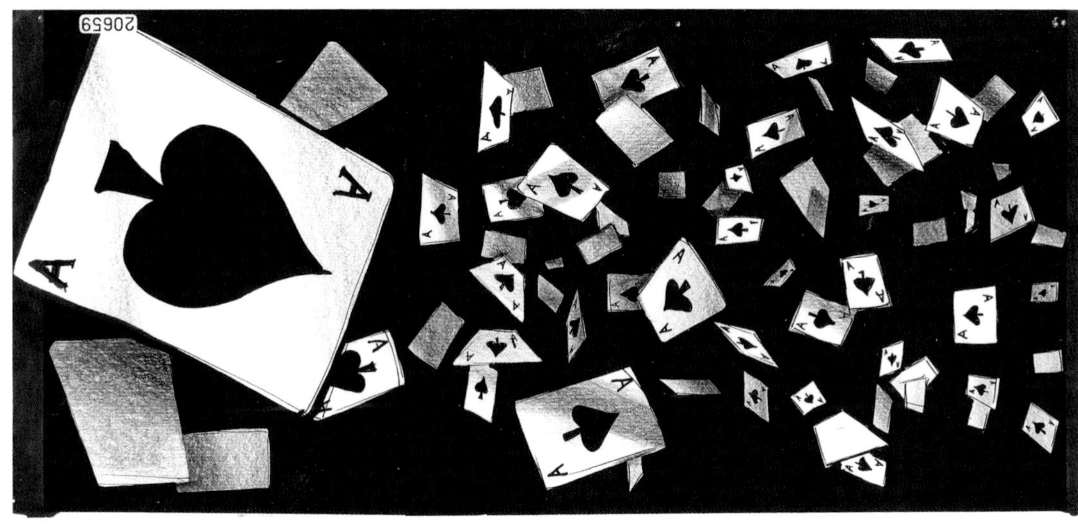

ABOVE: *Joe Ranft's drawing of a magician's playing cards.* OPPOSITE: *John Musker's moving storyboard tribute at Pixar's "A Celebration of Joe Ranft's Life," September 17, 2005.*

retreat in Mendocino, California. He was accompanied by two "peace warriors" from Watts: Eric Fryerson, age thirty-nine, whom he personally sponsored, and Elegba Earl, age thirty-two, whom, thirteen years before, had stopped gang warfare between L.A.'s Bloods and Crips.

The two men and Ranft were "worlds apart," says Luis J. Rodriguez, a teacher at the retreat. "But in the men's conferences, they shared stories, poems, ideas, emotions, and visions. They became fast friends and peace collaborators."[14]

Su was on an errand when her husband and the men departed. "So I didn't get to kiss Joe good-bye," she later said.

Somewhere along the way Ranft traded places with Earl, allowing him to drive. About 3:00 P.M. on a tight curve eleven miles from their destination, the driver lost control of the car. It swerved and fell 130 feet over the side of the road, overturning twice before landing where the Navarro River meets the Pacific Ocean. Fryerson escaped through the crushed sunroof. But suddenly the current caught the car with its two remaining occupants and overturned it in fourteen feet of water.[15]

A memorial for Joe Ranft was held at the Mill Valley Community Center on August 21, 2005, with eulogies from grief-stricken family members (including his wife and sister), neighbors, and colleagues Steve Jobs, Ed Catmull, John Lasseter, Henry Selick, Brenda Chapman, Lee Unkrich, and Andrew Stanton, among others. On September 17, "A Celebration of Joe Ranft's Life" was held at Pixar Animation Studios with remembrances in stories and pictures by many of Ranft's coworkers at Disney and Pixar, including Pete Docter, John Musker, and John Lasseter. Both events were extremely emotional, full of tears and laughter as the participants expressed scores of poignant and funny remembrances of Ranft.

The shock and sadness of his family, friends, and colleagues continues to reverberate. To those who knew him personally, recalling Joe Ranft's loss feels like a sharp frisson in the midst of a sunny day. His creativity affected audiences around the world, and he positively touched everyone fortunate enough to come into contact with him. To lose such a uniquely gifted and good person in his prime shows how unfair life can be. His constant mantra—"Trust the Process"—is small consolation in accepting his loss.

At Pixar Animation Studios in Emeryville, among the shrubs and plants on the left of the allée leading to the main building, there is a young tree growing. It was planted in 2005 in Joe Ranft's honor "so we can remember him," John Lasseter told me recently. "I look at it every day and remember Joe."[16]

The tree was chosen because it is native to California and symbolizes the towering, ever-blossoming creativity, the physical size and long-lasting legacy of Joe Ranft.

The tree is, of course, a sequoia.

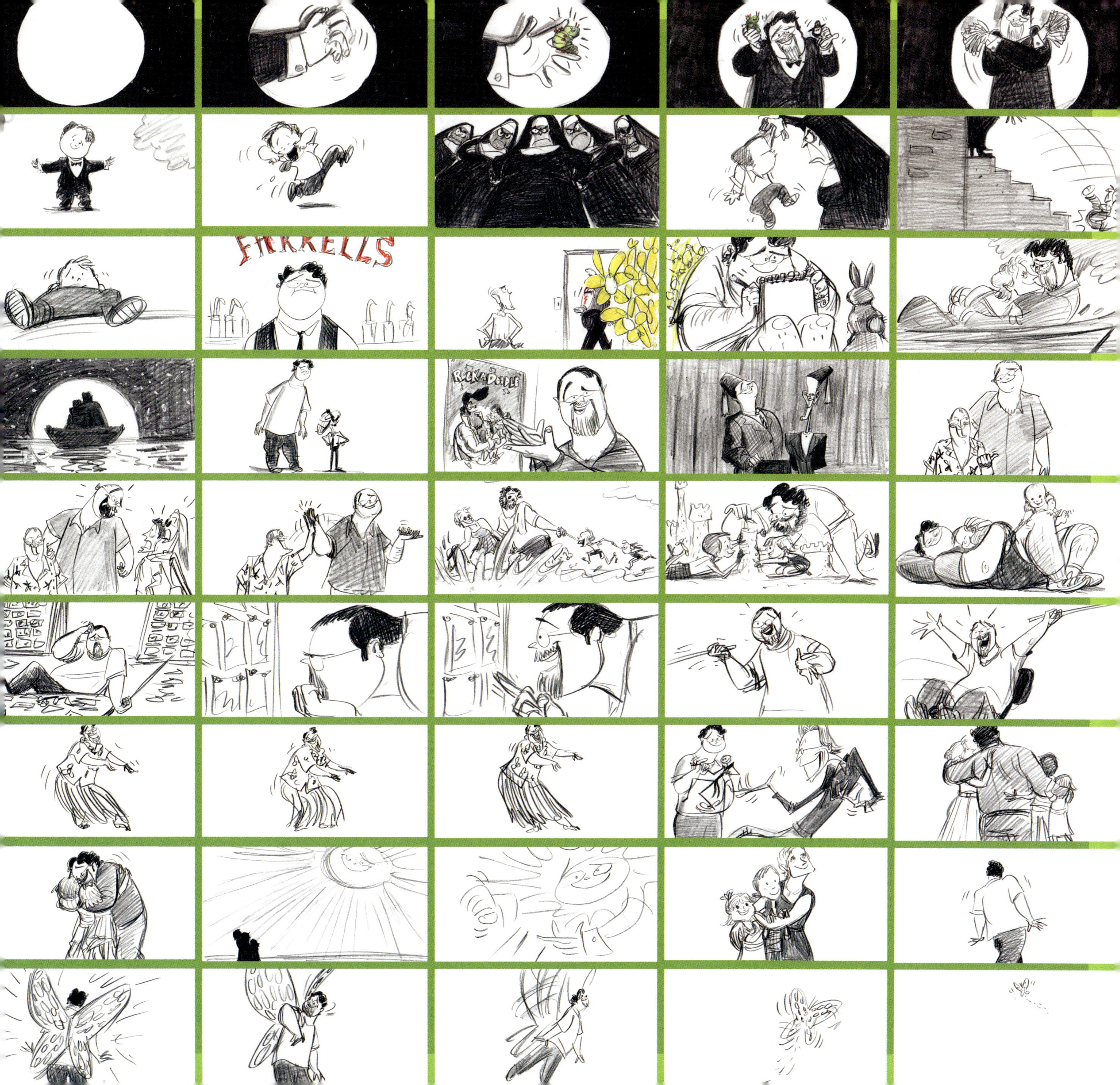
ROCKADOODLE

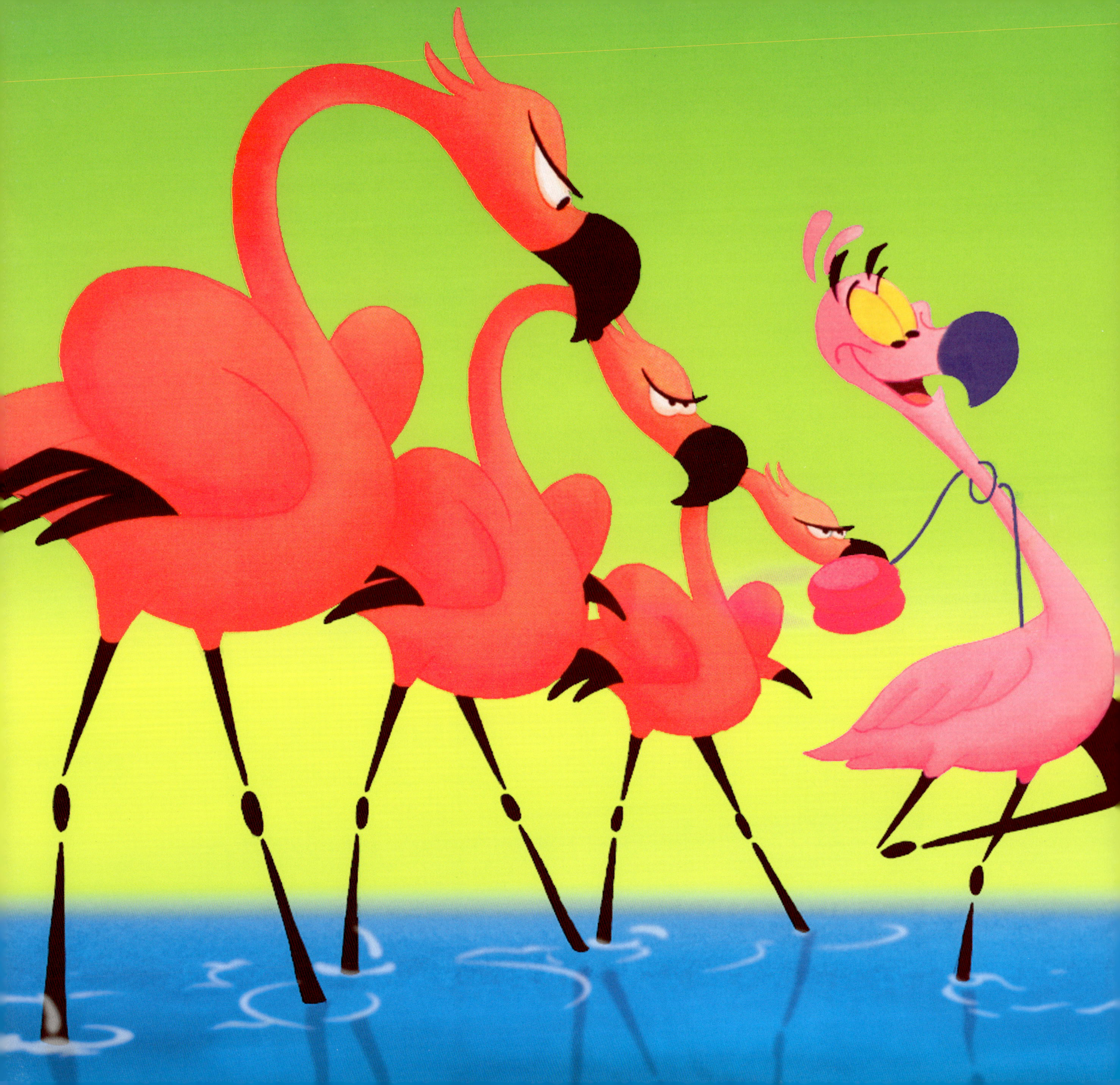

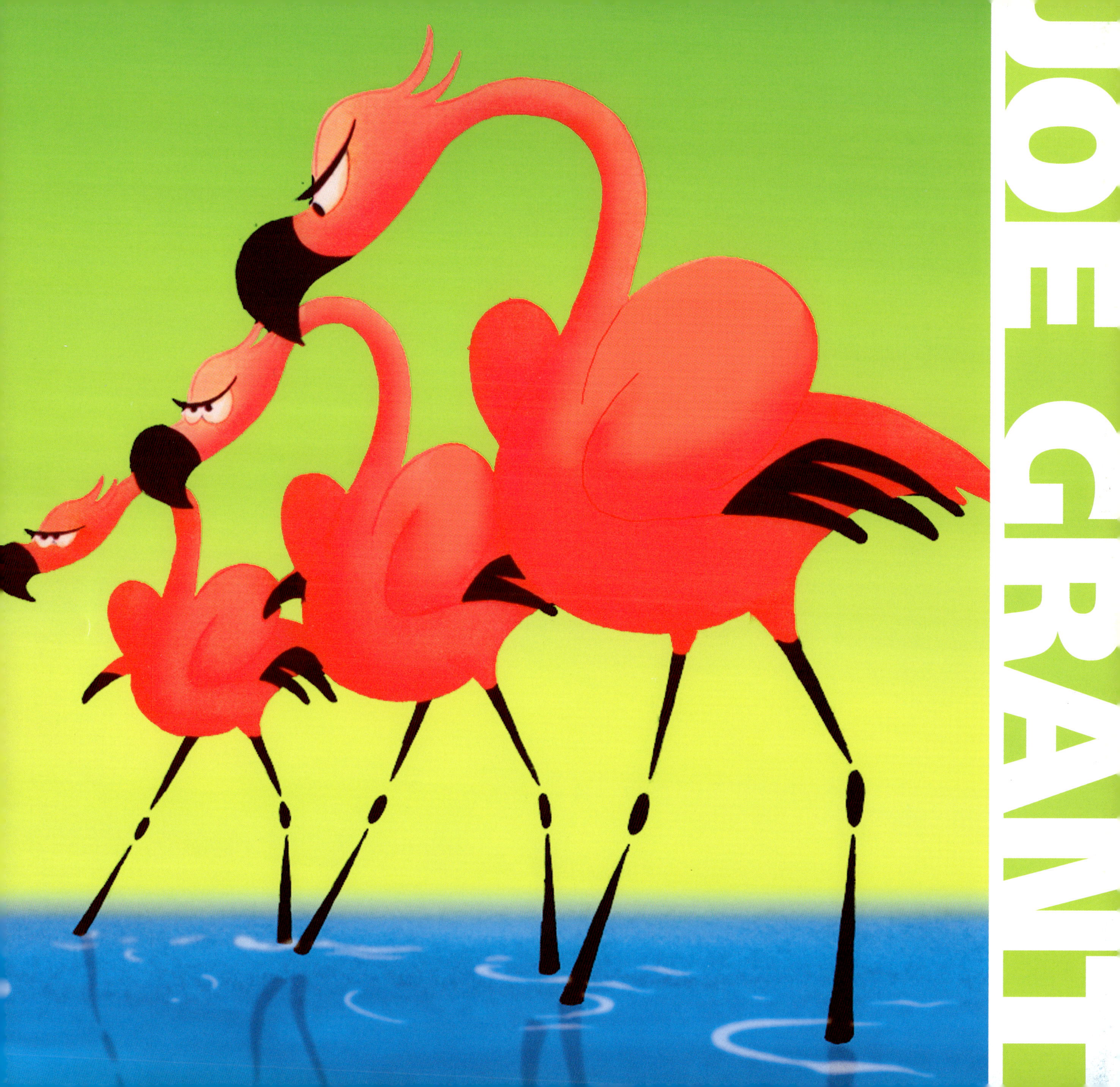
JOE GRANT

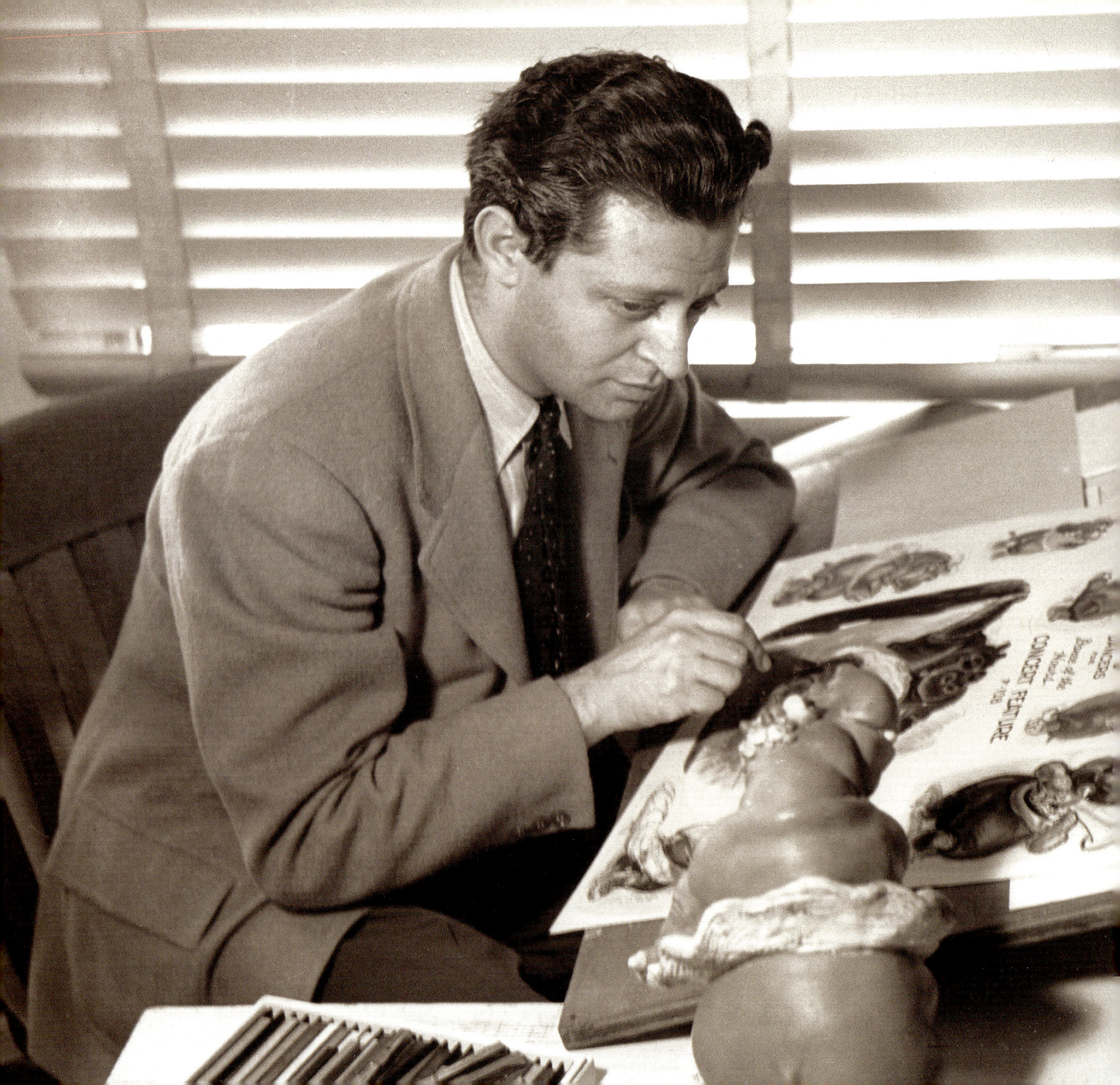
DANCERS
CONCERT FEATURE

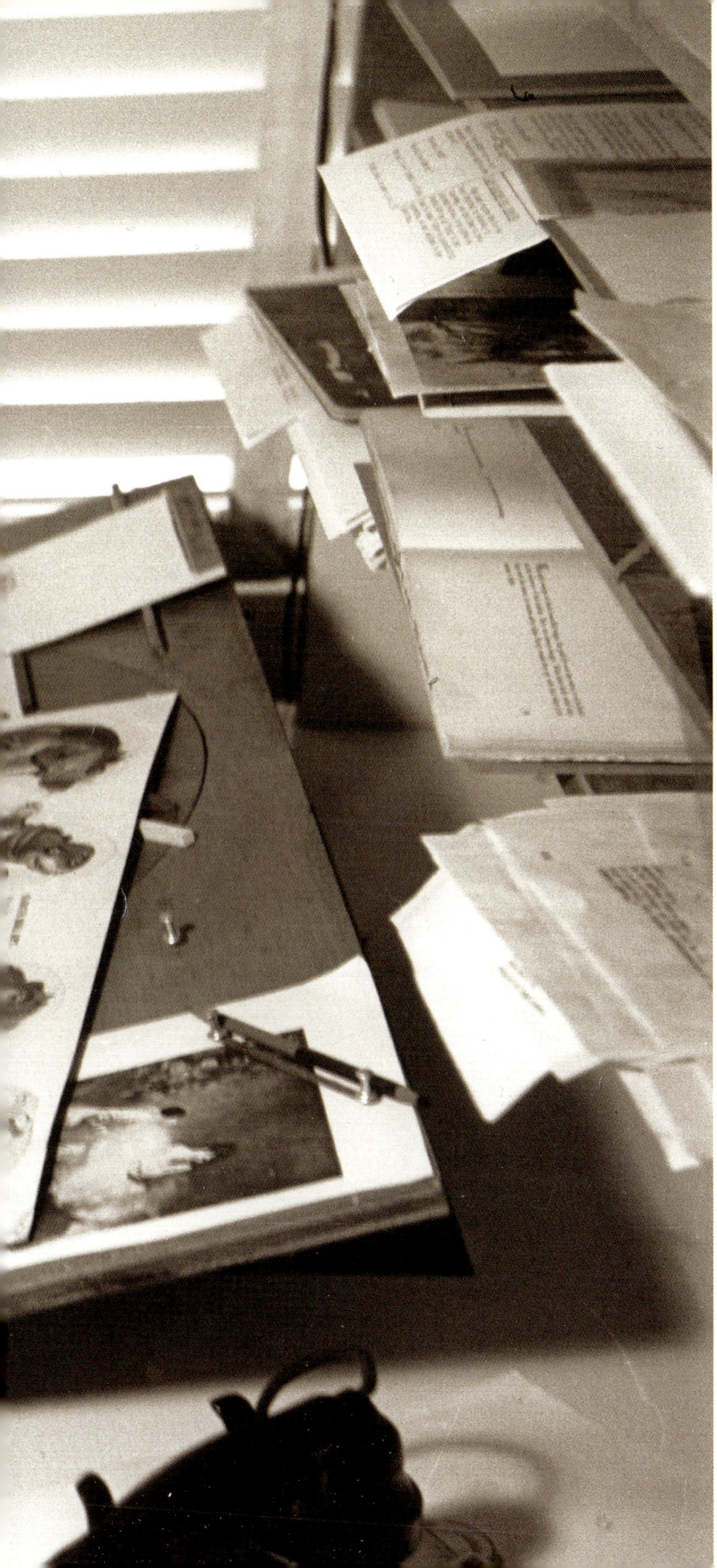

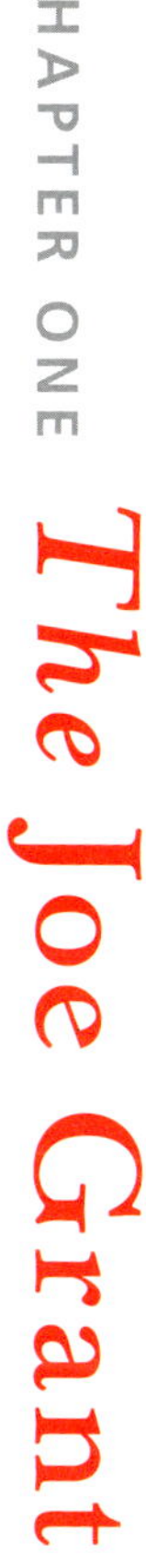

CHAPTER ONE

The Joe Grant

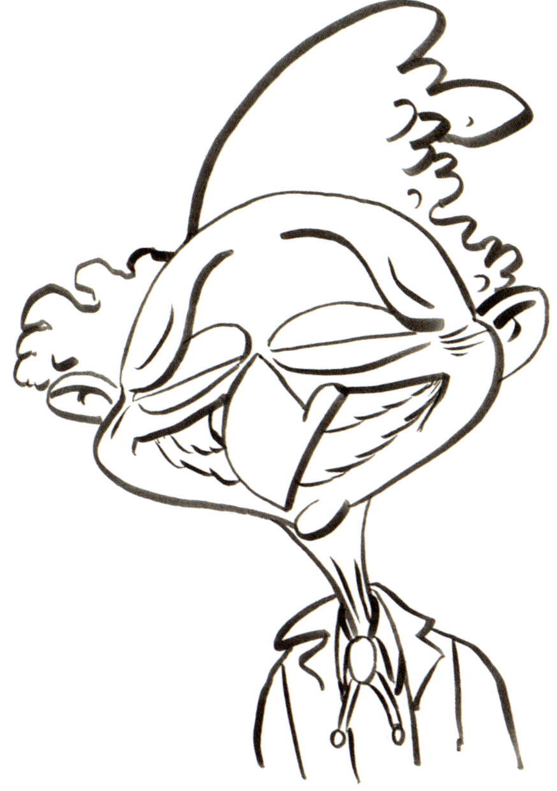

Suddenly, the old man was there.

He appeared one day in 1989 at the Walt Disney Feature Animation building, looking like the apprentice's sorcerer, with leonine white hair, a full mustache beneath a prominent nose, and inquisitive hooded eyes. Calmly perusing storyboards stacked in corridors. Showing up at story meetings for every project in the pipeline. Depositing "idea drawings" each morning at the offices of producers, directors, and animators, he seemed to be everywhere.

Among the predominantly young artists working on *Beauty and the Beast*, *Aladdin*, *The Lion King*, *Mulan*, and other films in progress, his presence was incongruous, to say the least, and apparently at odds with the studio's current zeitgeist: a short-lived second flowering of Disney animated features after years of artistic doubt and corporate turmoil during the 1970s and early '80s.

LEFT: *Thirty-two-year-old Joe Grant in 1940, when he was head of Disney's Character Model Department.* ABOVE: *Grant in his nineties, a caricature by John Musker.*

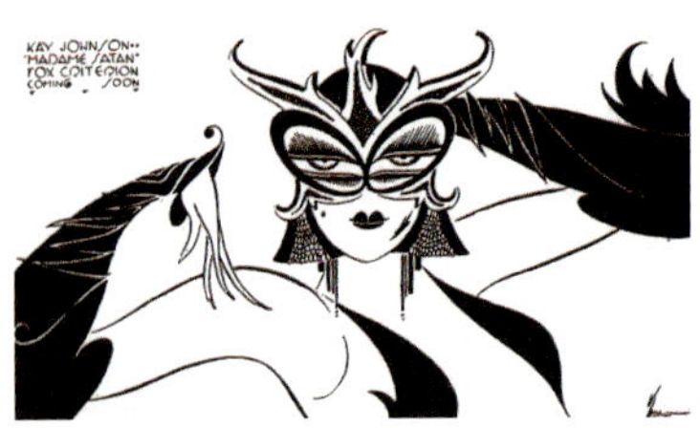

The studio's upcoming release, *The Little Mermaid*, had generated great excitement within the animation division. With a host of other features in development, this new Team Disney sought to create its own version of the studio's legendary "Golden Era" of the 1930s and '40s.

Who was this placid elderly gent in their midst?

His name, he said, was Joe Grant.

"I don't think anyone ever introduced Joe to me," Don Hahn, then the thirty-four-year-old producer of *Beauty and the Beast*, remembers. "He just started showing up at my door," or left sketches of ideas on Post-its on Hahn's desk, chair, or the middle of his carpet. "I thought it was a funny coincidence that he had the same name as the guy who used to run the Character Model Department for Walt."[1]

It was no coincidence.

He was indeed *the* Joe Grant, Walt Disney's right-hand man and most trusted confidant from mid-1933

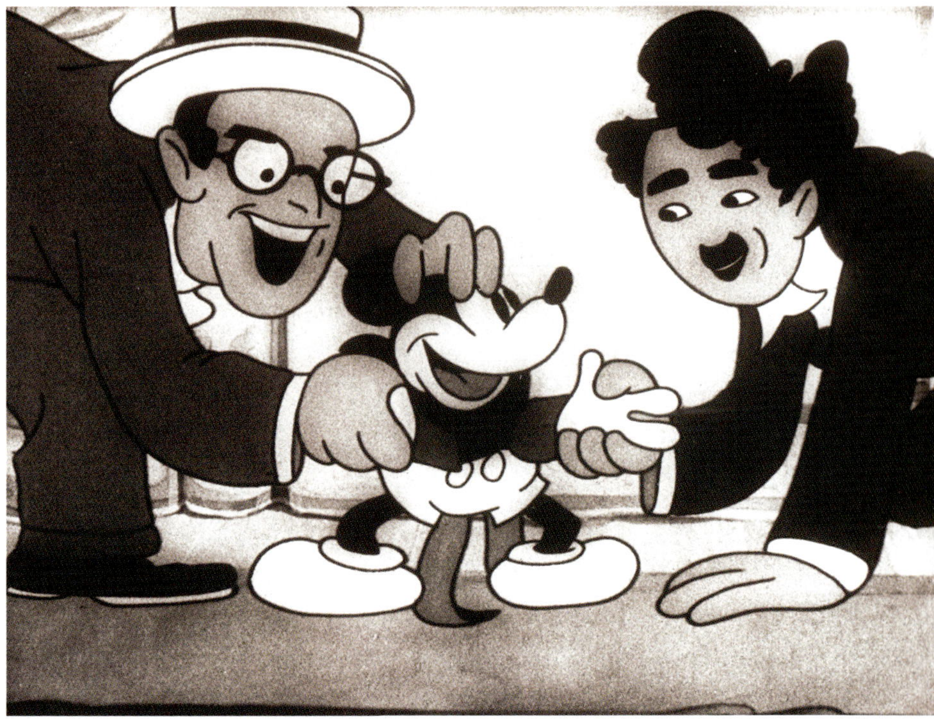

through 1949; *the* controversial Joe Grant, who was in charge of a Disney "think tank" called the Character Model Department, whose influence was envied by many; *Joe Grant*, a brilliant Los Angeles newspaper caricaturist who became a major creative contributor to several of the greatest animated films of all time, including *Snow White and the Seven Dwarfs*, *Pinocchio*, *Fantasia*, and *Dumbo*.

When the studio youngsters realized who was working among them, it was as if they had discovered a human coelacanth.

"Our jaws dropped because, first of all, he's alive?" recalls director Mike Gabriel. "Then they dropped further when we realized he's like a fifty-year-old, so vital, clever, and smart. He was on top of everything. This *is* Joe Grant!"[2]

Grant wore his eighty-one years well. He was fit, energetic, and youthful in outlook. Endlessly curious about the world beyond animation, up-to-date regarding the latest foreign film, *New Yorker* magazine essay, book, TV series, or art gallery opening. His quiet-spoken opinions were witty and straightforward.

ABOVE LEFT: *Joe Grant caricature of "Madam Satan" in September 1930 Los Angeles Record newspaper.* ABOVE: *Grant's movie star caricatures in Disney's Mickey's Gala Premiere (1933).* BELOW: (LEFT TO RIGHT) *Grant, Walt Disney, unknown, and Roy O. Disney during a rough cut screening of Pinocchio (1940).*

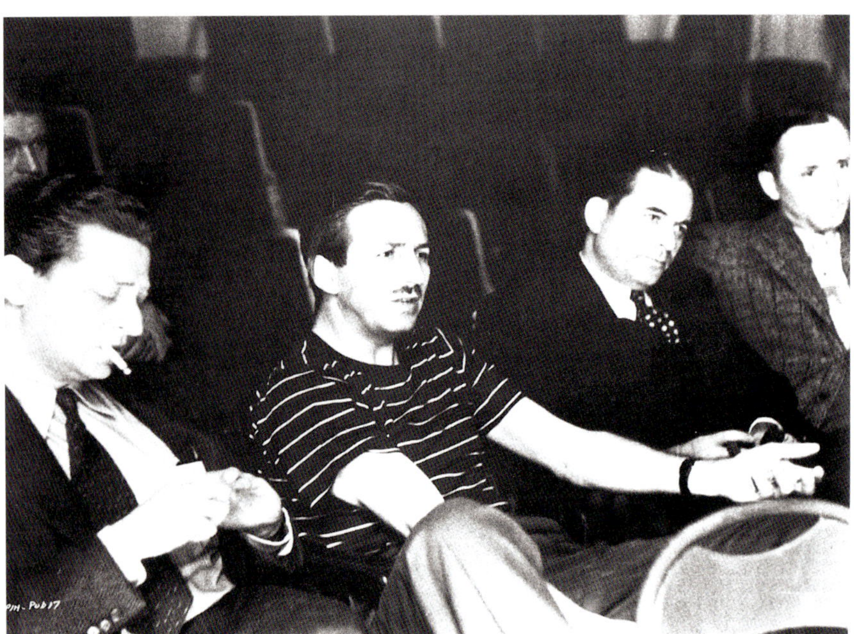

"Joe was a very modern guy," says animator/director Eric Goldberg. "He always saw the latest art house pictures when they were released. I'd feel like a yutz! I couldn't keep up with him."

Grant even had opinions about rock and roll. Thomas Schumacher, then senior vice president of Disney Feature Animation, will never forget when the rock band Hootie & the Blowfish won Best New Artist at the 1996 Grammy Awards. "The next morning," Schumacher says, "Eighty-eight-year-old Joe walked into my office, as he constantly did, talking and shaking his finger: 'You know why the kids love Hootie? I'll tell you why they love Hootie!'

"Joe was not locked in his time at all," Schumacher marvels.[3]

Grant's contemporaries were either deceased or retired—including the famed Nine Old Men, Walt's favored phalanx of animators. So, it seemed incredible to the current Disney staffers that they were in the presence of a man who was a vital link to the legendary period they hoped to emulate. Joe Grant: the closest the new generation would ever get to the creative mind and spirit of Walt Disney.

However, those seeking out Grant as a nostalgic talisman quickly discovered his interests lay in the present and future. Questions about his long career and personal life were deflected by claiming not to remember, pretending his hearing aid was on the fritz, or simply by his disarming wit.

"What was it like at the studio back then as compared to now?" elicited the retort: "It was a lot like now . . . (pause) . . . but we all drew better!"

Ba-da-boom! Next subject.

Questions regarding why he left the studio and what he'd been doing the last forty years brought vague replies. "He had a real defense rhythm," Pam Coats, then executive vice president of Creative Affairs, says. "He had a rhythm of someone who survived and just kept going." He could be a generous mentor "*if* you took the time," Coats emphasizes. But "you really had to take the time with Joe." Those who did, like Gabriel, Pete Docter, Dean DeBlois, Eric and Susan Goldberg, and Andreas Deja, among others, developed a deep respect for his wisdom and inspiring creativity.

"I admired his collaborativeness," Hahn says. "He wasn't this ivory-tower guy. He wanted to get his hands dirty—get in and draw those drawings!"[4]

Others at the studio, says Coats, "didn't want him around." Some directors and producers resented his

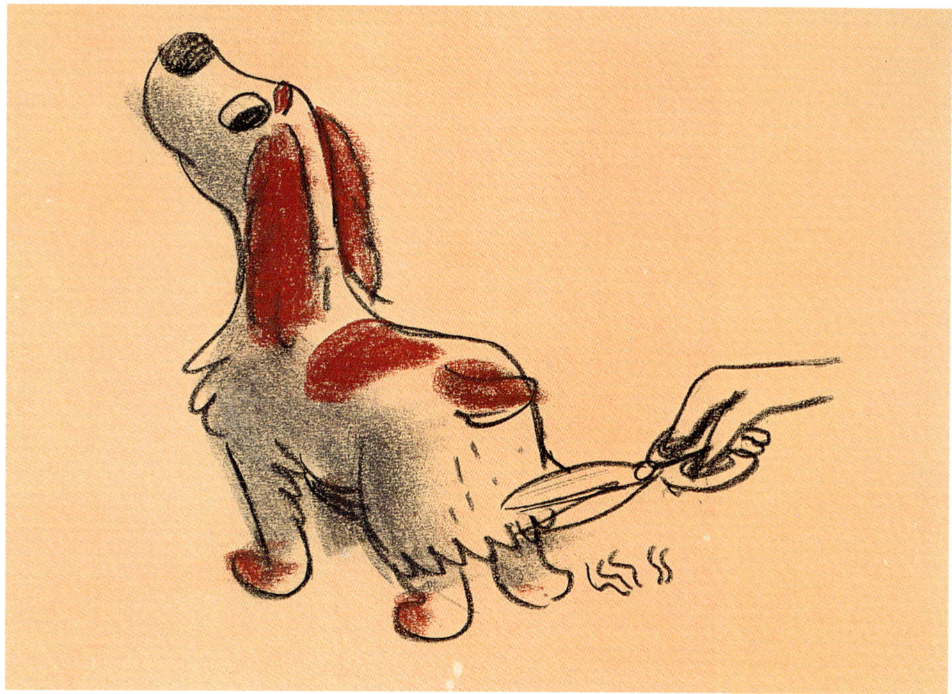

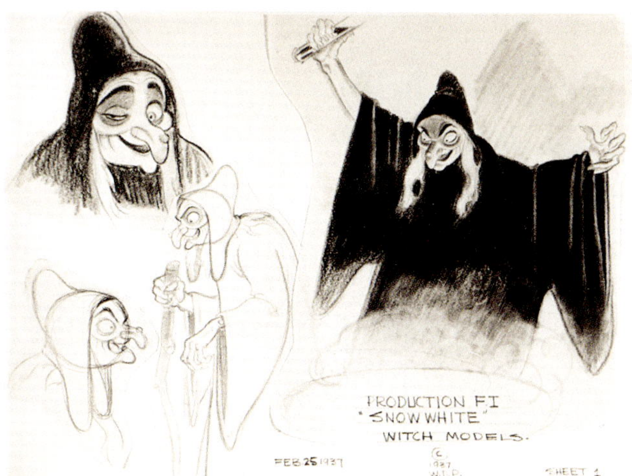

ABOVE: *Joe Grant's early concept for Lady in* LADY AND THE TRAMP *(1955).* BELOW: *Grant's design for the witch in* SNOW WHITE AND THE SEVEN DWARFS *(1937).*

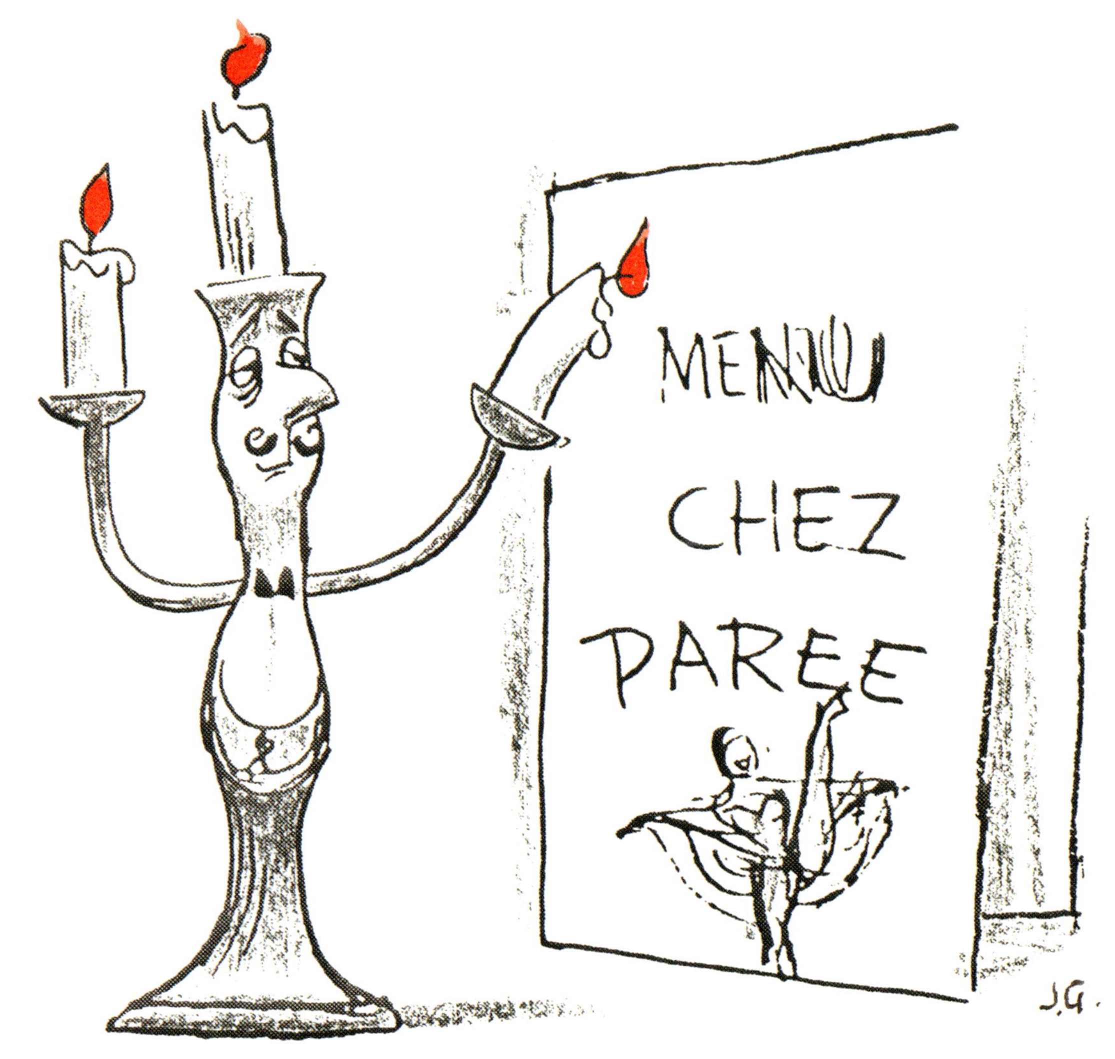

SUGGESTION FOR OPENING 'BE OUR GUEST' (SONG)

CANDELABRA AS MAITRE'D LIGHTS UP THE MENU .. MENU SWINGS OPEN PAGES BECOME THE BACKDROP FOR ENTERTAINMENT PERFORMED BY DINNER SERVICE.

THE MENU IS KIND OF BEAT-UP .. IT'S BEEN OUT OF USE FOR SOME TIME.

THE SONG ENDS WITH AN OFF-STAGE GROWL AND THE APPEARANCE OF THE BEAST ... THEY ALL SCATTER, LEAVING MAURICE ALONE.

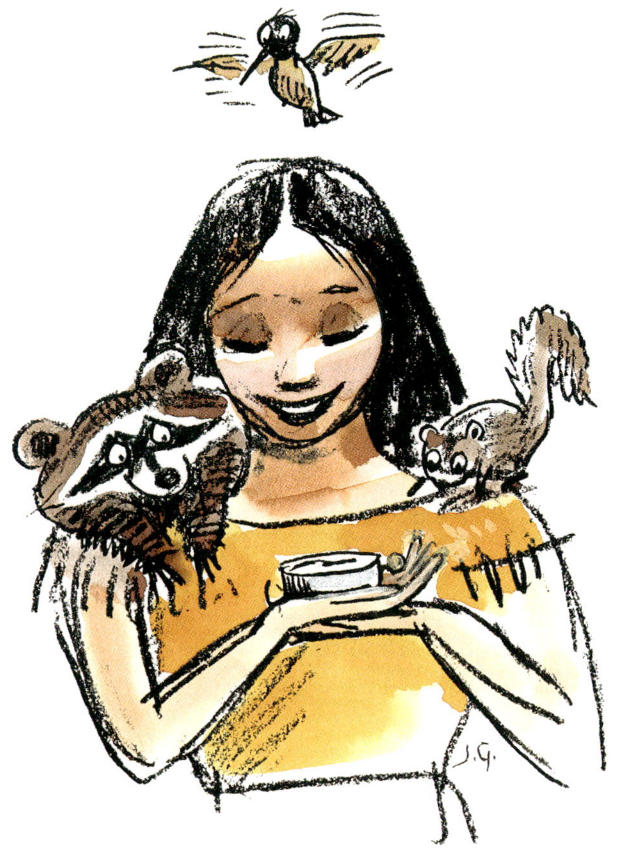

Smith's compass

age, style, working method, dogged persistence, and easy access to power. He could (and did) walk into the offices of Roy E. Disney (then chairman of Feature Animation), Schumacher (who brought Grant back), Coats, and other executives to present his ideas whenever he pleased. Ironically, these were some of the same reasons Grant was controversial during his first sixteen years at the studio.

What Joe Grant did make clear is that he had returned to Disney to work—period; to create animated films with the same drive and purpose he had once before brought to the studio.

"Get To Work" he wrote in distinctive calligraphy on a note taped to his office door. It was an order he obeyed with admirable discipline. "Creating was his oxygen," Gabriel observes.

Early in his career, his superbly styled caricatures blossomed in the *Los Angeles Record* newspaper and attracted Walt Disney, who personally brought Grant into the animated-film world. Grant's intelligence and imagination poured forth a perpetual stream of ideas for characters, gags, dialogue, and stories that significantly influenced Disney's films.

He spent the forty years between his Disney stints (1949–1989) running his own ceramics and greeting-card companies. Grant's bottomless well of creativity proved undiminished when he rejoined the studio as an octogenarian.

Grant's idea drawings subtly affect every phase of production because they feed animation, story, characters, and relationships, all the way through.[5] Walt Disney discovered in Grant a storyteller extraordinaire; he was a unique, intellectually rich resource of new ideas and possibilities for the art of animation and inspiring others. Both he and Grant had creative minds and a shared passion for this new medium of storytelling. Kindred spirits, they were simpatico in energy, drive, and ambition.

Alice Davis, wife of master animator Marc Davis, knew both Disney and Grant well. "Walt loved to ask you to do something that he knew you didn't think you were capable of doing," she observes, "and he would force you to grow. With Joe, Walt had to force himself to keep up with Joe!"[6]

"My personal belief is it's not the destination, it's the journey," Grant said in 1995. "I'm being curious and competitive. I have a vast area to look back on, a resource that's of some value here.

"The drawings I make are not storyboard drawings," he explained. "They are inspirational drawings. I always like to have an idea in each drawing, so if they look at it they can say that's a possibility. We can build on that.

"I think that's my function. Always has been."[7]

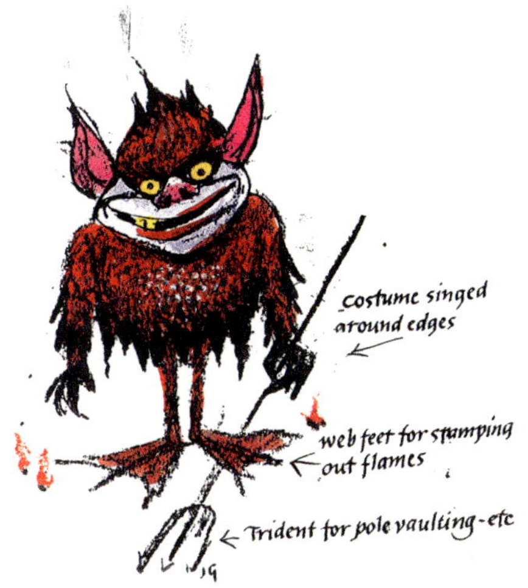

OPPOSITE: *Joe Grant suggests a haughty candelabra for* BEAUTY AND THE BEAST *(1991).* LEFT: *Grant's ideas for animal companions in* POCAHONTAS *(1995).* ABOVE: *a demon for* HERCULES *(1997).*

CHAPTER TWO

A Mobile Existence

He was always "Joe Grant."

His full name was Joseph Clarence Grant, but on his birth certificate, George and Eva Grant's newborn is listed simply as "Joe Grant."[1] He was born May 15, 1908, on New York City's Lower East Side at 139 Delancy Street. The building stood within sight of the Williamsburg Bridge in a teeming multiethnic neighborhood of mostly Eastern European Jews.

Many came to America in the late nineteenth-century wave of immigrants escaping the anti-Semitic pogroms sweeping Russia. Joe's father, George Albert Grant (January 1885–September 13, 1938), emigrated from Poland in 1890 at age five with his parents, Nathan (anglicized to Nat or Ned, b. 1860) and Fannie née Freund (b. 1861), who were married in 1883.[2]

"My father's father came from Poland," Joe Grant told an interviewer, not mentioning that his own father also was born there.

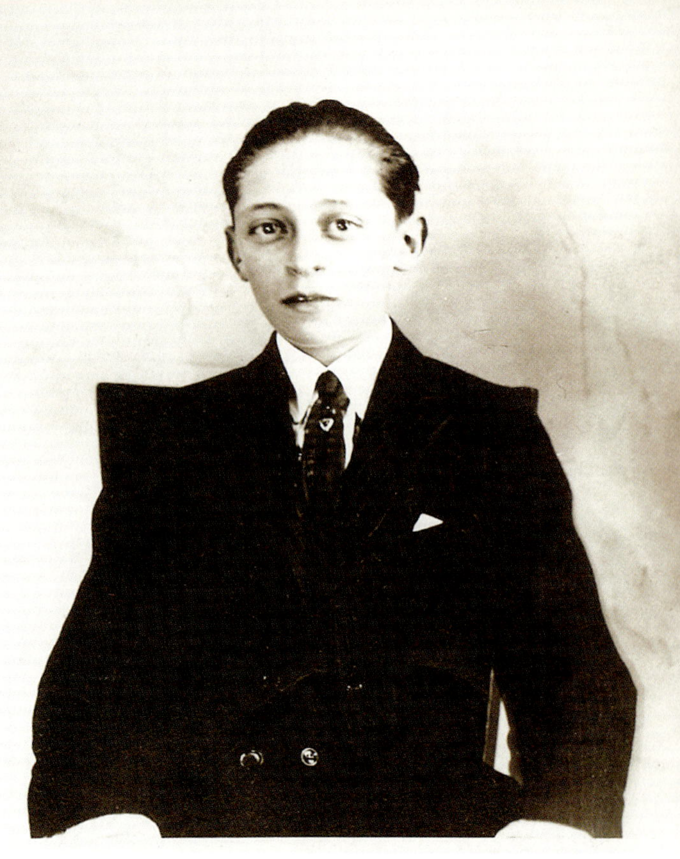

STATE OF NEW YORK.
CERTIFICATE AND RECORD OF BIRTH
OF

No. of Certificate, 40003

Name of Child	Joe Grant		
Sex	Male	Father's Occupation	Artist
Color	White	Mother's Name	Eva Grant
Date of Birth	May 15/1908	Mother's Name before Marriage	Eva Freunde
Place of Birth, Street and No.	139 Delancy St.	Mother's Residence	139 Delancy St.
Father's Name	George Grant	Mother's Birthplace	Russia
Father's Residence	139 Delancy St.	Mother's Age	21
Father's Birthplace	U. S.	Number of previous Children	—
Father's Age	24	How many now living (in all)	1

Name and address of person making this report. Signature, [illegible]
Residence, 150 Henry St.

Date of Report, ______190

Yes, they were Jewish, but they were non-Jewish. When they came here, some generations ago, [they faced] the problem of race shame. Because of the prejudice around. So they didn't remain religious in any way. Some cases it's good, sometimes bad. In this case, it was convenient."[3]

Nathan adopted the family surname "Grant" supposedly because he admired Ulysses S. Grant.[4] It seems an odd choice for a Jew, but Nathan was unaware that the famous Civil War general and president issued notorious General Orders #11 in December 1862 expelling all Jews from Kentucky, Tennessee, and Mississippi, "the most blatant official episode of anti-Semitism in nineteenth-century American history," according to the American Jewish Historical Society.[5]

Nathan's original surname of "Gumolinsky" (what family members believe it was) probably was altered upon entering the U.S.A.[6] Joe's wife, Jennie, joked that if her husband was "Joe Gumolinsky" she'd never have married him.[7]

"They all wanted to be Americans as quickly as possible. And they did," Grant said. The wish to assimilate quickly into American culture and downplay their Jewish heritage was hastened by memories of the pogroms as well as the obvious and insidious anti-Semitism in their new homeland.[8]

Nathan, Fannie, and George settled briefly in Philadelphia. Nathan's occupation is listed in the 1900 census as "musician," but where he played is unknown. By 1905, he is a musician at the Grand Opera House in downtown Los Angeles. Years later he put down his violin and returned east to New York to open a candy store; by 1930, he is back in Los Angeles, a cigar "retail merchant."[9]

Longevity coupled with productivity ran in the Grant family; the 1930 census notes "Nat" Grant working at age seventy. He lived nineteen more years (surviving Fannie by more than a decade), dying in a nursing home in 1949.[10]

Nathan Grant greatly influenced Joe's self-discipline.[11] Joe learned to read by attending silent movies every Saturday morning and reading the subtitles aloud to Grandpa Nat. The old man was learned and corresponded extensively in Russian, Latvian, German, and Yiddish. "He was a man of high moral character, self-disciplined, and very loving, especially toward his grandson Joseph," Jennifer Grant Castrup, Joe's daughter, says.

Nathan touted the importance of eating oatmeal, chewing food twenty times, and exercising daily.[12] Years later when a young animator asked Joe "how have you been able to maintain your creative energies for all these years?" he leaned forward "as if to protect his secret" and "spoke softly . . . 'Eat your oatmeal.'"[13]

George A. Grant, Nathan's son, displayed precocious talent for drawing as a teenager. He attended art classes "when in short pants" taught by Howard Pyle (1853–1911), illustrator and founder of the Brandywine school of painting, and gained solid drawing technique. In 1901, at sixteen, he enrolled in the Pennsylvania Museum School of Industrial Art (PMSIA), where he studied "industrial drawing" and sculpture classes and received a certificate the following year.[14]

Success came early. By 1904, George worked as an illustrator for William Randolph Hearst's *Los Angeles Examiner*, which Hearst had founded the previous year to assist his campaign for president.[15] Later, Grant contributed illustrations to the *Saturday Evening Post* and became art director for Hearst's *New York American*. The ambitious young man traveled between coasts on assignments. He was, Joe said, "as close to Hearst as I was to Disney."[16]

The December 23, 1906, *Los Angeles Times* noted that twenty-one-year-old George Albert Grant exhibited more than thirty "very delightful" sketches at the first annual exhibition of works by the Press Artists' Association of Los Angeles.[17] His draftsmanship was masterful; his photorealistic portraits are remarkable in their precise detailing and tactile humanity.

On August 3, 1907, the marriage of twenty-three-year-old [sic] George ("a native of Russia") and twenty-year-old Eva Green ("a native of New York") was announced.[18] The couple, "residents of Los Angeles," honeymooned at the Coronado Hotel, a luxurious Victorian beach resort across San Diego Bay. Nine months later, on May 15, Joe was born.[19]

Eva Green Grant was born in November 1887. Her father, Abraham I. Scheider, a tailor (May 26, 1862–January 28, 1941) and mother, Lena Wallak (who was thought to be born in 1867 and died before 1930), were both born in Russia and married in 1881. Three years later they immigrated to America

GH--WORLD'S MOST VI

AL LEADER
ES PROGRAM
SARMAMENT

r Declares England's Loyalty
Nations Imperiled by Present
; Prosperity for Island Empire

avid Lloyd George
er Premier of Great Britain

May 11.—(By Cable)—Whatever
come of the forthcoming general
t will make one thing evident:
men and women of this country
to see Liberalism perish. Its faith
d survived triumphantly, the al-
strain of the last four years.
e electoral system (which must be
Liberal statesmanship to rectify)
ing panic induced by the "Red
nine months of Socialist govern-
n them the result in 1924 of almost
iberal party from parliament.
party while contesting only three
rty seats polled just under three

es at the polls found no reflection
iberalism in the country. Its mis-
istead as a stimulus and an oppor-
ervatives and Socialists tried for
abandoned the effort a year or
Liberalism by the suggestion, and
ne time to persuade the electorate
again be found for Liberalism on
m. Both maneuvers have failed,
vatism has been alienating by its
rtisan supporters while the edifice

it must
the Lib-
s ideas.
ast four
left its
the stat-
recom-
official
the pro-
by both

gh that
her par-
in the
country
ernment
pired by
ns, sus-
al faith,
rience in
istration
Liberal
esses.

have a strong government it can only be a Liberal government.

But why is a strong government needed? Because in the first place a government is needed that will work for peace.

BALDWIN FLAYED

Building of Warships Denounced

NO ADMINISTRATION could have proved feebler and more vacillating in its handling of this all important question than Mr. Baldwin's. It has allowed the initiative in regard to our foreign policy to pass from this country to others. It has lost sight of our major objectives in pursuit of th...

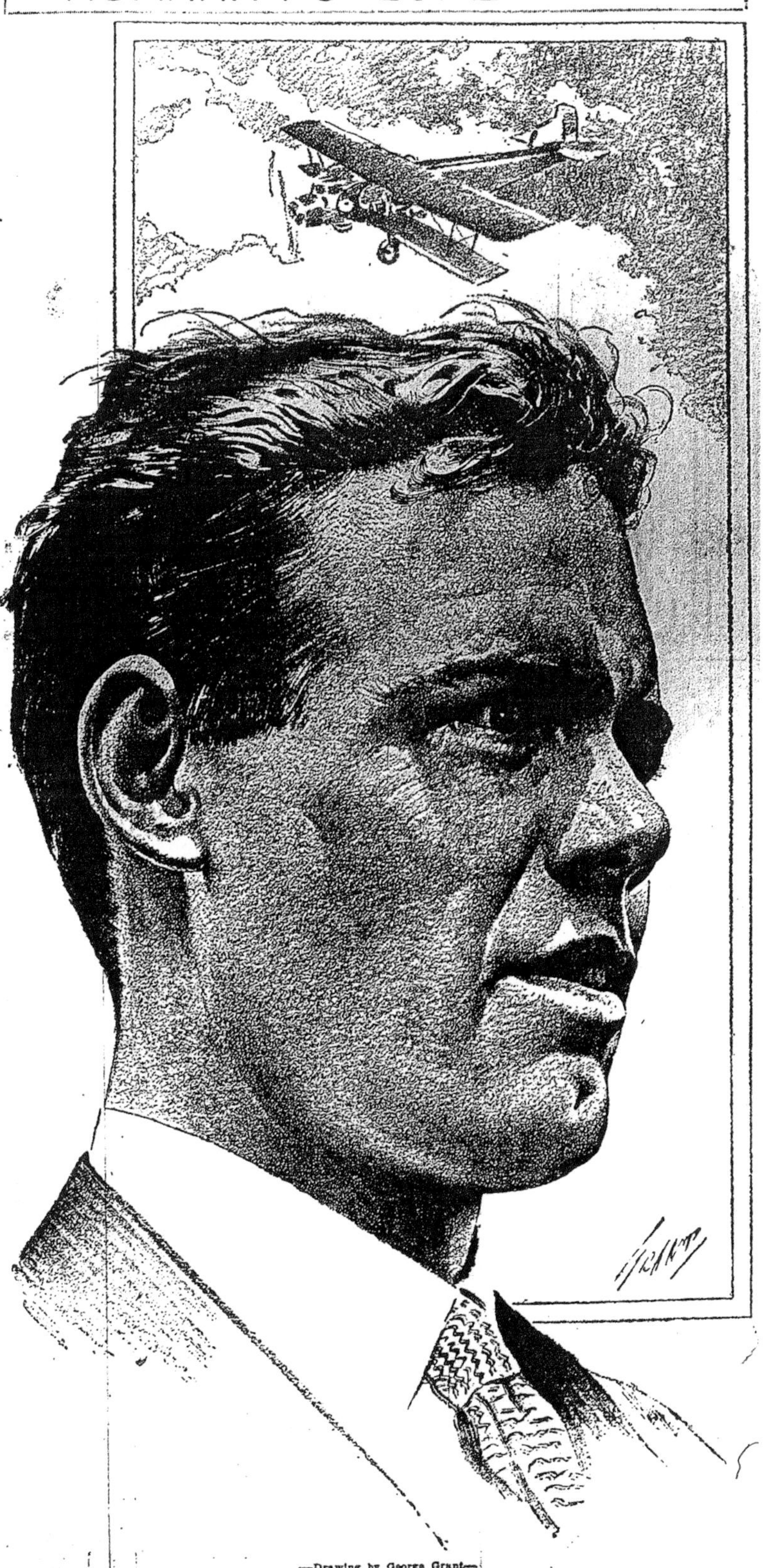

HUMANITY'S 'LONE EAGLE'

—Drawing by George Grant—

CHARLES AUGUSTUS LINDBERGH, the former air mail pilot, who won a place among the immortals by his flight from New York to Paris two years ago.

with their newborn son Joseph.[20] "Scheider" was changed to Green (and sometimes "Greene") either upon arrival in New York or later when in California. It may never have been legally changed; Eva listed Scheider as her maiden name on Joe's birth certificate. Six of seven children born to Abraham and Lena in New York survived: Charles, Eva, Louis, Annie, Sophie, and Ruben.[21]

By 1900, the Greens lived in San Francisco where Abraham was a successful tailor. After the 1906 earthquake he relocated his family and business to L.A., where his store of ready-made clothing was a favorite among studio executives and their wives.[22]

George Grant was renowned for his charm and his attire—always in necktie and spats; Eva, pretty, petite, from a prosperous family, was an excellent cook specializing in Jewish cuisine. Her granddaughters remember lean briskets and traditional matzoh ball soup made with chicken feet.[23] "The most wonderful cooking in the world," says Carol Grant Grubb, Joe's eldest daughter. "She cooked like my father drew."[24]

Eva was a perfectionist. At Thanksgiving, the kosher butcher's face turned red when he saw her. If last year's turkey wasn't good, he'd hear about it. As the butcher exploded, tiny Eva stood her ground saying, "I don't want another tough turkey!" In restaurants, if a steak wasn't done correctly or the coffee was a bit too old, back to the kitchen it went. When family members were sick, whether with simple colds or devastating tuberculosis, Grandmother Eva was always the one who took care of them. Her strength and stern demeanor were her way of showing love.[25]

Eva traveled back and forth between the East and West coasts with George.[26] In New York, Eva and George lived on West 136th Street near Riverside Drive. There, on September 11, 1912, their daughter,

Realistic line portraits by George A. Grant, Joe's father, in the Los Angeles Examiner. OPPOSITE: *Charles A. Lindbergh (May 12, 1929).* RIGHT TOP: *Asa Keyes (January 16, 1929).* BELOW: *Dr. Hugo Eckener (August 26, 1929).*

Geraldine, was born. By that time, however, Eva was intermittently separated from George.

Years later, Joe delicately mentioned his family's "domestic strife." His parents, it seemed, were out-of-synch personalities trapped in a troubled marriage. Eva, stern and proper, strove for a balanced home life with regular, elaborate meals with the whole family. George, bohemian in temperament, ambitious for his art and career, worked irregular, long hours alongside hard-drinking newspaper cronies. "He had a very interesting life," Joe gingerly said of his father's alcoholism. But "it was a little too liquid."

George often arrived home at 2:00 A.M. heavily fueled, with or without friends in tow, and played Mozart, Schumann, or Chopin piano pieces—loud! "He kept people up," Joe laughed. "But he played beautifully." Poor Eva suffered through his mood swings.[27] It was not the steady bourgeois life of her childhood, nor what she desired for her children. Asked if his mother was artistically inclined, Joe answered, "No." Then added, "Culinarily, yes."[28]

Hearst allegedly sent George to San Simeon to dry him out. This may have occurred in the early 1920s; San Simeon was built in 1919, and by 1924 George Grant was no longer exclusively employed by Hearst's *Los Angeles Examiner.*[29]

In a scene out of movie melodramas, Eva periodically sent her young son out at dinnertime to locate her husband in saloons.[30] "[George] was an excellent artist and quite a man, but, you know, alcohol had 'im," Danielle Workman, Joe's niece, says.[31] Joe claimed his parents married and divorced twice. Eva was granted a final decree in 1934, four years before George's death and about five months after Joe signed with Disney.[32] But for years the mismatched couple parted and reunited numerous times. Every time there was a problem, Abraham Green summoned Eva and her children to Los Angeles. Sometimes she remained east and Joe went west with his father. "It was sort of a mobile existence," he said of his family.[33]

Joe loved both parents but feared his mother, the disciplinarian, whom he spent more time with.[34] George was less rigid regarding behavior, so whenever Joe came to Los Angeles with his dad, he "lived the life of Riley." George gave Joe tickets to Venice Beach Amusement Park, and that made him very popular with his young friends. When Eva arrived, Joe's undisciplined freedom was abruptly cut short.[35]

Joe was fascinated by his father's artistry. "Just seeing the magic of his hand on the drawing board," he recalled. He constantly observed him drawing at home and in newspaper offices.[36]

George knew many famed cartoonists. He regaled Joe with tales of visiting the Sheepshead Bay, Brooklyn, New York, home of Winsor McCay (1867–1934), the great pioneer comic strip and animation artist who joined Hearst papers in 1911. George was fond of McCay and his beautiful color epic comic strip *Little Nemo in Slumberland.* "Comic strips meant something in those days," Joe said. McCay's friend George McManus (1884–1954), creator of *Bringing Up Father,* piqued George when the cartoonist helped himself to dozens of the newspaper art department's expensive Bristol boards.[37]

George and Joe were closest to Milt Gross (1895–1953), often visiting him at home, which had a strange tobacconist's smell because he discarded old cigar butts by placing them inside books.[38]

They admired Gross's simple, loopy, laugh-provoking cartoons, a wild style accompanied by a parody of Yiddish dialect (as in his 1926 books *Nize Baby* and *Hiawatta: Witt No Odder Poems*). "Marvelous," said Joe Grant of Gross's work. "And it wasn't offensive. It was just funny. His drawings were *him.* He had that wonderful comic sense. And Milt

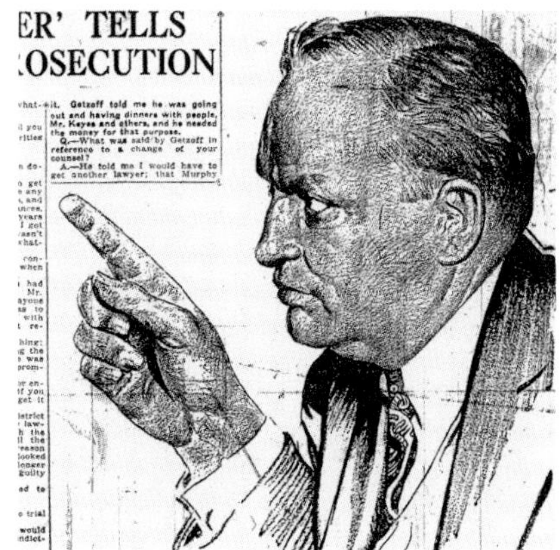

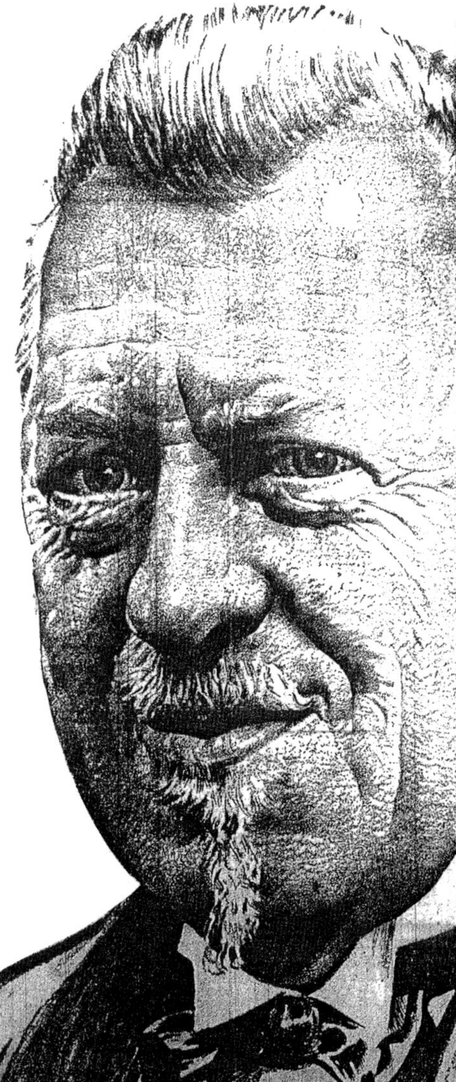

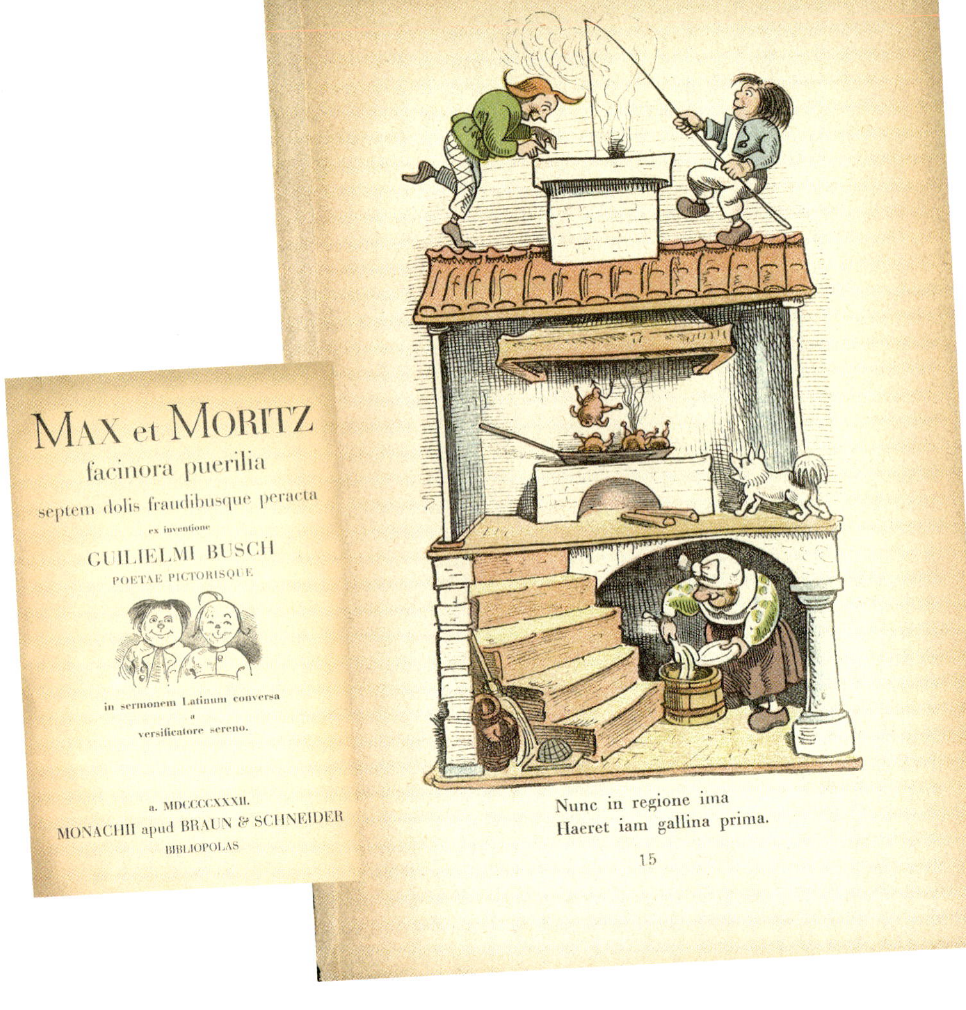

TOP: *Two Wilhelm Busch illustrations for* MAX AND MORITZ *stories.* BOTTOM: *Walter Trier sketch for Till Eulenspiegel's baptism.* RIGHT: *A 1914 book of caricatures by Olaf Gulbransson.*

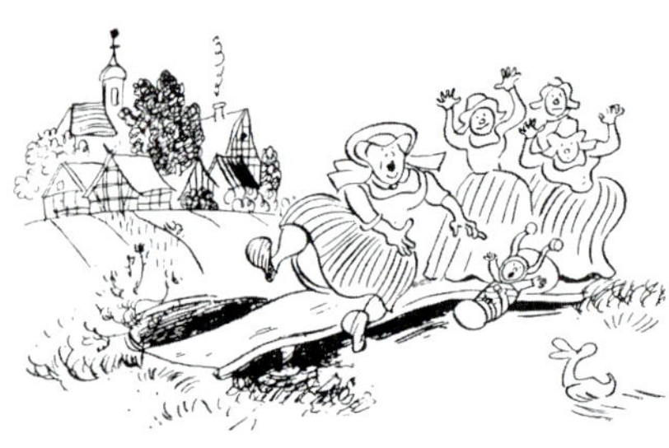

was very influential in animation, his style. I don't think he's been given half the credit for what has been appropriated from his work."[39] Gross had a strong personal impact on Joe's style, humor, and thinking regarding storytelling drawings.

Joe's father's collection of art books of European caricaturists and artists, such as Honoré Daumier, Gustave Doré, and Ludwig Richter, "overwhelmed" the youngster.[40] George was particularly fond of German artists: the stylish, precise caricatures of Olaf Gulbransson; the witty sequential cartoons of Wilhelm Busch, whose *Max and Moritz* stories are precursors of the modern comic strip; and he subscribed to the German satirical weekly *Simplicissimus*, featuring Thomas Theodor Heine, Walter Trier, and a panoply of illustrators whose modern graphics matched the magazine's acerbic political commentary.

There was also Heinrich Kley (1863–1945) and his brilliant, sculptural scribblings of anthropomorphic alligators, hippos, and elephants, and mythical beings (devils, centaurs, fauns). George Grosz wrote of Kley's "remarkable observation of movement":

> His sure rapid line roped in the grotesque creatures—parodies of humanity in animal forms, and people generally clad only in Adam's costume and struggling to escape their fates—who are at one and the same time the inhabitants of the world of his imagination, and the prey of his whirling, flying line . . . Like Walt Disney, he humanizes his beasts.[41]

George gave a first edition of Kley sketches on handmade paper to Joe, who years later brought the book to Walt Disney to inspire artists and animators working on *Fantasia*.[42]

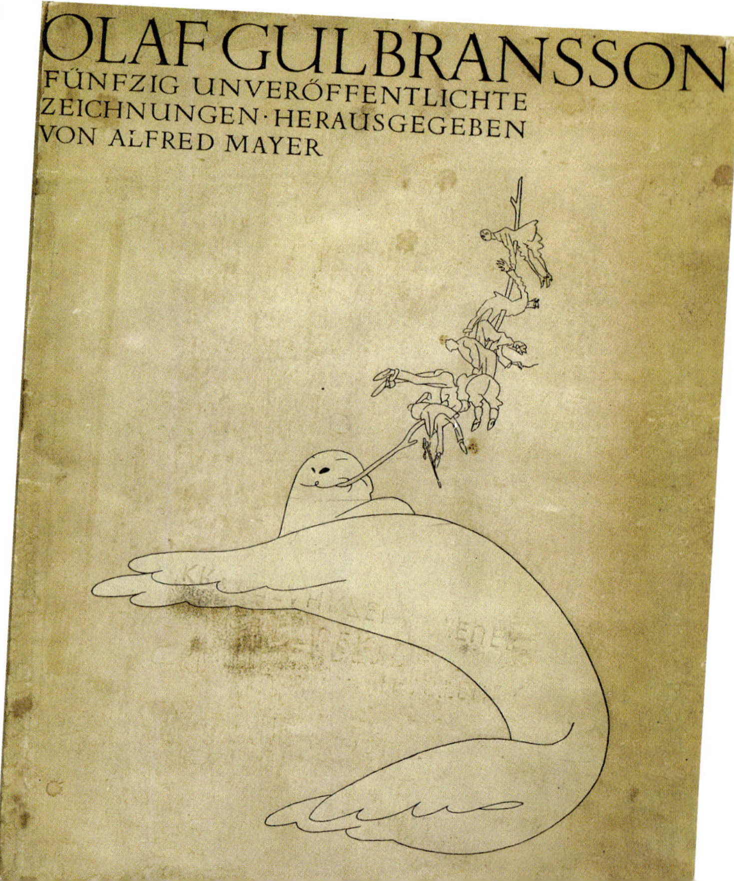

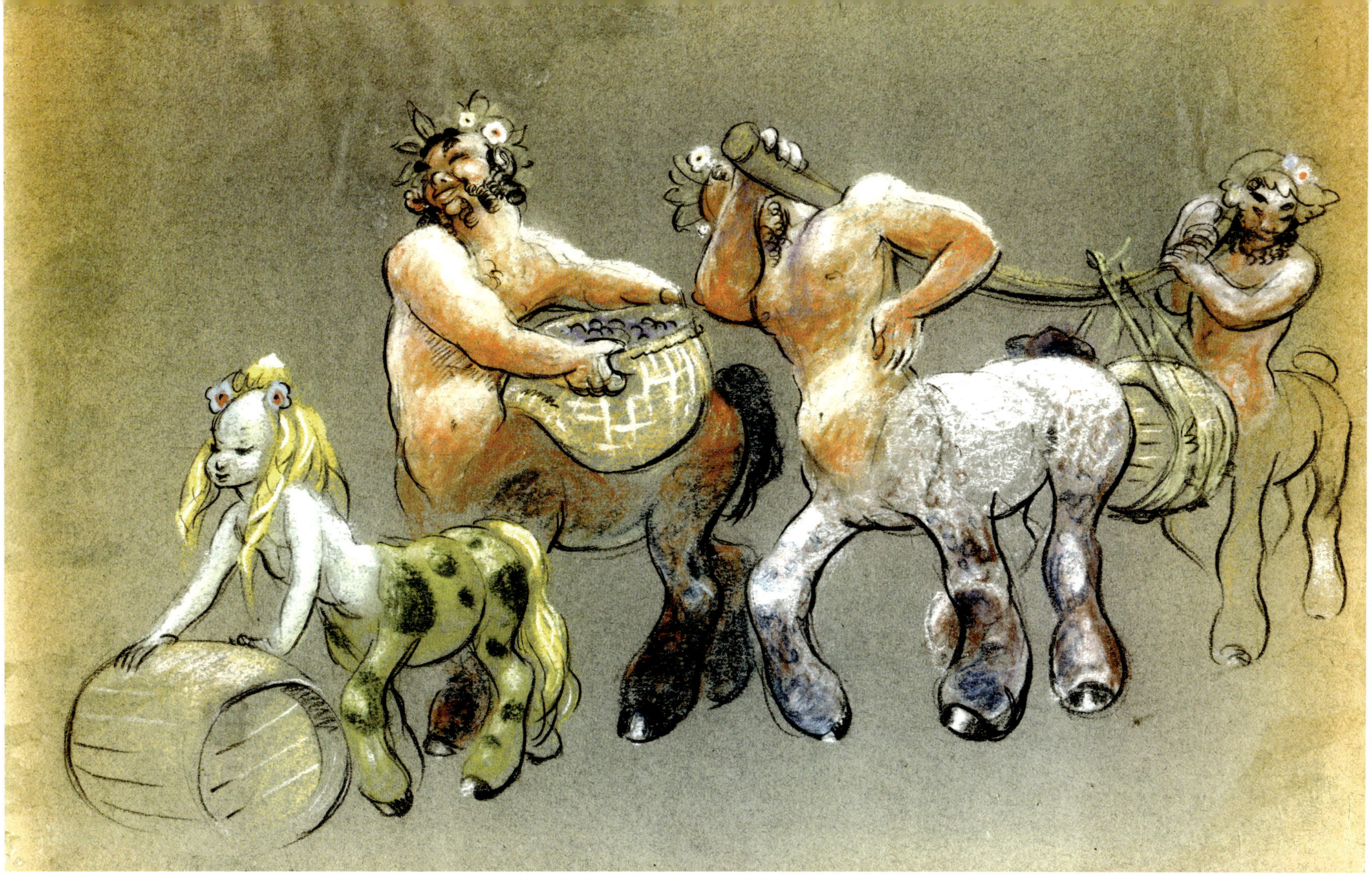

ABOVE: *FANTASIA's centaurs (pastel by James Bodrero) were inspired by Heinrich Kley's mythological drawings* (BELOW).

George's artistic guidance was offhand, nothing academic. He mentored by example, through his magical draftsmanship and work ethic. Despite personal problems, he churned out quality portraits daily to meet newspaper deadlines. His eclectic art books inspired Joe, the nascent artist, exposing him to eye-popping, imaginative visual stimuli.

Joe's father instilled in him a lifelong love of reading and literature. George subscribed to the premier literary/cultural magazines with a cosmopolitan viewpoint, *Vanity Fair* and its rival *The New Yorker*. In addition, whenever George dried out he would read Charles Dickens while eating boxes of chocolate-coated almonds.

George's tacit encouragement contrasted with Eva's family regarding art as a career. His uncles attacked Joe, claiming artists never got anywhere. "But I stuck it out," Joe said.[43] Garment merchant Abraham Green and sons looked down on the Grants, Carol Grubb notes, "'cause they didn't have a lot of money."[44] They surely disapproved of George's drinking and its effect on Eva. In turn, Nathan Grant disliked his daughter-in-law, unfairly blaming Eva for George's drinking.

In 1916, Joe Grant, age nine, began to make money in the arts, namely film; and ironically it was through Grandfather Green.

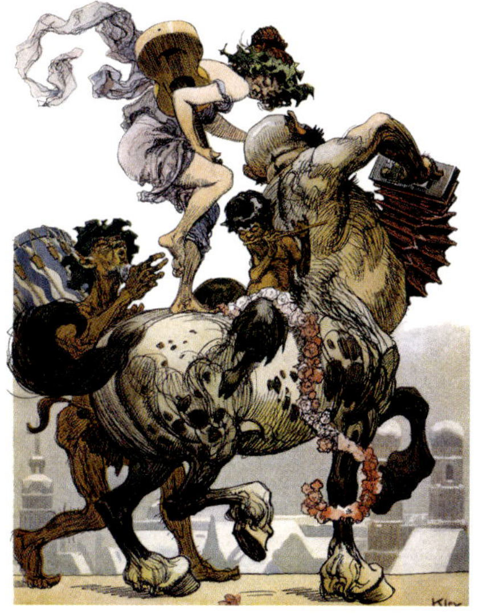

CHAPTER THREE

Kewpies, Caskets, and Shoes

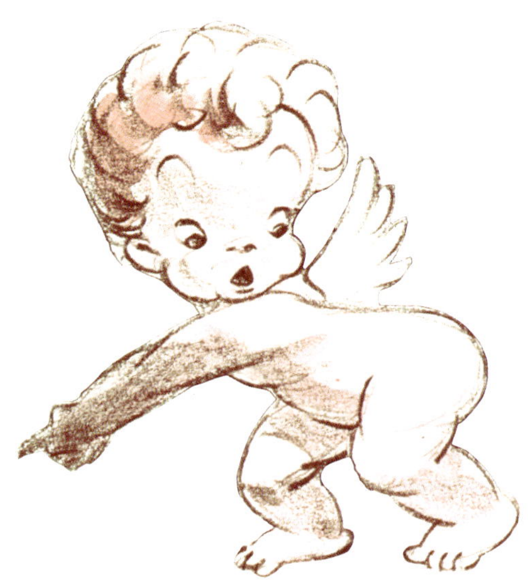

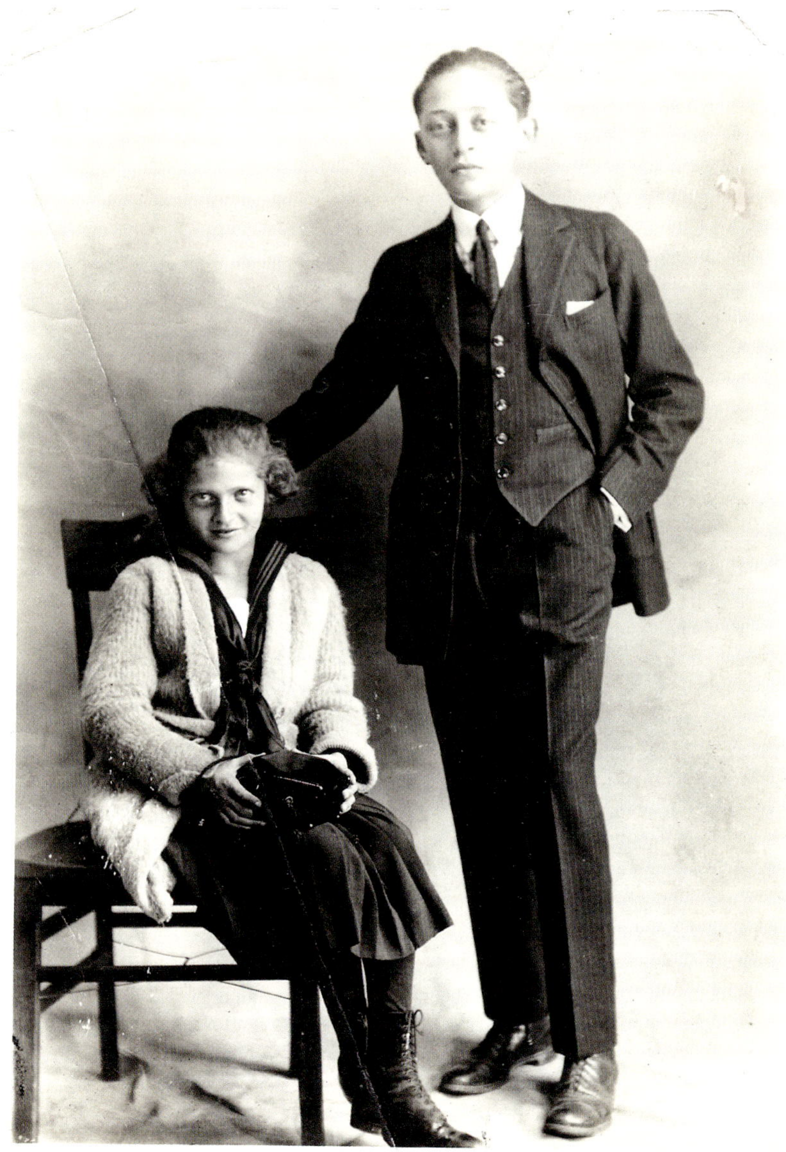

ABOVE: *A cupid from* FANTASIA *(1940).*
RIGHT: *Joe Grant and his sister, Geraldine.*

A Fox Film Corporation general manager, a friend of Abraham Green, hired nine-year-old Joe as a "featured player" for $35 a week, "work or not." He appeared unbilled in feature-length juvenile stories directed in 1917 and 1918 by Sidney and Chester Franklin, including *Jack and the Beanstalk*, *Treasure Island*, and *Fan Fan*, adapted from *The Mikado*.[1]

Life in the movies could be dangerous. In one film, Grant was hung on a clothesline and spun; in another he jumped off a ship's plank. More than eighty years later, he recalled the nearly eight-foot giant hired for *Jack and the Beanstalk* who proved terrifying on and off the set. Equally monstrous was another kid's mom who believed her tot was being ignored. The prototypical stage mother dragged Joe behind the scenery to pull off his costume and put it on her own son. Eva stopped her just in time.[2]

Sidney Franklin later produced *The Barretts of Wimpole Street* (1934), the Academy Award–winning *Mrs. Miniver* (1942), and *The Yearling* (1946), among other prestigious films. In April 1937, he transferred rights for Felix Salten's novel *Bambi: A Life in the Woods* to Walt Disney. Grant was present at an early meeting between Disney and Franklin, now a polished MGM producer/director. When Grant reminded Franklin of the humble juvenile films he directed, Franklin appeared stricken, and "we had a very cold evening, I must say," Grant recalled.[3]

By January 1920, eleven-year-old Joe was back in New York with seven-year-old Geraldine and mother, Eva, age thirty-three, described in the 1920 census as "single." They were boarders on West

113th Street along with Eva's sister Sophia, a recently divorced cloak saleswoman. The "head of the household"/owner of the boarding house was a fifty-one-year-old dressmaker.[4]

Joe remembered Eva feeding him and his sister hoop cheese and noodles, while the dressmaker ate an entire chicken by herself. "And she didn't offer them anything," Carol Grubb says. "He never forgot that." He creatively turned the name of the woman into "Osowitz," a synonym he employed to admonish his daughters if they acted selfish. "So, anytime we did anything that wasn't up to snuff, [he'd say] 'Osowitz, Carol! Osowitz!'"[5]

The Green sisters tried to make it on their own away from their West Coast families and former husbands. Sophie was tough, entrepreneurial, and known for her critical eye. Described as a black-haired "spitfire," by 1930 she was in business in Los Angeles with a partner, Lillian Eisinger, specializing in millinery with lace trim; her second husband, Joseph A. Zuboff, joined the company in the mid-1930s, and throughout the 1940s, movie studios commissioned hats from the Sophie Green Veil Company. Ann, the third Green sister, "married a man who bought practically all of Wilshire Boulevard," according to her niece Carol. "My grandmother was the one who had nothing. They [Eva and her two children] had nothing."[6]

By June 1922, Eva and the kids were back in Los Angeles. Despite disruptive public school attendance on both coasts, "Joseph Grant" is listed in the junior high class roll entering Venice Union Polytechnic High School. Eva and the children may have lived at George's bungalow at 2512 Ocean Front in Venice. George's career and life were deteriorating. He stayed with his parents on First Street downtown near the *Examiner* building and Nathan Grant's cigar store.[7]

"We lived at Venice on the beach, and that was a real trampy situation," Joe remembered. When the tide was high it surrounded their house. The town's canals, built early in the century by tobacco mogul Abbot Kinney, were muddy and in decline, and the famous pier was being rebuilt after another devastating fire.

When Joe stayed there with his father, newspaper characters would show up at all hours of the night and party. Young Joe stayed up, too, and attended school the next morning with dark circles under his eyes. Often he skipped school to tag along with George when he went to work.[8]

That, of course, did not happen with Eva. But at school, Joe said, he did little in his classes. Instead, he drew illustrations of Vesuvius and Pompeian relics for the principal, archaeologist Edward W. Clark, and did commercial work also "for his benefit," he said. "I was quite a pet all the way through."[9]

He may not have gone all the way through. In June 1926, the names of many of Joe's classmates are among Venice High's graduating class, but his is not.[10]

George saved on expenses by living with his parents, Nathan and Fannie, while Eva and their children lived with her parents, Abraham and Lena. Young Joe felt an urgency to contribute to the family income.

One of his earliest jobs, a so-called artistic effort, was painting eyes on Kewpie dolls. "I was hired because I wore an open collar and the guy said you look like an artist," he joked. Illustrator Rose O'Neill's popular Kewpies were modeled on classical paintings of the baby Roman god of love. (So, too, the cupids in *Fantasia* that Grant's Character Model Department later designed.) He graduated to painting lips, but the smell of wet plaster pouring into molds and half-baked dolls was sickening. Eva soon rescued him.

At one point he made drawings of caskets for a mortuary and advertisements for "a couple of places in Beverly Hills that liked my stuff." He squeezed in

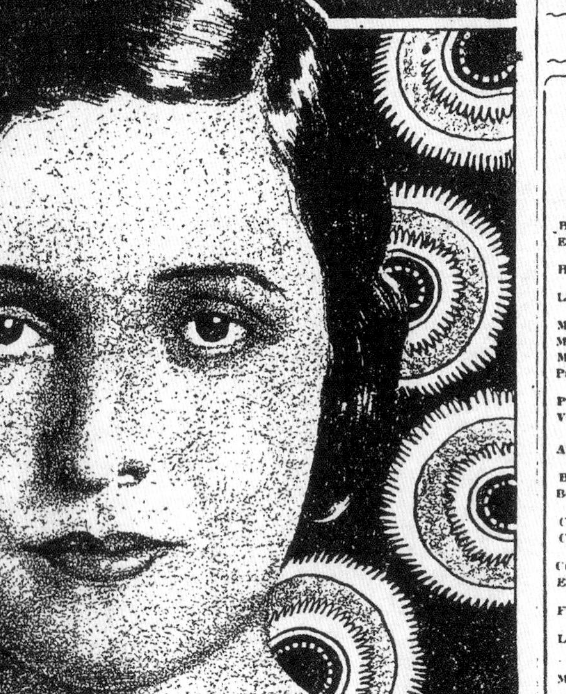

LOS ANGELES, SATURDAY, OCTOBER 13, 1928

Theater Guide

THE PLAYS

Belasco—"The Squall."
El Capitan—"The Shannons of Broadway."
Hollywood Play House—"The Best People."
Lincoln—"Up in Mabel's Room," with all colored cast.
Majestic—"The Desert Song."
Mayan—"The Marriage Bed," Oct. 17.
Music Box—"Tarnish."
Pasadena—"The Great Broxopp." Oct. 16.
President—"The Wooden Kimono."
Vine Street—"On Approval."

THE FILMS

Alhambra—John Gilbert in "Four Walls."
Biltmore—"Simba."
Boulevard—"Our Dancing Daughters." Boulevard revue.
California—Films and vaudeville.
Chinese—"White Shadows in the South Seas."
Criterion—Jannings in "Patriot."
Egyptian—Colman-Banky in "Two Lovers."
Figueroa—Gaynor-Farrell in "Street Angel."
Loew's State—Buster Keaton in "The Cameraman." Texas Guinan in person.
Manchester—Sunday, Monday, Tuesday, "Four Walls." Wednesday, Thursday, Friday, "Street Angel." Saturday, "Love Over Night." Sol Lowe and band.
Metropolitan—Barthelmess in "Out of the Ruins." Henry Busse. Publix revue.
Shrine—"The River Woman," Oct. 16.
Sunbeam—Sunday, Monday, "The Show Girl." Tuesday, Wednesday, Thursday, "The Docks of New York." Friday, "Love Over Night." Saturday, "Caught in the Fog." Vaudeville Saturday and Sunday.
Tower—"The Terror."
United Artists—Norma Talmadge in "The Woman Disputed" replaces Dolores Del Rio in "Revenge" Oct. 17.
Uptown—"Four Sons." Juanita Connors and her girl friends.
Warner Brothers—Al Jolson in "The Singing Fool." Larry Ceballos revue.

THE VARIETIES

Hillstreet—The Great Nicola, Mary Haynes, "Undercurrent," Hal Yates and Cooper Lawley, Jack Hanley, Gerber's Gaieties. On screen: "The Whip."
Orpheum—Lou Holtz, Donald Brian, Miss Juliet, Norette, Paul Yocan

…e Joyce, famous screen and stage actress, who will be co-starred with Owen Moore in The Marriage Bed," new play by Ernest Pascal, which opens next Wednesday night at the Mayan theater. Sketched by Joseph Grant, Record staff artist.

Dick the Younger

We call Richard Barthelmess Dick the Younger because he looks younger in every picture. He's starring now in "Out of the Ruins," at the Metropolitan.

evening drawing classes at the Chouinard Art Institute, determined to make a living as an artist.

By 1927, however, nineteen-year-old Grant was an "assistant branch manager" for the Zinke Rebottoming Co., a shoe sales and repair store.[11] Along with administrative duties, he designed window displays of shoes, and he lived with Eva and his sister at Abraham Green's home. "He was very strange," Joe once said of Grandfather Abraham. "He couldn't write [English, only Yiddish], but he was the businessman."[12]

The Greens thought they "saved" Joe from the insecurities of a life dedicated to art. He was gainfully employed in a steady job in a reliable business (everybody needs shoes), and his wasteful artistic impulses found expression in occasional window displays of the latest in shoe leather.

Despite the Greens' animosity toward George, Joe remained close to his father. Within a year, George afforded his son an escape from his "shoe prison" and initiated the real beginning of Joe Grant's artistic life.

Joe Grant loved the denizens and "clownish" atmosphere of city newsrooms. "They were a wild bunch, fun and hard-drinking," Grant recalled.

Fast-talking reporters out of *The Front Page* leapt onto desks melodramatically denouncing the paper's management.[1] Cartoonists and illustrators matched their colleagues' anarchy with raunchy, funny drawings spilling over desks and tacked to bare walls. Cowbells rang when pretty women were sighted, and the jolly fellows never lost an opportunity to poke fun at visitors, even a colleague's kid.

For years, Joe tagged along with his father when he was art director at the *Los Angeles Examiner*. When George Grant first arrived in 1903, the editorial offices were housed in a six-story building at Broadway and Fifth Street in downtown Los Angeles.

In 1915, the *Examiner* moved south to Eleventh Street into a block-long Mission-style building designed by architect Julia Morgan. William Hearst declared the ornate structure—with its great arched spaces and columns, patterned tiled floors, and friezes—"thoroughly practicable for all newspaper demands."[2] Joe was an unofficial office boy, an eager bug-eyed kid who ran errands, fetched cheese sandwiches for the city editor, and endured practical jokes with good humor. Newsmen cajoled him into running fool's errands to the composing room to fetch a "bucket of vanishing points" or the layout department to locate a "paper stretcher." "I grew up on newspapers," he boasted.[3]

In turn, Grant soaked up the news craft, watching writers bang out stories on typewriters meeting tight deadlines, observing photos retouched and Intaglio zinc-plate engravings turned into illustrations. He saw teams working together making stories come alive. "Kind of learning the ropes," he said. "I got all my education in the early days on the job."[4] Later, his stored knowledge found an outlet in animation's assembly-line processes, and when he produced ceramics and greeting cards. Newspaper jargon infiltrated his speech: "Give me the headline," he'd say, demanding a quick report from his family.[5]

Most important, the kid learned drawing techniques looking "over my father's shoulder." Watching George draw detailed portraits with crowquill pen, ink, and Conté crayon on textured white Bristol was a veritable master class. "He was a master at it," Joe marveled more than seventy-five years later. "No one's ever come close to him."[6]

Except George Grant's son. By the time Joe was nineteen, it was difficult to differentiate his artwork from George's without looking at the artist's signature. The kid absorbed and emulated to an uncanny degree his father's photo-realistic style. Obviously ready for professional work, Joe, George felt, was wasted as a shoe store window dresser. The political cartoonist/art director of the *Los Angeles Record* needed an assistant; George suggested he hire Joe.

The *Record*, part of E. W. Scripps' West Coast Group, "was a daily newspaper," wrote Adrienne Tytla, "the darling of liberals, intellectuals, the disenchanted, and the avant-garde because it was less conservative than either [Harry] Chandler's *Los Angeles Times* or Hearst's *Examiner*."[7]

Los Angeles Record

J. GRANT

STAFF ARTIST

TUCKER 1121

OPPOSITE: *The October 11, 1928,* LOS ANGELES RECORD *featured portraits by both Grants, demonstrating Joe's ability to emulate his father's graphic style. Actress Alice Joyce was by Joe, and actor Richard Barthelmess was done by George. Joe, a "staff artist," is mentioned in a caption, but his father, a freelancer, is not.*
RIGHT: *Joe Grant's 1928* LOS ANGELES RECORD *business card.*

The hardscrabble *Record* didn't have Hearst's large circulation, nor a prestigious location in a fancy building. It was several blocks removed from the *Examiner* in a two-story outfit of cramped quarters next to the Pacific Electric Railroad elevated tracks. When asked why his father didn't find him a job on the *Examiner*, Joe replied, "I don't think he thought I was ready for it."[8]

Perhaps he was *too* ready. George Grant, now a struggling alcoholic freelancer, drew detailed illustrations *and* less elaborate cartoons for both the *Examiner* and the *Record*. He was willing to help his son move ahead, but not on his turf. For his part, Joe wanted to prove himself, and the *Record* was fertile soil to set down roots and grow.

Twenty-year-old Joe Grant began at the *Los Angeles Record* in June 1928 at $10 a week.[9] His superior draftsmanship was soon showcased on the front page: on August 22, 1928, a pen, ink, and crayon portrait of presidential hopeful Alfred Smith appeared. The sports page contains a second Joe Grant photo-realistic portrait, of football-player-turned-wrestler Jim McMillen. Both drawings are spitting images of the look and technique of Grant's father, whose work appears in the same issue.

On the movie page, George Grant is represented by a cartoon illustrating a cliché: a smiling waiter labeled "Producer" serving "John Q. Public" a film reel on a dish tagged "Greater Movie Season." The sketch is well drawn, but far from his realistic style. Perhaps George, feeling protective, wanted his son's launch to enjoy center stage without direct comparisons to his own well-known draftsmanship.

Through the early fall of 1928, Joe kept busy drawing detailed portraits for the sports page (boxer Joey Sangor on August 27), drama page (Jeanne Eagels' stage appearance on August 25), film page (Ronald Colman in *Two Lovers* on September 1, Joe's first movie-star portrait), and often the front page ("vice baron" Albert Marco on September 7). The September 15 issue features on-site sketches of a murder trial by "Joe Grant, a *Record* staff artist." Though less detailed, the drawings remain realistic.

From October 1 through October 9, 1928, Joe illustrated a daily serial about reforming the prison system. Titled "Caged! by Convict No. 23319 (Ben Clegg)," minimally detailed drawings, each containing an idea pertinent to the dramatic story, are his earliest attempt at sequential visual storytelling.

Both Grants were on the same page of the *Record*'s film/stage section the next week (October 13): George offered a strong portrait on a white background of Richard Barthelmess in *Out of the Ruins*; Joe presented Alice Joyce in a play (*The Marriage Bed*), drawn as realistically as his father's illustration but against a sunburst abstract background.

The portraits were based, as usual, on publicity photos. Occasionally, the Grants varied their formulaic style. Impressive is George's November 1 plug for *Beggars of Life*: a detailed Wallace Beery, cigarette dangling from his lips, looms large and forbidding over line drawings (no shading) of Louise Brooks and Richard Arlen. Joe, on November 29, promotes *The Loves of Casanova* in pure line delineating three actors, saving detailing for the patterned costumes.

At the end of 1928, Joe had gained considerable experience and a salary increase by taking on every assignment thrown his way. In his first six months, editors used his artwork on theater, film, sports, and society pages, a dramatic serial, on-site reportage, and front-page stories about politics and crime. The more knowledge he gained, the more he struggled to move beyond George's style and find his own artistic voice. At first he used messy charcoal instead of the clean Conté crayons his dad preferred; noticing his son's blackened hands, George teased him by calling him "old black Joe."[10]

An editor called it Joe Grant's "iron dog period." His "elaborately, lovingly, and laboriously shaded sketches" looked fine as originals, but after reduction for printing, "the lines thickened, and more than once a beautiful blond looked a trifle like Al Jolson in blackface when the proof was taken."[11] Sometimes Grant substituted pen and ink crosshatching instead of crayon for textured detail, merely a variation of his father's variations.

"My father was traditional," Joe said. "At that time, I had to do something different. I toyed around with caricature early in my life, used my mother as a model—which was sacrilegious," he joked. A lifelong compulsive sketcher, he filled notebooks with exaggerated images of celebrities and newspaper colleagues.

One day Llewellyn Miller (1899–1971), the *Record*'s drama-desk editor who sat in the next cubicle, noticed them. Miller was an experienced writer/critic on film, theater productions, and performers; in addition, she assigned articles and was herself a skilled caricaturist. In Los Angeles in the 1920s, live theater thrived alongside motion pictures, and Miller's drama/film page sparkled with stories on operas, local repertory companies, vaudeville, and touring shows as well as the latest movies.

On October 6, 1928, two of her cartoons (Al Jolson in *The Singing Fool* and actors in a comedic play) bracket a brooding realistic portrait of opera baritone Lawrence Tibbett by Joe Grant. Miller's caricatures are simple in design, direct in staging, and visually appealing. In a few lines she captures Clara Bow's insouciance, Gloria Swanson's insolence in *Sadie Thompson*, and Charlie Chaplin's haplessness before a lion in *The Circus.* Soon, however, Miller's writing and administrative duties took precedence, and so the *Record* sought another caricaturist.

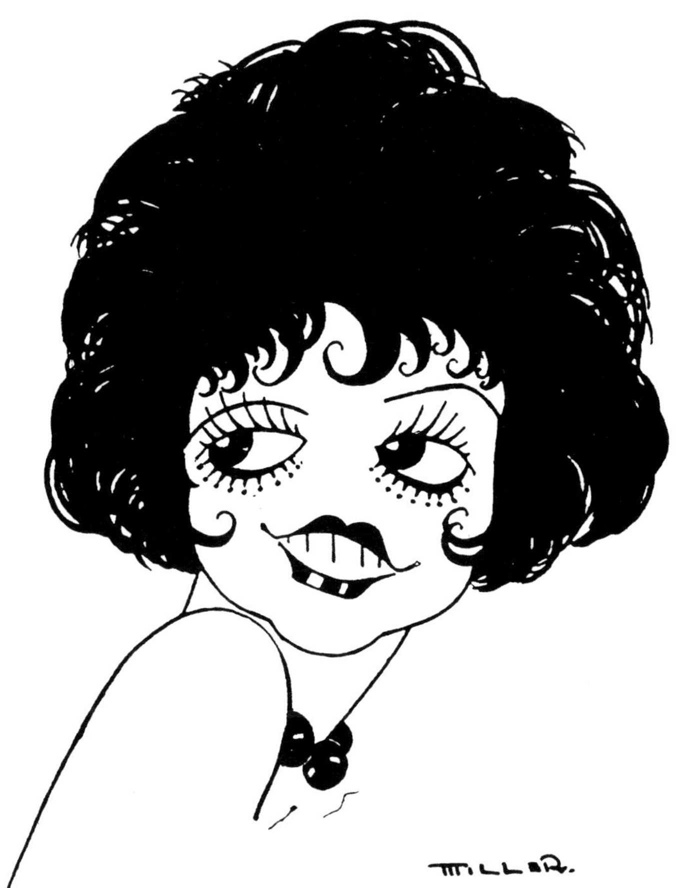

Llewellyn Miller's caricature of Clara Bow, Los Angeles Record, c. 1928.

First, with much fanfare, management brought in John Decker, a hard-drinking, party-throwing German émigré and painter of celebrities; but his weak and misshapen *Record* caricatures lasted only a few months.[12]

In June 1928, Russian artist and teacher Victor Mall approached caricature as art deco meets constructivism, minus humor. Soon he, too, was gone.[13] Occasionally, Theodore Langguth, a Hearst engraver and art department head of *The San Francisco Examiner* for forty years, contributed line portraits; but his style was basically realistic. Xavier Cugat, before he became the "Rumba King" bandleader, contributed sardonic stylized caricatures to the *Los Angeles Record*. He did become a resident caricaturist for a year, but at the rival *Los Angeles Times*.[14]

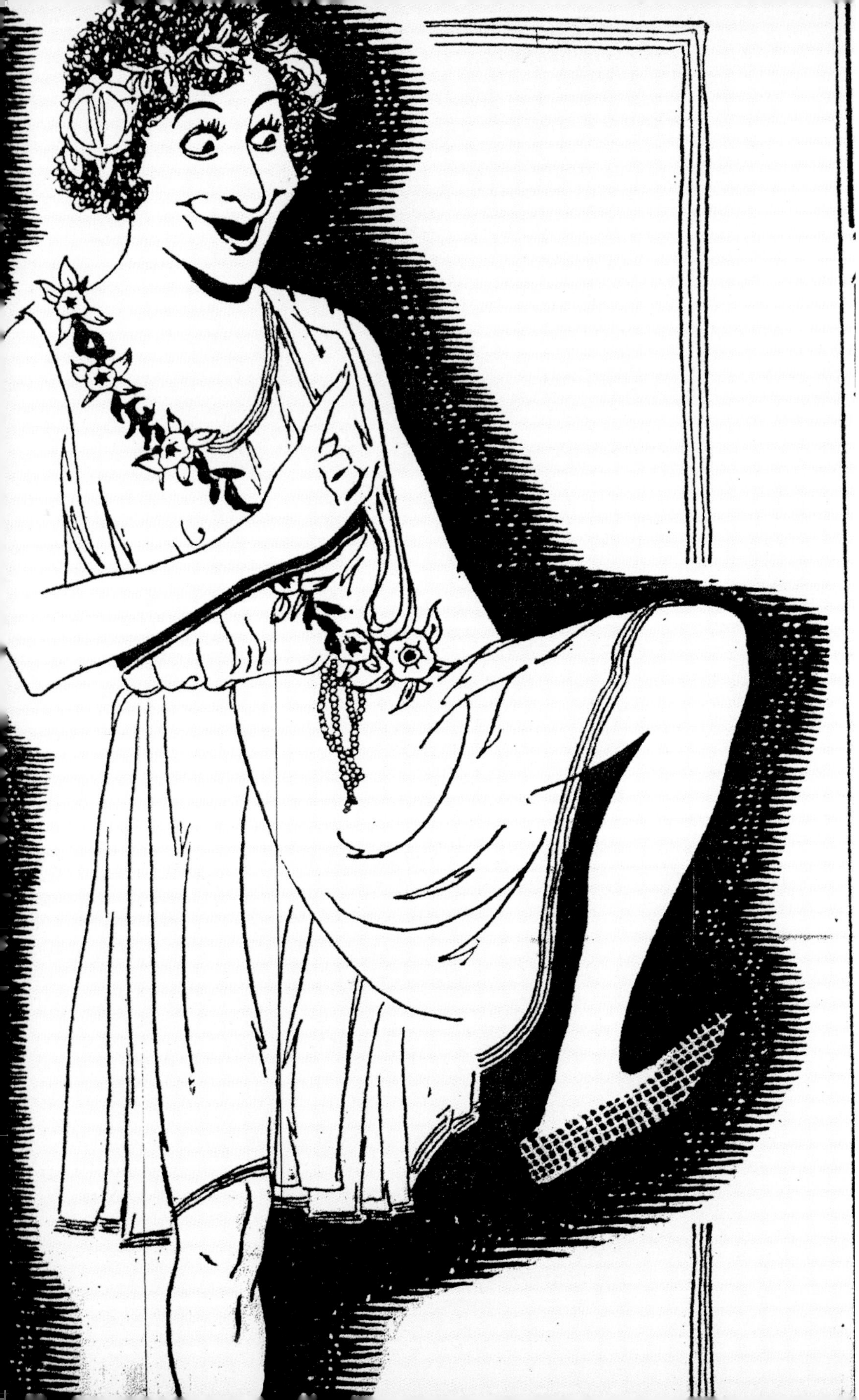

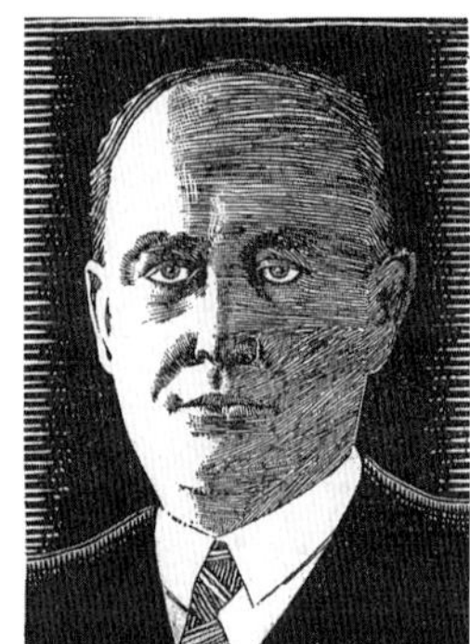
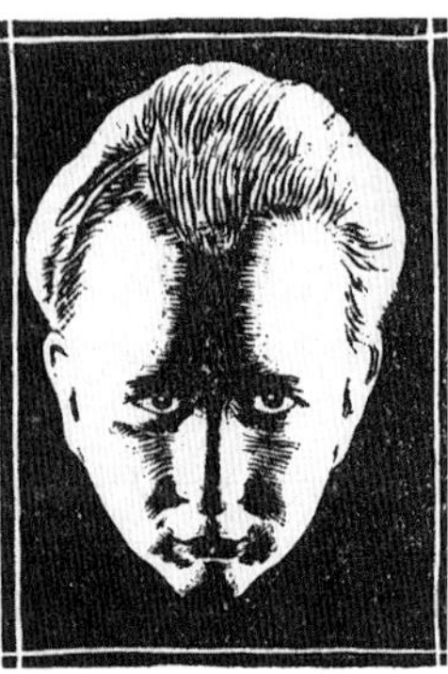

Joe Grant's style experiments (LEFT TO RIGHT)*: comedienne Fanny Brice (December 29, 1928), industrialist Hiram S. Brown (December 28, 1928), and conductor Leopold Stokowski (December 27, 1928).*

George Grant attempted an occasional caricature, though this was not his forte. In a December 1, 1928, drawing of Charlotte Greenwood, the eccentric dancer kicks a long leg out of a bathtub. George merely attached a realistic head (barely resembling Greenwood) drawn with little detail onto a similarly rendered body. A tiny fish swept up in the swing of the comedienne's limb doesn't make this stilted sketch amusing.

"I became friendly with the drama editor who was in the next booth to me," Joe recalled. "She did a few caricatures and . . . she said, 'Why don't you try some?'"[15]

A week after his father's unsuccessful caricature attempt, Joe took tentative but decisive steps toward simplification and distortion in his drawings. On December 8 he plunged in, discarding detail and hyperrealism for a lighter approach: James Gleason playing a saxophone (in the play *The Shannons of Broadway* at the El Capitan Theatre) is white against a black background as tiny white musical notes float upward in an imaginative, stylish design. On the film page, Joe employed an exaggerated style reminiscent of cartoonist T. S. Sullivant: actor Guinn Williams (in the film *Noah's Ark* at Grauman's Chinese Theatre) with oversized head and tiny loinclothed body carrying a cord of lumber.

More conventional portraits of conductor Leopold Stokowski (December 27) and Hiram S.

Brown, RKO's new president (December 28), were based on publicity photos. But this time Grant used playful crosshatching for texture, alternating black and white patterns for posterlike rather than photographic imagery.

He ended 1928 with a full-length image of Fanny Brice in the film *My Man*, performing her signature dance to spring; or "Sprink!" as the caption says, mimicking her faux Yiddish accent (December 29). The picture's photographic roots are obvious, but Grant continued loosening up. There is less detail than ever on the figure and a black abstract pattern outlining Brice's white form, particularly her gawky leg in midjump.

The new year began with a breakthrough: on January 4, 1929, the *Los Angeles Record* published Joe Grant's first true caricature: comic actor Edward Everett Horton looking quizzical with worried brow and small, twisted mouth.

It is "a real full-blown portrait caricature," comments Wendy Wick Reaves, curator of prints and drawings at the National Portrait Gallery of the Smithsonian Institution and author of *Celebrity Caricature in America*. "It's abbreviated, it's in a linear style; he's using a geometric stylization so the elements of the head, face, and the hair are triangular. He also uses a heightened black-and-white contrast. It's a very punched-up graphic style."[16]

Grant's joy in successfully transitioning into artful caricature is apparent over the next four years. He'd found a magic key to unlock his own creative spirit. Although he continually experimented with witty graphic variations, the actors' star qualities remain intact and recognizable.

When asked in 2003 what makes a good caricature, Grant joked, "Someone with a lot of wrinkles." Then he got serious. "It has to be a face that has character," he continued. "That you can see

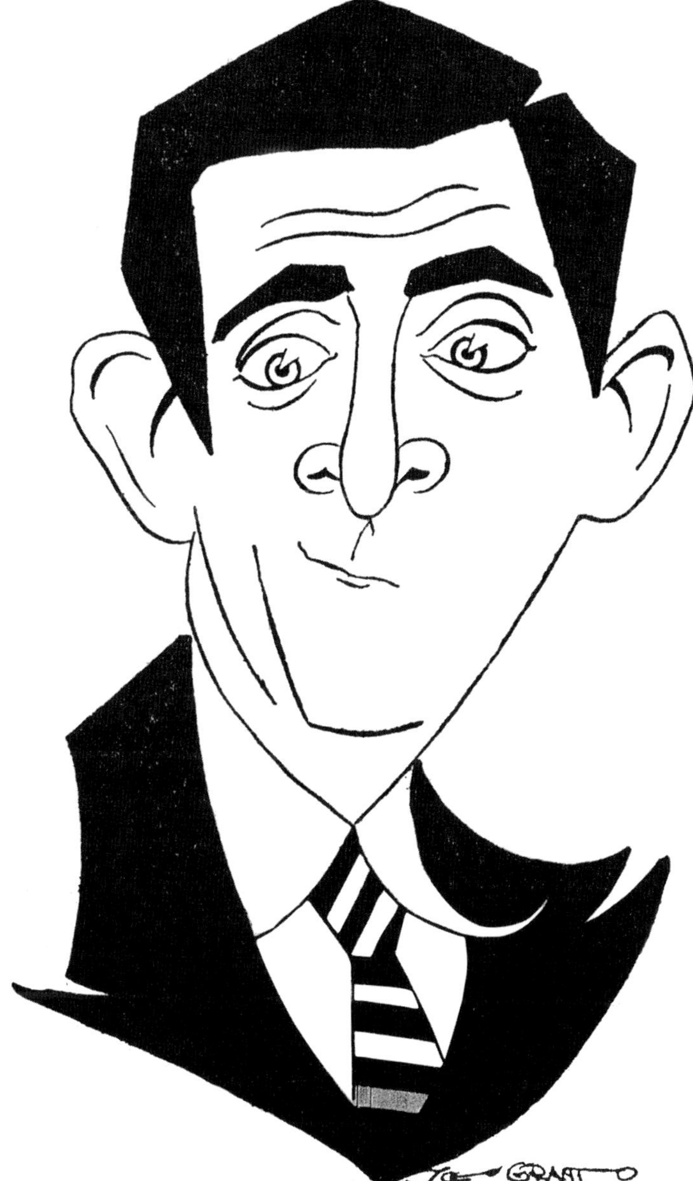

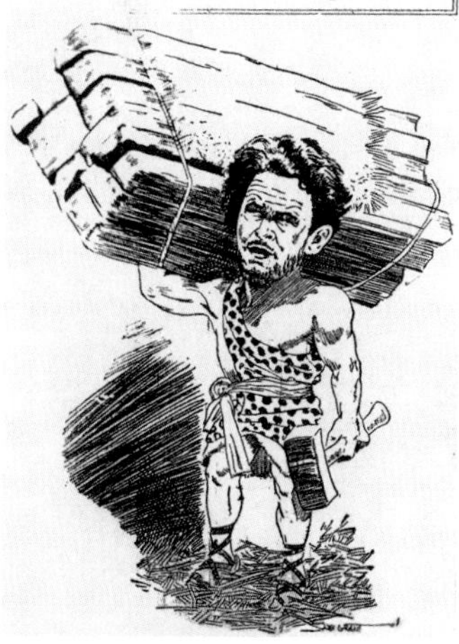

LEFT: *The first true Joe Grant caricature: Edward Everett Horton (January 4, 1929).* RIGHT: *actor Guinn Williams in* NOAH'S ARK *(December 8, 1928).*

and recognize. There are people that are impossible to caricature. Mostly beautiful women."[17]

Nevertheless, he successfully caricatured Greta Garbo several times. His first Garbo (August 10, 1929) had sultry eyes and sensual lips floating in white space (minus an anchoring nose) framed by cascading hair; her V neckline becomes the panel surrounding the cartoon. Stronger is Grant's high-style Garbo of January 23, 1932: hair hidden under a skullcap, head in three-quarter view against black accenting a high cheekbone, mouth a plump bullet, and heavy-lidded eye topped by a single brow line; a bold gray stripe

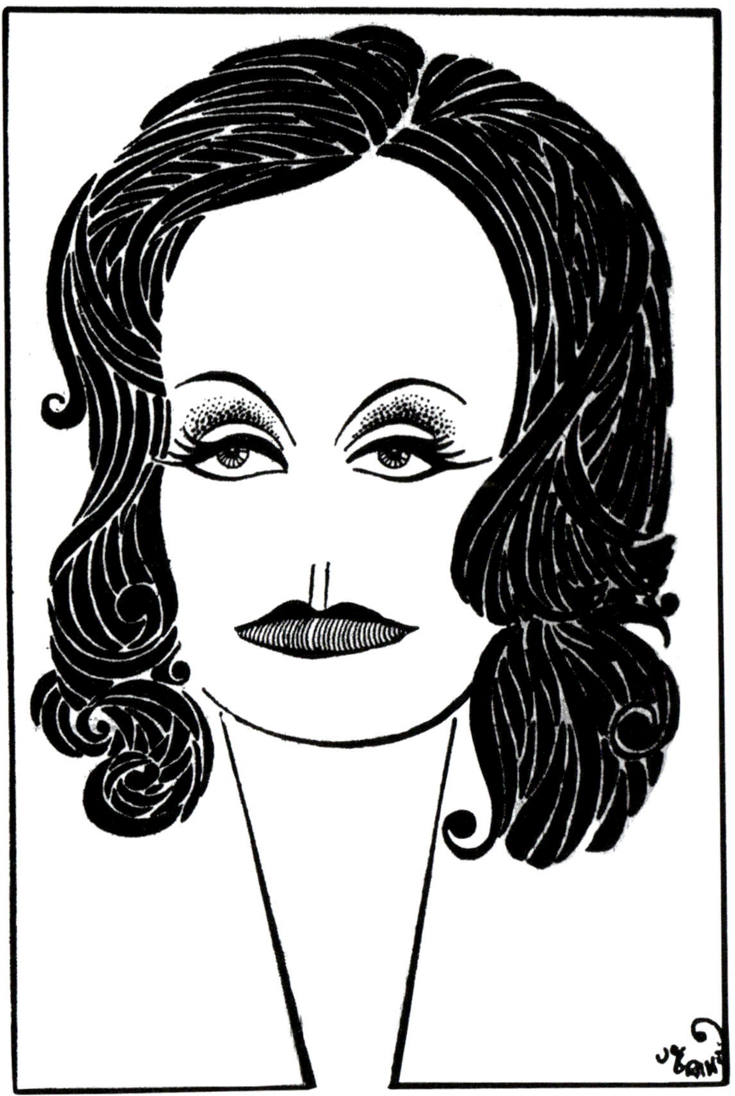

Joe Grant variations on Greta Garbo. THIS PAGE, LEFT: *August 10, 1929.* RIGHT: *February 13, 1932.* OPPOSITE: *January 23, 1932.*

inside a white face line indicates the ghost of a nose. A month later, Garbo appeared in the center of a page containing five other Joe Grant drawings, each in differing styles; some (Garbo, Barbara Stanwyck, and Helen Hayes) are more representational in appearance than the highly caricatured comedians Roscoe Ates and Joe E. Brown.

"Garbo you could do a million different ways," Grant said. "Something so decorative about her face. And just her qualities. There was something sort of slithery about her, her movements and everything. Very graceful person. Best one I did of her was in *Queen Christina*."[18]

When Grant drew the torsos of celebrities, their poses reflect their personalities; be it casual, confident cowpoke John Wayne (October 2, 1930), electrifying monster Boris Karloff in *Frankenstein* (January 2 and 14, 1932), or goofy Charlotte Greenwood's elongated form playfully squeezed into a thin panel along an entire page.

"This business of getting a likeness," Reaves observes, "not every caricaturist had it to the same degree. I think Joe Grant did have it. And it's a fairly subtle kind of sensibility. He didn't do so much of the full figure, but he seemed to have a sense of the essential thing to capture in the face to make it recognizable."[19]

An early caricature of young Joan Crawford (August 22, 1929) captured the "flaming youth" qualities of the pretty bobbed-hair starlet, recognizable by virtue of her large intense eye (in profile) and determined chin. As her persona developed, Grant dug deeper; in a later (undated)

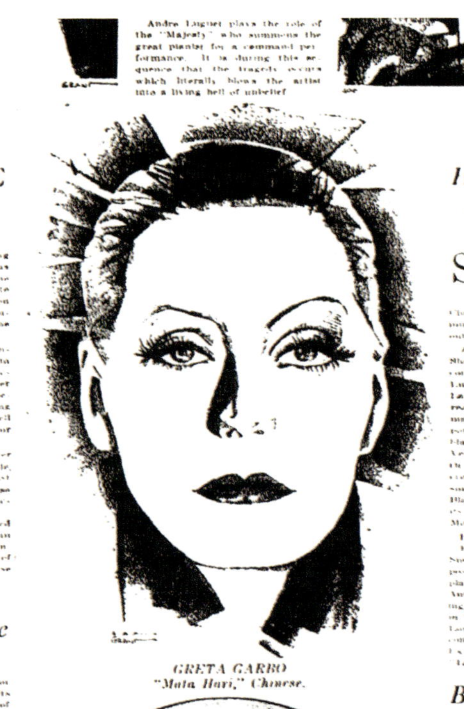

S FAME
'ERAL
ES

Not Have
orries

HELL
STU
C

Being
Job

GRETA GARBO
"Mata Hari," Chinese.

portrait, Crawford faces us, kohl-rimmed eyes glaring, single-line eyebrows angry. She has no nose to flare, but her wide, frowning mouth shape amusingly mimics the huge bow around her neck. Grant tapped into Crawford's star persona, making it frighteningly funny.

"You usually start straight, in other words, representational," Grant said of his methodology. "Then you work on it. Sometimes, even without being aware of it, a caricature comes out. Let me put it this way: it's very simple. You struggle from beginning to end!

"When I saw my first stuff being produced, from that point on I was on my way," Grant recalled. Soon five of his drawings appeared each Saturday on the *Record*'s drama/movie page, and others were spotted in various sections throughout the week. The clever, proliferating caricatures "by Joe Grant" attracted the public's attention. Equally importantly, the movie industry took notice.

In addition to his salary, Grant earned extra money weekly ($10 per drawing) from film studios (MGM, Warner Bros., Fox, among others) when he drew a caricature spotlighting their upcoming movie.[20] "You have to remember I was selling," Grant said. "Because the publicist[s] were very anxious to get me to do these things. So they could get space in the paper. The drama editors would take a drawing, but not a photo [because] anybody could do that!"

"I was art director," he said of his developing power at the *Record*, "but art director of one person. Myself!"

Out of necessity he became involved in the paper's technical processes. "I had an inebriated engraver," Grant explained, who got drunk and sat reading humor magazines. He was "well smashed" when he received Grant's zinc-plate drawings for routing (digging out and cleaning up the lines). "He'd dry rout

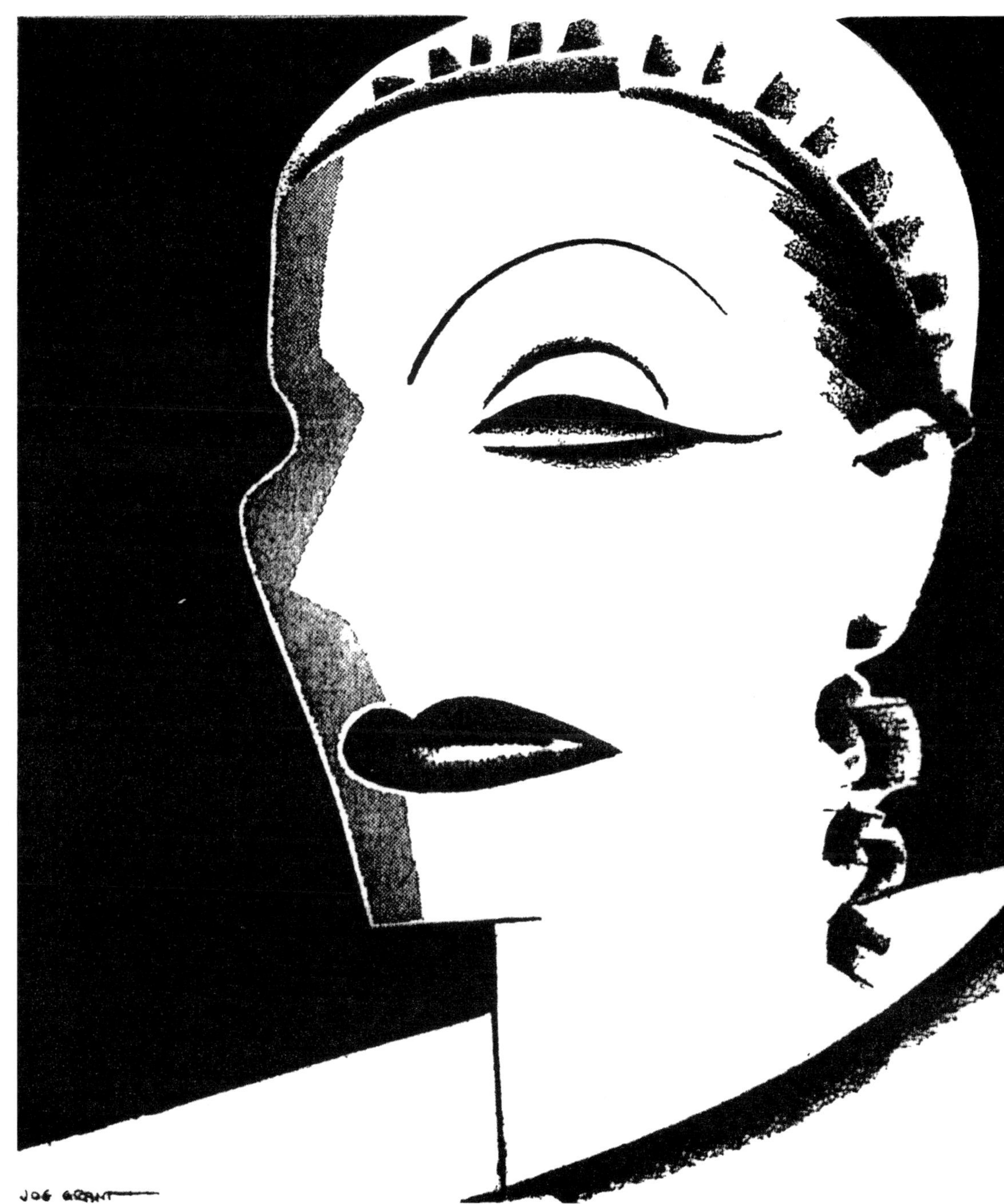

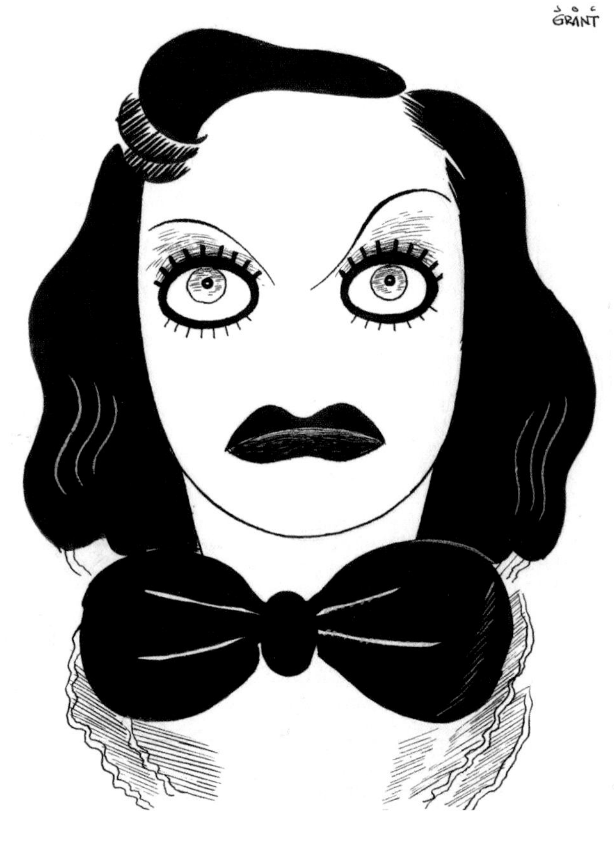

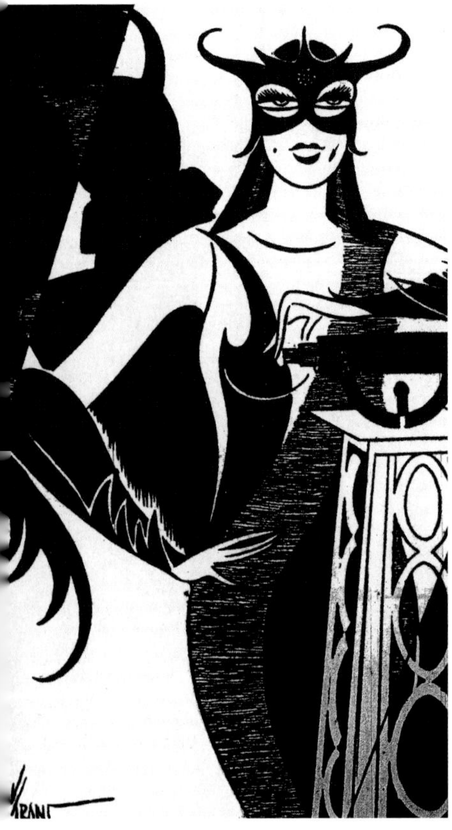

CLOCKWISE FROM RIGHT: *Joe Grant's 1933 Joan Crawford caricature for Sardi's Hollywood; Marlene Dietrich, February 3, 1932; Kay Johnson, star of C.B. DeMille's* MADAM SATAN, *September 24, 1930.*

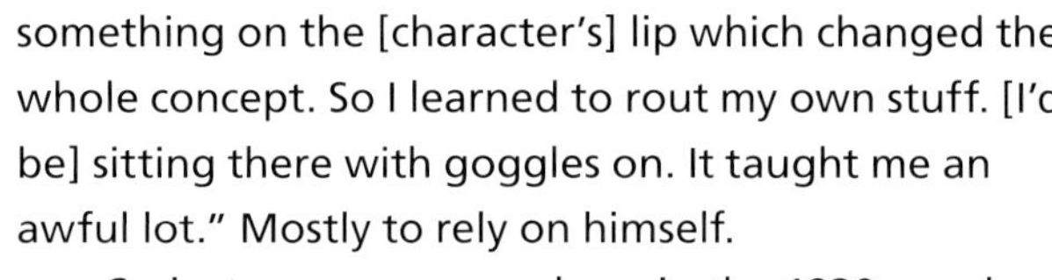

something on the [character's] lip which changed the whole concept. So I learned to rout my own stuff. [I'd be] sitting there with goggles on. It taught me an awful lot." Mostly to rely on himself.

Caricature was everywhere in the 1920s, and Grant restlessly tried on and discarded graphic elements of other caricaturists. "Why does everything I [draw] look different? Because I'm an adventurer," he explained. "And I do want to make everything different. I can't possibly do, as [Al] Hirschfeld does, the same banana fingers. There's always something new to find in each subject. Sometimes I do, sometimes I don't."

In Grant's caricatures are glimpses of Miguel Covarrubias (1902–1957) ("He was completely overpowering," said Grant), William Auerbach-Levy (1889–1964) (who published in *The New Yorker*, *Collier's*, and *Ladies' Home Journal*), Al Frueh (1880–1968) ("a nice simple style"), Al Hirschfeld (1903–2003), and elegant, witty Ralph Barton (1891–1931). "Technique-wise," Grant said, "I was very influenced by Ralph Barton and a number of others of that period. But Barton influenced me most. I admired his style and approach. Sort of an Oriental quality to it, in his characters. I didn't appropriate. I was just influenced."[21]

"You see these echoes in Joe's work," Reaves concurs. "But, that said, he was very inventive. That imagination does come through very clearly. He's got a whole banquet of techniques to draw from because there's so much published in the '20s. But he uses them very cleverly.

"The other thing that is absolutely key for caricaturing is understanding the accents that you have to grab hold of in order to get a likeness. He was very good at that, and that's more than draftsmanship."[22]

In August 1932, thirty-nine of Joe Grant's caricatures illustrated *Hollywood Follies—Tattle Telling on the Stars* by Sonia Lee, a book of "incidents and incidentals about the great of Hollywood." Llewellyn Miller reviewed it for the *Record* with affectionate hyperbole ("Joe Grant Does Brilliant First Book"), recapped Grant's career to date, and predicted a bright future for her protégé.

> Four years ago, almost to the day, *Record* readers who were gifted with the ability to see into the future said to themselves, "Ah! Here begins another brilliant career!"
>
> There was a Joe Grant drawing on the front page. It was a picture of Al Smith done in the early Grant manner . . . Then those clairvoyant spirits who had been watching his work had another thrill. Grant's first caricature appeared. . . . The book is a brilliant milestone on a career, which is just beginning, for this young man

of 24 years is destined to be one of the most spectacular of American illustrators.

Watch this young gentleman whose pencil is loaded with the dynamite of laughter—he is on his way up![23]

What did George Grant think of his son's switch to caricature? "A little shocked," said Joe, "because he thought I'd go down his road and I didn't. He soon became accustomed to it. 'If he wants to do it let him do it.' Liberal."

In 1929, the Grants had attempted a brief reconcilation. Once again George, Eva, Geraldine, and Joe lived under the same roof in a rented house on Coolidge Avenue. Eva's father lived nearby in the $6,000 house he owned.[24] It was an unhappy, volatile situation for both sides of the family. Eva filed for divorce on April 8, 1930, and moved back to her father's house with seventeen-year-old Geraldine.[25] George became a lodger at a Ninth Street hotel.[26] During this personal turmoil, a photo of George A. Grant, unsmiling in glasses, appeared in the April 6, 1930, *Los Angeles Times* with six other artists, including Norman Rockwell, judging an Easter poster contest sponsored by the Hollywood Bowl.[27]

Eva's action was exacerbated when twenty-two-year-old Joe moved out and married. His growing local fame and increased earnings as a caricaturist bolstered his independence. He first met June Hershey (1909–2000) at Zinke's shoe store. One year younger than Joe, she was a lyricist who, in 1941, would write the words to the song "Deep in the Heart of Texas." In 1930, the newlyweds rented their home for $35 a month on Norton Avenue, far from Joe's parents.

Joe described June as "a nice person," Jennifer Castrup says. "They both realized that they were too young and had little in common for a lasting relationship."[28] Eva strongly disapproved of the shiksa who stole her son away. "Grandma didn't like her," Carol Grubb says. "Daddy said Grandma made it so difficult." June filed for a divorce on January 29, 1932.[29]

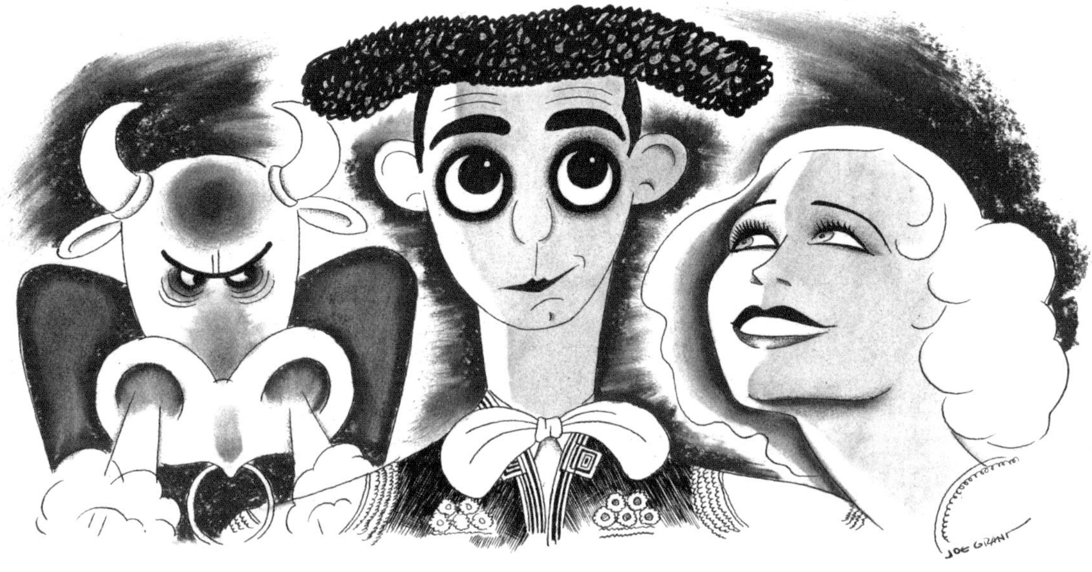

Eddie Cantor and Lyda Roberti in THE KID FROM SPAIN, *released November 1932.*

In November 1932, Joe was part of "an exhibit of the works of outstanding newspaper artists" at the F. Suie One Art Gallery in Los Angeles.[30] There were other important developments in 1933. He married again, this time to Jennie Miller, a true soul mate; and he was hired to contribute caricatures to two movie productions.

For Paramount's *Design For Living*, he drew three cartoons of Napoleon in various stages of undress down to his underwear. Director Ernst Lubitsch invited Grant onto the set to sketch Gary Cooper and Fredric March for a scene in which Miriam Hopkins draws the two men sleeping. "That was a wonderful week," Grant said.

Another studio needed caricatures of Hollywood stars for an animated cartoon. "I hadn't the slightest idea I would ever work there," Grant recalled of the day he walked down a corridor to meet Walt Disney.[31]

CHAPTER FIVE

Mickey and Jennie

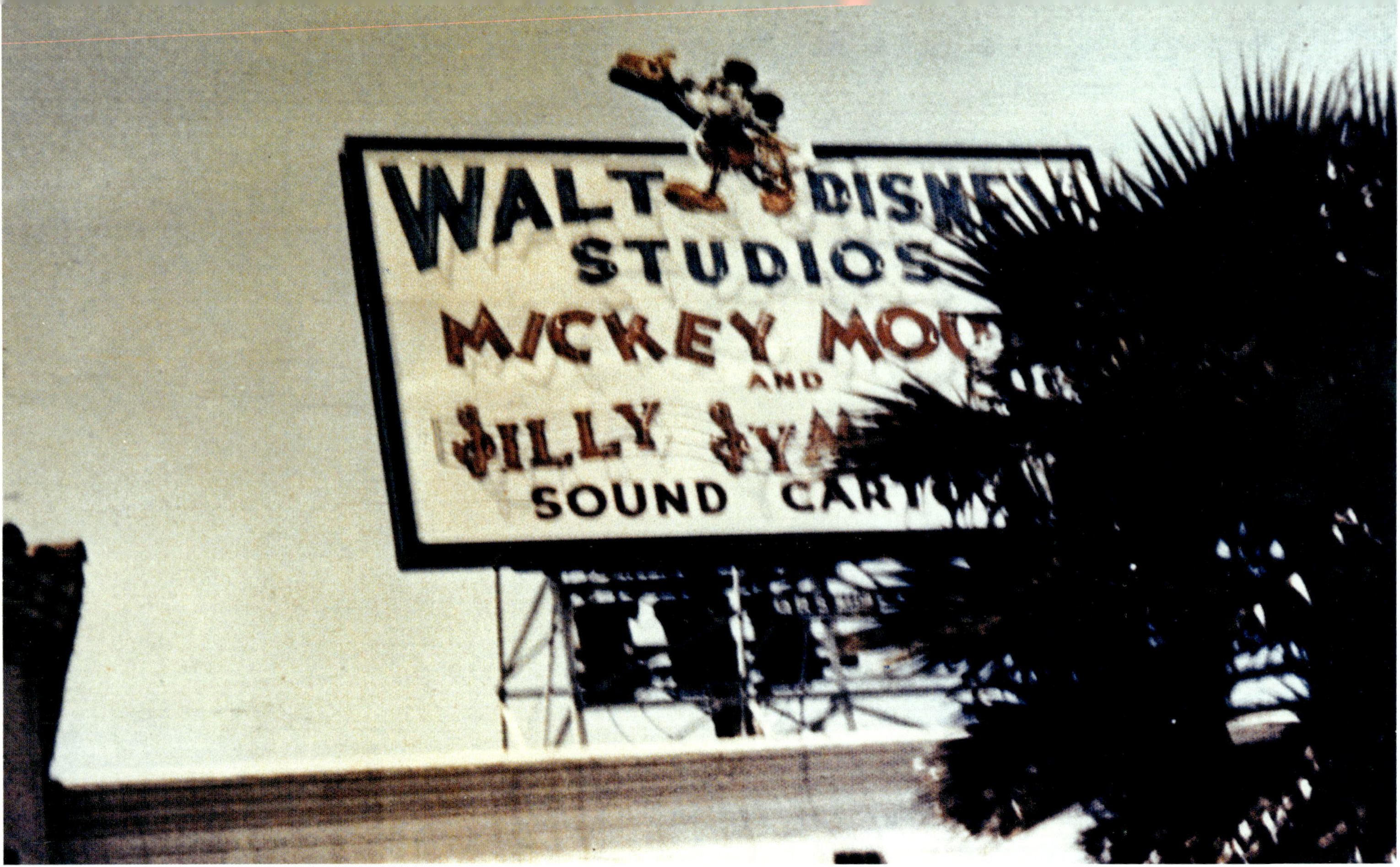

Disney's Hyperion Avenue studio neon sign.

Ground zero of the animation world in spring 1933 was the Walt Disney Studios at 2719 Hyperion Avenue. Since his invention of Mickey Mouse in 1928, Walt Disney had become a world figure. His drive and creativity revolutionized the animated cartoon with innovative sound tracks, color, and characters whose empathetic personalities leapt off the screen.

The success of the action-oriented Mickey Mouse shorts engendered a second, primarily musical series in 1929 called Silly Symphonies. By October 1932, *Motion Picture Herald,* an exhibitors trade paper, celebrated Mickey Mouse's fourth birthday by claiming his "'shorts' are now more important than Gandhi's and cover a lot more territory!"

In 1932, the Academy of Motion Picture Arts and Sciences gave its first award for a cartoon to Walt Disney for the Silly Symphony *Flowers and Trees* and a special award for the creation of Mickey Mouse.[1] By 1933, Disney's ideas for a full-length animated cartoon feature began to crystallize in his mind.

Disney's success and ambition led to rapid growth in his personnel (two hundred employees in 1934, one hundred more in 1935), necessitating a physical expansion. Additions were constructed and additional space requisitioned in bungalows across the street. This optimistic development is remarkable considering it occurred as America was weathering the Great Depression.

As Joe Grant headed toward Disney's office, he heard strains of "Who's Afraid of the Big Bad Wolf," a theme song from a Silly Symphony-in-progress titled *Three Little Pigs.*[2] No one imagined at the time how hugely popular the song and film would become when released in May 1933. The cartoon was a breakthrough in personality animation, but the symbolism of a wolf at the door of three innocents resonated with the average citizen's plight enduring

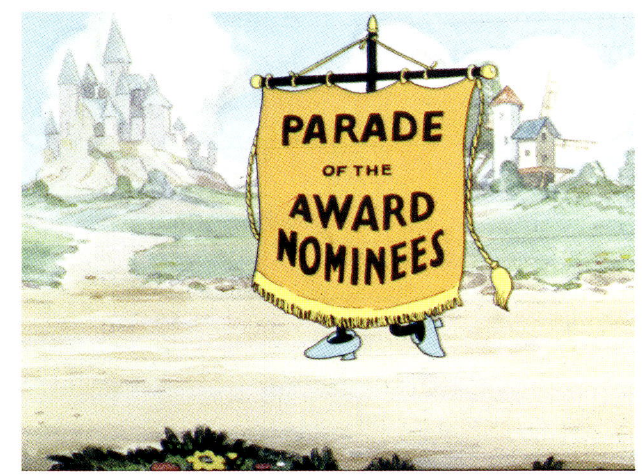

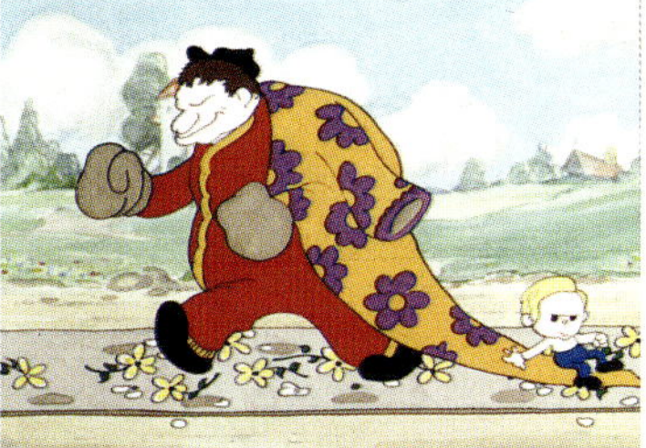

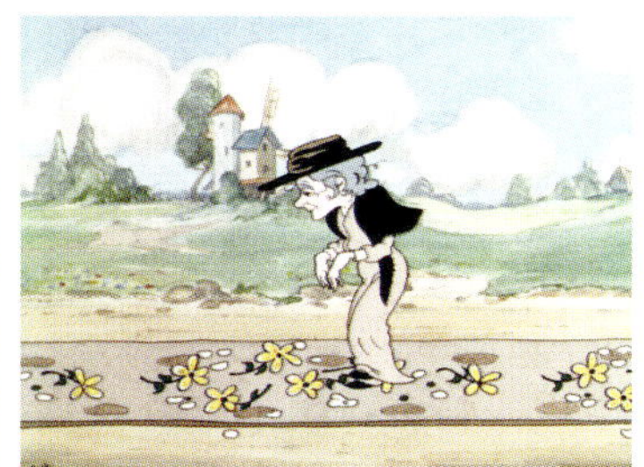

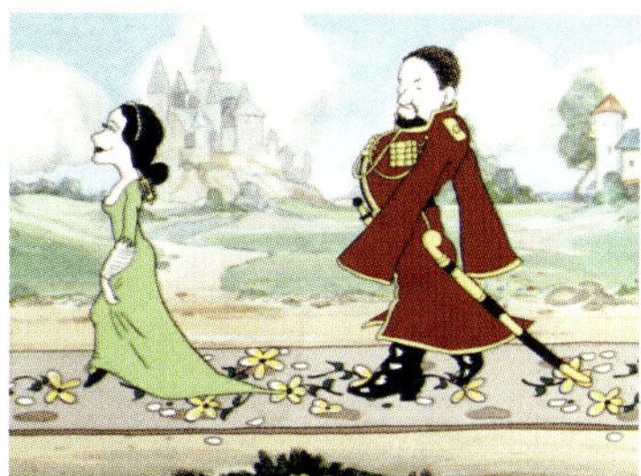

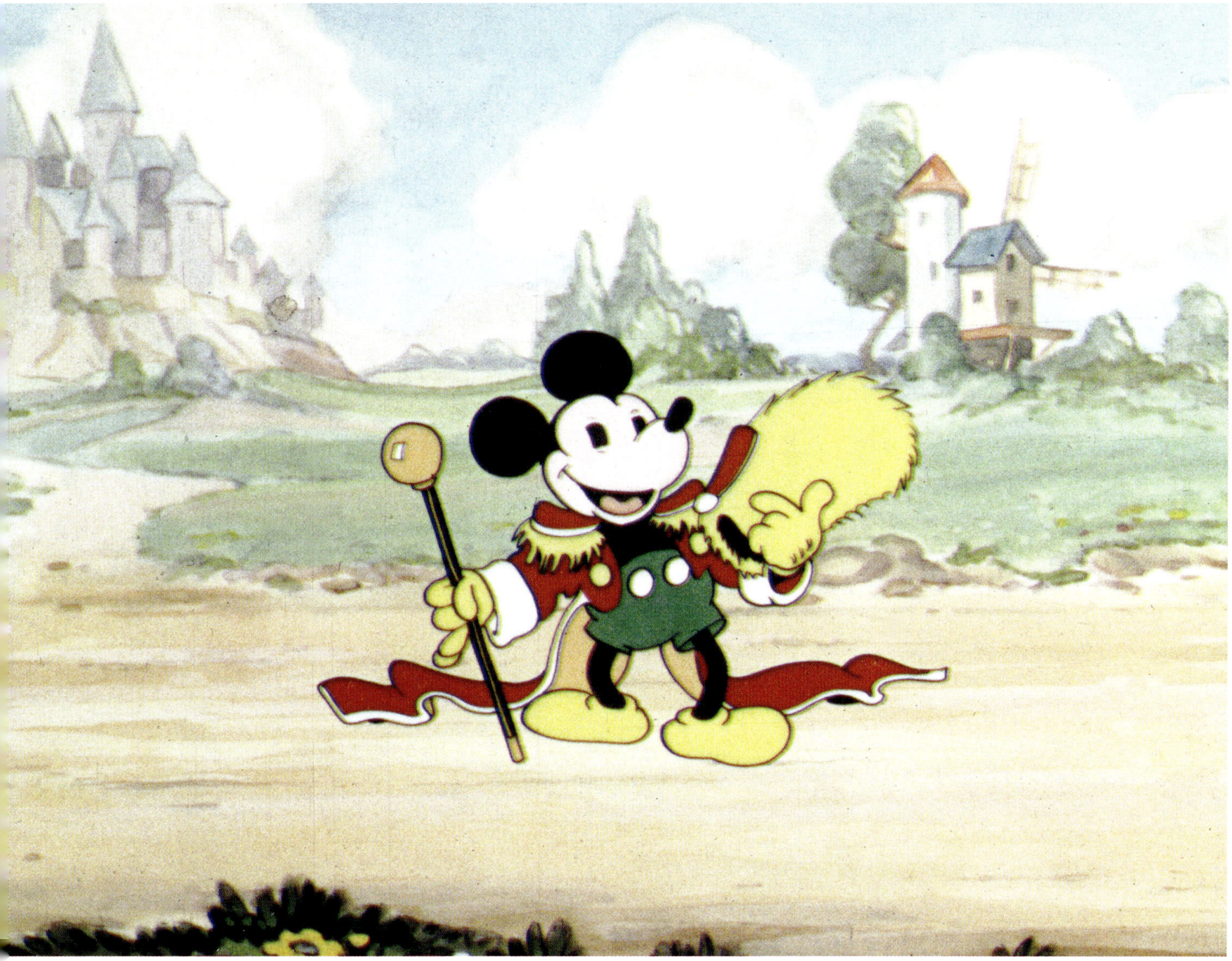

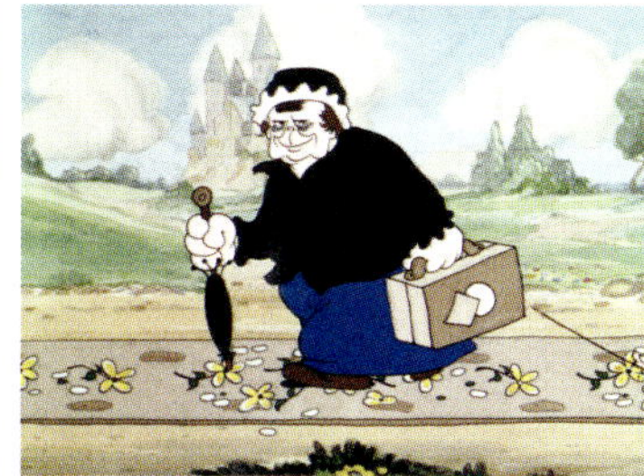

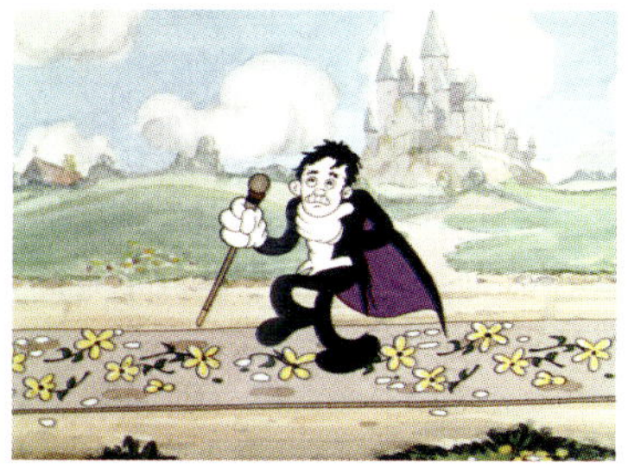

A special color cartoon made for the 1932 Academy Awards ceremony "borrowed" designs from Joe Grant's newspaper caricatures of (CLOCKWISE FROM TOP LEFT) *Wallace Beery, Helen Hayes, the Lunts, Marie Dressler, and Fredric March.*

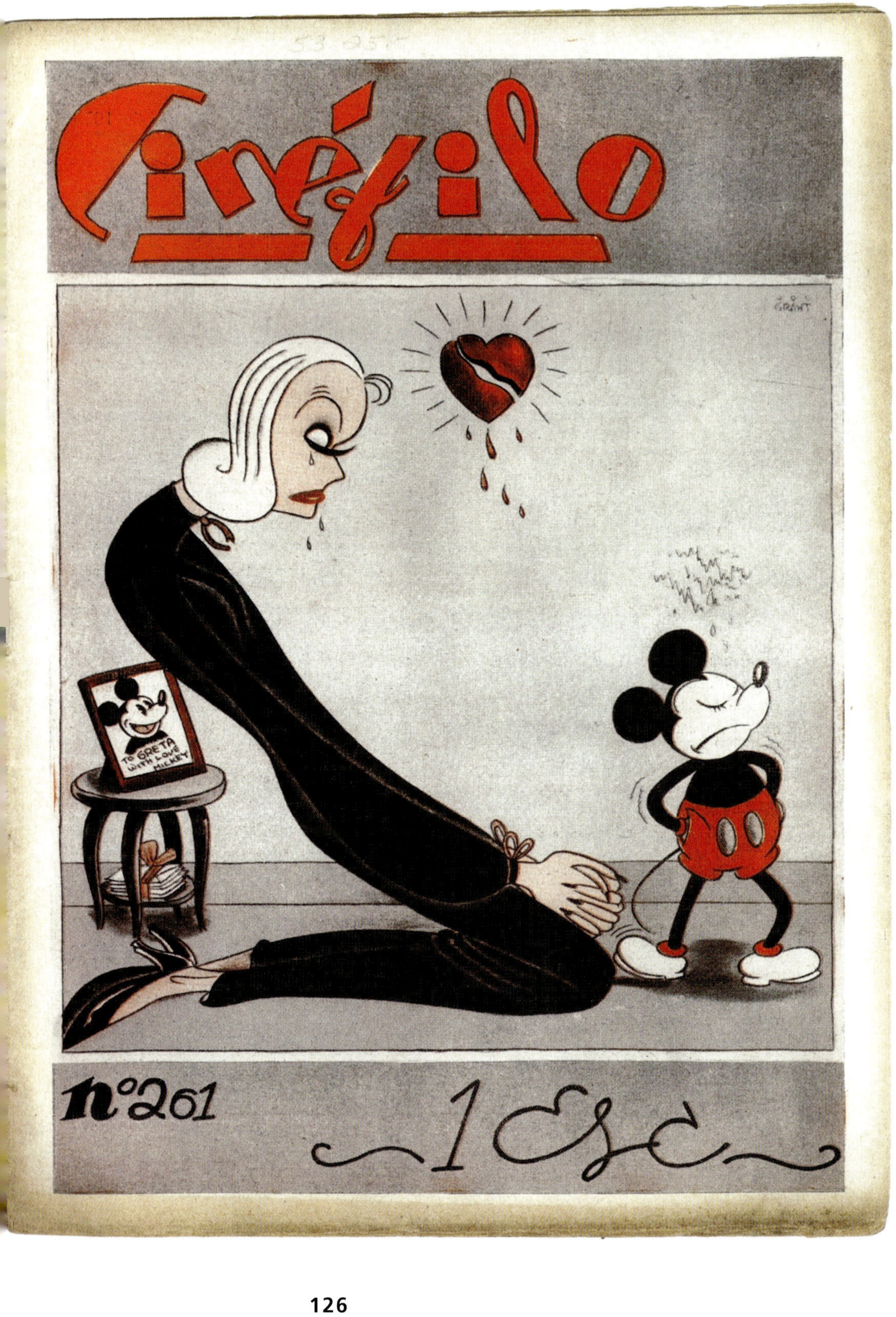

Cinéfilo

TO GRETA WITH LOVE MICKEY

nº261

1 Esc

America's economic troubles. Both song and film became a "stirring manifesto of hope," wrote Stephen Watts in *The Magic Kingdom*, and encouraged Americans to "pull together to defeat a common, ferocious enemy."[3]

Grant immediately felt at home at Disney, which resembled newspaper art departments. It was "essentially a drawing factory," artist Martin Provensen said. "You waded up to your waist in drawings!"[4]

Grant knew newspaper colleagues now employed there, including Charles E. Philippi in Scene Layouts and Hugh Hennesy of the Scenic Department, and two chums from Venice High, animators Dick Lundy and Leslie (Les) Clark. Al Zinnen, a political cartoonist for Hearst's *Examiner*, would join the Disney Layout Department in September.[5]

"The atmosphere was relaxed but exciting," Grant said. "I was terribly impressed."[6]

When he stood before Walt Disney, he felt "so overwhelmed with just his presence." The boss, however, proved to be "unassuming" and "such a likable guy" that the two quickly hit it off and began a long talk.[7]

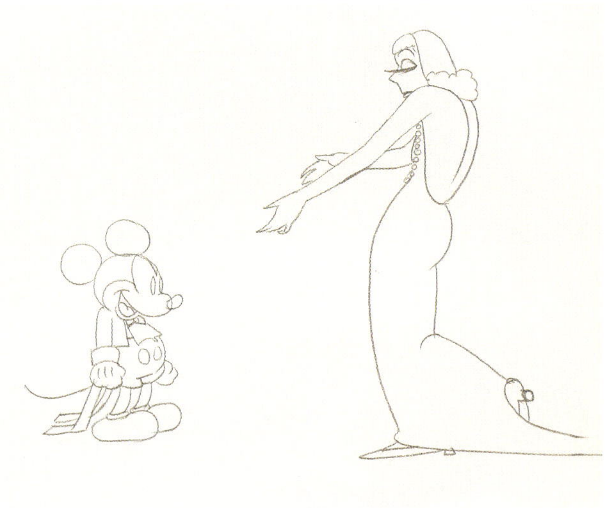

Grant was flattered that Disney admired his work in the *Record*. In fact, his caricatures were referenced—without credit or compensation—in *Mickey's Parade of Nominees*, a special color cartoon produced for the 1932 Academy Award ceremony. *Mickey's Gala Premiere*, a new short in production, required many caricatures of Hollywood stars and celebrities, and this time Disney went directly to Grant for model drawings.

During their conversation, Disney expressed keen interest in incorporating more "caricature" into his films. He was thinking of reaching beyond merely drawing movie stars, and talked of bringing artful exaggeration into all aspects of animation production: design, writing, and motion.

In a 1935 memo, he set down thoughts on the subject in a veritable manifesto. "The first duty of the cartoon," Disney wrote, "is not to picture or duplicate real action or things as they actually happen—but to give a caricature of life and action." He called for a "study of the actual . . . so we may have a basis upon which to go into the fantastic, the unreal, the imaginative—and yet to let it have a foundation of fact, in order that it may more richly possess sincerity and contact with the public."[8]

Grant would play a part in the development of "a sense of caricature" that Disney was reaching for. For now, he eagerly accepted the freelance assignment.

In *Mickey's Gala Premiere* (released July 1, 1933), Mickey Mouse presents a new film in grand Hollywood fashion: powerful carbon-arc lamps light the skies, crowds of fans cheer behind barricades, and limousines disgorge Hollywood celebrities. All the stars, including Wallace Beery, Marie Dressler, the Marx Brothers, Laurel and Hardy, Mae West, Maurice Chevalier, Joan Crawford, Gloria Swanson, Constance Bennett, Douglas Fairbanks, Harold Lloyd, Adolphe Menjou, Joe E. Brown, Eddie Cantor, Jimmy Durante, Edward G. Robinson, Clark Gable, Buster Keaton, and Charlie Chaplin, are wildly enthusiastic about the mouse and his movie. Late in the film, the crowd parts as Greta Garbo enters to plant a kiss on Mickey. In the end, it's all revealed as a dream when Mickey is "kissed" awake by his dog Pluto.

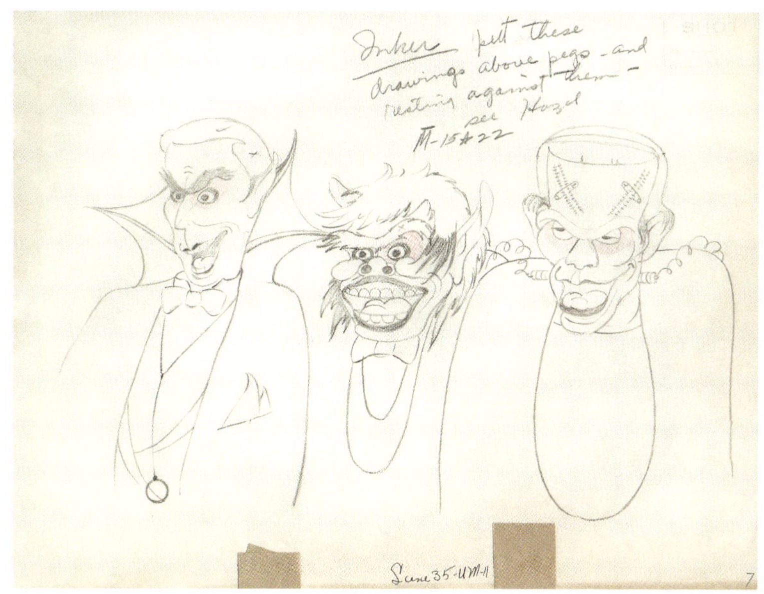

The aw-shucks ending doesn't disguise Disney's real-life ambitions, evident throughout the film. The cartoon producer wanted his films accorded respect and attention on a par with live-action studios. Four years later, Disney realized his dream with *Snow White and the Seven Dwarfs*' grand premiere.

Grant met with Disney and his story staff to develop gags based on his caricatures. In one witty gem, three movie monsters—Dracula (Bela Lugosi), Mr. Hyde (Fredric March), and Frankenstein (Boris Karloff)—sit in the audience and laugh simultaneously with ghoulish glee. (*"M-m-m-uaaaaaaa-haaaaaa-haaaaaaah!"*)

Grant enjoyed his indoctrination into animation's mysterious processes. However, some animators balked, complaining his designs were not "workable." Newspaper caricatures are viewed in one set position, but animators need dimensional designs; heads and bodies must turn, yet still resemble the celebrities. "They'd picked a profile, which was a likeness," Grant explained. "As soon as they'd turn it,

OPPOSITE, LEFT: *Greta Garbo and Mickey Mouse illustrated by Joe Grant for a 1933 Portuguese movie magazine.* OPPOSITE, BOTTOM: *an animation drawing of Mickey greeted by Garbo in* MICKEY'S GALA PREMIERE *(1933).* ABOVE: *monster stars Bela Lugosi (Dracula), Fredric March (Mr. Hyde), and Boris Karloff (Frankenstein).*

it was lost. Except for Jimmy Durante, who had a big nose, so that was simple enough."[9]

Grant was stubborn and uncompromising. "I knew that would be the work of the animator, to translate what I did. And I really made very little effort to accommodate them," he said, laughing. "All I was interested in was the impression, the emotion."

Grant's cavalier condescension was unwise; he was off on the wrong foot with the animators, foreshadowing future misunderstandings and hostilities.[10] Disney, however, was more than pleased with Grant's artwork. "He realized I had something," Grant said years later.[11]

Disney was also intrigued by the intellectual grasp of this young man, seven years his junior, whose casual art and literary references were wide-ranging, urbane, and erudite. Perhaps Disney recognized something of himself in Grant's background: both men endured difficult family situations while growing up, both had limited formal educations, and were "saved" by cartooning from mundane careers and lives. Most importantly, Disney felt akin to Grant's restless, creative imagination and sparkling ideas for animation.

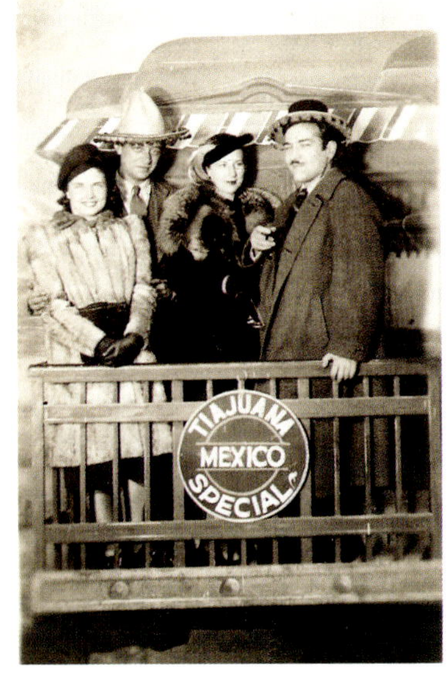

Jennie and Joe Grant (LEFT) with friends Adrienne and Bill Tytla.

One day Disney phoned to ask Grant to join his Story Department full time. "This was the opportunity for me," thought Grant. "Music, color, drawing. It was everything!" But before accepting, Grant discussed the offer with his new wife.

Jennie Miller Grant (1913–1991) was a beautiful, intelligent, petite (five-foot) brunette nearly six years younger than her husband. She was born November 16, 1913, of Catholic Irish/German stock, the younger of two daughters. Her father, Charles, was a New York accountant, an intellectual who read Goethe to Jennie in German.[12] Though a proud American who changed his family name "von Falkenstein" to "Miller" and considered Teddy Roosevelt his personal hero, he also subscribed to a German paper. America's virulent anti-German sentiment at the beginning of World War I forced the Miller family to leave the United States. For the war's duration they lived in the farming community of Bonaventure, Quebec, Canada, then returned to New York.[13]

Jennie was eleven when her diabetic father died of a stroke in 1924. She, her mother, and sister settled in Los Angeles on steep Fargo Street, where her father's sisters, Carrie and Emma, also lived. Jennie's mother, Lucy (née Lucille McMinanin), remarried, but died from tuberculosis when Jennie was a teen.

Jennie's two German aunts, educated and independent-minded, became surrogate mothers, nurturing her intellectual gifts by encouraging her to read classic literature. Upon graduation from high school in 1931, Jennie was offered a full scholarship to the University of Washington, an unusual opportunity for women in those days.[14]

Instead, "she took on the challenge of Joe Grant," says Jennifer Castrup.[15]

They met through Joe's sister, Geraldine (Gerry), Jennie's closest high school friend. Jennie helped Gerry with her studies and, in turn, ate many a meal at the Grant house. Eva was so fond of her, she became another surrogate mother, teaching Jennie her delicious recipes.

Occasionally the two teenage girls visited Zinke's shoe store to ask Gerry's brother, Joe, for money to see a show. "She [Jennie] was garbed in a middy and bloomers. I didn't think much of the situation," Grant said in 1994. But Jennie was smitten.

In 1932, when Grant and his wife split, Geraldine arranged for nineteen-year-old Jennie and twenty-four-year-old Joe to meet again. "My sister was quite a matchmaker," Grant admitted.[16]

Remembering the kid in bloomers, he was reluctant at first and quite unprepared for Jennie's transformation into a beauty. From a piece of gray wool, she sewed a slim, long-sleeved dress accessorized with suede pumps and silk stockings, and staged a grand entrance down a staircase. On her appearance, Grant took a second look.[17]

"We became close," he said. "Very."[18]

They were engaged on March 7, 1933, and married in Los Angeles on March 13. Because Joe's divorce wouldn't be officially granted until the next year (April 12, 1934), Jennie insisted they remarry. "For my mother everything had to be right. He thought it was funny," Carol Grubb says.

When Disney's offer came, Joe sought Jennie's counsel as he would for their nearly six decades of married life. Grant hesitated because under his new contract, his caricatures were also appearing in a Chicago newspaper. But he also knew that his mainstay, the *Los Angeles Record,* was going to cease publication on October 30, 1933, the nadir of the Depression. (The paper reemerged as the *Los Angeles Post-Record* in November, before finally folding in 1934.)

Also, the market for caricatures was dwindling. Theaters were closing, and newspapers were disappearing or merging. Newspaper feature components were now bought from syndicated sources, bypassing the local columnist or caricaturist.

"There was also the question of fashion," Wendy Wick Reaves comments. "The wonderfully drawn covers in fancy 1920s magazines and in advertising are, in the 1930s, getting more photographic coverage. That geometric stylization and abbreviation of crisp art deco lines seemed in the '20s terribly fashionable. It fit with the urban sensibility. By the '30s, that was no longer a snappy new look. Joe Grant was beginning to pick up on that."[19]

Jennie saw Disney's offer not only as a lifeline, but as a great opportunity. Disney was a young company on the rise with possibly bigger successes to come. Jennie believed her husband could be an integral part of that.

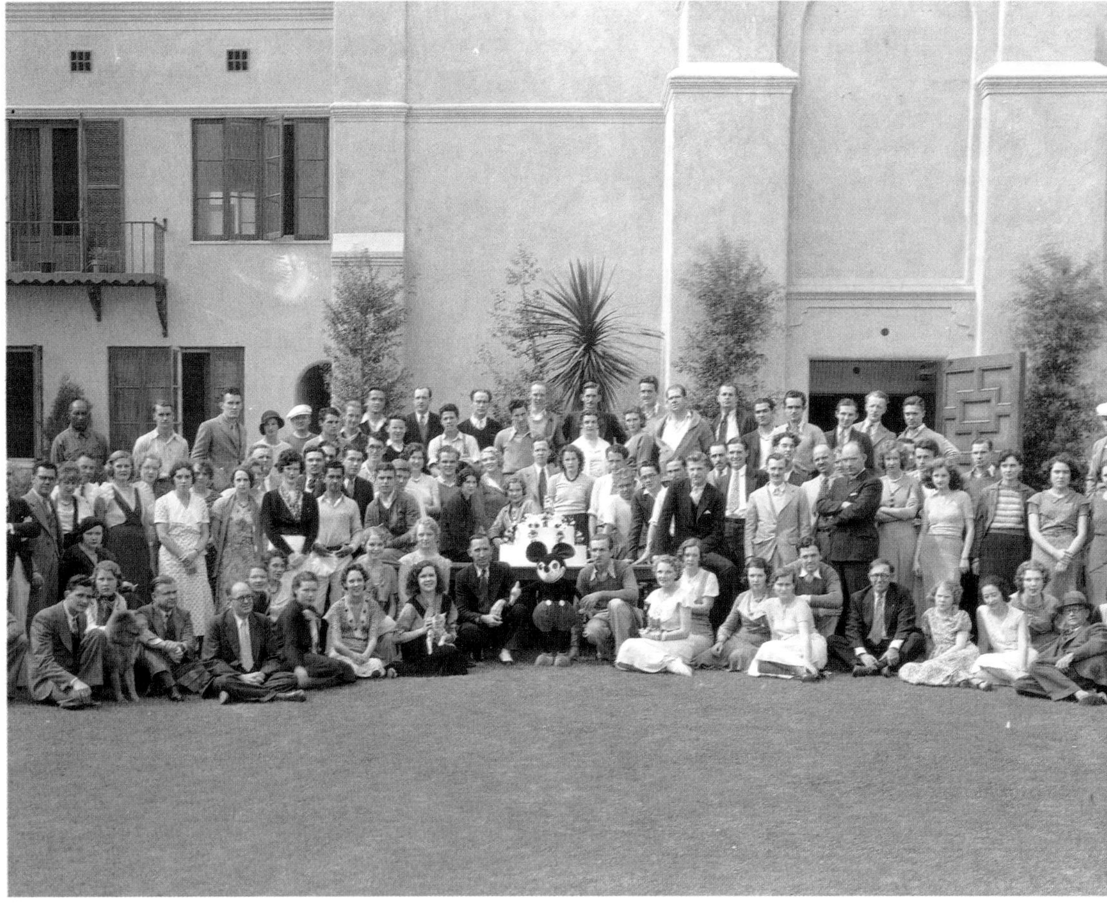

Disney's Hyperion Avenue studio in the early 1930s.

Ultimately, the decision to join Disney was Joe's. He was truly infatuated with animation and the creative potential he found at the Disney Studio with its amazing leader. He signed with Disney on September 9, 1933.

"I had fallen in love with the studio," he said more than half a century later. "I had fallen in love with the idea [of animation], particularly the *idea* and then him later because, God, he was—he *was* the idea!"[20]

Of Wrens and Witches

"**I honestly feel** that the heart of our organization is the Story Department," Walt Disney wrote in a December 23, 1935, memorandum.[1] "If the story is good the picture may be good, but if the story is weak, good color, music, and animation cannot save it."[2]

In 1931, Disney organized animation's first discrete story unit. Previously, creating stories for cartoons was casual and haphazard. Animators were responsible for film "plots," usually consisting of strings of gags. Disney separated the storytellers from the animators. "Walt was the first cartoon producer to appreciate the special talents of the individual artist," wrote Ted Sears, Disney's first head of Story, "and allow him to concentrate upon the thing he did best."[3]

Sears, a gag man and "scenario editor" from the Max Fleischer animation studio, led a team consisting of Webb Smith, a droll former newspaper cartoonist for Hearst's *Los Angeles Examiner*; Pinto Colvig, a brash former circus clown, writer, and cartoonist on the *San Francisco Bulletin*; and Albert Hurter, a Swiss-born animator with European academic training in architecture and fine art.

Hurter's unique function in the Story Department was to create "inspirational sketches." When new projects were proposed, he was "given free rein to let his imagination wander, creating strange animals, plants, scenery, or costumes that might serve as models for the forthcoming production."

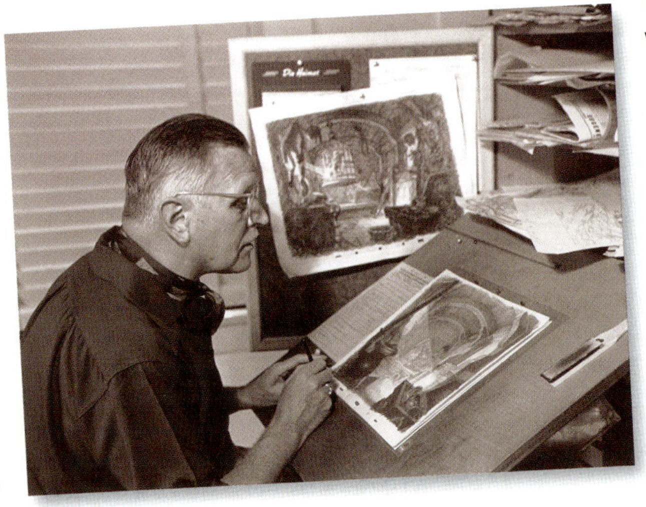

Albert Hurter, Joe Grant's mentor at Disney.

Driving this eclectic little group was Disney himself, whose own storytelling gifts were formidable. "We must have good stories," he demanded in a memo to Sears. Ideally, people "who cannot only think up ideas, but who can carry them through and sell them . . ."

Between 1932 and 1934, the Story Department increased to a dozen. Joe Grant, one of the new recruits, shared a small airless room with two cigar smokers, Hurter and sketch man Bob Kuwahara. Grant smoked Players cigarettes and later a pipe before quitting altogether. "It's a wonder I didn't get lung cancer in there."[4]

His colleagues reminded him of the oddball practical jokers he knew at newspaper offices. Colvig (the voice of Goofy, Grumpy, and Sleepy) played a trombone that was attached to a chain around his neck because "I almost swallowed one of these things!" Grant often observed Sears dropping off to sleep while pondering a storyboard, his large head resting on his hand. When his finger hit his hairline, he'd wake up with the perfect solution. "It was magical," Grant attested.[5]

The boss was in his early thirties and the staff was mostly twenty-somethings (like Grant); fifty-year-old Albert Hurter was considered an old man. But Grant was "overwhelmed" by Hurter's talent, and thought him "a genius—what a privilege he was." He admired the calm, methodical way Hurter turned out page upon page of fantastic, beautifully realized idea drawings daily.

"He had a cigar in his left hand, a magic wand in his right."[6]

The quiet older gent with a middle European accent was "extremely knowledgeable" about fine art. Hurter introduced Grant to obscure Dutch painters and the German/French illustrator Hermann Vogel (1856–1918). Both admired the work of Kley and *Simplicissimus* cartoonists, and Grant brought in books of their art. Grant felt an affinity with Hurter. ("My background was one of experimenting and developing.") And he was Grant's tacit mentor.[7] Grant was the new boy, in awe of Disney's dream factory, eager to find his niche and justify Walt's faith in him. "Your whole focus was appealing to Walt to stimulate him," he said. "And also to raise yourself in his esteem."[8]

He recalled Walt saying more than once that artists were a dime a dozen. "Now that sounds rather crude and cruel," Grant admitted. "But what he meant was he wanted a *thinking* artist, an artist with ideas, not somebody who was literal, but somebody who had imagination."[9] Grant was determined to become Walt's standout thinking artist.

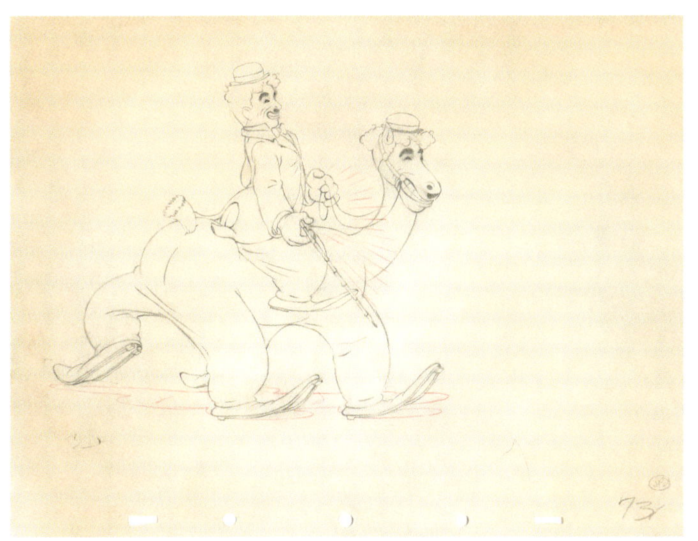

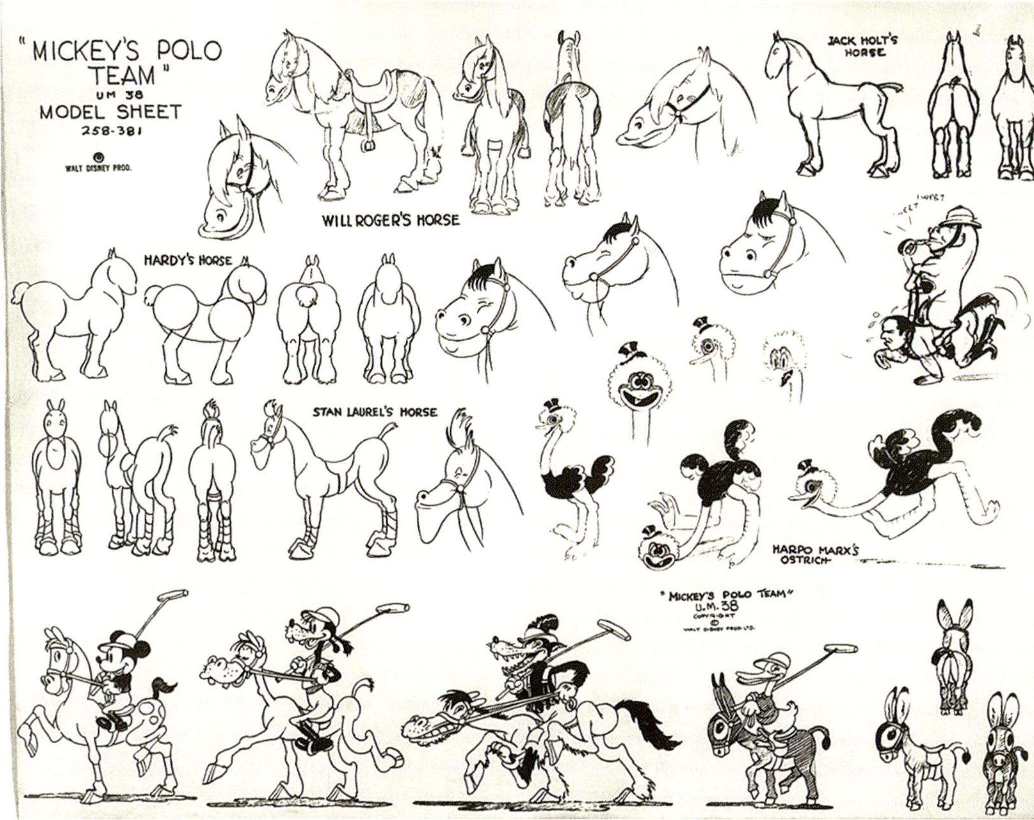

Mickey's Polo Team (1936), whose character designs were based on Joe Grant caricatures.

At home, he prepared elaborate sketches to present to Walt the next day. His first claim to fame was a large drawing for *Gulliver Mickey* (1934) showing a giant Mickey Mouse surrounded by Lilliputians, with each figure performing specific actions. "That was what appealed to Disney, " he explained. "I was bringing a little thinking to the sketches."[10] The drawing went over well. "I realized then that that's what he [Walt] needed for inspiration," Grant said. "I made quite a fetish of it after that, all the way through."

When a drawing stimulated Disney, "you were proud of your achievement. A story might grow out of the idea." The *Gulliver* sketch was "in a sense what he had in mind. I was just lucky to come up with it."[11]

Grant's caricatures for *Broken Toys* (1935) and *Mickey's Polo Team* (1936) impressed Walt, who sent a gift of "Christmas cheer" expressing his

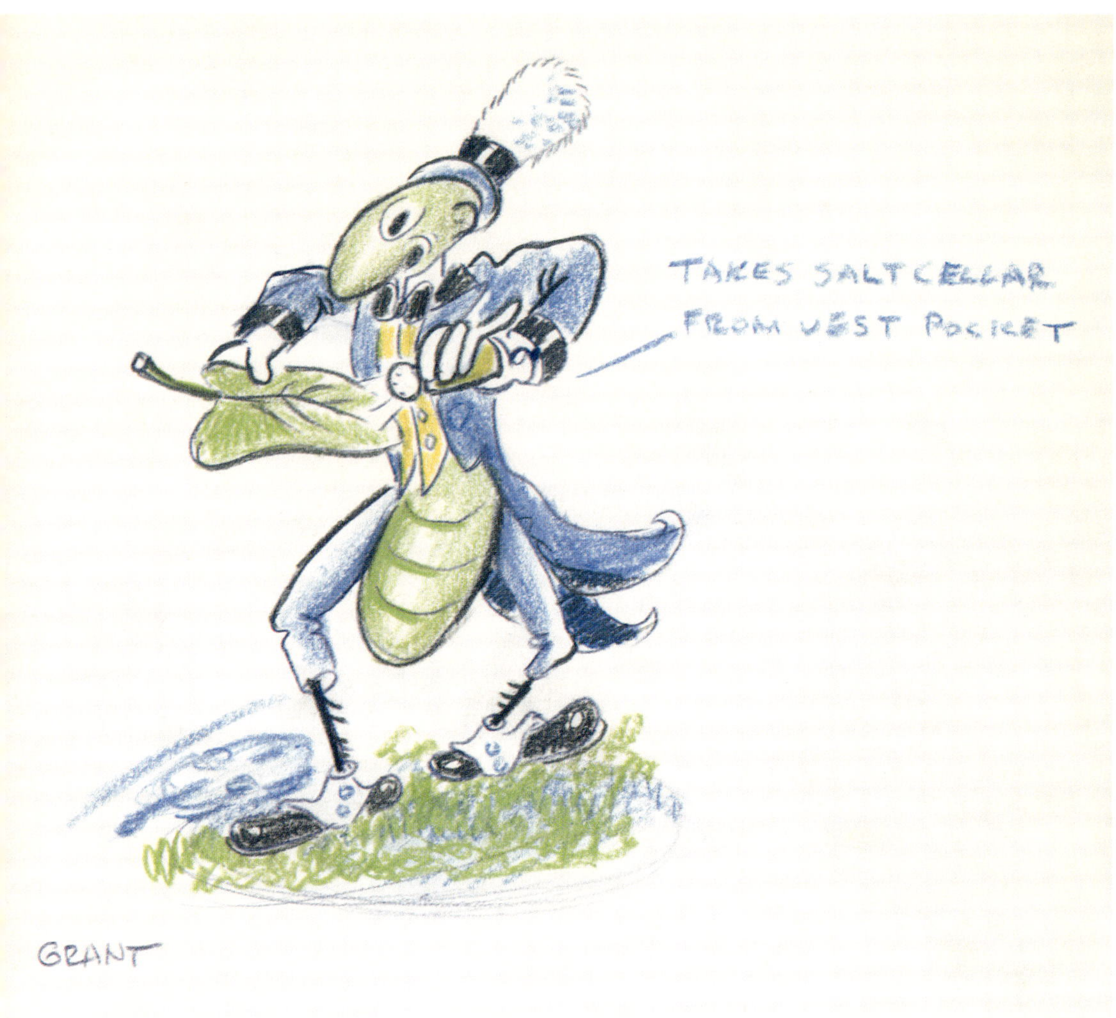

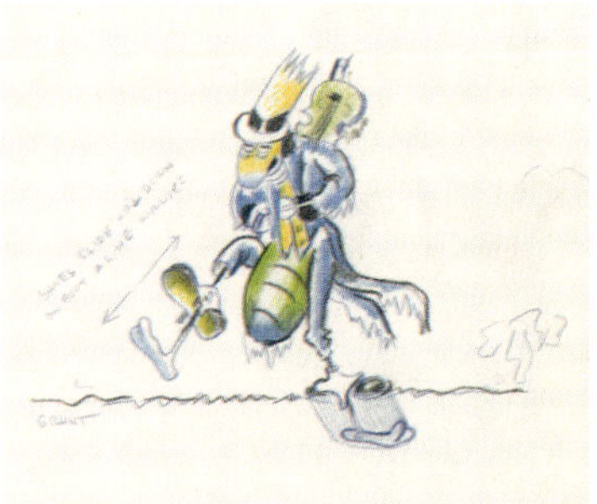

Joe Grant idea sketches for the Silly Symphony GRASSHOPPER AND THE ANTS *(1934).*

"appreciation to you for the marvelous caricature of Jack Holt," who appears in the polo short. "Jack was tickled to death with it, and it is occupying a very prominent place in his home."[12]

Disney's intuitiveness fascinated Grant. "It was very magical to be with him. He always seemed to know ahead of time what you were thinking. And he could outpace you very quickly. He had better ideas, but he did use you . . . the idea of the bee going around getting the pollen." Grant also noted, "He did have a sting though!"[13]

Presenting a storyboard to Walt Disney was stressful. "There was a certain power when he came into a room—electrifying!" remembered Grant. "A story meeting was like a court trial. You were either going to be executed or receive a life sentence."

"You got his full attention," said story man Vance Gerry, "and he worked very closely with the characters and what they would do and what they would say. It was very easy for him to change his mind, which he did. But he was always looking for something better. If he was in the right mood, people would be very excited, and he would excite people by how he would act things out or the suggestions he would make."[14]

A man of mercurial moods, he might offer stinging sarcasm or unbridled enthusiasm. Bianca Majolie, the Story Department's only woman, was not spared. At a January 23, 1939, meeting on *Fantasia*'s *Nutcracker Suite* sequence, Walt complained to Majolie that he didn't "think the continuity is right" and "doesn't approve of what you're doing with [the Sugar Plum Fairies]. The possibilities are here," he said, referring to her drawings, "but they're not developed yet, Bianca!" After the meeting Majolie vomited, as she often did after sessions with Walt.[15]

Disney signaled impatience and displeasure by tapping his fingertips. "That made a helluva racket," Grant remembered. "They beat out a tattoo that was almost a Morse code: 'This no damned good!'"[16] Bill Peet found it "unnerving" to pitch storyboards as Walt leaned forward in his chair like a tiger about to pounce, with a deep scowl and one eyebrow cocked at a precarious angle.[17]

Grant contributed story sketches and character designs to *Grasshopper and the Ants* (1934), *The Tortoise and the Hare* (1935), *The Golden Touch* (1935), *Water Babies* (1935), and *Alpine Climbers* (1936) along with other artists. "You [would] find yourself in and out of all these things somewhere or another, because they were all in the same room and they were trying to move them through . . . the whole group was working together, and you'd just be shoved around. So everybody was working on everybody's stuff."[18] He attracted more attention by experimenting with colored Nupastel sticks, which are harder and cleaner than traditional pastels. Sometimes he presented an entire storyboard in color or spotted color sketches throughout. His work sparkled and pleased Walt. Color began appearing on others' storyboards.

Then Disney paired the impressive Grant with William (Bill) Cottrell (1906–1995), an equally impressive writer, who was two years Grant's senior. They became the studio's first story team. "Cottrell was very intelligent in his approach to things," Grant said admiringly.

Cottrell, who hailed from Indiana, moved to Los Angeles in 1923 and attended Occidental College, majoring in journalism. He worked as sportswriter/cartoonist on the *Orange County Plain Dealer* and submitted continuity dialogue and ideas to George Herriman for his *Krazy Kat* comic strip distributed by Hearst.

Joining Disney in 1929, Cottrell became an animation cameraman and editor of foreign versions of the shorts—replacing English titles and signs with foreign inserts. He found both experiences "very helpful" when he moved into story. "I knew how to do it mechanically . . . ideas of how to accomplish something that you wouldn't think of doing before without the knowledge" of camera work and editing.[19]

A talented wordsmith handy with a typewriter, Cottrell contributed continuity ideas and gags to *Three Little Pigs* and other films. When Disney combined Cottrell's literary talents with Grant's visual imagination and drawing ability, wonderful films resulted, including *Three Little Kittens* (1935), which won Disney his fourth Academy Award; *Pluto's Judgement Day* (1935); and *Three Little Wolves* (1936).

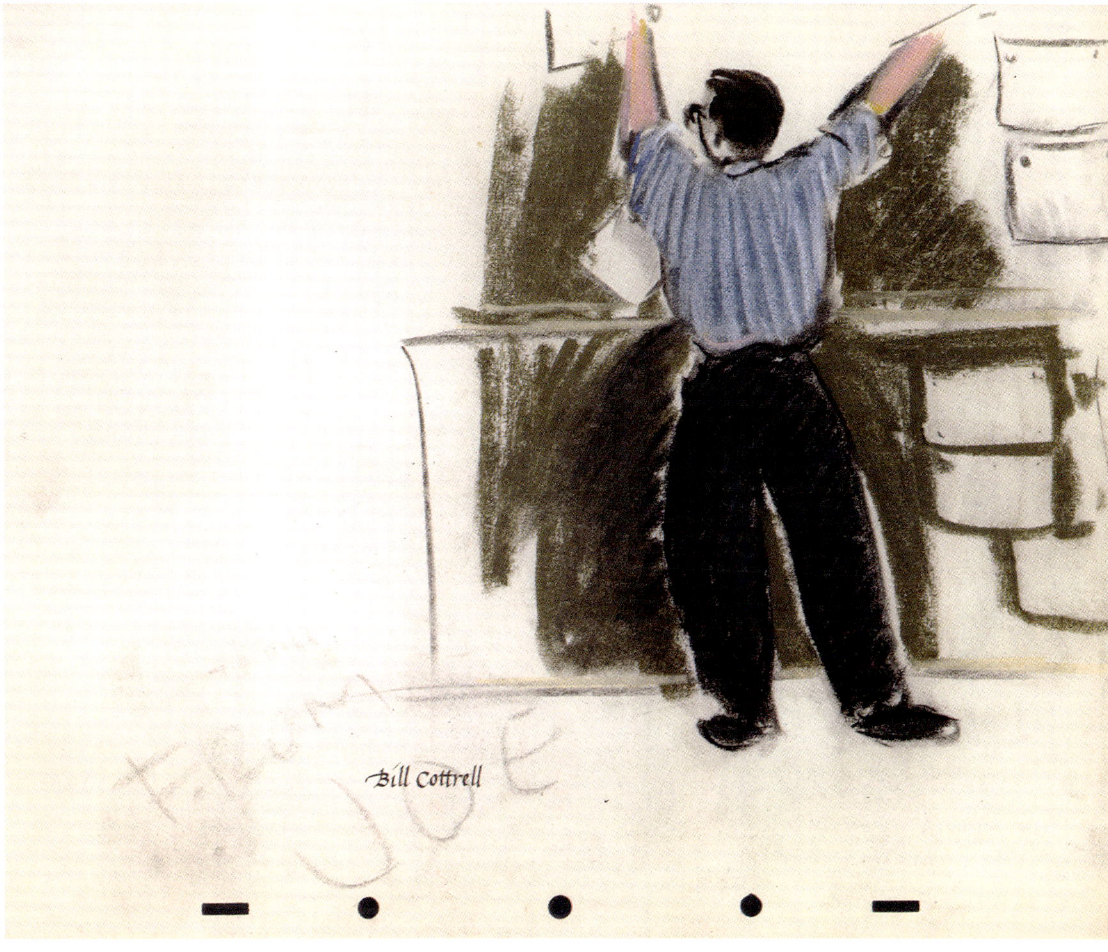

Cottrell, Grant claimed, moved Mickey Mouse, the Depression-era hero, into the middle class when he asked Walt, "Why does Mickey have to sit on a stool with a broken leg, and why does the plaster have to be coming off the wall in every scene? Why does he live in such abject poverty?" Cottrell, said Grant, was "very modest and shy about these ideas, but he was very close to Walt."[20] In 1938, Cottrell married Disney's sister-in-law Hazel Sewell; years later he became an executive at WED, the Disney theme park organization, and eventually president of Retlaw, a Disney family company, retiring in 1982.

Bill and Joe shared newspaper backgrounds as well as "an intellectual bond" and a "wonderful rapport" tossing ideas back and forth all day. Their partnership, Grant said, was "probably one of the most enjoyable times I had."[21]

ABOVE: *Joe Grant caricatures his story partner Bill Cottrell.* BELOW: *Cottrell as animation cameraman in 1929.*

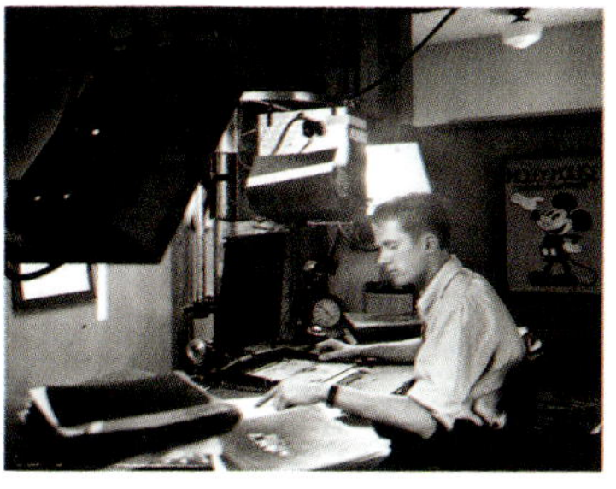

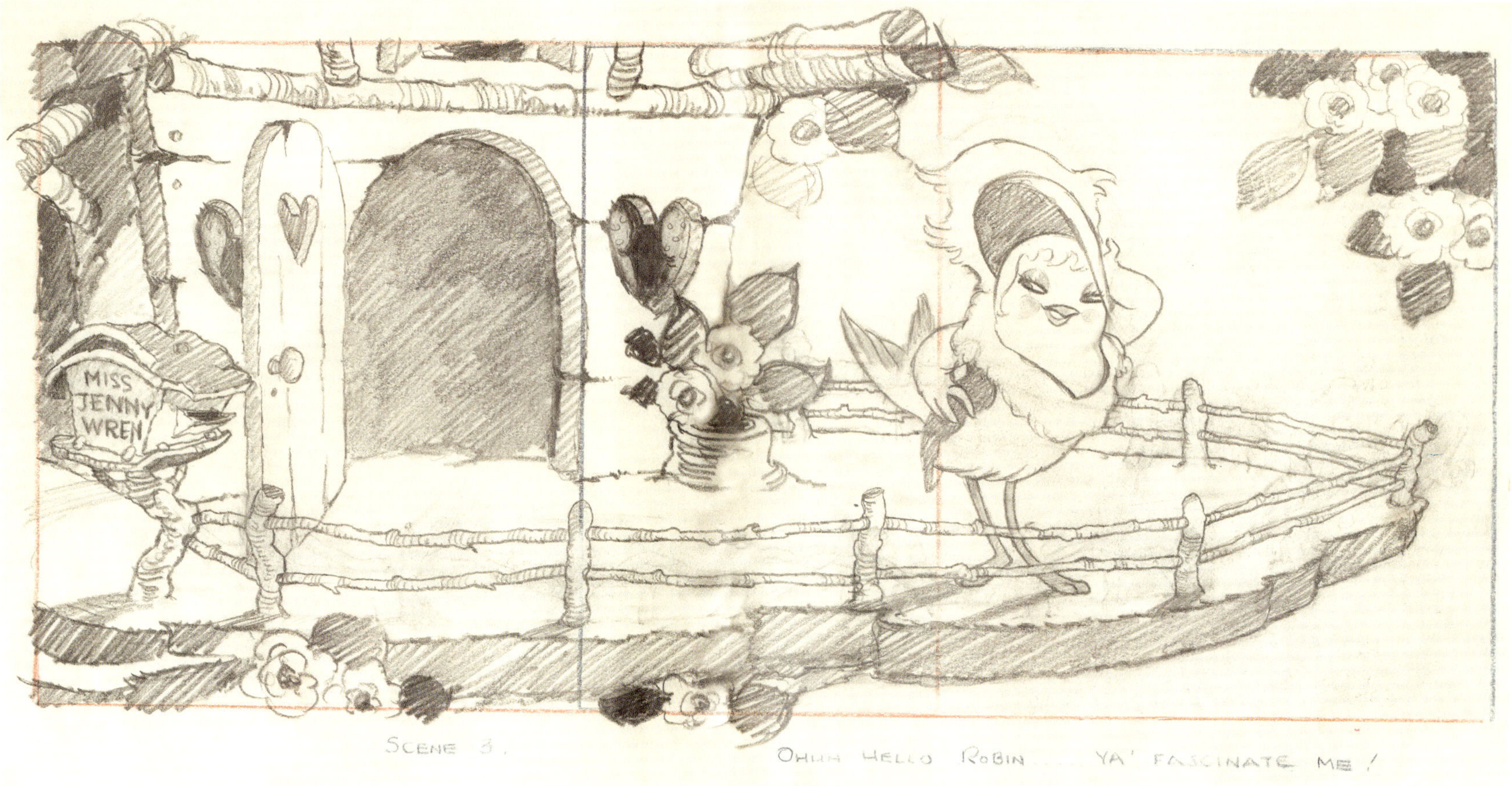

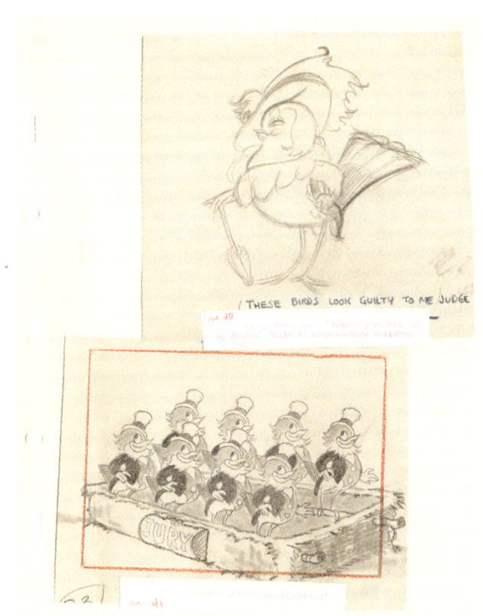

Who Killed Cock Robin? (1935) starred Jenny Wren as an avian Mae West caricature by Joe Grant.

Like Neil Simon's *The Odd Couple*, Cottrell was "Felix" to Grant's "Oscar." At day's end, "everything was askew and all over the place" on Grant's desk. Next morning, thanks to Cottrell, the mess was gone—desk clean, papers filed. It was "sort of a shoemaker and the elves type of thing," Grant remembered. "He was wonderful."[22]

The two bubbled with ideas. Disney memoed Sears that Cottrell and Grant "are very anxious to do the story of Wynken, Blynken, and Nod. I think it is fine . . . [and they are] quite enthused over this Hollywood idea where all the personalities of Hollywood are gathered together in bird and animal form in a big wood called The Hollywoods. . . ."

"We worked well together," Grant said of their partnership, "because I could picture what he had in mind and also ideas of my own. He was a great inspiration to me." Cottrell "brought gentleness and good taste to all his work," wrote Robin Allan, "a foil to [Joe Grant's] satirical sharpness."[23]

Their most attention-grabbing collaboration was the 1935 Silly Symphony *Who Killed Cock Robin?* A witty satire of jurisprudence, *Cock Robin* was an adult-oriented antidote to the more saccharine Symphonies. "We got into the more high-class stuff," as Grant put it.[24] "We were really on our way."[25]

The film contains clever cinematic transitions, such as cross-dissolving from a policeman's truncheon whacking a prisoner's head to a judge's gavel pounding his desk for order in the court to move the plot along. Cottrell suggested Gilbert and Sullivan–like rhymes for the jury. "The satire is dark and brutal, but also mercurial and unpredictable," write Russell Merritt and J. B. Kaufman in *Walt Disney's Silly Symphonies*. "An altogether remarkable film, arguably, along with *The Band Concert*, the most intricately designed short film Disney ever made."[26]

Grant and Cottrell hoped their modern approach in *Cock Robin* would lead to other sophisticated stories, "but it didn't [happen]," Grant said. "Disney couldn't turn the whole studio around to take that view . . . he might have disappointed a lot of his followers."[27] *Cock Robin*'s characters allude to contemporary celebrities, the most direct being voluptuous Jenny Wren, modeled on Mae West. Compared with his tight design of West in *Mickey's Gala Premiere* two years before, this malleable version of the sexy star demonstrates Grant had learned to create flexible freely moving forms.

Grant used bird anatomy selectively to bring forth more Mae West. Her feathered décolletage accents a generous bosom; a large tail gives her body sultry sways. Jenny slowly struts her bodacious stuff, always moving, weaving into and out of West-ian poses (one hand on hip, the other patting her hair); talking seductively out of the side of her tiny mouth; pointing her parasol to insinuate and excite the judge (an old owl) and jury (lustful as bald-headed men in the front row of a burlesque theater).

Something magical happens when Jenny Wren appears. Grant's design and Hamilton Luske's subtle animation encouraged Disney that he could make a feature with believable, credible cartoons. Grant's eye-appealing animation designs registered strongly with Disney.

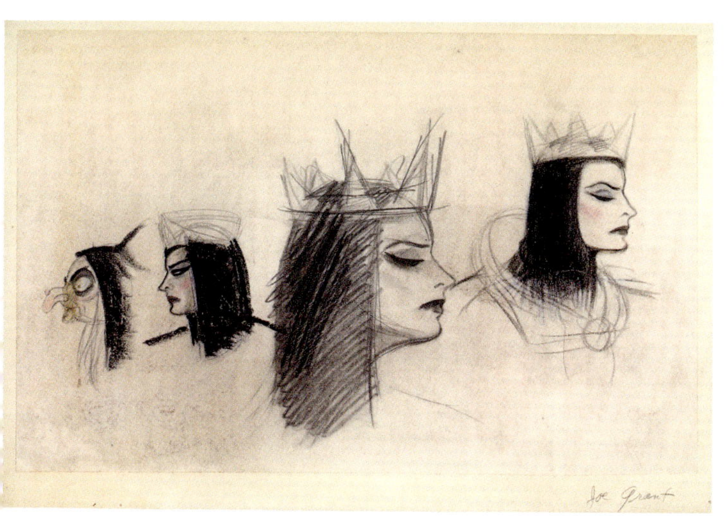

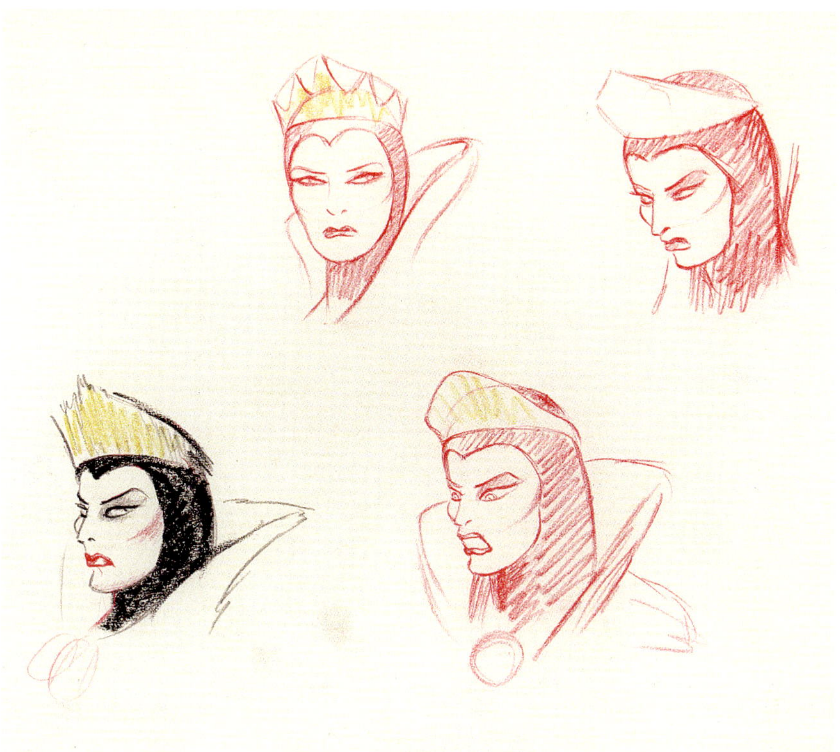

By 1936, Grant and Cottrell were developing the narrative for *Snow White and the Seven Dwarfs*. Grant often suggested visual accents emphasizing mood or action; for instance, in a June 25, 1936, story meeting when Disney suggests the huntsman draw his knife while moving toward Snow White, Grant comments: "We just get a flash of the knife as it is being pulled." Walt repeats the suggestion ("We just flash on the shining article . . ."), giving it his blessing. The histrionic touch appears in the film. [28]

Cottrell and Grant were assigned the "witch" sequences: the evil queen's transformation into a hag. "Maybe we just had a flair or interest in the melodramatic," said Cottrell, the sequence director.[29] For mood they referenced Hermann Vogel, whom they referred to as "Hank Bird," playing off the English translation of his surname.[30] Shakespeare's witches in *Macbeth* inspired the bubbling potion that changes the queen into a toothless crone.

Grant's queen—high cheekbones, cruel mouth, elegant bearing—was modeled on Joan Crawford,

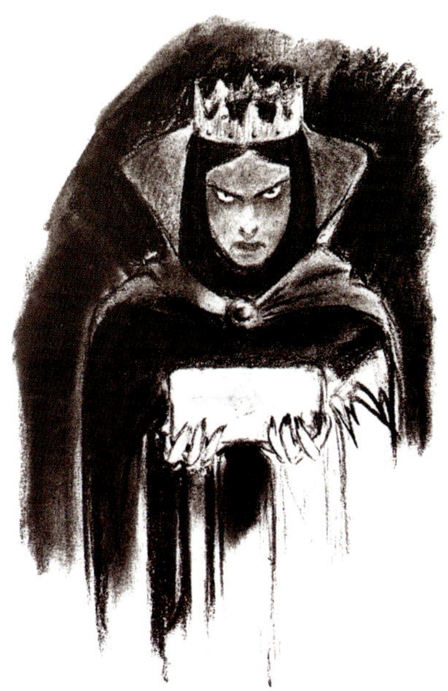

Joe Grant's concept drawings for the wicked queen in Snow White and the Seven Dwarfs *(1937).*

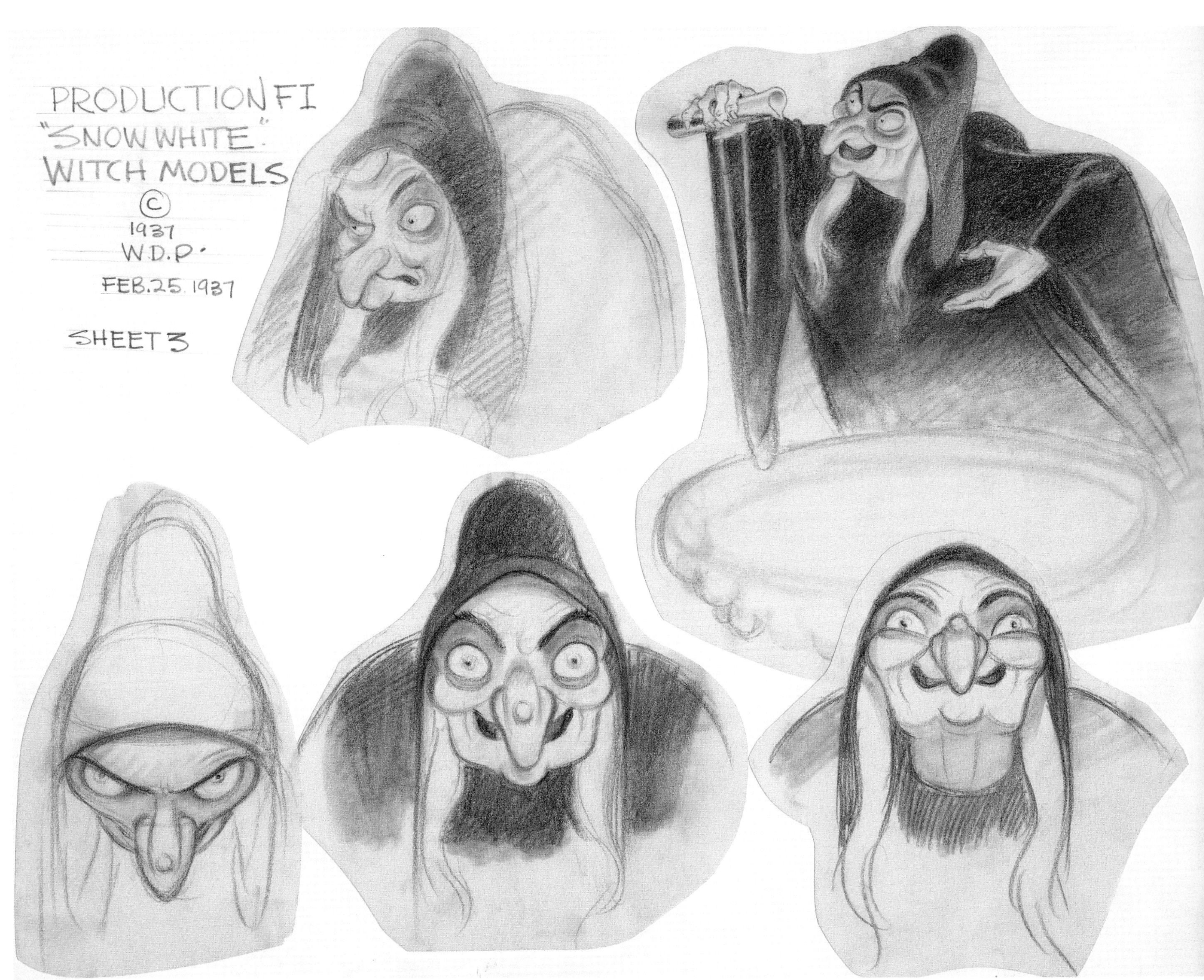

ABOVE AND OPPOSITE: *Grant's designs and idea sketches for the witch in* SNOW WHITE AND THE SEVEN DWARFS.

Katharine Hepburn, Helen Gahagan (as the immortal queen in *She* [1935]), and papier-mâché masks by W. T. Benda. The crone's influences were more eclectic, from Lionel Barrymore's granny drag performance in *The Devil Doll* (1935) to an elderly neighbor with a warty nose who lived across the street from Grant. "She had a basket and used to pick persimmons," Grant said. "I changed persimmons to apples."[31]

Veteran actress Lucille La Verne's performance in *A Tale of Two Cities* (1935) as "The Vengeance" also inspired. In fact, she recorded the voices for *Snow White*'s queen *and* hag, the latter performed with juicy gusto after removing her teeth!

Only Grant and Albert Hurter received "Character Designer" screen credit in *Snow White*. Grant's queen and witch stylings are permanent symbols of "evil" in Disney iconography; after seven decades, they still scare the curds and whey out of children.

Animators continued to grumble about Grant. He "was always drawing stuff that we couldn't do," said one. "It was always pastel." Grant infuriated them and (they felt) undercut them when he'd ask Walt disingenuously, "Why can't the animators do this?"

Animator Ollie Johnston voiced a common suspicion of Grant: "I think he had his personal agenda." Johnston's colleague Frank Thomas recalled, "He had these drawings always ready to show Walt at an opportune moment [and he'd] wait till Walt was talking about something that wasn't quite coming off. 'Well, uh, I was working last night, Walt, and, uh. . .' Walt'd say, 'Whatcha got there, Joe?' Out would come a little pastel sketch from Joe's inside pocket. 'Yah! Hey guys. Come look at this!' We'd say, 'Well, Walt, ya can't . . .' Well, you didn't say can't or don't or won't to Walt. You'd say with gritted teeth, 'Yeah, that looks pretty good. Heh-heh.'"[32]

Some directors and production managers resented Grant's closeness to Walt the Sun King. After a long day, he'd invite Joe to discuss (over sherry) current and future productions and (it was assumed) personnel. "Joe Grant really had [Walt's] ear," observed one artist, "and he could sell him stuff any time he wanted. He could just walk in on Walt any time he wanted. Joe was very good and brash enough to do this and lucky enough to get away with it."[33]

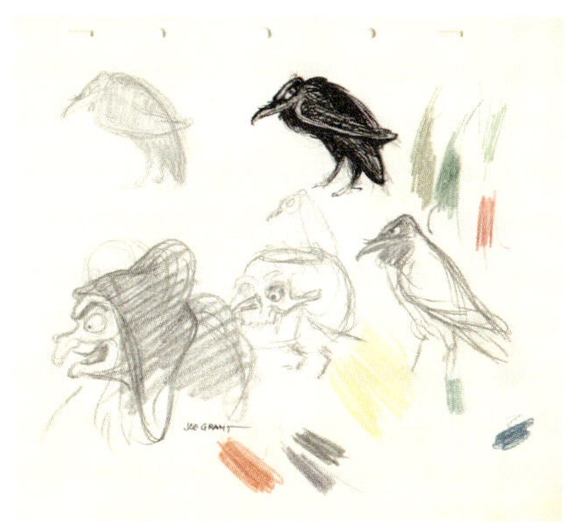

Among the rank-and-file animators, Grant was considered an empire builder and power seeker. A whiff of casual anti-Semitism was in the air. "He was the one guy in the studio I could compare to the

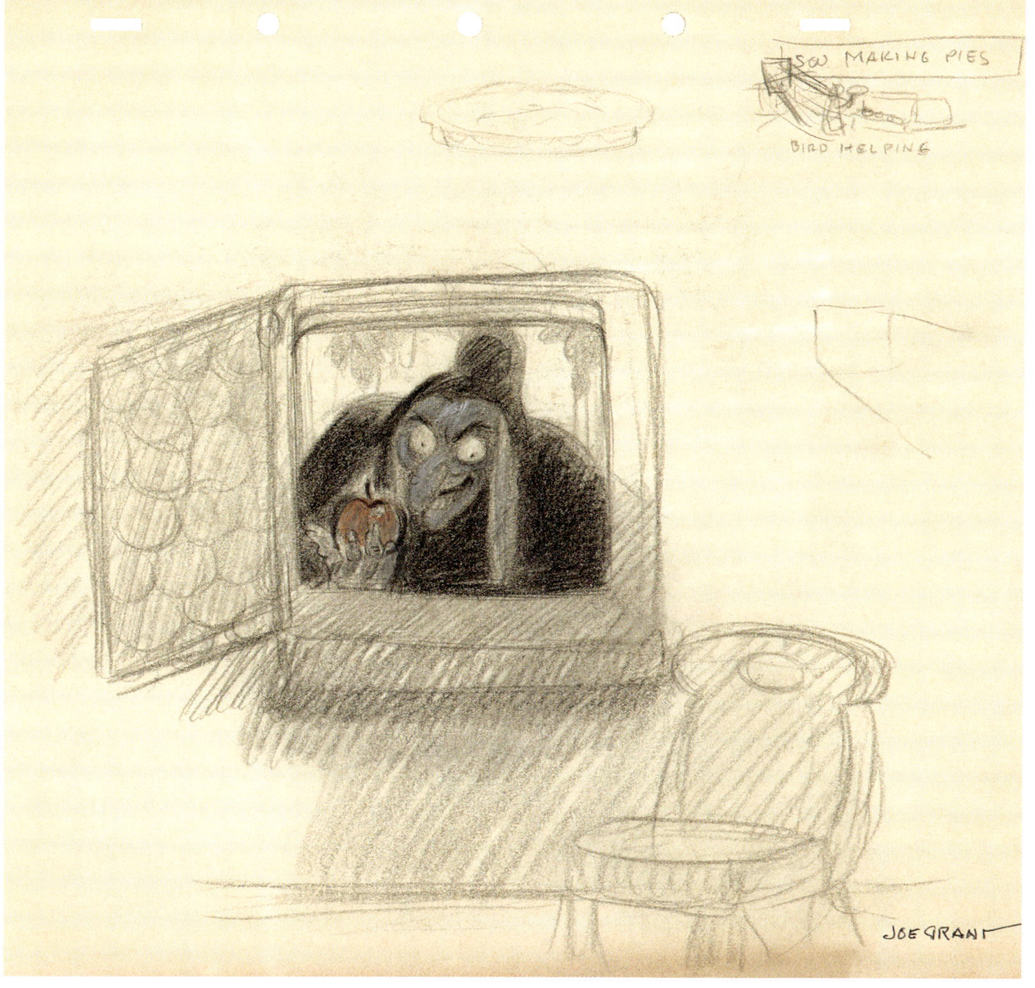

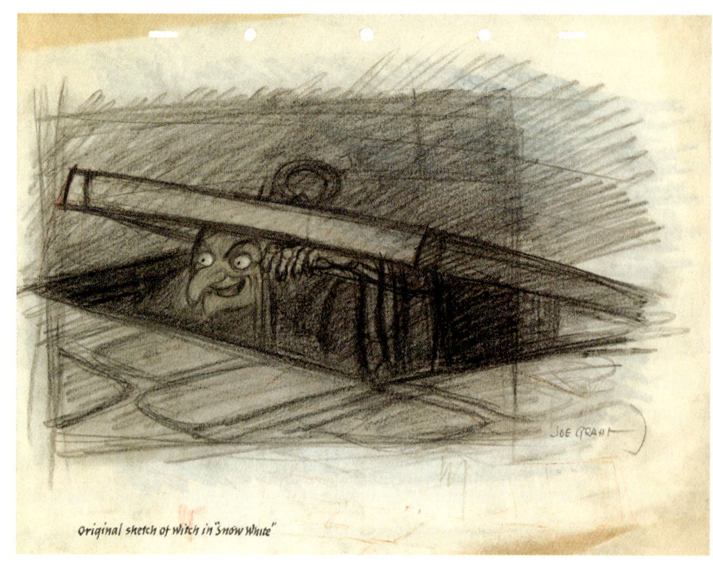

legendary Sammy Glick," animator Ward Kimball said. He referred to the protagonist of Budd Schulberg's 1941 novel, *What Makes Sammy Run?*, an uneducated newspaper copyboy who spurns his Jewish heritage and backstabs his way to become a top Hollywood screenwriter. "He was a born operator," Kimball said of Grant. "He was very ambitious."[34] Disney's next move exacerbated the seething jealousy of Grant.

In 1937, before *Snow White* opened, Disney "came down the hall and said, 'Joe, what are we going to do for an encore?'" It was his Delphic way of asking (ordering) Grant to set up a new department of "inspirational sketch artists," a "think tank" to develop stories and characters. The Character Model Department began on October 11, 1937, as indicated on Grant's personnel record. For his new duties he was paid $200 a week, a high salary for the time. In less than a year it was raised another $100.[35] Grant was excited by the new opportunity, but saddened that Disney had other plans for his friend Cottrell. "He didn't include Bill in it," Grant said. "He just decided I was the one to take it over, so that was it. But it was typical of him to divide and conquer."

Grant felt it was characteristic of Disney's management style to prevent challenges to his power. "Disney had something within him that if we got too chummy, too close, and maybe too successful, he'd break it up."[36]

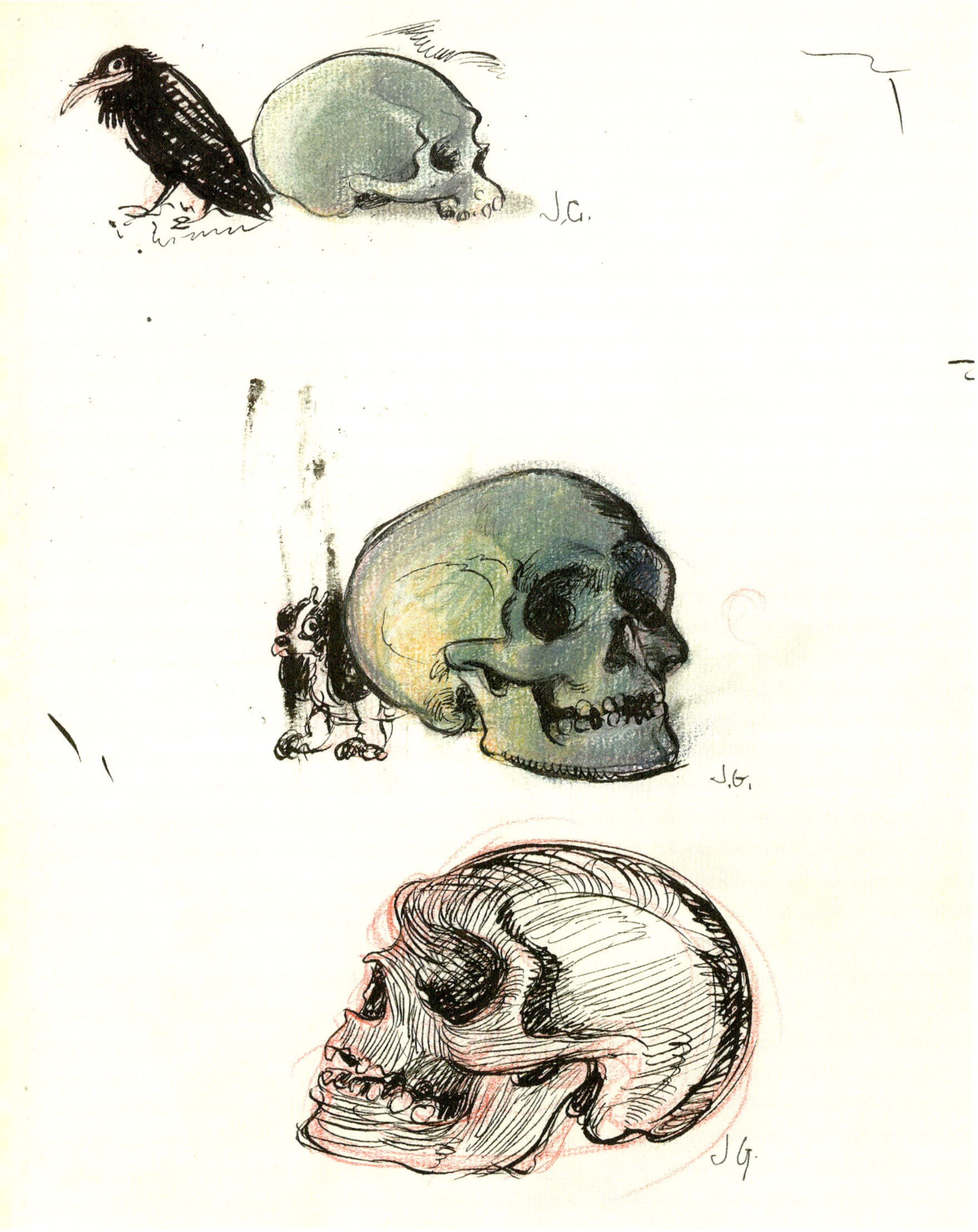

THIS PAGE AND OPPOSITE: *Snow White and the Seven Dwarfs' raven, witch, and Magic Mirror mask, designed by Joe Grant.*

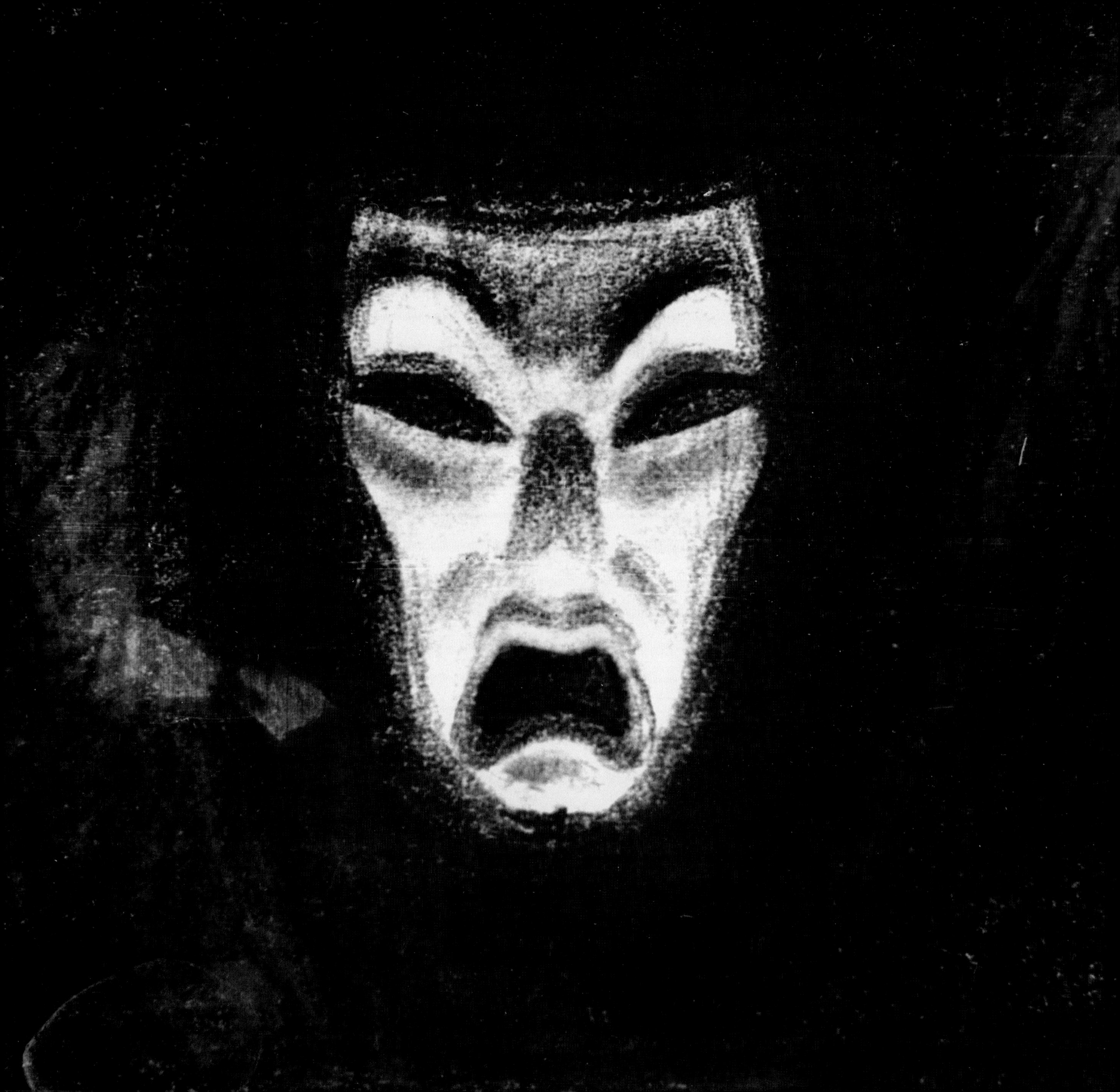

CHARACTER MODEL DEP'T.
O.K. by JG DATE 12-16-38
NUMBER M162-C
MODEL SHEETS SUBJECT TO RECALL
WITHOUT NOTICE
© Walt Disney Enterprises

Grant's ambitions for his Character Model Department were high. He saw it as a means to advance his and Disney's vaulting, expansive dreams for the art of animation.

"I was enthusiastic as hell about [animation]," Grant said. "I thought it was the greatest thing. I couldn't think of anything beyond it. All the great art of the past, all the achievement, there couldn't have been anything like this. I imagine people who did tapestries in the seventeenth century felt the same way. You know, 'Look what I'm making!'"[1]

The new department initially consisted of three people researching fairy- and folk-tales, children's books, short stories, and novels. It grew "one by one," Grant said, "as talent came up, why we'd grab 'em off. We could be very selective and get the best people." The main qualification was imagination and the ability to draw anything easily. He hired an eclectic group of marvelous graphic artists, illustrators, and sculptors from inside and outside the studio, including John Parr (Jack) Miller, Bob Jones, Martin Provensen, Campbell Grant (no relation to Joe), John Walbridge, Fini Rudiger, Charles Cristadoro, Helen Nerbovig, Duke Russell, Del Connell, Earl Hurd, Bill Wallett, Wah Ming Chang, Tom Codrick, Mary Blair, Aurelius Battaglia, James Bodrero, Albert Hurter, and, among others, Kay Nielsen, estimable designer of deluxe European fairy-tale books.[2]

The studio was bursting at the seams. Walls were demolished in a bungalow across Hyperion Avenue to accommodate the new department. Story meetings for *Pinocchio* began in late 1937 and Walt, flush with profits from the success of *Snow White*, soon okayed a "Concert Feature" (*Fantasia*, to be produced concurrent with *Pinocchio*) and (later) a feature about a baby elephant named Dumbo.

For *Pinocchio*, Grant's department drew suggestions for characters, props, costumes, and settings to guide layout and story artists and animators. "Their first challenge was to define the appearance of the main characters," wrote sculptor/puppeteer Bob Jones. Pinocchio alone took twelve artists (including Jones, Joe Grant, Campbell Grant, Jack Miller, and Martin Provensen, and animators Frank Thomas, Ollie Johnston, Fred Moore, Les Clark, and

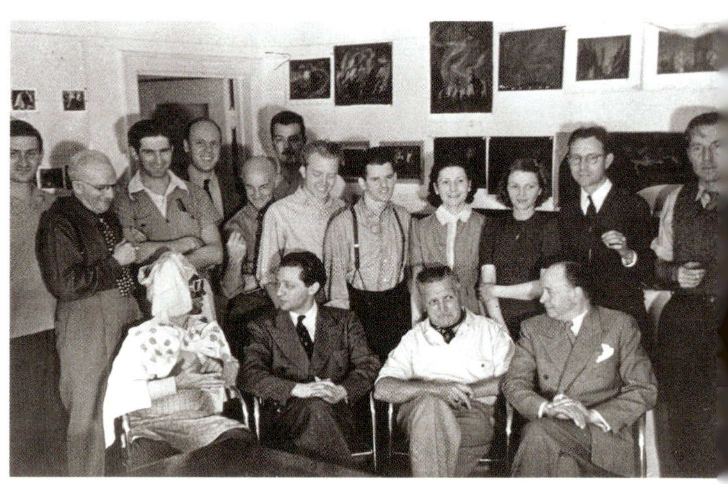

Members of Joe Grant's Character Model Department celebrate his thirty-first birthday in 1939. STANDING LEFT TO RIGHT: *James Bodrero, Earl Hurd, unknown, Bill Jones, unknown, Duke Russell, Martin Provensen, Jack Miller, Helen Nerbovig, unknown, John Walbridge, and Bill Wallett.* SEATED LEFT TO RIGHT: *Campbell Grant, Joe Grant, Albert Hurter, and Kay Nielsen.*

Milt Kahl) and eighteen months to "transform a stiff wooden figure into the lovable little character" finally seen on the screen. Disney considered the first design "too brash and lacking in appeal," so animation was delayed. The final version (dated February 20, 1939), based on drawings by Kahl, also served as model for a Pinocchio marionette made by Jones, Cristadoro, and Chang for animation study and publicity purposes.[3]

Hurter drew Geppetto's *gemütlich* toy shop containing rococo cuckoo clocks and mechanical dolls, various other characters, a village setting, even a giant anthropomorphic tree who was Pinocchio's real "father" and resembled Geppetto. The tree doesn't appear in the film, but it's an example of Grant's department's imaginative explorations. Jack Miller (later a beloved Golden Book illustrator) designed the children in Pinocchio's village; Campbell Grant fashioned Stromboli the evil puppeteer, Figaro the cat, and Cleo the goldfish. Joe Grant kept his hand in "inventing peripheral characters like Jiminy Cricket," said Martin Provensen; or rather *reinventing* the cricket who was killed early on in the original story. Grant's cricket wasn't as cute as Walt wanted, so it was redesigned by the cricket's animator, Ward Kimball. When Aurelius Battaglia drew a funny speculative sequence with fox and cat comic villains, Grant showed it to Walt, and it was immediately picked up for development. "It was through things like that," Provensen said, that the Model Department quickly "became a story department."

Grant made sure his department was integral to Disney's storytelling process. Several features released through 1955 originated or were developed there. Some never progressed beyond exploratory sketches, such as *Don Quixote* or Hans Christian Andersen's *The Little Fir Tree, The Emperor's New Clothes,* and *Through the Picture Frame.* Nor did several witty original stories devised by Grant,

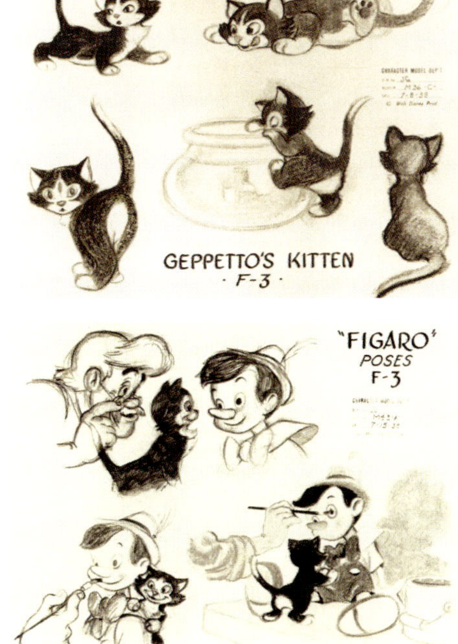

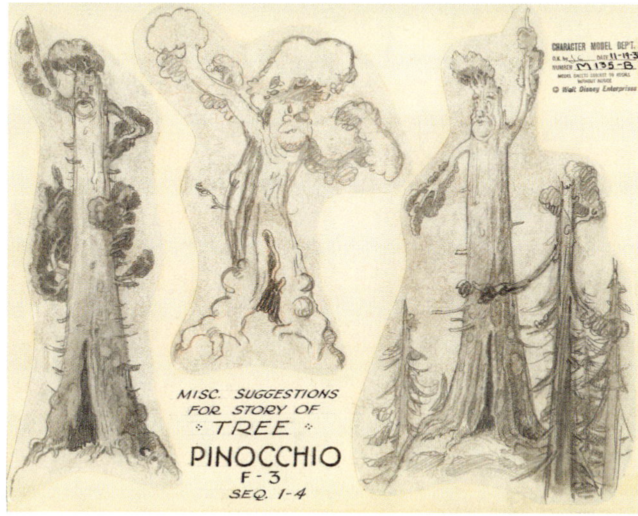

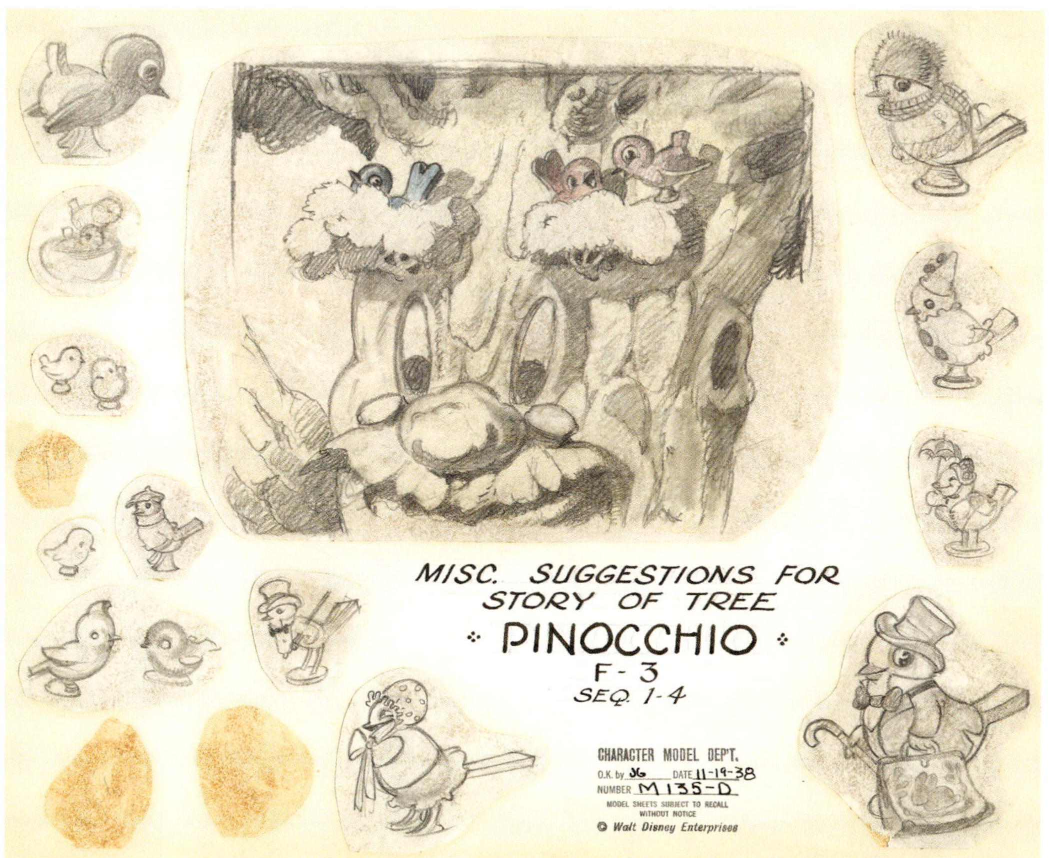

Model sheets approved by Joe Grant for Pinocchio *(1940).*

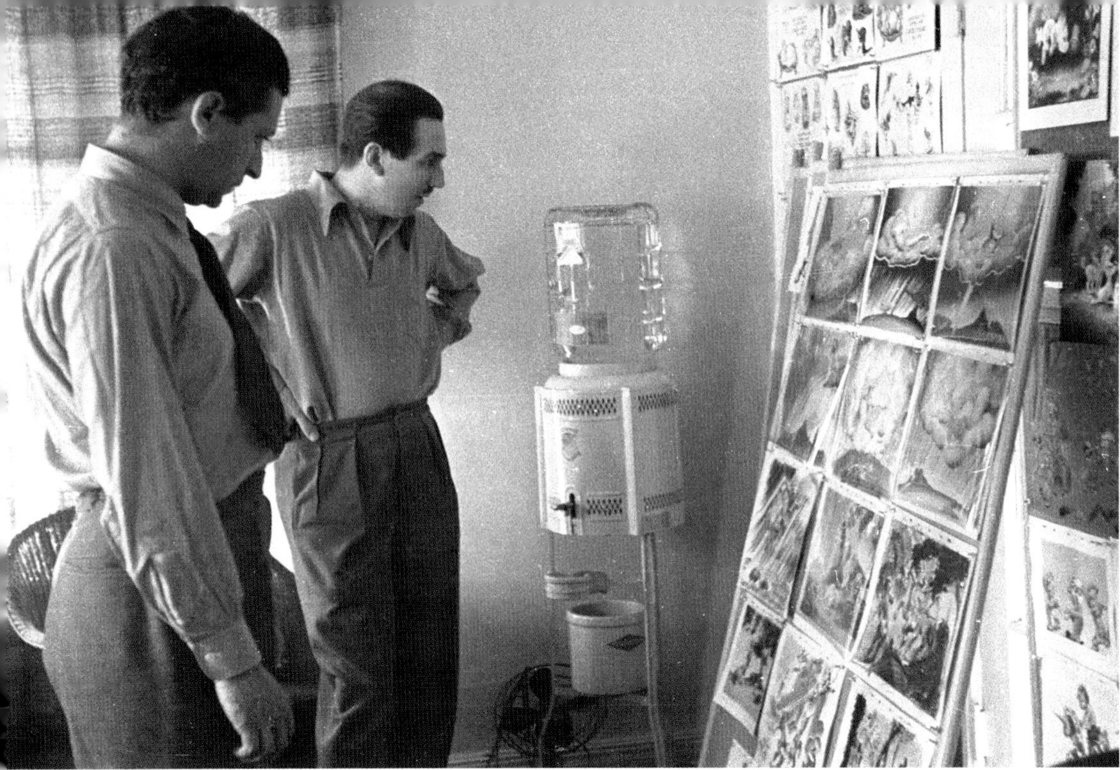

ABOVE: *Joe Grant* (LEFT) *and Walt Disney, c. 1939, assess concept art for the "Pastoral" sequence in* FANTASIA. BELOW: *Character Model Department artist Martin Provensen.*

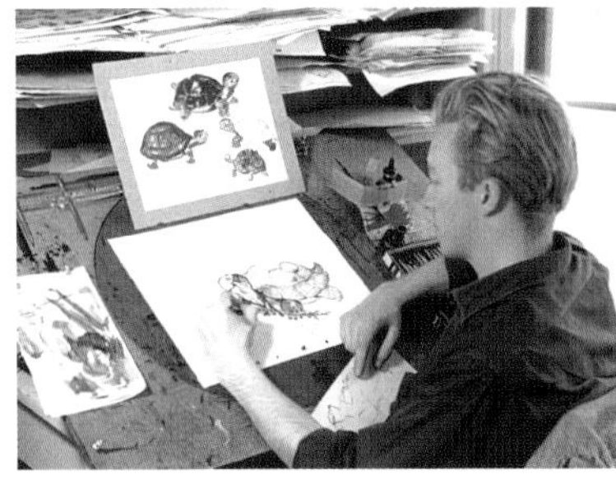

including *Roland the 13th* (a World War I pigeon spy) and *The Square World* (about conformism and totalitarianism). *Alice in Wonderland*, *Peter Pan*, *Wind in the Willows*, and *Lady and the Tramp* appeared years later.

In Character Model, ideas poured forth in evocative gouache, oil, watercolor, pastel, and charcoal drawings. Once, the artists experimented with magnetized white silhouettes animated in stop-motion on a black magnetized sheet. "We tried all kinds of things," Grant said proudly.[4]

Martin Provensen recalled that drawings were everywhere and individual drawings "had no particular value or meaning."

> [Drawing] was seen as the currency of the day. It was like words with writers, you know? . . . the raw material and you poured these drawings out. Looking back now, I realize it was the best training in the world for an illustrator because you were endlessly visualizing, on paper, every kind of possible idea . . . [The studio] would throw things at you that would, on the face of it, seem impossible to draw . . . And you found a way, somehow. Somebody would find a way to do it.

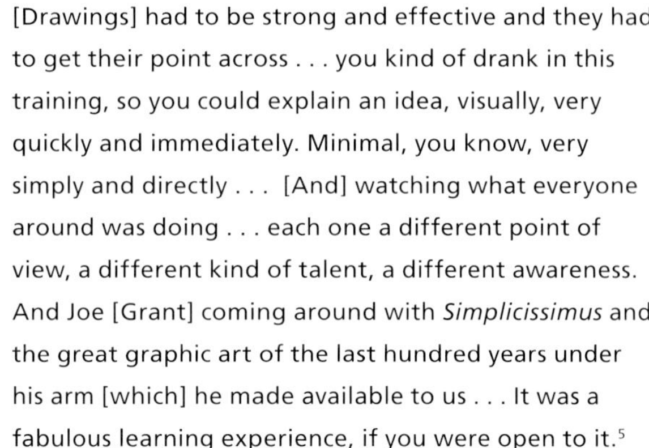

> [Drawings] had to be strong and effective and they had to get their point across . . . you kind of drank in this training, so you could explain an idea, visually, very quickly and immediately. Minimal, you know, very simply and directly . . . [And] watching what everyone around was doing . . . each one a different point of view, a different kind of talent, a different awareness. And Joe [Grant] coming around with *Simplicissimus* and the great graphic art of the last hundred years under his arm [which] he made available to us . . . It was a fabulous learning experience, if you were open to it.[5]

Grant inspected all work and selected key poses, which were cut out and mounted onto cardboard to become "model sheets" for copying and distribution to production units. "No model sheet of characters was official until it bore the seal, 'OK, J.G.,'" wrote Frank Thomas and Ollie Johnston in *Disney Animation: The Illusion of Life*, acknowledging Joe Grant as "the studio's authority on the design and appearance of nearly everything that moved on the screen, and his taste and judgment were largely responsible for the pleasing style that identified the Disney product."[6]

The Model Department became Walt Disney's playground. He crossed Hyperion Avenue to visit two or three times daily. "Because that was a brain trust where he could try out new ideas," Grant said.[7] He would "sit down and look at a drawing and come up with an idea. Or he would say we can put this here and put that there and so on. It was a think tank. And we were happy with that."[8]

Grant described his brainstorming with Disney as "competitive" and "a ping-pong game."[9] Grant analyzed and accommodated Walt's mind. "Walt was a brain picker," he said. "If you came up with a good novelty idea . . . he would grow with it. This we made a point of doing. I didn't allow them to just make random sketches. Each thing had to be significant. It may not have been in continuity, but they would throw him off on another track and that always excited him. And us, too, for that matter."[10]

Campbell Grant, later an illustrator and Native American rock-art expert, remembered Joe's "tremendous faculty of being very simpatico with Disney, who admired his mind. Joe could always talk to him, which was not always easy. In half an hour he could throw at Walt six or seven ideas and maybe half of them sounded pretty damned good. He had a very fertile mind, and he was always coming up with strange and interesting ideas."[11]

Well organized, Grant ran his department "quite loosely," allowing his artists considerable autonomy. "Every three or four days, he'd breeze in and say, 'Well, what have we got to talk about?'"[12] To Martin Provensen, Grant was "first of all, a very clever man."

> He was much more sophisticated, aesthetically, than a great many of the people [at the studio]. He introduced all of us to many European artists, like Walter Trier and Gus Botha . . . He was up on the stuff. He knew about it and none of the rest of us did . . . He had an omnivorous curiosity about graphics. . . .

Overall, Provensen thought Joe "was a remarkable man, and Disney never knew how to use him very well because he wasn't in the mainstream of the Disney cartoon point of view. He was more European, more . . . interested in peripheral aspects of drawing . . . and I think he might have done the studio a lot of good if he had had the opportunity to pursue that."[13]

Disney's cryptic remark ("The model sheets establish what the character looks like, but something else is needed.") triggered expansion into three-dimensional models ("maquettes"). Bob Jones, a puppeteer, suggested hiring sculptors, and Grant subsequently employed Ted Kline, Lorna (Shirley) Soderstrom, Duke Russell, and Charles Cristadoro to model small figures in clay and plasticine. Helen Nerbovig and other Ink and Paint Department women painted them.

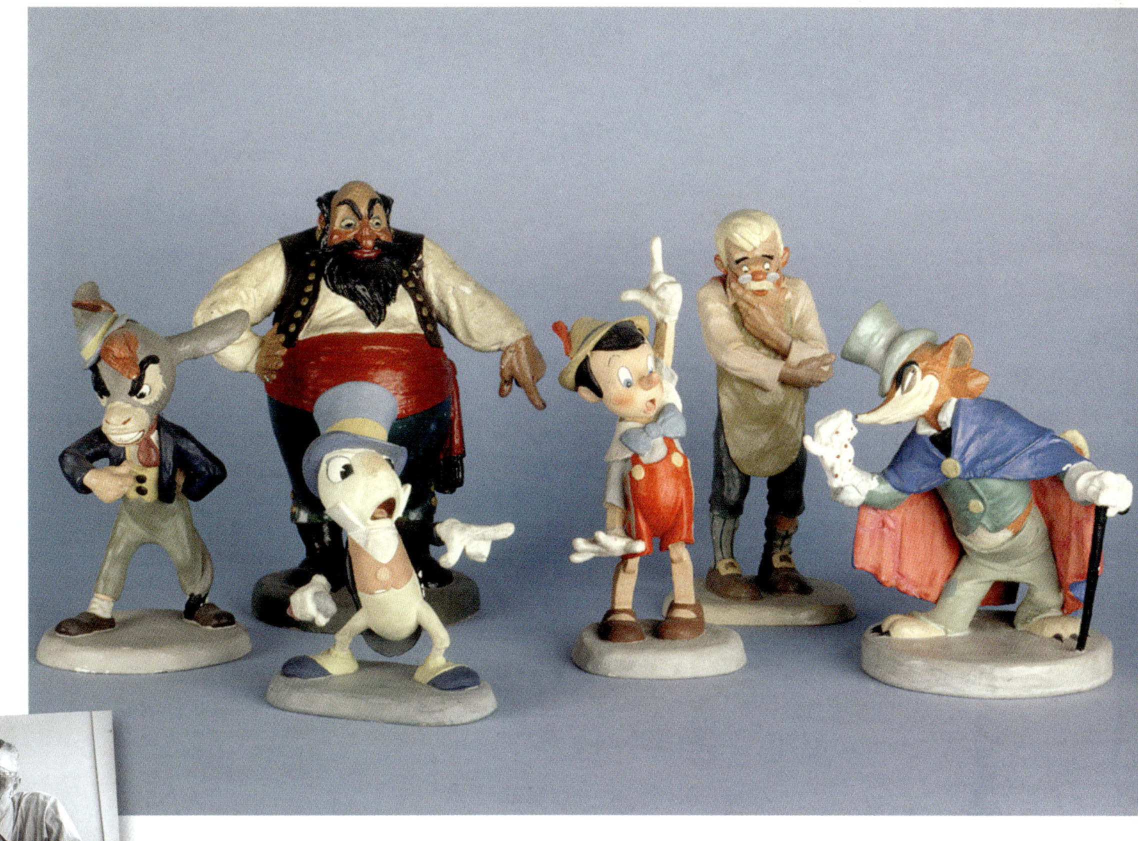

ABOVE, *Pinocchio character maquettes.* LEFT: *Character Model sculptor Charles Cristadoro.*

Grant was fascinated with making terra-cotta ceramics; during *Snow White*, he made a 3-D model of the hag that Disney admired. Grant installed a kiln in his backyard and on weekends shared his hobby with Miller and Provensen, who dropped by to sculpt, bake, and glaze fantastic creatures.

Bob and Bill Jones managed the maquette area, which resembled a magic toy shop. The Joneses also built three-dimensional props—cuckoo clocks, a Gypsy wagon, fully articulated marionettes, and a whale (outside and inside its belly) for *Pinocchio*; planets, volcanoes, and a miniature earthquake set for *Fantasia*'s special effects. The department supervised costumes and makeup for the live-action cinematography of actors and dancers that animators used for reference.

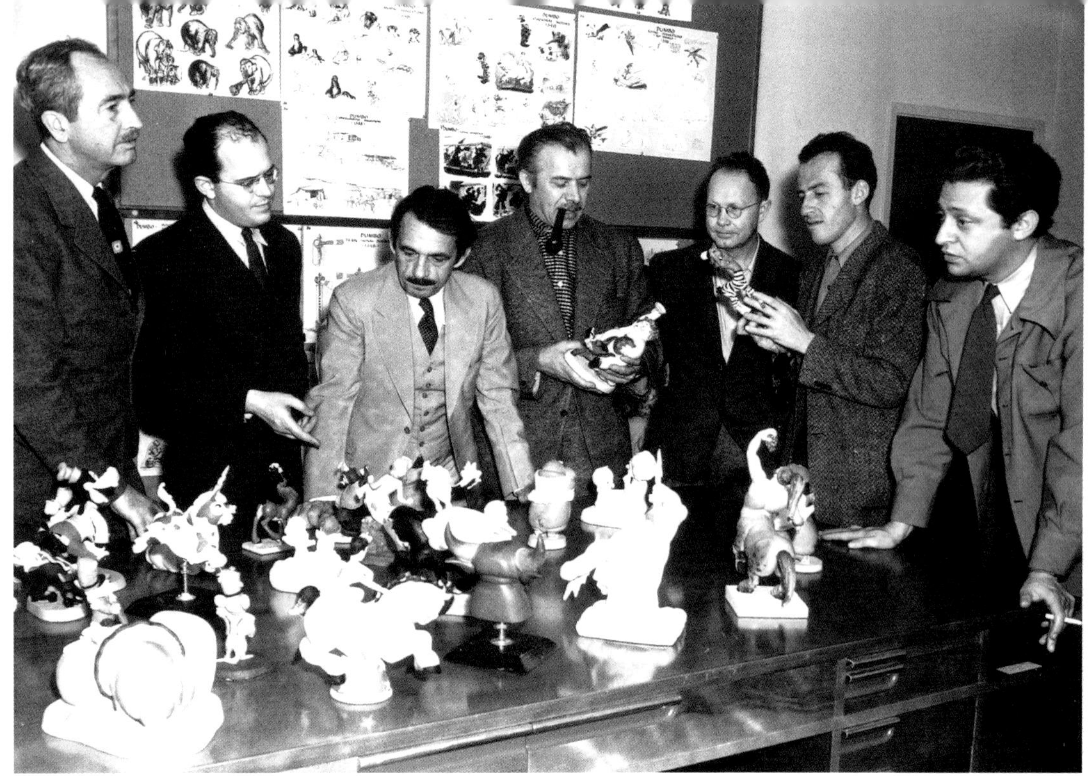

ABOVE: *Joe Grant* (FAR RIGHT) *meets with Associated American Artists members visiting the Disney Studio in May 1940, including* (LEFT TO RIGHT) *George Biddle, Reeves Lowenthal, Thomas Hart Benton, Ernest Fiene, Grant Wood, and George Schreiber.* BELOW: *Dick Huemer* (LEFT) *and Grant confer with* FANTASIA *narrator Deems Taylor.* BELOW, RIGHT: *Huemer as seen by Grant.*

As *Pinocchio* moved through the pipeline, Disney assigned Grant to the concert feature taking shape. The oak that became *Fantasia* started as an acorn: a Mickey Mouse short based on Paul Dukas's *The Sorcerer's Apprentice*. Leopold Stokowski conducted the score and Disney's expansionist instincts were excited. He decided to string classical pieces together to form a movie concert.

Grant became *Fantasia*'s "story director," in addition to supervising the Character Model Department. He would help Disney, Stokowski, and music critic Deems Taylor select the music and concoct visualizations. Disney partnered Grant with Richard (Dick) Huemer (1898–1979), ten years his senior and a self-described "disappointed novelist."

Huemer was an animation pioneer. His career began as a teenager in the Bronx, New York, at Raoul Barre's, the first animation studio. At Max Fleischer's studio in the 1920s, Huemer gained a reputation as one of his generation's finest animators. He "helped build the early framework of animation," wrote a peer.[14]

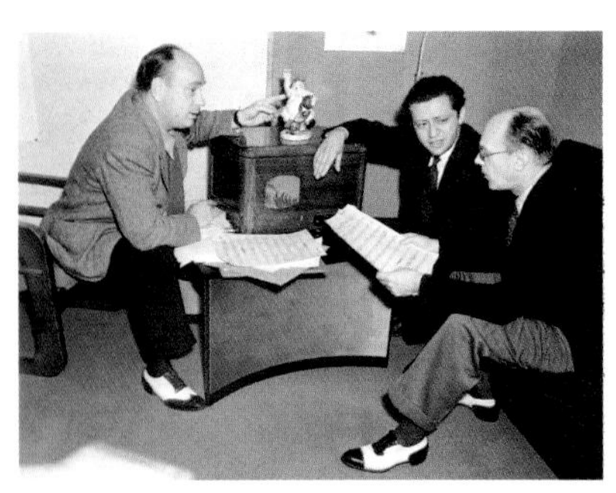

Huemer started at Disney in 1933, happy to be "associated with a genius." He contributed animation to twenty-five Mickey Mouse and Silly Symphony shorts, directed two shorts, plus a discarded sequence in *Snow White* and the opening scenes in *Pinocchio*. His and Grant's task for *Fantasia* was to "get this monster off the ground."

"Walt came over," Grant recalled, "and said, 'I've got Dick Huemer here. Anything you can do with him?' I found out he could use a typewriter and we went from there. We got to talking story and began developing [*Fantasia*]. We had a good relationship."[15]

In fact, Grant found this partnership as creative as his earlier one with Bill Cottrell. Again there was an intellectual kinship. "[Huemer] was a wise and witty man, a droll man who, in a quiet way, pulled rugs from under pompous and false heroes, transformed giants into pygmies and inauspiciously extracted teeth from snarling paper lions," wrote animator Grim Natwick. It is a description that could suffice for Grant as well.[16] Both men were urbane bootstrappers who grew up in big cities and supported themselves as young men. Each cast a gimlet eye on life and shared a sense of humor alternately cynical and warmhearted. Both enjoyed literature and the sophisticated wit of *The New Yorker* and *Vanity Fair* and were knowledgeable regarding art, history, and music. Huemer studied violin, and Grant's grandfather was, as noted, a violinist and his father a pianist.[17] "Not only was Dick

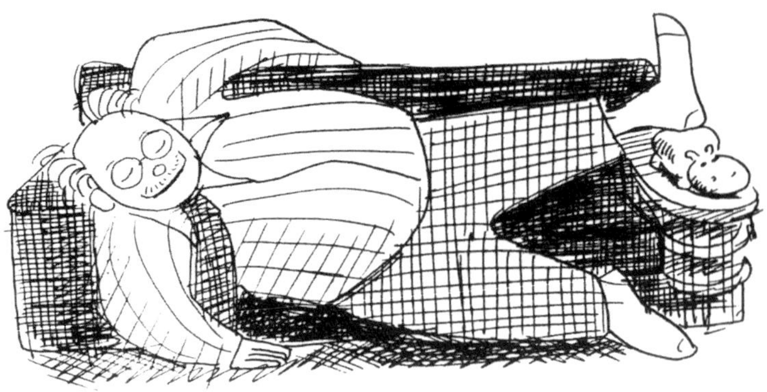

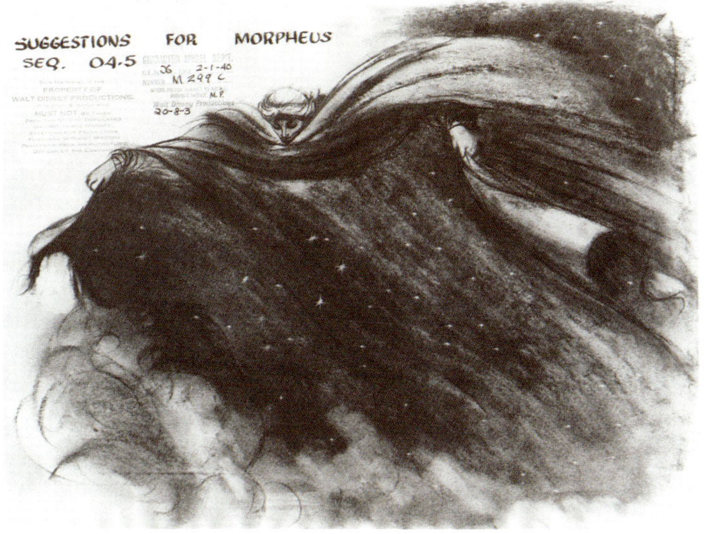

a great animator," said animator Shamus Culhane, "he was also a gourmet and a true bon vivant. Why he even went to the opera!" The latter fact was Disney's reason for assigning him to *Fantasia*. "Meet Dick Huemer. He goes to operas," was his bumptious way of introducing him to studio visitors.

In September 1938, Grant and Huemer attended story meetings with Disney, Stokowski, and Taylor, listening to recordings of classical pieces day after day "until our ears were stopped up with it." They sought "story music," something in a composition suggesting a visualization. "There's always a good story in a good piece of music," Grant believed.[18]

Grant and Huemer accompanied Disney to Philadelphia, where Stokowski and the Philadephia Orchestra recorded Bach's *Toccata & Fugue in D*, Stravinsky's *Rite of Spring*, Beethoven's *Pastoral* Symphony, Tchaikovsky's *Nutcracker Suite*, Moussorgsky's *Night on Bald Mountain*, Ponchielli's *Dance of the Hours*, and Schubert's *Ave Maria* in "Fantasound," an early version of stereo. Before and after the sound track recording, enchanting drawings appeared on Character Model drawing boards. Fauns, Pegasus, Sugar Plum Fairies, a tyrannosaurus, the devil on Bald Mountain, hippos in tutus, alligators in cloaks, Bacchus, Zeus, and balletic mushrooms were some of the creatures that found their way to the screen. Grant and Huemer guided the phantasms from conception to story.

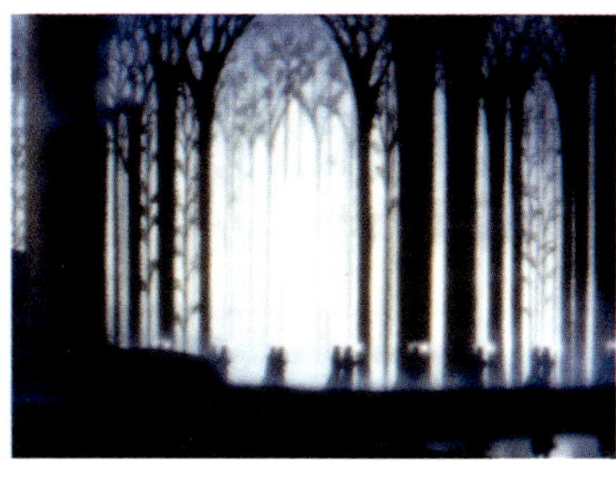

ABOVE: *Ave Maria's cathedral forest.* LEFT: *model sheet for Morpheus in* FANTASIA. BELOW: *Joe Grant's ideas for* FANTASIA*'s sorcerer.*

Grant, as always, contributed ideas. He fashioned concepts for the eerie wizard in *The Sorcerer's Apprentice*, suggested that the devil's wings unfold atop Bald Mountain, and that the forest in the *Ave Maria* finale resembles stained glass windows. He continued to be the go-to guy for caricatures, as seen in *The Autograph Hound* (1939).[19] But Grant's administrative responsibilities as Disney's confidant/adviser on all projects often prevented him from

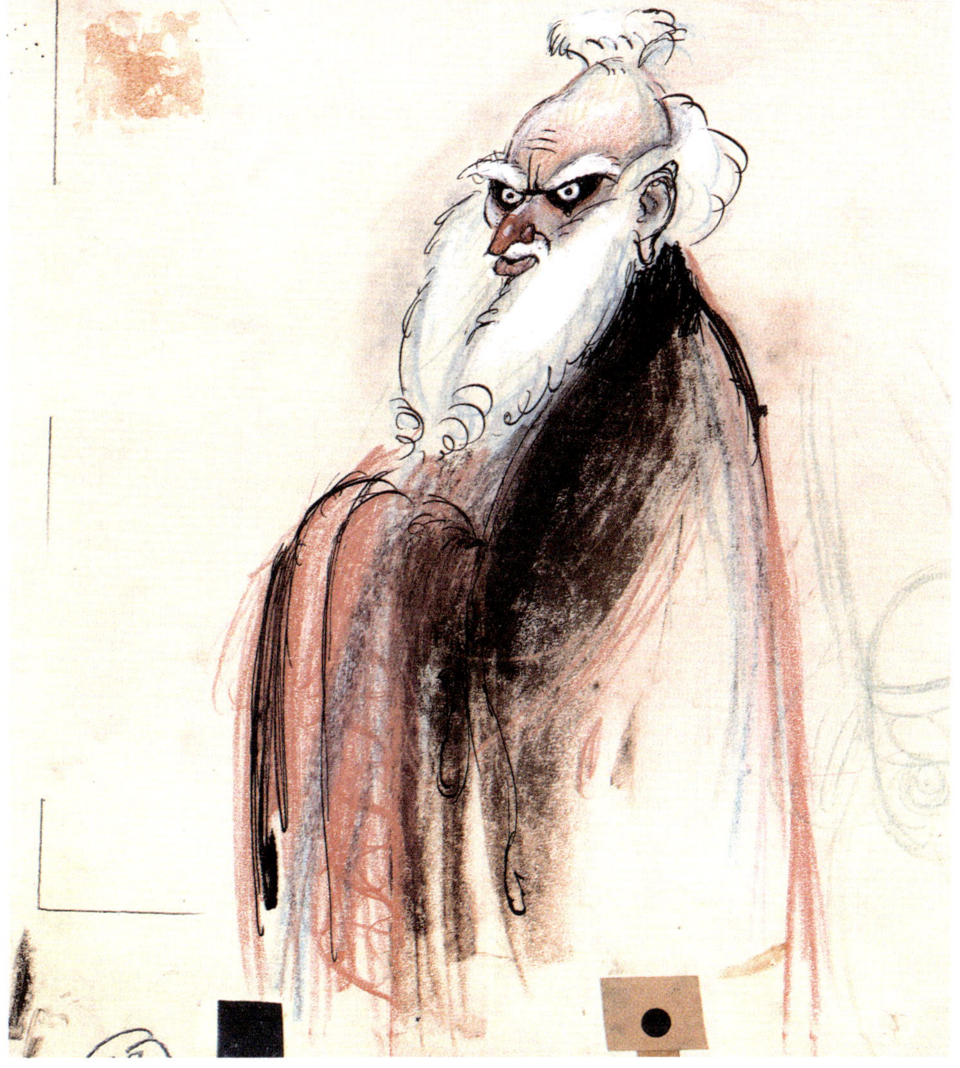

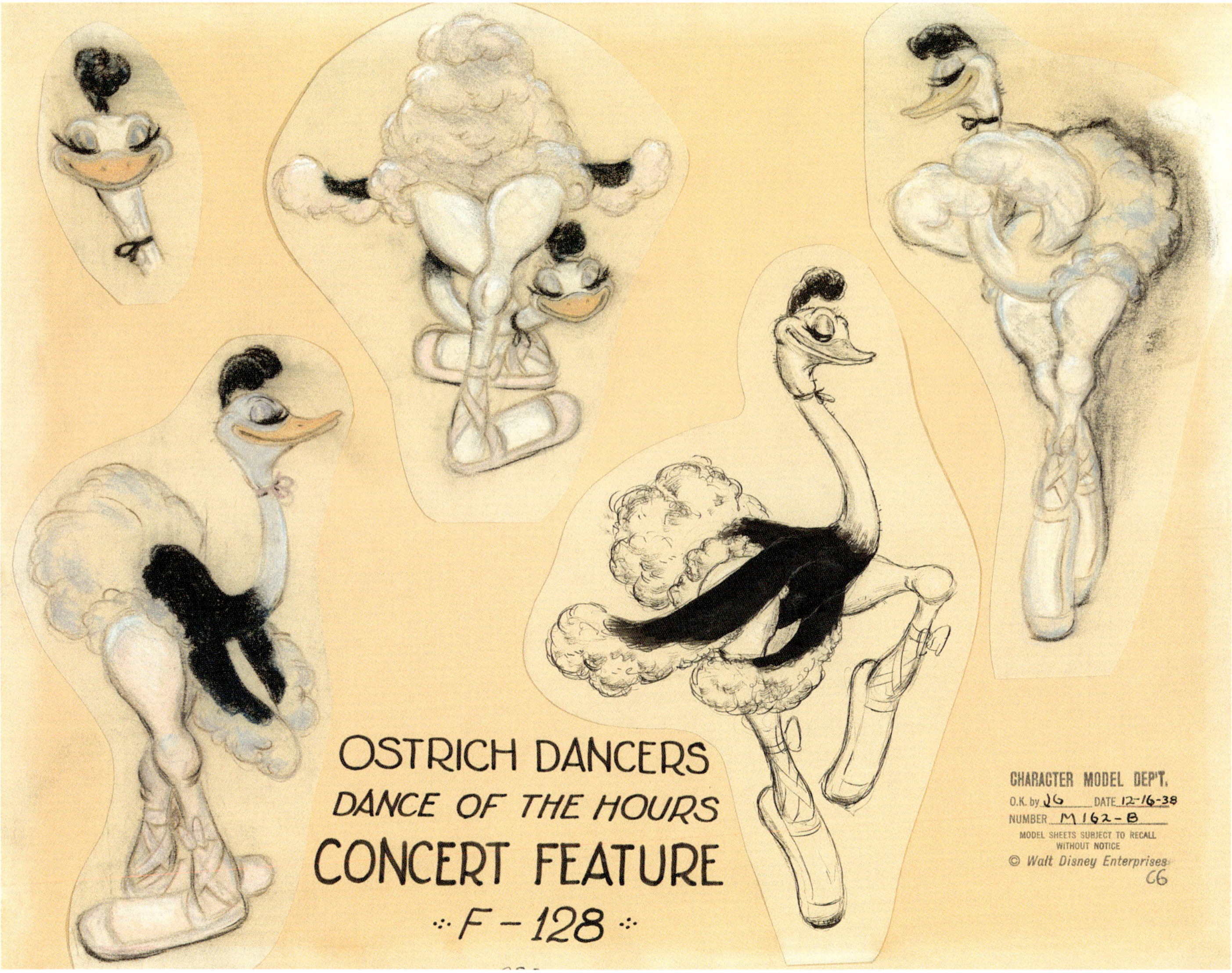

Model sheets approved by Joe Grant for FANTASIA.

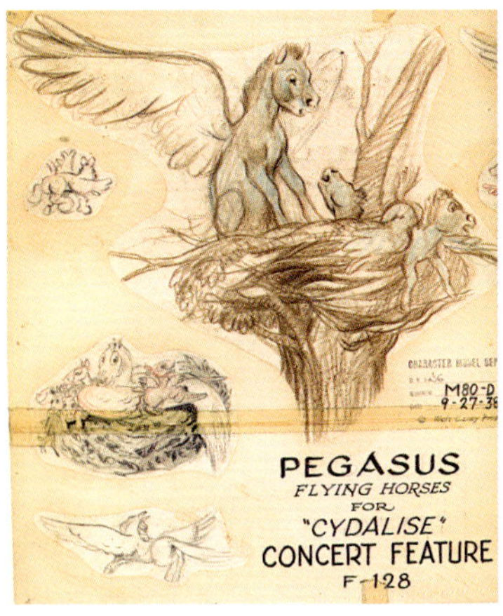

keeping his drawing hand in. Newcomer T. (Thornton) Hee designed caricatures for the 1938 short *Mother Goose Goes Hollywood*.

While *Fantasia* was in production, two major events occurred in Grant's personal life. On September 13, 1938, George A. Grant, living alone at the Hotel Diplomat at 108 West Forty-third Street, off Times Square in New York City, died of a stroke. When and why he returned east is unknown, as is the state of his relationship with his family. Two days later he was buried at Beth El Cemetery in Westwood, New Jersey, with funeral arrangements handled by a cousin, Grace S. Pleckner, "acting for wife Eva who phoned permission from Cal [sic]."

On his burial day, The *New York Journal-American* noted that George Grant was "for many years art director of the *New York American* and a widely known illustrator . . . His wife, Eva and a son, both of who are in California, survive." There was no mention of his parents or daughter. No immediate family members attended. Eva, it is assumed, preferred not to; circumstances may have prevented Joe. The unexpected death and burial within twenty-four hours, as required by Jewish tradition, occurred during the intense *Fantasia* story and music meetings that he was an integral part of.[20]

A happy event occurred the next year. On June 20, 1939, Jennie gave birth to the Grants' first child, Carol. Another daughter, Jennifer, was born in 1944. With fatherhood, Joe's responsibilities increased at home in addition to the studio. He and Jennie continued supporting Eva, who lived with them until Joe provided her with a house in nearby Eagle Rock.[21]

When war began in Europe in the fall of 1939, the studio's financial prospects began a frightening downward spiral. The European market was severely reduced, and profits from *Snow White* were devoured by a new $3 million studio in Burbank and two costly features. *Pinocchio*, released in February 1940 at a cost of $2.6 million, was a box office disappointment; so was the experimental, equally expensive *Fantasia* ($2.3 million), which opened in November. Layoffs and pay cuts began.

In early 1940, however, story and visual development proceeded on *Alice in Wonderland* and *Peter Pan*, and Grant/Huemer began a treatment about a baby elephant. Grant's Model Department was the first to move into the new studio in early 1940, but it continued to attract resentment and jealous sniping. "He kept building his Model Department," Ward Kimball fumed, "until . . . he had one whole wing, with assistants and stenographers, and this was his kingdom!"[22] Some referred to the department as a "playboy salon."

In their "little sanctuary," Grant's people were said to "float" through the day drawing freely, with none of the grinding pressures the animators faced. Grant was a tolerant boss who indulged his imaginative crew when they, for instance, improvised a play based on the tale of Sweeney Todd, laughed and kidded around, then drew the incidents they'd just invented.

The animators had production managers looking over their shoulders, goading them to turn out hundreds of drawings on tight weekly deadlines. Animators and managers were personally responsible for their work, which was directly critiqued by Walt. Character Model artists, by contrast, were shielded by their cool and laid-back boss, Grant, who ran a low-pressure department that tended to be condescending toward the grunts enmeshed in production, especially the animators.

> Dick [Huemer], and myself, and Martin [Provensen] and Jim [Bodrero]—these people had read, they were intelligent, they knew music and literature, and they were good conversationalists. They were universal people in their knowledge. I would admit that we were great snobs, that we looked down upon these guys [animators] as a hundred per cent yokel. There was no changing them. We were roundly hated for it.[23]

He thumbed his nose at his critics. "And another thing," Grant said in 1988, "every time I'd go back east with Walt, alone with him, it was all, 'What the hell? What is this guy?' The *What Makes Sammy Run?* kind of thing."

This quote indicates that Grant was aware of the anti-Semitic undercurrent toward him among a few studio staffers. But he did not know how deeply those few resented him. He did not see, for example, an August 1940 entry in one animator's diary that noted some of "the boys" musing about what they'd do "the day before we quit" the studio. In addition to throwing pies, spraying seltzer in executives' faces, and putting skunk oil in the air-conditioning, they would paint the word *Jude* on Joe Grant's car. This odious comment was made at a time when the Nazi persecution of Jews was well known.[24]

"All I was doing," said Grant of the poison aimed toward him, "all I could contribute, and was anxious to do that—these projects to me were just precious. Get them going! I didn't care what the hell they said!"[25]

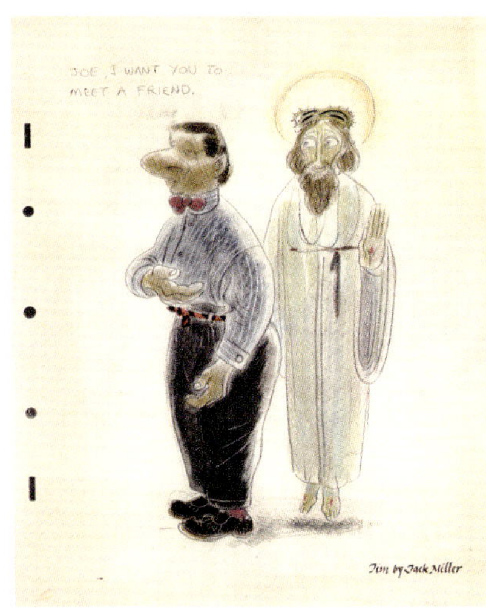

Character Model artist Jack Miller's caricature of James Bodrero (who claimed to know everybody) introducing "a friend" to Joe Grant.

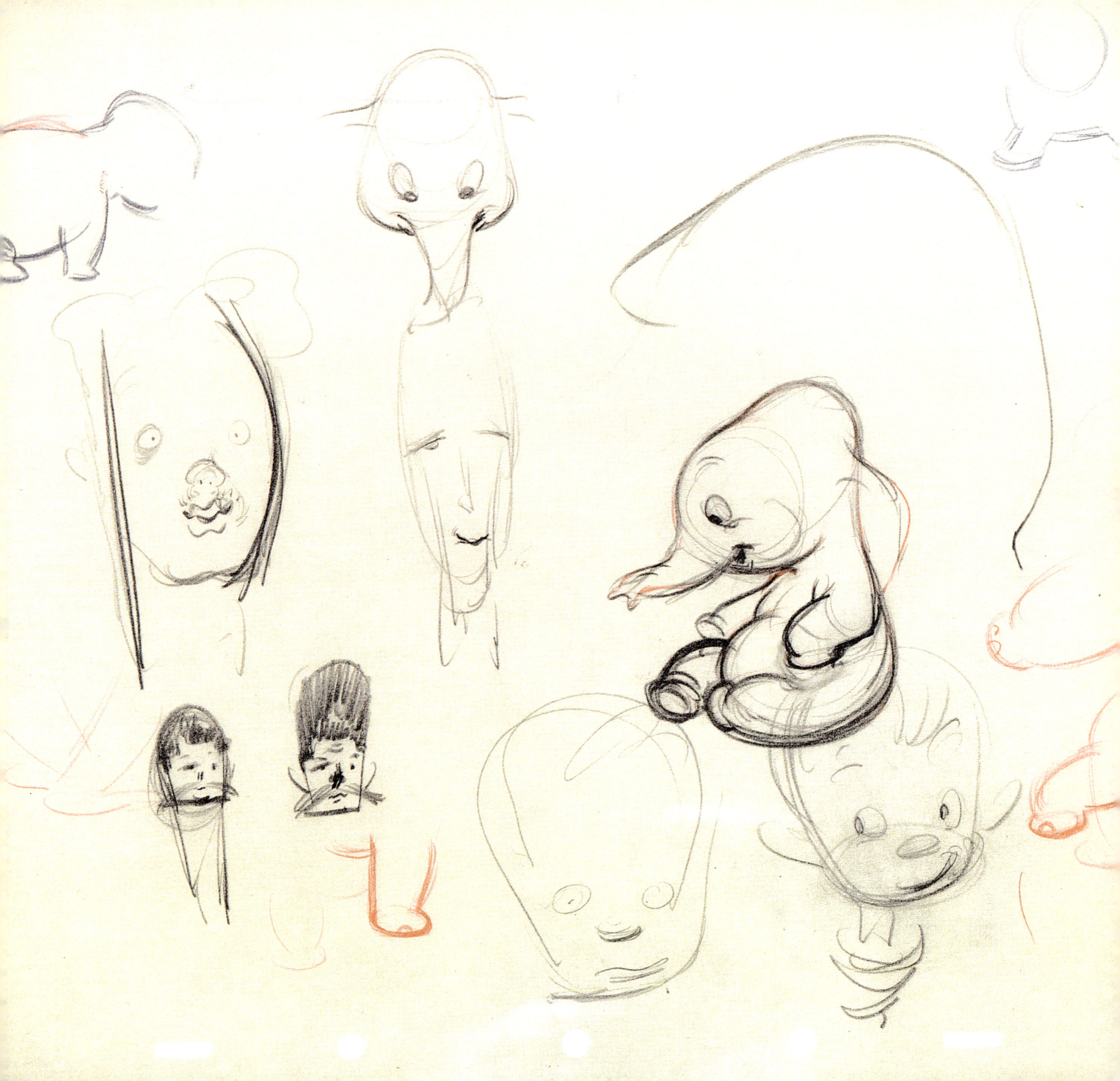

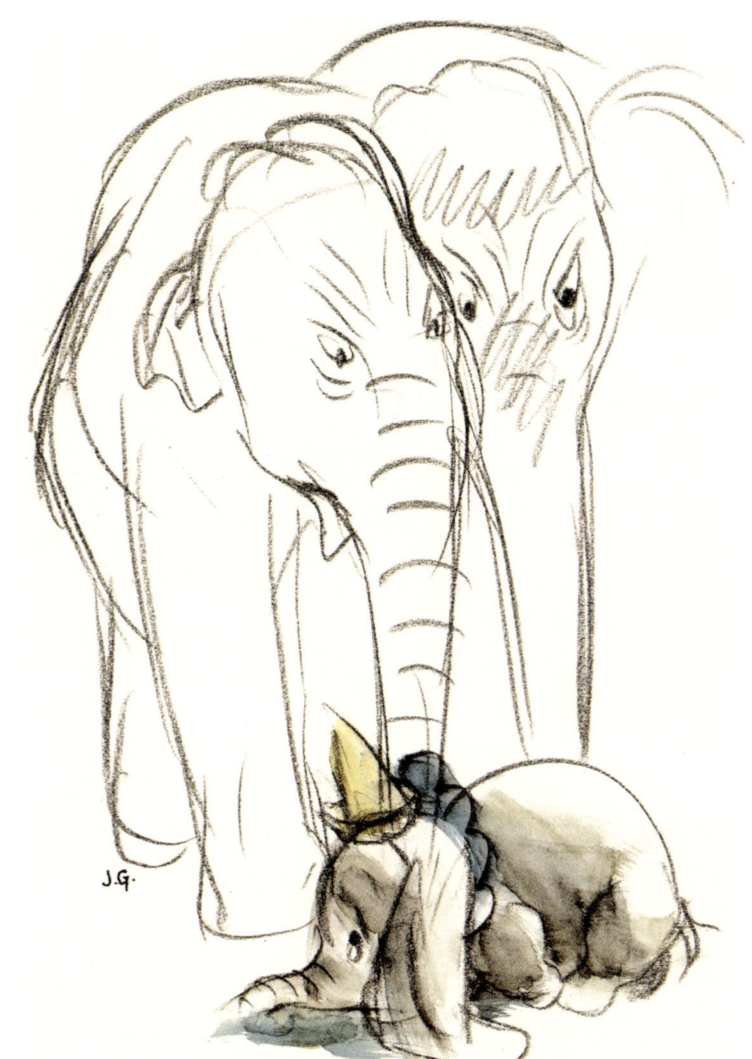

OPPOSITE: *Dumbo in animator Bill Tytla's exploratory sketches.* ABOVE: *a Joe Grant idea sketch for* DUMBO.

Walt Disney's *Dumbo*

was based on a book by Helen Aberson and her husband, Harold Pearl, with sixteen pen-and-ink sketches by Helen Durney. Roll-A-Book, a Syracuse, New York company specializing in boxed scroll-formatted books, published *Dumbo, the Flying Elephant* in 1939.

It was Roll-A-Book publisher Everett Whitmyre who contacted the Disney Studio, which immediately responded to the story of the big-eared baby elephant. The Pearls, in a hasty move later regretted, signed away all rights to the property to Disney for screen credit and $1,000.[1]

In a June 1939 letter to Disney soliciting work, illustrator Durney wrote, "You will have lots of fun immortalizing [Dumbo] for he is a most adaptable and loveable subject." Disney replied in December: "As you predicted, he has proven to be a swell little character to work with, and we are having a lot of fun making the picture. I only hope that the finished production will live up to your high expectations."[2]

Dumbo was planned as a short until Disney tossed the project to Grant and Huemer for feature-length development. The team brainstormed ideas, quickly conjuring the now-famous pink elephants and stork-delivery sequences. They changed Dumbo's mom's name from "Mother Ella" to "Mrs. Jumbo," referring to the famed Barnum & Bailey Circus pachyderm. They riffed on elephants' alleged fear of mice, replacing a wise robin named "Red" with a wiseacre sidekick named "Timothy," a tiny mouse with a big mouth and an even bigger heart. They invented a "rusty black crow" (expanded to five in the film), who advises that psychology and a "Magic Golden Feather from the Sacred Woozle-Bird of Persia" might convince Dumbo that he can fly.

Between January 22 and March 21, 1940, Grant and Huemer wrote a charming 102-page outline, which became the film's template. Disney was intrigued by their playfully teasing him with a few pages daily that "kept the suspense," Huemer said.

For example, when Dumbo accidentally springboards into a pyramid of elephants, the Disney team added a teardrop to the synopsis page:

> Dear Reader: If you are at all faint-hearted or impressionable, we earnestly advise you to stop right here!! Read no further! Do something else! Go to the movies—or to bed—anything!—But skip the rest of this chapter!!![3]

"It was a case of bringing logs to the head beaver for him to build his dam," Huemer explained. "We thought it was a good way to intrigue him." As Grant

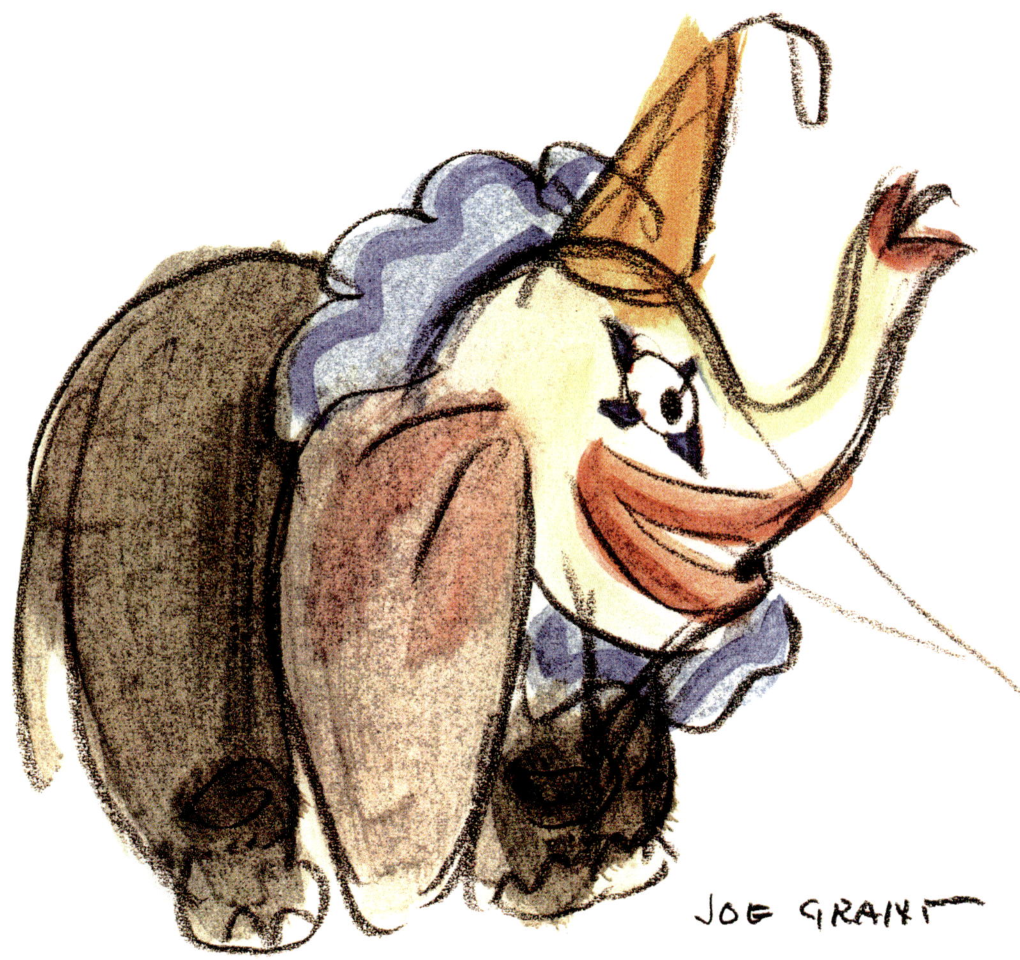

well knew, "Walt was very susceptible to stimulation. People would show him drawings and he'd light up and get enthusiastic," Huemer said. "And we'd be off and running with his approval."[4]

When Disney green-lighted *Dumbo*, Grant's department got busy in a hurry. Character Model "lit the fire" with conceptual sketches that the Story Department turned into continuity storyboards.[5]

At the same time, the Character Model Department "began to dwindle." Its artists were now dispatched to sequence directors to develop idea sketches as needed. "Whatever picture, we'd send somebody into the unit to work with them," Grant explained. Also, when America entered the war in December 1941, studio personnel shrank, not merely because of box office and market loss, as men were drafted or volunteered for services.

Two Dumbo *drawings* (ABOVE) *by Joe Grant and* (RIGHT) *a watercolor by Mary Blair.*

Another reason the Character Model Department was gradually disbanded was that Grant and Huemer "were now star writers," as Grant put it, busily writing for various projects. "[It] changed the concept completely. We were glad to get out of it [Character Model] 'cause it was a chance to identify yourself with a complete story from beginning to end."

Grant still supervised the department, but writing now took precedence. He found originating product more creative. Equally important, it kept him close to Walt, who believed story was the heart of his organization.

Writing also provided an escape from the anonymity of being an administrator. Grant chafed at the responsibilities but minimal glory of a department head. As a "star writer" he might regain the public celebrity he had when he was on the staff of the *Los Angeles Record* eight years before.

Time magazine obliged. It shone a spotlight on Grant and Huemer in a December 29, 1941, article on the success of *Dumbo* (released in October):

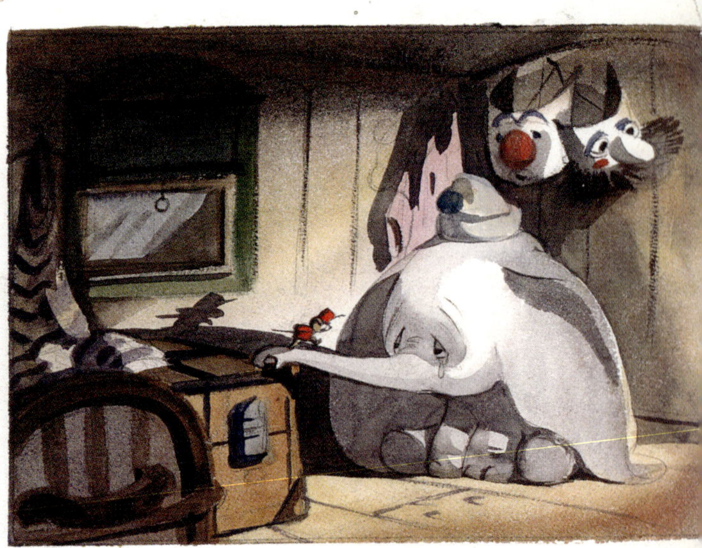

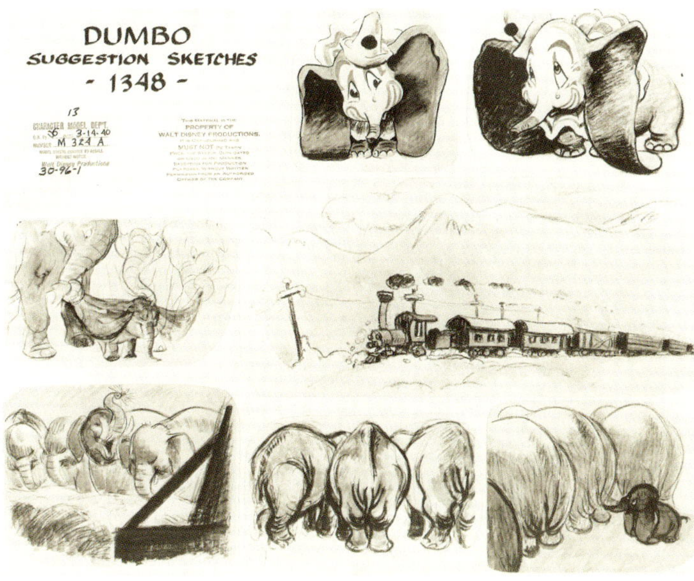

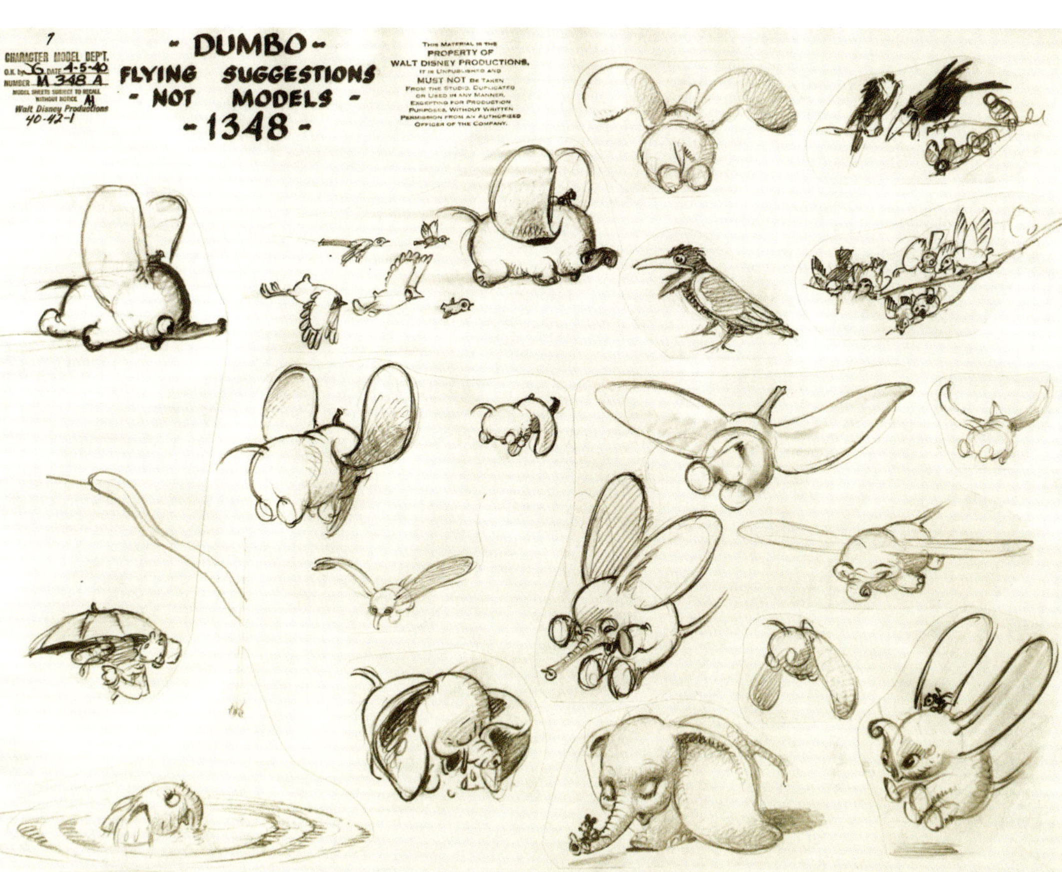

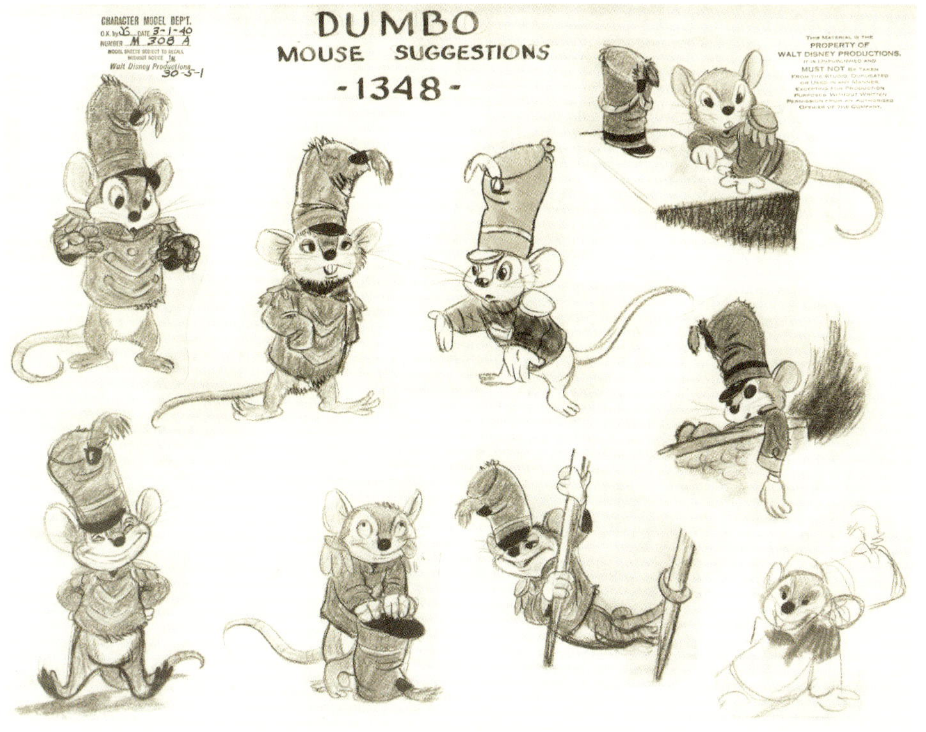

Dumbo model sheets by (CLOCKWISE FROM ABOVE) *unknown, Albert Hurter, and Jack Miller.*

> At length, [Disney] turned the little elephant over to one of his best writers, moody, sad-eyed Joe Grant, to see what he could do.
>
> That was what Grant and his happy-go-lucky partner, Dick Huemer, were waiting for. . . . They were scarcely a quarter of the way through their story when Disney steamed into their office one morning, the latest installment bunched in his hand. "This is good!" he sputtered. "What the hell happens tomorrow?"
>
> The Grant-Huemer script . . . had the germ of every important episode of the final screen version. . . .

Time's public tribute to Grant and Huemer backfired, however, tarnishing the two "stars" in Disney's eyes. "After Walt read the article," Huemer said, "he met Joe Grant and myself in the [parking] lot and indicated his displeasure. He didn't think it was a very good article, not particularly flattering to him. As he turned away he said, 'What the hell, didn't I have anything to do with the picture?' which is what the write-up sounds like, I admit.

"But in a sense it was partly true," Huemer continued. "He didn't have as much to do with it as he did with his other pictures."[6]

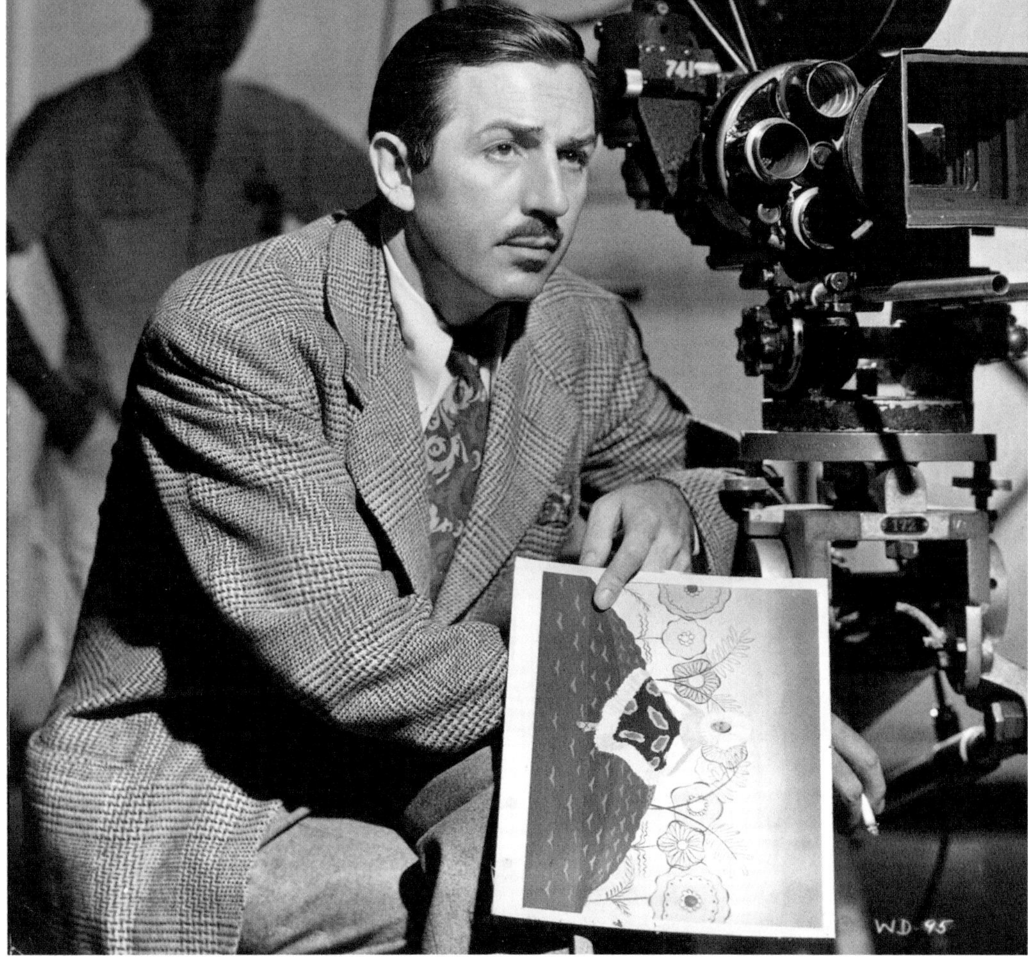

Walt Disney, c. 1945.

Walt Disney was suffering through a tumultuous time. In May 1941, a third of his employees—upset by layoffs, low wages, no bonuses, or job security, all exacerbated by the European war—began an acrimonious strike that lasted through September. During it, Disney was in South America (from August to October) with several artists researching future films. The trip was encouraged at the behest of the U.S. government's "Good Neighbor" program, specifically Nelson Rockefeller's Office of the Coordinator of Inter-American Affairs, which sought to promote friendly relations among all American nations when the European war spread. "At that point I would have gone to China to get away from it all," said Disney.[7]

Company men Grant and Huemer did not join the strike line. All executives and directors stayed in, as did top-echelon animators, with two exceptions: Art Babbitt and Vladimir Tytla. The pair accosted Grant each morning outside the studio gates hoping to convince him to join them.

Grant never liked Babbitt: "I didn't like his politics," which were unapologetically progressive.[8] However, Joe and Jennie were close with Tytla and his wife, Adrienne; the couples vacationed in Mexico, and Grant was best man at their wedding. "I had a lot of friends out there in the strike, and there were a lot of threats and whatnot," Grant said. "It was kind of a shambles."[9]

At one point, Tytla and others suggested Grant replace Walt as studio head. "It was a horrifying thought," Grant said. "I said, 'I don't want to hear that voiced again. That's absolutely ridiculous.' They were just grabbing at straws. They wanted a champion inside. I would have been sucker number one![10]

"That strike was so stupid to me! Because I had given up a wonderful career on the newspaper to come there, because I love [animation], and now I'm going to go out on a strike? They couldn't understand it, but I could."[11]

The strike was "a great imposition" to animation's development because it had the effect of a stroke on Disney, Grant said.[12] "Walt never got over it. [It] destroyed his momentum. You discouraged him to the point where he lost faith in humanity . . . [he thought all] people are not trustworthy in a sense."[13] Grant felt the strike crippled Walt in his "thinking on politics and things in general."[14] *Time*'s implication that *Dumbo* sailed through production without him made him suspicious of his "star writers."

"Even though *Dumbo* has always been regarded as one of Walt's better pictures, he hated it," said Huemer. Using an odd analogy for a city boy, he explained that Disney "had to 'own lamb.' Until the mother licks the lamb clean and makes it hers, she won't nurse it."[15]

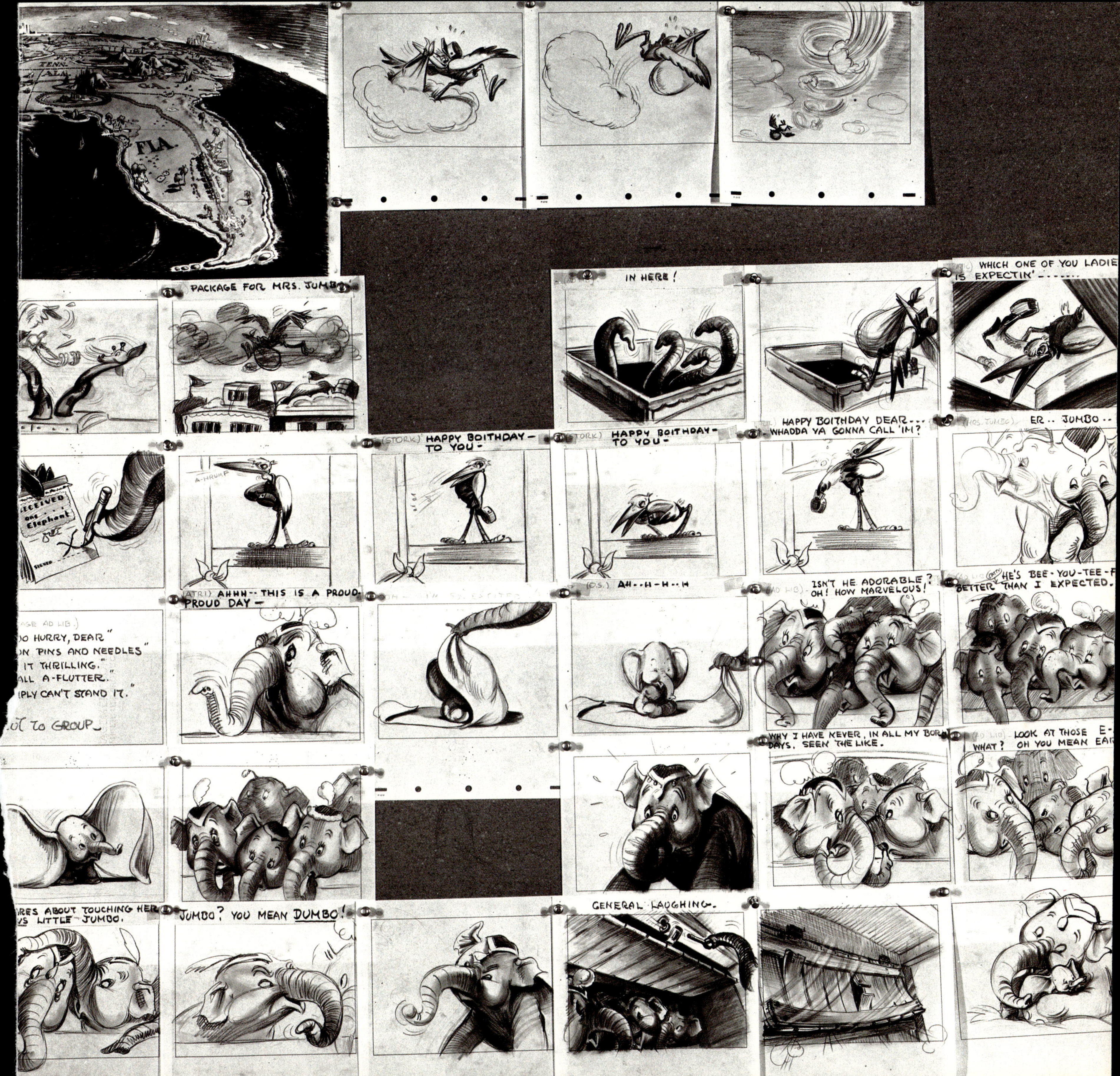
TENN.
ALA.
FLA.
PACKAGE FOR MRS. JUMBO
IN HERE!
WHICH ONE OF YOU LADIE
IS EXPECTIN' - - - - - - -
RECEIVED
One
Elephant
SIGNED
A-HRUMP
(STORK) HAPPY BOITHDAY -
TO YOU -
(STORK) HAPPY BOITHDAY -
TO YOU -
HAPPY BOITHDAY DEAR...
WHADDA YA GONNA CALL 'IM?
(MRS. JUMBO) ER.. JUMBO..
AGE AD LIB.)
DO HURRY, DEAR"
ON PINS AND NEEDLES"
IT THRILLING."
ALL A-FLUTTER."
IPLY CAN'T STAND IT."
UT TO GROUP
(ATRI) AHHH -- THIS IS A PROUD-
PROUD DAY -
(O.S.) AH--H--H
(AD LIB) - ISN'T HE ADORABLE?
OH! HOW MARVELOUS!
(AD LIB) HE'S BEE-YOU-TEE-F
BETTER THAN I EXPECTED.
WHY I HAVE NEVER, IN ALL MY BORN
DAYS, SEEN THE LIKE.
LOOK AT THOSE E-
WHAT? OH YOU MEAN EAR
RES ABOUT TOUCHING HER
US LITTLE JUMBO.
JUMBO? YOU MEAN DUMBO!
GENERAL LAUGHING.

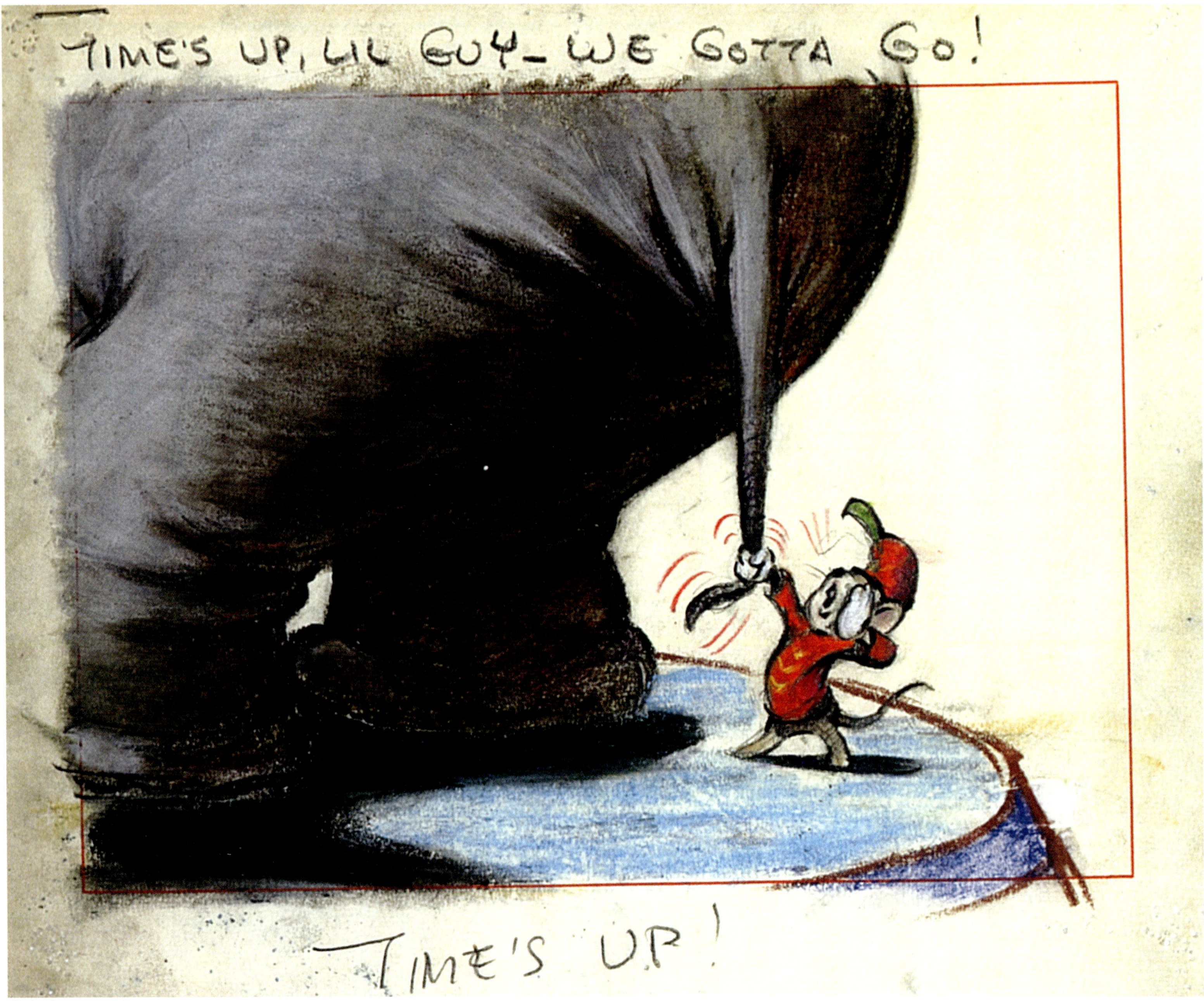

A DUMBO *story sketch, artist unknown.*

Huemer believed his writing partner "set himself up as a rival to Walt" and "Walt became aware of it. He had a little espionage system and he heard about Joe's arrogance. So he got to hate our little department." Perhaps Disney's spies saw Grant's casual in-house caricatures as a case of self-promotion at the expense of Walt. In one, Grant and Huemer in formal dress are catered to by beautiful women, while in the background a neon marquee flashes "*Dumbo*—A New Grant-Huemer Musical!" Grant, cigar in hand, shouts into a phone, "What Character Model Department?"

Maybe Walt's sycophants saw Roy Williams's cartoon of an apron-clad Walt scrubbing floors late at night at "Grant-Huemer Productions." "Dick and I had just finished *Dumbo* and we were pretty cocky," Grant admitted.[16] "We were beginning to feel our oats. We wanted to be identified. Who were we?"[17]

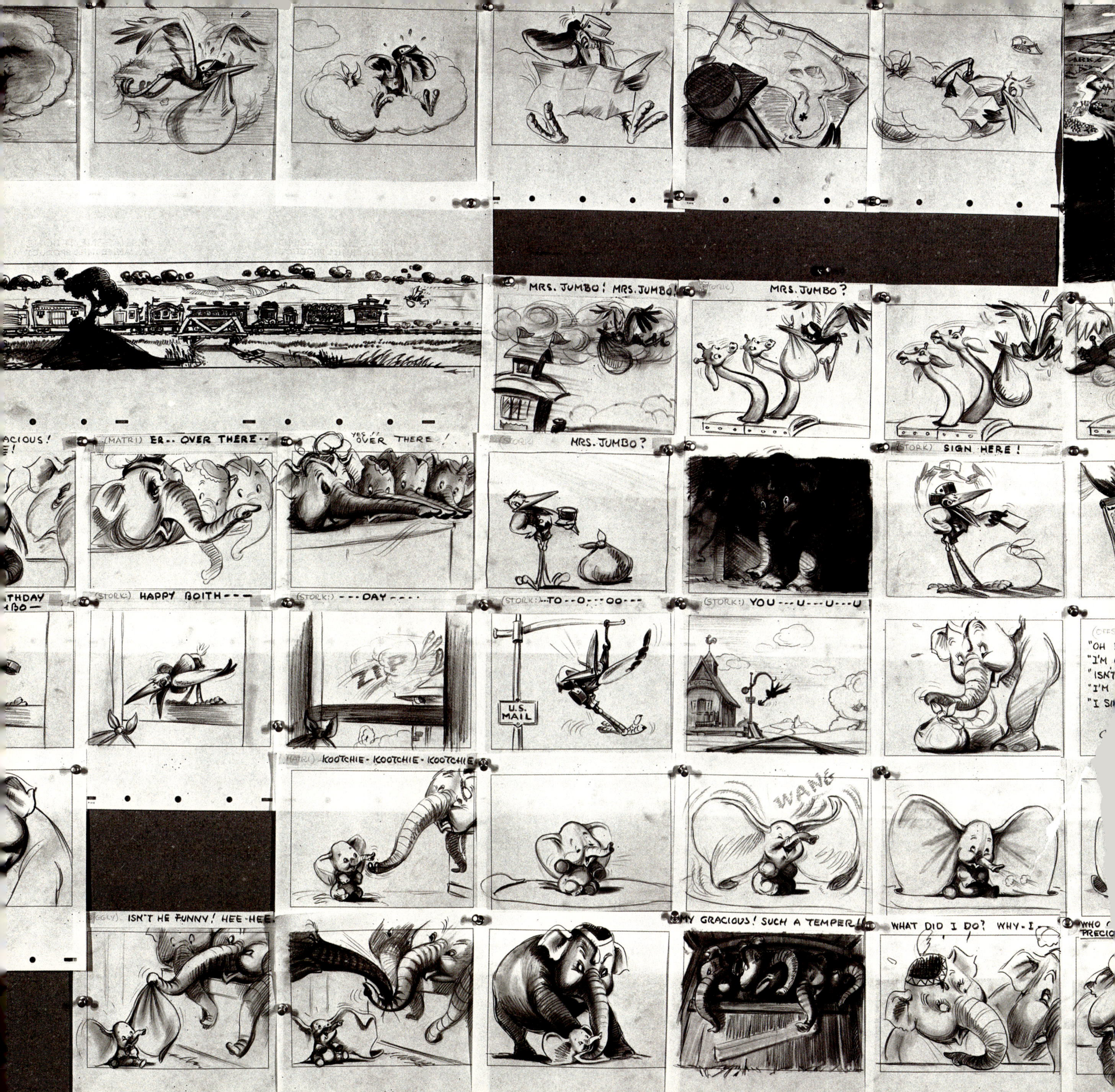
MRS. JUMBO! MRS. JUMBO!
(STORK) MRS. JUMBO?
(MATRI) ER-- OVER THERE--
YES !! OVER THERE !
(STORK) MRS. JUMBO?
(STORK) SIGN HERE!
(STORK:) HAPPY BOITH---
(STORK:) ---DAY----
ZIP
(STORK:) --TO--O---OO---
U.S. MAIL
(STORK:) YOU---U---U---U
(MATRI) KOOTCHIE-KOOTCHIE-KOOTCHIE
WANG
ISN'T HE FUNNY! HEE-HEE.
MY GRACIOUS! SUCH A TEMPER!!
WHAT DID I DO? WHY-I

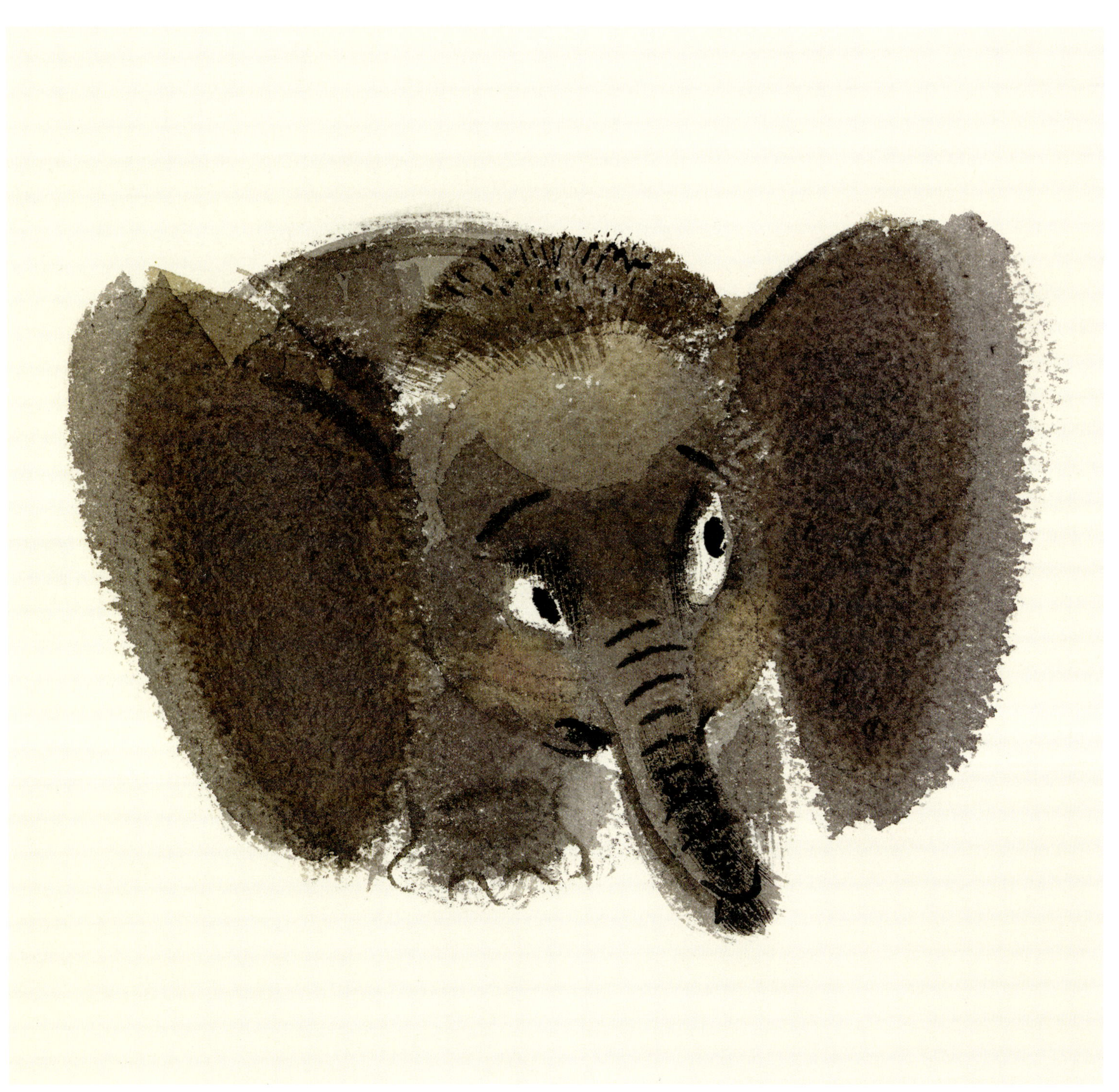

Joe Grant sketch for Dumbo; *following foldout pages are* Dumbo *storyboards by various artists.*

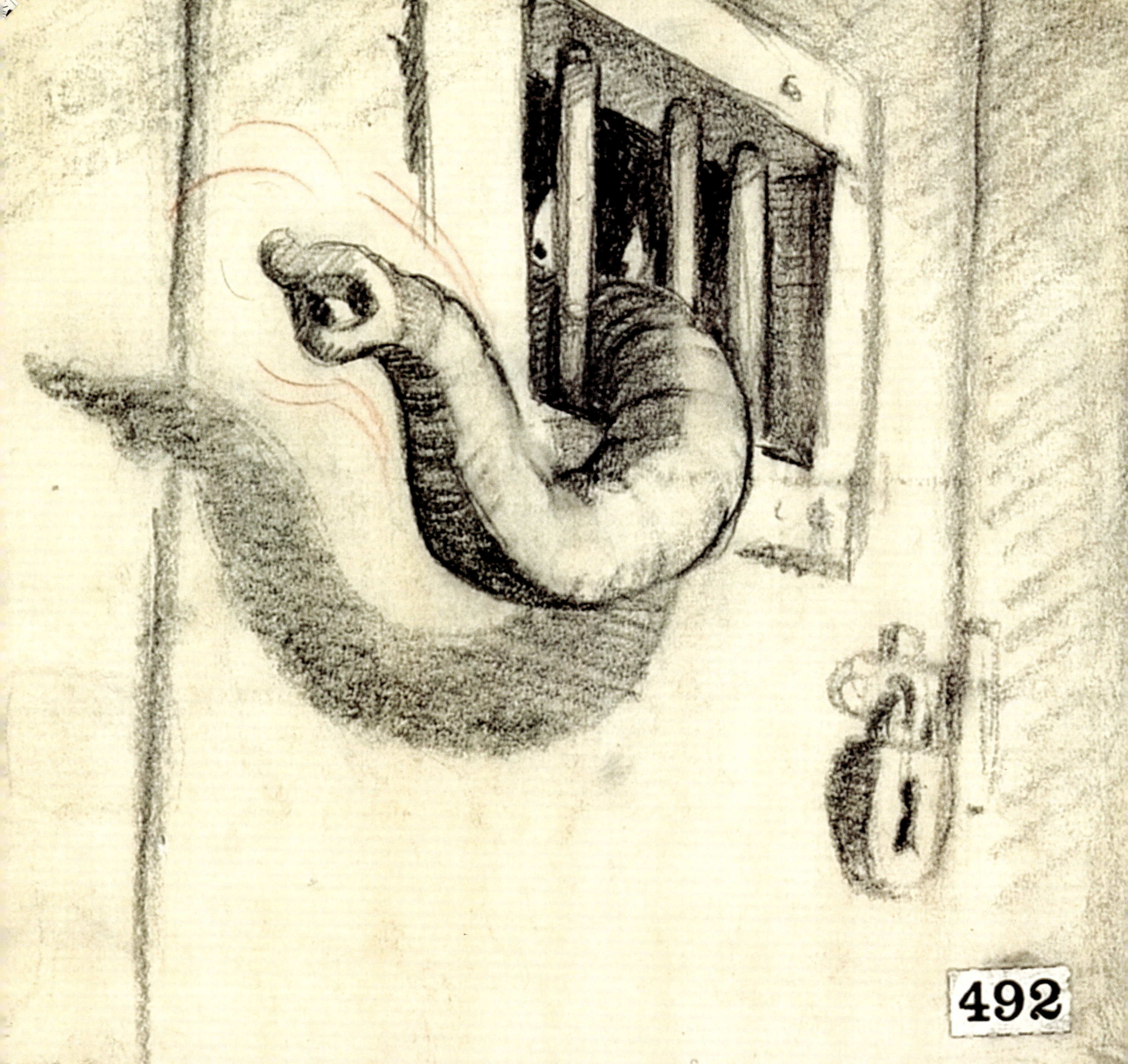
492

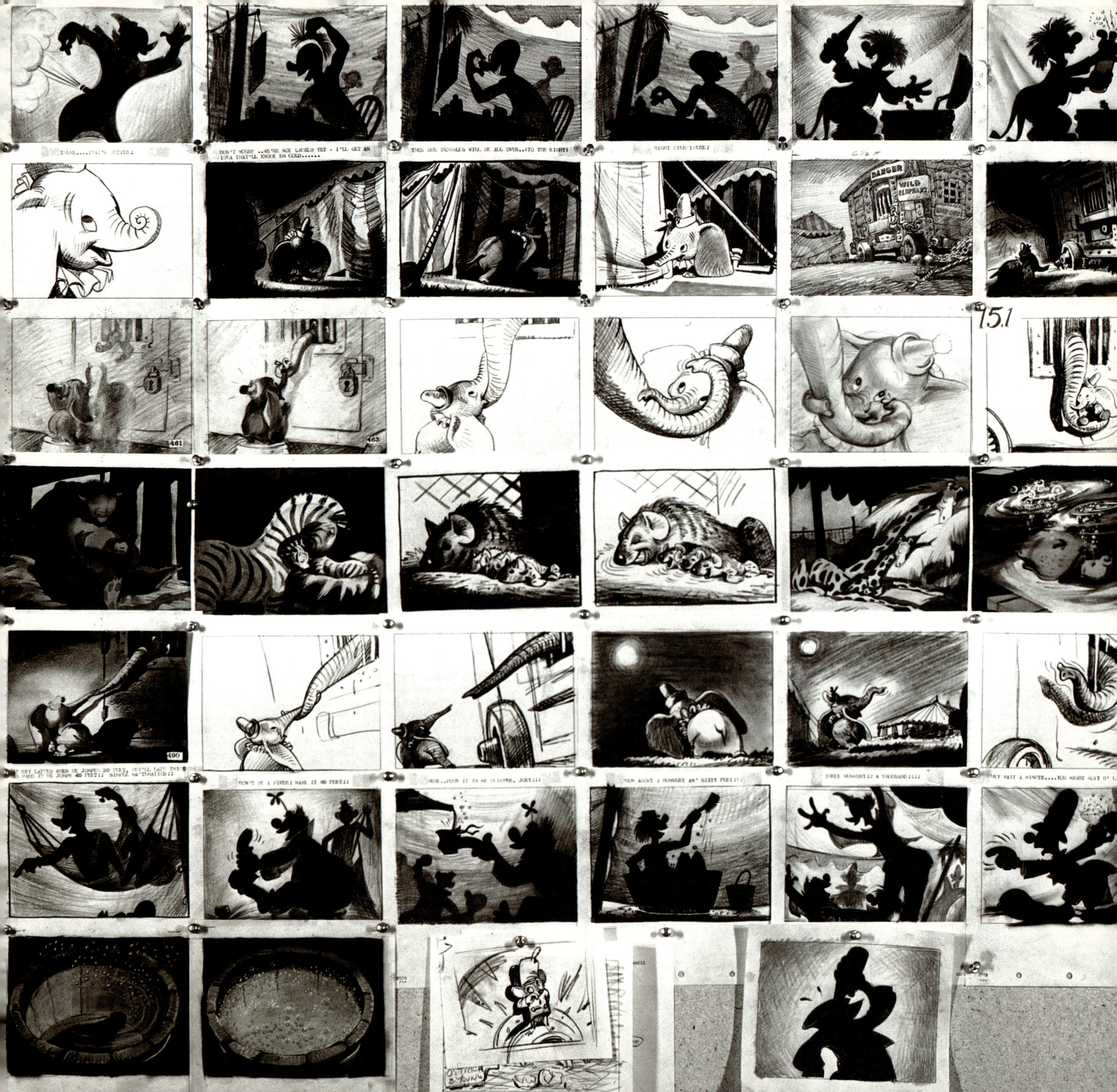
DON'T WORRY ..WE'RE NOT LICKED YET - I'LL GET AN
IDEA THAT'LL KNOCK EM COLD......
THEN OUR TROUBLES WILL BE ALL OVER..(TO THE RIGHT)
RIGHT OVER THERE!
DANGER
WILD ELEPHANT
461
463
15.1
490
DON'T BE A PIKER! MAKE IT 80 FEET!!
THREE HUNNERT!! A THOUSAND!!!!

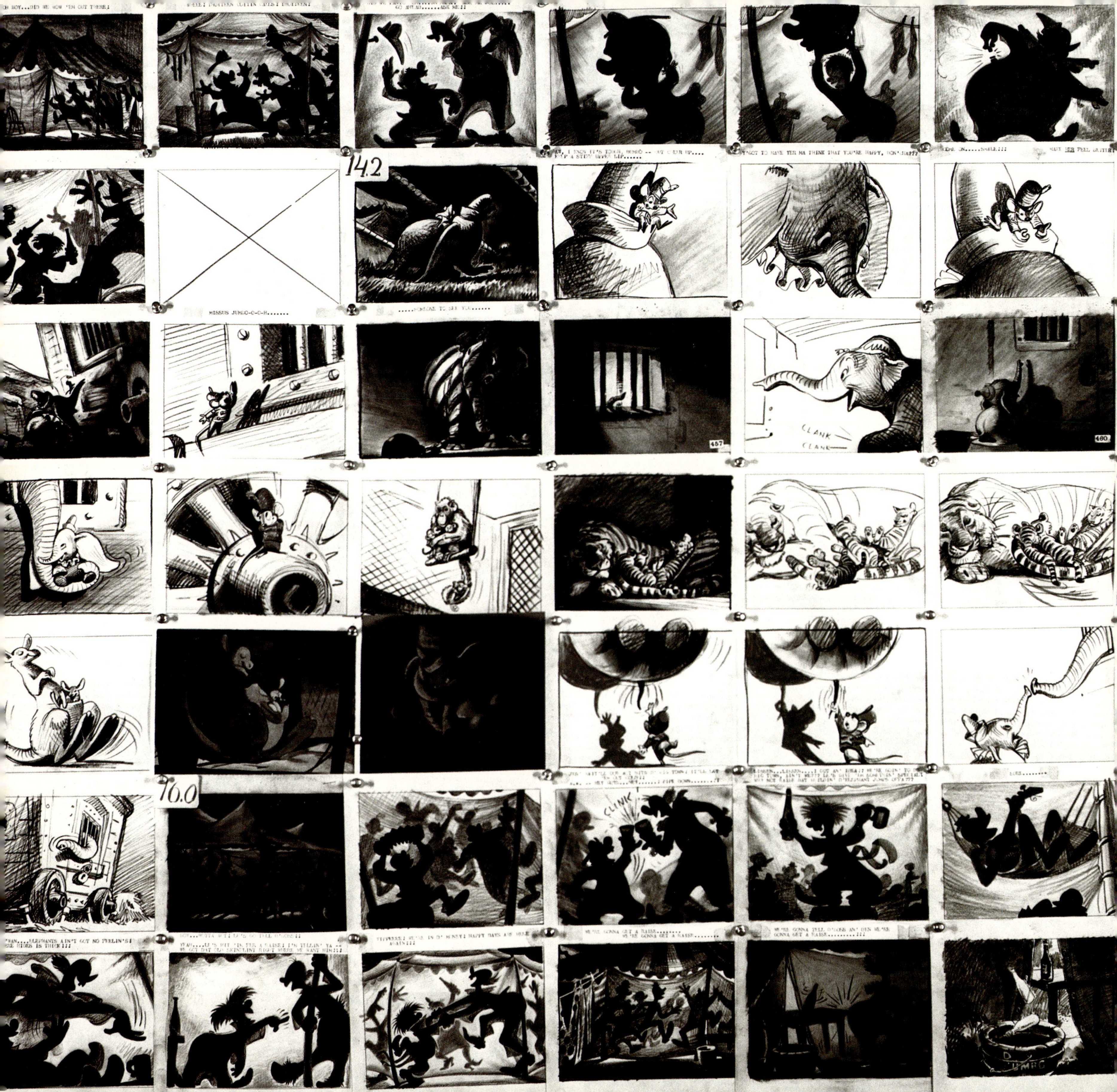
142
MISSUS JUMBO-O-O-H.......
457
CLANK
CLANK
480
76.0
CLINK

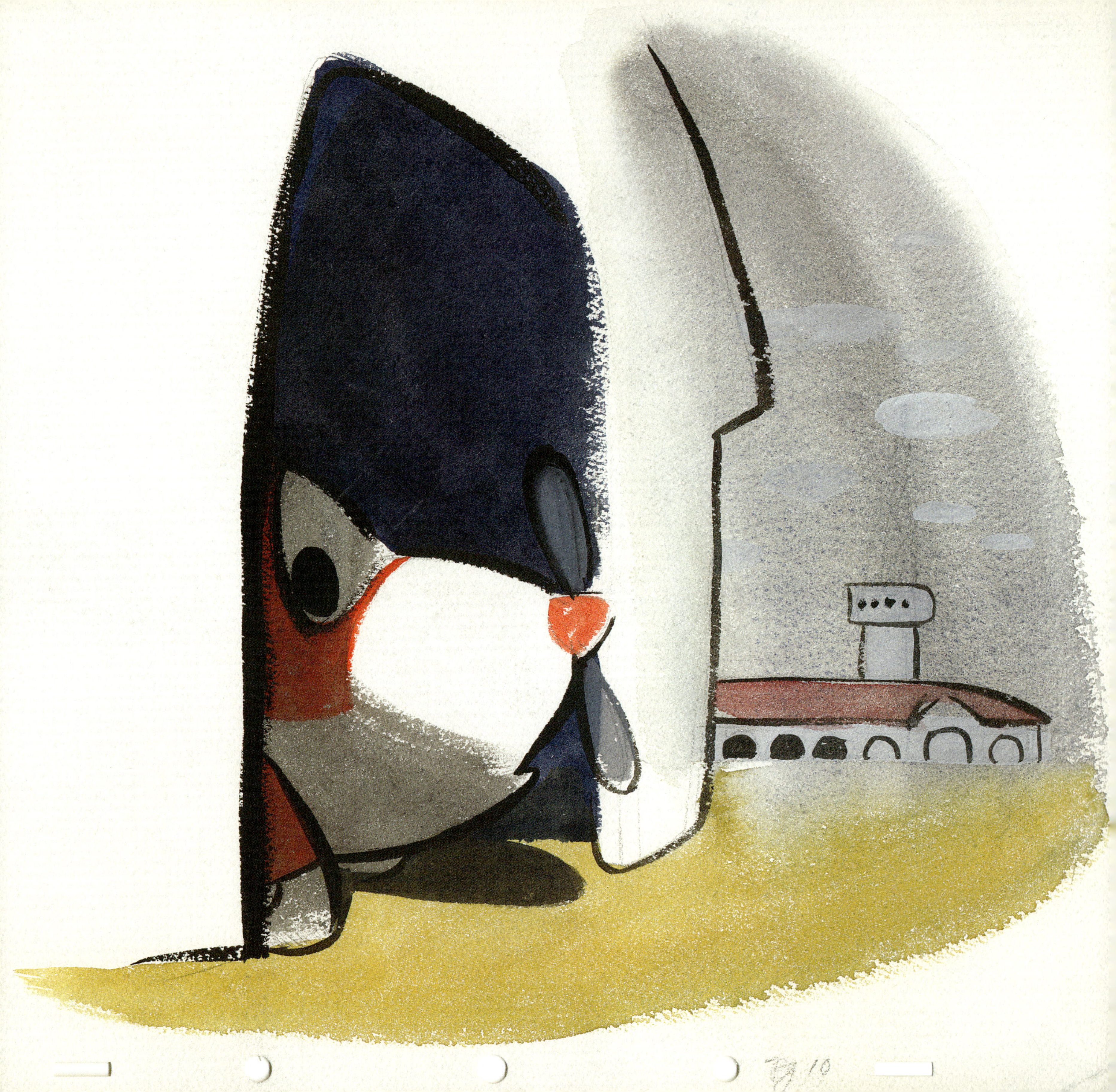

On June 20, 1941, in the middle of the strike, *The Reluctant Dragon*, a live-action feature with animated segments, was released. Quickly produced to generate much-needed cash, the film is, ironically, a sunny guided tour of Disney's new studio, purportedly filled with happy workers cheerily revealing animation's "secret" processes.

For a Story Department sequence, Huemer and Grant offered "Baby Weems," a wry tale about a precocious infant who composes and conducts symphonies and discusses relativity theories with Einstein. "Baby Weems" is a most un-Disney-like parable about the enticements and pitfalls of celebrity and the American public's miniscule attention span. It is presented as story sketches (wonderfully rendered in Nupastels by Jack Miller) with limited animation. Baby Weems's design was based on Grant's sketches of his two-year-old daughter, Carol.

Again, Walt's star writers garnered special praise. "The hit of the show is unquestionably the 'Baby Weems' sequence," said *The Hollywood Reporter* on June 16, 1941. "The preview gang was completely won by Baby Weems, written by Joe Grant, Dick Huemer, and John Miller . . . brilliant satire." In addition, Doubleday Books published an illustrated book, under Grant and Huemer's byline, adapted from the film. The *Los Angeles Times*'s book reviewer praised it as "a hilarious satire [that] gave me more laughs" than three other books.[18]

The prolific pair kept busy. When *Saludos Amigos*, Disney's first Latin American compilation feature (released February 6, 1943), needed another story, Grant/Huemer quickly provided an adaptation of one of their old stories.[19] They Latinized "Petey O'Toole"—a baby airplane attending flight school who makes his first solo flight across a southwestern prairie and over "Old Thunderhead," a dangerous mountain. Petey became Pedro, a novice mail plane in Chile, who flies through dangerous weather over Aconcagua, the highest mountain in the Americas. Grant, Provensen, and Miller provided concept drawings.

For *The Three Caballeros* (1945), another compilation feature, Grant/Huemer contributed "The Laughing Gauchito," which never reached the screen. Nevertheless, they were paid $500 for "assignment of all rights" to "Laughing Gauchito," "Pedro," and "Baby Weems."[20]

For the time being, Walt Disney sheathed his feelings regarding his "star writers." They were talented, prolific generators of original stories. Though obviously ambitious, they were loyal. Now that America was at war, the studio kept afloat filling government contracts for propaganda and training films. In that arena, Grant and Huemer would prove even more stellar.

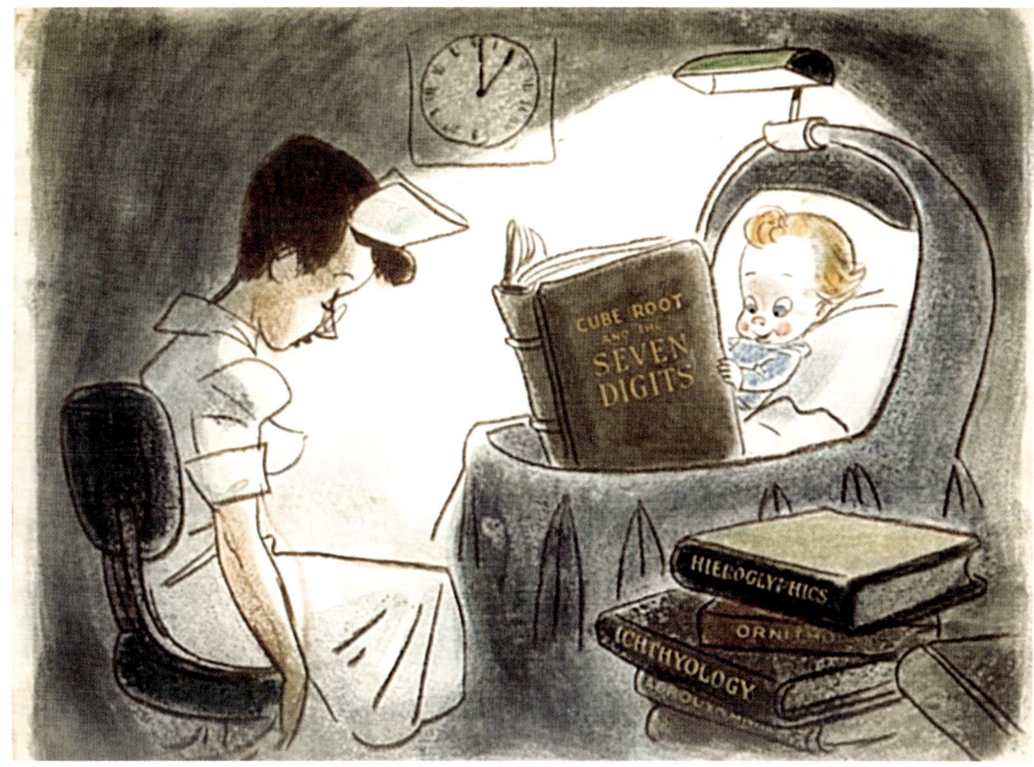

OPPOSITE: *Watercolor concept sketch for Pedro from* SALUDOS AMIGOS *(1943).* THIS PAGE: *Jack Miller's drawing for the "Baby Weems" segment from* THE RELUCTANT DRAGON *(1941).*

By mid-1942, more than ninety-three percent of Disney production was engaged in government-contracted propaganda and training films. Joe Grant and Dick Huemer had a hand in the best of these films designed for the home front: *Reason and Emotion* (1943), *Chicken Little* (1943), *Education for Death* (1943), *Der Fuehrer's Face* (1943), and the most widely seen of all of Disney wartime films: *The New Spirit* (January 1942).[1]

Grant and Huemer accompanied Walt Disney to Washington, D.C., for meetings with government officials, including Secretary of the Treasury Henry Morgenthau, who had commissioned *The New Spirit*, which stressed the importance of paying taxes to support the war effort ("Taxes to Beat the Axis!"). Tax payments were due March 15 and the government order came late—on December 18, 1941, a week after the attack on Pearl Harbor—so enormous pressure was put on Disney and his staff to meet what director Wilfred Jackson described as "an absolutely ridiculous, completely impossible deadline."[2]

In Washington, D.C., Walt Disney (with pointer), Dick Huemer (FAR RIGHT), and Joe Grant (SECOND FROM RIGHT) present storyboards for THE NEW SPIRIT (1942) to Henry Morgenthau, U.S. Treasury Secretary.

On December 20, Grant and Huemer handed in a story treatment. In it Donald Duck talks to his radio about paying his taxes after waking from a nightmare in "Axisland." (Most of this would be used in *Der Fuehrer's Face*.) The final narrative for *The New Spirit* was quickly pulled together through intense story conferences after Disney, Grant, and Huemer returned from Washington.

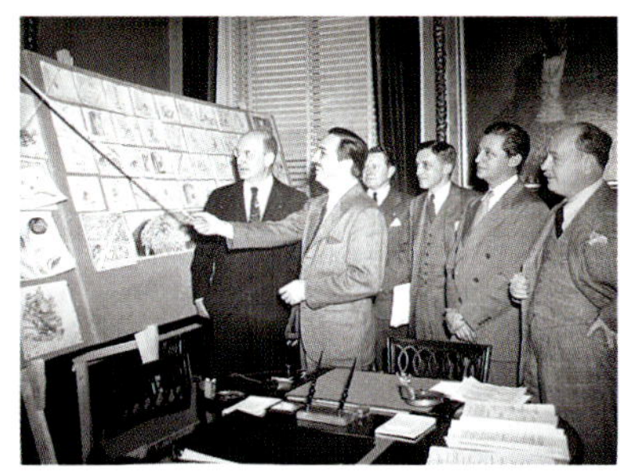

At a meeting two days before Christmas 1941, Disney rallied his creative staff. A conference transcript reveals how well Disney and Grant worked together. Concept sketches for *The New Spirit* were on storyboards when the four-hour meeting convened with Grant, Huemer, producer Ben Sharpsteen, director Jackson, musician Ollie Wallace, Character Model artists Martin Provensen and Aurie Battaglia, layout artist Ken O'Connor, and story artist Bill Peed (who later changed his name to "Peet"), among others.

Disney opened the meeting by telling how he had proposed that Donald Duck be portrayed as "a little guy, symbolizing the average American." Morgenthau preferred a human character to represent John Q. Public, but Disney says he convinced him that the Duck could be "very effective." As Donald listens to a radio broadcast, he visualizes "a terrific menace" through "the power of the cartoon medium, just the same as your editorial cartoon."[3]

At the beginning of the meeting, Walt and Joe riff on each other's suggestions in what reads like a private conversation:

JOE: You want to show what you get back for your income tax. You get protection.

WALT: Do you suppose we could open without even mentioning Donald Duck?

JOE: We were wondering if we could open right on this menace, then come back to Donald, who is listening with his feathers all standing up.

WALT: You dissolve into the radio, and come back and there is the Duck sitting there.

JOE: Doesn't he have guns and all sorts of things laying [sic] around, to protect himself?

WALT: As he listens, he gets stirred up to a point where he will do anything.

JOE: You have one angle, where he ran out to enlist, then came back dejected. He has flat feet.

WALT: Does he have to go out and enlist?

JOE: We didn't like it. It takes too long.

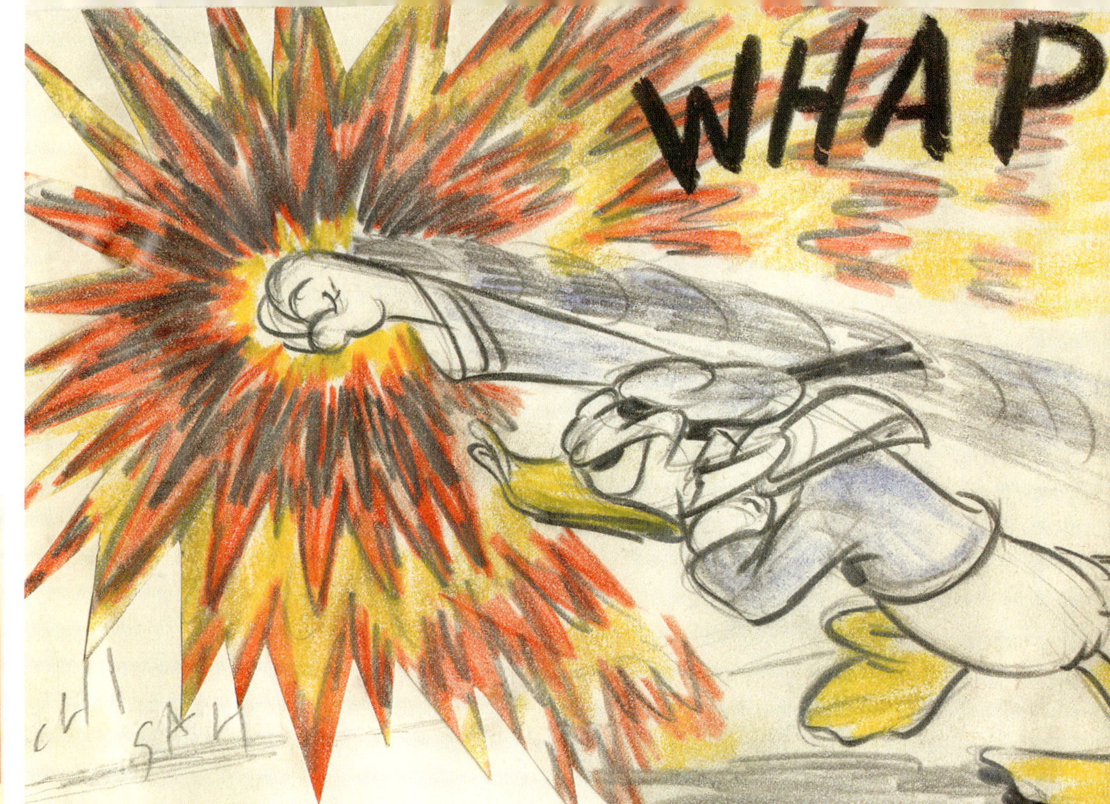

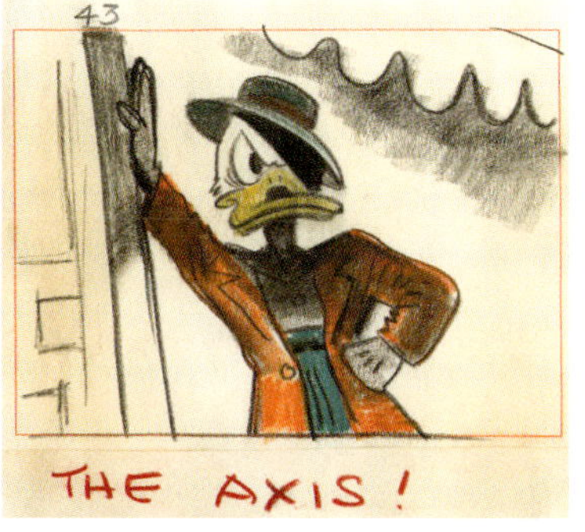

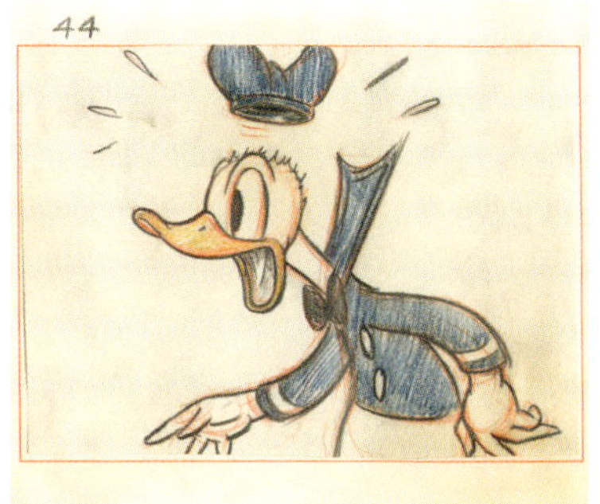

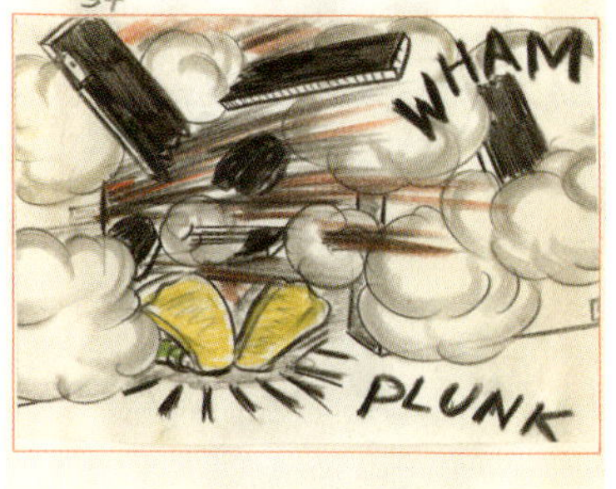

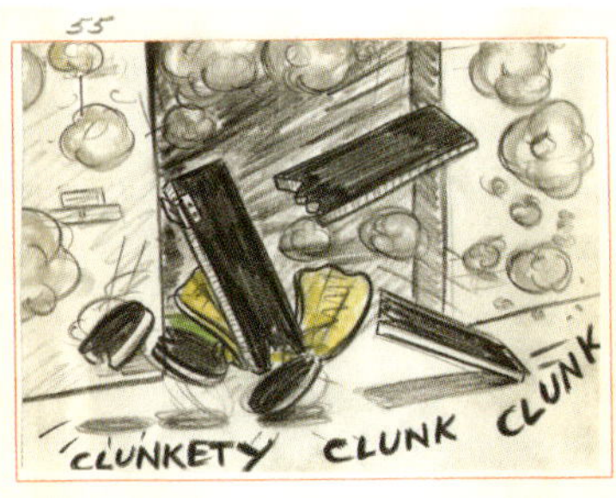

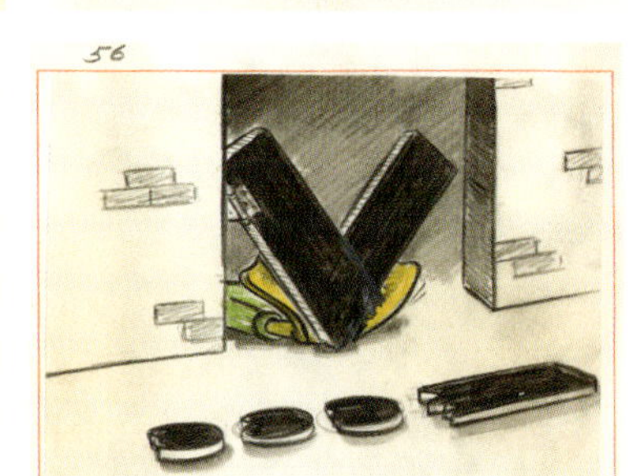

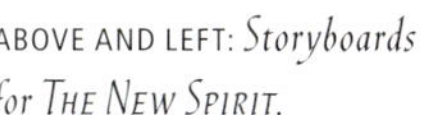

ABOVE AND LEFT: *Storyboards for* THE NEW SPIRIT.

Grant suggests funny visual gags throughout. "On Donald's dollar, instead of an eagle, could it have a duck?" he asks. And later: "He has a sword and a gun. He is running around like a tank, with all this stuff on him, and he gets just to the door when the radio stops him." When Donald drops his tax form in a mailbox, Grant suggests he is "about eighteenth in line and he runs under all the feet and puts his in first." Walt immediately agrees: "That would give it that Donald Duck flavor!"

Grant steers Walt, praises others' ideas, repeats suggestions for clarification and confirmation, and moves forward with Walt's preferences. Grant points out Peet's "good thought" regarding an eagle rolling up his sleeve, then suggests moving into close-ups of the factory, asking if Walt approves the stylized arms and hands pounding out wartime machinery. "Yes, I like it," Disney replies. "That's what we want. A certain force. A very graphic way to represent something."

Shorts at Disney normally required about six months in production; *The New Spirit*—from phoned-in script approval by Washington to film negative delivery from Technicolor—was completed in only four weeks, "the fastest time ever made on any cartoon," Disney wrote to Undersecretary of the

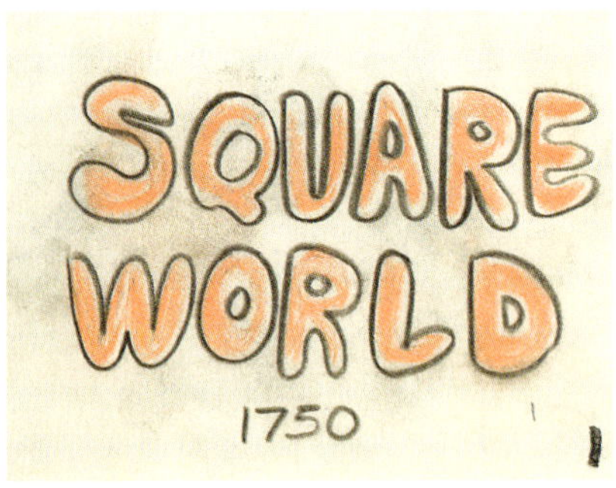

THIS PAGE AND OPPOSITE: *Story sketches and ideas for* THE SQUARE WORLD.

Treasury George Buffington.[4] The government offered the film to 12,000 theaters free, and it quickly became a hit. *The New York Times* film reviewer called it "the most effective of the morale films yet released by the government." It was nominated for an Oscar, and within six months a sequel, *The Spirit of '43*, was ordered.

Meanwhile, Grant and Huemer plunged into other war-related shorts, including the Academy Award–winning *Der Fuehrer's Face*. It was originally titled *Donald Duck in Nutzi Land*, and the two writers loaded the narrative with satirical visual puns. Poor Donald is oppressed and depressed living in a nightmarish totalitarian country. Sharply parodied is the Nazi habit of incorporating swastika imagery into home décor and landscaping; in Nutzi Land, shrubbery, trees, and houses are shaped like broken crosses or contain Hitler's mustache and forelock.

Donald awakes each dawn to a sour oompah band, an alarm clock raising a one-arm "Heil Hitler!" salute, a bayonet's sharp point. He subsists on fake food for breakfast: wooden bread, aroma of eggs and bacon, and coffee made from a single bean. He toils on a bomb factory assembly line inspired, Grant said, by Charlie Chaplin's *Modern Times*. Tightening shell casings between obligatory salutes to images of Hitler at ever-increasing speeds, Donald goes mad in a wildly surreal sequence reminiscent of *Dumbo*'s Pink Elephants section.

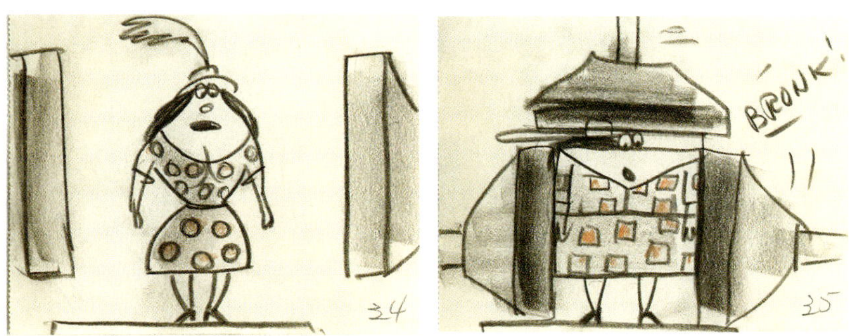

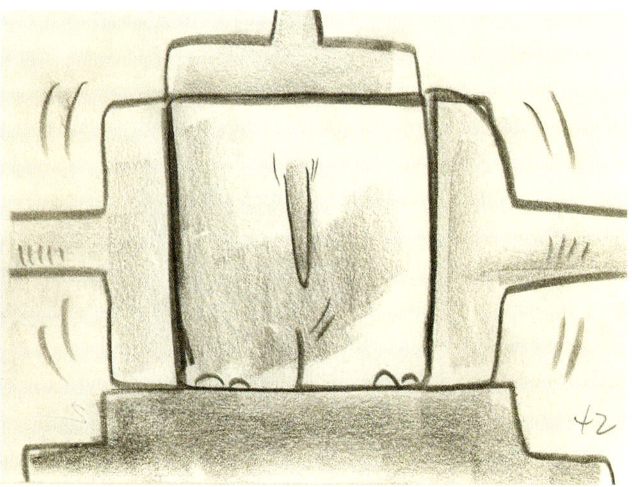

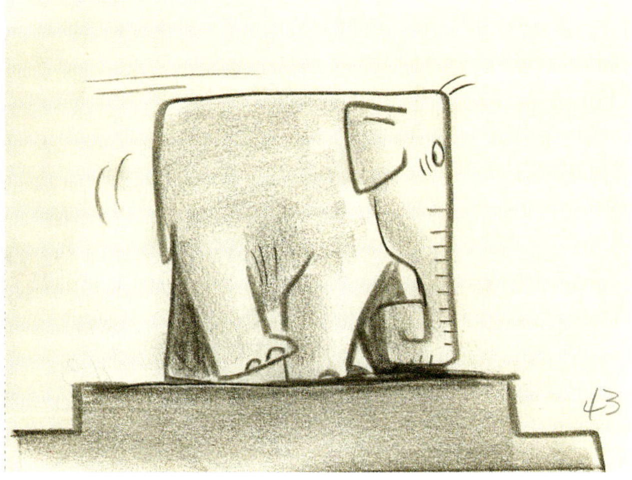

The Square World, another Grant/Huemer protest against totalitarianism, racism, and loss of personal freedom, reached only a preliminary stage. The allegorical tale concerns people in the land of What's-Its-Name, who, like everyone, have many shapes. Mighty-Highty-Tighty, the megalomaniacal ruler, is squat and square. He declares, "I do not like so many shapes. My shape is the right shape!" His soldiers set forth to remake the entire world into square shapes, including people, buildings, cars, trees, even chickens and their eggs. When babies continue to be born in a diversity of shapes, Mighty-Highty-Tighty commits suicide.

The imaginative puns are in a modernist, childlike stylization unusual for Disney, resembling European poster graphics, which United Productions of America later adopted for their shorts, such as *Gerald McBoing Boing* (1951). It would have worked well in limited animation, but Disney wasn't interested. Its theme is similar to *Der Fuehrer's Face*, and Grant heard from the legal department. "They thought it was too communistic."[5]

Grant and Huemer's experimentations wandered far from the familiar, tried-and-true Disney formulas.

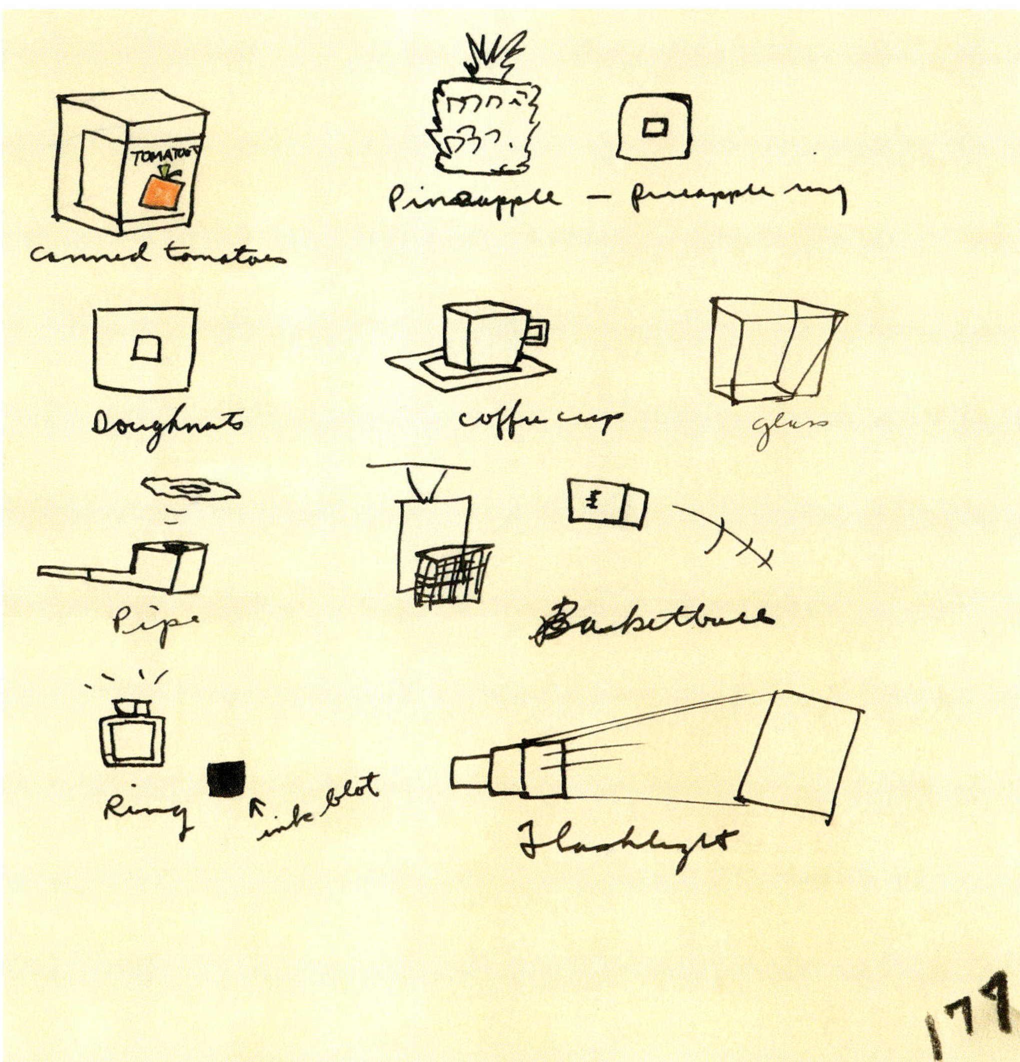

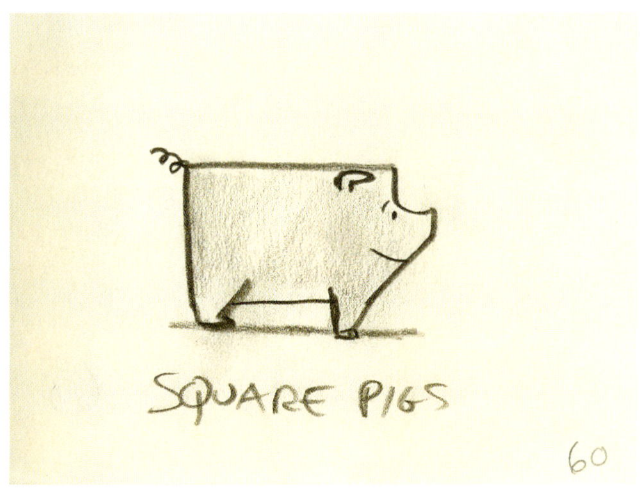

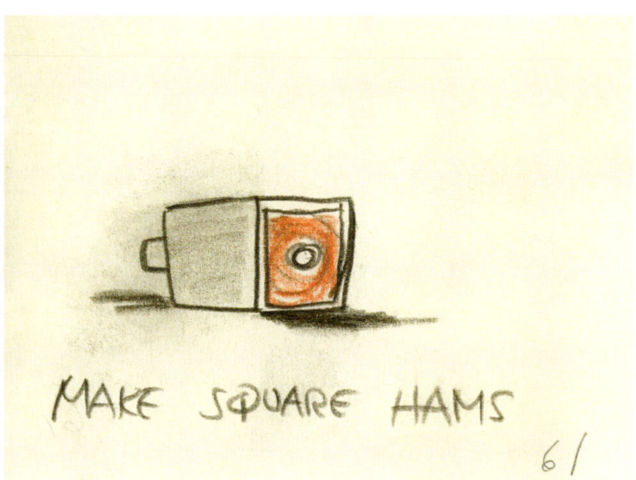

Disney's preference was for traditional fairy tales, not original, outré morality politics. Though war projects took priority, Disney planned for a return to full-length animated films. In September 1943, before market conditions allowed, he assigned Grant/Huemer to *Cinderella*, a project proposed in the 1930s (as were *Peter Pan*, *Alice in Wonderland*, and *The Little Mermaid*).

Roy Williams drew a cartoon of Disney visiting one story man's room after another with Cinderella's glass slipper. When he slips the shoe onto Grant's foot, he yells, "It fits!" as Grant holds his nose.[6] "That sort of picture didn't appeal to me at all," Grant admitted. "I never liked pictures where you knew

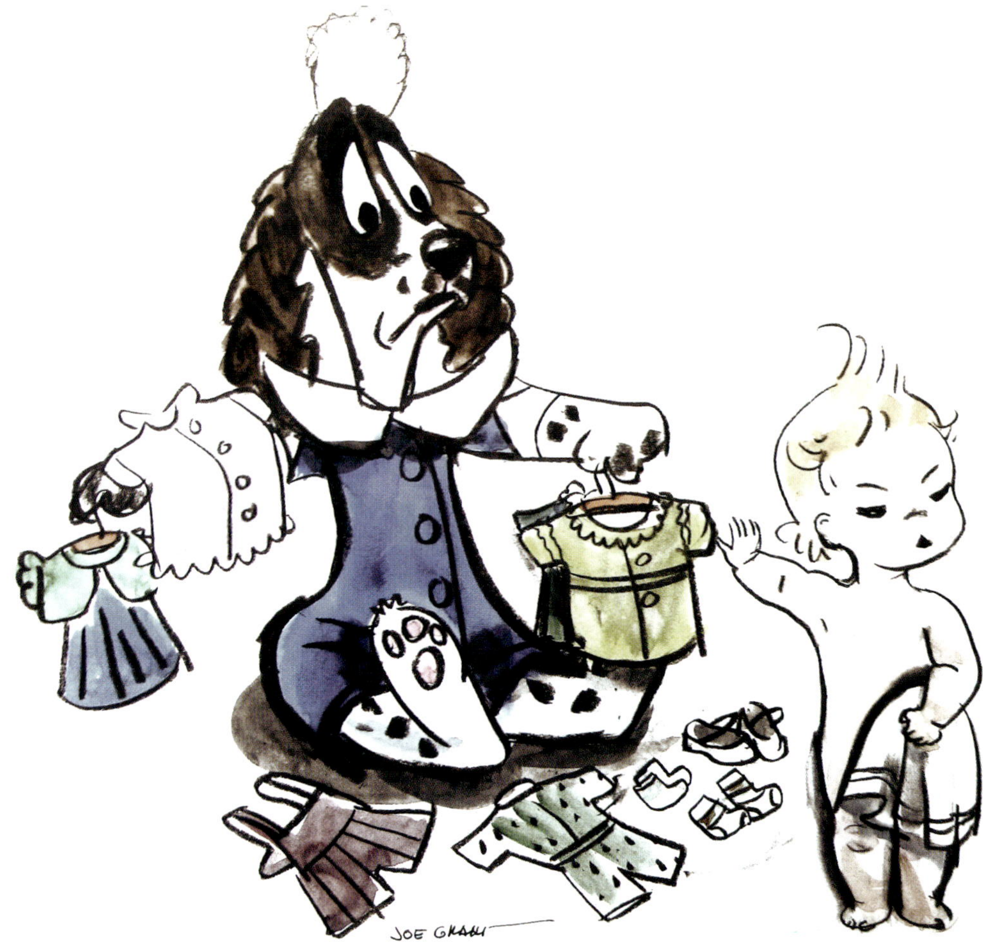

aunt with two Siamese cats. On a visit to the Grant home, Disney, always searching for story material, noticed the Lady drawings.

"Joe, why don't you make a storyboard of that?" Walt asked.[8]

Dutifully, Grant, Jack Miller, and Mary Blair drew and painted "possible business" for Lady's adventures. Scripts were written from July through December 1939, and in 1940 and 1941; then the war intervened.

However, *Lady* drawings appeared in Grant's solo art exhibit at the Chouinard Art Institute (from April 19 through May 20, 1942) and were reviewed by the *Los Angeles Times*:

> Gayest art show in town just now is by Joe Grant—a Walt Disney animator who gets in the groove and stays there . . . Grant exemplifies the Disney flair for cartoons that are both funny and beautiful. Dogs of all sorts, bachelor girls, babies and flowers flow off his crayon or pen alive and moving and touched off with just the right accent.

The review cites as "extra good" Grant's illustrations "for a story about Norah, a canine nurse who has a towheaded baby in charge." Exhibiting pseudonymous "Lady" drawings was Grant's quietly

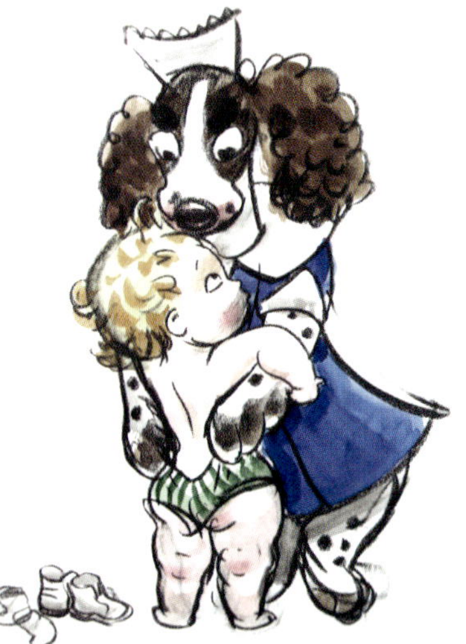

Joe Grant sketches, c. 1939, of the family dog, Lady, as nursemaid to his daughter Carol.

how it was going to end. We wanted to be original as we could be, but we were far from [being] always right, believe me." In 1938, Dick Huemer had suggested to Walt that he produce J. R. R. Tolkien's *The Hobbit*, first published in 1937. But Disney "couldn't see it."[7]

A preliminary *Cinderella* storyboard was halted in 1945, then sputtered up again in 1946 with other writers; the next year, writing and storyboards began in earnest for the film that in 1950 became Disney's feature animation comeback.

Another recurring assignment proved more to Grant's liking because he provided the original story. *Lady and the Tramp* originated in 1939 soon after the birth of Grant's daughter Carol. He sketched the baby with the family's springer spaniel, Lady Nell the Second; he soon built a cartoon world around Lady, including a Highland terrier neighbor and a haughty

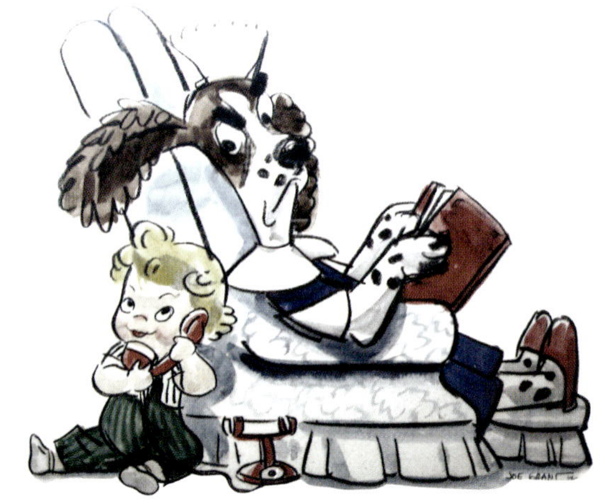

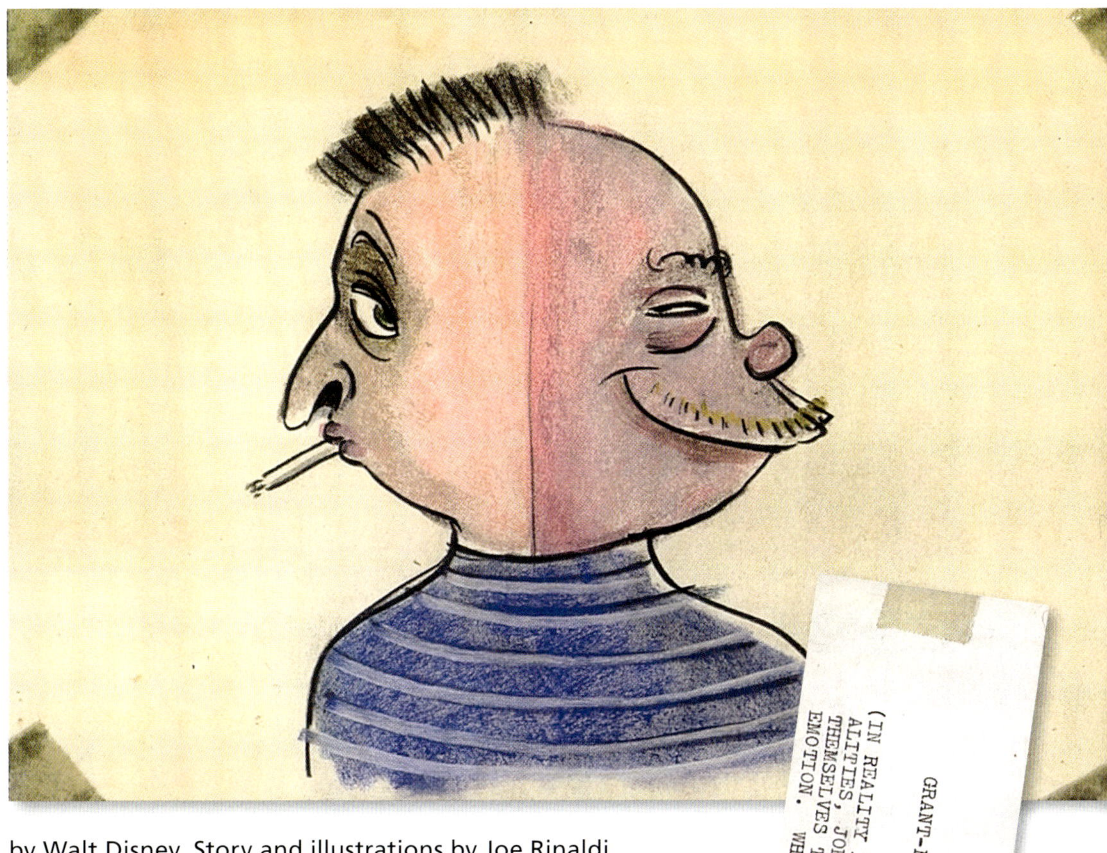

Joe Grant and Dick Huemer, Disney's star writers.

defiant way of continuing to promote the project to Walt. If he didn't see the exhibit, Walt certainly would not have missed Grant's lauditory review.[9]

In 1943, *Lady* leapt back to life with a Grant/Huemer script. The cost for six weeks' work preparing the story script ("Phase 2") included "direct salaries" of $1,530 for Grant and $1,020 for Huemer.[10] Their story proved dull, except for two territorial skirmishes: comical between Lady and the two cats, and melodramatic when Lady protects the baby from a rat. Disney disliked the script, but continued to be intrigued by the dog theme and characters.

In 1945, Disney read a *Cosmopolitan* magazine story titled "Happy Dan, the Cynical Dog," a fable for grown-ups by Ward Greene. Seeing dramatic/romantic possibilities in combining Lady's soft personality with a hard-edged male, he bought the story's rights. In August, outside writers discussed *Lady* with Grant and Disney, now to include a new dog named (at one time or another) Homer, Rags, and Bozo, before becoming Tramp.[11]

A June 20, 1946, memo from Grant to Disney indicates *Lady and the Tramp* was in consideration as a thirty-minute "featurette":

> The new song "I'm Free As the Breeze," will be ready for you to hear on Monday. Also an acetate of "The Lady and the Tramp," with new lyrics. We all think that the new "Dog Opera" idea of handling "Lady" has breathed new life into it.[12]

The unpredictable Disney "suddenly decided that the picture we make should come from a book," Grant said. "And it drove Dick and I crazy!" The idea "in his [Disney's] mind . . . gave it authenticity." In 1953, four years after Grant left the studio and two years before *Lady and the Tramp* was released, a novel was published titled *Lady and the Tramp—The Story of Two Dogs* by Ward Greene, with a foreword by Walt Disney. Story and illustrations by Joe Rinaldi were from storyboards for the film-in-progress. "There was no originality there," Grant commented.

To Grant's great dismay, he received no screen credit for his essential contributions. Rubbing salt in his wounds, studio publicity circulated stories that the film's inspiration was a cocker spaniel puppy Disney gave to his wife wrapped in a hat box. "Somebody said, 'Well, Walt had a dog like that.' It turned out he had two poodles, which had nothing to do with it. They were all frizzied up," Grant scoffed.

Lady and the Tramp, Grant said in 1995, is "a real tragedy as far as I'm concerned as far as the credit for it. This I never forgave Walt for. He knew damn well where all this stuff came from!"[13]

Public recognition of Grant's creativity was important to him. In January 1944, he participated in an art exhibition at The Little Gallery in Beverly Hills with eight other Disney artists, including Mary Blair, Jim Bodrero, Marc Davis, Phil Dyke, Virgil Partsch, Bill Peet, Elmer Plummer, and Martin Provensen. According to the *Los Angeles Times*, Grant stole the show:

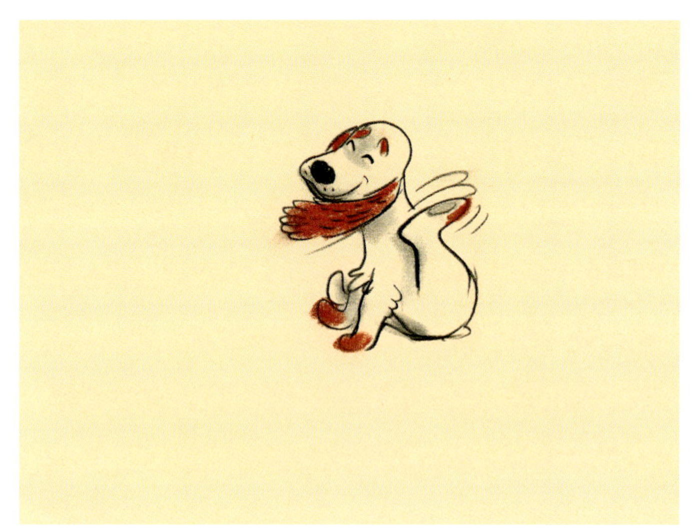

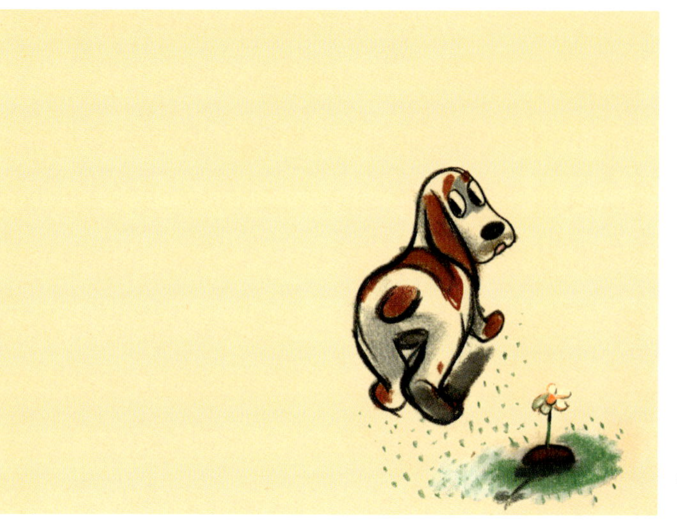

Joe Grant's idea sketches for LADY AND THE TRAMP, *c. 1939.*

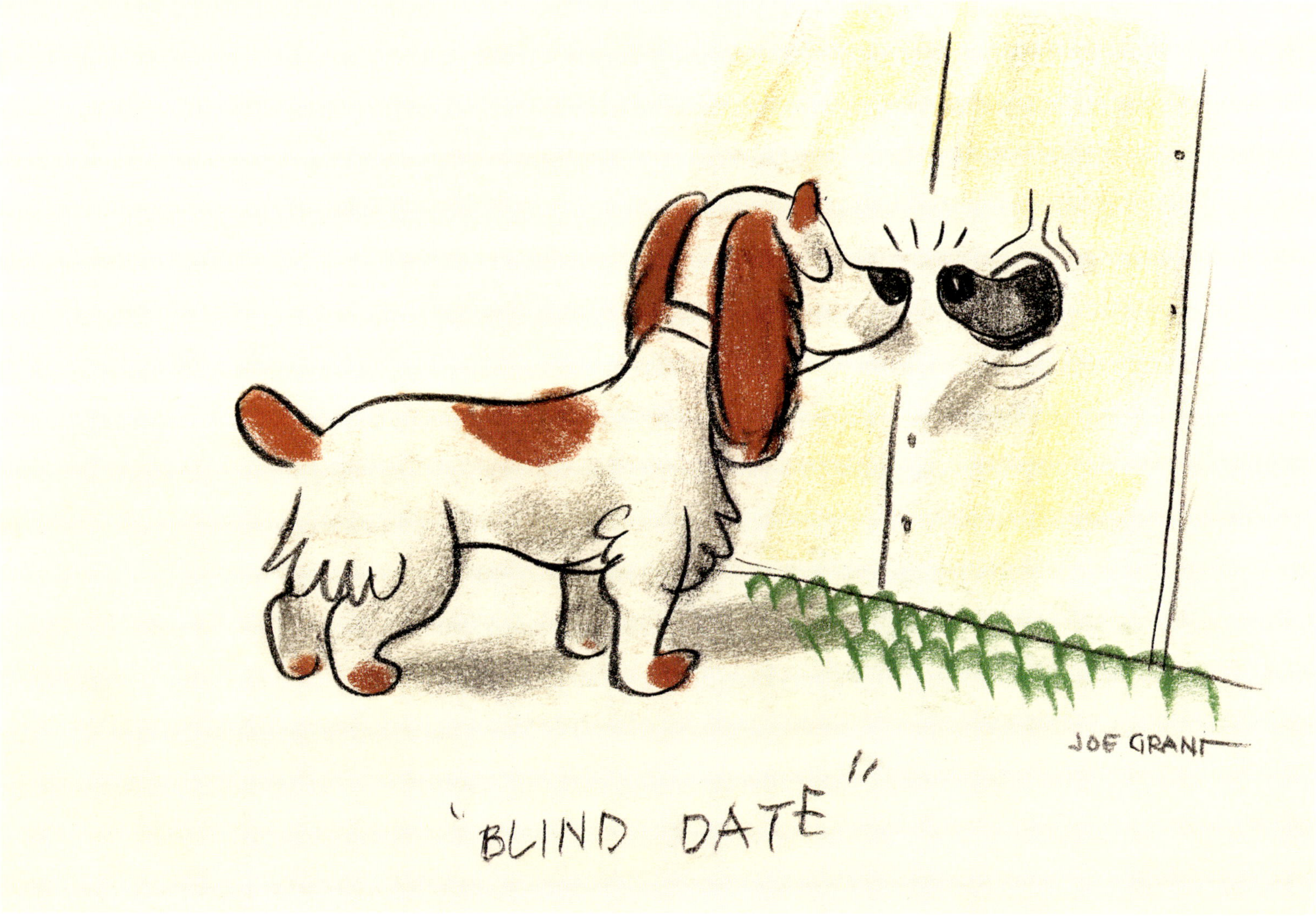

JOE GRANT

"BLIND DATE"

> Joe Grant leads the fun. He paints pert little nudes or models them in colored ceramic. See his Anne Boleyn—before and after she lost her head. And if you like your humor more weird, his triangular people on roofs might suit you.[14]

The review was a balm on the stressful balancing act he performed at the studio, dealing with a temperamental boss and petty jealousies of coworkers, while trying to contribute creatively to an art form he loved. "A sort of exhaustion set in" during this period, Grant admitted. He feared his talent as an artist "was beginning to fade, and I was depending on other people for things I could delineate as well or better.

"And another thing, too, is the anonymity," he said. "I had come from a newspaper in which my name was in the paper almost every day. And I was known as a person!" He felt an "ache to get back to my caricatures and newspaper illustrations, magazine, whatever I had going."[15]

"During the war," Dick Huemer recalled, "Joe Grant and I were finally at odds with Walt and he with us, and we thought we ought to leave."[16] One day they drove to Culver City to talk to MGM executive Fred Quimby about joining his cartoon division, home to *Tom & Jerry* and *Droopy Dog*. "We asked ourselves, what kind of films will we make there?" Grant recalled. "What kind of stories? It won't be the same or as good, and we don't like the films these guys make anyway. So we talked ourselves out of leaving."[17]

Disney learned of their restlessness because during the war, Huemer said, "You weren't allowed to change jobs, and employers were obliged to tell a competitor when men were thinking of changing jobs, which Quimby did. Or at least Walt found out somehow and he forbade us to leave. So we finished out our contracts."

They reconciled themselves to a strained situation with Walt, who by the end of the war was "ill-tempered to the point of acrimony," wrote Steven Watts in *The Magic Kingdom: Walt Disney and the American Way of Life*. "This work-driven, temperamental man, operating under mounting stress, became increasingly cranky, even bitter, and lashed out with greater frequency and intensity at his employees," who called him "the wounded bear" behind his back.[18]

Secretly, away from the studio, Grant and Huemer formed their own company (Grant & Hume) and sought legal protection of cartoon characters and products of their own devising. They applied for a design patent (on January 8, 1945) for Oogle, a pop-eyed elephant-like creature they planned to market as a doll, a comic strip, and a book of seven short stories. Grant & Hume commenced a patent search on the name "Surrealism" as applied to toiletries for a grotesque perfume bottle they designed—a Venus de Milo with a globe head in a brick pattern.

Other Grant & Hume ideas: "Brush Off" lint remover for clothing; plates imprinted with babies' hand- or footprints by licensees, such as child photographers; kids' stories illustrated by figures created by arrangement of typography; illustrated stationery for little boys and for little girls; a toy Indian teepee as a cover for a child's chamber pot; and chewing gum for travelers containing an anti-motion-sickness ingredient.[19]

"You know, I can't figure you out, Joe," Disney once said to Grant, who replied, "Isn't that good?" Grant surmised he meant, "Where do I fit in here, what am I doing? So I said, 'Well, you're still buying the ideas, aren't you?'" "Yeah," Disney replied.

"He wanted to pigeonhole me, as he did with most people," Grant said. "Because he couldn't, he was very frustrated."[20]

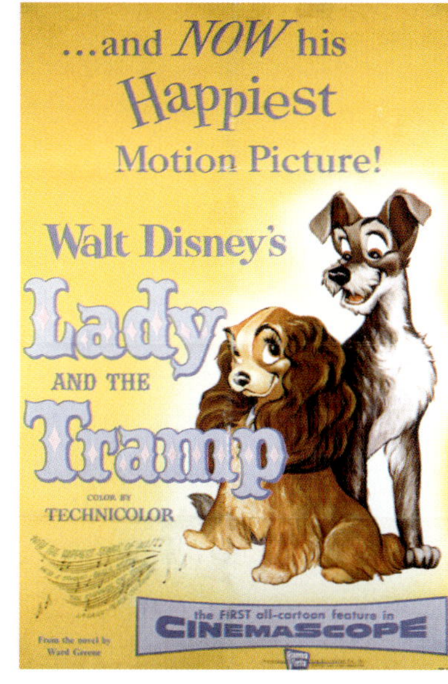

Lady and the Tramp poster (1955).

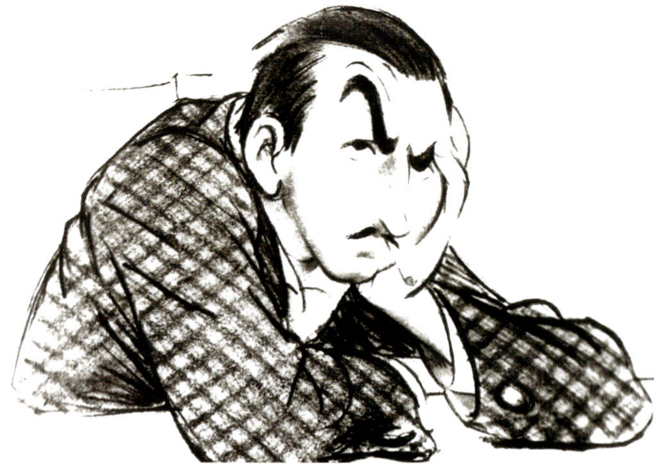

In the summer of 1946, nearly 500 Disney employees were laid off and *Alice* and *Peter Pan*, among other features, were postponed indefinitely. The studio, scrambling to regain its prewar footing, diversified into live-action combined with animation, such as *Song of the South* (released that fall), and "package" features consisting of cartoons linked by music, such as *Make Mine Music* (released in August). For the latter, Huemer was on the story team and Grant was production supervisor, in effect its producer although Walt was "the ruling voice and he made the decisions."

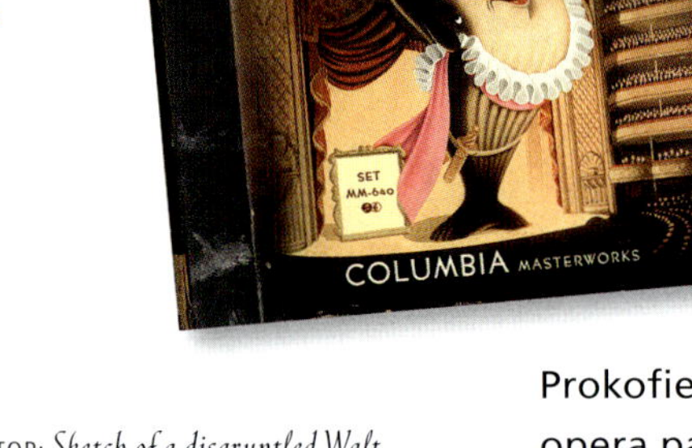

"I was really involved up to my neck in that thing," Grant said of producing a "roughneck *Fantasia*." In *Make Mine Music*, ten pop music segments were visually interpreted in ways brilliant to bathetic. Among the successful: Benny Goodman's playfully surreal sections ("After You've Gone," "All the Cats Join In"), a charming interpretation of Prokofiev's "Peter and the Wolf," and an imaginative opera parody, "The Whale Who Wanted to Sing at the Met." The film's nadir is "Ballade Ballet" with David Lichine and Tatiana Riabouchinska (of the Ballet Russe) dancing among a flock of insipid Cupids in syrupy settings to Dinah Shore warbling "Two Silhouettes." Disney "felt it needed a sentimental piece to slow it down," Grant said, "but it was out of place for me."

TOP: Sketch of a disgruntled Walt Disney, artist unknown. ABOVE: A record album from a segment of MAKE MINE MUSIC *(1946). RIGHT: an elaborate neon marquee in New York.*

Grant felt zero enthusiasm for the project. "I felt this was second-hand stuff, just putting a bunch of shorts together." In any case, "as [with] all producers there, it's Walt's production and you had to follow through." If Grant was unhappy with a sequence director, he had to "go in on Walt's coattails and put him in front of you [to say], 'This is what I don't want done.'"[1]

During impromptu hallway conversations or in Disney's office after work, Grant gingerly brought up problems. Sometimes Disney would say, "Joe, I don't agree with you. I think it's fine the way it is." And that would be that. "Just so it wasn't at the point where you were running around snitching on somebody," Grant explained. "You had to force your ideas the best way you could." Disney agreeing with him proved problematic, too; often he expressed Grant's opinion

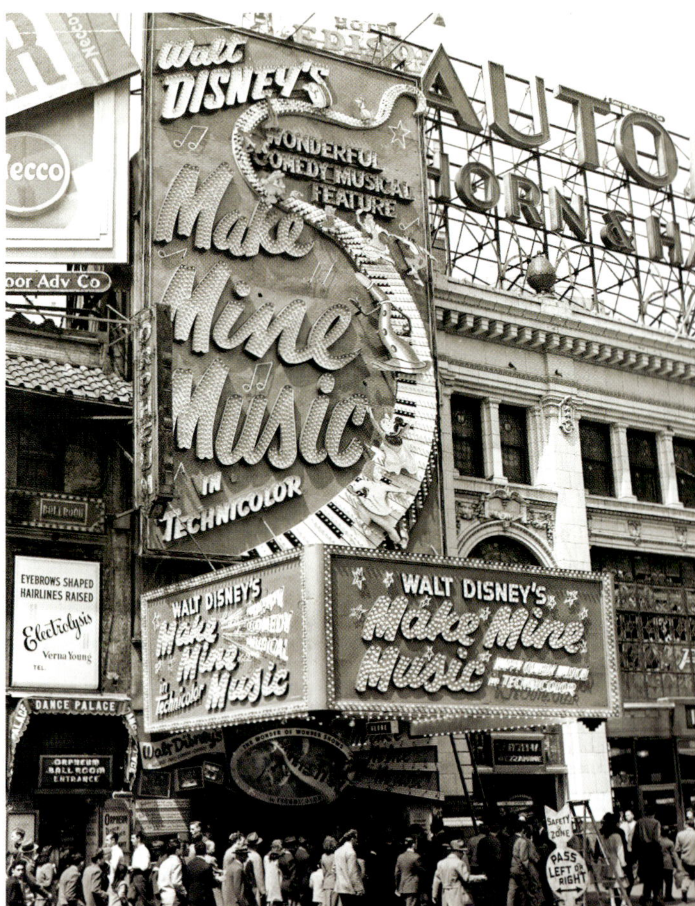

bluntly: "Joe doesn't think this is right!" Embarrassed, Grant could "see the director burning."[2]

Make Mine Music made a small profit but was disdained by most reviewers. Disney, Grant thought, "was kind of noncommittal" and distant about the film. "And I didn't feel completely appreciated for all the work we did."[3]

In early 1946, Disney hired Salvador Dali to create conceptual art for *Destino*, a surrealist short. Although it was soon shelved (and not produced until 2003, thirty-seven years after Disney's death), Grant was encouraged by Disney's sporadic interest in expanding the borders of mainstream animation.

He attempted to interest him in contemporary writer/illustrators, such as Ludwig Bemelmans and James Thurber. "We wanted 'Unicorn in the Garden' before UPA got it." It was a story from Thurber's 1940 book *Fables for Our Time & Famous Poems Illustrated*, which UPA produced in 1953. Unfortunately, Thurber hated the Disney executive sent east to make a deal for that property as well as for Thurber's other books, *Many Moons*, *The White Deer*, and *The 13 Clocks*, all, Grant believed, "good feature material. I felt if we sent somebody back there with a little more artistic approach to it and let [Thurber] dream a little bit with it, we would have gotten it."

Don Quixote was another property the studio "never got anywhere with," Grant said. "A lot of that stuff was, in a sense, beyond Walt. It had to be simple enough and an opportunity for humor for him to really feel it. Every script or treatment of it didn't seem too exciting. [Though] it had a possibility for romance in it and two good characters to follow through [and] two animals to use." Grant and Huemer were part of a small "heretical bunch...that wanted to do something more sophisticated all the time."[4]

Instead, Disney tossed them a 1930 short story written for *Cosmopolitan* magazine by Sinclair Lewis called "Little Bear Bongo," about a circus bear cub who escapes to a life in the wild. Grant and Huemer spent two weeks investigating the feature possibilities, then candidly wrote Disney a negative assessment:

> . . . we find Bongo himself too shallow to build on. As for the background of the story, we find it terrifically limited . . . the whole plot and situation fails to register as an adult idea, the desire for which you yourself expressed so well when you said that adults are always looking around for some little kid to take in to see our pictures. We . . . have for some time been convinced that the future of this business lies in the finding of new ways to intrigue adult audiences.

Disney bullheadedly made *Bongo* as part of *Fun and Fancy Free*, a weak compilation feature in 1947. Grant and Huemer were next assigned to *Alice in Wonderland*.

"*Alice* was nothing but a problem, always a problem," Grant moaned. In the late 1930s, he participated in futile story meetings in which Disney tried to find "entertainment," "warmth," and funny business in Lewis Carroll's stubbornly intellectual tale. A March 15, 1939, story conference transcript reveals Walt's frustration with the project:

WALT: (To Joe) Have you been through *Alice in Wonderland* lately?

JOE: No. I've been through the script though. I think there are some pretty good situations in this.

WALT: Yes, and some, too, that are not so good.

JOE: I like the stuff on the disappearing cat—swell possibilities in that.

WALT: Yes. Let's see. What are the good situations?

JOE: The tea party stuff is good.

WALT: Yes, the tea party is to me the best . . . You

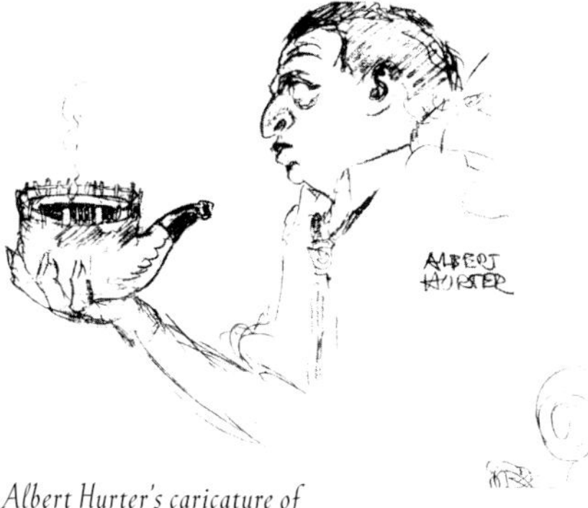

Albert Hurter's caricature of a pipe-smoking Joe Grant.

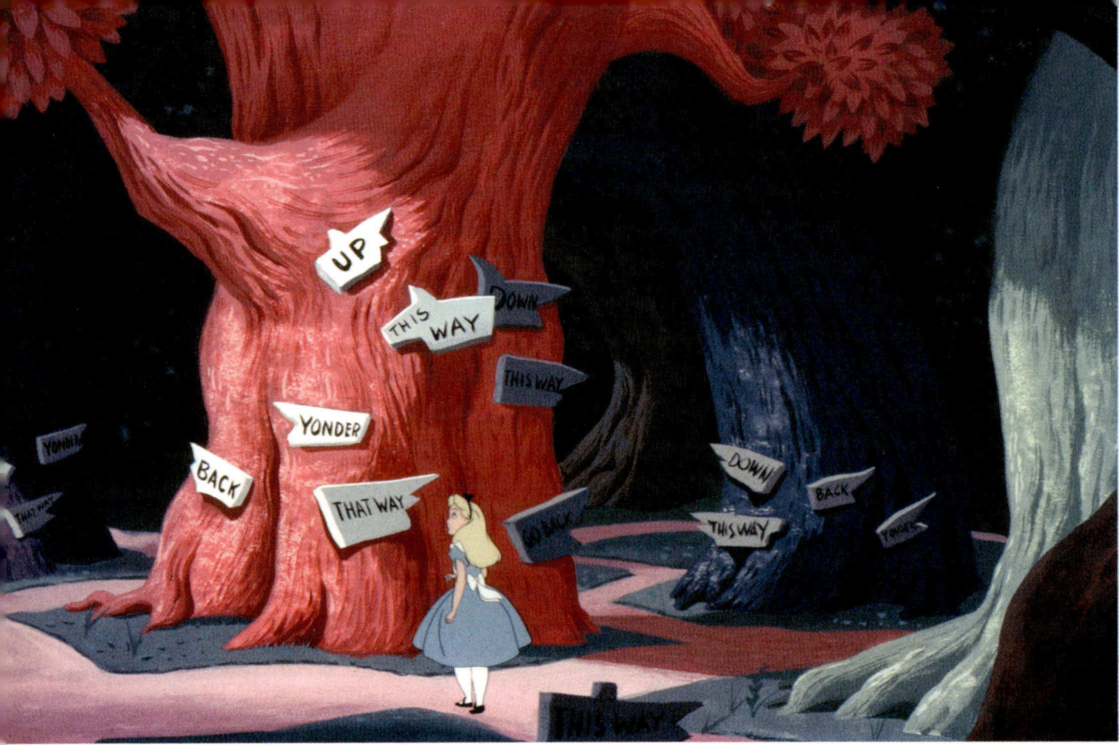

Alice in Wonderland (1951).

> know, I think we're missing a hell of a lot in the stuff that is our medium. . . everything isn't dialogue. Talk, dialogue business that depends on dialogue, hinges on dialogue.

Disney then tore into an unfortunate writer named Dana Coty.

WALT: I'm saying that to you because I think maybe you're the one that's responsible for a lot of silly business that has no basis on anything funny.

DANA: Well, in the duchess's house, I wrote that very loosely to begin with, Walt.

WALT: I don't give a damn how you wrote it. It's what we're driving at. If it hasn't got a basis for something funny, don't write it! There's no use writing the thing and then alibi-ing for it afterwards. It just throws us off the track. Don't just write anything to fill up some pages. We had the same criticism, the last time we were together.[5]

A decade later nothing had changed.

"I think it was over his head," Dick Huemer commented. "He muffed the whole idea of it. To me, it's one of the greatest books in the English language. It's much too good for children. And Walt was unsubtle."

"All the underlying ideas and satire in it was Victorian," Grant explained. "And it was hard to translate and bring up to date. Going into the story was something [Walt] wasn't happy to do." Regarding Alice, Grant noted that "she's an observer. She doesn't do anything except be a victim. And you just set her up there to see a bunch of funny characters and that was it. It was a variety show and the only link was the White Rabbit running back and forth. This seemed like a trivial way to do it."

In November 1945, Disney brought British novelist Aldous Huxley, author of the science fiction classic *Brave New World*, onto *Alice* briefly. *Alice and the Mysterious Mr. Carroll* would combine live-action with animation, as in *Song Of The South*; *that* film's child actor Luana Patten would be Alice.[6] Huxley attended five meetings and wrote a script, which Grant said only "compounded the confusion." It included leisurely dialogue between Alice and Charles Dodgson (Lewis Carroll's actual name).[7]

At story meetings, "every time [Huxley] started to say anything," Huemer recalled, "he never got anywhere because Walt did all the talking and had all the ideas." The partially blind author piped up once; as Walt explained a character's entrance, Huxley said, "Ah yes! I can see that! Hail the Conquering Rabbit comes!" Disney grunted, and Huxley soon disappeared as rapidly as the White Rabbit.

"Walt was always very conscious of publicity and the effect of things," Huemer explained. "This seemed to be a good gesture, to have one of the great living English writers do the great English classic." But "Huxley contributed not one thing to our *Alice in Wonderland*."[8]

Walt was determined to return to full-length animated features despite opposition from his brother Roy O. Disney, the studio's business head. After brotherly arguments and a competitive presentation of storyboards, the less problematic *Cinderella* won out over *Alice*. Story man Bill Peet noted "*Cinderella* was such a simple tale that there weren't any great deviations in it to begin with. Actually, it was a matter of how you worked out the sequences to interlock the cat and mouse situations."[9]

Grant ruefully likened the story's ending to the sinking of the *Titanic*: "You know how it's going to wind up."

Nevertheless, his survivalist instincts said to get more involved in, and enthusiastic for, the chosen feature. He sold Disney on the idea of bringing *Cinderella*'s supervising animators temporarily under *his* supervision in the nearly defunct Character Model Department. As animators developed the characters, Grant proposed, he would make suggestions regarding their design. Then, based on early animation pencil tests, Grant-approved model sheets would be distributed to the animators.

Unfortunately, the first senior animator selected was his bête noire Ward Kimball, assigned to animate a cat. Kimball, who made no secret of his intense dislike of Grant and envied his closeness to Walt, was "really pissed off. This was degrading to me," he said, "going into a bull pen with other Joe Grant slaves," he said. "I thought, I'm supposed to be a talented, experienced supervising animator, and I have to sit here and develop characters under Joe's tutelage? Something rebelled inside of me."[10]

So Kimball spent two weeks drawing a single cat's head in great detail, adding a whisker in the morning (between long coffee breaks) and a whisker in the afternoon, ending up with "a medical drawing" resembling "an old-time lithograph."

"What the hell are you doing?" Grant said. "You've been up here three days and you haven't done a god-damned thing! What the hell is this? Come on, give us some of that old Ward Kimball stuff." Kimball, sadistically playful as a cat, said, "Joe, in order to develop a character, you have to start out with a realistic approach. You have to know what's anatomically correct and analyze it, realistically. I have my own way of working." Grant cursed and walked out.

And then there was Walt, whose interest in animation had waned considerably from the time of the strike onward. True, he wanted to return to making animated features, but his laser focus was now on diversification into live-action features, nature films, television, and amusement parks, not animation. "We were very narrow-minded about everything," Grant said years later. (Grant often spoke of himself using the first person plural.) "We thought [Walt] should do nothing but cartoons. And when he went into anything else, we felt a betrayal.

"But he had that vision, and he was going to complete it," said Grant. "Once he had an idea to do something, even if he found all kinds of obstacles in his way, he did it."[11] As a producer, Grant was earning $400 a week, an excellent salary in 1949.[12] But so dispirited was he by life at the studio, when he handed his paycheck to Jennie (as he always did), he called it "blood money."

"I began to feel sour. Something was amiss."

Long gone were "the glory days" when he said he "couldn't wait to get to work in the morning."[13] Now he was "angry almost all the time," according to Nick Grubb, his son-in-law. "Something was going on. He was very, very upset. Basically he couldn't get them to do what he wanted them to do." He would come home "ranting and raving" saying, "'Jesus Christ, I've got to get the hell out of there!'"[14]

On April 13, 1949, Joe Grant was released from his contract.

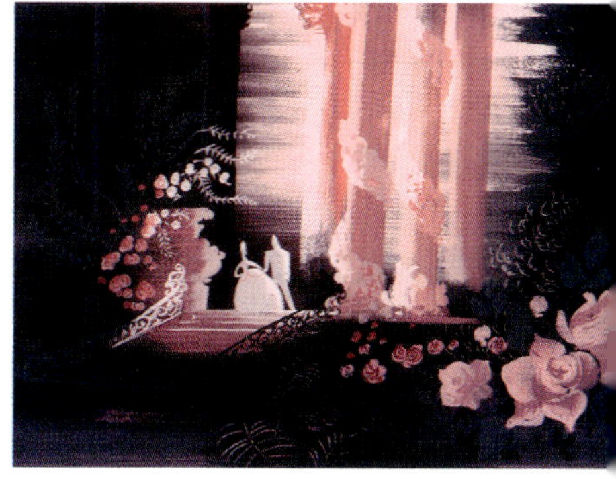

A Mary Blair concept painting for Cinderella *(1950).*

Good-bye to Pixieland

Why did Walt Disney's closest, most trusted, and most powerful colleague leave? Was he fired or did he quit?

Grant never revealed exactly why, but he offered clues. For instance, he shared with friends a bittersweet lament "written in a moment of pique" around 1949 (excerpted below) titled "Good-bye to Pixieland—Chapter One":

> . . . The rivers of fun have long ago dried up. The gales of laughter no longer sweep through the gingerbread towers and set the bells of folly a-tinkling. Some of the pixies in a fit of mournfulness have laid the hands of violence upon themselves. Some laughed themselves to death with broken hearts. Some perished of pernicious ennui. Many fled in time. Others were expelled, kicked out by the royal boot. Some stayed on to the end and watched the slow disintegration of a fabulous and phoney [sic] fairyland. I am one of the latter. . . .[1]

With the diminishment of Character Model personnel, Grant's enemies outnumbered supporters. He was a figure of authority, a studio manager with unique access to Walt Disney, who relied on and trusted his advice regarding films, story, design, and personnel. This did not sit well with those who did not enjoy similar privileges, such as the animators. Envy was inevitable.

"I didn't play the good fairy with all these things," Grant said, admitting he advised Disney on hiring and firing. "There were some people that were not too valuable to the department."[2]

For example, he didn't support Oskar Fischinger (1900–1967), the great German master of abstract animated films, hired for a brief, troubled time in *Fantasia*'s special effects department. "When I had the Fischinger stuff [test animation] run off for Walt, he didn't like it at all," Grant recalled.[3] "As much as I admired the Bauhaus and all I knew about it, [Fischinger] escaped me, too," Grant said in 1994.[4] Within nine months, Fischinger was kaput.

Likewise, Grant found little merit in conceptual watercolors for *Alice in Wonderland* by David Hall (1903–1964), who worked at Disney for nearly a year starting March 1939. Grant claimed "there was no business" in Hall's beautiful drawings. "They were just straight illustrations. Which to him [Walt] would be useless." Disney made final decisions regarding his employees, but Grant's lack of enthusiasm ensured their dismissal.

Though close professionally, Grant and Disney were never friends. Disney, sympathetic for the most part to Grant's ideas, sought his opinion on all studio matters, especially storytelling. "Wherever we went," Grant recalled, "we talked story."[5] He remembered walking with Disney down New York's Fifth Avenue in the midst of the Easter Parade. Crushed fedora on the back of his head, hopping with one foot on the curb, Disney was oblivious of his lopsided gait, so engrossed was he in telling Grant all about *Jack and the Beanstalk*. "He

Dewdrop fairies cavort in "The Nutcracker Suite" segment from FANTASIA.

was involved twenty-four hours a day with whatever the project was."[6]

When Disney visited Grant's home, it was always work-related, even when his two young daughters accompanied him. Not only did Disney discover the story of the dog, Lady, there, but he found *Mary Poppins* and *Winnie-the-Pooh* when Jennie read them to his and the Grants' children. "He wasn't interested in [*Poppins*] right away, but that's the first time he heard of it," Grant said.[7] "It wasn't much later I found out they optioned all that stuff, which, of course, if I had any brains, I would have done that!"[8]

Ward Kimball, in sulfurous interviews, claimed it was he who convinced Walt to "fire" Grant because "he is doing more damage than he is doing good." He wildly accused Grant of being "a freewheeling villain," of "trying to take advantage of Walt . . . with dazzling footwork" and "taking credit" for other people's ideas.[9]

Only once did Kimball experience the kind of professional intimacy with Walt that Grant did on a daily basis for nearly sixteen years. It occurred on a brief train trip they shared to the Chicago Railroad Fair in 1948. Plied by Walt's questions about employees, his tongue loosened by Scotch from Disney's cut-glass decanter, Kimball said he "hated Joe so much . . . I really unloaded, because Joe was another person who was doing the place harm."[10]

Basically, Kimball accused Grant of accumulating power by taking credit for others' ideas. The latter charge is ironic and questionable considering Grant's lifelong creative fecundity. "Bill [Peet] will tell you," claimed Kimball, "that when he was doing story sketches for *Dumbo*, Joe would never tell Walt it was Bill's work." However, Grant claimed it was Aurelius Battaglia of the Character Model Department who "did the great work on *Dumbo*. Beautiful drawings," which Grant did tout to Disney. Peet "wasn't in my department at the time."

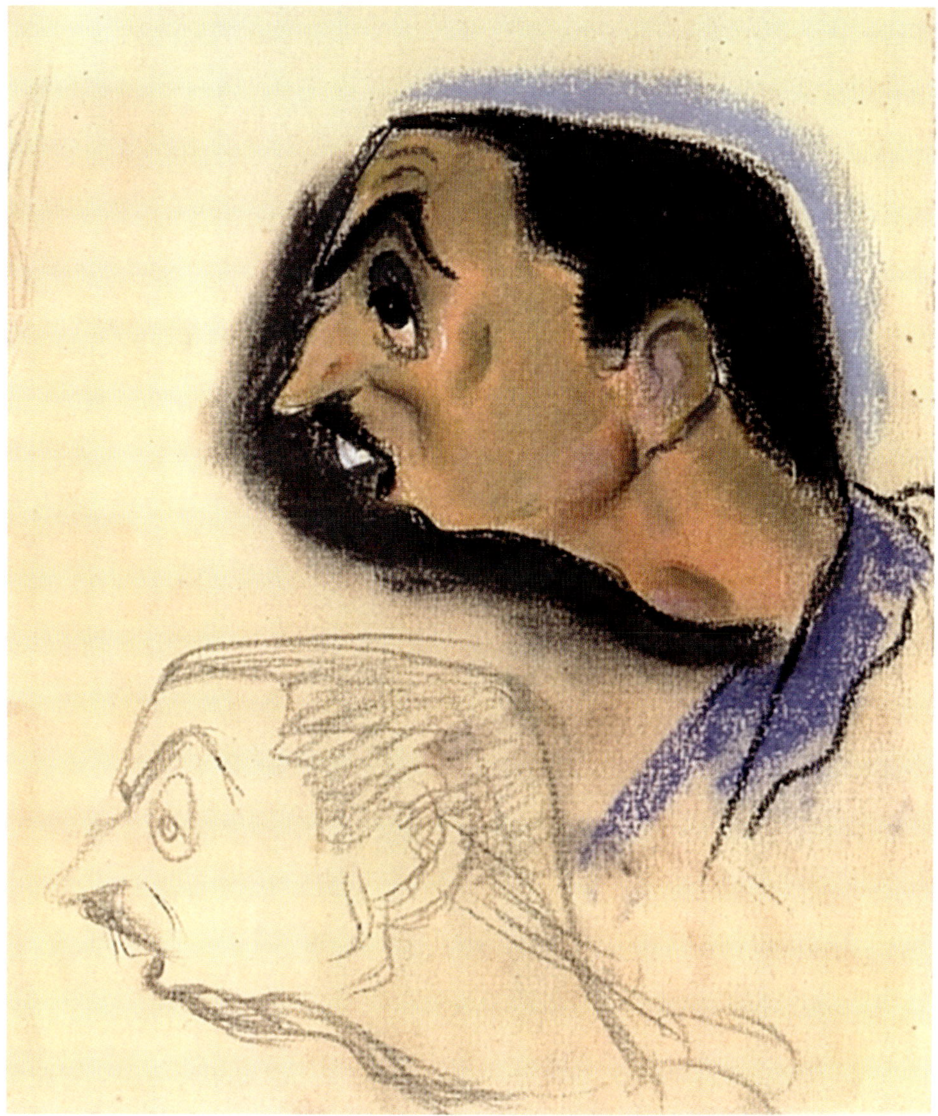

Walt Disney, pastel by Joe Grant.

In *Bill Peet—An Autobiography,* Peet affirms Grant's statement. "Otto Englander, the [story] supervisor of *Dumbo*," wrote Peet, "was familiar with my work on *Pinocchio* and gave me a large part of the story to develop on my own. . . ." Further, Peet notes he did not toil anonymously: "I contributed so much to the production that Otto allowed me to present my storyboards to Walt one day . . . I was greatly relieved to make it through the boards without faltering and find Walt relaxed and smiling. But then Walt was enthusiastic about all my boards on *Dumbo*. . . ."[11]

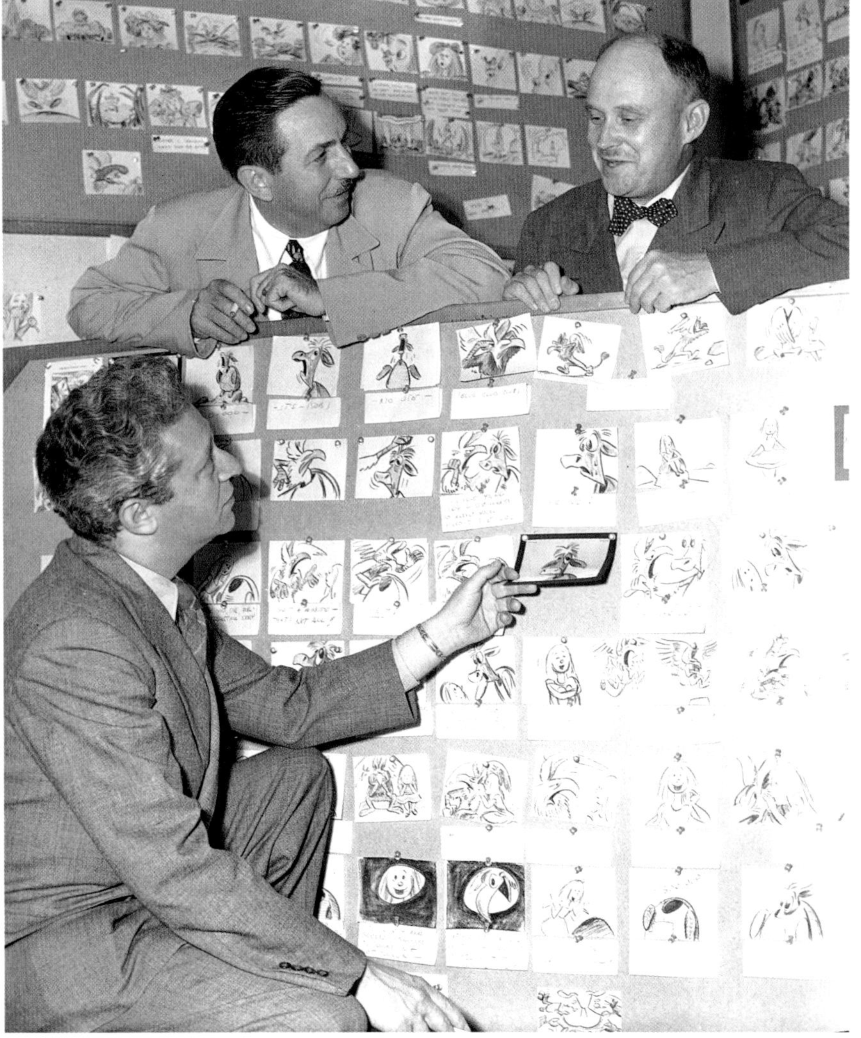

Joe Grant, Walt Disney, and Barnard College professor William C. Greet, speech consultant, discuss storyboards for Alice in Wonderland *on July 18, 1947.*

Grant said in 2003 that "there was a time when Bill Peet was acting up and Walt said, 'You'll never be a Joe Grant!' Of course," Grant claimed, "Peet hated me from that day on."[12]

Grant, as noted, ran an "idea department"; that is, he accumulated concepts, designs, and ideas from *many* artists. Because he had entrée as few others did at the studio, he brought ideas directly to Walt Disney's attention. And sometimes, as happens in large corporate cultures, an individual source went uncredited. "You always have this problem when ideas are being pitched [of] who's getting credit for it," Tom Schumacher observes. "Lot of people get credit for things they didn't create."[13]

For Grant, the most important thing was to bring any and all ideas to Walt's attention, in order to move things along into production. Grant's attitude was, as stated, "These projects to me were just precious. Get them going! I didn't care what the hell they said."

He was confident and energetic, a force to be reckoned with. His cool arrogance and disdain toward the animators, the perceived privilege and aloofness of his department, the jealousy his closeness to Walt engendered, and his cavalier gathering of ideas added fuel to his enemies' fire. Even Dick Huemer complained in his 1974 oral history that Grant was "very unpopular" because "he had the habit of taking other people's work and running to Walt with it as if he had done it." Huemer said he experienced "a lot of friction with this guy for that reason."

But Huemer immediately recanted his statement saying, "I enjoyed working with him . . . He wasn't too bad with me, actually. It's others who have more of a complaint."[14] For his part, Grant felt compelled to take the lead in his relationship with the laid-back Huemer. "Dick was never what you'd call a powerhouse," Grant said. "He's not going to get up and say, 'Do this, do that.' He would be very easy-going . . . Dick was not what you'd call a follow-through man."[15]

Huemer suggested to interviewer Joe Adamson that he "question Bill Peet on the subject [of Grant taking credit for his work]. But stand well back!" When I interviewed Peet in 1997, the irascible story man grumbled about Grant always "saying the right things" to Walt, but he didn't mention *Dumbo*. He did claim that during *Cinderella*'s pre-production stage, Grant took an idea of Peet's to Walt. During a subsequent argument, Grant allegedly "fired" Peet, who immediately brought to Walt's attention this usurpation of his powers. "It took a while" but, according to Peet, that was the act that led Walt "to can Joe Grant."[16]

However, there were larger issues beyond studio jealousies, squabbles, petty backbiting, and rumors that led to Grant's departure. He could have survived all that, *if* he and Walt were still on the same page regarding the Disney Studio's future. But they were not.

"To me it was anathema for him to be doing live-action," Grant said in 1994.

> Here we had the greatest medium in the world. I guess he just got tired . . . Could get rushes on a live-action [film] overnight. Just looked like an easier way out for him in a sense . . . He wanted to move faster. Animation right up to today is a tremendously slow process. It does not move. It looks like still water all the time. He was, in a sense, a Henry Ford. Whatever he was doing he would expand and expand. And if it didn't suit the tempo of his expansion, he'd do something else.[17]

"Having been close to him for quite a while," Grant said, "knowing his nature, there's that expansiveness which is always there . . . he wanted the novelty of something new. And anything technologically that came along he was interested in. He had such a fertile imagination." Grant described Disney as generally "light-headed," meaning that adversity, challenges, and problems rolled off his back. Competitive animation studios, such as UPA or Warners, didn't affect him. "He still had his vision of what he was going to do, and he did it."

Disney "understood the cycle of life," Grant said. "Things come back. What goes around comes around. I've never known him to be desperate about anything."

In 1949, it was clear that Disney's interest lay in forms of entertainment other than animation. But Grant ardently loved animation and its great potential. Walt did not.

Like a disaffected lover, Grant admitted feeling "very cynical about it after a while. Because you ask yourself, 'What's this for?' And I don't know, you could go on for hours analyzing yourself as to why you did the things you did, what was affecting you.

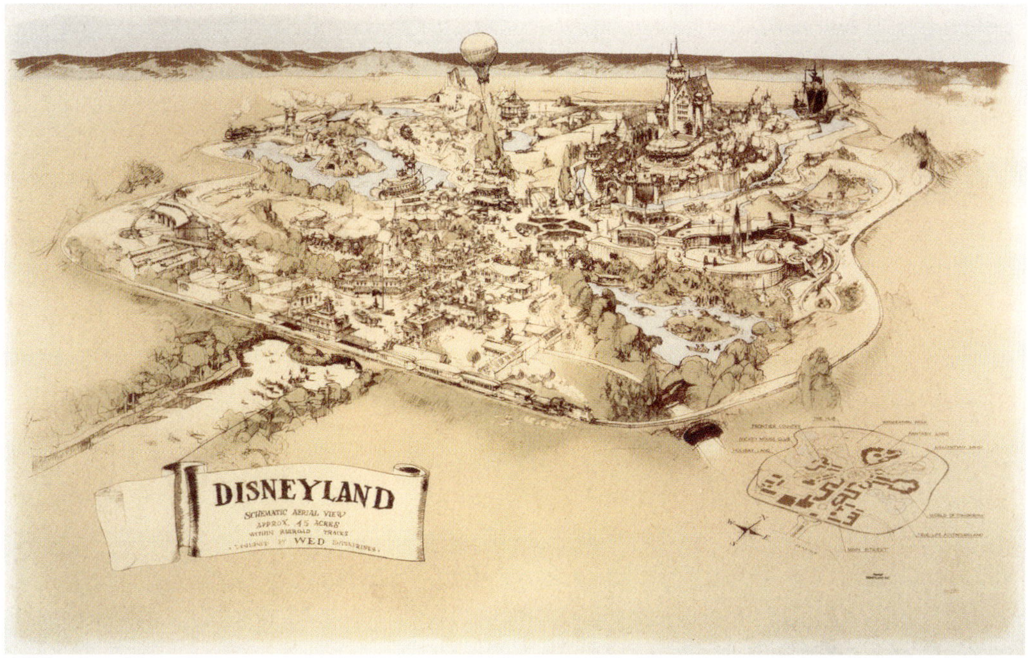

"And I think, too, it was trying to find yourself as an individual. And that was my real big problem."

Grant harkened back again to his early fame as a caricaturist. "If I hadn't had that [recognition] before," perhaps, he mused, he might have continued sublimating himself for the studio's greater good. "You know, we have people at the studio that have never had another job," he said derisively. "They've lived here all the time from beginning to end. I mean, to me that's a pretty dull journey. I wanted some interests beyond that.

"I was beginning to run down. And also I had other ideas of my own. Because I did feel we were more or less becoming disengaged in the whole, great, wonderful adventure."

And so, the two gentlemen parted company.

"I didn't realize he was a genius until after I left," Grant said years later of Walt Disney. "You know you're working with a man every day, he's just workmanlike and he has his way of expressing himself and you were in awe of him, but you didn't realize all of the dynamics behind him.

"He could inspire you, and he could let you down."[18]

ABOVE: *An early map of Disneyland.*
BELOW: *a Joe Grant ceramic design.*

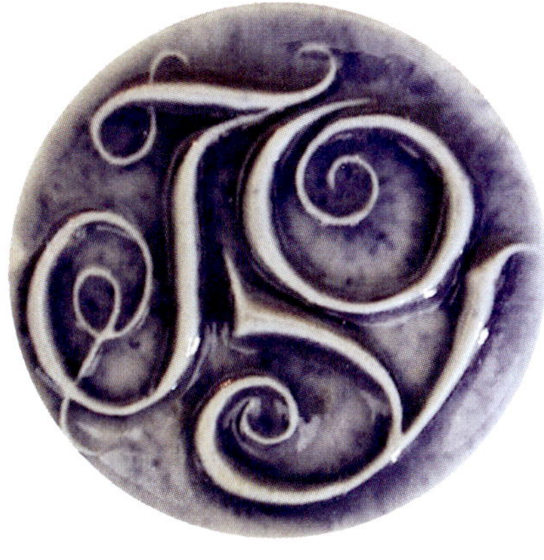

Moving On

Joe Grant separated from the Disney Studio a month shy of his forty-first birthday. On his own after sixteen years, he felt newly energized. His life was before him—and little did he know how lengthy it would be: nearly sixty more years.

"He was not one to wallow in self-pity or express misgivings about his life," Jennifer Castrup says of her emotionally contained father.[1] Indeed, he had much to be grateful for in 1949, starting with Jennie, his loving, supportive wife, and their children, ten-year-old Carol and five-year-old Jennifer. Thanks to Jennie's years of wise money management, they owned the two-acre property she found and the house she designed on Opechee Way in Glendale. "His home gave him a tremendous amount of rootedness," Castrup says.

A Joe Grant painting of himself playing hide-and-seek with daughter Carol, c. 1940.

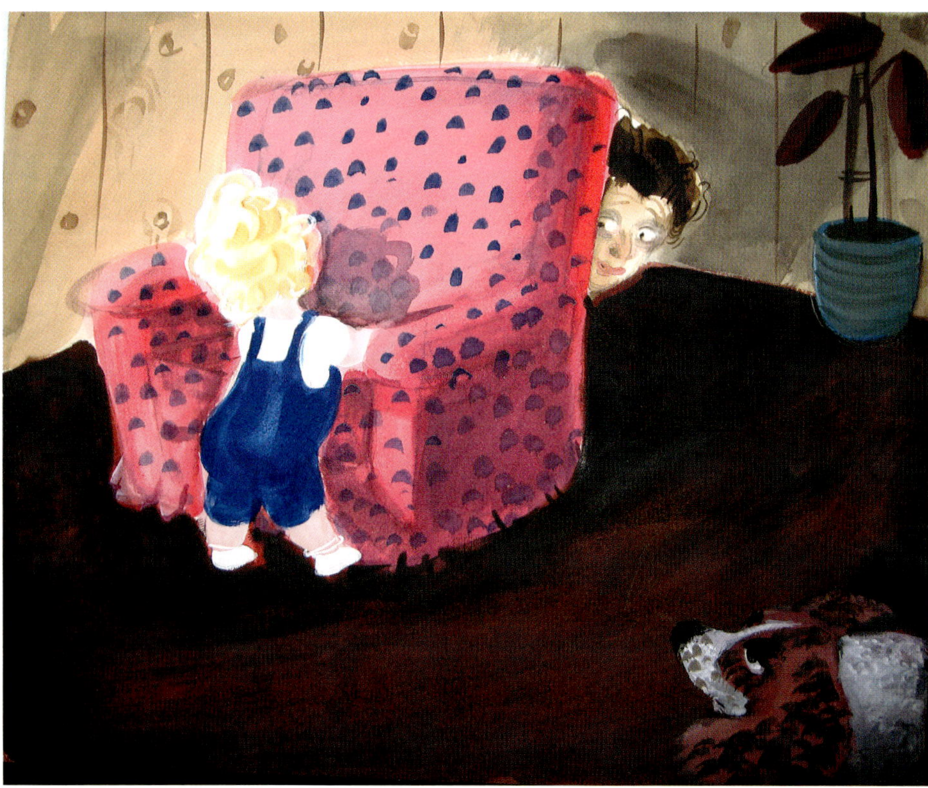

Grant continued supporting Eva, now in her early sixties. "He took care of his mother all her life and so did Jennie," recalls Danielle Workman. Eva helped women as a "practical nurse," caring for them upon their release from the hospital. (Eva Grant died on July 21, 1965.)[2]

Jennie encouraged Joe to follow one of his dreams. Using his backyard kiln, he set up a ceramics business designing and firing plates, tiles, and sculptures. Jennie managed accounting books and became the company's charming saleswoman. The children were delighted. "It was heaven on earth having both parents at home and my dad in overalls out there, playing," Castrup says.

Grant realized from the beginning that the woman he married "is not just a wife" but one "with a brain" who is "a good friend." Together, they made, sold, and shipped ceramics all over the country. "It was clumsy in a way because it was a heavy industry. But we did succeed in it. We had fun."

"It *was* fun," Castrup concurs; however, "for a few years it was a very hard way to make a living. But they sold their lamp bases to some of the finest stores [along with] the plates, tiles. And he invented a way to transfer photography onto plates, and wound up with an article in *Popular Mechanics*. Very inventive man."

Another Grant idea was drawing sequential narratives on "story plates." Plate one, a man sits on a bench, woman going by; plate two, she drops her handkerchief; plate three, he picks it up and they meet, and so forth. "Silly simple stuff," Grant said.[3]

Why ceramics? "He was really a man of the earth," Castrup explains, who "loved working with his hands. As sophisticated as he was in other ways—he could look and be so dapper—at the same time be so comfortable in his overalls moving boulders around. Multifaceted man." As noted, Grant sculpted caricatured busts during his newspaper days, but he

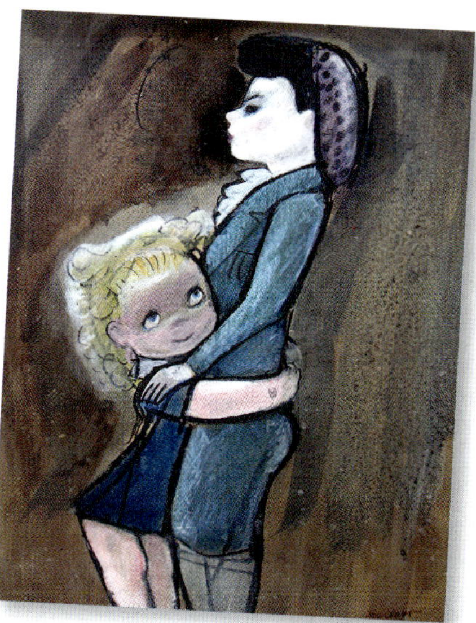

really learned from artists he hired at Disney, such as sculptors Bob Jones and Charles Cristadoro.[4]

Grant didn't abandon sketching. He stashed paper and pencils in plastic bags all over his property should inspiration strike. He drew during business meetings and casual conversations; he drew on restaurant place mats and napkins; he kept cut paper in shirt pockets.[5] An associate described his right hand as "a separate entity" from the rest of him. Drawing was his major means of communication, to comment on events and happenings, to explain, sometimes to apologize. "It has to be an obsession," Grant told Don Hahn. "You have to do it because you can't not do it."[6]

His flow of idea drawings found a perfect outlet when he bought into a greeting card company owned since 1936 by Rudolph Falkenstein, Jennie's uncle, for $10,000.[7] Grant proceeded to create years of witty, visually appealing designs. Anthropomorphism abounds and objects often form the text in baby shower, luau, and tea party announcements; bridal shower and wedding invitations; and holiday greetings. Grant's profuse imagination is amazing.

He immersed himself in graphic reproduction processes (echoing his self-taught engraving at the *Los Angeles Record*). He delighted in solving the mysteries of leaf embossing, thermography (raised text and imagery), silk screen, letter press, and offset—the various qualities of papers and inks. He developed a passion for calligraphy, which became a strong influence in the card designs. Once again he became "art director of one person. Myself!"

"Starting with announcements, invitations, and thank-you notes, we moved into Christmas cards," says Morey Lawton, part of the small staff Grant hired at Castle, Ltd. "Our creations became the 'industry standard' and most emulated."[8] The company won awards, attracting industry-wide attention in the 1950s. In 1961, Williamhouse, Inc., a large paper-conversion company seeking to enter retailing, bought the company. Grant stayed on for a while as head designer.[9] He developed cellophane packaging for note cards with a clip and special rack, instead of boxes, to make them more accessible. He especially enjoyed working in three dimensions, designing packages and boxes.

As he moved toward retirement age, Jennie eased him into travel and seeing the world. "My mother was wonderful at planning next stages," says Castrup. "Both of them were. They worked together [making] very well-planned trips, always [orchestrated] around art." One of their first trips was to England, Carol Grubb recalls. "In the 1970s, they traveled to Japan, then the Netherlands, and a Russian trip. Went to Norway, Denmark, and Sweden. Hawaii. Spain in 1980. They did see the rest of the world."

Jennie began studies at Otis Art Institute and created expressionistic collages. When grandchildren Michael Grubb and Diane Castrup came along, Jennie and Joe became very involved in their rearing. They faithfully attended school functions, and Jennie made elaborate breakfasts for the grandchildren; but Joe insisted they eat a bowl of oatmeal first, passing on his grandfather Nathan's belief in cereal's life-prolonging properties.[10]

In the early 1970s, Joe, Jennie, and daughter Jennifer started Opechee Designs, a ceramics company that produced pots and plaques. Grant hand-carved designs in plaster, with St. Francis a

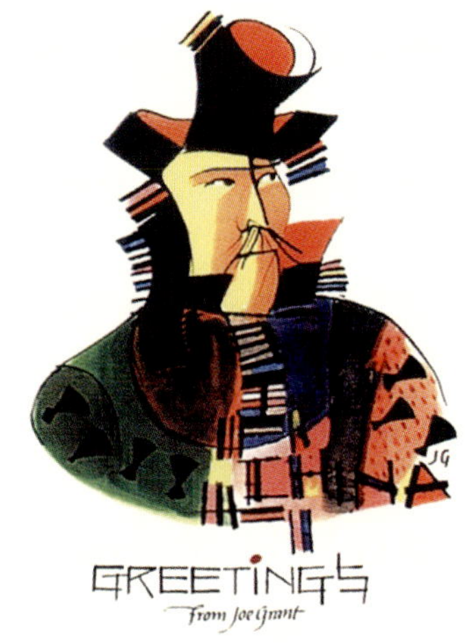

TOP: *Carol and her mother, Jennie, in a painting by Joe Grant.* ABOVE: *a Joe Grant Christmas card.* BELOW: *Grant playing with daughter Carol.*

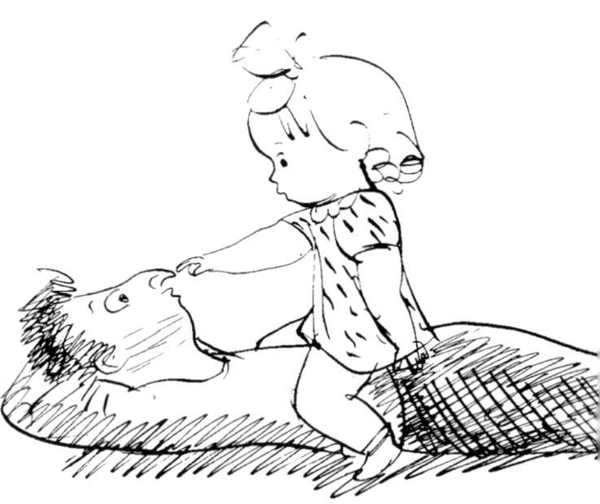

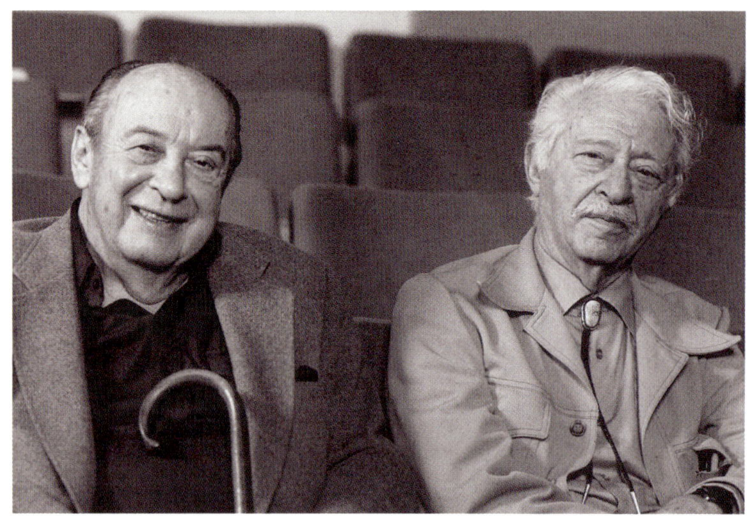

ABOVE: *Old friends Marc Davis and Joe Grant.* BELOW: *Ollie Johnston and Joe Grant.*

favorite subject. The products sold well to Catholic retreat houses and California missions.

In 1985, ASIFA Hollywood, the Los Angeles chapter of The International Animated Film Society, awarded Grant (and seven others) the Winsor McCay Award "for distinguished lifetime contributions to the art of animation." Grant stayed in touch with a few former Disney colleagues, mainly Bill Cottrell, Jack Miller, and Martin Provensen.

In the late 1950s, Joe and Jennie rekindled a friendship with animator Marc Davis and his wife, Alice. One of Disney's famed "Nine Old Men," Davis had admired [Grant] and his friendship since the *Snow White* days, Alice recalls. "If [Joe] was your friend, you had a friend for life. To the day Joe died, he looked up something new and would pass it on. He was very young between the ears, never talking about the past [but about] the future. Very much like Walt. I think [Joe and Walt] were constantly competing with each other and didn't know it."[11]

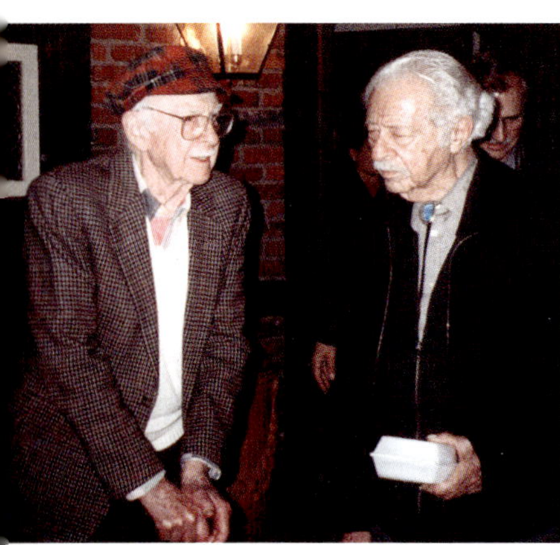

After Grant left the studio, he and Walt Disney never spoke again. "I was too busy, and I'm sure he was," Grant commented late in life. "Once," he remembered, "[Walt] made a remark to somebody who could pass it on: he wondered why Joe didn't visit. But that was just a reaction. When I get into something new, I mean it's 100 percent or 200. And that was the last thing I was interested in at that time."[12]

When Disney died in 1966, Grant felt "sad," but did not regret his long separation from him and the studio. "I had ceramics, greeting cards, and a world of my own."[13]

"Daddy had a hard side to him," Carol Grubb comments. "That's why he was successful. He never let emotions get involved [or] get away [from him]."[14]

Grant always praised Walt Disney to interviewers, never maligned him. Two years before Grant died, for example, he spoke eloquently of Disney's charisma:

> His vitality fills the room. When he talked to you, you found yourself responding visually to everything he was saying. He was a tremendous spellbounder [sic] and a great salesman . . . he was a man who could think on many levels at once. And, also, he had intuition . . . he seemed to know everything ahead of time and he was really amazing.[15]

In old age, Grant adopted a placid, Zen-like attitude toward his former Disney associates, never uttering an unkind word about them. Removed by time and circumstance from the studio's internecine politics and competitiveness, old "rivalries" dissolved. Occasionally he dined with master animators Frank Thomas and Ollie Johnston and their wives.[16]

Grant even praised Ward Kimball, citing "the new spirit" he brought to the studio in 1934, "the remarkable humor that he had," and his musical sense of animation. ("He felt movement to music."[17]) Kimball remained implacable. Once when Kimball visited the studio cafeteria for lunch with a friend, he spotted the elderly Grant passing through and dove under a table.[18]

Bill Peet, another supposed "adversary" from the old days, often phoned Grant to chat. Peet, who quit Disney bitterly in 1964, subsequently enjoyed a second career as an extraordinary children's book writer/illustrator; he also suffered from strokes, throat cancer, and alcohol abuse.[19] When Peet's autobiography was published in 1989, Grant could tease its author: "I told him it should have been retitled, *For the Love of*

Peet!"[20] After Grant returned to Disney in the late 1980s, he suggested to young people he mentored that they should visit Peet, who was recovering from his second stroke, as a gesture of respect.[21]

Grant did not reconcile with his former writing and business partner Dick Huemer, whom he considered a "soulmate" at Disney. "The only time I began to feel a part of anything is when I had Dick Huemer and we wrote together," he said.[22] At some point they stopped communicating. Huemer left Disney after a staff cut in 1948, then returned in 1951 to write special shorts and television and print projects until his 1973 retirement. He didn't contact Grant because, as noted, he had mixed feelings about him; he felt dominated and outpaced by his partner, ten years his junior, who teased the older man by calling him "kid."[23]

That Grant regretted not remaining friends might be intuited from his recollection of a dream in 1979 in which he was alone "in a basement" when suddenly Huemer's presence "passed me by . . . and I said, 'So long, kid.' The next day it was in the papers that he was dead."[24]

A colleague who did stay in touch was story man/director Jack Kinney (1909–1992). Kinney joined the studio in 1931 and often worked with Grant; he directed *Der Fuehrer's Face* among other shorts, and was sequence director on various features, including *Dumbo*'s Pink Elephants and *Make Mine Music*'s Benny Goodman sections.

In 1988, Kinney published an unauthorized account of his early years, *Walt Disney and Assorted Other Characters*. At that time, the new talent at Disney's Feature Animation division was trying to re-create the story development process based on how it had functioned in the 1930s and '40s under Walt Disney. Roy E. Disney, Walt's nephew, sent Charlie Fink, head of creative development, to visit Kinney.

Kinney was in poor health, so his wife asked his friend Joe Grant to attend the bedside meeting and help answer Fink's questions. "Jack was sick and out of it," Fink recalls. "Joe was shy about his credits and deferential because it was Jack's meeting." However, Fink was so impressed by Grant he went back to Disney raving about "the youngest old guy I ever knew."[25]

Tom Schumacher, who was in the middle of his first year producing *The Rescuers Down Under*, invited Grant to view the work-in-progress. Curious as always, Grant agreed to visit the Disney lot for the first time in nearly forty years.

Later, while lunching with Schumacher, *Down Under* codirectors Mike Gabriel and Hendel Butoy, and story head Joe Ranft, Grant burst forth with "a million ideas," Schumacher recalls, "none of which were do-able." One suggestion was, "The giant bird shouldn't be an eagle, but something extraordinary, magical. When its wings beat it should play music, on and on. He just gave us all these ideas at lunch." The young men were mesmerized by his imagination and energy. "He was so on top of everything," Gabriel remembers.[26]

Schumacher recalls Grant theorizing that a movie is a clothesline to hang gags on. "Joe always thought everything is business and bits." He was impressed by Grant's essential questions for filmmakers: Where is the film's heart? Who are the characters you can identify with and care for? What's special about your film? What's fresh, unique, surprising? What will make the audience laugh immediately when they see it? What does the audience take home? What can we give them to think about tonight, tomorrow, and years from now? "So, we invited him back a few times," Schumacher says.[27]

The first drawing Grant gave *The Rescuers Down Under* crew was of a bird playing a harplike feather on its head with its foot. "It was colored and

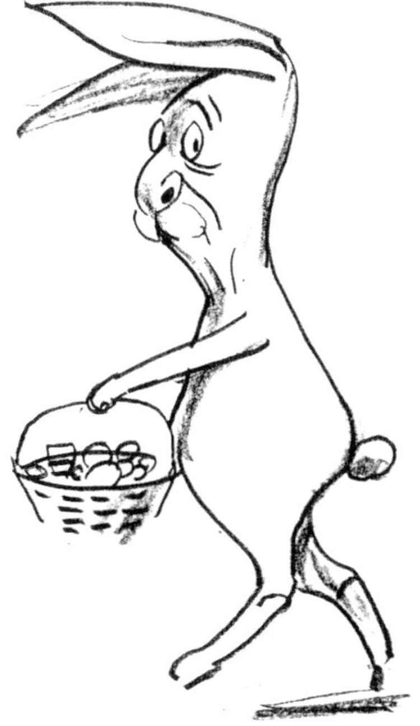

Joe Grant as the Easter Bunny delivering ideas at the studio.

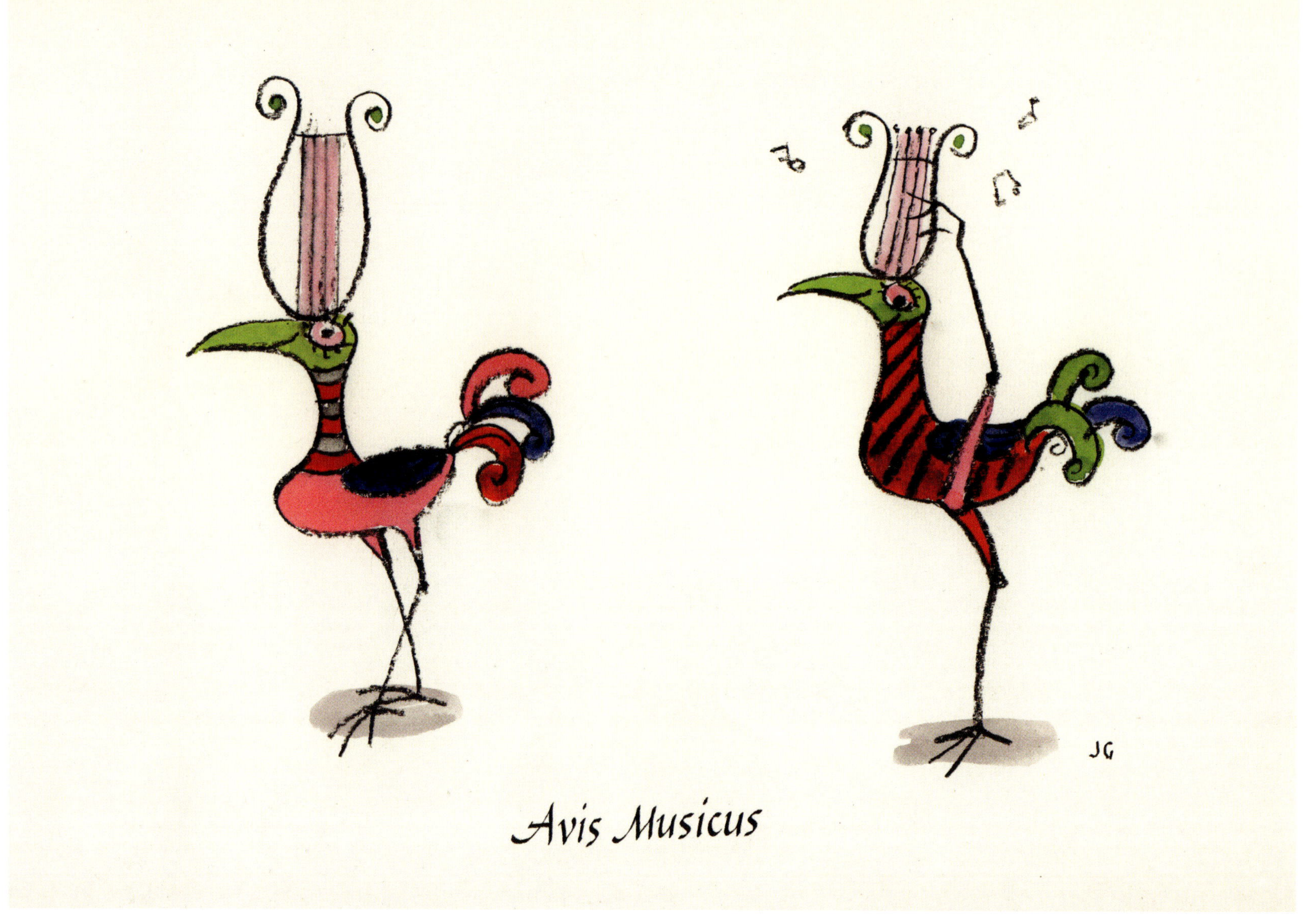

A Joe Grant concept for a magical bird in THE RESCUERS DOWN UNDER.

beautiful and I looked at it a long time thinking, how do you come up with and execute an idea so cleanly and directly?" Gabriel says. "Such a direct statement! He can do this today? He's got this in him? Wow! So we asked him if he could contribute some ideas" on a part-time basis for new projects.[28]

But Grant was leery about returning to the Disney fold after so many years. As in 1933, he asked Jennie for her opinion. And as before, she encouraged him to try it: "My wife said, 'You *should* go back!'" He did. Then, in 1991 (at eighty-three), when Schumacher offered him full-time employment at Disney, Jennie encouraged him to accept.

By that time, Jennie was gravely ill with a lung ailment that had lingered for three years. When she succumbed on June 10, 1991, Grant was devastated.

"But," says Jennifer Castrup, reflecting on her parents' long, loving union, "I think when you have a really wonderful marriage, a rich relationship that isn't focused on each other but looks out into the world, when one partner passes it doesn't mean that the other partner has to pass away, too. And I think they both wanted that for each other."[29]

Eventually, Grant rallied. "We've got an awful lot to do," he told his daughter Carol. Then he accepted Disney's offer.

CHAPTER THIRTEEN

Master of the Big Idea

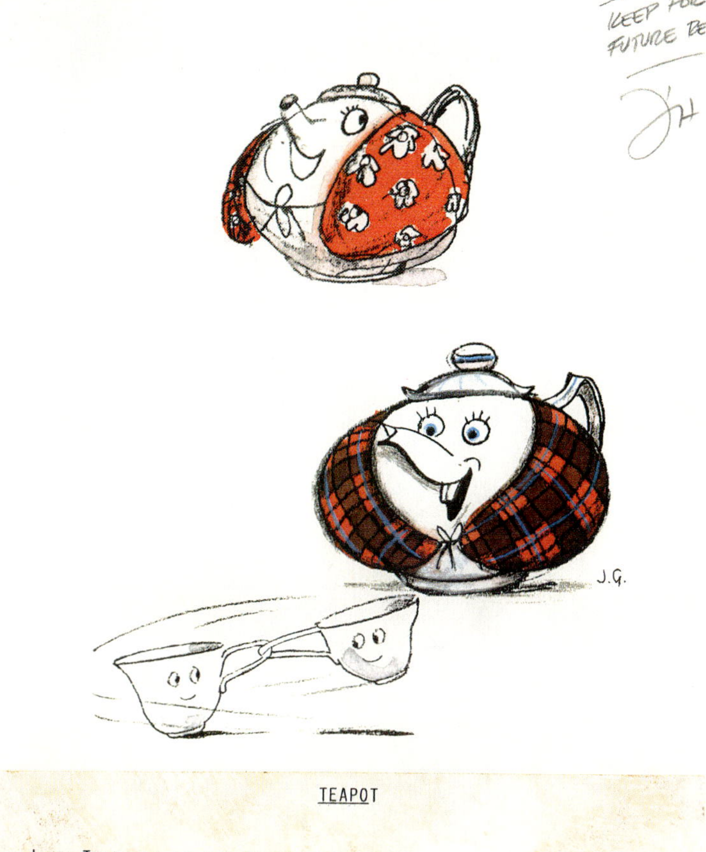

TEAPOT

LADY TEASDALE IN HER PLAID COZY, SURROUNDED BY HER CLATTERING CUPS AND SAUCERS -- CHARACTER NOTE: LIKE A MOTHER HEN "EVERYTHING CAN BE SETTLED, NO MATTER HOW BAD, "BY HAVING A NICE CUP OF TEA!"

ABOVE: *Joe Grant's idea for the motherly crockery that became Mrs. Potts* (BELOW) *in* BEAUTY AND THE BEAST.

When Joe Grant returned to visit Disney in 1989, he referred to himself as "Rip Van Winkle." Unlike Washington Irving's eighteenth-century protagonist who slept for twenty years and awoke to a world of profound changes, Grant thought "not much" had changed over the last forty years in getting an animated feature to the screen.

Except: "It's become big business. It's a little too big, that's the problem," Grant said.[1]

When he left, Disney was a small studio teetering on the brink of financial disaster. It was a place with only one boss, not layers of authority figures. "When Walt was there he had control," Grant remembered.

Now the Disney organization was huge, and hugely successful. Grant found he had to sell ideas to a Hydra of young production and marketing heads. "At one point after *The Lion King*," historian Charles Solomon comments, "there were more vice presidents at Feature Animation than animators."[2]

Survival instincts intact, Grant zeroed in like a heat sensor on individuals with varying degrees of power—from studio executives Michael Eisner and Jeffrey Katzenberg; to animation heads Roy E. Disney, Tom Schumacher, and Peter Schneider (and later David Stainton); to production colleagues in story, direction, and design, such as Mike Gabriel, Burny Mattinson, John Musker, Eric Goldberg, and Don Hahn, among others. Using a home Xerox machine and Post-it notes, he peppered the studio daily with drawings of ideas for characters, gags, situations, and dialogue. He was determined to be heard and to affect the films.

"You've got to stump for your ideas," Grant once explained, laughing. "You've got to be totally annoying, instead of being rude."

"If you listened to Joe, you couldn't help but adore him," Pam Coats, Creative Affairs vice president, says. But sometimes he was "like a pesky little mosquito you just wanted to swat away for a while."[3]

"Joe's way of presenting ideas was insidious, but wonderful," producer Don Hahn recalls. During the initial stages of *Beauty and the Beast*, Grant would drop by Hahn's office unannounced with drawings of a teapot wearing a cozy scarf; if Hahn was out, he'd leave them on a chair or desk. "At first I would think, 'A teapot? This will never work, she's just a hopping head.'" But, like a time bomb, the idea would slowly "fester in our brains until we couldn't live *without* the idea of having a talking teapot in our movie!"[4]

Grant also left teapot drawings with the film's directors and head of story. "He was tirelessly persistent in getting his ideas across," Hahn says. "Then the idea would surface probably from someone else: 'Oh, a teapot!' because Joe's genetic material had been spread around so much."[5]

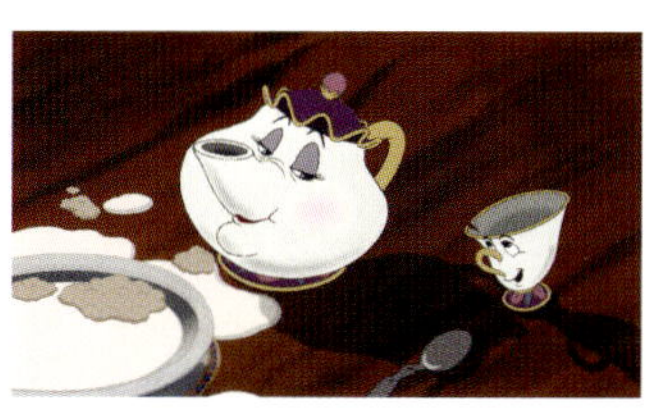

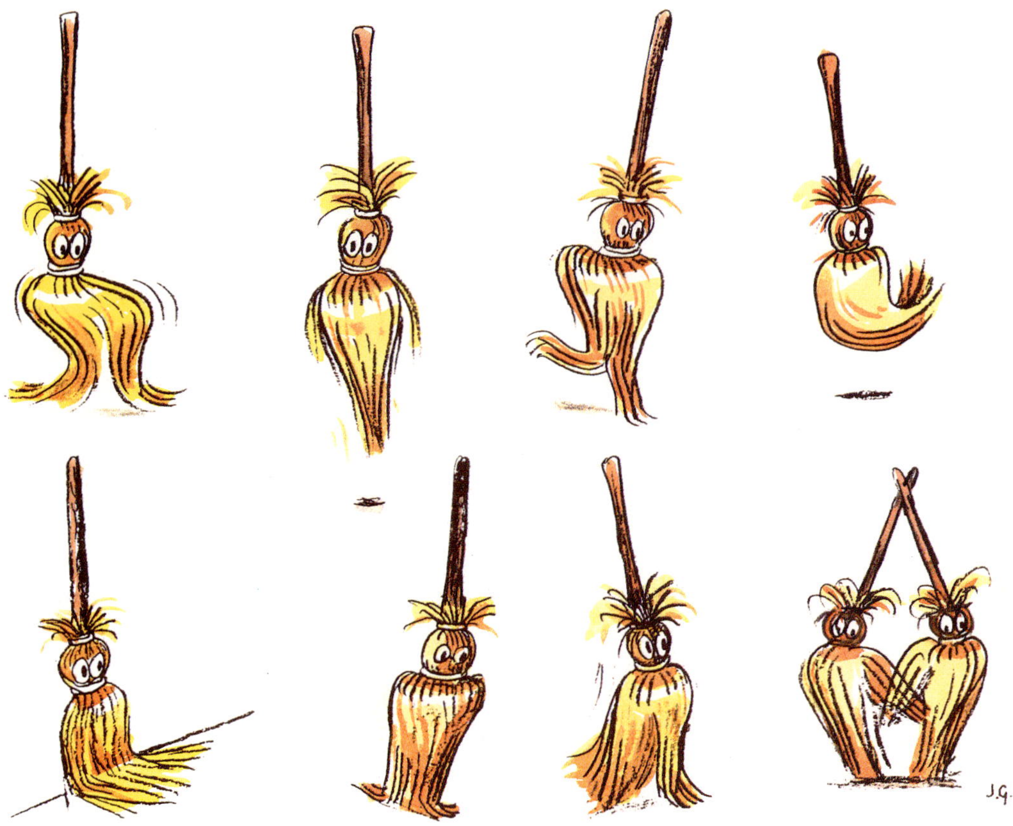

ABOVE: *Joe Grant's ideas for anthropomorphic brooms in* BEAUTY AND THE BEAST. BELOW: *a message to producer Tom Schumacher regarding* THE LION KING. RIGHT: *Grant's yo-yo-loving ostrich.*

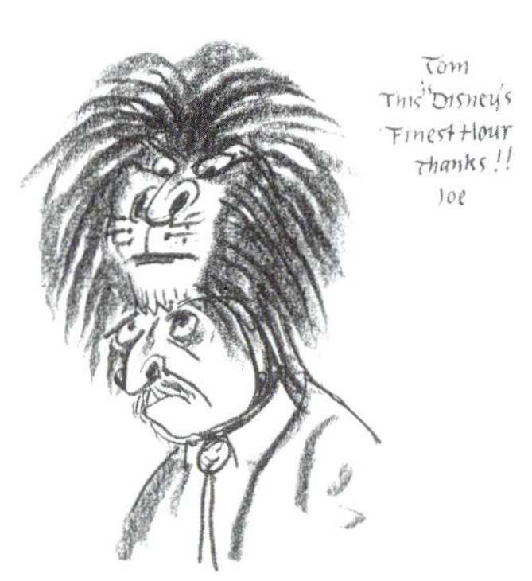

Hahn thought of Grant as "master of the big idea, usually hidden in his pocket. He embellished the *Beauty* characters," Hahn says, "such as the candlestick, and later on [with] *The Lion King* he did amazing drawings of lions and baboons. Truly inspirational art."

Grant worked on *The Lion King* when it was called *The King of the Jungle*, "a film that no one wanted to work on," says Hahn, who produced it. "He'd slip drawings to the directors of abstract lions, and a baboon carrying a staff, and of a little bird that would flit around and give advice to one of the main characters, the lion king," all of whom ended up in the final film. "[Grant] was always there lobbing in his ideas, like grenades, usually in the form of tiny but powerful little drawings no bigger than your fist."[6]

For *Aladdin*, Grant suggested treating the magic lamp as a character and he invented Abu, a small thieving monkey, as Aladdin's sidekick. Top studio executives, whose careers began in live-action, preferred a human buddy and outside scriptwriters were brought in. But when directors John Musker and Ron Clements came onto the project, they went through the movie's script and "threw out the live-action approach," Musker says, making it "more of an animation thing." Grant's monkey was back (and nearly steals the picture). Although his lamp-with-personality idea did not make it, its anthropomorphism was transferred to the Magic Carpet.

"Joe was all about entertainment, animation, visual whimsy, bring the animals into it," Musker says. As in the old days, Grant brought in books such as *Tenggren's Golden Tales from the Arabian Nights*, illustrated by his *Pinocchio* colleague Gustaf Tenggren, to inspire the designers. "The styling was great," Musker recalls. "We made copies of it."

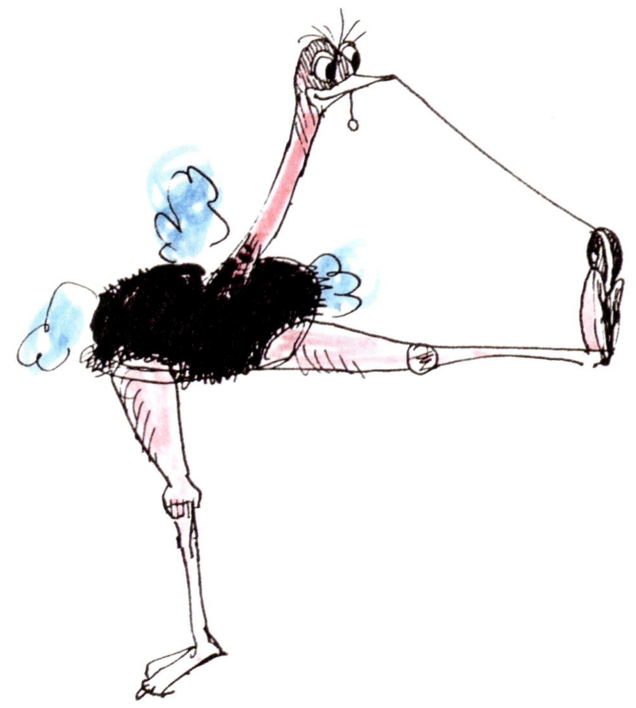

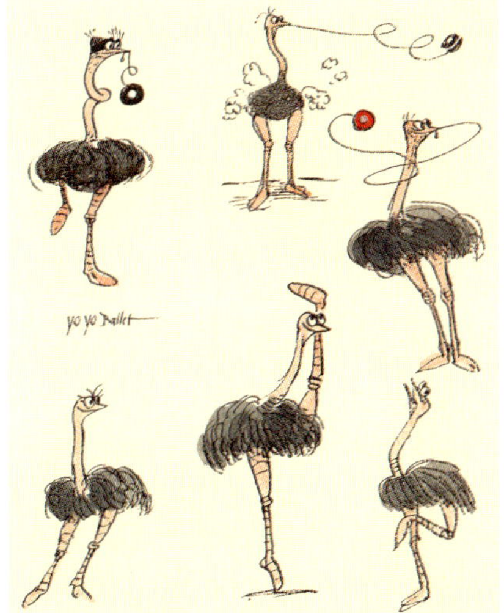

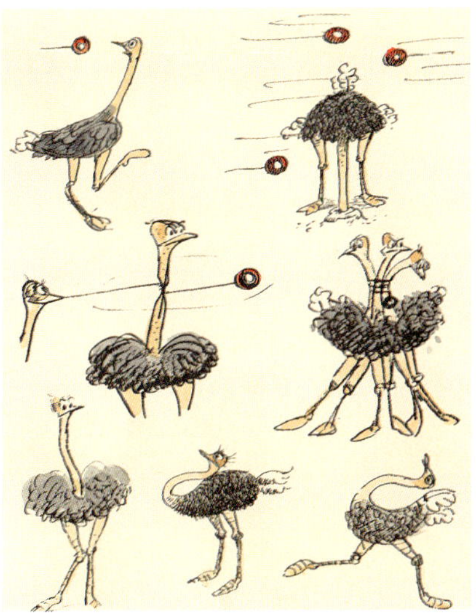

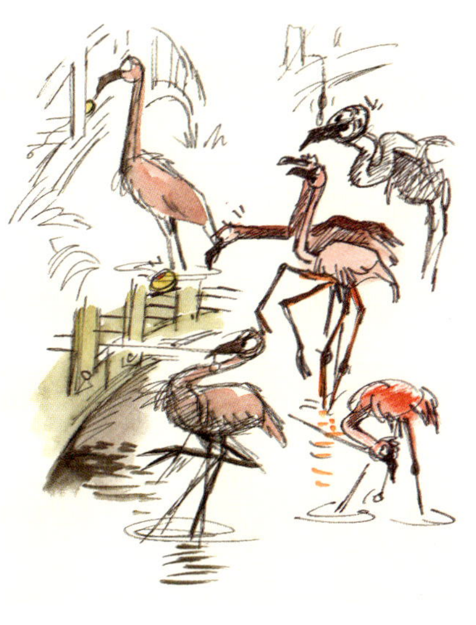

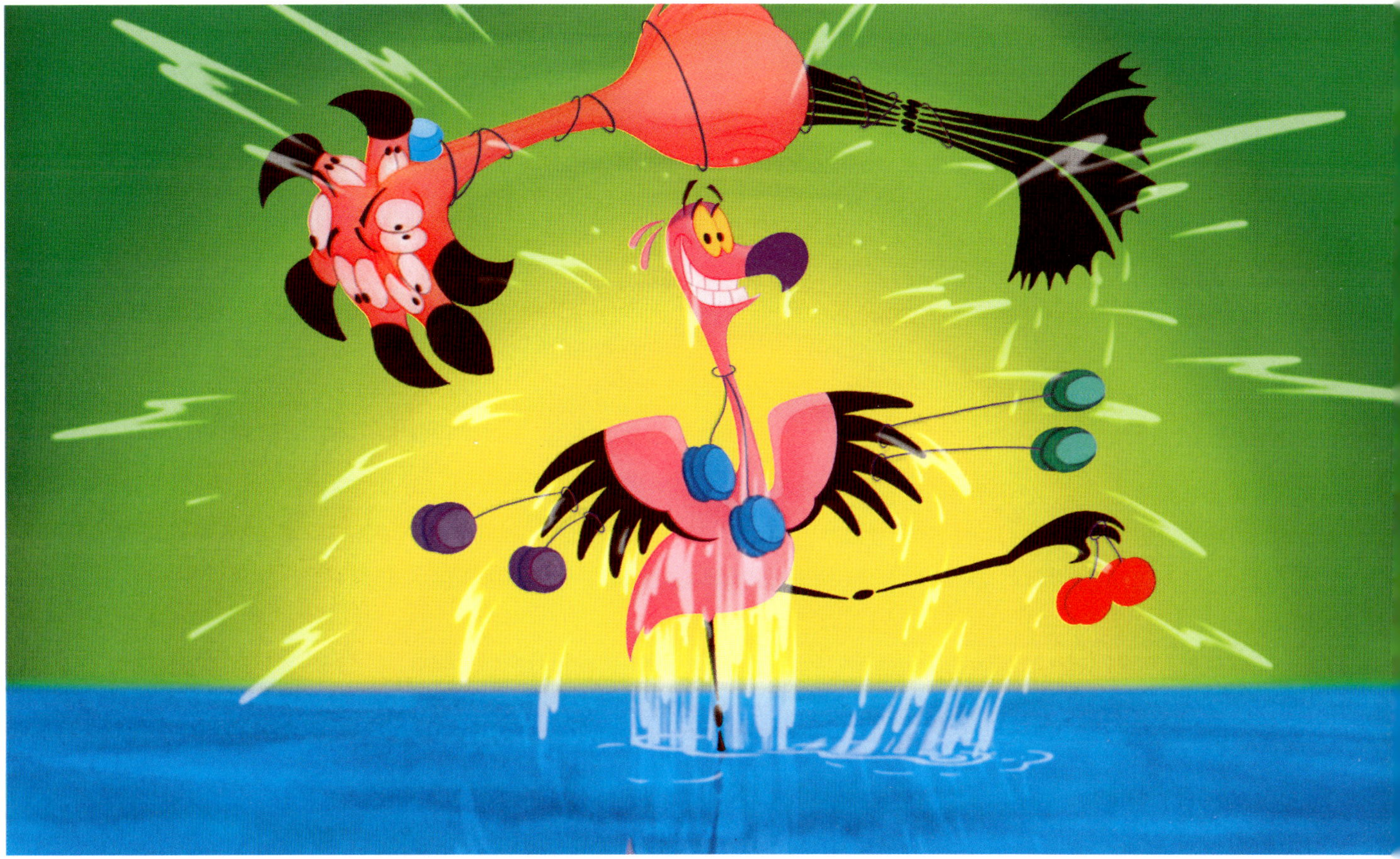

Joe Grant's ostrich sketches (LEFT) were changed to flamingos in FANTASIA/2000.

"Joe was a nuclear generator of ideas," says Eric Goldberg, who single-handedly (and brilliantly) animated the *Carnival of the Animals*, a sequence in *Fantasia/2000* based on Grant's "nutball concept" of ostriches playing with yo-yos. CEO Michael Eisner inserted himself into the process by suggesting flamingos, instead of ostriches. "Michael was entranced by flamingos as potential characters," says Roy Disney.[7]

Susan Goldberg, Eric's wife, art directed the sequence using hundreds of handmade watercolors of flamingos for each drawing. "We convinced [management] that the technique was going to work, which is very difficult to do with a huge studio like this," Eric says. "It wasn't going to look cheap." Because of his eclectic tastes, Grant was delighted and supported the technique. "He was our guardian angel for the process."[8] (Many staffers interpreted the nonconformist flamingo—creatively playing while thwarting his uptight rivals' militant sameness—as artist-versus-management.)

For *Pocahontas*, Grant "had this nutty idea for a wise old willow tree," Hahn recalls. "She had a sawed-off stump on top of her head and would reach up and point to her rings and reminisce about this year or that. She's in the movie."[9]

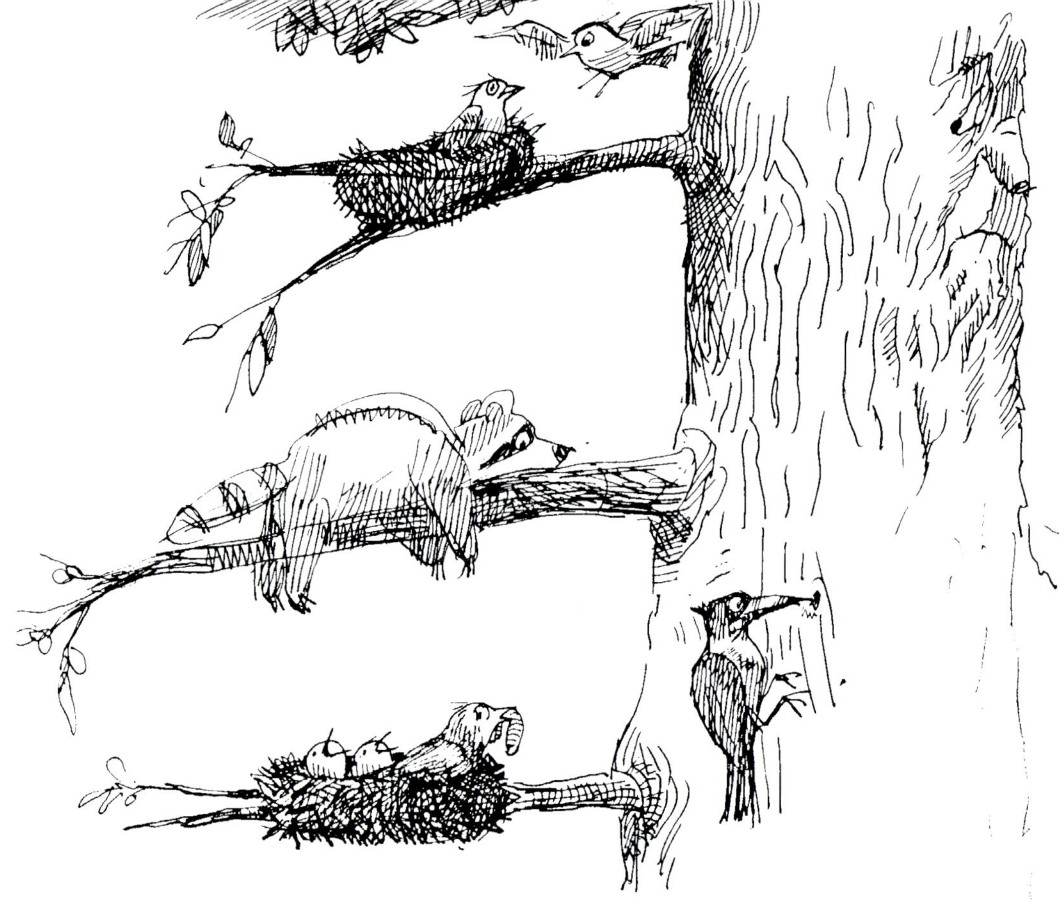

Joe Grant's designs and gags for Grandmother Willow in POCAHONTAS.

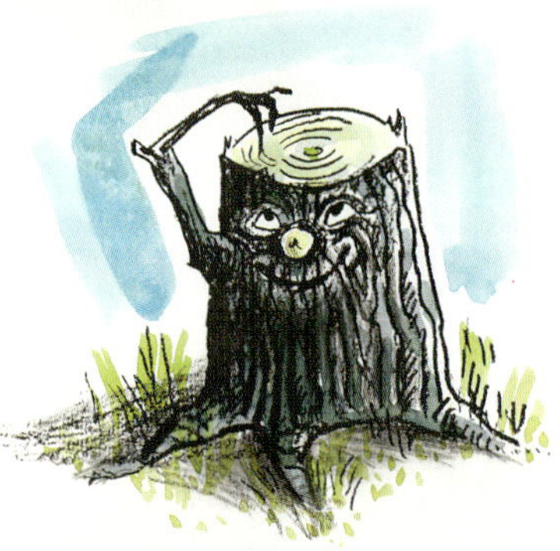

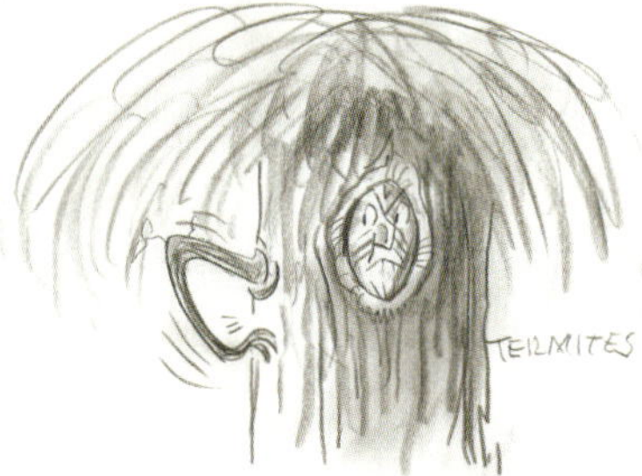

Mother Tree as narrator

Veteran story man and director Burny Mattinson (born in 1935 and hired at Disney in 1953) shared an office with Grant after the latter's return. Mattinson became as close a creative partner and sounding board for Grant as William Cottrell and Dick Huemer. "I'd say Joe and I were a team," Mattinson says, from *Pocahontas* on.

"I'd just come onto the picture and Jeffrey [Katzenberg] wanted to get rid of Grandmother Willow. He didn't like her because she was ordinary, unfunny. They were having [story] problems, some of the story men were bolting. Peter [Schneider] said I want you to get over there and work in there." Mattinson was given a section to storyboard of Pocahontas sitting on the tree stump, delivering straight, dull dialogue.

"One day Joe came in with these cornball sayings" for Grandmother Willow. "'My bark is worse than my bite,' 'The roots of all problems,' 'They're barking up the wrong tree' (spoken to termites), one gag after another. He says, 'Use these.'

"Are you kidding?" Mattinson said. "I have to pitch this [storyboard] tomorrow and you want me to use these?"

"Yeah, yeah. I think these are good. You use them."

"No. I'm not gonna do it, Joe. Forget it!" Mattinson protested.

Grant walked out and went home. Mattinson thought about it and decided he *would* put all the corny sayings in and pitch it tomorrow "just to show Joe how bad they are."

Early next morning, Mattinson showed Grant the board interwoven with his corny sayings. "Yeah, that's good. These are wonderful," he said. Mattinson remained skeptical but went to the story meeting and pitched.

"Everybody loved it!" Mattinson recalls. "All of a sudden: 'Oh, I want her in!' 'Let's build her part bigger!' So Joe saved Grandmother Willow. And Joe did that constantly. He would come up with little ideas, little touches like that."[10]

"All the side characters in *Pocahontas* are Joe's," Tom Schumacher says. "Grandmother Willow, Meeko the raccoon, Flit the hummingbird, they were all his." The incidental characters enliven a bland, walking-on-eggs, politically correct script tied slavishly to a live-action approach. "They relied so heavily on the script," Grant said. "Things were

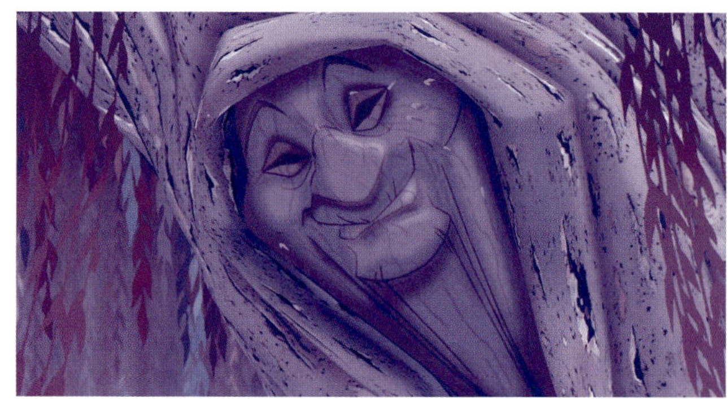

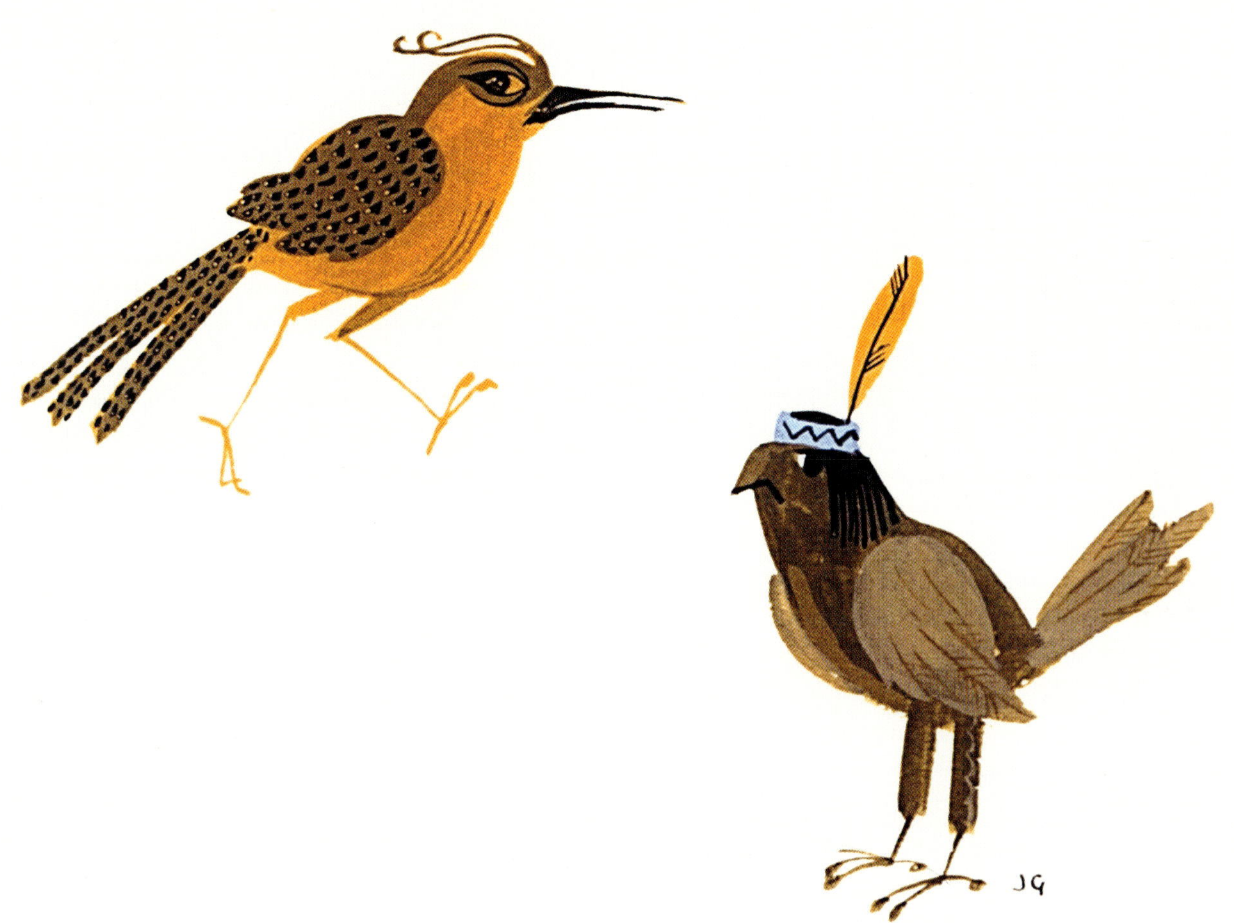

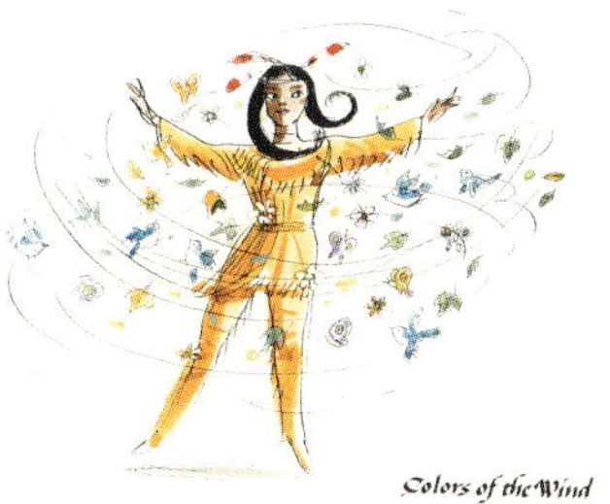

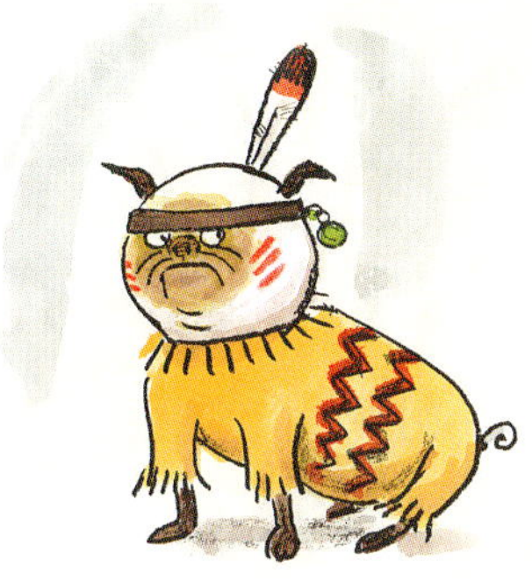

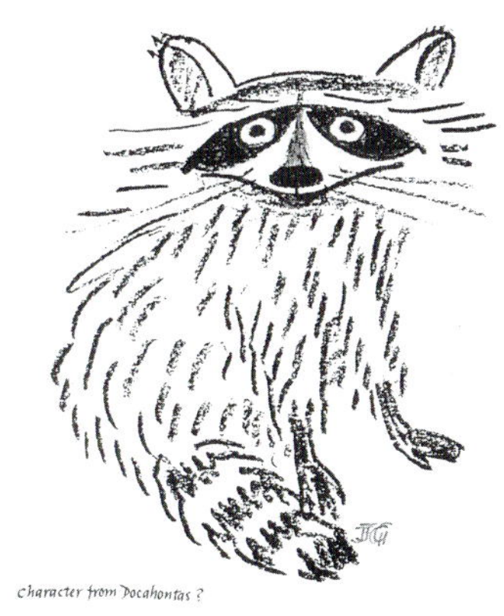

Joe Grant's concepts for colors of the wind and companion critters for POCAHONTAS.

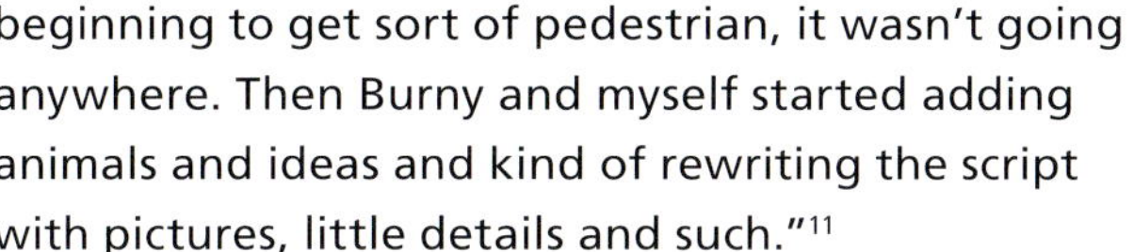

beginning to get sort of pedestrian, it wasn't going anywhere. Then Burny and myself started adding animals and ideas and kind of rewriting the script with pictures, little details and such."[11]

Schumacher remembers Grant's "big idea [was] that when [Pocahontas] talked with the animals, they could talk to her. A talking animal movie. Very much in the tradition of an expanded Snow White or Briar Rose [in *Sleeping Beauty*]. Jeffrey hated it. Too babyish, too young. It needs to be more like a live-action movie. The irony is Jeffrey never liked Joe's ideas until Jeffrey left [the Disney studio in 1994]," Schumacher says. "Then he was always hounding Joe to work for him." Grant liked Katzenberg's energy and drive. "He did a pretty good job. When he left we lost a really good driver. He wasn't Walt, but he had that same love of the medium."[12]

"Joe was so prolific," says Eric Goldberg, who codirected *Pocahontas* with Gabriel. "Every day there'd be two or three sketches slid under your door with different ideas. Consequently Mike and I had a burgeoning 'Joe drawer.' When we were stuck we'd open up the drawer, find one of Joe's drawings, and go, 'Oh yeah!'" Grant's suggestions brought charm to the picture and visual stimulation, like the swirling leaves around Pocahontas, or shadows on storm clouds as warriors clash. "When you see the final film, you realize how much of Joe really is in it," Goldberg says.

Mike Gabriel worked with Grant before and after *Pocahontas*, and they developed a close friendship.[13] They first partnered on *Swan Lake*, a feature ultimately shelved. For four months, the oldster and the younger man (born in 1954) sat at opposite ends of a desk talking and drawing ideas. In the afternoon Grant would go home, type up their ideas, and make more small drawings spurred by their conversation. Gabriel remained at the studio drawing *his* visualizations. Each day they met and went at it again.

"We developed the story and plot for *Swan Lake* into written form, and Joe said this is exactly how Dick Huemer and he always worked," Gabriel says.

> [Joe] was great sitting in a room and running with an idea. You never had awkward moments. He had such a fertile mind . . . I never heard Joe say, "No, that's not a good idea." He'd say, "Yeah. Yeah! That's good. That's good! Y'know, another thing I was thinkin' we could try is . . ." Just keep it rolling. He was so funny. Plus his notes were so gorgeous in that calligraphy.[14]

Gabriel and Grant's outline went to the studio's writer/advisers for review ("the live-action guys," says Gabriel) and came back with scathing comments: "This is the most amateurish, worthless nothing. There is no movie here, no story." The old way of developing a story for animation—moving organically back and forth between concept sketches, written outlines and treatments, and story drawings—was no longer acceptable. It was considered inefficient and slow. Now, The Script came first.

"We never had scripts per se," Mattinson says of the older, more fluid process of story development. "We would just have an outline of an idea handed out, sequences to be developed by the story guys involved." Eventually a final script evolved. "Now we had live-action people in charge of the studio," Gabriel says, "and they considered live-action screenplay writers the real thing."

Grant soldiered on, determinedly doing things his way despite the current studio system and its political dynamics. "He was keenly aware," Schumacher says, that there was a contingent of writing teams, developers, and directors who "didn't want him around."

"Joe didn't make art based on other people's art," Pam Coats says. "Joe made ideas and art based on the vision of what he wanted to do. Both Michael [Eisner] and Jeffrey [Katzenberg] would try to make art based on last week's success. Michael never 'got' Joe. Because he was old and you had to listen to him."

Coats says she had "enormous pressure from Michael" for high concepts and scripts.[15] "He wanted *the* idea. There was so much demand from Michael to just put stuff on. Like spaghetti theory: prepare all day and throw stuff against the wall and see what stuck with him, a constant churning of big concepts. So you were trying to juggle what Michael wanted and you were trying to listen to Joe."

As noted, Grant worked best one-on-one tossing ideas back and forth; or dropping off drawings to individuals. ("I called him 'Dripping Water,'" Coats says, "which wears through anything.") Used to being his own boss, he did not fit comfortably within the studio's group system.

Grant had access to studio heads, producers, and directors "merely by the fact that he would walk in. He did it to me, too," Coats says. "So, Joe operated on that level, knowing that he shouldn't. Just because that's what he was used to. I think he manipulated the system because he didn't want to be bothered. Think about it: the guy was eighty when I met him."

Some young staffers didn't "really give him a chance," Coats says, because he didn't do continuity storyboarding or come up with a narrative through line for the entire story. "Joe was an idea guy. That's what he did. Came up with bits and pieces of ideas. Within that system it took me a while to relax into Joe and go, 'Oh, this is how this guys works.' As opposed to being too busy to really listen to him."

"He would interrupt story meetings," Schumacher says. "His style was so informed by the fact that he wasn't following the dialogue in the room. It was kids talking very fast. His hearing was bad, he would never go with the group dynamic. He was never on track with anything. *But*, left to his own devices . . ."

To finish his sentence, Schumacher silently reveals a simple line drawing by Grant. It is of Quasimodo, the squat, stout, hunchbacked bell ringer from *The Hunchback of Notre Dame*, staring dumbfounded at his reflection in a large elongated bell. In his stretched likeness, he is tall and straight, a reversal of fun-house mirror alterations. "After he polishes the bell," Grant wrote on this tiny but emotionally powerful drawing, "the distortion makes him whole."

"Beautiful," Schumacher says quietly. "Why didn't we use *that*?"

It was merely one in a torrent of shimmering ideas Grant tossed off each day. Warm, witty, imaginative windows into characters and their inner lives that didn't get on the screen. "He always built stories from the character out," Hahn observes. "I don't think he cared about plot all that much."

"He was an idea man," reiterates Mattinson, recalling arguments with Grant about dropping ideas at random into a storyboard. Although the banter was friendly, Grant disdained the difficulties of the storyboard process. "Well, that's why I'm the idea man and you can do the grunt work. It's your job!" Grant told him.[16] "Joe was this unbelievable font of stuff," Schumacher says, but "hard to integrate" into the studio system.

A Joe Grant idea for THE HUNCHBACK OF NOTRE DAME.

"You had developers who worked to keep Michael [Eisner] happy," Coats says. "I had to assign them [to] Joe Grant. I'd say, 'You need to sit down and listen to his ideas.' Because Joe always had ideas. He was active and persistent. And by the way, if you didn't listen and manage the man, he dropped his drawings right on Roy E. Disney's desk. So you needed to pay attention to him even if you didn't like him. And if you liked him, then you could learn from him."

"Joe was keenly aware of what was going on around him," says Schumacher. A producer "would come to me and say, 'You know Joe's driving the boys crazy,' referring to certain directors. 'Can you keep him out of the room?' In turn, Grant would come to Schumacher saying, "They're having a meeting about that [sequence] today. They didn't invite me. Should I go?" And then he would just turn up. "He had a way of just going to meetings."

Despite these problems, Grant continued to produce invaluable work, such as designs and business for Philoctetes the satyr and other

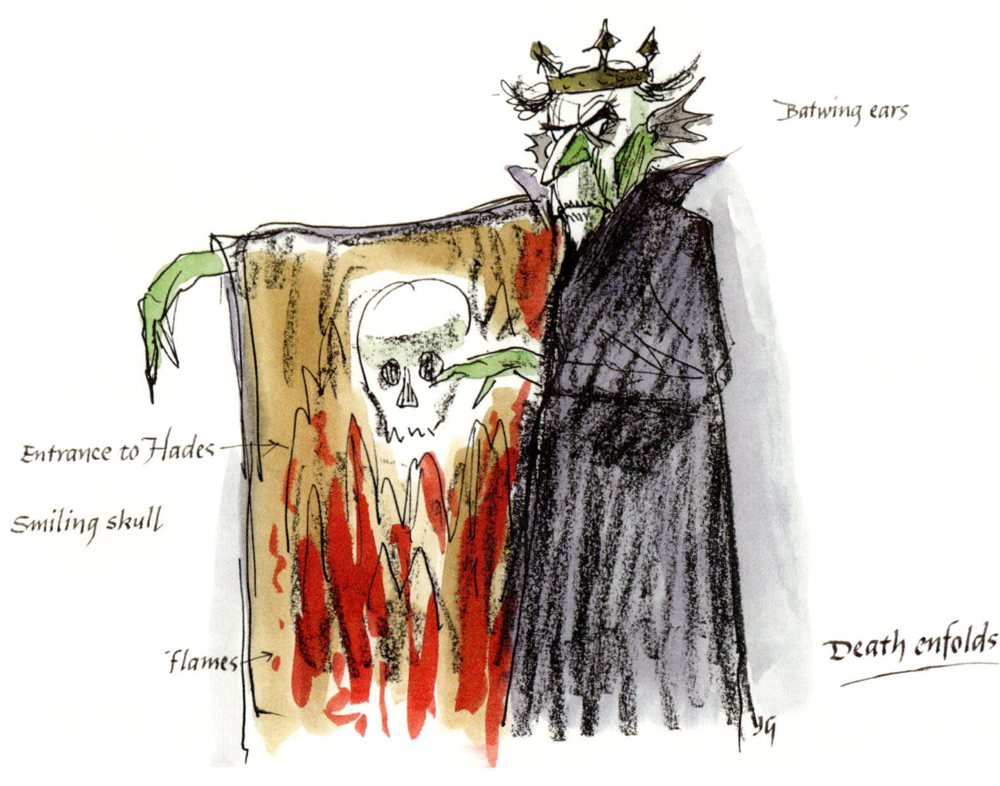

Mythological monsters by Joe Grant for HERCULES.

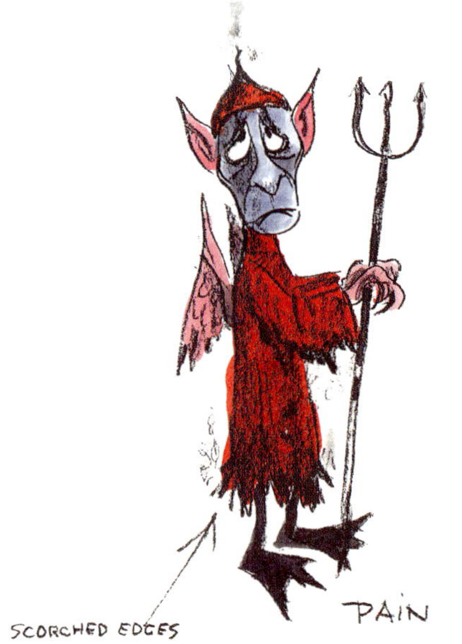

mythological creatures in *Hercules* as well as the cricket and dragon in *Mulan*. Many young animators, directors, and designers continued to gravitate to Grant. "They liked him a lot 'cause he would come up with ideas they could use in their pictures. He was interested in what they were doing," Mattinson says. "They felt Joe was an important factor around here. And he was. An inspiration for a lot of people."[17] Don Hahn's office was next to Grant's. He watched a daily parade of visitors "from film directors and corporate presidents to children who wanted to meet Dumbo's daddy. It was like having a priest and a confessional next door."[18]

Pete Docter often traveled from Pixar to visit and consult with Grant, who offered the title *Monsters, Inc.* for the 2001 feature Docter directed. "As I developed *Monsters*," Docter says, "I pitched Joe a bunch of things. He would take the info, shout out ideas, but in the mail there'd come this beautiful calligraphy [saying], 'Pete, I had some thoughts. Joe.' There'd be these drawings of monsters in various situations, or intriguing visual ideas." Docter phoned Grant on weekends to compare production notes. Grant kept Docter's number next to his phone. "In case of emergency, I guess, or a good story idea, call Pete Docter."[19]

Grant pushed his bosses toward properties he originated or adapted. The latter included *The Abandoned*, a Paul Gallico tale about a boy who changes into a cat, and *Mr. Popper's Penguins* by Richard Atwater. *Bitzi* was a story Grant and Jennie developed; it was about an elephant from India trying to make it big in Hollywood and ends up working in a used-car lot and falling in love. Considerable time and effort was spent by Grant, Mattinson, and story artist Vance Gerry developing all three of these projects, but none came to fruition.

In August 2000, a *Los Angeles Times* reporter, Jeffrey Gettleman, told of Grant and Mattinson pitching *Bitzi* to "the suits" who "sat as stone-faced as gargoyles as Grant told jokes and Mattinson worked the boards, with a flourish, but with no more effect than a fishing lure that had lost its shine." After they had pitched for twenty minutes, one executive "suggested that if *Bitzi* were to work at all, it would be better as a live-action movie." Grant was "furious," wrote Gettleman. "Walt would have backed it immediately, no questions," he complained to the reporter.

Gettleman described Grant as "a vulnerable old man who aches to tell love stories. He just happens to do it with animals." The frustration of the rejection of the *Bitzi* project "sometimes trigger[s] the unsettling realization that he's in the sunset of his life, that so much is behind him and only a thinning sliver lies ahead. 'Sometimes, I can hear this little voice saying there's so much more that I want to do,' Grant said. 'When I hear that, I have to tell myself, 'Shut up, Joe, let it go.'"[20]

"I had to give him something to do," Schumacher explains about allowing Grant to work on *Bitzi* and *The Abandoned* even though there was little chance they would be produced. "Joe didn't have enough to do and people were really anxious about him being in their way. I just couldn't get traction with either [film]. Nobody wanted to make these movies. They seemed of a different era. The plot's sticky, and no one could quite get the idea."

"I'll be honest about *Bitzi*," Pam Coats says. "It's a cute idea, but it sounds like an idea that had had its time and the take on it didn't feel pertinent anymore. We tried with that. It didn't feel like it would have made a big movie."

The same thing happened to *Mr. Popper's Penguins*, even with Roy E. Disney's strong interest.

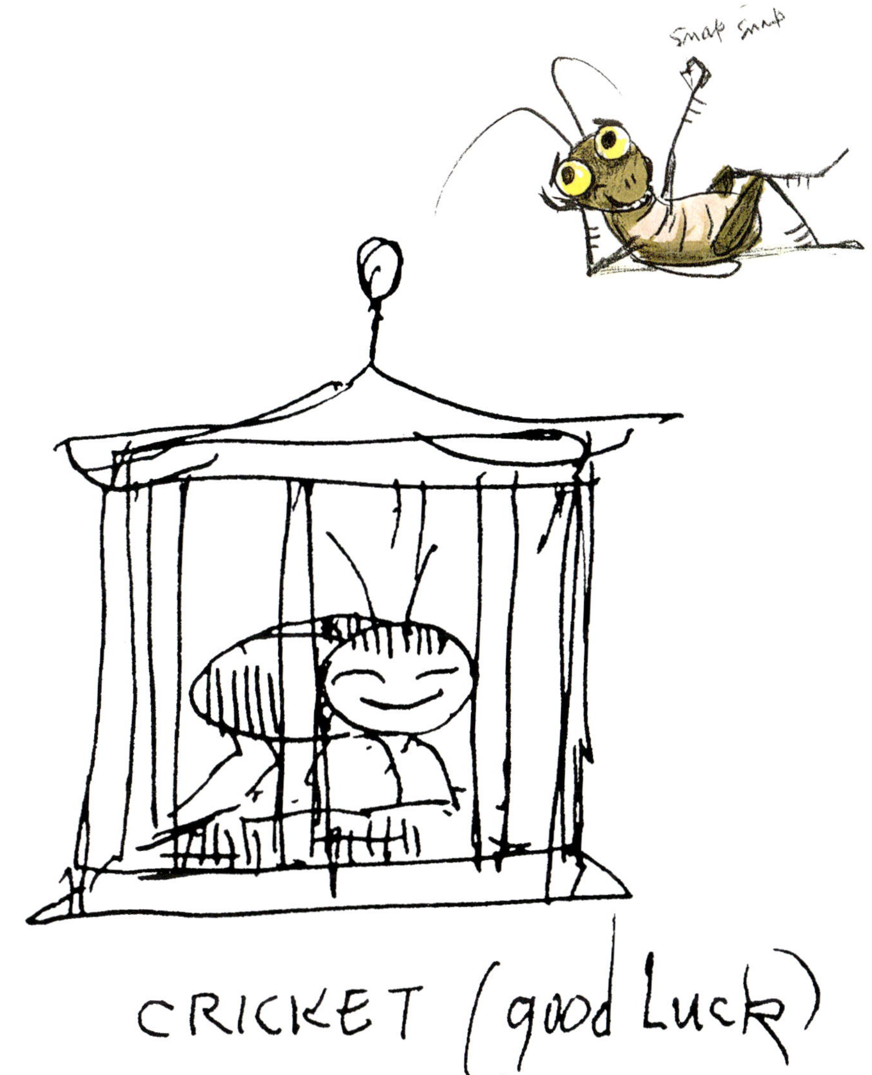

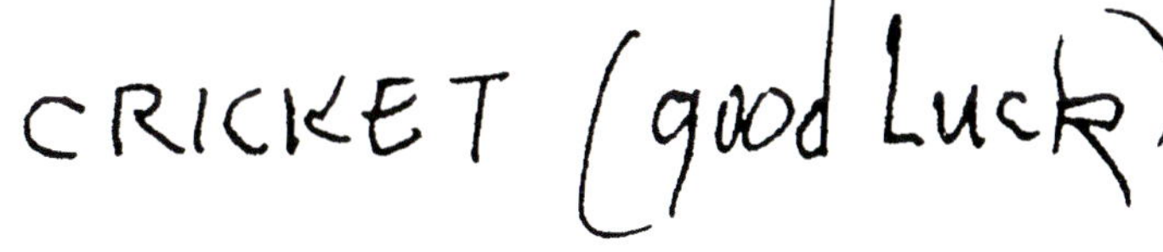

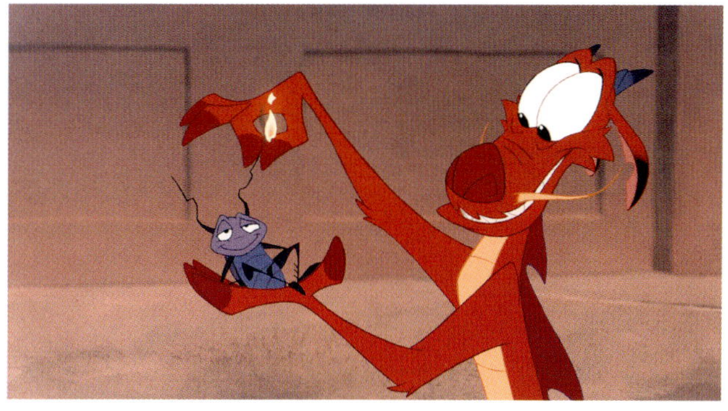

Joe Grant's lucky cricket for MULAN.

Coats recalls Eisner and Stainton saying it "needed to be hip, needed to be set in New York, the penguin needed to perform. Joe had no interest in making the story more present. He also had great ideas that we could never get our hands around and figure out how to make them." One was about dead pets. "Joe was a huge animal lover. He had an idea in his head about his dog dying and then coming back to guide him," Coats explains. "Initially it was like, Joe, we can't do a story in a happy animated movie where a dog dies. He was insistent, so we worked on that for a while. I think it's a great idea, though in its initial germ it was an old-fashioned idea."

Grant said he was "surprised" when Schumacher once told him regarding *Lady and the Tramp*, "Joe, we'd never make that picture again or one like it." Grant said he didn't really believe that. He preferred stories that are "not too realistic. I come from *Dumbo* to *Lion King*," he explained. "The animal stuff in *Pocahontas*, that's where I live. To me that's the cartoon biz."[21]

"I think he was frustrated by the process and felt a little blown off in his later years," Hahn says. "He wasn't given the forum to present his ideas in a way he thought was meaningful. He felt people would meet with him, say, 'Oh, that's great, fantastic, let's get going.' Then everything would fall apart." Grant referred to management as "The Wall."

Meantime, Disney pursued the fickle teen market with fast-paced animated films full of "hip" contemporary attitude and references, but poorly thought out, soulless scripts and characters, such as *The Emperor's New Groove*; *Atlantis: The Last Empire*; and *Treasure Planet*. In 2004, to compete with Pixar, Michael Eisner threw out Disney hand-drawn animation in favor of CGI, a misguided baby-with-the-bathwater decision that led to even more flailing about.

Grant's one-line reviews of the studio's recent offerings were popular among the artists. *Home on the Range*, starring three cows, was dismissed by him as "milk duds." The 2005 CGI feature *Chicken Little* led him to question, "Where are the yolks?" Caught napping during another film's premiere, Grant quipped to the director: "This picture has no middle."

Friends and colleagues who had lost their jobs when computers replaced handmade animation came by his office to unburden themselves. While deeply saddened for them, Grant believed digital technology was the future, and Disney needed to be involved. In 1995, he found *Toy Story*'s "new developments very exciting. Technology is running ahead of us right now. We've got to catch up with it with some good ideas."

After a 2001 preview of Katzenberg's *Shrek*, he said, "It's time to burn the pencils," which (as in days of old) irritated some animators. "I had my arguments with Joe about CGI," says Andreas Deja, one of Disney's finest animator/draftsmen of recent times and Grant's friend and admirer. "He would say, 'Walt would embrace this and make it work.' I would argue, 'Would he cut off hand-drawn animation? Isn't Walt known for adding to his expression? When we got into live-action, he didn't stop animation. When he went from shorts to features, he kept the shorts going for a long time.' Joe said, 'That's true. I'd forgotten about that.' I would tease him in a loving, joking way. I said, 'Joe, just because you're a certain age doesn't mean you have to prove constantly that you're hip!'"[22]

When Grant referred to Walt Disney, it was always with respect and admiration.[23] In 1993, reacting to charges in a forthcoming book that Disney was anti-Semitic, the studio prepared a packet of rebuttal material. Grant wrote and signed a declaration stating:

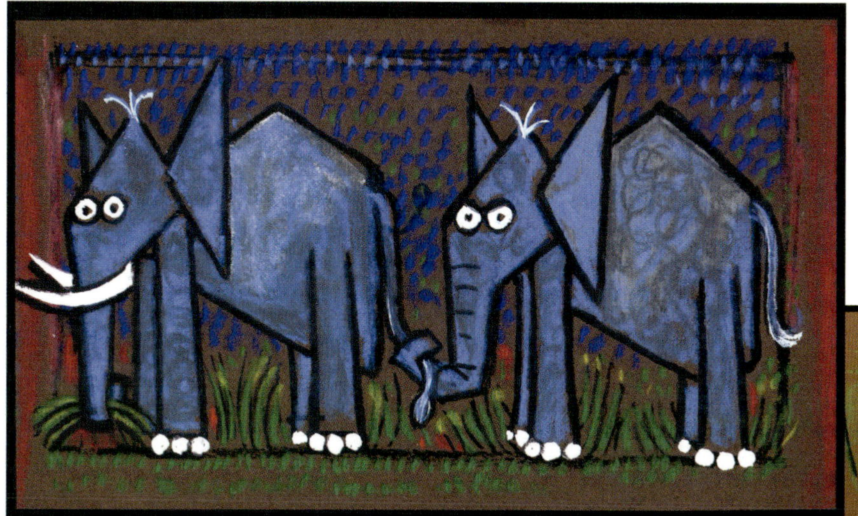

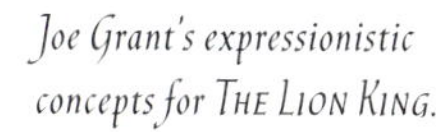

Joe Grant's expressionistic concepts for The Lion King.

> I am a member of the Jewish faith and can, from my own personal knowledge and experience, deny categorically that Walt Disney was anti-semitic [sic].[24]

Considering how little Grant identified with religious worship in general and his Jewish heritage in particular, his loyalty to Disney in this instance, forty-four years after their last strained meeting, is touching.[25]

Ironically, while "The Wall" was constraining Grant's creativity at the studio, his reputation in the outside world had grown to iconic proportions. In 1992, he was named an official Disney Legend at a ceremony on the studio lot; the National Cartoonists Society presented him with a Ruben Award in 1996; over seventy of his *Los Angeles Record* caricatures found a permanent home at the National Portrait Gallery, Smithsonian Institution; in France, he was honored with a celebration of his life and work at the 1998 Annecy International Animation Festival; and in 2002, the Los Angeles Film Critics Association presented him with a Special Achievement Award. Pixar showed their affection and respect by naming the cookie-box circus-wagon in *A Bug's Life* after Grant.

As he approached the century mark, numerous periodicals featured him; for example, "May He Stay Forever Young," in *The Times* of London; and a *Los Angeles Times* cover story, "A 'Toon Man for the Ages."

The publicity was generated by Howard E. Green, Disney vice president of Studio Communications, who became as close as family to Grant during his last fifteen years. "It was fun getting him some attention in later years," Green says. One of his happiest memories is of accompanying Grant to France in 1998. "You'd think that would be a rough trip for a ninety-year-old, jet lag and all. But next morning in Paris at seven A.M. he's on the phone saying, 'Are you ready? Ready to go?'" They toured seven museums in three days. "He was like a kid in a candy store. I never saw him so excited. It was hard to keep up with him."

Grant's newfound celebrity, he said, was sometimes "fun, sometimes laughable, sometimes it's sad."[26] Dean DeBlois once glimpsed his essential loneliness. Visiting Grant's home studio, he noticed a photograph of Jennie. "She was smiling, full of life. It was taken in the corner of his studio which had a little daybed and trinkets arranged at the window. And I looked over and that space was completely undisturbed. The only thing missing was her. It was like a little shrine."[27]

Another visitor, Jonas Rivera, remembers the notes Grant left for himself around the house. "One said, 'October 5, 1983. Earthquake happened today,' written in beautiful calligraphy. Another was the day his wife died: 'Jennie passed away.' His house was like his diary," Rivera notes. "He was an artist constantly observing and making notes and just leaving little trails of his thoughts."[28]

When he reached his ninety-sixth year, Grant reduced his time at the studio to four days a week. He stubbornly continued to drive himself to the studio, as family and friends joked nervously about how terrifying he was behind a steering wheel. "He didn't like being helped," Howard Green remembers. "He resented being old. That his body was letting him down. He didn't want people to see that. Very proud."

After one-too-many minor auto accidents, Schumacher arranged for a car service to bring him to and from work. "I just loved him to death," he says. "He also reminded me of my family." In his final year, Grant reluctantly used a wheelchair to get around studio corridors; Mattinson joked he was "Joe's pusher."

In 2004, a short film derived from an idea of Grant's was produced by Don Hahn with design/direction by Mike Gabriel. *Lorenzo* was based on "Lorenzo the Magnificent," a story Grant had originated sixty years before in the Character Model Department concerning a selfish blue cat whose tail takes on a life of its own after crossing paths with a mysterious, magical black cat.

Grant "sold" his story to the studio in his inimitable way. "Joe started to pin up drawings in his room of a blue cat who was tormented by his tail," Hahn remembers. "The drawings multiplied like rabbits. And as many times as I went into his room, he never mentioned all the drawings of the blue cat. There were five, then ten, then twenty." He filled a storyboard outside his office with blue cats. People started to ask what it was. Hahn used his clout to "ramrod things through the development process and to say, 'Here's a great short. Let's get it done!'" Gabriel signed on immediately, and "it was like a little Joe Grant unit on the side that would do his bidding for him."

This happy collaboration culminated when *Lorenzo* was nominated for an Academy Award for Best Animated Short, and Grant and Gabriel attended the ceremony. "He was very proud of Mike. He thought of him as a son," says Diane Castrup, who pushed her tuxedoed grandfather in his wheelchair onto the red carpet. Well-wishers in the crowd

THIS PAGE AND OPPOSITE:
Joe Grant's final concepts for the Disney Studio: LORENZO, a short film about a spoiled blue cat whose tail had a life of its own. The short was nominated for an Academy Award.

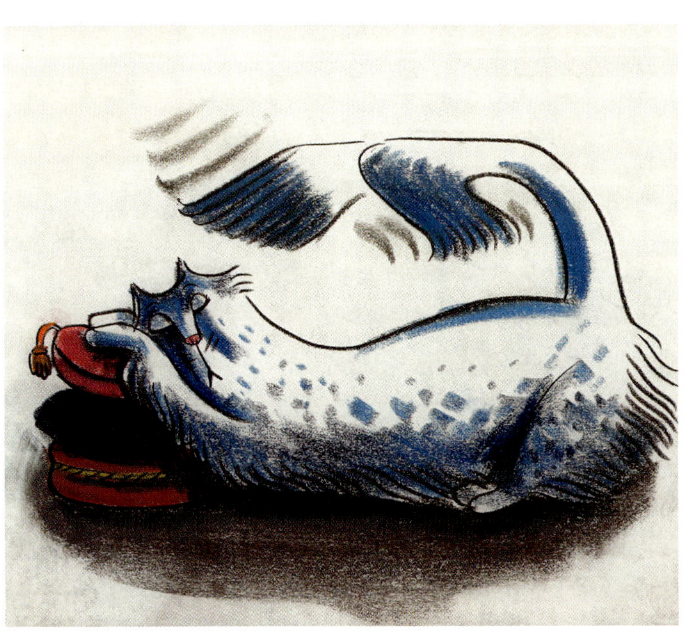

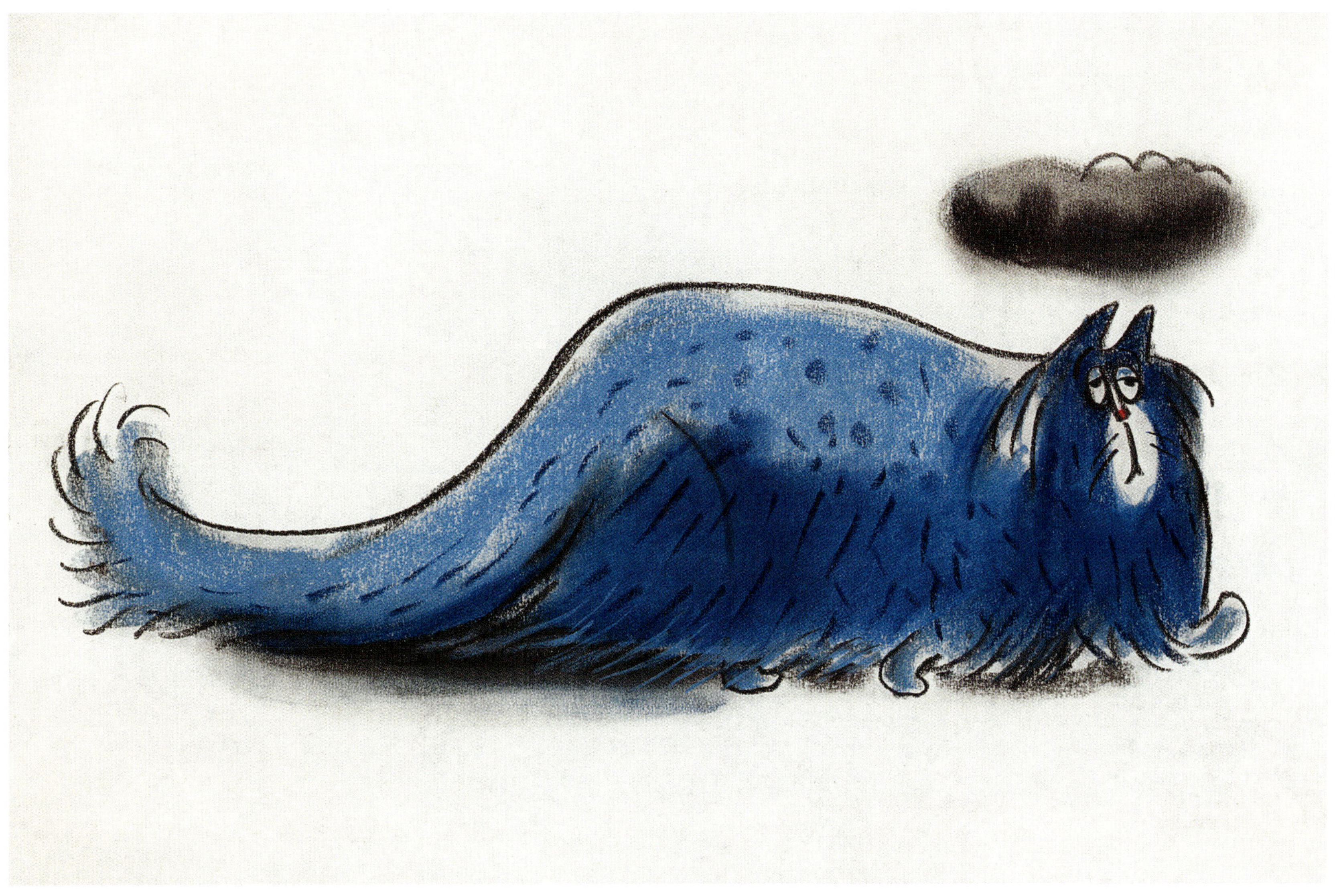

shouted "Joe" as photographers' cameras clicked. Grant was thrilled, and although the film did not win, it was a proud and triumphant moment in both filmmakers' careers. The film proved to be Grant's last hurrah, but a fine one full of his charm, wit, and sass.

"Joe, we made it to the Oscars, baby!" Gabriel said to his mentor. "He looked so good and he had so many funny lines that evening," Gabriel recalls. "Joe said that from his perspective in the wheelchair, it was a night of cummerbunds and cleavage!"

On May 6, 2005, Grant awoke when Ketta, the housekeeper, arrived. She put foodstuffs together for him because he liked to cook for himself. "This is going to be a wonderful day," he said. After his obligatory oatmeal breakfast, he went outside and sat under a tree to read the newspaper. "It was a morning ritual," Jennifer Castrup says. "On his special bench. I'd talk to him on the phone and he'd say, 'Well, I'm not in it.' Not in what? 'Oh, the obituaries.'" Father and daughter would laugh and then "on with the day."

When Joe Grant's fatal heart attack occurred later that morning, he was seated at his drawing board, hard at work.

NOTES

JOE RANFT

CHAPTER ONE Joe! Put in the Teeth!

1. Pete Docter interview by John Canemaker, 17 August 2007.
2. Andrew Stanton interview by JC, 17 August 2007.
3. Darla Anderson interview by JC, 13 August 2007.
4. Lee Unkrich interview by JC, 13 August 2007.
5. "*Antz* vs. *Bugs*. The inside story of how DreamWorks beat Pixar to the screen." *Business Week*, 23 November 1998. < http://www.businessweek.com/1998/47/b3605013.htm >; *Antz* opened 2 October, 1998; *A Bug's Life* opened 25 November 1998.
6. Jerome Ranft interview by JC, 15 August 2007.
7. Joe Ranft phone interview by Charles Solomon, 1 December 1998. Courtesy Charles Solomon.
8. *The New York Times* film review by Janet Maslin, 25 November 1998.
9. "Dog Bites" column "as told to Laurel Wellman," *San Francisco Weekly*, 20 August 2000. When a memo turned up deeming nine former Mondrian staff members "too ethnic," the U.S. Equal Employment Opportunities Commission made Schrager pay each of the complainants $120,000.
10. John Lasseter at Joe Ranft memorial service, Mill Valley, California, 21 August 2005.
11. Brenda Chapman at Ranft memorial service, 21 August 2005.
12. Bob Peterson interview by JC, 17 August 2007.

CHAPTER TWO The Best Storyboard Guy in the Business

1. John Lasseter quote in Joe Ranft obituary, *San Francisco Chronicle*, 18 August 2005.
2. Ibid.
3. Ed Catmull interview by JC, 13 August 2007.
4. Letter from Joe Ranft to Disney executives "Re: Story Training Ideas," 18 December 1995. Courtesy Su Ranft.
5. Ibid.
6. 21 May 1999, "Story Development" document. Courtesy Su Ranft.
7. Brad Bird interview by JC, 17 August 2007.
8. John Musker interview by JC, 25 July 2007.
9. Jerry Rees, phone interview by JC, 21 September 2007.
10. Henry Seleck, *Hollywood Reporter*, 18 August 2005.

CHAPTER THREE Spitting at Nuns

1. Lasseter at Ranft memorial service, 21 August 2005.
2. Joe Ranft interview by JC, 23 July 1997.
3. Ruth Ranft phone interview by JC, 1 October 2007; Jerome Ranft, 15 August 2007.
4. Su Ranft interview by JC, 16 August 2007.
5. Ruth Ann Ranft, Joe Ranft's sister, memorial service, 21 August 2005.
6. Ibid.
7. Su Ranft interview.
8. John Tschudin interview by JC, 15 August 2007.
9. Ruth Ranft interview.
10. *The New York Times*, 13 November 2007, "Studies on Pupils Say Bad Behavior is Not Dooming" by Benedict Carey.
11. Joe Ranft interview by JC, 23 July 1997.
12. Mark Kirkland began studying in the Experimental Animation Program at CalArts at age 17; as of 2005, he had directed more episodes of *The Simpsons* than any other director.
13. Joe Ranft interview with Charles Solomon, 1 December 1998. Courtesy Charles Solomon.

CHAPTER FOUR The CalArts Experience

1. "The *Fantasia* That Never Was" by John Canemaker, *Print*, January/February 1988.
2. Bob Thomas, *Walt Disney: An American Original* (New York: Simon & Schuster, 1976), pp. 331–332.
3. CalArts Web site: <http://muse.calarts.edu/schools/film/faculty/engel_jules.html>
4. 30 May 2005, Nancy Beiman Web site: <http://madcartoonist.blogspot.com/2005_05_01_archive.html>
5. Tony Anselmo e-mail to JC, 20 September 2007.
6. Joe Ranft interview, 23 July 1997.
7. Musker interview.
8. Anselmo e-mail.

CHAPTER FIVE Disney Daze and That Big Crazy Kid

1. John Canemaker, *Walt Disney's Nine Old Men & the Art of Animation*, Disney Editions, 2001, pp. 54–81.
2. Ojai Animation Conference, California, 22 July 1995, <http://www.awn.com/mag/issue1.1/articles/kroyer.html>
3. *Burton on Burton*, edited by Mark Salisbury. Faber and Faber (London, Boston, 1995), p. 13.
4. John Taylor, *Storming the Magic Kingdom* (New York: Knopf, 1987), p. 21.
5. *Walt Disney's Nine Old Men & the Art of Animation*, p. 79.
6. Ibid.
7. Brad Bird interview by JC, 17 August 2007. In *The Family Dog*, a TV half hour directed by Bird in 1987, there is a visual reference to "The Rat's Nest" in one scene. See also: "A Disney Dissenter Shuns Song and Dance" by John Canemaker, *The New York Times*, 8 August 1999.
8. "11 Animators Quit Disney, Form Studio," *The New York Times*, 20 September 1979.
9. Darrell Van Citters phone interview by JC, 27 November 2007.
10. Henry Selick at Ranft memorial service, 21 August 2005
11. *Storming the Magic Kingdom*, p. 23.
12. Ibid, p. 24
13. Tom Wilhite phone interview by JC, 14 September 2007.
14. *Burton on Burton*, pp. 11–12.
15. Ranft/Solomon interview, 1 December 1998.
16. *Burton on Burton*, p. 10. "I was very strange back then. [I would] do weird things like get my wisdom teeth out and bleed all over the hallways." See photo of young Burton and Ranft, c. 1980, on Steve Hulett Web site: <http://www.animationguild.org/_ReuseLibrary/blogart/randyc/Joe_Tim.jpg>
17. Michael Giaimo interview, 28 November 2007.
18. Henry Selick at Ranft memorial service, 21 August 2005
19. Floyd Norman writing in *Jim Hill Media*, 5 June 2007. < http://jimhillmedia.com/>
20. Six years later, after many other changes (including the verb in the title), the film became the hit *Who Framed Roger Rabbit*.

CHAPTER SIX Improvisation

1. Besides Ranft, Eddie Show performers included Mike Giaimo, Darrell Van Citters, Mike Gabriel, Chris Buck, Brian McEntee, Sue Mantel, Shawn Keller, Bret Thompson, among others.
2. *Drawing the Line*. Tom Sito, University Press of Kentucky, 2006. pp. 263–276.
3. Lee Unkrich to JC, 13 August 2007.
4. The Groundlings Web site: http://www.groundlings.com/start.htm
5. Joe Ranft letter to Disney execs re Story Training Ideas, 18 December 1995.

CHAPTER SEVEN Love and a Toaster

1. Tom Wilhite phone interview by JC, 14 September 2007.
2. Lasseter at Ranft memorial service.
3. Jerry Rees phone interview by JC, 21 September 2007.
4. "Toon Story: John Lasseter's Animated Life" by Mike Lyons, *Animation World Magazine*, issue 3.8, November 1998.
5. Tom Wilhite e-mail to JC, 19 September 2007.
6. *Toy Story—The Art and Making of the Animated Film*. Text by John Lasseter and Steve Daly (New York: Hyperion, 1995), p. 14.
7. Pixar's Magic Man" by Brent Schlender, *Fortune*, 17 May 2006, CNNMoney.com.
8. Ibid.
9. Lasseter at Ranft memorial service.
10. "Pixar's Magic Man," *Fortune*.
11. Brenda Chapman at Ranft memorial service.
12. Jerome Ranft interview.
13. Michael Giaimo phone interview by JC, 30 November 2007.
14. http://www.webagarretson.com/weba/Current.html
15. Michael Giaimo phone interview by JC, 14 December 2007.
16. http://religiousmovements.lib.virginia.edu/nrms/life.html
17. http://en.wikipedia.org/wiki/Lifespring#_note-Perso

CHAPTER EIGHT We Gotta Get Out of Here

1. Su Ranft interview.

2. Henry Selick at Ranft memorial service, 21 August 2005.

3. Tom Wilhite phone interview by JC, 14 September 2007.

4. Tom Wilhite e-mail to JC, 12 September 2007.

5. *The Brave Little Toaster* CD sound track brochure. Percepto Records.

6. Su Ranft interview.

7. The operation cost the couple only $1,800 instead of $18,000 in the States. Joe Ranft to JC, 23 July 1997.

8. Ruth Ranft phone interview by JC, 1 October 2007.

9. Joe Ranft to JC, 23 July 1997.

10. Rebecca Rees phone interview by JC, 21 September 2007.

11. The *Toaster* production crew included Mark Dindal, Randy Cartwright, Chris Buck, Mike Giaimo, Dan Haskett, Rob Minkoff, Steve Segal, Kirk Wise, Steve Wahl, Charles Richardson, among others.

12. Jerome Ranft interview.

13. Joe Ranft to Charles Solomon, 1 December 1998.

14. This section regarding teaching storyboarding is compiled from Joe Ranft's personal notes courtesy of Su Ranft and discussions, shared material, and interviews the author had with Joe Ranft.

15. Brenda Chapman at Ranft memorial service, 21 August 2005.

16. Brenda Chapman phone interview with JC, 12 September 2007.

17. *Storytelling in Animation—The Art of the Animated Image*, Volume 2, An anthology edited by John Canemaker, American Film Institute, 1988, pp. 71–82.

18. Tom Schumacher to JC, 27 May 2008.

19. Joe Ranft letter to JC, 8 August 1988.

20. Joe Ranft letter to JC, 17 April 1989:

> Dear John,
>
> It's Friday afternoon and I'm burnt out after a busy day of work on *The Rescuers Down Under.* I can't bring myself to draw one more damn story sketch, so I thought I'd write to you and send you some goodies that have been sitting on my desk since before Christmas. They're some [copies of animator] Freddy Moore Timothy Mouse [drawings from *Dumbo*]. And I just love them. There [sic] so simple direct and fun. What a natural unpretentious draftsman! I hope you enjoy them.
>
> Congratulations on your [HBO] project [*You Don't Have To Die*] I haven't seen it yet but I hear good things about it. It's been a good year for me Very buisy [sic] too!
>
> I went to Australia to do research for *Rescuers Down Under* (Mickey paid the bill). Bought some aboriginal artwork while I was there. What a beautiful place the outback is! I also went to the Ottawa Animation Festival and gave a talk/workshop on story. It was fun (and I lived thru it). I'm back teaching at CalArts one night a week. And have been serving on the Disney review board since January. So I'm buisy [sic] and subject to animation burn out periodically.
>
> After the Academy Awards Richard Williams took all of us who worked on *Roger* [*Rabbit*] out to lunch and we got to hold the Oscars. And drink. I hope all is well with you, John. Keep in touch,
>
> Your friend, Joe Ranft.

CHAPTER NINE Nightmare

1. Letter from Joe Ranft to JC, 1 January 1991.

2. DeviantArt Web site: <http://handyrand.deviantart.com/art/Buttocks-revised-76835027>

3. Joe Ranft letter to JC, 4 April 1991.

4. Bird had nothing to do with the *Family Dog* TV series, which he dislikes. "I gave Joe grief about it," Bird joked recently. "He was a little defensive because he knows my feelings toward it. If I wanted to get him, that's where I'd go: Hey, what do you know? You worked on the *Family Dog* series." Brad Bird interview by JC, 17 August 2007.

5. Brenda Chapman phone interview by JC, 12 September 2007; Jerome Ranft interview.

6. Joe Ranft letter to JC, 4 April 1991.

7. John Lasseter at Ranft memorial service.

8. John Lasseter interview by Karl Cohen, *ASIFA San Francisco Newsletter*, November 1995, p. 5.

CHAPTER TEN Toy Stories

1. Darla Anderson interview.

2. *Toy Story—The Art and Making of the Animated Film*, p. 44.

3. Salon.com, 23 November 1999.

4. Lee Unkrich interview.

CHAPTER ELEVEN The Ultimate Collaborator

1. "Toy Story: From Plastic to Fantastic" by Rita Kempley, *Washington Post*, 22 November 1995.

2. "Computers 'Toy' With Us, Pixar-animated Dazzler for all ages" by Peter Stack. *San Francisco Chronicle*, 22 November 1995.

3. Jeff Kurtti, *A Bug's Life—The Art and Making of an Epic of Miniature Proportions* (New York: Hyperion, 1998), p. 11.

4. Kelly Asbury e-mail, 3 January 1998.

5. "Peach Fuzz," EW.com, posted 26 April 1996.

6. Ibid.

7. Lane Smith phone interview by JC, 2 January 2008.

8. *A Bug's Life—The Art and Making of an Epic of Miniature Proportions*, p. 27.

9. Ibid, p. 38.

10. Bob Peterson to JC, 17 August 2007.

11. "'Toy' Story Man" Salon.com, 23 November 1999.

12. Joe Ranft to Charles Solomon, 23 July 1997.

13. Darla Anderson interview.

CHAPTER TWELVE An Amazing Mentor

1. "Mickey [Mouse] is always signing the checks," Joe Ranft said in 1997. "He was always a Disney employee," corroborated Su Ranft recently. "When he worked at Skellington on *Nightmare*," explained Su, "he was an employee of a limited partnership. So he didn't make buckets of money. Then he went to work at Pixar [on *Toy Story*], which was a limited partnership, so he was paid by the partnership. Then, when he went back over to Skellington on *James and the Giant Peach*, his full-on Disney employee contract was about to end." Joe Ranft said, "On Pixar [films] it was [called] Hi Tech Toons, the company they set up for *Toy Story*. Even Disney produced *Brave Toaster*. I have no agent. I always work for people I went to school with or met in the early days at Disney."

2. Courtesy Su Ranft collection.

3. Lee Unkrich interview.

4. *Toy Story* was nominated for, but did not win, Academy Awards in three categories; Ranft and six colleagues were nominated for "Best Writing, Screenplay Written Directly for the Screen." John Lasseter won a Special Achievement Academy Award.

5. Memo dated 4 June 1998 from Randy Nelson, Pixar University, courtesy Su Ranft; Joe Ranft prepared a how-to list of instructions for pitching storyboards called "Presentation of Storyboards by Joe Ranft" as follows:

"Ideally, you've worked long and hard on your sequence and it's ready to be presented.

"You think it's entertaining and it's something an audience is going to enjoy.

"The main thing to keep in mind when presenting is to communicate the board clearly to your audience.

"Don't do anything to distract from the entertainment. Do everything possible to let the board play clearly.

"Here are some suggestions to think about before pitching a board.

> 1. Prepare. Know the board and dialogue, rehearse with your fellow artists before a big presentation.
>
> 2. Do character voices if you're comfortable doing them. If not, your own voice will do fine.
>
> 3. Take a moment to establish a connection with your audience. Make eye contact before you begin.
>
> 4. Face your audience. Don't stand with your back to them.
>
> 5. Stand so that everyone can see the sketches. Don't cover them up with your body.
>
> 6. Speak clearly, don't mumble or talk to the floor. Project vocally to your audience.
>
> 7. Pace your presentation so that your audience gets a feel for what the final movie could be like. Don't slow down to over-explain screen directions and logistics at the expense of pacing.
>
> 8. Don't rush through action or fast-paced sequences at the expense of clarity. Use lots of energy but be clear. Don't overact and distract from the board.
>
> 9. Getting up and talking in front of people is one of the number one fears we human beings have. So if you happen to be a human being, you probably will experience stage fright. One way of alleviating this tremendous fear is to have a point of concentration. In other words focus on the material. The more you concentrate on it, the less self-conscious you will be.
>
> 10. Remember to keep breathing and just be yourself."

6. Darla Anderson interview.

CHAPTER THIRTEEN Trust the Process

1. "Toy Story Man," Salon.com, 23 November 1999.
2. Ibid.
3. Andrew Stanton interview.
4. Ed Catmull to JC, 13 August 2007; another viewpoint regarding storytelling at Pixar as compared to Hayao Miyazaki of Ghibli Studio in Japan (an animation filmmaker John Lasseter greatly admires) was offered in January 2008 at <GhibliWorld.com>.

   Pixar story artist Enrico Casarosa talks about Miyazaki's influence on his work and contrasts the ways Pixar and Ghibli tell their stories.

   > " . . . the process [at Pixar] is very much one of doing and redoing, making things better step by step. It involves a willingness to pick apart the movie and its themes. This constant editing and refining can be frustrating at times. The huge difference is that at Ghibli, storyboards are done by the director and they are followed without exception. So you find a very different way of doing things there, the studio and its artists are following the leader's vision without deliberation, editing, or feedback necessary . . . In this setting though, Miyazaki is free to go on his own journey finding the movie he wants to tell, bit by bit. The result are stories that are more fully personal and hold an authenticity and uniqueness which is close to impossible to achieve in the US, where a story, in the best case scenario, is well-crafted by several gifted people while in the worse case scenario is made by committee. I think that's what is great about many projects coming from Japan, with their own merits or faults, they possess an unwavering will to stick to their director's vision. The stories are allowed to be more idiosyncratic that way and that is what I personally find inspiring and refreshing."

5. Jorgen Klubien phone interview by JC, 7 January 2008.
6. Brad Bird interview.
7. Jonas Rivera to JC, 17 August 2007.
8. Darla Anderson interview.
9. *The Bear and the Bow* is scheduled for release Christmas 2011.
10. Brenda Chapman phone interview by JC, 12 September 2007.
11. Joe Ranft e-mail to JC, 7 June 2005; Jordy Ranft was attending summer camp.
12. I received two final messages from Joe: a handwritten note dated 19 July 2005 on *Cars* storyboard paper:

    > Dear John, Here are some [color copies] of Vance Gerry [story]boards for you. Thanks so much for the Monstro [the Whale from *Pinocchio*] drawings. I had a great visit with you in NY and loved our time oogling your animation art collection! The girls are doing well. Sue is fully recovered and Jordy's home from camp. Best, Joe

    The last message was an e-mail dated 11 August 2005, five days before he died:

    > Hey John, Thanks for the Monstro [story] board. Did you get the Vance Gerry boards I sent? Sue and Sophia are doing fine. They were sorry to miss seeing you although I don't think I would have seen as much of you[r] fantastic animation art collection had they been there. By the way I love your article for *The Wall Street Journal* ["Disney Erases Hand-Drawn Animation," 9 August 2005]. Perhaps 2-D will someday return to the halls of Disney.

13. Tom Schumacher to JC, 27 May 2008.
14. www.luisjrodriguez.com, 25 August 2005.
15. *The Hollywood Reporter*, 18 August 2005.
16. John Lasseter phone interview by JC, 15 January 2008.

JOE GRANT

CHAPTER ONE *The Joe Grant*

1. Don Hahn, "A Tribute for Joe's Memorial Service," Joe Grant Life Celebration, 14 May 2005.
2. Mike Gabriel to JC, 25 July 2007.
3. Tom Schumacher to JC, 27 May 2008.
4. Don Hahn to JC, 26 July 2007.
5. Tom Schumacher to JC, 25 July 1995.
6. Alice Davis to JC and Joseph Kennedy, 7 February 2008.
7. Joe Grant to JC, 24 July 1995.

CHAPTER TWO A Mobile Existence

1. State of New York Certificate and Record of Birth, 15 May 1908, #40003; 1910 U.S. Census. I am grateful to Joseph J. Kennedy's diligence and skill as a researcher for information derived from census records, birth and death records, city directory, and voter registration sources in New York and Los Angeles.
2. 1900 U.S. Census.
3. Joe Grant to JC, 11 November 1994.
4. Ibid.
5. The American Jewish Historical Society Web site chapter 27: <http://www.ajhs.org/publications/chapters/chapter.cfm?documentID=215>
6. "They had great difficulty pronouncing his Polish name," Joe Grant said. "And all he got was stares for his name, so he . . . simplified it." Joe Grant to JC, 11 November 1994.
7. Carol Grant Grubb to JC, 23 July 2007.
8. Joe Grant Oral History by Charles Solomon, March 2000. Courtesy Charles Solomon.
9. 1905 Los Angeles City Directory; Lance Bowling, 13 February 2008 e-mail to JC; 1930 U.S. Census; Carol Grant Grubb, 23 July 2007. There are no records that Nathan Grant played with the L.A. Philharmonic or the L.A. Symphony.
10. "Ned" Grant's birth date is listed as May 1859 in the California Death Index; Carol Grant Grubb interview by JC, 7 February 2008.
11. Jennifer Grant Castrup to JC, 24 July 2007.
12. Jennifer Grant Castrup e-mail to JC, 2 October 2007.
13. Dorse A. Lanpher, <http://www.drawn2gether.com/blog/2008/06/05/eat-your-oatmeal/ >
14. <http://www.churchman.org/7howard_pyle.htm>; Joe Grant Oral History: "And he [George A.] was in short pants in life [drawing] classes. So you can imagine he was pretty well advanced in many ways (laughs)." Pennsylvania Museum and School of Industrial Art catalog, Sara J. MacDonald, Public Services Librarian e-mail to JC, 25 January 2008.
15. Sara J. MacDonald; Los Angeles 1904 City Directory.
16. Joe Grant to Robin Allan, 30 May, 25 June 1985, and 14 August 1986.
17. *Los Angeles Times*, "Art and Artists" by Anthony E. Anderson, 23 December 1906.
18. *Los Angeles Times*, "Marriages," 3 August 1907.
19. Jennifer Grant Castrup: "August 5, 1907 is the date of their honeymoon"; Amy Booth Green found the newlyweds' signatures in the hotel's 1907 guest registry. The Coronado Hotel was featured in the film *Some Like It Hot* and was the design model for Walt Disney World's Grand Floridian Resort and Spa.
20. 1900 U.S. Census. Census dates are notoriously inaccurate; in this case Lena may have been a child bride of fourteen years when she married Abe, whose dates on the 1930 census indicate he was born in 1863, which would have made him eighteen when he married.
21. Ibid.
22. Jennifer Grant Castrup to JC e-mail, 2 October 2007.
23. Jennifer Grant Castrup to JC, 24 July 2007.
24. Carol Grant Grubb to JC, 23 July 2007.
25. Danielle Workman to JC phone interview, 22 August 2007.
26. *Los Angeles Times*, 30 May 1909, "Some Notable Festivities Incident to Society During the Past Week—Miss Greene to Receive."
27. Joe Grant Oral History.
28. Joe Grant to JC, 11 November 1994.
29. Los Angeles City Business Directory, 1923.
30. Carol Grant Grubb to JC, 7 February 2008.
31. Danielle Workman to JC phone interview, 22 August 2007.
32. "Divorce Decrees Granted," *Los Angeles Times*, 20 February 1934.
33. Joe Grant to JC, 11 November 1994.
34. Carol Grant Grubb to JC, 7 February 2008; Jennifer Grant Castrup, 24 July 2007.
35. Joe Grant Oral History.
36. Ibid.
37. Ibid.
38. Ibid.
39. Milt Gross directed two MGM animated cartoons in 1938.
40. Joe Grant Oral History.
41. *Walt Disney and Europe—European Influences on the Animated Feature Films of Walt Disney* by Robin Allan. John Libbey & Co. Ltd. 1999, note #30, p. 172.
42. "I'd say introducing me to the works of artists was the most useful to me later, particularly at Disney," Joe recalled in 2000. Joe Grant Oral History.
43. Ibid.
44. Carol Grant Grubb to JC, 7 February 2008.

CHAPTER THREE Kewpies, Caskets, and Shoes

1. Joe Grant Oral History.
2. Jennifer Grant Castrup to JC, 24 July 2007.
3. Joe Grant Oral History.
4. 1920 U.S. Census.

5. Carol Grant Grubb to JC, 2 February 2008.

6. Carol Grant Grubb to JC, 7 February 2008.

7. 1922 L.A. City Directory. Within a year George's parents moved to 274 E. Forty-eighth Street and George moved to 1118 Colton Street, which was around the corner from 1103 First Street and close to the *Examiner* offices on South Broadway. 1922 Voter Registration Records.

8. Joe Grant to JC, 11 November 1994.

9. Joe Grant Oral History. In 1925, the school was annexed to the city of Los Angeles and the name changed to Venice High School.

10. I am grateful to Joanne Samija, researcher for Don Hahn's forthcoming documentary film on Joe Grant, for this information.

11. 1928 Los Angeles City Directory.

12. Joe Grant Oral History.

CHAPTER FOUR Art Director of Myself

1. Joe Grant to JC, 11 April 2003.

2. *Julia Morgan Architect* by Sara Holmes Boutelle (New York: Abbeville Press, 1988), p. 174.

3. Joe Grant to JC, 24 July 1995.

4. Joe Grant Oral History.

5. Carol Grant Grubb phone interview, 25 March 2008.

6. Joe Grant to JC, 11 April 2003.

7. *Disney's Giant and the Artist's Model* by Adrienne Tytla. Self-published, 2004, p. 137.

8. Joe Grant to JC, 11 April 2003.

9. Joe Grant to JC, 11 November 1994. 8 June 1928, may have been his start date, based on an image of the *Los Angeles Record*'s front page of that date on Grant's "Staff Artist" business card.

10. Carol Grant Grubb to JC, 23 July 2007.

11. "Joe Grant Does Brilliant First Book" by Llewellyn Miller, the *Los Angeles Record*, August 1934. Courtesy Jennifer Grant Castrup.

12. John Decker (1895–1947) painted commissioned portraits of Greta Garbo, Chaplin, and John Barrymore (a close drinking buddy); he caricatured Harry Langdon in the *Los Angeles Record* on 11 February 1928 and the cast of *Chicago* on 18 February 1928, among other pages; for a biography of Decker, see *Bohemian Rogue: The Life of Hollywood Artist John Decker* by Stephen C. Jordan, Scarecrow Press, 2005.

13. Victor Mall (1901–1989) taught at the Hollywood Academy of Modern Art and later became an ad agency art director; he drew the cast of *Companionate Marriage* on 2 June 1928 in the *Los Angeles Record*. <for bio info: <Askart.com>

14. Ibid for bio info; in the 28 August 1928 *Los Angeles Record*, Langguth drew a "study" of actress Baclanova. Xavier Cugat (1900–1990) contributed a 28 October 1928 drawing of L.A. Philharmonic conductor Georg Schneevoigt that amuses for what is missing (M-shaped hair nearly outlining a face of free-floating features assembled around a straight line nose) as it does by what is there (diamond-shaped belly in a tux on two straight lines for feet).

15. Joe Grant to JC, 11 April 2003.

16. Wendy Wick Reaves to JC, 11 March 2008; Llewellyn Miller once wrote that she considered Grant's first pure caricature to be "a drawing of [actor] Robert McWade, and indicated in a maze of lines and a tangle of shading the power, the incisive humor, the gentle ruthlessness and the economy of means which were to make Grant, at the end of two years, the leading caricaturist of movie people, second to no one in the nation." "Joe Grant Does Brilliant First Book" by Llewellyn Miller, the *Los Angeles Record*, August 1934.

17. Joe Grant to JC, 11 April 2003.

18. Ibid.

19. Reaves interview.

20. Receipts from Fox West Coast theaters and Warner Bros. Theaters Inc. courtesy Jennifer Grant Castrup.

21. Joe Grant Oral History.

22. Reaves interview.

23. "Joe Grant Does Brilliant First Book" by Llewellyn Miller, the *Los Angeles Record*, August 1934. Clipping courtesy Jennifer Grant Castrup.

    Llewellyn Miller later moved to New York and became the first woman officer (vice president) of the Society of Magazine Writers, later the American Society of Journalists and Authors, Inc. (ASJA). She was described as a "beloved and kind-hearted *grande dame*" who "was never rich, always struggling to make it come out even." After her death in 1971, the Society named the Llewellyn Miller Fund for financial aid to writers after her. *ASJA*, vol. 48, #9, October 1999, "Bloom Steps Down from Miller Fund."

24. 1929 Los Angeles City Directory.

25. *Los Angeles Times*, "Divorce Suits Filed," 8 April 1930.

26. 1930 U.S. Census.

27. *Los Angeles Times*, "Hollywood High Girl gets Prize—Jury of Artists Selects Easter Poster of Girl," 6 April 1930, p. A2.

28. Jennifer Grant Castrup e-mail to JC, 2 October 2007.

29. Carol Grant Grubb to JC, 23 July 2007, 7 February 2008. Divorce papers filed in the Superior Court of the State of California.

30. *Los Angeles Times*, 14 November 1932, "News Artists Will Exhibit."

31. Joe Grant to JC, 11 November 1994.

CHAPTER FIVE Mickey and Jennie

1. Bob Thomas, *Walt Disney—An American Original* (New York: Simon & Schuster, 1976), p. 119.

2. Joe Grant to JC, 11 November 1994.

3. Stephen Watts, *The Magic Kingdom—Walt Disney and the American Way of Life* (Boston, New York: Houghton Mifflin, 1997), p. 80.

4. Martin Provensen to J. B. Kaufman, 21 November 1985.

5. *Motion Picture Herald*, 1 October 1932.

6. Joe Grant to JC, 11 November 1994.

7. Ibid.

8. 23 December 1935 memo, Walt Disney to Donald Graham.

9. Joe Grant Oral History.

10. Ibid.

11. Joe Grant to JC, 11 November 1994.

12. Jennifer Grant Castrup to JC, 24 July 2007.

13. Carol Grant Grubb to JC, 23 July 2007.

14. "More Students Will Graduate. Exercises in High School Due Tomorrow." *Los Angeles Times*, 17 June 1931. Jennie Miller was among 173 pupils who graduated from Belmont High on 18 June 1931.

15. Jennifer Grant Castrup e-mail to JC, 2 October 2007. Carol Grant Grubb to JC, 7 February 2008.

16. *Los Angeles Times*, "Vital Record—Intention to Marry, White—Miller," 13 August 1932.

17. Carol Grant Grubb to JC, 23 July 2007.

18. Joe Grant to JC, 11 November 1994.

19. Reaves interview.

20. Joe Grant to Robin Allan, 14 August 1986.

CHAPTER SIX Of Wrens and Witches

1. John Canemaker, *Paper Dreams—The Art & Artists of Disney Storyboards* (New York: Hyperion, 1999), p. 70.

2. Nancy Naumberg, ed., *We Make the Movies*, "Mickey Mouse Presents" by Walt Disney (Faber & Faber, 1936), p. 256.

3. Albert Hurter, *He Drew As He Pleased* (New York: Simon & Schuster, 1948), unpaginated.

4. Joe Grant to Michael Barrier, 14 October 1988. Courtesy of Michael Barrier.

5. Joe Grant to JC, 11 November 1994.

6. Ibid; Joe Grant to JC, 6 September 1994; Joe Grant Oral History.

7. Joe Grant interview, TV is OK Productions, 1997.

8. Joe Grant to Michael Barrier, 14 October 1988.

9. Interview by TV is OK.

10. Joe Grant to J. B. Kaufman, 21 November 1985. Courtesy of J. B. Kaufman.

11. Joe Grant Oral History.

12. Letter to Joe and Jennie Grant from Walt Disney, 24 December 1935. Courtesy Jennifer Grant Castrup.

13. Joe Grant Oral History.

14. Vance Gerry to Charles Solomon, October 1993.

15. *Before the Animation Begins*, p. 104.

16. Charles Solomon, *The Disney That Never Was* (New York: Hyperion, 1995), p. 12.

17. Bill Peet, *Bill Peet: An Autobiography* (Boston: Houghton Mifflin, 1989), p. 113.

18. Joe Grant to J. B. Kaufman, 21 November 1985.

19. William Cottrell to Jay Horan, 10 August 1983.

20. Joe Grant to J. B. Kaufman, 21 November 1985.

21. Joe Grant to Michael Barrier, 14 October 1988; Joe Grant to JC, 11 November 1994.

22. Joe Grant to Charles Solomon, Oral History.

23. *Walt Disney and Europe*, p. 33, note #19.

24. *Before the Animation Begins*, p. 56.

25. Joe Grant Oral History.

26. Russell Merritt and J. B. Kaufman, *Walt Disney's Silly Symphonies* (Germona, Italy: La cineteca del Friuli, 2006), pp. 22–23.

27. Joe Grant to J. B. Kaufman, 21 November 1985.

28. *Disney Animation: The Illusion of Life*, p. 384.

29. William Cottrell to Jay Horan.

30. Joe Grant to JC, 7 January 1995.

31. Joe Grant to Mike Lyons, 20 October 1999.

32. *Before the Animation Begins*, p. 63.

33. Campbell Grant to Michael Barrier, 2 February 1977. Courtesy Michael Barrier.

34. Ward Kimball to Michael Barrier, 2 November 1976.

35. The raise is dated 5 September 1938. Joe Grant personnel record, Walt Disney Archives.

36. Joe Grant to JC, 11 November 1994.

CHAPTER SEVEN OK, J.G.

1. Robin Allan, "Still is the story told," *Storytelling in Animation—the Art of the Animated Image*, Vol. 2, ed. John Canemaker (Los Angeles: American Film Institute, 1988), pp. 83–92.

2. For biographical information on many of the Character Model artists, see *Before the Animation Begins: The Art and Lives of Disney Inspirational Sketch Artists* (New York: Hyperion, 1996) and *Paper Dreams: The Art & Artists of Disney Storyboards* (New York: Hyperion, 1999).

3. "Walt Disney's Pinocchio—Creating a Most Famous Puppet Character" submitted by Bob Jones, 23 January 1989. Walt Disney Archives.

4. Joe Grant to JC, 7 January 1995.

5. Martin Provensen to J. B. Kaufman, 21 November 1985.

6. *The Illusion of Life*, p. 208. At some point Del Connell cut out and mounted the art and signed Grant's initials and the date in the rubber stamp space containing the "OK" "because [Grant had] already okayed the art." Connell referred to Grant as "JG the OK guy."

7. Joe Grant to J. B. Kaufman, 21 November 1985.

8. Joe Grant Oral History.

9. Joe Grant to Don Peri, 22 February 2003.

10. Joe Grant to Robin Allan, 14 August 1986.

11. Cambell Grant to Michael Barrier, 2 February 1977.

12. Ibid.

13. Martin Provensen to Michael Barrier, 4 July 1983.

14. Grim Natwick, *Cartoonist Profiles*, #45, March 1980.

15. Joe Grant to JC, 11 November 1994.

16. Natwick, *Cartoonist Profiles*.

17. For more information on Richard Huemer, visit the family Web site: <http://huemer.com/animate1.htm >

18. Joe Grant to Mike Lyons, 20 October 1999.

19. Joe Grant to J. B. Kaufman, 21 November 1985.

20. 13 September 1938, NYC Death Certificate; *NYJ-A*, 15 September 1938, "Last Rites Held for Geo. Grant."

21. Danielle Workman phone interview with JC, 22 August 2007. Grant's sister Geraldine, described as "for playing and fun and not real serious," married Jack Turner Strock at an early age and had a daughter (Danielle) in 1934. Danille spent considerable time being cared for by Grandmother Eva, Uncle Joe, and Aunt Jennie, and she considered all three her surrogate parents.

22. Ward Kimball to Michael Barrier, 2 November 1976.

23. Joe Grant to Michael Barrier, 14 October 1988.

24. Diary research courtesy of Amid Amidi.

25. Joe Grant to Michael Barrier, 14 October 1988; see also: Michael Barrier, *Hollywood Cartoons—American Animation in Its Golden Age* (Oxford University Press, 1999), pp. 256–259.

CHAPTER EIGHT The Star Writers

1. "The Long Flight of Dumbo," by Dick Case, the (Syracuse) *Post-Standard*, 5 May 2002. Helen Durney's papers and drawings for *Dumbo* are in the special collections of Bird Library at Syracuse University.

2. Ibid.

3. *Dumbo* manuscript by Joe Grant and Dick Huemer, 1940, p. 35. Walt Disney Archives.

4. Recollections of Richard Huemer: An Oral History of the Motion Picture in America. Interviewed by Joe Adamson (UCLA/AFI, 1969), p. 168.

5. Joe Grant to Michael Barrier, 14 October 1988.

6. Richard Huemer Oral History, p. 154.

7. *Time*, 29 December 1941.

8. Joe Grant to Robin Allan, 14 August 1986.

9. Joe Grant to Don Peri, 22 February 2003. Courtesy Don Peri.

10. Joe Grant to Robin Allan.

11. Joe Grant to Michael Barrier, 14 October 1988.

12. Joe Grant to Don Peri, 22 February 2003.

13. Joe Grant to JC, 11 November 1994.

14. Joe Grant to Don Peri, 22 February 2003.

15. Richard Huemer Oral History.

16. Joe Grant interview by TV is OK Productions, 1997.

17. Joe Grant Oral History.

18. *Los Angeles Times*, "I'll Be the Judge, You Be Jury," 14 June 1941.

19. Richard Huemer UCLA Oral History.

20. Letter dated 31 March 1942 from Hal Adelquist, Walt Disney Productions' Personnel Department, to Joe Grant and Dick Huemer. Courtesy Jennifer Grant Castrup and Richard Huemer, Jr.

CHAPTER NINE The War Without and Within

1. Richard Shale, *Donald Duck Joins Up* (Ann Arbor, MI: UMI Research Press, 1982, 1976), p. 27; several war shorts are on the DVD collection *Walt Disney On the Front Lines*.

2. Ibid.

3. Story conference notes "Defense Picture," 23 December 1941. Walt Disney Archives.

4. *Donald Duck Joins Up*, p. 28.

5. Joe Grant to Michael Barrier, 14 October 1988.

6. Ibid.

7. UCLA Oral History.

8. Joe Grant to JC, 24 July 1995.

9. *Los Angeles Times* "The Arts." "Disney Artist Has Gay Show" by A.M., 16 January 1942.

10. Estimated cost on *Lady* story script memo dated 5 November 1943. Courtesy Jennifer Grant Castrup.

11. Inter-Office Communication, 13 August 1945, from Jack Lavin to Joe Grant and Hal Adelquist. Courtesy Jennifer Grant Castrup.

12. Inter-Office Communication, Joe Grant to Walt Disney, 20 June 1946. Courtesy Jennifer Grant Castrup.

13. Joe Grant to JC, 7 January 1995.

14. *Los Angeles Times*, "Artists Have Fun" by A.M., 16 January 1944.

15. Joe Grant Oral History.

16. Richard Huemer UCLA Oral History.

17. Joe Grant to JC, 18 January 1997.

18. Steven Watts, *The Magic Kingdom: Walt Disney and the American Way of Life* (Boston, New York: Houghton Mifflin, 1997), p. 263.

19. Richard Huemer, Jr. to JC, e-mail, 25 June 2008.

20. Joe Grant Oral History.

CHAPTER TEN Something Was Amiss

1. Joe Grant to Michael Barrier, 14 October 1988.

2. Ibid.

3. Joe Grant Oral History.

4. Joe Grant to JC, 7 January 1994.

5. *Alice* conference notes courtesy Walt Disney Archives.

6. *Los Angeles Times*, 19 November 1945, part 1, page 11.

7. Aldous Huxley *Alice in Wonderland* script, courtesy Robin Allan.

8. On 7 July 1947, Disney engaged Professor William C. Greet of the English Department of Barnard College, Columbia University, as a "speech consultant" on *Alice in Wonderland*, which was not to be an all-animation feature. Greet met with Kathryn Beaumont, the final choice for the role of Alice, on 8 August 1947. Joe Grant, Walt, and Prof. Greet posed for photos on 18 July 1947. Disney Studio press release and Walt Disney's desk diary, courtesy Robert Tieman, Walt Disney Archives.

9. Bill Peet to Michael Barrier, 15 August 1978.

10. Ward Kimball to Michael Barrier, 2 November 1976.

11. Joe Grant Oral History.

12. Joe Grant personnel file. Walt Disney Archives.

13. Joe Grant Oral History.

14. Nick Grubb to JC, 23 July 2007.

CHAPTER ELEVEN Good-bye to Pixieland

1. "Good-bye to Pixieland" by Joe Grant

> A long farewell, and good riddance.
>
> I shall shake the star dust out of my hair. I shall comb the whimsy out of my beard. I shall set my doddering footsteps upon the road back to sanity and reason and never once look back with regret.
>
> I had a high old time in Pixieland. In fact I can now admit that I was a pixie myself for quite a while. Longer than I care to remember. I was

an initiate into the inner circle of the pixie court and a close associate of the "Grand Panjandrum" himself. I know whereof I talk when I say that the G.P. was as odd a fish as you ever heard of. Who else on the eve of war would have shouted, "War? That's a lot of hooey! There won't be a war!" Or on the subject of women who else would have swept the whole argument away with the assertion, "Women? Women are all constipated!"

A rare fellow, the "Grand Panjandrum." You would never suspect it to meet him when he was on his good behavior or holding high court amidst starry-eyed admirers (who often times included some of the biggest names of the civilized world). At such times he was wont to affect a coy boyish-ness and naiveté which had a strange affect upon those workers of Pixieland who were unfortunate to be standing around. The effect was principally in the region of the stomach. But the visitors from the outside world of the commonplace loved it and he knew it. And he gave it to them like the clever man he was. It was good business.

They say the dog reflects the master. And they, whoever they are, speak truly. Just so did all Pixieland reflect the character and crotchets of the Grand Panjandrum so that there was assembled for a space of time as peculiar an aggregation of individuals as may never be gotten together again. It is all over now. The Grand Panjandrum no longer rules in state over his giggling myrmidons. The rivers of fun have long ago dried up. The gales of laughter no longer sweep through the gingerbread towers and set the bells of folly a-tinkling.

Some of the pixies in a fit of mournfulness have laid the hands of violence upon themselves. Some laughed themselves to death with broken hearts. Some perished of pernicious ennui. Many fled in time. Others were expelled, kicked out by the royal boot. Some stayed on to the end and watched the slow disintegration of a fabulous and phoney [sic] fairyland. I am one of the latter. And now if you like I will take you by the hand and lead you staring and breathless through this once great kingdom of mirth through the labyrinth of intrigue, through the crooked winding streets of incompetence, over the bridge of sighs, into the grand hall glittering with false brilliance . . . up . . . up . . . to the foot of the "Grand Panjandrum" himself. And you shall see what you shall see.

2. Joe Grant to Michael Barrier, 14 October 1988.
3. Ibid.
4. Joe Grant to JC, 11 November 1994.
5. Joe Grant to JC, 24 July 1995.
6. Joe Grant to TV is OK Productions, 1997.
7. Joe Grant to Michael Barrier, 14 October 1988.
8. Joe Grant to Don Peri, 22 February 2003.
9. Ward Kimball to Michael Barrier, 2 November 1976.
10. Ward Kimball to Michael Barrier, 12 December 1986.
11. Bill Peet, *Bill Peet—An Autobiography* (Boston: Houghton Mifflin, 1989), pp. 111–113.
12. Joe Grant to Don Peri, 22 February 2003.
13. Tom Schumacher to JC, 27 May 2008; Michael Barrier on "reputations": "It's hard for me to think of anyone who was in any way a *boss*—director or producer—in animation's golden age who hasn't been the target of negative stories. (After all, who has been the subject of more venomous gossip than Walt Disney?)" <michaelbarrier.com>, 30 April 2008.
14. Dick Huemer UCLA Oral History.
15. Joe Grant to Michael Barrier, 14 October 1988.
16. Bill Peet to JC, 13 January 1997.
17. Joe Grant to JC, 7 January 1994.
18. Joe Grant Oral History.

CHAPTER TWELVE Moving On

1. Jennifer Grant Castrup e-mail to JC, 2 October 2007.
2. Danielle Workman phone interview with JC, 22 August 2007.
3. Joe Grant to JC, 11 April 2003.
4. Bob Jones (Robert M. Jones) (1913–1990) was on the Disney staff in Special Effects from 6 July 1937 to 2 February 1941; little biographical information is available. Charles C. Cristadoro (1881–1967) was a sculptor of figures for the 1914 Panama Pacific International Exposition in San Francisco and during the 1930s puppets for the WPA Federal Theatre Project in Hollywood and a dinosaur modeler for the 1933 film *King Kong*. Grant hired him for Disney's Character Model Department in March 1938 to render three-dimensional models of *Pinocchio* characters. Information courtesy of David R. Smith and Robert Tieman, Walt Disney Archives.
5. Diane Castrup to JC, 4 October 2007.
6. Don Hahn to JC, 26 July 2007.
7. Jennifer Grant Castrup to JC, 24 July 2007.
8. Morey Lawton letter, 2005. Courtesy Jennifer Grant Castrup.
9. "Acquisition of Castle, Ltd., twenty-five-year-old Los Angeles manufacturer of greeting cards by Williamhouse, Inc., New York, was reported by Joe Grant, president of the local company." *Los Angeles Times*, "Castle, Ltd. Acquired by New York Company," 7 September 1961.
10. Diane Castrup to JC, 4 October 2007.
11. Alice Davis to JC, 7 February 2008.
12. Joe Grant Oral History.
13. Joe Grant to Don Peri, 22 February 2003.
14. Carol Grant Grubb to JC, 7 February 2008.
15. Ibid.
16. In their 1981 book, the two animators said that in the old days Grant's handling of "flashy" drawing mediums, like pastel, was "always a source of annoyance, and envy, to the animators, who were restricted to line drawings and flat color." Frank Thomas and Ollie Johnston, *Disney Animation: The Illusion of Life* (New York: Abbeville Press, 1981), p. 208.
17. Joe Grant Oral History.
18. Howard Green to JC, 23 July 2007.
19. "Bill Peet," said Burny Mattinson, "Joe used to talk to him all the time, a lot after [Peet] left [Disney in 1964]. They kept in contact an awful lot. It was initiated by Peet, who would call [Joe]. Course [Peet] would be a little loaded sometimes." Burny Mattinson to JC, 25 July 2007.
20. Joe Grant to Don Peri, 22 February 2003.
21. Dean DeBlois to JC, phone interview 4 June 2008.
22. Joe Grant Oral History.
23. *Paper Dreams*, pp. 160–165.
24. Joe Grant to Don Peri, 22 February 2003; Dick Huemer died 30 November 1979 at age 81.
25. Charlie Fink speech at Joe Grant Life Celebration, Alex Theatre, Glendale, California, 28 June 2005; Fink was Disney Feature Animation Creative Development head from 1986 to 1991.
26. Mike Gabriel to JC, 25 July 2007.
27. Tom Schumacher to JC, 27 May 2008.
28. Undated thank-you note. Courtesy Tom Schumacher.
29. Jennifer Grant Castrup, 24 July 2007.

CHAPTER THIRTEEN
Master of the Big Idea

1. Joe Grant to Don Peri, 22 February 2003.
2. Charles Solomon to JC, 22 July 2007.
3. Pam Coats phone interview with JC, 3 June 2008.
4. Don Hahn at Joe Grant Life Celebration, 28 June 2005.
5. Don Hahn to JC, 26 July 2007.
6. Don Hahn, Joe Grant Life Celebration.
7. John Culhane, *Fantasia/2000—Visions of Hope* (New York: Disney Editions, 1999), p. 102.
8. Eric Goldberg to JC, 25 July 2007.
9. Don Hahn, Joe Grant Life Celebration.
10. Burny Mattinson to JC, 25 July 2007.
11. Joe Grant to JC, 7 January 1995.
12. Joe Grant to Don Peri, 22 February 2003.
13. Van Eaton Gallery brochure, September 2007.
14. Mike Gabriel to JC, 25 July 2007.
15. For example, Jeffrey Katzenberg said *Pocahontas* was "the *Romeo and Juliet* we've been trying to get off the ground." Mike Gabriel interview 25 July 2007.
16. Burny Mattinson to JC, 25 July 2007.
17. Ibid.
18. Don Hahn, Joe Grant Life Celebration.
19. Pete Docter to JC, 17 August 2007.
20. "A Touch of Gray in Hollywood" by Jeffrey Gettleman. *Los Angeles Times*, 27 May 2000.
21. Joe Grant to JC, 7 January 1995.
22. Andreas Deja to JC, 25 July 2007.
23. Joe Grant to JC, 11 November 1994.
24. Declaration of Joe Grant, 7 July 1993. Courtesy Jennifer Grant Castrup.
25. Charles Solomon recalled Iwo Takamoto, a skilled Japanese American draftsman, was hired on the spot by the Disney Studio soon after his release from one of America's World War II internment camps. "Disney didn't care what color you were," Takamoto said, "if you could draw well enough." Charles Solomon e-mail to JC, 25 July 2008.
26. Joe Grant to JC, 7 January 1994.
27. Dean DeBlois to JC, 4 June 2008.
28. Jonas Rivera to JC, 17 August 2007.

INDEX

ACKNOWLE

My first debt is to Joe Grant and Joe Ranft, who through the years offered me numerous conversations and formal interviews as well as the gift of their trust and friendship.

For their full cooperation and warm support of this exploration of two extraordinary artists and human beings, I am most grateful to the Grant and Ranft families: Carol Grant Grubb, Jennifer Grant Castrup, Michael Grubb, Nick Grubb, Diane Castrup, and Danielle Workman; and Su Ranft, Jerome Ranft, Adrienne Ranft, Ruth and James Ranft, and Ranft family friend John Tschudin.

Not for the first time, my research was again greatly aided by my knowledgeable friends at the Walt Disney Archives: David R. Smith and Robert Tieman, who also checked the manuscript for factual errors; many rare original artworks were found by my tireless friends at the Walt Disney Animation Research Library: Lella Smith, Ann Hansen, Mary Walsh, Doug Engala, and Fox Carney; and at the Disney Photo Library, where my friends Ed Squair, Rick E. Lorentz, Andrea Recendez-Carbone, LaToya Morgan, and Mike Buckhoff diligently provided numerous photographs.

At Pixar, I received equally expert help from new friends, including archivists Peggy Tran-Le, Elyse Klaidman, Janet Vrcic, Kat Chanover, and Christine Freeman, Juliet G. Roth, and Heather Feng, John Lasseter's chief assistant.

Valuable information was provided by Lisa Falk, senior librarian, Los Angeles Public Library History and Genealogy Department; Wendy Wick Reaves, curator prints and drawings, National Portrait Gallery—Smithsonian Institution; Sara J. MacDonald, public services librarian, The University of the Arts University Libraries and Archives, Philadelphia; Lynn Dougherty, UArts registrar; Joanna Samija, researcher for Don Hahn; Lance Bowling—Cambria Master Recordings; Carol Merrill-Mirsky, Ph.D., director/curator, Hollywood Bowl Museum; Arvind Manocha, Los Angeles Philharmonic Association; and Ann Butler and Marvin Taylor, curators of the John Canemaker Animation Collection in the Fales Collection at Bobst Library, New York University.

During the course of my research, many people shared their impressions and memories of the two Joes with me. Among them, I am most grateful to Darla Anderson, Tony Anselmo, Kelly Asbury, Brad Bird, Ed Catmull, Brenda Chapman, Pam Coats, Andreas Deja, Pete Docter, Mike Gabriel, Michael Giaimo, Eric and Susan Goldberg, Howard E. Green, Don Hahn, Richard Huemer, Jr., Jorgen Klubien, John Lasseter, Burny Mattinson, John Musker (who also generously supplied several of his brilliant caricatures to help illustrate this book), Bob Peterson, Jerry Rees, Rebecca Rees, Jonas Rivera, Thomas Schumacher, Lane Smith, Andrew Stanton, Lee Unkrich, Darrell Van Citters, Tom Wilhite, and Richard Williams.

Once again I offer deep thanks to my fellow animation historians for their generous support of my work, including Amid Amidi and Jerry Beck of CartoonBrew.com, Jeff Kurtti, Kuniko

DGMENTS

Okubo, Michael Sporn, Ted Thomas, and Stephen Worth of the ASIFA-Hollywood Animation Archive. A special thank-you to Mark Johnson, King Features archivist, who prepared a special video for me of early caricatures in animation; and to Leonard Maltin, who supplied Grant caricatures from his personal collection as seen in the newsletter *Leonard Maltin's Movie Crazy*.

I am deeply indebted to historians Michael Barrier, J. B. Kaufman, and Don Peri, whose sensitive and probing personal interviews with Joe Grant yielded much valuable information. Of particular help was my good friend and esteemed animation historian Charles Solomon for his invaluable Joe Grant oral history recorded in 2000, which now resides in the Margaret Herrick Library of the Academy of Motion Picture Arts and Sciences.

For various kindnesses extended to me during the course of my work, I express my warm thanks to Nancy Beiman, David Bohnett, Dennis Frahmann, Steve Heller, Jeanne McCafferty, Tim Palin, Imogen Sutton, Heidi Leigh, Suzi Mattmiller, Shelley Mithun, Sheila Saxby, Eugene Salandra, Ken Martinez, Monica Lago-Kaytis, Scott Johnston, and Roger Viloria.

Robert Cornfield performed yeoman service not only in his usual capacity as my literary representative, but as a keen-eyed editor of the manuscript in its early stage; his scrutiny of and suggestions for the text were of enormous value.

This is my fifth project with the estimable Wendy Lefkon, vice president and editorial director of Disney Editions, who, before there was a manuscript or even a proposal, enthusiastically and warmly championed the idea of this book; as always, she has been a bedrock of support and positive energy. Wendy assembled a fine team to bring the work into print, including Jon Glick, whose page designs sing.

Joseph Kennedy, the Joe with whom I share my life, is an excellent writer and editor who patiently perused all five versions of the manuscript and made countless cogent suggestions that influenced my writing greatly. In addition, he expertly and painstakingly researched Joe Grant's genealogy and personal history in New York and Los Angeles, providing many heretofore-unknown details about the artist's life. He is, and always has been, a reliable sounding board and provided loving support.

I have dedicated this book to Howard E. Green, who for over thirty years has been an invaluable ally and friend at the Disney Studio to me and many other animation historians. Howard is a beacon of human warmth and generous help in a sometimes cold and bureaucratic corporate entity. In addition, his love of animation has extended to a number of elderly master animators, on whom he lavished much personal attention and care and placed them and their accomplishments in a public spotlight, such as Frank Thomas, Ollie Johnston, Marc Davis, and Ward Kimball. He was especially close and attentive to Joe Grant, who, despite their age difference, were best buddies.

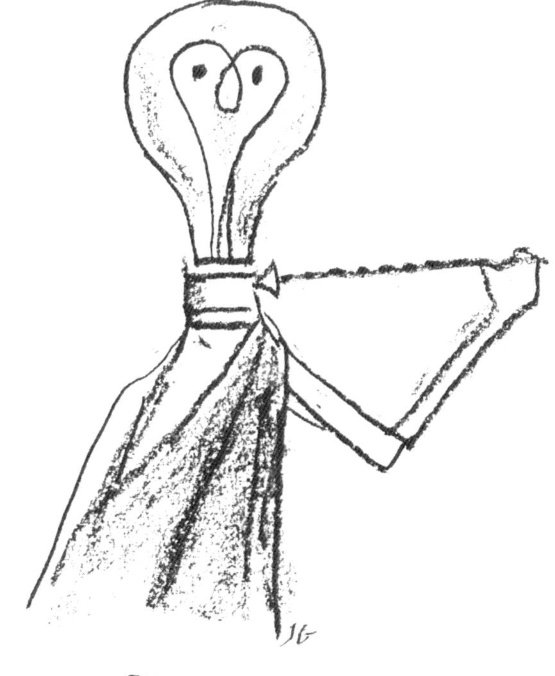

Tom
The lights on!
What's next?
Joe

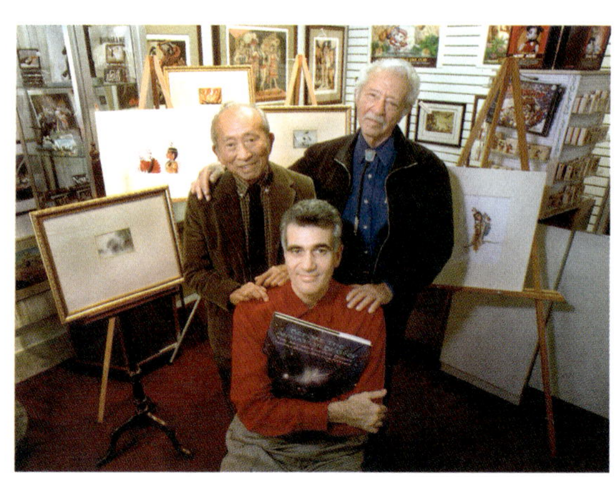

TOP: *Tyrus Wong (BAMBI concept artist), John Canemaker, and Joe Grant in Burbank, California, 1996.* BELOW: *John Canemaker with Joe Ranft at Pacific Film Archives, Berkeley, California, 2004.*

John **Canemaker** is an internationally renowned independent animator, animation historian, and teacher, whose films have been honored with multiple awards, and whose writings express deep understanding and sensitivity about the art of animation and its artists.

Canemaker won a 2005 Academy Award and an Emmy Award for his animated short, *The Moon and the Son: An Imagined Conversation*. Since 1974, he has produced more than a dozen personal animated films and documentaries, and has designed and animated sequences for feature films, commercials, and Peabody– and Academy Award–winning documentaries.

He has written ten books about animation and more than one hundred essays, reviews, and other articles, for *The Wall Street Journal*, *The New York Times*, *Time* magazine, *Print* magazine, and other periodicals.

Canemaker is also a tenured full professor and executive director of the animation program at the Tisch School of the Arts Kanbar Department of Film and Television at New York University. The John Canemaker Animation Collection, part of the Fales Collection in Bobst Library at New York University, is an archival resource established in 1989 that is available to all scholars, researchers, and students.

He is much in demand as a lecturer on animation history and has given talks and screenings at New York's Museum of Modern Art, the Los Angeles County Museum of Art, Pacific Film Archive, Smithsonian Institute, American Film Institute, and numerous other museums, universities, and film festivals around the world.

He lives in New York City and eastern Long Island.

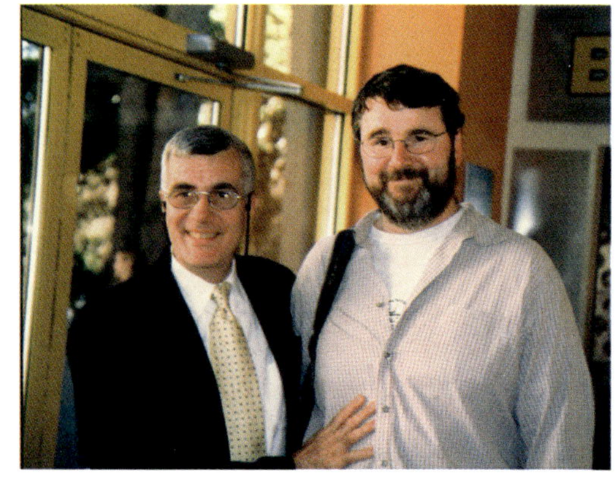

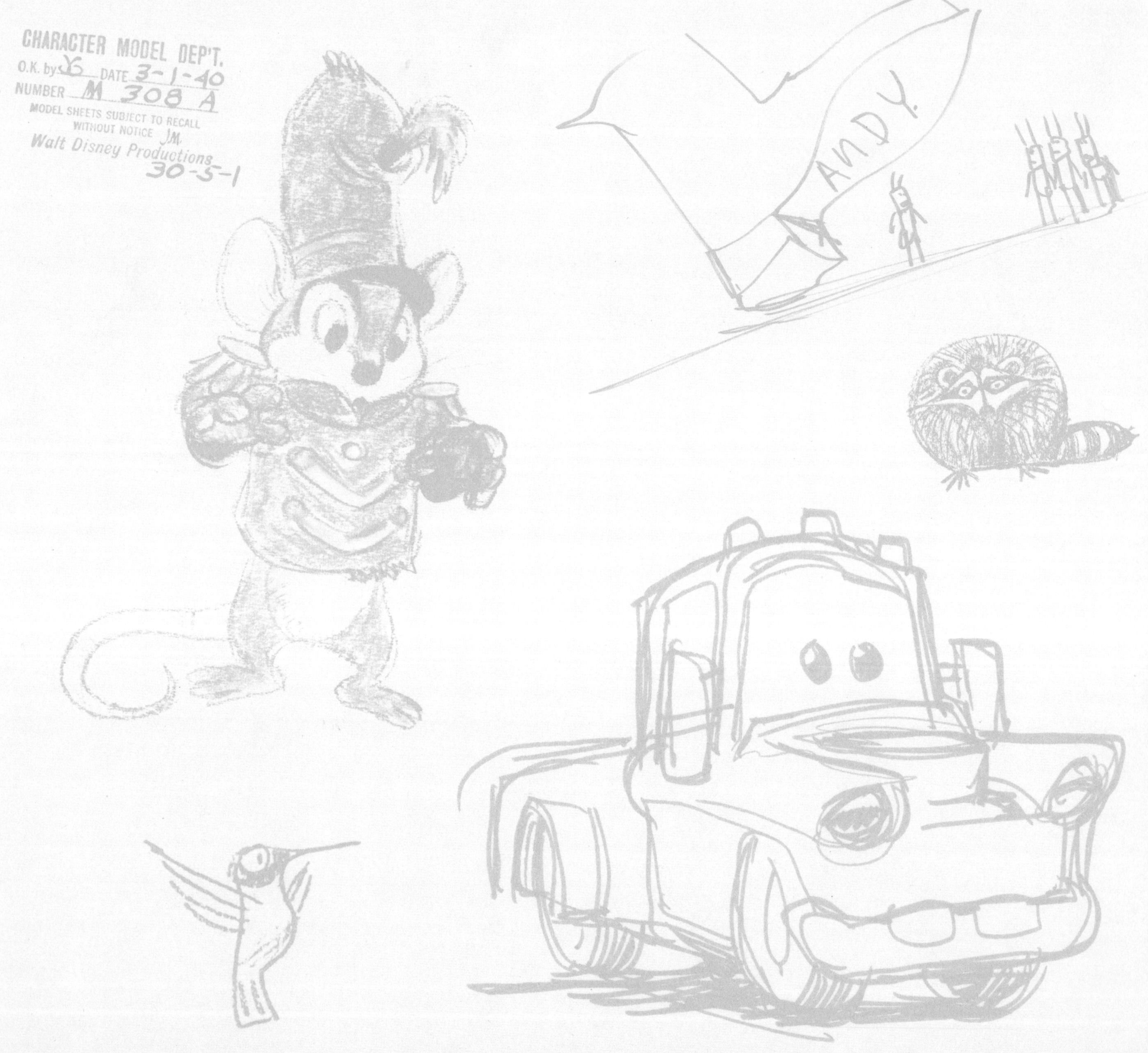
CHARACTER MODEL DEP'T.
O.K. by YG DATE 3-1-40
NUMBER M 308 A
MODEL SHEETS SUBJECT TO RECALL
WITHOUT NOTICE JM
Walt Disney Productions
30-5-1
ANDY